PRAISE FOR JOHN J. DWYER'S *STONEWALL*

"In this remarkable novel, John Dwyer brings the character of Stonewall Jackson to life. The colorful and paradoxical man who was both an ardent opponent of Southern slavery and a loyal defender of Southern liberty, who was both a gentle teacher of the Scriptures and a fierce master of artillery, and who was both a forthright gentleman and a wily field commander vividly comes to the fore.

"Dwyer has a knack for dialogue, for action, and for presenting the paradoxes of both that great age of conflict and that great man who so dominated it. He has simultaneously painted with broad brush strokes and with an eye for intricate detail.

"This is a sumptuous, sprawling, and scintillating historical novel that you'll want to curl up with for many hours."

—George Grant
Author of *The Blood of the Moon* and
Grand Illusions

"In his novel *Stonewall*, John J. Dwyer makes one of the great heroes of American history accessible to modern readers."

—*The Daily Oklahoman*

"*Stonewall* put me to thinking about what it takes to lead a moral life . . . The world is a dangerous place for souls, and as we make our way in it, we could do worse than take advice from a Christian soldier."

—H. W. Crocker III
Conservative Book Club

"In John Dwyer's *Stonewall*, you'll find a riveting story of war, an absorbing history, and a tender love story. But, above all, *Stonewall* is the story of a man who could truly lead . . . because he was a man of character."

—Penna Dexter
Point of View Radio Talk Show

"I have rarely read a more compelling biographical novel. Dwyer's writing keeps the reader coming back for more."

—Howard G. Hendricks

978-0-8054-1663-3

Published by B & H Publishing Group,
Nashville, Tennessee

Dewey Decimal Classification: 813
Subject Heading: HISTORICAL FICTION
Library of Congress Card Catalog Number: 98-8712

Front cover illustration from the original painting by Mort Künstler,
"Jackson at Antietam," © 1989 Mort Künstler, Inc.

Library of Congress Cataloging-in-Publication Data
Dwyer, John, 1956–
        Stonewall / by John Dwyer.
                p.   cm.
        ISBN 978-0-8054-1663-3 (alk. paper)
        1. Jackson, Stonewall, 1824–63—Fiction. 2. Generals—Southern States—
Fiction. 3. United States—History—Civil War, 1861–65—Fiction. I. Title.
PS3554.W925S76   1998
813'.54—dc21
                                                                                98-8712
                                                                                CIP

6 7 8 9 10 11 12 13 14 15   11 10 09 08 07

STONEWALL

A NOVEL

JOHN J. DWYER

BROADMAN
&HOLMAN
PUBLISHERS
NASHVILLE, TENNESSEE

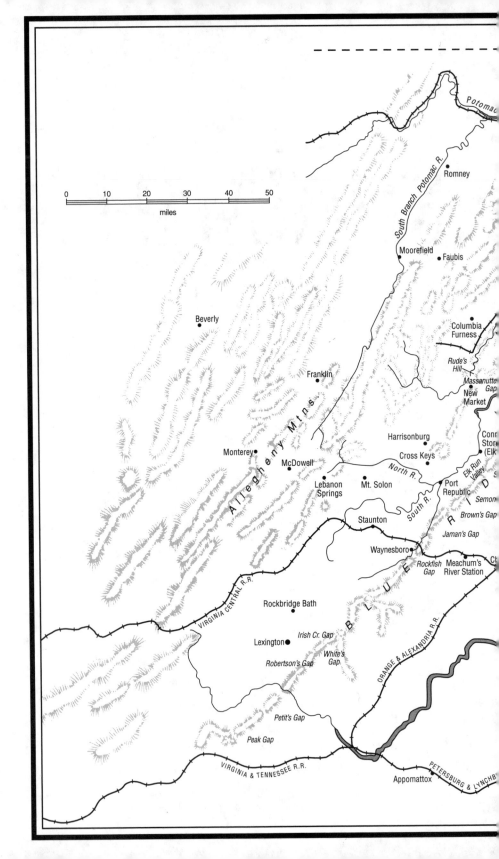

0 10 20 30 40 50
miles

Potomac R.

Romney

South Branch Potomac R.

Moorefield
Faubis

Beverly

Columbia
Furness

Rude's
Hill

Massanutte
Gap

Franklin

New
Market

Harrisonburg

Conr
Stor
(Elk

Monterey
McDowell

Cross Keys

North R.

Elk Run
Valley

Lebanon
Springs

Mt. Solon

Port
Republic

Semon

A T l e g h e n y   M t n s.

South R.

Brown's Gap

Jaman's Gap

Staunton

Waynesboro

Rockfish
Gap

Meachum's
River Station

Ch

B
L
U
E

R

Rockbridge Bath

VIRGINIA CENTRAL R.R.

Lexington

Irish Cr. Gap

White's
Gap

Robertson's Gap

ORANGE & ALEXANDRIA R.R.

Petit's Gap

Peak Gap

VIRGINIA & TENNESSEE R.R.

PETERSBURG & LYNCHB

Appomattox

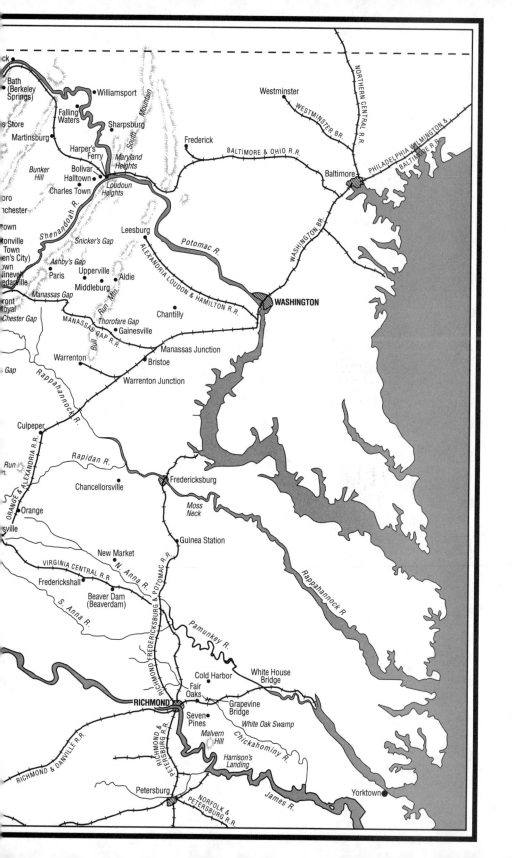

For my beloved wife, Grace

From the sessions of sweet, silent thought,
I summon up remembrance.
—*Shakespeare's Sonnets*

PROLOGUE

EACH YEAR WHEN GOD AGAIN BREATHES HIS SUBLIME SPRING into the Valley, it bids me look back in remembrance of that great and awful day. Can it really be seventy-five years ago tomorrow?

How often have I wondered if that day would have come had he lived.

Everything is so different now, for which I am very thankful. You will never have to see your loved ones killed or maimed, Katie Helen, your home, mementos, and every earthly possession stolen or destroyed, your dreams dashed, and your hopes left wanting.

No, I would not wish on you and yours what Providence offered to us, but I would not trade it to you for anything on earth, either. For it all happened, and it was God's cup for us, and I am thankful that those I knew and loved took it and drank it down and complained not.

I can no longer see the walls around me, but I see every flower, every shutter, every blooming branch of what was then. Each has its own story to tell. And I hear the voices of them who were but are no more.

Will you walk once more with me, Katie, beloved child of my child, down these hallowed lanes? If you will let your pretty eyes watch for me, and your young ears listen, then maybe—maybe—he shall come to us today as he did to them long ago.

For I have been young but am now old and am soon to go and meet them, all of them. Soon to go and meet him, whom I never knew. But Mama told me about him. She loved him.

The amazing thing was that she and the Yankee both came to love him. And they were both here that day, after he was gone.

I remember two things above all else the day the soldiers came to Lexington: the plinking sound Martha's fingers produced on the pianoforte keyboard and the cursing of the invaders. I had never heard such language, Katie, so I was not upset about it. Mama was, though. And I was upset about Martha's pianoforte playing. I never liked to play, and never liked it when she did.

She knew the keys and how to play, but somehow I could always tell, even without being in the room, when it was Martha who was on the pianoforte, mounds of blond curls spilling down in her face and onto her shoulders, because the music sounded like her mind was really somewhere else, which of course it usually was.

That's probably why she was the last one in the house to hear the cannon fire, even though she was on the main floor, continuing to plink. My brother Herbie and I were down in the cellar, getting a quick bath in the porcelain washtub that my father, Colonel John Preston—your great-grandfather—had freighted in from New York. Mama knew the Yankees would likely come through Lexington because of what they had done to the other towns up and down what she called "Virginia's loveliest valley, hushed in her embracing hills." Her Valley. The Shenandoah.

Margaret Junkin Preston—Maggie—Mama—possessed a stubborn mix of spunk and pride. And even though she had no love for the Yankees, though she had been one herself, she would not have dared allow any of the Preston children to turn out with dirty faces and grass-stained clothes for anyone—even the Yankees. Since Herbie, nearly three, and I, almost six, were the only members of the family with dirty faces and grass-stained clothes, we were the ones who got tossed into the washtub. At least it was a quick wash.

Herbie and I shared another distinction. Unlike Papa's other seven children, our mother was Maggie. Theirs was Sally Preston, my father's first wife, who had died eight years before, in 1856.

Anyway, the Yankee cannon blasts grew so loud that all of the china and crystal and windows and glass photographs in the house began to tinkle and rattle, as did the cans and jars down in the cool cellar with us. Even in that cellar, our ears began to ring from the noise. In fact, little Herbie shook and cried. I remember this made Mama very angry. The Yankees were supposedly just bombing our Virginia Military Institute (VMI), a couple of miles across town to the east, from the high ground on the other side of the Maury River. (The Maury is how Colonel Preston, who had a Yankee bounty on his head, escaped with some of the family valuables the day before. We named the high ground Hunter's Hill after the invasion. It is called that to this day.) Later, however, we learned that the Yankee commander Hunter would lob an occasional shell into the town at random, just to put the fear of God into folks. He wouldn't have known that most of us already feared the Lord God plenty, and he would someday too. Fortunately, the shells themselves killed no one, though I heard old Mrs. Cobb had a stroke during the shelling and one family had a couple of people injured when some shelves in their cellar collapsed on them from the shock of a nearby explosion.

The pinions of fear never gripped me tighter than when I heard the cannonball blow up right outside in our yard, not fifty feet from the colonnaded front porch. It shook the whole house. I don't know how, with all the jars and cans falling and Herbie and me screaming and crying, but somehow, in an instant, Mama had us scooped up, dressed, and one of us under each arm as she went bounding up the stairs.

Mama. In a way it's hard to talk about her, even now. And yet I have so much in my heart I want to say. She gave me—everything. Five feet and a hundred pounds of power and grace, seasoned with redheaded salt. But her strength came from somewhere within.

Women did not write and publish back then—but she did. Women did not start black Sunday schools back then—but she did (he got all the credit, but it was really her idea). Women did not *see* things back then. Nor did anyone else. Not like she did.

I'm not sure when she started loving him, but I think it was very early. She also did not like him at first, not at all.

Anyhow, Martha had finally stopped playing the pianoforte and was standing by the window in the parlor when Mama rushed into the room with Herbie and me in tow. The explosion outside had spattered the window glass with rich brown wads of Virginia soil. Martha stared out at the black smoke that was both near and far away—she herself was somewhere else again—when Mama, still toting both us boys, reached her and grabbed her by the arm. Mama herded the three of us into the hall. She still had Herbie stuffed under one wiry arm like a little ball of sobbing blond dough. My elder half sisters Phebe and Elizabeth and half brother John were in the hall, too, but cousin Martha's eight-year-old sister Mary wasn't at first, and Mama was hollering for her. (The supposed short visit of Martha and Mary—their mother an invalid and their father dead at Sharpsburg—had become quite extended.) Then Mary came screaming from the sitting room, hugging her doll—her favorite one, the soft pink one she liked to chew.

That was when Papa's painting of General Washington crashed to the floor in the parlor. It sounded louder than the explosion a few moments earlier in the front yard. I shall never forget the general's eyes. As they looked up at me from that other room, I felt the strangest sensation that they were staring straight through me.

Did he somehow know that at that very moment his namesake, Washington College, which he had helped found as a gift to Virginia, was being sacked and plundered, its contents stolen, smashed, or emptied out onto its lush tree-shaded green carpet, which lay just yards from the VMI? (Papa's own grandfather had been President Washington's secretary of state.)

Everyone got very quiet then, even Herbie. The only sound in the house was the resolute *click-click-click* of Great-grandfather Preston's giant walnut grandfather clock, coming from Papa's study. I believe it was the first time I had ever heard it.

The Yankees shelled the towns to scare the people and chase away the soldiers. It worked. They did it much worse to Fredericksburg, Richmond, Winchester, Harrisonburg, Staunton, and Leesburg than they did Lexington, though.

Mama gathered us all up like a furtive hen collecting her chicks under her wings, then hustled us back down into the cellar.

General David Hunter. "The Villain of the Valley," we called him. A Virginian who went with the Union. He wasn't the only one. But there was no one else like him. "Black Dave" his own men called him. A true hater of slavery. And a true hater of us.

But it was the scar. He got it from a Confederate minié ball at First Manassas. He was nearly killed when his brother Virginians, their backs against the wall, reversed the rout and the course of history and chased the Yankees across the Potomac and back into Maryland. I always felt the scar Hunter carried on the inside was deeper than the ugly one across his face. How else could a Valley man destroy his own land, devastate his own people?

When I was younger and wilder, I would have enjoyed finishing the job those boys at Manassas started on David Hunter. I had my chance once. I saw Hunter in a train station late at night in Richmond ten years after the war. It was late, dark, and cold, and nobody was around. I had my gun. But I was a Christian man by then, and he looked old and unhappy and his scar had become even uglier. I felt like he would surely answer for what he did to my Valley. Besides, Jubal Early had finally run Hunter back into West Virginia, which tainted any glory he sought to take with him from his marauding. So,

I actually felt sorry for him. I heard a few years later he had died of the palsy up North. He won the war, but he could never come home to the Valley.

Oh, that day! Day of our sorrow, day of our shame. Hunter and his Northern legions had swarmed up the Valley, destroying or sweeping aside everything in their path. And now they stood on the emerald heights above Lexington, poised to enter. Our tattered remnant of malnourished, mostly barefoot Confederate troops in the area had left tearfully the day before, as they knew that to remain in town would incite a bloodbath from which we by now knew the Yankees would not shirk, even if it meant the total destruction of the town and every man, woman, and child in it. Such were the policies of Grant, Sherman, Sheridan—and David Hunter.

I was first to hear the women screaming. One was sobbing in the next house. Smoke wafted across the town from the artillery barrage. I was told that the Millers' attractive servant, Mrs. Johnson, sent her two young boys over to the VMI cemetery to lay their bodies across *his* grave, even though it didn't yet have a marker, to protect it in case the Yankees tried to dig it up. Everyone already knew the Federals badly wanted his sword, and they thought it might be buried with him.

I can still feel the shudder that ran through me like the first dark unexpected slash of winter as I saw the invaders spill over the hill just north of Lexington and flow down into the town like rich blue molasses, trodding over my sacred ground, beneath or near which all that was ever dear to me now lies.

On they came, thousands of them. First the cavalry, riding several abreast at a fast trot over this very street upon which we now walk, which ran in front of our house. (Did you know, Katie, that street is now named Preston Street?) Two hours it took them all to pass! Only then came the uncounted legions of foot soldiers.

I saw Lylburn Downing standing on the sidewalk, holding his Bible in one hand and looking tall and handsome like always in his frock coat, collar, and hat. Two of the young girls from his colored folks church were scared and hanging on to him. He watched the Yankees closely as they passed, choking dust and all, but I couldn't tell what was in his heart.

We all clung to Mama at the front door like a cluster of grapes on the vine as the first foot soldier opened our white picket gate. She shooed us upstairs. The bluecoats were dirty, sweaty, and scavenging for food. She invited them into the kitchen. I don't think she realized how many would come in, though.

I looked down from a front window and saw the whole yard filled with them. They filled the street, too, and all of the other yards, as well as our fields north of the house. Numerous Yankee cavalrymen thundered across that acreage, foraging for food and animals. We had earlier secreted most of our livestock out into the country. The Federals found it all later, though.

Downstairs, they were cleaning out the cupboards and pantries as fast as they could take the food and cram it down their throats. Those that couldn't get into the kitchen scrambled through the house, taking what they wanted. Some of them fought over individual items. One soldier had lifted the painting of General Washington off the floor when one of his comrades grabbed hold and attempted to wrest it away from him.

The second soldier was larger, but the first one was a tough little red-headed Irishman who wasn't about to let it go. They struggled, finally falling to the floor cursing, where the little Irishman's knee, driven by the weight of the two men, snapped the heavy portrait cleanly in two.

The next thing I knew, Mama burst into the bedroom where Phebe (cradling the again-crying Herbie in her arms), Elizabeth, John, Martha, Mary, four Preston slaves, and I huddled in a corner like frightened puppies. She had that lovely flush she always had when excited about something.

"Quick, Phebe," she said, rushing across the room to us. "Let me have it back. You take the others and run and stay with Grandma Preston in her room."

Phebe's once dimpled blushing cheeks hung pallid and slack. You see, Katie, her handsome fiancée lay beneath a large plot of Gettysburg, Pennsylvania, earth. Two hundred fifty other Virginians and North Carolinians provided his earthly remains companionship. Phebe's smile, and other outward evidences of emotion, rarely showed. She was now twenty-four—three years older than her beloved Danny when double Yankee canister felled him at thirty yards during that gallant and tragic charge up Cemetery Ridge with George Pickett. Like so many others, her savaged heart continued beating only out of duty to her God and her Virginia.

She handed Herbie to Elizabeth and retrieved a magnificent long, gleaming stainless steel sword from beneath her frayed hoop skirt. She passed it to Mama, who quickly stuffed it under her own worn dress.

"Come, brothers and sisters," Phebe said, guiding us toward the door, "let's go see Grandma." Then she turned back to Mama, who was positioning the sword under her skirt.

"I—I wish *he* were here. Don't you, Mama?"

Mama opened her mouth, but no words came. Instead, after a moment, we heard the sound of china shattering downstairs.

"You take them and run along now, Princess," Mama said, pushing Phebe, with the rest of us in tow, out of the room and into the hall.

The sounds came too fast now to understand. The one thing I knew from birth in my Southern home was that men who would storm and damage your house were men to be killed if possible, and otherwise steadfastly avoided.

Down the stairs Mama bounded. On the first floor, troops were wolfing down chicken legs and bread and carting valuables out of the house. They swarmed around her as she made her way toward the kitchen.

She maneuvered around a towering corporal and the heavy brass lamp he lugged, then stepped into the kitchen in time to see a soldier hoist a coffee (chicory, by then) pot aloft and drain its remaining dregs down his throat.

Her eyes gazed in amazement around the room, which was already swept clean. Cupboard cabinets were flung open and spilled flour powdered the kitchen. Through a now-grimy window, she saw troops hauling food outside from our cellar.

"Where's the key to the smokehouse, Reb?" a mustachioed sergeant snarled. Then, Colt revolver in hand: "Unless you want us to burn your lovely Secesh palace to the ground."

Mama turned to him and replied, "Yes, we are at your mercy." She drew a deep breath and looked heavenward in concentrated silence, impervious to the clamor around her. When she turned back toward the sergeant, her words came soft and even: "Go ahead and burn it down—but I'll not give you the keys."

Crimson shock streaked the sergeant's face. A long moment passed. The sergeant's dark eyes simmered as he glared down at her. Mama heard shouts and chatter from outside. "Look, boys! Over here! The corn crib!" Finally, the sergeant uncocked his pistol and holstered it.

"Well then, we'll just kick in the door," he said with a smirk. "And we may indeed fire the house, when we're finished cleaning it out." Two other soldiers followed him quickly out the back door.

Just then, a burly, blond, bearded Yankee, his mouth full of food, lifted an enormous box that appeared to contain the remaining contents of the kitchen, and headed for the front of the house.

Aflush, Mama grabbed the soldier's beefy arm and jerked him around to face her. He was a foot taller and perhaps 120 pounds heavier than she.

"I'll be asking you to leave this food here, soldier." Her eyes burned like twin cobalt torches. "There are ten of us under this roof, black and white, including seven females and seven children. And after this box of food, we have nothing to eat but a few packages of crackers. Nothing!"

The blond looked around nervously. A couple of other soldiers laughed at him.

"You've cleaned out the smokehouse," Mama stormed, "the corn crib, the cellar, everything in our home. Now I demand, for the sake of your own mother, if there be a shred of decency within you, put back that box!"

A few nearby soldiers now began chiding the blond out loud. He blushed deeply. Mama's jaw dropped open as she realized, *They are speaking German!* The blond whirled away, grunting something inaudible—in German—to Mama.

Her shoulders sagged and her head bowed. She began weeping where she stood.

Across town, at that VMI gravesite, two young black boys, eyes wide with fear, stared up at a cluster of approaching Union troops.

"That must be it!" one soldier exclaimed.

Nearing the verdant spot, which boasted no headstone, the soldiers stared down in silence at the two trembling youths.

"You fellows can run along," a corporal said. "We've only come to pay our respects."

A rugged, leathery-faced sergeant stepped to the front of the throng. "We loved him too."

Back at our house, Mama heard a piercing shout flavored with an unmistakable Irish brogue. "Come lads, they're burning that nest of Rebel vipers, the Virginia Military Institute!'"

She looked up with a start. She wheeled toward our open front door. One soldier merrily whistled "Wait for the Wagon" as he jerked the curtains off of the windows, but she didn't even see him. Several other men hustled out the door just ahead of her, carting our family valuables and rushing toward the next event.

Did any of them know how well Mama knew the face of war? Did they know she had one stepson buried at Manassas, another buried on the grounds at VMI, and yet another still fighting with the VMI cadets after having lost an arm at Winchester? And her husband—a colonel—fleeing the Yankees somewhere between Lexington and Richmond, his considerable properties "confiscated" and his thick bush of hair turned from black to white during three years of war?

Mama walked as if under a spell out onto the portico and down all the polished, hedge-trimmed front steps. Moving toward the street, her eyes glazed, she thought of other days and other faces, all now gone, every one of them.

"No, not the VMI," she whispered.

Another soldier almost knocked her down as he rushed past her, a sheet stuffed full of our family belongings slung over his shoulder. "Serves you right," he hooted, "mean way you Rebs treated Dr. Junkin—your own pa, no less!"

Stunned, she watched him shove past a couple of other soldiers who grabbed for his booty.

"Margaret, Margaret dear!"

It was Mrs. Pendleton, wife of the Episcopal rector and Confederate brigadier general, much of whose gospel the past three years had been preached through the potent mouths of the Rockbridge Artillery battery he founded—cannons named Matthew, Mark, Luke, and John. The Pendletons' brilliant twenty-four-year-old son Sandie, himself already an adjutant general, lay buried in a fresh plot three blocks away in the Lexington cemetery.

"It's not only the VMI, Margaret," Mrs. Pendleton cried. "They're burning all of the faculty homes too!"

The distraught woman rushed down the street as Mama halted in stunned stupor.

Then, the crash of more breakage behind her. She turned to see a gangly teenaged private making his way precariously down the steps with a stack of china piled high in his arms. She gasped as another dish slid free and burst into tiny pieces.

Her fire and flush returned.

"Why, you young Yankee hoodlum. What use have you for such finery?"

The youngster stopped in his tracks at the foot of the stairs, his face smitten with a sheepish gawk.

"You turn right around and march back into that house and leave what's left of Colonel Preston's family china!" Mama shouted.

As the acned teenager pondered his next move, two other soldiers, each stocky and swarthy in complexion, quickly approached him. One got down on all fours behind the boy, and the other shoved the youngster over the first, while grabbing for as much of the china as he could reach.

Mama recoiled in horror as half of the china crashed to the ground in pieces. The other half either fell but remained intact or was secured by the laughing soldier who did the shoving. The teenager and the other soldier began fistfighting in the midst of the china that was on the ground, rolling around and mashing the ancient Old World treasures into tiny pieces.

Mama grabbed the laughing china bandit as he attempted his getaway.

"Let me go, lady," he urged, his accent thick. "Come on, let me go!"

"You're not taking anything else," she cried. "You all are nothing but a bunch of dirty, thieving animals!"

"Pick on someone your own size, lady," one Yankee jeered. "Carlucci's no match for you!"

As other soldiers laughed, she latched onto Carlucci's arm for dear life, then grabbed a handful of his oily, jet-black hair. He cried in pain. Then, the bluecoat raised one arm to strike her while cradling the china in his other arm.

"I sure don't have to take this from no Secesh colonel's wife!" he hollered.

"You touch her, soldier, and I'll shoot you dead."

Dark sooty smoke now billowed across the front yard, ferried by a breeze, from explosions in surrounding neighborhoods and from the burning buildings and houses on the other side of the small town. Mama, her formerly laughing foe—his arm still upraised—and the soldiers around them squinted to see from whom the last words came.

After a long, tense moment, a gust of wind swept back the black cloud and revealed a Union officer. Handsome and possessed of a hearty brown beard, speckled with traces of gray, he wore a black eye patch strapped over his left eye.

The officer held a cocked Colt .45 revolver in his hand. It was pointed at Carlucci's heart.

Shock on the china bandit's face gradually dissolved into shame, and he bowed his head as the other men quickly dispersed. He peeked at Mama, then turned and headed back up the steps, across the porch, and into our house, with the remaining plates and dishes.

The teenager, his nose bloodied, began to collect the few undamaged pieces strewn around him on the ground. That done, he too returned quietly into the house.

The officer holstered his handgun and stepped toward Mama.

"You all right, ma'am?" he asked.

She glowered up at him, blue eyes afire and chin quaking.

His eye broke contact with hers and flickered toward the ground. Then he pivoted and walked back to his horse, which was tethered to the white picket fence encompassing our front yard. He pulled an object from one of his saddlebags and returned to Mama.

"Your late brother-in-law showed me many things—most importantly, this," he said.

Surprised, Mama reached out to take a thick, worn volume with the barely recognizable words *Holy Bible* embossed on its cover.

She stared at the book, then opened it. Words were inscribed in a flowing hand.

> To the finest young man I know, with my
> fervent prayers that your bright future shall soon be
> illumined as will that holy city of which the sainted
> apostle wrote, "had no need of the sun, neither of the
> moon, to shine in it: for the glory of God did lighten
> it, and the Lamb is the light thereof."

Mama looked up with a jolt.

"*You*," she gasped.

The officer's eye was wet.

Then, a clink against the sidewalk. The officer noticed the glimmer of steel protruding from her frayed, hooped skirt. For a long, long moment, they stared at one another.

"I—I had no other way to thank him," the man with the eye patch said softly, his words cushioned with gentleness. After another moment, he drew his sturdy frame erect and said, "I'll post a guard here." Then he touched his hat in respect. "God bless you, Maggie."

He turned and left. Mama clutched the Bible tightly to her chest with one hand and stabilized the sword with the other, her eyes glistening. Waves of coughing racked her as new billows of smoke swirled around her and around our beautiful, defiled home.

Across town, flames blazed from the entire VMI complex, as well as the homes in the faculty neighborhood, choking the surrounding areas and turning the bright spring noon to black midnight for the entire village.

As the Yankees swarmed through Lexington, looting many dwellings and trashing Washington College—which was founded with a fifty-thousand-dollar grant from the father of the Federal troops' own country—the Coullings' three young daughters stood weeping in front of their flaming home as soldiers continued stoking the fire. Their mother grabbed an officer.

"Please, sir, all our earthly possessions are in there," she cried. "Please let me bring out my baby things—"

The officer pulled away from her, and she collapsed to the ground on her knees, sobbing.

What fear we? thought Mama. Tiny Mama, with crown and soul of fire, her pen so much bigger than she. She too would gain immortal renown. For her words would never die. The Poetess of the Confederacy: "See Jackson—his sword in his hand, like the stern rocks around him, immovable stand."

The next street over, Federal troops carried Mr. Robertson, feet-first, out of the doorway of his home, where he had been felled by a fusillade of Yankee gunfire. Nearby, blankets were pulled over the lifeless bodies of the two bluecoats he had blasted with his .10-gauge. They had shouldered their way into his small frame home and were rummaging through his family's valuables, heedless of his plaintive beseechings for them to leave. When one insulted his fourteen-year-old daughter with lewd remarks, Robertson grabbed his shotgun down from the wall.

That daughter, four others, and his wife now watched, wailing with grief and under Union guard, as their protector was carried away.

Mama glanced around as the remaining Yankees hustled out of our yard and house, many of them headed toward the fires, their faces painted with mercenary glee. Safe, she repositioned the sword under her skirt.

She turned and started back up the concrete steps toward our portico. The pockmarked teen who had carted the china out a few moments before was coming down.

Halfway up, Mama encountered him, his head cast down. When he looked up, tears smeared his sooty face. He glanced at Mama, then looked away, his chin quivering.

Head bowed again, he choked, "Ma'am, I'm . . . I'm real sorry, ma'am. My Ma . . . she didn't never have no . . . I'm sorry—" That was all. He rushed down the steps, through the yard and into the swirling blue throng. Mama watched after him for a moment, pity filling her eyes, then continued her slow certain trek back up the steps.

One final young Yankee emerged smiling through the door, pulling a handsome gray Confederate officers' greatcoat, several sizes too large for him, over his shoulders. Colonel Preston had paid nearly fifty dollars for that coat.

We children all burst through the doorway just as Mama reached it. We screamed of how the Yankees had stolen our breakfasts right up off the dining room table. We clutched her desperately and began weeping as never before. I still remember the softness of her worn yellow dress and the sweet smell of lilac on her skin and how she held me tight and safe.

Back at the cemetery, the Johnson boys remained draped across the unmarked plot. Hundreds of the Northern invaders filed without word past that grave that day. None trifled with it, nor with its brave sentinels.

No name? No record? The thought fired Mama as the wails of crying children filled her ears, and her eyes swept across our devastation. *Ask the world; the world has read his story.*

And now, precious Katie, before eventide comes, I shall tell you that story. A story of a different world, a different people. An imperfect people, a distant people, a vanished people of land and time and place and family and community. Things of which you know little.

For as you will one day understand, those things are mostly now gone, gone with those who fought to preserve them. There would have been no "Black Dave" Hunters, Katie, and no shells in the front yard, and no Yankee defenders-of-Virginian-virtue in eye patches had what was described soon after the war by the Catholic bishop of New Orleans not occurred.

"O Lord," the bishop petitioned, following the prayer the occupying Union forces constrained him to utter for President Lincoln, "when Thou didst decide to defeat the Confederate States of America, Thou first had to remove Thy servant, Stonewall Jackson."

This is his story, Katie Helen. This is your story.

CHAPTER 1

THEY SAID JOHNNY APPLESEED HIMSELF PLANTED THE TREE out front.

Thomas Jackson remembered that tree and the huge sculpted fruit that hung in crimson clusters from it, before dropping onto the soft green padding below.

He remembered the clean, sweet, wide mountain air that went on forever. And first and foremost he remembered the smiles and the suppers around the table with his mama and his pa, sister Elizabeth, and brother Warren.

His parents, Julia Neale and Jonathan Jackson, were a handsome couple, both well schooled—especially for their time and area—and the Jackson clan from which Jonathan hailed was perhaps the most distinguished family west of the Allegheny Mountains. The Jacksons had made their mark as counselors of law, merchants, and political leaders.

Life together had looked promising for Julia and Jonathan when they married back in 1817. Jonathan's pioneer father had endowed him with significant land holdings. But the winsome son did not possess the rugged father's strength, resolve, or judgment. A man who was appealing to women and liked by men, Jonathan's tastes ran too much to cards, socializing, and, most damagingly, the assumption of others' financial obligations.

Julia was different. She possessed a sweet but determined spirit and strong religious convictions. She deeply loved Jonathan. His quick step and twinkling blue eyes were magic to her. And she admired both motivations for his financial entanglements—desire to help others and to better provide for his own family.

His mounting list of assumed debts, however, troubled her as she knitted and rocked in the old chair that Grandmother O'Neale had brought with her across the sea from the north of Ireland. During these times, after the children had been put to bed, Proverbs 11:15 often returned to her mind: *"He that is surety for a stranger shall smart for it."* But she trusted God, she loved Jonathan, and she prayed. Knitting and rocking in the evening, with the worn family Bible open on her lap, she would feel the pressing vicissitudes of her life waft away. And she would sleep deeply and in great peace.

She would need the peace, as one chilly morning in early spring of 1827 seven-year-old Elizabeth lay prone in a sweat, eyes closed and her pa at her side nursing her. Thomas discerned, though only three, how strong his mother seemed, doing her knitting and rocking in her wooden chair at the foot of the bed even at such a serious time. Warren and the family's gentle black giant, Uncle Robinson, stood nearby.

Thomas did not know what *fever* meant then. And he could not have pronounced *typhoid*. But he knew his father was worried about Elizabeth.

The tousle-haired boy never knew his mother's thoughts, other than that she was always there and had a sweet voice that soothed him when he was sad or afraid. He sometimes wondered if she was the way she was because of the small old book she seemed always to have with her.

"Please, Little Bit, please don't go yet," his father pleaded, his perspiring face inches from Elizabeth's. "Please!"

Julia Neale Jackson rocked in her chair. Thomas saw how huge her stomach was with the next baby. He looked at his mother's face. It wasn't as nice looking as his father's and her forehead was creased with some lines on it, but it seemed content.

"She be in a better place now, Jonathan," Julia said to her husband, in her soothing way.

Only now could Thomas see his father's face was gray and ghost-like. Jonathan wept deep racking sobs as he pulled Elizabeth's limp little body to his.

Thomas looked up and saw that Uncle Robinson had tears streaming down his face. He loved the big man's whole head. It was large and nice to look at, and Thomas always thought it looked like a big black lion's head with bright white teeth. But a gentle lion Uncle Robinson was.

Warren's eyes were wet, but he stood quiet and still.

"Warren, Tom, you come here," Julia said, her knitting on her lap and her arms extended toward them.

As little Thomas entered his mother's embrace, he peered out through wide baby blue eyes at his father and the sweet kind girl the sweat-soaked man clutched against his chest, the one who had always played with Tom during the times he was sad.

Thomas Jackson remembered dark clouds and thunder the day Jonathan lay dying a few weeks later. He also remembered that as his pa grew sicker, the house didn't stay neat and clean like it usually did. And the rocking chair was empty all the time.

The room was darker this time, and Tom, spooked, could hear the wind whooshing through the apple tree outside, and through the dogwoods and pines farther out from the cabin.

Julia was now enormous. She was sitting on the bed where Jonathan was before, and he was lying where Elizabeth had been. Perspiration beads cascaded from his face in determined ranks, and he was talking, talking a lot, but his eyes were closed. Julia rubbed the cloth over his forehead, then wrung it out in the basin next to the bed.

Her face held no expression, but her eyes looked tired. All of a sudden, something hurt her—she grabbed her engorged abdomen and gasped. This scared Tom. Warren put his arm around Tom's shoulder and gave him his sure, winning smile. Uncle Robinson was there again. That made Tom feel a little better. Tom remembered Uncle Robinson asking his mother if she was all right. She nodded. Whatever was wrong with her stomach was OK now, and she turned back to Jonathan.

Warren leaned over and whispered in Tom's ear, "I think Pa's going to go be with Elizabeth."

Tom looked up at his big brother, surprised and confused, but he didn't say anything because even a three-year-old, especially one as intuitive as he, could tell it wasn't a time to talk.

They laid Jonathan next to Elizabeth in the grove near the cabin. Tom never saw Warren go near the graves, and he only saw his mama do so once, to set Elizabeth's little wooden cross back up after a winter storm howled down from the mountain the next year and knocked it over. However, Tom visited the graves nearly every day. Sometimes he just stood and looked down at them, not thinking about anything. Other times, he would sit and think about Pa and Elizabeth and maybe even talk to them. He remembered them better because the crosses were always there, close to home.

Once in a while, mainly in springtime, Tom would sneak daisies and forget-me-nots from the long rolling meadow that stretched out behind the grove and put them on the graves. He watched carefully, to insure that no one saw him, because he knew that putting flowers on a grave was something that girls might do, but a real man never would.

He did not know that, in that mystical manner mothers have forever had, Julia often saw him at his task. And when she didn't, she would soon notice the newly picked flowers on the spots 'neath where her beloveds lay. And she would treasure up those moments watching Tom, and others remembered about her beloveds, and her heart would swell until she thought it would burst. Then she would remember the Scripture in Job: *"The LORD gave, and the LORD hath taken away; blessed be the name of the LORD."* And she would cry until she could not cry anymore or until one of the boys came in or little Laura Ann needed milk. And then she would pray for Warren, Tom, and Laura Ann, who was born twenty-four hours to the minute after Jonathan's passing. Then for Tom again, that the sensitive boy would have a good, strong heart and be equal to the perturbations of love and loss and life.

The little wooden crosses marking the final earthly resting places of Jonathan and Elizabeth still stood lonely sentinel one especially intoxicating May dusk in 1830. As the sweet smell of clover, mint, and pine permeated their nostrils, Mama's new husband, Blake Woodson, and Tom's uncle Brake Jackson faced the darkening woods out back of the old Jackson homeplace.

"Come on, Tom Jackson!" Woodson shouted. "Come on out of there, you hear? Your aunt and uncle have got to be going now!"

"I declare, for a six-year-old boy, that young Tom knows his mind," Uncle Brake said.

Warren and Uncle Robinson, standing nearby, glanced at one another.

Julia had worked with all the energy her heart and body could muster to provide for Warren, Tom, and little Laura Ann. However, her judgment in some ways did not match her piety. After learning that most all of the estate owned by the generous but thriftless Jonathan was to be claimed by creditors (of others, for whom Jonathan had provided surety) and bill collectors, she rejected the petitions of her family and married another man possessed of both legal training and dubious financial sense.

Woodson's financial lot, in fact, proved to be even worse than Jonathan's.

But it was Julia's tired, worn old frontier body of thirty, now pregnant again, that was most to blame for the situation that had caused Tom to be huddled in the spooky, animal-infested tangle that ran down from behind the cabin.

Sadness and frustration filled Woodson's face.

"Poor little guy," he said. "I don't know what else to do. Been looking since sunup and nothing. You and Aunt Jennie are already late leaving, Brake. And he's fixing to be in there with the mountain lions."

The group heard sounds behind them. It was Julia, limping from the house with the help of Uncle Brake's wife, Jennie. Three-year-old Laura Ann trailed behind them, sucking her thumb and carrying a small, tattered wool blanket. Pain sliced Woodson's face as he rushed to support his wife's tottering frame.

"Why Julia, sweetie," he said, "you shouldn't be out of bed. You can hardly walk. You know the doctor said you—"

She ignored his proffered hand and squinted out into the silent woods. The paleness of her once-ruddy complexion caused Uncle Robinson to wince and half-shake his head.

Julia swallowed hard. "Tom. Tom Jackson," she said. "I love you, honey."

Shivering behind a thick tree trunk in the deepening shadows, his face streaked with tears and dirt, Tom choked back more sobs. He flinched as a wild beast screeched from somewhere in the woods.

"Tom, honey," the charmed voice continued, "please come out now, before it gets dark."

Oh no, what to do? Tom thought, uncertain. Too many emotions. Too much to think. He began to weep wrenchingly, chewing hard on his small grimy fist to muffle the sound.

"Tom, I promised Uncle Brake and Aunt Jennie you'd be good for them."

Got to be good for her, Tom thought with a grimace. *Don't want to disappoint her. She's the only one that matters anymore. Everyone else important leaving. Don't want her to go too. Not fair, God, not at all.*

The dark silence descended like a black canopy. Then, a small lonesome figure emerged from the thick brush. When Tom reached his mother, he collapsed sobbing into her arms. Mother and son clung to one another as though never to let go.

"Why, Mama? Why do I have to go away?" the boy cried.

She stroked his thick, mussed chocolate hair. "It's for your best, Son. Your aunt and uncle are much better able to care for you now than am I."

"But Mama, I just want you."

Tears rolled down Julia's face. For the first time, a guttural moan sounded from deep within her. Warren bit his lip.

Uncle Robinson's large, clear raven eyes glistened. He had known much pain in his life, having been separated from his own mother when he was a boy. His debt-ridden white owner had become deathly ill and with tears in his eyes had sold young Robinson to put food on the table for his own children. The gentle giant had always been partial to little Tom, and now he felt more so. *It don't seem right, Lord. Some things just don't seem right, Sir.*

Julia brought Tom back in from the woods, fed him, and bedded him down. Despite his hurt and pain, his exhaustion drove him to deep slumber within seconds of his head hitting the frayed feather pillow. But his mother's eyes did not close all night. She alternately tried to sleep in the bed, then rocked and knitted in the chair.

Around 3:00 A.M., she rose, put on her old threadbare gray shawl, and went outside.

The golden moon shone high and bright in the silent sky, and the myriad of constellations above her sparkled with clarity. There was the Big Dipper, which Tom still remembered his pa showing him and to which the boy referred as "Pa's Dip." Off to the east, over the mountains, a shooting star arched across the horizon.

The sweet, pastoral fragrance was so rich in her nostrils that she felt she could almost drink it down her throat like the cold, clear mountain stream water that ran down from above on the other side of the grove.

Poor Tom, she prayed. *What a fine boy I know he'll be, Lord, with your protection and help. Elizabeth is gone, Warren will handle whatever comes, but little Tommy . . . You have made him special; O Lord, I have known that since the very night he was born. He has a heart that is . . . different. He is a rare jewel, Lord, I know he is. Please bear him up under Your mighty wings. Be his shield and his buckler and let me never cease to faithfully pray for him. Someday, I believe You shall shine Your power and Your glory mightily through my little boy. I believe it as I believe You are here with me right now, Lord.*

The mountains were peaceful now, but she knew what a hard country it had been, and in many ways still was. Johnny Appleseed was not the only one to have traveled the area in the early days. Just after she and Jonathan had moved out to this beautiful, audacious, barely tamed back corner of western Virginia, her first husband had found a pile of old arrowheads. Later, under some brush she had finally goaded him into clearing out for a garden, he came across two human skulls, a knife, a tomahawk, and a soft, frazzled stuffed doll, or what was left of it. This far land could be unforgiving. You could give and give and it just took—your husband, your children, finally you.

It also poured forth some of God's most beautiful handiwork. Like strange, bright flowers at odd times of the year. Like— *Oh my, the graves,* she thought. New flowers had appeared on the graves. She stared for a moment, then walked toward them, pulling the shawl tighter against the chill.

Blue, green, orange, and red flowers. Right where Tom always placed them. She whirled toward the cabin. It was dark. Even from here, she could faintly hear Tom's distinctive, soft snores. And she had heard them almost from the moment she laid him down. *He could not have placed these flowers. Then who*—wait, someone was on the ground in the shadows, over by the grove. *Uncle Robinson.* She walked to him.

Like everyone else, he was exhausted. Normally a light, alert sleeper, he did not even stir as she approached. In the old days, he would have been a quick scalp on this night, as would the rest of them. *In the old days, you couldn't afford a deep sleep,* she thought.

Then she noticed something else in the luminous moonshine—a wad of blue, green, orange, and red flowers in Robinson's huge black hand.

No one said anything when Uncle Brake guided the buckboard out a few hours later. It was sad, and mountain folks knew better than to suffer words when none were of use.

As they pulled out, Tom watched his mother from the back of the wagon. Her face looked whiter than ever. A horrible thought stung him like a pine needle: *What if I never see her again?*

Little Laura could take it no longer. She broke free from her mother and began to toddle, fast, after the buckboard, holding forth a handful of crumpled daisies in her hand. Tom melted as he watched her. Her desire to reach him was so strong that he feared she would topple forward at any second and plunge face first into the dirt.

"Tommy! Tommy!" she cried. "Come back, Tommy!"

Tom watched his little blond darling chase him, his eyes full. His compact chest swelling, he forced his quivering lips together. *I won't cry, not again. Cried too much already.*

Late the next November, Laura and Tom, together again, joined Uncle Brake and Uncle Robinson to go see Mama for the last time. The day dawned snowy and cold, mountain cold. Warren had been moved two months after leaving Mama, to a house on the other side of Clarksburg to live with one of the Neale families. Tom and Laura had not seen him in the four months since. Tom especially had missed him, nearly as much, he guessed, as he missed Mama.

The boy never liked Uncle Brake. He wanted to be with his mother. It didn't help any that his uncle seemed to wish for Warren to be with him rather than Tom. It caused the loneliness in Tom's heart, cold and heavy, to grow even stronger.

Snow blanketed the apple tree, the bitter wind shaking its fragile, white-powdered branches, as Uncle Robinson pulled the buckboard up to the snow-piled cabin.

Uncle Brake stepped into the dwelling and lanky Uncle Robinson helped the two children down. His small mittened hand dwarfed in Uncle Robinson's enormous one, Tom grimaced and bowed against the swirling, stinging ivory flakes, which were now turning crystalline.

The quiet black giant led Tom and Laura into the cabin. Shaking off, Tom thought, *It seems different than I remember.* He noticed the home was in a complete state of disarray. Then he followed Uncle Robinson into *that* room. *That dark, cold, dread room where people go when they are leaving and never coming back.* He wasn't sure he wanted to go in there—but there was Mama. *Oh!* She did not even look like Mama anymore. She looked, um, old. Old and very, very white, like a ghost. She lay on the bed.

The boy scarcely saw Warren standing nearby, or Uncle Brake, or a Neale aunt whose name he could not recall. Or Woodson, who could not muster a living for Tom or the rest of his family, kneeling by the bed at his wife's side. Or sweet, fuzzy-headed two-month-old Wirt, being suckled by his mother Julia.

Tom shrugged loose from Uncle Robinson and walked across to the bed, as if in a hypnotic trance. He stared at his mother.

She turned toward him. Her lips were blue. But when he saw the countenance of her face straight on, it was different than he had first thought. Yes, different. She looked like—an *angel.*

She summoned a weary smile, then reached her hand to his cheek. The gentleness that had calmed many rushing rivers in Tom's life remained in that hand. But now the boy felt the hand trembling. He remained stoic, but his chin began to quiver.

"Oh, my dear, sweet, good Tom," she said. Soft words. Words he could barely hear. Words that meant the whole world. "You've been through so much, my darling."

Tears began streaming down Tom's cheeks, but he stood in silence.

Julia swallowed, with effort. "Now I'm going to go away, Tom. But there is no reason to be afraid. I'm going to be with Pa and Elizabeth, so I'm going to be very happy."

An excited three-year-old girl tramped across the room to the bed. "Mama, Mama, Mama." Little Laura. Bright eyed, a happy smile lighting her cherub face, her gaze trained on Julia.

Warren ground his teeth together to keep from bursting into tears, his eyes watering over. Uncle Robinson covered his mouth with the back of one hand, his face already painted with tears.

Julia swallowed hard again, her eyes misting over as she stroked Laura's golden hair. Then she turned back to Tom.

"Jesus will come and be with you," she said, "when you ask Him to cleanse your heart from wicked thoughts and deeds and when you embrace Him and His death on the cross in trust and faith for the forgiveness of your sins. He will guard and protect you until God decides it's time for you to come and be with us."

Wirt cooed, causing Julia to pause.

"But first," she continued, "the Lord has some things that He wants you to do here. Some good and exciting and wonderful things. Then, when He brings you to be with us, we'll all be able to celebrate the fine things you did on earth. Does that make sense to you, Son?"

No, Mama, but if you say so, he thought, beginning to nod. Julia paused, closing her eyes and catching her breath.

"Now, Son, can you remember a couple of things for me?" she continued after a moment.

Another slow nod. Then Tom felt a tug on his leg. It was Laura, hugging him, her sweet upturned face radiant with love and affection. He put his arm around her and pulled her close.

Deep coughs racked Julia. Then Wirt sputtered and squirmed. Finally she continued again, with difficulty.

"Tom, Son, you must be generous to all," she said, "especially those less fortunate than yourself. You must love the Lord with all of your heart and all of your soul and all of your mind, and other people as yourself. These are not just words, Son; they must be your life." She summoned all of her strength and grabbed her rapt son's arm.

"And Tom, you must always remember that no matter what obstacles or problems you run up against in life, if you try and try and never, ever give up"—she rose to one elbow and delivered the last with force and passion, looking straight into his face, her eyes alight—"*you may be whatever you resolve to be.*"

Tom stared at her, his lips parting just a bit. The room was hushed. Julia drew deeply for breath. A weak smile crept across her now quiet face. She cupped Tom's chin in one hand, little Laura's in the other. After a few seconds, her arms were shaking so hard she had to pull them back.

Wirt burst out crying and Woodson lifted him away from Julia. Then she bid Warren, Tom, and Laura each in turn to stand by her with their heads bowed as she offered fervent and passionate prayer for their protection and guidance all through life.

Tom, his arm still wrapped around Laura, split open his eyelids and cast a surreptitious peek at his mother through the tiniest of openings as she prayed for the children.

Her eyes are barely open and I can't understand all of her words, but she—how can it be?—she looks like she is beginning to glow!

As his eyes widened in amazement, Julia prayed with calm a few verses from Psalm 118: "'Let them now that fear the LORD say, that his mercy endureth for ever. I called upon the LORD in distress.'" The words began to trail and to come farther apart. "'The LORD answered me . . . and set me . . . in a large place.'" Weaker now, beginning to go away. "'The LORD . . . is . . . on . . . my . . . side . . . '"

"'I will not fear: what can man do unto me?'" Uncle Robinson finished the verse, eyes swimming and voice cracking, but a brilliant ivory gleam lighting the handsome, distinguished face. "Miss Julia be with the Lord Jesus now, honeys."

For a moment, all was silent. Then Woodson began to sob until the sounds of his grief filled the chill room. The aunt, also in tears, took the sleeping Wirt. Uncle Brake shook his head. Warren buried his face in his hands.

"Is Mama sleeping, Tommy?" asked little innocent Laura.

Tom stared at his dead mother. Then at Uncle Robinson, the venerable cheeks again wet. Then, back at his mother. Her face was at peace.

No one stays; they all go. They all leave me. Even Mama. I know that now. No one can I trust. They all break their word and leave me. Going to be strong, ready next time. Never, ever going to cry again, either.

A strange sound interrupted Tom's thoughts. He and the others turned to see. The wooden chair, now in a far, dark corner of the death room, held Mama's knitting things, coated along with the rest of the chair by a layer of dust. The chair rocked to and fro, as it had from Tom's earliest recollection. One thing was different this time: nobody was within ten feet of it.

CHAPTER 2

TOM NEVER KNEW HER BY ANYTHING BUT GRANNY NANCY. After his Grandma Jackson and his aunts all died off or moved away, Granny Nancy was the only female at Jackson's Mill, the enchanting spread owned by Tom's uncle Cummins Jackson. The mill, which boasted a functioning, water-powered wheel set next to a deep, sparkling pond and seven thousand acres of rich green western Virginia bottomland, was where the boy eventually landed in his orphaned travels.

Granny Nancy was also the oldest person by at least thirty years at Jackson's Mill and the only adult who owned or read a Bible.

It was said her father was a younger brother of Crispus Attucks, the Negro slave killed by the British in the infamous Boston Massacre of 1770. He was hunted by the Crown later in the War for Independence, along with his white master, for their involvement in the ambushing of a British payroll wagon. Both were caught and hanged in the town square in full view of their families and friends.

Nancy was supposedly a baby when all this occurred. After her grieving mother died of pneumonia the same year, the New England family who had owned her parents raised her. She had three children of her own before she was sold by the family to Cummins' father to settle an unpaid debt of merchandise. Also, slaveowners in the North were coming under increased persecution, so it seemed that the smart—and economical—thing to do was unload them at a profit to Southerners, whose cotton and cash crop farms were booming. That way, one could be in good shape financially as well as morally.

One of Nancy's children died as an infant. That was no uncommon occurrence among black or white children, but it was sudden, unexpected, and Nancy felt as though her very heart had been cut out of her body with a dull knife. The other two children lived, but one was kept by the Northern family when Nancy was sold. This rendered the bereaved woman ill and scarcely able to function. But, as she had given life, the child who went with her to Virginia and the Jacksons gave life back to her. Young Nathan, for the next several years, provided Nancy's only reason for taking her next breath. She regained her health while loving him with what strength of heart remained in her, all the while shivering against the looming specter of his loss. His life was happy and secure.

Nathan was killed when Shawnee Indians raided the Jackson homestead during a barn raising. It happened so quickly that he suffered neither pain nor fear. For that, at least, Nancy was thankful.

Man, woman, and child—of any color—were the targets in the desperate war of survival between new and native Americans. Nine-year-old Nathan, four white men, and two white women fell that bloody day in a hellish nightmare of guns, tomahawks, and knives before the bloodied Shawnees were driven off.

With this final, violent loss, Nancy was inconsolable. She would not eat or drink. She could not sleep. The bracing image of her beloved Nathan, his head scalped and his throat cut nearly clean through, drove her to the brink of death. It wasn't until Rosa Lee, the other female slave on the Jackson spread, spoke to her of the Bible and of finding peace and eternal salvation through belief in the person of and obedience to the teachings of Jesus Christ, that Nancy began to think again that she might rather live than die. When Rosa Lee convinced Nancy that her two children, not yet having known of their own sinful condition and thus unable to embrace God's plan of deliverance through forgiveness in Christ, were all in the rapturous, joyful presence of the Almighty, the weary woman determined to be a follower of the Lord for the remainder of her days.

Since then, peace and contentment had been her constant companions, even when she suffered through having been raped behind the mill building by one of Cummins's no-good Tennessee cousins from the Johnston wing of the clan and then a subsequent miscarriage.

Cummins—tall, barrel-chested, rough-and-ready—tracked the violator through snow, storm, and flood all the way to Kentucky when he learned of the vile act. There, he shot him, then hanged him for good measure.

The rape and subsequent loss made Nancy wish all the more for heaven and caused her to live all the more like it where she was. She began to tell others, black and white, about the Good Book and Jesus and the better way they offered. She began preaching at the mill to whomever would listen, which wasn't many. Cummins, his two brothers, four male cousins, and two nephews were not interested. The women on the place—Cummins' two sisters and Rosa Lee—were her only audience. And of the women, one sister and Rosa Lee eventually died, and the other sister and her husband, Cummins's cousin Cale Connagher, headed west to Kentucky, along the route Cummins had taken on his trail of vengeance.

The men at the mill were mostly good boys, but not given to piety. Cards, horses, and John Barleycorn were their preferred religion. They worked hard at the mill and the land around it, especially in the early days, and they recreated hard afterward.

Thus it was that Granny Nancy and young Tom Jackson arrived at a great fondness for one another after the boy's arrival at Jackson's Mill in 1833. Both had lost nearly everybody and everything. Tom had been bounced around from one relative to another in the nearly two years since his mother's death.

For the preceding few months, Tom had abided with Uncle Brake and Aunt Jennie. Like before, he and Uncle Brake had clashed almost from the start. Uncle Brake, being of a similar determined disposition as Tom but without the boy's innate sensitivity and concern for others, had not and did not provide an enjoyable roost for his young nephew. This time, Tom was through with the man for good. Accompanied as he was during each leg of his journey by Uncle Robinson, the boy returned to Jackson's Mill.

"I have quit Brake," the nine-year-old announced at the door that evening to the gape-mouthed clan, resolve stoking the flashing blue eyes. "And I shall not return to him."

Godly old Nancy took a particular liking to Tom because he alone would sit at her feet as she told stories from the huge Bible on her lap (which she could not read). He would listen with wide-eyed wonder as she rocked her chair by the fireplace and opened up new worlds for him that he had never explored. Worlds of brave warriors, giant men, beautiful queens, huge whales, mammoth boats and floods, and people and God performing miracles. Nancy also recognized in young Tom that familiar restlessness of one who had had what he counted on taken from him—again and again.

Tom loved the hardy life at Jackson's Mill. Making it even better was Laura's arrival a few months after his. The aunt with whom she had been staying had died. The boy worked the stock, fished, and after a couple of years, began to serve as Cummins's jockey in the races his uncle scared up regularly around the county. For some reason, Tom was Cummins' favorite, over any of the others at the mill. Sometimes Tom had a queer, strong notion that Cummins reminded him of someone else, but he could not figure whom.

Despite his rarefied surroundings, Tom developed an ailment, or group of ailments, that was difficult to diagnose, but seemed to center around digestive tract irregularities. He sought advice from old Doc Brian, who was in the nearest town, Kimmerling, ten miles away, and tried various diets to deal with the condition. At times he felt as though everything from his circulation to his vision to his hearing to his bowel movements were affected. The symptoms never got much better or much worse; they just came and went. Cummins never said so, and Tom was the one person on the place for whom he had a true soft spot, but the hulking landowner suspected perhaps a touch of hypochondria, though he did not know a word existed to describe the condition. In any event, Tom, on the brink of puberty, didn't grow much for a couple of years.

One thing that his assorted ailments did not affect was Tom's fishing acumen. He enjoyed fishing, and he enjoyed his standing, and exclusive, agreement to provide any fish he caught to local gunsmith Conrad Kester for fifty cents apiece.

One lazy June day, the fish seemed to be fighting for the honor of taking Tom's hook. After several nice catches, he hauled in a real prize: a meaty three-pound pike. He slung the fine string over his shoulder and hustled off for town.

Along the way he passed a large plantation manor belonging to Colonel John Talbott, a hero of the American War of 1812 with Great Britain. The colonel, a short, barrel-chested man with bright red, almost orange, hair was just back from a ride with his dogs.

He stepped down from his horse and called to Tom. "Looks like you made quite a haul there today, Tom." He approached the boy, leading his horse by the reins.

"This one appears to be a good three pounds," Tom beamed.

"Why, I expect you're right about that, son," Talbott replied. "How would you like one dollar for that big one, Tom?"

"One—a whole dollar, sir?"

"That's right."

The boy's face split clean in half with an ear-to-ear grin. "Golly, Colonel Talbott, that's really—" Then a cloud advanced across his countenance. He fell silent for a moment. Talbott stared, wondering if he had missed something.

Tom shook his head, "No sir, I can't do it."

"What? Well, why not?"

"Well, Colonel, I've got an agreement with Mr. Kester to sell him any fish I catch."

The colonel's cheeks flushed. "Ah, Tom, lad, you've got three or four other nice ones on that string. Tell you what, I'll give you a dollar and a quarter for it. No way that Kester will top that. And besides, he'll never know you let loose of one fish, anyway."

Tom shifted his feet and glanced at the string. His words were soft. "That's not the point, sir. This fish is sold."

"Well, what's he pay you for the fish you catch, Tom?"

Tom blanched. "Fifty cents apiece."

"Ah, for goodness sakes, Tom," Talbott scoffed. Now Tom could see the veins on the colonel's thick bull neck jutting out. "That beaut's worth more than any old fifty cents, boy."

"Well, he's paid me fifty cents for many a fish that was worth a lot less than that, so I reckon I won't take him for the fool, now that I've got him a good one." Azure sparks were starting in Tom's eyes, and his young jaw was set like granite.

"All right, boy," Talbott cried, lifting his hands in surrender. "Will you at least let me hire you at the rate of seventy-five cents per fish for all your future catches?"

"I'd be happy to consider that, sir," Tom replied as Talbott's face broke into a much-relieved smile, "as soon as I find out whether Mr. Kester would care to match the offer."

"Confound it, boy!" *This was too much!* "And I thought your clan of Jacksons more Irish than Scots."

"Oh, you'd be mistaken, Colonel," Tom said, turning to leave with his catch, "mistaken indeed, sir."

In addition to listening to Granny Nancy's Bible stories and fishing, something else began to claim more and more of Tom's leisure time as the months, and years, drifted by at Jackson's Mill: the duties and responsibilities attendant to commanding the area militia.

His troops, ages six to twelve, consisted of a couple of younger cousins, two or three white boys from neighboring families—and a couple of their sisters—and two or three young black boys and as many young black girls.

But his most loyal soldier was his own sister.

"Tom! Tom!" the children would shout when they spotted him returning from a fishing expedition or errand to town. "Tom, it's time!"

"Fall in, men, fall in," Tom would shout, catching the long stick Laura tossed to him, the one he used to direct his troops.

"I get to be the hickory stick!"

"No, you goose, his name is Old Hickory!"

"I'm Davy Crockett!"

"I'm Daniel Boone!"

Behind him in the jabbering, giggling band were the cousins and neighboring white boys, then Laura and the other white girls, followed by the black boys, and finally the black girls.

Often, the formation was ragged and beset with stragglers. This in no way pleased its commander. *Laughing, then attacking the enemy before being given orders to do so. Not acceptable!*

"Straighten up that line, men," Tom would call. "Press up, men, press up!"

But he would turn and steal a wink at Laura, who would blush and become one giddy blond smile. Then the troops would respond to the familiar command by falling into instant lockstep formation.

"All right," Tom would bark, turning back toward the front, "at the quick-step, now!"

And on they would march. On to victory and glory—again—against the British. The next day it might be the Cherokees, or maybe the French. Always with stern, confident Tom leading the way. Always as the fast-marching foot soldiers of the sovereign state of Virginia, one of the grand and glorious united states of America, subject to no government before its own in Richmond.

Little Laura became the apple of her brother's eye. Wrapped in her cute petite frame was a precocious, headstrong girl. Her temperament was sweet, but, oh, could she work the male population at the mill. To witness the many, varied items that grown men would fetch and do for a sweet, eyelash-batting young girl was an amazing experience. But it was Tom she idolized from the start.

Granny Nancy was the one person who knew how much Tom would hurt when Cummins decided one day it would be best, with no white women remaining at the mill, for Laura to return to her uncle Alfred Neale over near Parkersburg. Uncle Alfred, like most of the clan, no longer went by O'Neale, as it was a long time before any attachment of Irish—even Scotch-Irish—heritage to oneself was considered advantageous in America. Granny Nancy knew nothing about such bigotry toward the Irish or anyone else. She only knew things had been a certain way, were that way now, and in the providence of the Almighty, likely would remain as such. She also discerned that Laura was curious, sensitive, and possessed of a heightened sense of justice and fair play, like Tom. And Granny Nancy knew that these things, along with the siblings' shared early perturbations, had bonded them tightly.

Tom wanted to run and hide the day Uncle Alfred arrived in the wagon to take Laura away. *It hurts again, like before,* he thought. *When will they all stop going away?*

After Uncle Cummins, Granny Nancy, and some of the others had hugged the pretty ten-year-old, Tom embraced her. He did not let go for nearly a full minute, as if it would allow him to hold onto Laura and everyone and everything else dear to him.

When he finally released her, he stepped back, rubbing his eyes and fighting the flood that was forming in them. *Someday there will be no more tears and no more partings and no more being left alone.* He longed for reunions and homecomings that would forever supplant farewells. He turned and ran to the woods and, despite himself and his vow, wept bitterly.

Springs arrived and autumns departed. Though dogged both by his physical infirmities and the relentless, gleeful kidding about them that came from his male relatives, Tom bested the ailments well enough to grow strong in body and mind. And he came to love his western Virginia mountains, with their tall pines and cedars, sweeping vistas, and brightly painted flowers and blossoms of every hue.

On the days when he was not leading drills for the garrison, and when his chores and work were finished, Tom would grab his two favorite books and retire along about midafternoon to his favorite spot. Tom's place-of-places lay at the foot of a soft, grassy hill that rose gently from the mill pond on the side opposite the main house. From this carpeted station he would observe the clean, fresh air—enriched more often than not with the sweet aroma of Granny Nancy's omnipresent kitchen chimney—pure cool water, and verdant foliage. He could see across the pond to the main house a quarter of a mile away, but a thick line of pines, cedars, and maples lined the perimeter of his view on all sides except on the hill that ascended at his back.

Here was where the seen merged with the unseen for Tom. Where life was breathed into past and present alike. Where that life led into dreams—dreams that might chart destinies. Nestled into this quiet place away from the mill, Tom would stretch out on nature's royal rug and open the Holy Bible or *Swamp Fox, the Military Exploits of Francis Marion*. Into the pages of the latter, an epic chronicling the exploits of the guerilla hero of the American Revolution, Tom had slipped a worn copy of William Cullen Bryant's famed *The Song of Marion's Men*.

> *Our band is few, but true and tried,*
> *Our leader frank and bold;*
> *The British soldier trembles*
> *When Marion's name is told.*
> *Our fortress is the good greenwood,*
> *Our tent the cypress-tree;*
> *We know the forest 'round us,*
> *As seamen know the sea.*
> *We know its walls of thorny vines,*
> *In glades of ready grass,*
> *Its safe and silent islands*
> *Within the dark morass.*

Plied with the wisdom of man and God, the thoughts and dreams would flow. Tom would be a fleet-footed sharpshooter in the woods. Then he would be on a jam-packed raft with the legendary Marion, his men, and their horses, crossing the Pedree River in South Carolina to ambush Colonel Banastre Tarleton and his well-ordered British troops. Into a world of fame and grandeur the boy would plunge. A world where the Jackson name would once again take its rightful place, its chosen place, as it had when Jacksons were practicing the law and governing territories and serving presidents. A world where that name had not fallen on poverty and death and ruin.

Sometimes a warm breeze would blow cold through his bones and his stomach would knot and the wrath would rise and his anger would boil toward his father and his stepfather and, God forgive him, even his mother. Anger for their respective roles in the saga that had brought the family name to, in Tom's eyes, a disgrace. It was then that he would shout, "I shall do it!" *I shall return the name of Jackson to its fair station among the names of men!*

More often than not, however, he would observe nature's unde-spoiled beauty. He would hear the proud sound of the American bald eagle and gaze upward to follow its majestic, soaring glide in the azure sky. Or his eyes would follow, not more than fifty feet away, the magnificent gray buck leaning over to drink from the chill dark pond. That buck had a peculiar way of never coming close to anyone at the mill but Tom. It was a wise strategy, as the mill was chock-full of crack shots.

The slight breeze would rustle the pages of Tom's books, and the buck would jerk his head up and look straight at Tom. For a moment their eyes would meet. Tom would look into the beast's large, gentle brown orbs and see splendor, strength, and vulnerability. *Why must such consummate beauty perish, often horribly? And why sisters and fathers and mothers, and their good name with them? This will take much searching and study and meditation. Perhaps someday I will know also why so much pain exists.*

Tom would then pull a small, worn, black-and-white sketch from his Bible and stare at it. Many thoughts and feelings were stored up in his full young heart as he looked upon his mother's likeness. *Mama.*

Suddenly, one golden late afternoon, there came a commotion from across the pond, back toward the main house. With gingerness, he returned the sketch to the Bible. Someone had arrived on horse-back, a familiar figure. The family began to swarm around him and shout. Tom glanced back at the buck. *Gone.* He blinked and gazed around the entire area. Gone. *Amazing.*

Then one word floated across the pond to him above all the others—*Warren.* Tom started to attention and peered across the tranquil pool. Yes, it was true! Tall, dashing, and leaping down off the big bay was eighteen-year-old Warren Jackson.

Tom jumped up, his books tumbling to the grass and out of sight. He raced away, not seeing the buck's soulful eyes following from a shaded hollow nearby.

The sweet sound of good mountain fiddling, "Won't You Come with Me to the Bower?," wafted into Tom's ears as he rounded the curve toward the main house. And there was his brother.

"Warren!"

"Tommy!"

Then Warren had one arm around Tom's neck and the other under one of his arms, locking the younger boy's head and thrusting it with a hearty laugh toward the raucous throng of kinfolk. As the fiddling grew quicker and louder, Warren swung Tom around several times, hooting all the while, before Tom got hold of a leg and twisted his strapping brother to the dirt.

Everyone, including Warren, laughed in surprise at Tom's determined move. In feigned distress, Warren cried uncle, and the brothers clambered up, hugging one another and dusting off.

From out of nowhere, two-hundred-forty-pound Cummins Jackson grabbed one brother's neck in the crook of each arm and playfully squeezed them until their heads looked like red cherries ready to pop open.

"Good to see brothers who ain't lost their liking one for another," Tom's hulking uncle bellowed. He then granted his gasping nephews reprieves after having reestablished his stature as true he-bull of Jackson's Mill. "But Warren, try to be a might gentler in the future with my junior partner here."

All Warren could rasp out was, "*Me* gentler?"

Warren was not as close to Tom as was Laura, but only because, in the younger brother's eyes, he resided on a higher plane. A plane such as the one from which his father had held—and, to a degree, continued to hold—court in Tom's life. It was a sublime and singular plane, reserved for that indomitable superior officer, protector, and friend for whom Tom had ever sought, unbeknownst to himself, to find, serve, and please. One who would help confirm in bold relief what was true and good and trustworthy, who would both order and create order for Tom's universe.

Now Warren carried the mantle. Warren, bursting with energy and freshness, schemes, plans, and ideas; never halted by the tragedies of the past or present—somehow, empowered by them. Tom moved inward; Warren, outward.

And there he was, returned with education. He had even run and taught at a small school. And all at eighteen years of age. Tom was no will-o'-the-wisp, but he would always heed the siren songs Warren played.

Laughing, lying, fiddling, fish frying, and cork-pulling comprised the Jackson's Mill menu for the remainder of the day and evening. Late into the night, Warren pulled Tom aside. Tom's current officer in command had an assignment. They would go to Parkersburg and see Uncle Alfred and Laura. Of course, Tom could but obey his superior.

And he reveled in the reunion. Yet, bright-eyed, pig-tailed Laura seemed even more thrilled to see him than he was her. While Warren sipped tea spiced with a mint leaf on the porch with the adults, Tom and Laura rushed through a field and along a wooded path to a beautiful green patch of clover. Her mouth was not able to move fast enough to tell him of all that was new. Of how nice her aunt and uncle had been, the new friends she had made, the bully Bobby Joe Tolliver down the road who would one day get his due, the sweet boy Jimmy McGuire over by the ford who brought her lilies of the valley. But, of course, none of the boys were as cute, smart, or strong as Tom.

The days passed. For Tom, it was a time of magic and renewal. Of barbecues, fiddle-playing, a house-raising, working with the animals, squirrel hunting with Warren, and more walks and talks with Laura. Memories of death and separation faded from the boy's thoughts.

Tom spent much of his time higher up the mountain from his uncle's cabin, with Alfred's newfangled contraption. It was an amazing glass device that magnified distant objects and brought them into visual focus. Tom had heard of such, but never seen one. The piece allowed him to draw even closer to the raw untamed world that was beginning to feel as though it were a part of his very own soul. For Tom felt better in his wild mountains, in spirit and in body. Even his various afflictions seemed to improve while there.

Just before dusk each evening, Tom sat and drank in the mountain mosaic opposite a steep valley from him. Bathed by warm autumnal sunlight, the scene offered him a breathtaking rainbow vista of every imaginable color—red, green, blue, yellow, orange, gold, brown, purple. And the boy never failed to note the presence of potentially strategic mountain passes, trails, and roads. For these would be critical if armies had to be moved through the area.

During one such communing with nature, Warren broke into Tom's world to impart his latest revelation—a crinkled, faded sheet of printed paper that announced: "Fortunes available for those men willing to work for them!"

Steamboats that traveled the Ohio River were paying men up to a dollar a day for cutting wood. The men lived on one of the river islands downstream and sold the cut wood to passing boats. The boat merchants bought all they could get.

Warren's gray eyes flickered. "Tommy," he breathed, his handsome, high-cheekboned face flushing and iron strengthening his voice. "You know what this means? Our chance to set up with a stake. The kind so's we won't never have to shuffle around to find folks to work for or help us again."

The kind to restore the name.

"Why, we'll start our own mill," Warren continued, "or no, we'll head out West and start up our own store on one of the rivers. Maybe we'll start a school, too—or two or ten. With me teaching and you keeping the books and doing the all around work the way you do for Uncle Cummins, it'd be a sure thing. We'll romance 'em, every one!"

Romance 'em, yes. Toothsome, fair-haired Warren could romance 'em, all right. As he had little brother Tommy so often. *The Ohio River—heck, the Pacific Ocean with Warren!—mills, schools, or fighting Cherokees. Anything with Warren.*

The news saddened Laura, but did not surprise her.

"But who will be going with you?" came her concerned response as Tom, with exaggerated ease and confidence, skipped rocks across the sparkling little pond that abutted the clover patch.

He turned to her as if slapped.

"*With* us? Why, nobody, little sister. Why should anyone come with us?"

"But isn't the Ohio big and dangerous?"

"Naw," he scoffed, leisurely skipping another rock, "not for Warren and me." Then he turned back and wrapped an arm around her shoulders and said, in a fatherly way, "You've got to understand, Laura; Warren and I have grown up. We're men now. I can ride, shoot, work—I could make it on my own if I had to. So," he shrugged, "it's time for me to break out, on my own. Only little girls and babies should stay around the homestead."

"Which is Uncle Cummins, a little girl or a baby?" Just a glimmer of mischief twinkled in Laura's eyes.

Tom turned crimson. "Well, older fellows can come back—after they've proven themselves out on their own, of course."

"Oh, I see," Laura replied, eyelashes fluttering. "So will you bring something back for me?"

"Why, sure." Tom sensed he was off the hook now, and was very glad to be. "What would you like?"

"Oh, anything, Tommy, anything at all."

"Consider it done. I'll bring you back the nicest item that I see."

"Oh, Tommy, you're wonderful." She leapt to hug him and kissed him on the cheek. Tom blushed again.

"Hey, Tommy—come on back," Warren called from near the house. "It's gingerbread cake!"

Tom's eyes widened. "Whoa, you didn't tell me there was gingerbread cake, Laura."

"It was a surprise," she giggled, "and I helped make it."

"Well, let's go, little sister."

And off he went, Laura trilling behind him. She was happy for both her brothers. For Warren, because she knew that was the way he was. And for Tom, because he would be serving with his commander. Yet just then, a strange feeling passed over her. It stayed only an instant before leaving, but it impressed her young heart that things would not again be quite as wonderful as they had been the past fleeting days.

As the statuesque mountains dividing that hilly western region of the Old Dominion from the larger remaining area of the state loomed in the distance, the beckoning call of Warren's voice rolled across the field again. "Come on, Tommy!"

CHAPTER 3

"LOOKS LIKE SOMETHING COMING UP," TOM SAID, SQUINTING into the golden late afternoon sun. From their perch on the upper deck of the steamboat *Chesapeake,* he and Warren could see a chunk of land bulging out into the river several hundred yards ahead. Even from that distance, gliding easily along in the center of the Ohio, they could tell it was a beehive of activity.

"Sure as shootin'," Warren nodded, grabbing his haversack. "Let's tell the captain this is where we get off."

Like other such outposts, Hamilton's Point did not prove to offer the fortunes promised on Warren's fading notice. As the boys disembarked and walked the hard dirt paths that passed for thoroughfares, Tom saw numerous frontier peddlers, a respectable merchant or two, an occasional family of settlers, and a scruffy mélange of speculators, adventurers, and swindlers. Of course, the youngster did not recognize these latter men as members of those particular persuasions, nor that many of them also followed the siren call of "Fortunes available for those men willing to work for them." He did quickly note, though, that no one seemed to have much use for him or Warren. Most of the passing steamboats either had their own crews cutting wood for them or were well stocked with kindling at their point of origin. This posed no obstacle for Warren, however. The boys would follow the rumors—and the fortunes—west to the mighty Mississippi.

"That's better anyway, Tommy," the older brother said, hope springing anew after the disappointments of the Ohio. "It'll mean more virgin territory no one else has covered."

"Sure," Tom smiled, "but isn't the Mississippi pretty far west?"

"Nah," Warren said with a nonchalant wave of his hand. Then he laughed. "Not much farther than we already come, anyhows. Why, the Ohio runs right into the Mississippi just yonder up the road a piece."

It still seemed to Tom a long time since they had left Cincinnati, though.

The torn, crumpled sheet the younger boy kept tucked in his pocket appeared yellower and grimier each time he pulled it out to look at it. As the days passed on the river, Tom frequently noticed a tattered line printed near the bottom of the sheet. It read: "Only the strong of heart and brave of soul should apply." Tom wondered almost every day if he fit those requirements. Looking back on the years of his young life, and the many fears and doubts attending them, as well as the mean thoughts he had held toward Uncle Brake and others—including God sometimes, though he would never tell that to anyone and, in fact, often apologized to God for it—he concluded he did not. Plus, he had certainly been frightened a number of times on this very trip, and for no good reason he could think of.

At least Warren was with him. Warren was surely strong of heart and brave of soul. If he could become more like Warren, he knew everything would work out in his life, and he might even be able to accomplish some fine feats and make Mama proud of him. He sometimes still wished he could see Mama, if just for a moment, though he never admitted this thought to Warren or anyone else. If he *could* see her, he would want her to give him a long, good hug like she used to give him. Although his memory of Mama was fading, he still remembered her hugs and how they melted his fears and hurts. It had been a long time since anybody had hugged him. The only exception he could remember since Mama was Granny Nancy, but even that was not the same. How much he missed Mama.

When the boys reached the Mississippi, the steamboats became rickety old barges and the rustic river towns, destitute hovels. The women disappeared and the men were more menacing.

Several days and a few hundred miles later, the Jacksons' current craft—old, weather-beaten, and waterworn—pulled into a landing known as Cherokee Strip. By now, cold, wetness, hunger, fatigue, and a state of near poverty had the boys immensely ready to secure information about the whereabouts of fortunes.

Within a few steps of disembarking, Warren and Tom recognized Cherokee Strip, to their dismay, as a smaller, rougher, seedier version of Hamilton's Point. The first man they saw sat atop an empty wooden barrel, whittling a piece of wood. The boys looked at one another, speaking in that silent pithy language of brothers who have traveled some of life's most important moments together.

Should we?

Got to start somewheres.

Let's go.

As they approached the man, he arced a potent amber charge of tobacco-laden spittle onto the muddy ground in front of the Jacksons. The brothers paused, shot each other a glance, then moved more slowly toward the grizzled, mud-caked whittler.

"Friend, could you direct us to where we might could find work cutting wood for the riverboats?" Warren asked. It seemed to Tom his brother's voice sounded a note or two higher than normal.

The whittler looked askance at the weary boys, then answered Warren's question by planting an amber missile onto the young man's dirty left boot. The brothers looked at one another again, then back at the man—his whittling, briefly interrupted, now resumed with aplomb.

"What was that you boys wanted to know about cutting wood?"

Warren and Tom whirled around to find a towering man possessed of a massive, gnarled mountain of red beard, glowering over them. Tom gasped at the sight of the giant's left arm, or what should have been his arm. It ended at the elbow. The right arm was more foreboding. It ended at the point of a huge, martial-appearing bowie knife.

The dumbstruck brothers looked away from the hulking red frontiersman as if ducking from a powerful blinding light. In unison, they backed slowly off as the huge man advanced menacingly toward them.

"Children oughtn't be this far west nohows," the hulk growled as he plodded ahead.

Ashen-faced and near shock, Warren and Tom continued their terrified, halting retreat. Just as they turned to break into a run, a thunderous "Boo!" boomed into their ears. Stunned, they half-turned and saw the grizzled whittler standing maybe two feet away.

The brothers broke into a frantic full run toward the heart (such as it was) of Cherokee Strip. Had their paralyzed vocal chords been capable, they would have been screaming as they ran. Their ears still aching from the whittler's withering yell, the sound of roaring laughter registered somewhere in the backs of their frazzled minds. It seemed to drift from the direction of the spot they had hastily left.

The fleeting thought struck Tom that some type of warm liquid was trickling down the back of his neck.

"Gentlemen! Gentlemen!"

Warren and Tom turned in midstride and saw a darkly handsome, clean-shaven man of about thirty-five calling them. His fresh, smooth buckskin coat and appearance contrasted sharply with the unkempt, shambling visages the boys had frequently witnessed on their Mississippi barge and at Cherokee Strip.

Pierre Lafayette "Lafe" Gremillion approached the panting brothers. Even on this dull winter day, his uncovered jet-black hair gleamed, and merry blue eyes and a wide ivory smile illumined his broad olive face. A polished corncob pipe protruded jauntily from his smile; it was the *pièce de résistance* for this intriguing character.

"Gentlemen, what happened back there?" Gremillion asked with concern in a rich, but fully American, brogue.

Warren and Tom looked at one another, then at the ground. Still shaking, at least on the inside, they were not sure what happened, much less what to say.

"Well, a fellow pulled a big, double-edged knife on us, biggest I ever saw," Warren mumbled sheepishly.

Gremillion shook his head and shot a look of disgust back toward the boys' antagonists.

"Scurrilous river vermin," the man groused.

Then the appealing face turned back to Warren and Tom and brightened. A strong hand reached toward the boys. "Lafe Gremillion." He spoke the surname with the silent-*I*, silent-*L*, two-syllable French pronunciation, emphasis on the latter syllable: Grim*yon*.

"May I treat you to some supper?"

Warren and Tom jumped at his invitation. Accompanying him to a nearby kitchen, the boys sat down to a feast of venison stew, sweetbread, and red beans. As they ate, Warren explained why they were heading westward. A knowing look joined Gremillion's chuckle.

"The west is yet a rough and untamed land," he said, smiling. "Boys like you can be easy prey."

Gremillion wiped his mouth and pushed his three-quarters empty plate aside. "But I have good news, boys. I am headed for an island ten miles farther down the river where fortunes are indeed available for those men willing to work for them."

The boys could scarcely believe their ears. In the weeks they had been traveling, they had gotten only colder, dirtier, broker, and hungrier. They had not so much as sunk an axe into wood.

"B-but," Warren stammered, "how do you know?"

"Why, I've only just come from there for supplies, of course! Now you boys look a little weather-beaten, but from sturdy stock, nonetheless." He paused for a moment to fire up his corncob pipe.

"I'll pay you boys twenty-five cents a day to come cut wood for me." Warren winked at Tom. "That's every day, so you will see it add up. As you get better, I might raise it some—maybe. And when you're finished and ready to move on, I'll let you take one trunk apiece with you of your own making."

Sporting their broadest grins since the trip began, Warren and Tom shook Gremillion's hand and thanked him for the opportunity— and their twenty-five cents apiece advance—as he left in haste to attend to other business.

"I told you, Tommy," Warren said as the brothers bedded down that night in a large room, stodgy with the aroma of smoke and whiskey. Against the wheezes, rasps, and snores of thirty or so men crowded onto the dirt floor of Cherokee Strip's best "boarding house," the elder Jackson smiled at something Tom could not see. When he spoke, his words conveyed a sense of awe and magic, as though he had stumbled upon a shining revelation, suspected but heretofore hidden. "Don't ever let anybody tell you that fortunes aren't available for the taking out West."

Tom reveled in the moment and in being with Warren. *How strange this life is,* he marveled. *Just when you think things are a certain way, they turn around on you. That can be good, but . . . what is there for a man to lean on when he needs more than what he has?*

"Do you really believe there's heaven after this world, Warren?"

"For the Christian, not for the infidel."

Tom watched his older brother pull his weather-beaten hat down over his eyes as he stretched out on the hard dirt. As usual, the boys used their bedrolls as pillows.

So sure he is. It never takes him more than a minute to fall asleep, no matter how bad the day has been or how uncertain the next one is. Tom knew that for a fact because he often watched, then sometimes took hours to go to sleep himself, so active and questioning was his own mind.

Fear rarely clutched Warren. And when it did he seemed to possess an audacious boldness even in the midst of it. Tom sometimes possessed the same, but he always knew bad things could happen without any notice or warning, bad things that could irrevocably change the world, no matter what anyone said or did in an attempt to change it back. Still, he didn't think about that as much as he used to. Warren and Granny Nancy had both helped him learn to face the future without fear because God had his whole life planned, and nothing would happen unless God intended or permitted it for good. Granny Nancy's favorite verse in the Good Book was Romans 8:28: *"And we know that all things work together for good to them that love God, to them who are the called according to his purpose."* That was what she always said in response to something she did not understand.

"So you think we'll all be together up in heaven someday, Warren—Mama and the rest of us?"

From behind his hat, Warren answered, "I'll be the first one to shake your hand and welcome you aboard, little brother."

Tom smiled and laid his dirty head atop his bedroll, then pulled his grimy hat over his face. *No one knew things the way Warren did.*

Lafe Gremillion seemed in the process of making a fortune with a vigorous woodcutting operation spanning a chain of small river islands ten miles south of Cherokee Strip. The January, Deep South climate proved mild, and Warren and Tom rejoiced in finally getting their stiff muscles working toward the prize they had long desired. With barely an interruption, they worked from sunup to sundown. Fortunately, pesky mosquitoes and other insects endemic to the region were in short supply due to brief, intermittent blasts of frigid air.

The work was exciting and vigorous, but it demanded a degree of bodily commitment the boys had never experienced, even in their rugged mountain upbringing. Searing pain stabbed at their every muscle. Some days—even as they cut and carried wood and even as men around them cursed and blasphemed and sometimes quit—Tom and Warren spat desperate, pithy prayers to God for the strength just to survive until the next break. Then, after those few precious moments of water and rest, involuntary groans escaped from the boys' lips as they struggled to their feet to face the work again.

But the resilience of arduous young bodies stands as one of God's wonders. Tom began to realize that as long as he was allowed occasional brief rests, his body could handle far more than he thought it could. And the result was a staggering amount of completed work. Not only that, but his performance would continue to improve beyond what he would have thought possible. And he noticed the various irritating ailments that plagued him during the normal times of less robust physical exertion would vanish.

Within a few days, despite the humidity and frequent runs of disease in the filthy camps, Warren's and Tom's sinewy physiques were already growing harder. And the relentless work ethic and hearty frontier constitutions of the strapping young Virginians caught the shrewd, learned eye of Gremillion. After a couple of weeks, he upped their wages to thirty cents per day. A few days later he named Warren supervisor over a log-cutting crew, which meant reporting directly to the camp foreman.

Despite the demanding work, the sturdy breed of Americans sweating for their fortunes on those remote Mississippi River islands were not the sort to curl up and sleep through the evening. No, the pleasures and benefits accruing from attaining one's riches did not need to be totally delayed when cards, whiskey, music, and tall tales were readily available.

As Warren and Tom washed up in the river after one vigorous workday, they saw a couple of the more adventuresome men in the camp preparing to squeeze in a logroll before the sun found its early winter way behind the horizon.

"Come on, Jacksons," a man on their crew hollered as he rushed past. "Them two big boats just left loaded with all the wood we cut so far, and someone will be back tomorrow with our first month's pay, so it's time for a hoedown!"

"Funny," Warren remarked to Tom as he wiped the water from his face and head, then combed back his thick dark hair, "I always thought you celebrated on the day you got paid, not the day before."

"So how much will we be getting, Warren?" Tom asked, bright-eyed.

"Well, I reckon we worked four full weeks, to the day. Two weeks of that, we got paid twenty-five cents a day apiece, and two weeks—"

"Hey Warren, come on, we been challenged!"

The brothers looked around to see Paul Cornell, an affable fellow Virginian shouting from the bank near the logroll where one man had just tumbled into the water.

Warren and the twenty-year-old Cornell had become card and wrestling partners, and now they intended to broaden their success to the logrolling competitions that rarely saw either of the competing two-man teams stay atop their wood for more than a few seconds.

The elder Jackson's steel gray eyes narrowed a fraction as he spotted the competition—the DeLozier brothers, a spunky pair of Cajuns from New Orleans. Davy and Danny DeLozier were short on build, long on élan, and powered most of the time by Louisiana Lightning rotgut. With the DeLoziers involved, whether the game be logrolling or tiddlywinks, excitement, if not trouble, could usually be expected.

"Maybe you can win some more money, Warren," Tom said.

The older brother shook his head. "Don't think so. Hardly any left in camp. Everyone's been paying it to Gremillion to buy food and supplies."

"How much do we have left?"

"Well, let's just say payday won't be coming any too soon, little brother," Warren smiled, tousling the fifteen-year-old's unruly shock of brown hair.

A boisterous throng of rugged, unshaved, and mostly unwashed men awaited Warren and Tom when they reached the logrolling area. Many of the men gulped whiskey from jars or jugs.

"The DeLoziers say they'll wager two dollars to one if we'll bet hard cash money and let them bet on credit against their tomorrow's wages," Cornell explained to Warren. "That's what most of the other men are doing."

Warren bit his lower lip and glanced around. The crowd was growing larger and rowdier as the light of day faded. A couple of campfires already popped and crackled. *This will be quite a night for the boys,* the Virginian mused.

"Where's Lafe Gremillion?" he asked Cornell.

"He left on one of the boats. Told everyone to yuck it up tonight because we won't have to start work again till he gets back midafternoon tomorrow. Then he's bringing back more free whiskey for everyone along with our wages."

Warren scanned the scene again. A fistfight broke out between an Irish Catholic and a Scottish Presbyterian, neither of whom took literally the scriptural admonitions against drunkenness and pugnacity. *Queer for a hard driver like Gremillion to leave camp, especially queer on a night like this. Queer to give us most of a day off. It's all queer. Be a good night to sack a ways out from camp.*

Warren now searched for Gremillion's camp ramrod, Rob Kubion.

"He went with Gremillion," Cornell said.

A jug crashed against a nearby rock.

Warren, half-smiling, shook his head at the folderol.

"You boys gonna have tea, or you gonna give us a chance to take your money?" Danny DeLozier chided, his high voice dripping with Cajun inflection.

"Yeah, start the match!" shouted another voice from the increasingly restive crowd.

"We'll take you all on, but I won't be a party to betting on credit," Warren said firmly.

"Aw, come on kid, everybody else is doing it!"

"Yeah, what's the matter, afraid your mama's gonna spank your bottom!"

Tom winced at that.

Davy DeLozier strutted like a peacock up to Warren. Barrel-chested and several years older, he still gave away four or five inches to the six-foot Virginian. The raucous crowd hushed. DeLozier stood so close to Warren, the latter could feel the sting of the Cajun's whiskey-soaked breath permeating his nostrils.

"Now you listen to me, you pretty, prissy urchin," DeLozier growled, "you put up that bet in hard American dollars or I'll take it offen you, and a hunk of bark out of your hide too."

Before Warren could respond, Tom barreled headlong into the startled DeLozier, taking him straight to the ground. The Cajun's pained moan and the thud of his body connecting with the mushy brown earth sounded in unison. Tom slugged away at the man's head and face with every ounce of strength in his being, his mouth silent but his blue eyes afire like hot anthracite.

Danny DeLozier grabbed a fistful of Tom's hair to pull him off Davy, but Warren tackled Danny and rolled over the spongy turf with him. The wave of men surrounding them broke into frenzied cheers and shouted bets—against the next day's wages—for the opposing teams of battling brothers.

As the brawl began to spread, Tom—still wailing away on top of Davy, who in a semi-drunken stupor merely tried to protect his face from the furious pounding—felt himself lifted straight up off his foe, then pitched through the air and into the river.

This drew a wild round of cheers from the euphoric crowd.

Tom came up sputtering and saw "Big Swede" Carlssen, a normally genial, blond mountain of a man, lift Davy DeLozier up by his collar and shake him.

"If you're a-gonna have a contest, then have the contest, but no bullying." With this, he shook DeLozier like a limp washrag. "And no forcing a man to bet, iffen he's not a-wanting to do so. Understand?"

"Y-yes, s-sir," DeLozier stammered.

Carlssen dropped Davy, then turned toward Warren and Danny, locked in a stalemate on the ground. The Nordic bull grabbed the neck of one combatant in each hand and jerked them both to their feet. Both were bruised, bloodied, and livid with anger.

"Now see here," the Swede barked, "we're a-gonna have a logroll now, fair and square, understand? Now, I want you boys to shake hands and start the match."

Warren and Danny glared at Carlssen, then at one another. The Swede tightened his grip on each neck, bringing reluctant handshakes from both combatants.

"Now," Carlssen smiled, gently releasing Warren and Danny, and glancing at the cowed crowd, "no more bets, please. Begin the match."

The whole camp roared. This was proving a far better show than any of them could have foreseen.

The teeming mass of men followed Warren as he started for the water. Then, a slashing pain shot through his leg from waist to toes. *My knee*, he grimaced.

"You get a gimp in that fracas?" Cornell asked.

"Blast, I think I wrenched it," Warren frowned, touching his knee tenderly.

"Can you go?"

Warren tried to walk, then sank dejectedly to the ground on his bottom. "I don't think so."

As a slip of muted sunlight peeked out of the low, heavy western horizon and the lumberjacks called for Warren to get up, he watched Tom clamber out of the water, soaked, winded, and coughing hoarsely. The DeLoziers slogged past the younger Jackson and into the water, laughing and cursing and forgetting their wounds. Then one of them elbowed Tom hard in the ribs and swore at him to get out of the way. Warren's steely eyes flashed and the solid square jaw firmed like flint. "Wrap it, Paul."

"Huh?"

"I said wrap it," Warren repeated, looking Cornell straight in the eye. "Tight."

"Hey, let's just forget it, Warren," Cornell shrugged. "If your knee's hurt, you can't work, and if you can't work, Gremillion will have you out of here on the next boat and someone else in your place, supervisor or not. And Tom too. Don't risk it."

Warren stared at him for a moment, then back at the dripping, shivering Tom, who hacked phlegm onto the ground as he approached.

"Sorry, Warren," Tom said, bowing his head in shame, "I sure fixed that one for you good."

"Come on, pretty boy!" Davy DeLozier yelled from the water, where he and Danny cockily handled the log they had chosen to use in the competition.

Warren placed his hand gently on Tom's shoulder. "Never apologize for defending a friend who's being attacked, Tommy. Mama and Pa would have been proud of you. And the Lord would not be displeased."

Tom looked up, eyes alight and his entire countenance transformed. *Warren*, he thought, *my captain!*

"Now, Tommy, will you wrap this here knee for me so I can put those DeLoziers in their place?"

"Sure, Warren!"

This befuddled Cornell. "You Jacksons amaze me. Come all the way from Virginia, through wind and cold and rain, nearly get yourselves killed, or at least maimed a couple of times, and now you're willing to risk it all on a silly logroll. I just can't figure it." He shook his head as the shoving, screaming crowd pressed around him, then smiled at Warren. "I don't understand it, but I like it—let's go teach those Cajun lizards a lesson."

The DeLoziers needed no prodding. Eager and seemingly sobered, they barely restrained themselves from lunging into Warren and Cornell as the latter pair strode into the waist-deep water.

"Pretty boy and his Virginia friend," Danny sneered. "We'll whip you a couple of different ways before the night's out."

Warren, who felt a strange shudder run through him that felt at once hot and cold and nearly caused him to swoon, ignored DeLozier, then flinched at the loud crack of a gun shot sounding over the noisy camp.

"He's lit out! Gremillion's lit plum out!" shouted "Gentleman Jim" Chandler, a Tennessean who was a poor attorney, a good bareknuckled boxer, and one of the few professional men in the camp.

A shocked hush gripped the entire camp.

Chandler, breathing heavily, shouted so all could hear. "I thought I recognized the skunk from a work crew back on the Ohio in '34. He worked us to the nub, then left us with two days' worth of rotgut while he departed with the cut timber. At wage-paying time a couple of days later, instead of receiving our several weeks' pay, we possessed only king-sized hangovers. Well, I just couldn't remember him for sure until now." (Quantities of mash whiskey in excess of one gallon per day for long periods of time have a tendency to cloud the memory of even the most astute mind.)

"What are you saying, dandy?" a rough voice shouted.

"I'm saying I followed Gremillion back to Cherokee Strip and watched him get paid for the wood we cut, then head upriver with that Kubion on a steamer. When I tried to stop them, someone gave me this knot on my bean from behind. I guess the lowlife charlatan has at least two friends, though I find that difficult to fathom."

The throng of dirty, drunken men assembled around Chandler comprehended little except that the Frenchman had evidently left with the wood they had cut and the money they had earned.

Tom heard only a hawk calling in the distance and the water lapping around him. *Whew! This water is freezing!* he noticed for the first time.

What followed still confused the boy years later when he would briefly think on it. One mighty, guttural roar rose up from the bowels of the enraged group. Tom felt the ground beneath him, though buffered by three feet of Mississippi River, shake more than he felt the pain in his ears. Then an unearthly scene unfolded which he would often remember. Men began to scream, curse, drink, fight, smash things, leap into the river, run into the woods nearby, fall and beat upon the ground, weep, and in some cases jump up and down where they stood, bawling like babies. It was a display of fierce, unharnessed energy unlike any Tom had ever seen or imagined.

Those men are dangerous now, he thought. *How fearsome they should be if their efforts were coordinated.* He suspected other large groups of crazed, potentially murderous men had similarly failed to direct their efforts with wisdom and shrewdness toward curtailing Mr. Pierre Lafayette "Lafe" Gremillion. Had they done so, he would not now be headed back up the mighty Mississippi much richer and with more jokes to tell his laughing confederates about the ignorant unwashed rabble left drunk and broke and lawless down on a cold, muddy, and now dark Louisiana riverbank.

As the mob spun into a hundred swirling, flailing knots, and one or two larger waves bowled over those before them, Tom thought, *What could I do with such men and energy who were disciplined and organized!*

A piercing scream nearby broke his train of thought. He turned to see cursing, sputtering Davy DeLozier scrapping to get his head above water, while a furious Danny, his hands wrenched around his brother's neck, did his best to hold it under.

And ole Lafe? Well, more than one river cut through the burgeoning frontier, and a slick, handsome Frenchman and his corncob pipe could take lots of time moving to the next. In fact, a trip to Europe could usually be worked in between projects, while things cooled down a bit.

Warren and Tom returned to Virginia in early spring. Tom had reacquired his various infirmities, along with a beautiful wooden trunk he himself had made for Laura. Warren toted a handsome collection of Indian beads and jewelry and a case of malaria, though that was not yet apparent. The boys were closer to one another than they had ever been.

Tom would often think back to the months he spent going down the Ohio and the mighty Mississippi, cutting wood with handsome, fair-haired Warren. But they made no fortunes, and the malaria would take Warren before his twentieth birthday.

CHAPTER 4

TOM GAVE HIMSELF THE MIDDLE NAME JONATHAN, IN HONOR of his father, when he arrived at West Point in the summer of 1842. His parents had given him no middle name. Now that he was set on a course of restoring the family honor of which his father was a part, Tom felt it right and proper to attach his sire's memory to that quest, since Jonathan Jackson had contributed all he could to it. Jonathan's failures were to be pitied, not derided. Therefore, Tom would carry his father's name forward with his own.

The efforts of two other Jonathans loomed larger in Tom's admission to the United States Military Academy, however. Those and the decision of another young western Virginian, the original academy congressional selection from Tom's district. That man, after spending several weeks at the institution in the late summer and early fall, decided its rigors were not for him and departed back to the Old Dominion.

At that point, a pair of talented young Virginia attorneys swung into action on Tom's behalf. Jonathan Bennett, a family friend of the Jacksons and Neales, and John Carlisle, a distant cousin of Tom's, asserted their budding influence in the political realm on their young friend's behalf. The fact that both these rising stars, in their midtwenties, proved such strong advocates for Tom strengthened his resolve that West Point was the correct course for him to take. Western Virginia congressman Samuel Hays recommended Tom for the appointment due largely to his respect for the work and word of Bennett and Carlisle.

It would not be the last time the winsome Bennett and the sturdy Carlisle would serve as Tom's emissaries.

The ascendency of the Jackson family name was not what impressed the small gathering of plebes that eyed the western Virginia mountaineer the first time he clomped through the doorway to the south barracks of the United States Military Academy. What a sight to behold for erudite young men such as George McClellan, George Pickett, Jesse Reno, and Dabney Maury, the latter three of them Virginians. Plain homespun clothing, massive brogans, a ridiculous wagoner's hat, and grimy saddlebags, slung over his shoulder—such fare did not grace their rarefied haunts.

Nor did it grab the fancy of Ambrose Powell Hill, who was of Culpeper County, but who coveted the Virginia society of Richmond and the Tidewater. To A. P. Hill, Jackson represented precisely that Virginian from which he wished to move as far away as possible, as quickly as possible. Jackson was not of the Virginia to which Hill aspired. *Stay away and don't get painted with the same brush as that buffoon,* Hill thought to himself as he and his unaffected young mates snickered at the passing hayseed.

"Here comes your fellow Virginian, Hill," the brilliant, diminutive, fifteen-year-old McClellan cackled.

No! Immediately connected with that fool, Hill thought, wincing. *Just what I don't wish. Must move away, stay away, brush his kind away like lice.*

"Don't blush, Hill," McClellan smiled. "If that unfortunate bumpkin lasts through the semester it will be a feat to rival any in the storied history of our beloved institution."

Tom strode, head down, past the group, which was now laughing out loud. His only salutation was a slight nod. After he passed, Pickett gave the group a slight nod of his own, then bowed out his legs, gave another nod, stooped over, nodded again, and marched a couple of mimicking steps after Tom, nodding—slightly—all the while. He grabbed a sack from the somber Hill and slung it over his shoulder.

"Why, I got all my earthly belongings in here, Hill," Pickett winked. "Just brung 'em up from the farm, don't you know!"

Several in the growing cluster of cadets began imitating Pickett. The whole area soon looked and sounded like a flock of clucking, quacking geese (for that was Tom's assigned persona), with necks stretched, heads nodding—slightly—and everyone grasping for something to pitch over their shoulders.

"What's going on over there?" a barrel-chested upper-class Ohioan inquired of a passing comrade as he stared from the other end of the hall at the animated commotion.

"I think they're welcoming that new fellow, Jackson, who just came in from the mountains out in western Virginia," came the reply. "He's supposedly quite the oaf."

The Ohioan's eyes narrowed. "They had best be circumspect. An oaf who has made it to this place—and two months late at that—from the mountains of western Virginia may be heard from."

The other man nodded. As he walked off, though, he thought to himself, *Ulysses "Sam" Grant is a good man, but he takes the oddest views on some things.*

"I got me some books in these here bags," Reno laughed with a thick backwoods inflection as the mockery continued, "but I don't know how to read 'em."

"I got me some lard in mine," McClellan retorted.

"Me, I ain't got nothin' in mine," Pickett said with a straight—nodding—face. "They's jest fer show."

"I don't know, Mac," Maury said, slowing to a flapping squat, a smile still painted on his face. "That fellow looks as though he intends to stay."

"Pickett, I will grant you," McClellan said, "that I have never seen a man with such big feet move so fast!"

At this, the entire group exploded into raucous, hooting laughter. All except for Virginian A. P. Hill. He was not laughing at all, and he stood quite still.

Tom knew he would not be the most prepared of cadets entering West Point with the class of 1846. He started a third of a semester behind everyone else and missed out on the rigorous summer training program on the plains outside the campus—and the introductions and bonding that accompanied it—as well as the first several weeks of the academic semester.

The real problem, however, lay in the spartan academic background the young Virginian brought with him to the institution. The fascinating thing was, despite his patchwork education, he had taught other youngsters for nine months in a one-room western Virginia schoolhouse. None of this came close to preparing him for what lay in store his first year at West Point.

While McClellan breezed to good grades and a satisfying, if demanding, freshman experience, Pickett breezed to bad marks, and Hill breezed to middling ones—and, initially at least, poor conduct—Tom Jackson fought for his academic life, in the classroom and out.

And the other cadets knew it. Some felt for him; others did not care; and a few made sport of the lanky, taciturn youngster whose awkward and abrasive unsociability masked shyness and complete social ignorance.

The latter group of cadets found daily entertainment in watching Tom's classroom performance. His inept, though dogged, attempts at the chalkboard became proverbial around the campus, and word of them spread beyond the plains of the Hudson.

With autumn chill washing the trees into a cornucopia of brilliant hues, Tom stood before his mates yet again one bright day, his uniform covered in chalk dust and his face beaded with hot perspiration.

George McClellan, now sixteen and seated near the front of the class, did not dislike the earnest, guileless Jackson. He just had difficulty comprehending how so ungainly and ill-prepared a hillbilly could qualify for the academy, or would even wish to subject himself to such continual humiliation.

Dislike was perhaps not the best word to describe the feelings of A. P. Hill, seated in the middle of the room, toward Jackson, either. Disdain and disregard would both have been preferable. Hill did despise the obsessive way in which Jackson seemed to conduct all his affairs, whether academic, martial, or personal. *Of course*, Hill thought to himself, *were I as lacking as he, I might act in a like desperate manner.*

"Psst . . . Reno," McClellan whispered across the aisle.

Reno, his eyes glazed over, turned to see McClellan grin toward Jackson.

Up front, the Virginian's trembling hand pressed the chalk against the board with such force that snowy white flecks of it fluttered downward. He grimaced in pain for an answer that would not seem to come, as though trying to expunge a hideous evil from his constitution. Or a lost family name.

The instructor, seated at his desk, noticed a drop of Jackson's sweat pat against the hardwood floor. The man glanced at his timepiece. Titters skipped through the class. The instructor looked back toward Tom, who maintained his earnest comportment. Then, the solemn youth inadvertently screeched the chalk across the board. A couple of cadets laughed out loud. A. P. Hill was embarrassed for himself. The instructor was embarrassed for Tom.

The lights went out each night at 10:15 for all cadets except one. That young man, eyes tired and bloodshot, would sit bolt upright on the wood floor in his small dormitory room. Sometimes Tom Jackson would extend his left arm straight up in the air. He did this because, in addition to the rheumatism, digestive problems, and hearing and vision difficulties he felt had worsened since his matriculation to West Point, his mind had grown increasingly certain that one side of his body was *heavier* than the other. By launching an arm upward, he could temporarily direct the blood flow of his body to provide a corrective for at least this problem.

Tom's nightly cerebral ceremony in no way aided the vision difficulty, the dim light of a coal-burning heater providing the only illumination in the room. The youth knew this, but he believed much must sometimes be sacrificed to achieve a greater good.

One frigid black midwinter night the young Virginian sat in his customary spot on the chilled floor. Near him lay a sheet of paper with a few lines of handwriting. He picked it up and read.

20 January 1843

> My dearest little sister Laura, I trust this correspondence finds you well from your recurrent ills. I must confess that I am almost homesick, and expect to continue so until I can have a view of my native mountains. I intend to remain in the army no longer than I can get rid of it with honor, and commence some professional business at home.

Tom grimaced in pain and grabbed his stomach. He reached for a compact metal kit on a nearby shelf. He opened it and pulled out several small bottles of medicine, took a slug from each, sighed, and returned the bottles to the kit.

Across the room, his slumbering roommate bellowed out a booming, bull moose snore. Tom turned toward where the cadet lay on his mattress, on the floor. Then the weary youth gazed at his own, empty, sleeping spot. *A few minutes, just a few, and then I could go a couple of more hours.* He yawned and stretched.

Now the words came back to him, as they often did this time of night, when it seemed so cold, so dark, so—hopeless. When it seemed as though the glances and snickers and forced friendliness were all merited. When it seemed as though maybe he should be back at the mill, swapping lies and slugs of corn mash and passing the years good-for-nothing.

You may be whatever you resolve to be.

She was with him, always, leading him. She had tried. She knew the name needed a champion. And she somehow knew he would be the one to champion it. He would carry her honor forward with him; and when the name was restored, he would dedicate it to her enduring memory. For she had given him everything.

He finished near the bottom in nearly all his classes that first year. Young George McClellan finished first in most of them, and first overall. But those few who stayed close around Tom began to see something beyond a homespun hayseed. He was not fancy; he was not fun. But they saw roots and still waters that ran deep. They saw a comrade who, when he was able to come up for air from his woeful academic struggles long enough to breathe, possessed an amazing concern and tenderness for their needs, an almost feminine sense of nurturing. Nearly everyone who knew him came to respect and admire the rough-hewn mountaineer.

Pickett and Reno entered Tom's room one evening when he was out. They intended to play one of their frequent pranks on him. This particular occasion, they planned to replace his underwear with some especially frilly female undergarments procured from a certain women's institution a few miles up the Hudson River. The pranksters were caught up short upon seeing a Bible verse written on a faded sheet of paper next to Tom's chest of drawers. It read, *"Blessed be God, even the Father of our Lord Jesus Christ, the Father of mercies, and the God of all comfort; Who comforteth us in all our tribulation, that we may be able to comfort them which are in any trouble, by the comfort wherewith we ourselves are comforted of God."*

"Since when did Tom Hick Jackson go getting religious?" Reno asked in surprise. Tom attended prescribed services and chapels, but little else of a religious nature.

"I don't know. He did bring blankets, soup, and medicine to Stoneman when he was sick," Pickett said.

"No fooling? I thought Stoneman played Tom Hick for the fool."

"He did. Before he got sick."

The two pranksters left Tom's room, female undergarments still in hand.

The second year, "Tom Hick" finished thirtieth in his class. The third, twentieth. The fourth, seventeenth. George Pickett finished last that year. Last was superior, however, to the status of A. P. Hill, who had contracted a severe case of venereal disease during a summer sojourn in New York City two years before, nearly died, and was forced to graduate with the class of 1847.

"My heavens," Reno said to McClellan as they prepared to depart from the academy, "if we had had one more year, Mac, Jackson would have finished ahead of you."

That, and Providence, had gone and arranged a war down in Mexico just for Thomas Jonathan Jackson—the man and the name.

CHAPTER 5

WITH SEPTEMBER 14, 1847, DAWNED THE CLIMACTIC DAY OF the controversial Mexican-American War for possession of modern-day New Mexico, Arizona, Colorado, and California. Was America's invasion of its neighbor to the south rank imperialism or manifest destiny? Opinions varied. Many, including a young backwoods Illinois lawyer named Abraham Lincoln, thought the effort was a reproach to the virtuous name of the young republic. Others thought that the effort was as natural and as necessary as the turning of the earth.

In any event, the recently and hastily graduated cadets—McClellan, Pickett, Reno, and the rest—knew to a man that if it weren't for Tom's actions that steamy day at Chapultepec Park, the American advance on the City of Mexico would probably have become a retreat, and the capital may not have been taken at all. A. P. Hill, squirming through his final, delayed a year back at West Point, knew it too.

That fateful mid-September day found lumbering but handsome twenty-three-year-old Tom already possessed of a significant war record. He had been promoted from second to first lieutenant back in April, while serving under Captain Francis Taylor, for his solid performance in leading his battery of artillery in pursuit of retreating Mexicans at Vera Cruz.

For several months afterward, however, as the Americans pressed the war on toward the unspeakably beautiful emerald valley whose lakes and marshes led to its crowned jewel, the City of Mexico, Tom languished behind the lines. Commissary and ordnance responsibilities were good experience, perhaps, but the family name would not be rebuilt by such duty.

Then one day, word passed through the ranks regarding openings for two lieutenants to assist in the command of a newly established battery led by one Captain John Bankhead Magruder. Magruder had distinguished himself in the battle of Cerro Gordo, another fight in which Tom participated. The flamboyant artillery chief actually captured the four cannons that comprised his new battery. Supreme American commander Winfield Scott, a Virginian like Magruder, awarded them to him for his gallantry.

The lieutenant positions were still open by the time word reached Tom because Magruder, who aspired to fame as a stage actor and was a fearless commander, was also a quick-tempered martinet who held no attraction as a superior for most junior officers. Tom was not most junior officers, however. What he saw in John Magruder was a uniformed rendition of Cummins Jackson—and a ticket to glory. He hurtled his way forward to secure the post.

However, day after day passed and he heard nothing. Guarding the army's lines of communications far from the sound of the guns seemed a rueful waste of opportunity for action and accomplishment. Tom sensed the opportunities of a lifetime parading past him while he languished. His gloom increased. He began to attend the local Catholic church in Tepeyahualco, where he was stationed, for solace.

One muggy July day, the lonely soldier felt particularly blue when he entered the church. He also felt confused. It seemed such a waste to have all the ideas he had rattling around up in his head about putting his military education to use, honoring the Jackson name, and building a record upon which to found a career in arms. (He had decided for the latter, as against the law, after finally tasting the thrill and thunder of battle.) At the same time, he was spending a fair amount of time conversing with Captain Taylor, a devout Episcopalian who had been Tom's superior ever since they shipped south from the States.

"You have the makings of a fine officer, Tom," the warmhearted Taylor had told him. "You're disciplined and not averse to boldness if the occasion warrants. But let me prod you a bit about a different matter."

Taylor rubbed his jaw as he eyed Tom. "Religion is a personal thing, a weighty consideration that each man ought to study for himself," the older man said in his gentle Vermont way. "I would challenge you with this question, Tom." Taylor discerned the younger man's confusion as his own eyes narrowed. "Does not it demand your solemn thought and investigation, to see where such a profound matter fits into your life? For if what the Bible claims is true actually is, had not we each best be prepared to offer satisfactory account to our Maker for our activities during this short time on earth?"

Tom determined to pursue the matter. That meant investigating the church closest to him—the Catholic. And on that muggy July day, a glad feeling he had done so enveloped him. The service, though simple like the folks attending it, was sublime and reverent. As Tom gazed around at the poor, humble, war-torn people of the land, giving thanks on their knees for what they did have, a strange thought struck him. What if the personal God whom Captain Taylor had discussed with him those past many weeks did not rank fame and worldly success as highly as he had supposed? What if those things actually ranked quite low? *I need to learn more about this God. And I think it would probably please Mama as well.*

"I throw myself into the hands of an all-wise God," he wrote Laura that night, "and hope that it may yet be for the better. Prolonged garrison duty may have been one of His means of diminishing my excessive ambition; and after having accomplished His purpose, whatever it may be, He then in His infinite wisdom may gratify my desire."

Prolonged garrison duty had also given Tom the opportunity to spend many weeks with Captain Taylor and the curious insights into matters both temporal and heavenly that he offered.

The next day, Taylor brought the word: Tom had orders to report immediately to Magruder, if he could find him. The man was a lion in the field, all movement and action, and it would probably take some doing to find to him. Taylor shook Tom's hand.

"Selfishly, I hate losing you, Lieutenant," he smiled. "I need more like you, not less." Then he paused and said, "You keep thinking on what I said about the Lord. You wrestle with it, and you ask Him to show you the way He has for you."

And then Taylor was gone. For a moment Tom lamented his separation from the man. He had come to enjoy, perhaps even to need, their nightly visits. But then the full import of the news struck him. *Lieutenant aiding in the command of a semi-independent battery! Perhaps there was a plan to all of this after all.*

Taylor had warned Tom about the high "terrible pass" of La Hoya. Slicing across the top of a mountain leading toward Puebla, its steep cliffs and thick foliage had stood silent watch through the centuries over the demise of many a traveler, outlaw, and, more recently, American soldier. But Tom had to cross it to reach Magruder.

The day he and his twelve-man escort approached La Hoya, the sky hung down even closer than usual, a charcoal gray canopy bulging with a vast load that it longed to deposit on the steaming hills below. Tom and the other men welcomed that prospect, their navy blue uniforms already soaked through with sweat.

The first sign of trouble was a rock slide at the apex of the pass, originating from the sheer heights above. Tom and the other soldiers dodged the debris hurtling toward them, though one man's horse threw him into the thick brush nearby.

As thunder crashed and rain fell, the thrown trooper screamed in pain. Tom assumed the man had broken a rib or collarbone or separated a shoulder. Then he heard the sharp report of musket fire echoing off the steep walls of the pass. He gauged, correctly, the nearness of the fire. Next he saw the two troopers riding point, shouting and waving for him and the main body of the squad to ride toward them. More musket fire crackled, and one of the point men flew with a jerk from his horse.

Then, chaos. Screaming Mexicans charged from right and left, most of them on foot and most of them in their army's tan outfits. A few wore sombreros and looked like the bandidos that had pestered Tom's cousins in south Texas for years. From above, the dam broke and the rain fell as from huge, bursting balloons. The deluge drenched Tom. Worse, the storm obscured the sun, and the loud, frantic scene turned nearly pitch-black dark.

The artillery lieutenant had no time to worry, though, as the Mexicans were on them. To Tom's mind, it all moved faster than he could believe; but to his body, his actions and everyone else's lumbered in slow motion. The first he knew they had shot his horse was when he himself hit the rocky ground with a thud. He sprang up, gunfire cracking all around him. He saw one comrade ride down a Mexican on foot and lance him with his sabre. Suddenly, a Mexican officer on horseback came straight for Tom, his own sabre held high. Tom grabbed for his pistol. Gone! He turned and saw it on the ground near his horse. No time, the officer was on him. *Bang!* The nearness of the shot deafened Tom. The Mexican officer flew from his horse and landed dead at Tom's feet. Tom turned and saw another dripping, dehorsed Yank, his nose bloody, standing next to him. He had fired the shot.

Now Tom could not see more than a few feet in any direction, the downpour was so heavy. He heard thuds, grunts, an occasional shriek. He saw slashing movements of blue and brown, and an occasional yellow flash of gunfire, but most of the men on both sides had either fired their single-shot loads or had wet powder. Then, a quick yelp and somebody piled into Tom, knocking him back down to the now-sloppy ground.

He scrambled to his feet and saw that a Mexican had attacked one of the Americans, and both had flown into him. They rolled around in the mud, struggling for control of a long hunting knife. *My bowie knife!* Tom whipped it from his belt just in time to duck a wild swing from the rifle butt of a charging Mexican soldier. As the man turned to swing again, Tom raised the huge, double-edged blade high across his own body, then slashed it wickedly back across the Mexican's throat. The man collapsed to the turf like a limp rag.

Tom saw a Yank sitting up against a dead horse, his blood-covered hands holding a stomach that was torn open. A wounded Mexican crawled toward the tangled forest nearby. Then he could hear no sound but the rain, and it began to subside.

Just like that, it was all over. A couple of Yanks approached Tom. One had a deep gash across his left cheekbone. Cool, clean rain cleansed it for him.

"They lit out, sir," the other soldier said.

"We've got a few prisoners, Lieutenant," the wounded man said.

Tom had never felt more alert and in control of his faculties. He gazed around. *Several horses left—some of ours, some of theirs.* A couple of men downed in the mud uttered agonized moans. "Let's load our dead and wounded and move," he said. "These hills are thick with them."

As he helped wrap a comrade's gashed side, Tom felt more completely a man than he ever had. Keen sorrow filled him for those who had fallen, especially his countrymen who had actually given their lives to provide him safe transit to his new command. A humble feeling surged over him with this thought. But an odd sense, stronger than before, clutched him that perhaps he was just where he should be, that maybe this was more than a stage or a stepping-stone to the law or some other respected field. Could it be that command of men and arms was his destiny? No, too much to make of a brief, though desperate, skirmish. But he noticed the daunted countenances of several of the other Americans. One was weeping; another shook as he climbed aboard his horse. Tom had known no fear during or after the fight. And for the first time since he began garrison duty, his arms, his stomach, his eyes, and his ears did not bother him.

From the beginning of their relationship, Tom admired the high-spirited Magruder, and the latter saw in the younger man an officer with salt and savvy. A fierce mid-August fight at Contreras during the

Americans' approach into the City of Mexico, the invaded country's capital, cemented this bond.

The two forces pitched the Contreras battle at coordinates designated by the U.S. Army's one-man scouting, surveying, and engineering party—a bold, middle-aged captain from Virginia named Robert E. Lee. Grapeshot raked the American lines. After it cut down a fellow officer, Tom acceded to command of his own section of guns.

"By thunder," Magruder boomed to his superior, General Pillow, a few days later, "the boy was a rock. Anytime, anyplace, you'd turn and there he was, blasting away. Give me more like him!"

Some of Tom's subordinates, meanwhile, thought him just a bit off his rocker. The blazing blue incandescence that fired his eyes in the heat of battle incited ambivalent feelings in those men.

Tom learned more lessons—and felt physically better than he had since childhood—at other fights. He decided that the traditional, European-style frontal assault against strongly fortified positions would not be a part of his command repertoire. He saw too many good men thrown on the ash heap of that venerable institution.

Reconnaissance, surprise, boldness, and the flank attack, on the other hand, won battles and wars.

The castle of Chapultepec loomed awe-imposingly down on the Americans' final stretch run into the City of Mexico. More than a massive fort on top of the city's highest hill, it symbolized national pride and power. It housed the Mexican war college and the palatial halls of Montezuma, the ancient Aztec king. Chapultepec would be Mexico's final stand, and the marshes and lakes around it would flow red with the blood of both sides.

Tom, promoted again to brevet (temporary, in time of war) captain, cared not about any of this as he and his men and hundreds of American infantry lay pinned down in ditches on either side of a shell-and musket-swept road a few hundred yards below the fortress. The slight hot breeze pushed clouds of white, gray, and black gunsmoke around the field of battle. In one place a man could see; in another, patches of smoke swirled like blinding blankets of impending doom.

Bold, not reckless, Tom winced as a ricocheting bullet kicked up a spray of dirt into his face. Caught in the excitement of a few American troopers finally breaking into Chapultepec after the days-long siege, and seeing enemy reinforcements about to enter the citadel, Tom had rushed his section up this road to ward off the hostiles. Perhaps he had rushed them too quickly; withering Mexican gunfire now savaged his men and others who had rushed forward. The horses that had transported his battery lay dead in every direction. There seemed nothing to do but hug the earth and pray that no direct hits would avail themselves.

After several moments, Tom began to boil with anger. *Nobody is doing anything. Have we come so far to cower in these lowly ditches, waiting for a weaker adversary on the brink of annihilation to pick us off one by one?* He ventured a look around. Across the narrow road, another American soldier screamed and fell dead. Names were not to be restored and reputations made—nor wars won—by such shrinking and cringing.

Tom Jackson leapt from the ditch and marched into the road, defying fate and the martial force of a world-class power whose dignity and very survival had been shoved up against its own back wall. Bullets sung by him on all sides. Dust kicked up in front of him, beside him, behind him. Then one Mexican sharpshooter honed in on him and drew a straight bead on his forehead. *Pop!* The Virginian stumbled forward over a rock, causing the shot to take off his cap rather than his scalp. The hat sailed, torn, back into the ditch near where Jackson had been. It landed in the lap of a seventeen-year-old Philadelphian named Wayne Marley.

Like everyone else, the callow, thinly handsome Marley was hugging mother earth. So far, Mexico had been everything he had hoped for, and then some. Traveling the ocean, traversing emerald valleys and splendid high mountains, observing how older men—*and soldiers at that!*—comported themselves, a curious feeling had lately come over him that in all of this adventure mingled with misery, he finally was gaining the father he had never known. He knew that did not make sense, but it was the closest he could come to defining the jumble of thoughts and emotions swirling inside him.

Seeing so many of his fellow soldiers die of dysentery, yellow fever, and other assorted ailments—many of their lives literally draining out of them through bloody diarrhea—did not brighten him. In fact, concern crept over him that he had become perhaps too quick in turning his head, tuning out the pleas of those in agony, and hiding behind some sort of barrier erected to protect his own sanity. But great buoyancy marks the young, and, other than witnessing the considerable suffering, Marley had mostly enjoyed his epic sojourn, God forgive him. Until now. There was no way to call *this* fun. His dirt-caked face flinched as a bullet whizzed by and a nearby soldier screamed and collapsed, his face a red sheet.

Darn that fool captain! Got us into this with his loony glory-seeking. Now look at him! Actually marching up and down the road in front of all creation, hair flying, shirttail flapping, waving at us, waving at the Mexicans, waving at everybody. He'll be dead in seconds. Darn the fool, then what will we do?

Marley clawed harder at the dirt.

Then, a young voice sounded over the din.

"Sir! Come back, sir!" A boy, little older than Marley, hacked away at the cords binding a light cannon to a heap of dead horses who had pulled it to the awful hellhole. Jackson ignored the boy's shouts and continued to parade back and forth, as if wondering what was keeping his men immobilized.

"Sir!" the youth repeated, "Sir, you'll be—"

A bullet punched a hole in the young man's canteen, the resulting gush drenching his private parts. This ended his concern for Jackson, and he dove for cover.

Those Americans in the ranks with enough salt or lurid curiosity to peek out as the fusillade continued saw Jackson, still defiant, turn his attention hard to his fellow troops. "Come on, men, there's no danger! See?"

Irritated at the lack of any response whatsoever, he turned and faced the Mexican guns, then the daunting castle up the hill.

"The man's plum *loco*," a mustachioed private huddling near Marley trembled.

Jackson planted his huge booted feet wide apart in the road and spread his arms as if in open invitation to the Mexicans.

"I don't believe it," shook another voice.

Bullets continued to ricochet all around Jackson. Then, in the midst of the chaos, he spotted a live cannonball on the ground a few yards ahead, rolling straight for him.

The ball seemed to slow down to a crawl.

"Look!" Marley gasped.

Jackson glared at the ball, blue eyes blazing, as if it were a high-stakes game of stud poker between him and the explosive. It came right for him and rolled between his legs, then off the road and into the ditch.

Peach-fuzzed Wayne Marley stared in silent wonder.

"*Loco*," the mustachioed trooper repeated.

"*Loco!* The tall *norteamericano* with the big feet is *loco!*" Mexican captain Emilio Rodgriguez sputtered to a pair of fresh-faced young lieutenants from their vantage spot behind a natural earthen embankment halfway up the gunblasted hill. Rodgriguez had fought against the liberal revolutionists in the early thirties, the Texicans after that, and some of those same Texicans up north in this war—the soulless and brutal Texas Rangers, who cared not who died in the wake of their bloody path. But never had he witnessed an act such as the one unfolding on the smoky road down below.

Rodgriguez lowered his field glasses and turned to Lieutenant Julio Garza. "Who is the best rifle you have, Garza?"

Without hesitation, "Juan Alvarez, Captain."

"Find him and place him in the rocks fifty yards below. His sole target is the *loco yanquis* on the road."

Rodgriguez failed to notice the trace of a smile that belied Garza's stoic countenance. And he failed to mention that the *loco yanquis*, in the midst of a hail of musket and cannon fire, had just stared down a live, moving cannonball, a cannonball that rolled between the man's *legs*. Rodgriguez had seen the tide of battle swing too often through the years through the extraordinary effort—though often unintended—of a single individual. He did not fear one foolish young fanatic who seemed immune to grape, ball, and canister. He did fear the effects that fanatic's actions could have on other, less brave men.

A good boy, Garza, Rodgriguez thought as the young man turned quickly to leave, *from a good family. When this war is over, I pray their loss is not too devastating.*

Julio Garza too had good eyes. As he turned to hustle off, two thoughts struck him. *How could a man stand as live ordnance rolled on hard rocky ground between his legs?* And, *The day of glory has arrived for my little cousin, Juan.*

Meanwhile, as American troops dove and scrambled to elude the runaway cannonball, it finally blew up in the ditch, sending earth flying and more smoke swirling.

To none of this did Jackson pay any heed. He waited only for the onslaught of support he knew would pour forth from the ditches at any second so that he could lead the charge up Chapultepec Hill and into the castle and glory. That support, however, was not forthcoming. Jackson's élan turned to square-jawed grit. His eyes recharged.

My cannon, he thought, eyeing the piece, now abandoned and nose-down back across the road. *We* will *take this hill.*

He stalked toward the fieldpiece like a thirsty man going for the water that would fuel the next part of a hot, dusty journey.

Marley could not fathom this. His mustachioed cohort and their leather-faced sergeant Calhoun appeared as baffled as he as they observed the spectacle.

"He's either the bravest or the most foolish man I've ever—," Sergeant Calhoun began. Another explosion, not far away, finished his sentence early and rained dirt and rocks down on the barrel-chested sergeant, who covered his head with his arms.

Marley was awed. *Never seen anything like this man. Maybe it is a good day to die. Maybe he's a good man to die with.* Ignoring the sod that covered him, Marley sprang to his feet, left his musket, and rushed toward the cannon Jackson had reached and was attempting, singlehandedly, to pull across the road.

"Marley!" Calhoun shouted. "Get back here, boy!"

But the Pennsylvanian was not listening. Smoke choked him, and bells and echoes rang in his ears from the din as he neared Jackson. Ducking his head, the boy shouted, "Can I help, sir?" Then he stopped cold. *My gosh, those eyes!* The captain's steely blues had turned white-hot. They possessed a strange, other-worldly luminescence. Marley was dumbstruck. *They know no fear.*

A thin smile curled its way across Jackson's lips, and he latched onto the cannon. When he spoke, calm and certainty steeled the words.

"We're taking this piece across the road and up onto that clearing, soldier."

Marley gaped at the unattainable position for just an instant. When a bullet pinged off the barrel of the cannon and slashed his left eye, he ceased thinking and began doing, ignoring the searing pain and the blood that seeped down his face.

A few hundred yards away, eighteen-year-old Mexican sharpshooter Juan Alvarez, a handsome, quiet boy with the eye of an eagle, quietly reloaded the second of his two percussion rifles. He had killed several men on this day and many more through the long sad months of the war. He had fought *norteamericanos, if you included the Tejas Rangers before this "official" war began,* since two days before his sixteenth birthday. He had not so much as been grazed by gunfire, though he had fought in many battles. He had been thrown through a wooden door by a tall Ranger in the terrible fight up at Granada, his own village. The force of that blow had knocked him out, which saved him from the slaughter of the vengeful *los tejanos sangrientes*, who screamed they were avenging the murders of some of their men. However, he had only a slight headache when he awoke, and no lasting effects. He was glad the *yanquis* he now fought did not seem so brutish as the Texicans. Of course, they had not been fighting his countrymen for nearly so long—or so desperately.

In a way, Juan hated the *norteamericanos*. Names like Goliad, the Nueces Strip, and the Alamo were distant and hazy to him. He knew not of the *yanquis* blood that had been spilled by the bucketful into ground on which those American settlers, many of them, had desired the new start to raise their families. Ground promised them by the Mexican government and unable to be conquered by centuries of Indians, Spaniards, and Mexicans. And he had never heard the words *Manifest Destiny*.

Juan had always been told by his father, grandfather, and uncles that the *norteamericanos* were arrogant and greedy and impossible to reason with. This miserable war had only confirmed all of that to Juan. Yet the Catholic upbringing his godly mother, rest her soul, had instilled in him, came back stronger now than it ever had been when he was growing up. Well he remembered the words of Father Benito the day he left the village to join the army. "Fight the good fight of the Lord, young Juan, but never forget we all reside in a fallen world. If the men you fight name the name of Christ, however unlearned they may be in their understanding of God or in their practices of that understanding, they are your brothers, and should be with you in heaven for eternity, which is much longer than the time you will fight them on this sad earth. Remember that as you fight, and not to hate them for the evil of the dark one, or their leaders, or even themselves. 'Vengeance belongeth unto me, I will recompense,' saith the Lord."

But sometimes Juan did hate the invaders. He knew some of the reasons they were here, but not all. He knew they had taken much land from Mexico and seemed to want more. He knew that because of them his poor country was now poorer, and in many cases, destroyed. He knew friends and relatives who had been killed or wounded. But he also knew that the Generalissimo de Santa Anna was a vain, proud man who had killed Alvarezes and others in his village. Why Santa Anna had again been allowed to lead Mexico, Juan did not know. He did know that he, Juan, fought not for any man, but for his country, his family, and his own honor. And he fought with all that he had, including the secret talent that God had bestowed on him to see clearly and hold a steady hand.

Still, it helped that he had such keen vision so as to kill the blue-coats from afar. *That way, they do not seem so much like men.* He did not know if his mother would like such thoughts. Suddenly, a strange surge of emotion rolled over him. He wanted to weep, but he did not know why. Then, the lieutenant appeared.

"The captain himself has asked for you to put an end to the *loco* man down on the road."

"The cannonball man, sir?"

"You saw too?"

Juan nodded, with a knowing smile. *Your grandfather's blood does run through me, too, hermano.*

Cousin Julio had been like a father, brother, and best friend all rolled into one for Juan ever since the youngster joined the army. It was Julio, also from Granada, who had paid off the district officials to let Juan in at his young age. It was Julio who had lifted Juan out of the miasma of his poor village and into this life that, though difficult at times, had given him a sense of purpose and resolution in life. Juan would stay in the army as long as Julio did, and his older cousin had already promised to take him with him wherever he went as he was promoted up the ranks. And with Julio being only two years older than Juan, already a lieutenant, and friends with many of the older officers, there could be many promotions in store.

"The removal of the cannonball man is very important to the captain, Juan. Very."

Moments before, Juan had missed his first shot of the day. A fluke occurring when the cannonball man stumbled over his own huge feet, which caused the boy's perfect shot to take off the soldier's cap rather than the top of his head. That shot had been made from a distance of 250 yards, through a momentary break in the multiple layers of swirling, eddying gunsmoke and dust. *I shall not miss again*, Juan calmly told himself.

The two shared a cryptic glance.

Could this be the day? Juan asked with bright doe eyes. Julio, who knew his younger cousin well, nodded. *The day of glory*, when Julio would be able to recommend promotion for Juan into the ranks of the noncommissioned officers. Juan did not come from as good a family as Julio—his mother, though a saint, had married poorly, unlike her sister, Julio's mother—but he would still serve well as a noncomm.

And that would always allow him easy posting with Julio through the payment of certain favors.

Plus, Juan was quite capable and a quick learner. He would never embarrass Julio. For even though the boy was family, honor came ahead of all, and Julio would never be able to take Juan where he went if the boy was not capable.

Juan needed no further prompting. They both knew what this meant. He sprang from the ground, grabbed his rifles and ammunition, and darted after Julio.

Calhoun and the other American troops cowering on both sides of the road comprised a rapt audience. Some peeked and others gawked at the farcical sight of the awkward, large-footed lieutenant and the skinny teenager rolling the cannon across a road being swept with the most devastating fire yet. A cannonball blasted the road not more than fifty feet from Tom Jackson's left shoulder. It peppered the Virginian's sun-burnished face with dirt and rocks, but he paid no mind.

Enormous and unrelenting, the Mexicans' gunfire grew more desperate in its attempt to chase the stalled but unwavering *yanquis* off the hill. Much of the fusillade, though, had shifted to the outrageous, hatless man who had been waving and shouting in the middle of the road and now attempted to push a cannon across it!

Lieutenant Julio Garza crouched down as he moved into place behind his cousin Juan. The stares from soldiers in the area had not escaped him, and he had seen the words passing through their lips when they saw the lieutenant and the fabled young marksman, Alvarez, position themselves on a line directly up the hill from the strutting *yanquis* peacock: "Ah, they're coming to get the cannonball man."

Still, as Julio squinted through his field glasses at the comedic smoke- and dust-obscured figure a hundred yards below, he shook his head in wonder. *The norteamericanos all around him, in much less exposed positions, they drop like thirsty men in a parched desert. So we aim our guns specifically for the loco man. Our bullets do not pierce him and our cannonballs do not explode near him. Why does he not fall?*

The thickening gray clouds of gunsmoke billowing around the field indeed provided Jackson's best cover. With Marley's aid, he guided the cannon to a small clearing just toward the Mexican line from the road.

"We'll stand here, soldier," he announced to the youngster.

As bullets whizzed all around him, Jackson grabbed a swab and shoved it down the throat of the large gun. Marley crouched frozen behind the cannon as one bullet after another ricocheted off the metal. This fact was not lost on the captain.

"Load."

Marley was paralyzed.

"I said *load*, soldier!"

As Captain Jackson appeared a more formidable immediate threat than did the guns up the hill, Marley decided to pull a ball from the box behind the barrel and stick it into the mouth of the cannon. Jackson rammed the ball home with the swab. Then he struck fire with a match and lit the fuse. Before the charge detonated, he pierced Marley with his anthracite eyes.

"Next time, you load *and* fire the fuse, soldier!"

Then, the cannon boomed forth its destruction and jerked backward two feet.

Up the hill, at that very instant, sharpshooter Juan Alvarez had Captain Jackson squarely in the sights of his .57-caliber long rifle. Now, in his workmanlike—and mortally effective—manner, the olive-skinned youth would bring to a sudden halt this attempted rally by the bloodied, bogged-down *yanquis*.

From this distance, Juan reflected without malice, *not even the loco man can stand.*

A fleeting thought of a girl from his village danced through his mind. Something about her had always stirred his blood. He had not understood the source of nor the resulting sensations that flooded over him when she came near. Now, since he had been at war and seen men with other women—some of those women had smiled at Juan and brought him fruit and drink—he thought he was beginning to understand. The first thing he would do after the war when he returned to the village would be to go see the girl. He felt sure now she had been waiting eagerly for him to do this all along.

Juan began his soft, deft squeeze of the trigger, which he had performed with fearful efficiency so many times before, including on this day. He never completed it. A single tiny piece of shrapnel from the explosion of Jackson's shot, which landed more than fifty yards away and inflicted no other casualties, plunked neatly through the middle of Juan's forehead. The boy collapsed onto his back like a sack of spilled feed. His loaded rifle landed on his still chest.

Lieutenant Julio Garza sprang to his feet in horror. He stared ashen-faced down at the gentle boy for whom he had so many plans—plans for glory, honor, and fame. A tear rolled off Julio's cheek onto the dusty ground.

Thus on small agate points do the balances of the world turn.

Back in the ditch, Calhoun shook his head at the spectacle before him.

"Those boys deserve medals," he said. "Here I come, Sanny Anny."

Then, to the surprise of the men around him, he stood and rushed across the road toward Jackson's cannon. The fleeting thought struck the mustachioed private that to pack such a bulk, the sergeant was a quick and nimble man. Halfway to his objective, however, a hail of fire chopped him down. He fell across the body of another dead trooper. Two more lay still nearby. Some of the bodies were already beginning to bloat in the suffocating heat.

In the ditch, Calhoun's men stared in stunned silence at their fallen leader.

At the cannon, Jackson and Marley were perfecting the system, and they sent another blast toward the enemy. This time, agonized screams followed the resultant explosion. Their unnerving shrieks carried down the hill.

"Captain Jackson!" Only a booming baritone voice like Magruder's could have been heard by Jackson, and even then only with the pre-cipitous, momentary decline in volume that occurred on the field. Just arrived and in a lather, Jackson's commander bellowed to him from the ditch across the road. His dead horse lay twenty yards behind him.

"Captain Jackson, retreat sir!"

It's Prince John himself, Marley thought as he peeked back while loading another ball. He glanced over at Jackson, who continued the loading process apace. *Is the man deaf?*

"General Worth's orders, Captain!" Magruder bellowed, "Pull back now, man!"

Marley stared at Jackson. *He* had *to hear him.* A second later, the burning eyes were again fixed on the lad.

"Fire the fuse, soldier."

Marley's mind emptied itself clean of thoughts of Magruder, generals, and retreats as he sent another volley screaming toward the entrenched enemy. Simultaneously, the Mexican barrage renewed its vigor. One shell exploded near Magruder's position, killing both the man immediately to his right and the one to his left. Miraculously, Magruder escaped unscathed, except for a shower of dirt. A second shell landed just behind him a few seconds later. This near miss drove him at last for cover.

Meanwhile, disconsolateness and restlessness pervaded the mustachioed private and Calhoun's other men. They felt they should do something, but weren't sure what. The answer came when one of them, a sweet-spirited, cherry-cheeked young towhead, was shot through the throat. He gasped desperately for a moment, then lay still. The mustachioed man stared at him, then at his dead sergeant, then over at Jackson and Marley, who were still firing, despite the hail of grapeshot and canister raining down around them. Across the road, two more U.S. soldiers fell dead.

Gonna die here anyhow, the mustachioed trooper thought to himself as he scrambled out of the ditch and into the road. A bullet hit and dropped him immediately. So fell the second soldier, then the third, but gradually, desperately, a few, then finally many made it across the road, through the other ditch, then up the hill toward the well-covered Mexicans.

Jackson, intent on keeping his gun firing, did not see his charging countrymen. Marley did.

"Captain, sir!" he shouted. "Captain!"

Now Jackson saw. He paused for the barest shred of an instant, a smile sneaking across his grim, grimy face. Then he slammed the swab back down the mouth of the cannon.

Thirty yards away, young Lieutenant Harvey Hill, waving his saber, exhorted three troopers as they wheeled another cannon across the road. "Come on, boys! Swing her into position, boys!"

Up the hill, the profuse Mexican fire tumbled a spate of onrushing bluecoats. Then the defenders began to break ranks. They appeared from behind all manner of bush and tree, and broke into headlong flight toward the castle above, waves of shouting, shooting *yanquis* in hot pursuit.

Jackson paused from his breakneck pace of cannon stoking just long enough to turn, luminous eyes still ablaze, and shout above the din to a sizable group of American troops huddled back across the road.

"Come on men, press on; don't miss this, your day of glory!"

After a moment's more hesitation, the soldiers charged screaming out of their ditch as one, across the road and up the hill.

Marley, continuing his part of the cannon chores, smiled at Captain Jackson. It was a strange smile because the boy's left eye was shut, the whole left side of his face was streaked with blood dripping onto his dirty blue coat, and because Marley thought this odd man and this whole surrealistic scenario themselves quite strange. It was also a young man's smile of newfound awe, perhaps even reverence.

Strange doings, however, had yet to run their course that violent, steamy Mexican day.

Tom Jackson realized something else quite strange. Each time he came under fire, he had a more perfect command of all his faculties—sight, hearing, smell, feeling, thought, and judgment—than at any other time. It seemed to him the speed and efficiency with which he operated increased in direct proportion to the intensity and volume of the guns on the field around him.

As Jackson hitched his cannon to horse-drawn wagons just arrived from the rear of the line, he noted the fire coming down from the hill had disappeared. That coming from the castle itself appeared much lighter. Then through the smoke he saw increased activity around Chapultepec. Looking through his field glasses, he saw scores of scaling ladders sprouting up around the walls. "From the halls of Montezuma . . . ."

"Let's get moving," he said to Marley. Eyeing the youth's sanguine condition, Jackson ripped off a large piece of his own shirt and tossed it to him. "You'll thank yourself one day as you rock by the hearth that you missed not a moment of this day, soldier." Then the Virginian turned and left. Marley, wincing against the pain now pounding in, wiped off as much of the blood as he could. He tied the shirt around his head and over the wounded eye, as tightly as possible, and followed Jackson up the bloody, corpse-strewn hill.

The fall of Chapultepec cut the heart and soul out of Santa Anna's army. The bitter realization set in on the commander in chief, mounting his white Arabian to retreat from the City of Mexico, that he was going to lose again to the Americans, as he had a decade before to Sam Houston's reckless barbarians at San Jacinto. Not all the scheming in the world, nor the largest chestful of medals that could bedeck the "Napoleon of the West's" magnificent habit could change this. But General Antonio López de Santa Anna chuckled as he remembered how the Indian-loving fool Houston had spared him, and how he had later escaped back to his own land. And how he had, after all, risen and fallen four times as leader of Mexico. He would rise again.

The Americans' pursuit continued northeast toward the final defense of the city itself. With growing energy and determination, and the speed of the four-team wagons that now drew his guns, Jackson soon returned to the front of the American advance. Even Magruder trailed behind.

"I say, Captain." Jackson, rushing forward on a horse commandeered from one of the wagons, turned to see a smiling officer riding up to him on the road. The rider showed no trace of dirt, sweat, or any other grime. *If that man has been near this battle, how does he remain so clean?* Jackson wondered as he glanced down at his own filthy, tattered, blood-spattered kit.

"Daniel Harvey Hill of South Carolina, sir, and my compliments, sir, on the inhospitable manner in which you chased those gentlemen out of their favorite castle back there."

Jackson returned the salute, but offered no fancy words. The uniform still amazed him. He did not realize Harvey Hill had rallied the next line of artillery and infantry up Chapultepec Hill, after Jackson's own.

"I've twenty men with me from the Fourth Artillery," Harvey said, "and forty or so from other units. I'd estimate we are a mile or more in front of our main body of infantry, sir."

"I'd have thought more than that, sir," Jackson replied.

Harvey stared at him.

"Lancers, gentlemen!"

Harvey and Jackson turned. A handsome, strapping officer their age or a bit older galloped up on a magnificent white stallion.

"Lieutenant Barnard Bee of South Carolina, at your service, gentlemen," the man saluted, his gauntleted hand clutching field glasses. "We had best position ourselves for a fight."

Jackson and Harvey ordered their guns and men into position just in time to meet a determined assault from a company of well-disciplined lancers. But the Mexicans had no chance. They could not get more than two horses astride one another on the narrow road. Shot and shell tore through their ranks. One assault failed, then a second, then a third.

Marley, ramrodding the next gun over from Jackson, saw the captain's countenance transformed anew with the heat of battle. *I am glad he fights with me and not against me.*

After driving off the lancers, Jackson and the others were joined by Magruder, with more infantry and guns.

"The generals can't figure you out, Captain," Magruder said with a cockeyed grin. "They're all wondering if you've been hit in the head."

Harvey and Bee laughed with gusto at that.

"My compliments, sir," Jackson replied with a straight face, "but the Mexicans are getting away as we stand here."

"Indeed they are, Captain Jackson," Magruder said, ordering the attack to continue.

Harvey and Bee looked at one another, then laughed out loud again.

CHAPTER 6

AMERICA WON ITS WAR AND ANNEXED ITS NEW TERRITORIES. IT would now begin in earnest the job of subduing a native population and land that the Spaniards and Mexicans had been unable to conquer. The task would be long, bloody, brutal, and laden with controversy. Thomas Jonathan Jackson would not be directly involved further in it, though in many ways at many times his indirect contributions would bear much weight.

After hostilities ceased in 1848, a ceremonial gathering of top-ranking American military officers took place in the Mexican capital's grand hall of the National Palace. When confronted with greeting young Jackson in the receiving line, Commander in Chief Winfield Scott stunned the audience by saying, "I don't know that I shall shake hands with Mr. Jackson."

Jackson, promoted faster and more often in the Mexican-American War than any other U.S. officer (two permanent promotions and two brevets), stood at attention with a dumb look and an extended hand. He had expected the latter to be shaken just as those of the fifty other highly decorated junior officers that preceded him in General Scott's procession down the receiving line had been. He had expected the glory and status gained through his valor on the field of battle and his adroit social contacts with some of Mexico's most highly placed families to find their *pièce de résistance* in this day of fame for the young warriors lined down the ornate gold and marble room.

Indeed, rare words of praise regarding Jackson's deeds from his superior Magruder on up through Generals Worth and Pillow and even Scott himself had flowed in a manner few officers in any army were ever so fortunate to engender, even in lifetimes of service. And months of study of the language, customs, and social graces of the beautiful, semitropical world in which the young Virginian found himself now basking had broadened him from the backwoods oaf once scoffed at by McClellan, Pickett, A. P. Hill, and the others. The process of social refinement was by no means complete, but it was at least begun.

Instead, with the broad-chested Jackson erect in a sartorial splendor that his modest resources could barely acquire, the towering, three-hundred-pound old warhorse sized him up through narrowed eyes, his own white-gloved hands clasped behind his enormous girth. As long seconds passed, the jolly room grew quiet. Curious glances passed between the crowd of senior officers; nervous ones, between the junior officers.

Jackson blushed as the mountainous Scott stared down on him with grave, steel eyes. Somewhere a glass broke. Jackson, stiff as a polished new caisson, nearly jumped out of his brilliant blue uniform. At this, Scott's eyes softened, though his voice did not.

"You may be able to forgive yourself for the way you slaughtered those poor Mexicans," the commander bellowed, his deep bass echoing off the high walls of the silent hall. "But I am not sure that I can."

Jackson's eyes nearly popped out of his head in horror, and as his face grew pale, his mouth grew open—wide open. Then somebody, but not Jackson, spied a grin peeling its way across Scott's huge, double-jowled head. A snicker escaped from that man. "Prince John" Magruder, splendid and dashing and standing nearby, began to laugh richly, for he could see the merry twinkle in Scott's eyes. Jackson couldn't, but Harvey Hill and Barnard Bee, a few places down the line of decorated junior officers, did, and they began to laugh, along with their comrades. In another moment, the high roof of the magnificent palace was all but rolled back with waves of laughter, clapping, and cheering from old and young officer alike.

When Scott seized Jackson's limp right hand in one bearlike paw and thumped his left arm with the other paw, his face splitting with laughter all the while, the truth finally dawned on the rigid junior officer that he was the butt of a precious, prized joke of admiration for which most of the other men in the room would have given large chunks of flesh and years of their lives.

After Scott had moved on and the official ceremony was completed, a pair of decorated officers, a few years older than Jackson, approached him.

"You're a good man, Tom Jackson," Sam Grant smiled, extending his hand, which Jackson took. "And I say with humbleness that I've always thought so."

"Well, thank you, Captain, sir," Jackson smiled.

"Please, 'Sam' will do," Grant said.

"Ah," the second man laughed, offering his hand, "call him Ulysses. It's still better than Hiram."

Jackson turned a quizzical expression on Grant.

"I dropped the Hiram a ways back," Grant said.

"I hear they're calling you 'Fightin' Joe' Hooker after the way you tore into the Mexicans at Chapultepec," Jackson said to the other officer.

"Didn't want you Virginians to get all the glory, Jackson," Hooker grinned, cockiness in his eyes. Then he turned to the other man. "Sam Grant, since when has the bar had to wait on you?"

Grant grinned again. "Be seeing you, Jackson."

In the following months, Jackson was afflicted with peace—his assortment of ailments gradually returned to him one by one, as the stimulation and vigor of battle receded from him—with a lifelong craving for lemons, and with a certain charming young *señorita* of *sangre azul*. The former could not be shaken; the latter, only with pain and a certain regret. A magnificent white steed purchased with a couple of months wages, handsome uniforms, and gay sessions of repartee in the native tongue brought the high-placed company that Jackson desired and that his tequila-drinking, card-playing associates could not begin to attain.

It also brought him the *señorita* who enchanted him above all others. But her flashing eyes, smooth tempting curves, and matchless Castilian countenance could never leave the land of her birth and placement. And when word came back from Laura (whose descent toward loneliness and illness had begun to evidence itself through her letters to her brother over the year) that she was now near death in the very flower of her young womanhood, and that final devastation certainly loomed for her were her brother not to return soon to his native mountains—from which he had even now been away so long—Jackson knew that *sangre azul* would never be his. For he could never turn his back on his beloved Laura, no matter how great or painful the personal cost, and no matter the anguished depths to which she plunged. In fact, he would visit her as soon as he returned to those mountains, to determine just what had been happening in her life to so bring her down. Unhappy marriage? (Why would not her husband's love and care sustain her? She had adored him when wed at seventeen.) The rigors of motherhood on what was still virtual frontier? The wear of ceaseless physical infirmity?

He ached with regret, but not doubt, as he wrote back to his sister shortly before he departed Mexico for good.

"If God has in His great wisdom afflicted you with disease incurable," he wrote, "then may He in His infinite goodness receive you into His heavenly abode, where though I should be deprived of you here in this world of cares, yet I should hope to meet with you in a land where care and sorrow are unknown: there with a mother, a brother, a sister, and yourself, and a father, to live in a state of felicity, uncontaminated by mortality."

He next turned with soberness to the issue of the glory that had suddenly found him, and was well known by now throughout western Virginia, through his deeds in battle.

Even through her tribulations, it concerned Laura. Was the compassionate, sensitive brother who had long helped to provide for her, no matter how mean his own financial estate, and whose letters had never ceased in their abundance and regularity through the years of his absence, a changed man? What of these stories of high adventure—and merciless violence—that had filtered back through newspaper accounts and word of mouth? All this and more she wondered about as she sat alone before the fire reading her brother's letter. Three-year-old Tommy, eighteen-month-old Elizabeth, and that man to whom she had given herself in marriage four years ago slept soundly in the other room. Had J. L. Arnold changed as much in those four years as he seemed to have done? Why was he so little like the man she thought she had married?

Or was it she who had changed? A chill gripped her. She ran her hand along the sides of her face. Her cheeks—the one facing the fire warm, the other cool—still seemed smooth; her hand, less so. She held both her hands out and looked at them. Sadness stabbed at her, nearly as palpable as the birth pangs she had three times felt. Her hands indeed betrayed the wear that was even more apparent in her heart. Was she destined for this loneliness, this high mountain toil? She had always loved spring and summer, and she did have strong feelings for the land that had long since become home, and its people. No, her sorrow welled up from something closer, more intimate. She wasn't quite sure what it was. Outside, the March snow continued to fall.

"My sister," Jackson's letter continued, "lest you find yourself dismayed at the numerous—and often inaccurate—reports you have received of my doings, allow me to assure you most earnestly of my ceaseless horror at the sight of our hospitals. I have, since my entry into this land, seen sights that would melt the heart of the most inhuman of beings."

As the wood crackled in the large fireplace and its heat warmed her against the chill draft sneaking in from the dark night, Laura grew more rapt in her attention to the letter.

"My friends dying around me," Jackson went on, "and my brave soldiers breathing their last on the bloody fields of battle, deprived of every human comfort—even now I can hardly open my eyes after entering a hospital, the atmosphere of which is generally so corrupted as to make the healthy sick."

Laura was surprised. She knew that war was no picnic, but this did not sound like the battles they had fought together while growing up at the mill and other places. She hoped never to see the face of war like this. She hoped her brother never to have to again either. His career "in arms" suddenly did not seem as grand or exciting to her. *Why on earth should he want to continue in it?* she wondered. She wanted him to come back to the mountains and stay.

"I would not live in a hospital a single week," Jackson concluded, "under the circumstances in which I have see them, for the whole of Mexico."

Laura put the letter down. She felt sad for her brother, but the night was tightening around her again, and others' feelings and concerns offered her no escape. She began to weep.

CHAPTER 7

THE CONCEPT OF DOUBT WAS AS FOREIGN TO DR. GEORGE Preston Junkin as the possibility that God had not charted every minute of his life from eternity past. Never had he known doubt in his life. When he recognized very early on that he needed forgiveness through belief in God, His Son Jesus Christ, and the shed blood of that Son, he entrusted his soul to that God and eventually began to proclaim these truths himself to others who needed to know them, first as an ordained minister in the small Associated Reformed Presbyterian Church of America, then, within a few years, the main Presbyterian Church itself.

But there were other things of which George Junkin was just as certain. He knew that the righteous would receive abundant reward in heaven, if not on earth, and the wicked, everlasting pain, judgment, and damnation. He recognized death not as an ending to all things but as a separation from all comfort and goodness. Those who died without Christ—rich or poor, slave or free—would indeed continue in conscious existence. But it would be a more horrific existence than mortal man could begin to imagine or comprehend. The Scriptures conveyed a sense of it when they spoke of hell as being a place of much weeping and gnashing of teeth, where the wicked—they being even the "good" who died without Christ—continued in everlasting conscious torment.

Junkin sometimes imagined the specter of an eternity spent in agony beyond all human description, with the great additional sorrow of the perfect memory of one's life on earth, memory that included the rejection of all presentations of the saving gospel of the Lord Jesus Christ by family, friend, or stranger. He tried to contemplate the unspeakable regret the lost man or woman must forever feel at having rejected the truth that his Bible assured him all, even the distant aborigine, would on some occasion be presented the opportunity to embrace. For a God who was both perfectly just and endlessly loving, would, according to His own Holy Word, create none without offering them the opportunity to accept His way to redemption, salvation, and deliverance. Being a staunch Calvinist, Junkin knew, of course, that many would opt against that wise choice. But it would be they—not the God who created them—with whom the blame would lie. By His very nature, as revealed in the Scriptures, Jehovah God was as incapable of meriting blame as man was of delivering himself from hellfire and damnation.

When he considered the multitude of poor, damned souls, which included by his calculation at least one of his own brothers, Junkin would sometimes burst into a pained, literally physical sweat. And he would vow anew that until his earthly body and mind ceased to function, he would take the heartfelt message of hope that God had so graciously entrusted to him to the highways and byways, to every corner and every venue where any would offer ear to listen.

There were yet many more things about which Junkin had no doubt. He knew that the holistic education of young minds was not an arena for Christians to abandon. To do so would mean leaving the realm to the infidel. He carried in his favorite, well-worn leather Bible, words his father had written with pen and ink before the eighteenth century had yet arrived: "I am much afraid that schools will prove to be great gates of Hell unless they diligently labor in explaining the Holy Scriptures, engraving them in the hearts of youth. I advise no one to place his child where Scriptures do not reign paramount. Every institution in which men are not increasingly occupied with the Word of God must become corrupt." Beneath the words was a simple attribution: Martin Luther.

This philosophy led Junkin into serving as president of several colleges and universities, the latest, in 1848, the Washington College nestled across beautiful, tree-spiced Lexington, Virginia, hills.

Junkin also felt quite certain that God had created the American nation as a sovereign entity, to be uniquely used to further His glorious kingdom on earth, in preparation for His later, completed, kingdom. That is, America was no accident of history, geography, or politics. It was no passing confederation of states or districts, some of which might eventually wander their own selfish way. Americans did not choose to be Americans; they were chosen by God and placed there, just as He chose His heavenly elect. With God, there were no accidents, as He was at the center of everything. America was—

designed to be—the very beginning of God's millennial kingdom on earth, to be founded on His holy principles, as she had been, and governed by His precepts and divine leading, as she had been, and would be.

It distressed Junkin that so few of the otherwise intelligent, often religiously enlightened citizens around him in small but erudite Lexington grasped the historical and spiritual significance of the American nation. This softness of conviction was a dangerous harbinger when considered against the many ill and divisive winds that continued to stir the country. Issues such as slavery, tariffs, and economic diversity and competition had long been sore spots between the nation's various sections: free, slave, border, west, and territories.

What most concerned Junkin were the many with power in the industrial North who seemed intent on forcing their will on the South— ostensibly for the worthy objective of eradicating slavery, but actually, he feared, at least in the case of many, for more mercenary reasons— and the growing number of the South's leaders who seemed bent on maintaining their region on a course of sectional self-determination, regardless of the effects that had on the rest of the nation. Also, whereas an increasing number of Southern leaders were coming to terms with the reality that slavery was both moral and economic suicide, a vigorous minority was growing more militant in its desire not only to retain slavery in the Southern states but to expand it into new areas as America's manifest destiny unfolded westward. Worst of all, this band of fools seemed to care not if their road led to divergent paths for the sections; though, Junkin feared, neither did some of the more ardent Northern slavery abolitionists. He had even begun to hear whispers from time to time suggesting the horrifying specter of certain states actually leaving the Union. Upon hearing such, he would shake his head in uncomprehending anger, then go to his knees in ever more fervent prayer for the future of his beloved nation.

He had needed much prayer through the years, Julia Rush Miller Junkin thought as she listened to her husband tutoring youngest daughter Julia in his study next door to the parlor, where she sat writing to her sister in Pennsylvania. Patient as he was, even with sixteen-year-old Julia and her stumbling Hebrew (Maggie and even Ellie had conquered both Hebrew and Greek through his home schooling in a decisive manner none of the four sons had done in the public schools), he seemed never to cease finding himself at the vortex of whatever controversy or righteous crusade held the day. The very practice he had persevered with through the classical educating of all three daughters was curious to many, disconcerting to some, and would perhaps have caused even more rancor in a day and place where ladies were to be ladies—but not necessarily or even preferably educated ones—had he not been so well regarded and had the end products not been so winsome and estimable. Indeed, in that two-college, two-girls'-school town of six thousand whites and six hundred blacks at the top of the Shenandoah Valley, the line of competent, literate suitors for the Junkin girls was constant and devoted.

She knew that George's dogged moral compass, fiery and overbearing as it could be, endeared him to her, even if it had sometimes wearied her as the calamitous disputes it caused between him and various boards of trustees had forced the growing family to move, in ceaseless near-poverty, from one campus presidency to another—and sometimes back again—through the years. This beautiful white-columned, red-bricked president's home halfway up the verdant hill at Washington College had offered virtually the only semicalm years of the forty she had spent with George Junkin.

As far back as she could remember, everyone had always called her Rush, even back through her childhood upbringing, which had been a wealthy, even luxurious, one in Philadelphia. She had been named for her father's close friend and business associate Benjamin Rush, who graduated from Princeton College at age fourteen, founded four universities, and served as surgeon general in the War of Independence and several presidential administrations. George loved all of this about the famed physician-scholar, plus the many quotes attributed to him such as, "If the Bible were ever to be taken out of schools—*though it would not be*—I lament we would be taking so much time and money to punish crime, we wouldn't have enough to prevent it."

Benjamin Rush also signed the Declaration of Independence.

To George, his beloved Rush was God's gift, and His living and abiding embodiment of grace, mercy, love—and God's holy and foreordained purpose for the sovereign American nation. The shaggy-haired giant in stature and spirit cowed to no man or institution, but worshiped and loved beyond death his wife and his God.

Washington College's board, faculty, student body, and even much of the town of Lexington were Old School Presbyterian and, as such, supportive of her husband and the battles he had won, and lost, on previous campuses and in previous pulpits. The school and town loved him. Oh, there was tension with Superintendent F. A. Smith and the Episcopals who predominated at the VMI just a few hundred yards away, but Rush sometimes wondered if most of that was not there by choice between the vigorous men who had built the respective schools. She suspicioned that were it not, the parties might have to take up other sports to replace it.

And the Valley! Never had she seen such lush beauty, even in the Cumberland from which George had sprung, back in Pennsylvania. Lexington, with its spruces, pines, oaks, and cedars painted over and around the town in lustrous and vivid richness from the Master's rainbow palette, seemed the loveliest place on earth to her. She truly hoped that, the sad practice of slavery notwithstanding, she and George might spend their remaining years together in this quiet, learned little village.

She heard singing from the next room. Today's instruction was completed, as Julia and her father were engaged in the hymn that closed each day's lessons. Today it sounded as though it were "A Mighty Fortress Is Our God." With Julia's age, the home lesson times were nearly finished. They had come to be such a regular part of the family's life for so many years—could it really be a quarter of a century since he had started Maggie, she studying Latin grammar and the Greek alphabet by age six?—that Rush had ceased to give them any more note than she had the tea times with the other faculty wives or the comings and goings of Lexington's four distinct seasons. But now she felt a sudden pang, as if with the realization that another of life's seasons was moving softly and gently to a close. That's how life's seasons usually did so, she thought, softly and gently and even without notice sometimes, until one day you looked back and a season was gone and now only a memory, and all the more precious for it. *Oh, memories!* She knew that her life's train was stocked full with far more than she had ever had any right to. A faithful and gracious God He was to have blessed her so. Oddly, the pain in her head that had become more frequent and acute these last few months, and which momentarily pierced her even now, made her even more jealous for the manifold precious treasures with which her loving Sovereign had blessed her. *Now here they come.*

"Woman," Dr. Junkin boomed even before he had reached the parlor—he most nearly always boomed—"did you not know that tonight was the night of the women's education debate at the Franklin?"

Of course she knew, as she knew that George's renown notwithstanding, the Lord had charged her with being the true spiritual rudder of the family.

"The blindness of this Union," he bellowed as his six-and-a-half-foot frame came through the door and an arm reached down around the smiling Julia's shoulder, "to ignore the treasure of its womanhood. Why, that redheaded spitfire," he continued, tossing his gigantic head in the direction of the second floor, "can run circles around anyone in this brood, or town, with word or pen, and in four languages to boot!"

Rush laid down her pen, as George would now be ready for his daily tea.

"Merely proves my point, and Luther's, anew," Junkin held forth, "that a nation that chooses not to imbue its education with its religion is a nation of fools headed for gigantic folly."

"Would you like your tea on the veranda, dear?" Rush asked with a smile.

Upstairs, her ninety-eight-pound form sprawled across her large bed, which was strewn with the latest issues of *Harper's*, the *Knickerbocker,* and the *Eclectic*, scarlet-trussed Margaret Junkin pondered her last verse:

> *I have gathered of the gladness,*
> *And the grief that fill the brook,*
> *Here some grace's shadowy outline—*
> *There some tender tone or look.*

It was coming slowly today, as it had been for this whole set. It had come with such ease and flow during her last book. She still marveled at what God had done through her tiny hand. Over one thousand copies in print of *Moonlight Revelations*—and she a woman!

She stared across at the lovely spring scene that presented itself to her in all of its burgeoning beauty outside her dormer. Just now, though, a bank of low thin clouds hung like a veil over God's handiwork. She jumped off the bed—*Mama wouldn't think that ladylike at all,* she mused—and bustled over to the glass.

Oh, why must I have been a woman! It was a thought that often rolled through her head, sometimes when writing was proving difficult, like now, and sometimes when she was on the kind of tear that had made her one of the best-known contemporary poetesses in Virginia, indeed, in the South. And with *Moonlight Revelations,* her reputation was beginning to seep into the New England of her birth. *Of course,* she frowned, *the field is quite narrow, is it not?* Few women had the education, the talent, the inclination, and the opportunity to write as did she.

Maggie turned back toward the sheet of paper on the bed, then the pile that cluttered her desk. She could not say that she had seen much of sorrow in her life—*unless,* she thought, *I count the fate of being exiled to this archaic backwoods slave kingdom with its fluttery women and its men whose violence pulses just beneath their courteous airs.* Her years had been—should have been—very happy, with all the brothers and sisters, who were so delightful, and Mama and Papa . . . and Ellie. Maggie's aqua blue eyes twinkled with merriment as nothing else could make them. *What had it always been about Ellie?* From that beaming spring day that shone brightly those many years ago, when she first glimpsed the pale, seven-pound bundle of happiness that seemed nothing but hazel eyes and a smile, the connection had been mystical and magical. Ellie had been her baby, her little sister, her best friend, her confidante. Hers.

She had told the whole world to Ellie, then often lived it through her. True, she had had to share Ellie to a degree. How could she not have? Everyone had always doted on Ellie. No, everyone had always adored Ellie. Ellie was different. Special. Set-apart. *She is too good for this sin-smeared old ball,* Maggie thought. *And that is certainly not a designation that I confer lightly.* Ellie was the prettiest and the wittiest and the kindest and certainly the happiest. The boys loved her, the girls loved her, the older folks loved her. Maggie would write; Ellie would do.

Melancholy enveloped Maggie as she returned to the desk. From where did such faith as Ellie's come? Why could not she herself have it? Why did she, the elder and more learned and certainly more knowledgeable of her Bible, doubt when Ellie in her innocence just trusted? She cringed when she thought of how different people must say the sisters were, as Christians and witnesses to their Lord.

She shook her head and dipped the pen again. If someday she could feel a trace—not just understand and give affirmation to, but really feel, believe, *trust!*—of Ellie's faith, she believed she might experience the abundant life Christ had promised. Until then, she would protect Ellie and guide her and make sure that she fell into no ill, nothing that was not worthy of her.

Now, at last, the words came flooding out, as though unleashed from long captivity and freed to herald their urgent messages of hope and fear, love and loss, to a waiting world that felt them as keenly as she but could never find a way to express them.

As Ruth among the reapers,
Memory, like a gleaner, strives
Thus to gather up a handful
From the harvest of your lives.

Like an exile in her sorrow,
Seeking midst the cast off leaves,
Golden grains of thought and feeling,
Dropped from out the garnered sheaves.

If she has not filled her bosom
With the full and ripen'd ears,
'Twas because her eyes were clouded,
And she could not see for tears!

CHAPTER 8

THE VMI CADETS TO WHOM TOM JACKSON BEGAN TEACHING artillery and natural philosophy (physics) in the fall of 1851 knew him to have been a hero in the Mexican-American War. They also considered him inept, a bore, and a fool as a classroom instructor. By the following spring, James A. Walker was convinced the man was all of these as he suffered through yet another interminable optics class under the clean-shaven twenty-seven-year-old professor already known to all as "Old Jack."

"Thus, we know," Jackson, whose agents Bennett and Carlisle had again championed his entrance into a respected military institution, intoned, "by this peculiar means of deduction and scientific application, that the amount of time required for light to reach from the planet of Mars to our own global environs is approximately three weeks."

Cadet Walker, handsome, redheaded, and full of South Carolina fire, grew less and less tolerant of Jackson's professorial lackings as he witnessed the instructor's daily regurgitations of the textbook. If a cadet dared ask for an explanation or clarification, "Tom Fool" would re-regurgitate, to the letter, his original soliloquy! On the artillery field, "Old Hick" Jackson was maybe tolerable. But in here—as Walker gazed around the horseshoe-shaped class configuration, nearly every cadet was either dozing or engaged in horseplay—*the man is a complete buffoon,* Walker thought.

Even straight-arrow Tom Munford, across the aisle, had had enough of it. Walker chuckled as he watched the usually studious Munford, head leaning against his hand, mouth wide open and eyes glassy, drift into space.

Enough is enough, Walker thought, as he saw Johnny Patton, across the room, zing a larger-than-usual spitball off John Mason's nose. *Gosh, that's the biggest one of those I've ever seen,* Walker mused, as the hulking Mason squealed in pain.

"Old Jack's lighting us up again today, huh, Munford?" Walker said, in a voice somewhere between a whisper and a scream.

Munford barely heard him, but Jackson turned immediately in Walker's direction.

"Mr. Walker, do not talk," the professor said.

"Why, sir, I was confused regarding what we know about how long it takes a light to get here from Mars."

Titters skipped across the room from those who were still conscious. One, a thoughtful North Carolinian named Irv Cullum, finished a lengthy scribbled stanza of verse on the back of his notebook cover.

> *'Tis said that Optics treats of light,*
> *But ho! believe it not, my lark;*
> *I've studied it with all my might,*
> *And still it's left me in the dark.*

Toward the rear of the class, Wayne Marley, still handsome despite the left eye patch he now wore, rolled the one eye he still had. He had heard this routine before, and many others similar to it, from Walker.

"We know by the peculiar means of deduction and scientific application just discussed that the amount of time required for light to reach from the planet of Mars," Jackson repeated, as one cadet in the back of the room, his head lolling against the palm of his hand and his eyes half-closed, mouthed the words in sync as Jackson spoke them, "to our own global environs is approximately three weeks."

"But, sir, I was confused regarding what we know about how long it takes a light to get here from Mars," Walker repeated verbatim with poker face.

As smiles spread across bored faces all around the room, a bellowing series of snores boomed forth from a cadet slumped on the front row, directly in front of Jackson. At this, the class exploded in long-suppressed laughter. Jackson stared in amazement at the slumbering student.

"Mr. Gay," the professor said, "you will wake up at once."

Mr. Gay's only response was a melodious rolling snore that reverberated off the young man's full, rubbery lips. The class's response was a bit more evocative, as the cadets began shouting and cajoling Gay from all over the room to rouse. Even the rigid Jackson sensed that the group did protest too much. *Since when,* Marley thought, shaking his head, *did this group give a hooting heck when one of their own slept through Old Jack's class?*

"Mr. Gay," Jackson repeated, blue eyes flashing this time on the unconscious lad, "you will wake up at once!"

Jackson's words echoed off the walls of the classroom, hushing the cadets for a moment. Then, halfway back in the class, a one-inch diameter iron canister ball rolled loudly across the wooden floor. Jackson craned his neck to catch sight of it.

Suddenly, Mr. Gay's head slid off his shoulder and onto the wooden desk with a loud thud, bringing him out of his dormant stupor. Bleary-eyed, stunned, and in pain, he gazed around at his classmates, who were now roaring—and pelting him with a hail of spit balls, assorted other paper wads, and pencils.

"Mr. Gay," Jackson shouted over the din, "consider yourself demerited and on report, sir!"

This served only to bring a cheer from the class and upraised arms from Mr. Gay, who turned toward his mates, nodding and smiling, as if in acceptance of a coveted honor.

"But why do you do it?" Marley asked Jackson as the two emerged later from the academic building. Jackson walked briskly with his inimitable long, loping strides. The younger man was nearly running to keep up.

"You walk three miles," Marley continued with feeling, "in the sleet and rain to wake that scoundrel Johnny Patton and apologize to him for counting him wrong on an answer when he was right—and he and the whole class mock you to scorn for it!"

Marley was waving his arms now.

"Then, you walk back up the hill every night to bring soup to a sick cadet who sleeps through your lectures even when he's healthy. I just don't understand it, sir."

"Our Savior would have done no less, only more," Jackson replied, never breaking stride.

Marley stared, then shook his head. "Well, whatever those buffoons think, I learn in your class." Jackson glanced out of the corner of his eye at the twenty-two-year-old cadet. "And I just want to thank you again for getting the scholarship grant for me, sir. My career in arms would be much stymied without it."

Meanwhile, James Walker was quite concerned about his own career being stymied—by Major Jackson. Walker had clashed with

Jackson almost from their first meeting on the parade ground eight months before. Both believed in themselves and their way, and there proved no room for give on the part of either. Nor did the Virginia Military Institute allow room for a second-year cadet to chart his own course.

While many a cadet had ridiculed and made sport of Jackson, both behind his back and in his classes, it was Walker who had refined the practice to a fine art. On the parade ground, while serving as a "horse" in the pulling of cannon, Walker began to prance, nicker, and kick, generating raucous laughter from everyone on the field—except Major Jackson, who put him on report. In the classroom, Walker would draw huge feet on the blackboard before Jackson's entry—and everyone knew who had the largest feet at the institute. And, he would push Jackson to the brink of bringing court-martial charges against him by questioning, albeit with ever-so-much finesse and panache, the instructor's judgment, teaching skills, and even his qualifications to hold the position he held. And around campus, it was Walker, who, upon sighting the awkward, loping professor marching straightaway to the destination of the moment, would charge to catch up with him, then march in lockstep one pace behind him.

On this particular bright April day in 1852, Walker, with Patton and Munford in tow, looked down from a third-floor window as Jackson and Marley approached on the sidewalk below.

"Look, Jimmy," Munford said, half excited and half terrified, "here he comes."

Walker and Patton exchanged glints. A nod from Walker signaled Patton to hoist a large pail filled with liquid from the floor. Walker took it and leaned out the window.

Jackson was proud as a peacock. "Why, it's a pleasure to offer aid to such a brave fellow artilleryman," he said, in reference to Marley's remark about the scholarship grant. He then turned to the younger man. "And one not ashamed to offer any sacrifice for what he knows in his heart and soul to be right."

From somewhere above came a gleeful shout.

"Tom Fool Jackson!"

Jackson and Marley looked up just in time for the free-falling pail of liquid to drench the professor and clatter off his head.

Jackson spewed liquid out and shook himself off. Then a quizzical look came over his face. "This doesn't smell like water."

Then the blue eyes flashed white-hot as they pierced Marley. The speechless cadet was pale. The only motion from his entire body was the twitching of his lone eye. But as suddenly as it had arrived, the professor's anger disappeared. His countenance loosened, becoming almost merry. The deep blue returned to his eyes and he winked at Marley.

"Let us pray, Mr. Marley, that should we ever again be forced to bear arms, that the aim of our men should remain as accurate!"

Marley relaxed, then laughed loudly as the two resumed their walking.

"They do not like your lectures, sir," Marley said, "but some of the men say that if ever there's a fight, it is you whom they should like to follow."

Jackson glanced at him again, then raised his left arm straight and high into the air. The spring in the professor's lumbering soggy step was a bit more pronounced as he marched on.

As he leaned his considerable girth back in the straight-backed wooden chair, it occurred to Judge John W. Brockenbrough that he had witnessed many a memorable sight during his twenty-two years of membership in the Franklin Society of Lexington. It pleased him that he had had a direct hand in shaping and molding the debating and literary organization into one that was recognized and honored throughout Virginia, including Richmond and the Tidewater, and even into neighboring states.

It did not hurt that, despite Lexington's compactness, its two esteemed colleges and its pair of fine girls' schools provided a well-spring of intellectual and oratorical competence. Never, however, had he seen such an event as was unfolding before his eyes this warm May evening as the Franklin convened for its monthly meeting in the Rockbridge County courthouse.

Moments before, the rotund judge had called upon the youngish Mexican War hero from the VMI to offer his arguments before the sartorially resplendent society membership. The ex-soldier was to speak in favor of advanced educational opportunities being offered for women rather than just for men, which of course was the normal practice. Brockenbrough had seen Major Jackson from a distance now and then around the village, and had even been once introduced to him after a Franklin meeting.

Jackson knew that the Society's format of debates and speaking provided splendid opportunity for education in a wide array of subjects, as well as a chance to meet some of the leading men in town and surrounding Rockbridge County whom he did not know through the VMI. And, it furnished him with the perfect situation to develop the skill of public speaking, at which he was woefully inept. The tall professor was not yet a member of the club—and if tonight was any barometer of his oratorical skill, he might never be—but he was a regular attendee.

Jackson had risen from his seat, stiff and ramrod-straight, when called upon, then lumbered in a near-trot to the lectern. At first, all had appeared normal. But not for long. Jackson had stared out at the sizable convocation, which was, if perhaps a shade to the dignified side, nonetheless friendly. However, cheerful expectancy on the part of that audience had turned first to embarrassment and then to tense, shifting uneasiness as Jackson had stood paralyzed and silent moment after agonizing moment, beads of sweat dripping from his face onto his well-pressed blue uniform.

Finally, just as the judge was about to stand and ask if Jackson might desire medical assistance, the professor began to stutter and stammer.

"It . . . er . . . it, that is, education is not a thing . . . that is, it is a wonderful thing and a . . . er . . . uh . . . an important thing that . . . well, its benefits should be avail-avail-available to all, because all have minds that need to be . . ."

A long pause. The tense group nearly leapt out of their seats as the bell atop the courthouse began to clang its hourly message.

"It is a g-good thing," Jackson stumbled, "for all minds, men and, men and . . ."

One minute, then two of thick, palpable silence.

"Women!" came a ringing shout from the rear of the room, followed by a snicker or two.

Now Jackson was irreversibly immobile and shut up. Men began to shift more nervously, then to whisper to one another.

Judge Brockenbrough had inherited much property and accumulated more in Virginia and out West, invested wisely and profitably in the stock markets, purchased two small businesses, been a respected judge for a dozen years, and built his own law practice in Lexington with several associates, clerks, and interns. One of these clerks was Joseph "Joe" Kennedy, the brilliant Washington College student whom the judge felt might someday go as far as the nation's gleaming White House on the Potomac up in Washington City. The law firm was the most thriving in the county; for that matter, in the upper Shenandoah region.

When Judge Brockenbrough felt he had something to say, he assumed it would be of benefit to whatever attendant audience he had at the time. In this case, it was Major Tom Jackson and seventy-five men at the monthly meeting of the Franklin Society.

"I hear that man is a professor," the judge bellowed, to no one specifically and everyone generally. "Why is he called a major?"

"He served under General Winfield Scott in Mexico," came an equally robust voice from across the room. It seemed good to the judge for someone to be speaking, for goodness' sake, since all these men had gathered together, some of them from the surrounding country and villages, despite their many commitments.

"Served with distinction," came a third voice off to the judge's left. "He was at the Point. Fearless they say."

The judge wasn't sure that he was buying that. "Man's scared out of his wits up there!" A sprinkling of (polite) titters skipped across the room as Jackson remained as stone stiff as the first president's statue out front of Washington College a few blocks to the north.

The judge was honestly befuddled. "How does he deal with those cadets at the VMI?"

"From what I hear, it's they who do the dealing, Judge Brockenbrough," a man said, leaning over from directly behind to speak into his ear. "They call him Tom Fool."

The judge shook his head. "Tom Fool."

Up front, Jackson was sweating. The few men nearest him could also detect a slight trembling. They could not know it was not sourced in the comments and mocking of the few men in the audience who reacted so to the strange professor. Jackson was not in the least aware of them or their reactions to his struggle. Nor was it due directly to stage fright. Oh, his initial reticence no doubt was. But he shook now because of a force inside him much more powerful and urgent than stage fright or embarrassment in front of one's peers (though he did not know most of the men in the room).

It was a presence, really, and it had been with him in large degree since a cold snowy day long ago when he was assured by a saintly dying woman that, "You may be whatever you resolve to be."

It had grown stronger since the deepening debt and commitment he had been feeling toward the Lord Jesus Christ, fanned by the gentle but persistent efforts of Captain Francis Taylor, had led to Jackson's being baptized a year after his return from Mexico. Since then, God and the Christian faith had proven an increasing reality for him. And the *presence* had grown stronger as well.

The presence now drove him to a degree of effort that had his eyes bulging out of their sockets and beads of perspiration dripping from his taut muscles. The Herculean obsession that every man seems to have lurking somewhere in his life, whether or not to love the wrong woman—or to love properly the right one—or to elude the bottle, or harness a profane tongue or a raging anger or a consuming ambition, Jackson faced on the floor of the Franklin in his first jagged attempts at public speech. There would be time enough for other, even greater, thorns of the flesh, but on this evening a cosmic battle waxed whose intensity none would ever know but Jackson himself, and he only through a glass darkly. For few were willing to allow God to take them to such a spiritual plane that they would ever experience the sublime purifying fire of inner warfare that blazed in Jackson as he gripped the lectern with such intensity that his knuckles glowed like white-hot wax.

Thus was Jackson's feeble mouth not opened in power for the sake of a speech. And thus in allowing such to be done, and done again and again and again, not allowing his mouth to be opened, but his heart, to the gentle but mighty shepherding of the Everlasting, was he made into what was not before and would not be again.

He spoke only, "It is true that God has designed different places and roles for men and women. But where He has not, let us not dare to do so, especially when He desires that all His created beings experience His fellowship and love, and when a proper Christian education can only serve to hasten and deepen that experience."

But God spoke to him: *"Hast thou not known? hast thou not heard, that the everlasting God, the LORD, the Creator of the ends of the earth, fainteth not, neither is weary? there is no searching of his understanding. He giveth power to the faint; and to them that have no might he increaseth strength. Even the youths shall faint and be weary, and the young men shall utterly fall: But they that wait upon the LORD shall renew their strength; they shall mount up with wings as eagles; they shall run, and not be weary; and they shall walk, and not faint."*

When Jackson finished, he strode back to his seat with the same determined gait earlier exhibited en route to the lectern. Judge Brockenbrough and the attorney seated next to him exchanged dubious glances. A doctor a few seats away covered his mouth with a hand to bury his laughter.

As Jackson sat down, the nervous men around him squirmed and looked away. Near the rear of the room, Captain Daniel Harvey Hill gazed with curiosity at the stiff-backed figure. Hill had always been a man of little contemplation and much action.

The members of the Franklin Society had plenty about which to talk as they emerged from the courthouse building later in the evening. Men joked, talked, and laughed as they descended the steep steps to the ground below.

"From what we saw tonight of our esteemed war hero," said one man, "I'm left to wonder if the Society has not exhausted the crop of qualified men in Lexington!"

The men around him broke into hearty laughter.

Just behind them, in full hearing range, stalked Jackson, left arm aloft and rigid. His placid countenance betrayed no evidence that the derogatory comments scored any impression on him at all.

"Major Jackson!"

The professor turned to see a polished, vaguely familiar figure coming through the door just behind him.

"Lucky for those pompous windbags you weren't firing the same ordnance on them you were on the Mexicans that afternoon up Chapultepec Hill!" Harvey Hill hooted, loud enough for anyone in the area to get the full effect.

Jackson looked askance at him, his left arm still pointed skyward, as he shook the smiling man's proffered hand.

"Captain Daniel Harvey Hill of South Carolina, at your service. I was there when you dragged the cannon across the road, when you stared down the cannonball, everything. We turned back those gallant but foolish lancers together."

A rare sparkle of the blue eyes. *The dandy*. "Ah, yes, a glorious day for our arms, that," Jackson said, relaxing.

"I'm at Washington College now," Harvey said, glancing at the Virginian's uplifted appendage, as they descended the steps.

"Yes, I remember seeing your name now," Jackson nodded.

"Jackson, I believe you're a bachelor."

The major eyed him.

"Well," Harvey continued, "a man has a duty to himself as well as to those he serves in his work. Jackson, I'd like you to join me for a little soiree tomorrow evening at the Reverend Dr. Junkin's home."

Raised eyebrows. "The Washington College Junkin?"

"There is only one clan of Junkins in Lexington to my knowledge, sir," Harvey said.

Jackson stared ahead, his already rapid gait quickening. The arm came down.

"I'm not one for seeming, sir," he uttered.

"Sir?" Harvey asked.

"Parties and putting on airs, sir."

Harvey gently grabbed Jackson's coat sleeve and stopped. "Jackson, do you like women?"

Jackson reddened, then glanced about to see if anyone had heard the words. "*Sir!*"

"Then I'll be by for you at seven o'clock," Harvey said. He grabbed Jackson's right hand and shook it, slapped him on the shoulder, then pivoted and strolled off into the evening.

Jackson stared after him for a moment in confusion. *Strange man, that. Never did get a spot of dirt on him, even after we turned back the lancers.* "It shall have to be 7:30," Jackson called out. "I've an optics lesson to prepare!"

A large banner was strung across the gleaming white columns of the president's house at Washington College. It read "Happy 60th, President Junkin." Those columns looked out to a spruce- and maple-draped lawn that sloped gently down toward town. It was a lovely tableau, so lovely that often, as Dr. Junkin would stand for a moment on the steps of the portico before making the short walk to his office, listening to the birds trilling and seeing the morning sun's long golden rays shooting through the trees, he would marvel that Eden—or the Eden to come—could surpass such serene matchless beauty.

Inside the handsome but utilitarian Georgian edifice, all was gay. The large group was noisy but well behaved, if not quite dignified in a Tidewater fashion. From the parlor came the melodious roll of a piano. Jackson gazed around. *The cream of Lexington society: church, business, military.* He knew a few of the men from the VMI. Over the din, Jackson could hear one powerful voice above the others. It resonated with confidence and resolution.

"But my dear fellow, Christians *must* be involved in education."

He stepped around a corner into a large room where he saw a powerful man to match the powerful voice.

"You must remember that a college is a religious, not a civil, institution," a towering hulk of a sixty-year-old bear boomed. The man was holding court in the midst of a throng.

"Sanders," he continued, as the target of his attention flinched upon hearing his name called, "you plant those seeds into the ground, then you pull them back out at harvesttime, don't you?" Sanders nodded. "But you don't create them, do you? Nor do I create the truths and principles that I teach. All creation comes from our heavenly Father."

Maggie Junkin watched her father's proclamations from the next room. A familiar smile creased her thin lips. Next to her sat her beloved sister Elinor, who at twenty-six, was her junior by five years.

Ellie giggled. "Well, Father is content on his birthday."

"With the requisite attentive and properly awestruck audience," Maggie agreed. Her thoughts ran a bit deeper. *At least as content as a man can be when his beloved wife of forty years lies dying in her bed upstairs.* She turned to her sister. Golden hair, luminous hazel eyes the color of a Tidewater surf that seemed to swim as such, clear skin, and *the glow*. Always she had seemed to have it. It had drawn the boys like flies to buttermilk since the start. If Maggie could scarcely aspire to Ellie's sure faith, perhaps she could to her easy winsome manner. She thought on that for a minute. *Hah.*

Despite the external and internal contrasts, the girls' dresses were identical and their hair prepared in the same fashion. Such was always the case, as was their cleared-eyed, slightly mischievous pertness. And the many men who had come courting rarely if ever saw one without the other.

Maggie was pretty; Ellie, beautiful.

Crash! From the opposite corner of the room, the sound of heavy shattering glass. Both sisters' eyes raced to where a solitary, rigidly-erect Tom Jackson had dropped a full pitcher of liquid onto an antique end table. And this, after having already spilled the pitcher's contents over the head of Mrs. Rodham—*Of all people, hee-hee, the old bitty!* Maggie giggled to herself—who sat on the couch next to the table, and on his own gray uniform.

Maggie noted the man's blushing crimson face as he felt the hard scrutiny of a roomful of surprised stares. She shook her head, half in pity, half in scorn. *What is such a fool doing here?*

Jackson grabbed a towel from a nearby servant and began wiping up the mess.

"Oh my goodness, Maggie," Ellie said with concern, "don't we know that poor man?"

"He attends the church," Maggie said.

"Shall we see if we can help him?" her sister said, moving in that direction.

People—most of all men—are so incompetent! Maggie thought, swishing her hooped skirt over to where Jackson held a soaked towel and offered an arm to help soggy Mrs. Rodham up from the couch. Around the room, conversations and piano playing resumed. From the next room, Junkin's discourse continued unabated.

Well, if you had to do it, sir, you did it to the right one, Maggie smiled, *and what an aim at that!*

Mrs. Rodham was not appreciative of Jackson's tendering of aid. "Don't come near me, young man," she crowed, "you've done quite enough already!"

Rather than dousing her fire, the drenching had stoked it. She glared at Jackson, her seventy-five-year-old body virtually springing off the couch. She stabbed a crooked, bony finger up into the humiliated man's face.

"Young man, you had best find yourself a wife to take care of you if you plan to attend further social functions around here."

Ellie and Maggie stifled giggles as the wizened old lady turned to waddle away. After several determined steps, she remembered that she had left her cane at the couch. Her limp immediately returned as she came back for the stick. She bent over slowly for it, uttering something between a groan and a grunt and flashing Jackson one last hateful dart.

Ellie gently wrested the wet towel from the mortified Jackson, while Maggie cleared off the victimized end table.

"You shouldn't pay too much heed to old Mrs. Rodham," Ellie said, attempting to soften the blow, while wiping up more liquid with another towel that the servant had supplied. She leaned a bit closer to Jackson and whispered, "She herself never married."

Jackson, the front of his uniform soaked, stared at Ellie in surprise.

"You must watch these women who get up into years without marrying," Maggie said—directing her words toward her sister, not Jackson—with a glint. "They may be awful to be around."

Ellie offered Jackson a charmed smile. "Why, just look at Maggie and me!"

What a sweet glow, Jackson thought to himself, as the oddly shining eyes twinkled at him. He attempted to smile, but before he could, the two sisters dissolved into giggles over Ellie's previous comment. After a moment, the major straightened his back again.

"Major Thomas J. Jackson, ma'am, of the VMI."

Ellie stared at him, then at Maggie, then the sisters again melted into laughter.

Maggie made an attempt to get serious. "Are you always so formal, Major Jackson?"

"Why . . . uh . . . I—"

Ellie shot a look at her sister and touched Jackson's arm lightly. "No need to answer that, Major Jackson. I am Elinor Junkin—"

"And I, Margaret Junkin—"

"And I do believe that we have seen you around the church."

That lady has some load of confidence, Jackson thought, *and grace.*

"Now you wait right here, Major," Ellie said, "while we go fetch something with which to wipe off your coat."

Jackson lowered his head and shoulders in a polite bow as the sisters swished away, giggling anew. He then resumed his customary iron-jawed, ramrod-straight standing to attention.

"And so tall and handsome!" Ellie responded to a comment from Maggie as they disappeared across the room.

Junkin was still holding forth. "Take that fine institution that was your brainchild, Colonel Preston." Colonel John Preston, forty-two, tall, debonair, exceedingly and darkly handsome, listened with respect. "I happen to know that at least one of your VMI professors has actually advocated secession from our sovereign Union should serious political pressure be brought to bear on the dominion to eradicate its slaveholding practices."

"Now, sir—," Preston began with earnest respect.

"My good man," Junkin cut in, "God made this government, its constitution, and our nation, and for anyone to brook the dissolution of His Union under any circumstance is to blaspheme the Almighty."

Ellie and Maggie passed through the room where Junkin orated as they swished back toward Jackson, clean towels in hand.

"You don't think anyone thinks ill of Father because he's a Northerner, do you, Ell?" Maggie asked.

"I think there shall always be those who think ill of Father," Ellie said, putting her arm around her sister's shoulder. "And there shall always be the majority of us who love and admire him."

They smiled at one another as they returned to Jackson's corner. He remained at attention as Ellie with care wiped off the front of his coat.

Maggie spoke again, mischief in her eyes. "They say that you are quite unpopular among some of your students, Major Jackson. Why is that?"

Ellie was honestly peeved. "Why, Maggie! Why would you say something like that to Major Jackson, especially when you've just met him?"

Maggie looked at Ellie, surprised.

"No, that's quite fair, ladies," Jackson interceded. "I must work earnestly to attain even a modicum of aptitude in the classroom. So, the analysis is quite fair."

Maggie looked back at Jackson, her eyebrows arching in surprise.

"It most certainly is not fair," Ellie said. She turned to Maggie. "Sister, when have you ever witnessed the major in his classroom?" Maggie blanched with embarrassment. "I thought so," Ellie continued. "See, I'm sure that you are a fine professor, Major."

"No, ma'am," Jackson insisted, without guile, "I'm really quite a poor instructor."

Ellie had no answer to this statement, so she twiddled with the wet towel she held. Maggie glanced down at the floor, saying nothing. *What a curiously strange individual,* she thought. After an awkward berth of silence, Jackson's left arm shot straight up into the air, as he remained rigid in his stance.

The sisters stared at him, then eyed one another. When no explanation or even acknowledgment was forthcoming, Ellie spoke again.

"Why Major, do you realize that your left arm is sticking straight up in the air?"

Maggie's blue eyes resumed their familiar glint. "Having so failed as the instructor, Major Jackson, do you now yearn to return to the role of a student?"

Whatever has come over Maggie? Ellie thought with a frown, surreptitiously pinching her sister hard on the arm. "Margaret Junkin, whatever has gotten into you? You apologize to the major immediately."

"No," Jackson said, "it is indeed a distraction to others and a thing that must be endured in order to even the flow of blood between my arms." The sisters gawked at him. "One arm is heavier than the other. It all stems from an alimentary canal problem."

Ellie had no idea what to say now.

Whatever has come over Ellie? Maggie thought.

"Jackson! My boy! Old hero of Chapultepec!" Harvey Hill, beaming, robust, and with an attractive woman at each arm. "Good to see you taking my advice to heart, old boy. And my goodness, *two* ladies, and those the lovely and quite eligible Junkin sisters, no less."

Jackson, arm still in the air, blushed anew. This time, so did Ellie and Maggie.

"Allow me to introduce to you the lovely pair that I have the honor to escort this evening," Harvey announced. "This is my wife, Isabella. And this, her younger sister, Mary Anna Morrison of Cottage Home, North Carolina."

Jackson executed a courteous, but stiff, bow to each woman before Harvey pressed on.

"And I believe you ladies are all acquainted," Harvey said. "The major here was a highly decorated war hero in Mexico."

Highly decorated? Ellie thought.

War hero? Maggie thought.

"Why," Harvey continued, "I myself was with him when he single-handedly turned the tide in the battle of— For goodness sakes, Jackson, what on earth is your arm doing wagging in the air like that, man? You look like one of the cadets raising his hand to ask a question in class!"

There, are you satisfied now? Ellie blurted at Maggie with her eyes. Now Maggie did not know what to make of this man.

"If you all don't mind, we'll go fetch another pitcher of punch," Ellie said. "Now Major Jackson, don't you go anywhere."

She grabbed Maggie's arm and they swished off again. Giggles fluttered back from them as they recrossed the room.

Ellie was enjoying this. "The major certainly is an odd character, is he not, Sister?"

"Yes, he is."

Very odd, Maggie thought as she stared back over her shoulder at Jackson. He remained stationary, his left arm thrust straight up toward the ceiling. *Very odd indeed.*

CHAPTER 9

SUMMERTIME RETURNED TO THE SHENANDOAH VALLEY. RICH verdant meadows rolled down to clear sparkling streams, which flowed along forests of white, pink, and red dogwood. Fertile green fields checkerboarded some of God's most richly arrayed farmland. Tall, stately pines wove a splendid tapestry through the entire wondrous tableau. This holy sanctuary of nature lay silent save for the busy chirping and chattering of a thousand birds of every shape and color. The Shenandoah Valley. Breadbasket of Virginia. Unbesmirched by the industrial revolution that now resounded through the great cities of the North while the agrarian South continued a leisurely outdoor life and thrived on the bounty of slave-produced cash crops like cotton, wheat, tobacco, rice, and sugar.

The jackrabbit heard them first. He cocked his head to listen more closely to the sudden break in the serene cycle surrounding him. In an instant he was gone.

The two horses were powerful thoroughbreds in the prime of their years. As usual, they raced side by side, mere feet apart. The countenances of the women upon them registered all the joyous tension that had ever been the product of these slashing gallops, which had begun sometime way back at the beginning in Pennsylvania, and of which Dr. Junkin had more often than not, at least in recent years, not been aware.

As the birds bursting into the immense bright azure sky unfolded into a dominolike canopy above, the bay and the black thundered and lathered across the meadows and the hills, leapt across Rockbridge Creek, then turned to race up Lexington Hill.

The terminus as always when the Junkin girls challenged this particular course was the enormous crooked hanging branch of the hulking oak that loomed as a faithful ancient sentinel over the crest of the hill.

The bay swept under the crooked branch, winner by half a heartbeat.

"I won, Sister!" Ellie Junkin shouted.

"This time, Sister, this time!" Maggie laughed back.

The girls reigned in their sweating mounts. As usual, they dressed identically. Unlike their mother, they had not ridden in the English sidesaddle fashion since childhood. This had been a good day. Before the ride, they had laughed themselves silly as Maggie recited her latest published poem, *The Step Mother!*, which chronicled the regrettable marriage of a woman of their approximate age and station upon her betrothal to a distinguished widower ten years her senior with seven children.

"Oh my," Ellie breathed.

She gazed across the narrow valley to the next hill. She saw beauty and opportunity.

"The VMI," said Maggie.

Hazel and blue eyes met in mischief and long knowing.

"Ha!"

"Ya!"

Slapping their horses with the reins, both tore out for the distant hill.

Major Thomas J. Jackson always seemed to do better on the parade ground than in the classroom. The cadets sensed his greater confidence and competence in the same fashion a horse discerns that of an accomplished rider.

This hot late-August afternoon, he directed a smartly bedecked group of cadets in the use of the bayonet.

"And thrust!" Jackson said. The youths plunged steel into invisible foes. "And thrust!"

Walker and Patton, at the rear of a group standing between exercises, grinned surreptitiously toward Jackson. Patton nodded as Walker lifted a large clod of dirt from the ground with one hand. His eyes beaming, the redhead reared back, then let the chunk fly.

"Yee-ah!"

Jackson turned toward the sound, just in time for the spinning clod to zing past one ear. He never saw it, though all the cadets did. He was, however, shocked to see a bay and a black—*each ridden by a screaming woman, no less!*—race across the field from the direction of Lexington Hill.

Jackson turned back toward the awestruck cadets.

"Men, never—ever—allow yourself the luxury of not having planned for every contingency the enemy may throw at you," he said. The booming sound of the usually soft, high-pitched voice riveted the cadets' attention back on Jackson.

"Conversely, be prepared to utilize any and all resources at your disposal to surprise, confuse, and confound him," he said. "Now thrust!"

Jackson had learned in his years in Mexico and since the importance of delaying the surprise component until just the right moment for maximum effectiveness. So embedded was this understanding in his mind that he wasn't even conscious of it at such times as this, when he took stock both of the continued rebellious antics of now-second-year cadet Walker and the large chunk of dirt that had just missed his left ear. And that was the one in which he already had frequent trouble hearing.

Brilliant, flashing ivory teeth adorned Ruthie Johnson's round, happy face. She now reigned over the Junkin household with a firm if benign hand. A healthy portion of vinegar spiced that hand.

A free woman granted her papers by her previous master (also a Presbyterian clergyman) on his deathbed, Ruthie often marveled at the irony that placed gentle people like the Junkins, with their absent-mindedness and evident near-complete lack of common horse sense, in a station above herself and others of her African race. These thoughts, too, were benign and free of even a trace of malice.

The Reverend Doctor's booming voice and its customary echo through the front foyer and hall confirmed for Ruthie that she once again had plotted with precision the timing of the family dinner. And what a sumptuous affair it was! Roast duck, ham, garden potatoes, snap beans, greens, snow peas, steaming hot rolls, cranberry sauce, and—if anyone had a spot left in his well-fed tummy, which of course they always would—Ruthie's intoxicating pecan pie.

Thank the Lord that voice and echo had finally returned to these halls, Ruthie thought. *Ever since Mrs. Junkin— Why, Lordy, Dr. Junkin sounds like he done brought the whole of Lexington home to supper with him tonight.*

Junkin strode into the large dining room, sons John and William on his heels like a couple of yapping whippets.

"Pa! Pa!" John exclaimed. "Tom Jackson brought us a copy of this month's *Harper's* back with him from New York!"

The elder Junkin stopped in his tracks and took the magazine John thrust toward him. His twinkling brown eyes grew wider the farther he leafed. One brow furrowed after a moment, and the eye beneath it peered over the periodical to see a nervous Jackson standing at stiff-backed attention across the room. *Poor fellow acts as though he'd never set foot inside a house before.*

"Ah, Major Jackson," Junkin said, "we're sitting down to a late dinner tonight. Hustle over here and join us, my boy."

Jackson started to reply, but Junkin, stuffing the *Harper's* into his coat, had already turned and marched into the dining room, John and William again on his heels.

"These publications," Junkin continued, "should be monitored not merely for their own merits, but in order to observe that which is occupying the thoughts and focus of the world around us that so desperately needs the Savior."

Ruthie's rotund figure belied her light-footed agility. And she was at her best in a crisis, which somehow supper time seemed nearly always to be around the Washington College president's house. She buzzed around the large mahogany dining table like a bee as the Junkins found their chairs. Here a cloth napkin was not placed properly on a lap; there a crystal glass of water was smudged.

"Let us return thanks now," Junkin said.

Somehow that always sounded more like an order than an invitation to Ruthie. Just before she bowed her head, she checked to see if everyone was in place. The Reverend Doctor at the head of the table, to his right twenty-eight-year-old eldest son John, son Ebenezer, son William, and that odd Major Jackson—*Why, he's sitting up straight as a board in his chair*—and to the Reverend Doctor's left, sixteen-year-old Julia, the baby of the clan, George Jr., and *two empty seats. Why, those girls!*

John, too, felt the weight of his father's proclamation, as it, effectively, cut off the question about to leave his tongue.

"Our gracious, sovereign Heavenly Father," began the sonorous prayer. "We praise you for your mercy in bringing back to this house those of us who now live away . . ."

The prayer sounded as clear at the top of the home's front stairs as it did down in the dining room. Ellie and Maggie, appearing not at all as gallivanting cross-country equestrians, giggled at one another's identical, and exquisite, lime silk dresses. Sometimes they just had the urge to wear the nicest things to supper with the family, while sometimes they thought it great sport to appear anything but the president's dignified young daughters at the nicest town soirees. They were never really sure what prompted such maverick tendencies, but it did seem to help the rest of life to be much more palatable.

"Oh, your hair looks beautiful," Ellie laughed. It was rare that Maggie fussed much over her flaming scarlet hair, but when she did, it was prepared identical to Ellie's, as now: cleaned, combed, and up in a neat bun.

"Shall we, Sister?" Maggie asked, extending an arm.

"We shall!"

They marched down the winding, red-carpeted staircase as their father's prayer rumbled on from the dining room. They hit the ground floor, Ellie merrily popping the walnut bannister rail with the heel of her hand, just in time to be snatched by two black hands and beset by a loud hoarse whisper.

"And just what do you young ladies think you're doing, showing up late for supper, and missing your father's thanksgiving, and you two already in trouble to boot!"

The surprised sisters found themselves staring straight into Ruthie's large brown eyes. Then they rustled toward the dining room, Ruthie helping them along with a swat on the rump.

At the dinner table, Junkin, finished with his eloquent, beseeching prayer, speared a slice of duck and passed the larger silver platter to John, who stared at the two empty seats across the table from him.

"So when do you return North for the medical practice, my—" Junkin noticed no answer was forthcoming from his preoccupied son. The older man nudged the younger in the chest with the large, heavy plate to help place emphasis on his next word, "*wise*, eldest son?"

The poke jolted John, who reddened, then took the platter. "Why, next Thurs—"

The swishing entrance of Ellie and Maggie curtailed his answer. John's and everyone else's eyes in the room, except Dr. Junkin's, followed the slender, splendidly arrayed figures of the girls to their seats.

The patriarch's eyes focused on the potatoes he was shoveling onto his plate.

"And George," he continued with aplomb, "I understand that youngster Willy Preston is tutoring your friends Anderson and Riley again with their Latin."

"Yes he is, sir," George Jr. returned.

"Bright boy, that Willy," Junkin said. "And his father, the colonel." Junkin passed the potatoes and looked down the right side of the table at Jackson. "In fact, I'm told that Colonel Preston and you go back to the late war in Mexico, Jackson."

Jackson at that moment possessed a mouth packed full of ham and snow peas. He entertained no immediate plans to be called upon, and it showed.

"Uh, yesshir. Goodsh friendsh we are, shir."

A burst of giggles escaped from the heretofore silent Ellie and Maggie. Their father shot a look at them that terminated the eruption.

"What is this Colonel Miller was saying about you spending all night waiting for him in his office?" Junkin proceeded.

A crimson flush rinsed Jackson's bulging cheeks.

"Why yes, Jackson," William said, "something about his excusing himself to attend to a matter while you were seated. Then he forgot you were waiting and went home."

"And the next morning, not having been dismissed, you were still waiting when he returned to his office." Jackson's brows arched at these baiting words, the first from Ellie's gay, enchanting voice. A mischievous hazel glint accompanied them.

Maggie glanced at Ellie, then at Jackson, then, fidgety, looked down and chased a lone remaining snow pea on her plate with her fork.

"Huzzah!" George Jr. whispered.

Silence held the room as Jackson shifted in his chair. Then he looked straight at Ellie.

"I find that a man's principal object in life should be the discharge of his duty," he said.

Ellie turned to Maggie, who half-glanced up at her. Junkin and John regarded one another. The barest trace of a smile curled up one side of John's mouth.

"Hmm," Junkin said. Then he spotted his own single surviving pea, stalked it, and finally stabbed it. Satisfied, he looked down the left side of the table at Ellie and Maggie. "And where did your duties take you ladies today?"

Now Ellie and Maggie did the squirming. They looked down, not answering.

Jackson eyed Ellie as he chewed. Then he peered at Maggie, who returned his gaze. Then his eyes returned to Ellie. There they stayed. Maggie saw. Ellie did not.

Ruthie bustled back into the room—to the rescue—silver coffee-pot in hand.

"So who'll have strawberries and cream this evening?" she asked. "Fresh-picked from the garden."

Junkin's eyes twinkled as Ruthie poured coffee, looking at everyone but him.

"John?" Ruthie asked. "Yes. Ebenezer? Yes. Ladies?" Ruthie gave a quick, disapproving shake of her head to Ellie. "Looks like everybody."

Then, she was gone as quickly as she arrived.

Her voice rattled on from the kitchen. "Young Moses! Up with them strawberries and cream, young man! Up with them now!"

Jackson scanned the table. *Brothers and sisters and father. Some giggling, some quiet, some drinking coffee, some whispering to one another. A family.* For just an instant, he saw his own smiling mother cutting his meat for him at the supper table. He gazed around to see Warren and Elizabeth again, giggling at one another. At the end of the table, his father chewed his food and winked, like a kindly king in his court.

"My dear Major Jackson." Junkin's clear strong voice snapped Jackson back, his eyes misty. Jackson cleared his throat. "Should you in future days have continued opportunities to gain acquaintance with the women of the Junkin house," the older man said, "you should be cautioned that they have a panache that, regretfully, most attribute to their paternal lineage."

Ellie and Maggie blushed anew and looked down. Junkin turned to the cherub-faced Julia, who sat immediately to his left.

"But the unbounding sweetness and compassion I thank our dear Lord each possesses," he said, "there can be no doubt from whence those came."

The lion-headed patriarch gazed down the table to the empty high-backed chair opposite him. The room was again quiet for a long moment, for the grand man was not in truth staring down an expansive oaken table, but rather the years and love of his life. The merest hint of wetness betrayed itself in his eyes.

CHAPTER 10

WALKER HAD PERHAPS SAT THROUGH ONE TOO MANY OF Professor Jackson's regurgitated optics lessons. But on this warm September day in 1852, the professor would offer little tolerance and brook no insolence. For a blond-headed, hazel-eyed slip of a girl had proved no little distraction to his normally rigid and effective lesson preparations. What feelings or concerns she was the source of he could not say nor even speculate. But he was wound up like a fisherman's knot and not obliged to suffer fools.

Thus ensued a considerable problem in that on this day one particular redheaded fool insisted on proving himself an even more formidable obstacle to the process of education and instruction than usual.

Jackson, who may have had every figure in every formula and equation (in a course full of them) committed permanently to memory, nonetheless possessed no manual dexterity, and consequently had an unfortunate inability to carry out even the simplest in classroom laboratory exercises designed to illustrate textbook theorems.

Walker knew this as well as anyone. He also knew that if one situation existed in Jackson's life bound to bring a smile and even a laugh to the austere instructor's face, even in front of his cadets, it was the utter collapse of yet another lab experiment. But Walker himself was in no laughing mood today. It was bad enough he could not seem to win the hand of Julia Junkin because of the complicating presence of Joe Kennedy, that smart-mouthed, lily-livered Yankee clerk of Judge Brockenbrough's. But knowing that Professor Jackson of all people occasionally dined at the same table with Julia—*Aah!*

Today's experiment progressed just about as usual. Jackson had the apparatus assembled on his table at the front of the classroom. His hands shaking as usual, he neared the climactic part of the experiment. *Just about now—yes!* Walker thought, watching closely. *Total collapse of the model, right on cue. And a bit of smoke today for good measure. That ignorant—*

"Tom Fool, he'll never learn, will he?"

Walker turned toward beefy Jimmy Mason, normally slumbering by this point in a Jackson lab exercise. Today Mason was not only wide awake, but had blurted out the very words about to emerge from Walker's own mouth.

A ripple of laughter skipped across the room. A ripple no greater or worse than many times before in a class of Professor Jackson's. But today, the prof's hands were singed, he was slapping out a small fire on his lab table, Ellie Junkin continued to invade his thoughts, and someone—*it sounded like the lazy Mason, but could it have been that sassy Walker again?*—was heaping on disrespect for the institute and authority in general and Jackson in particular.

"Mr. Mason, you will show respect in the future, sir," Jackson barked.

The class was strangely hushed. Jackson reddened.

It must have been Walker, he thought. "Mr. Walker, you will cease your constant displays of insubordination. They have ceased to amuse."

"Confound you, you ignorant fool," Walker shouted, the color of his face now rising to match that of his hair. "We sit in here every day and listen to your inanities and your witless repetitions and watch your idiotic failures at the lab table. Perhaps I must endure such an ordeal to graduate from this institution, but where I come from, sir, a man need not brook insult nor false charges from anyone, much less a fool."

After over a year, the showdown had finally arrived. The outburst stunned the class. No laughter this time. Some of the cadets lowered their eyes. Most, despite their usual amusement at the antics of both Walker and Jackson, now at the point of climax would gladly have found themselves almost anywhere else.

Marley gritted his teeth near the back of the room. He glared at the back of the carrot-topped head a few seats toward the front. *Stupid, hot-headed slaver.* The Pennsylvanian rose from his seat. *If Walker is so spoiling for a fight,* he thought, *he won't have to shame a professor to find one.* Abe Fulkerson, who occupied the seat behind Marley and knew the Mexican War veteran's devotion to Jackson, caught his arm. Marley's head whipped around.

"I think Jackson needs to handle this himself," Fulkerson whispered. "The worst thing for him would be to lose more respect."

Marley thought on that for a moment, then slid reluctantly back into his chair. But he was ready. And the men around him, who knew Jackson did not fire that cannon on the Chapultepec road alone, and unspokenly held the eye patch and its wearer near a state of awe, knew also that they wanted no part of Wayne Marley even in a classroom scrap. Fulkerson breathed out a soft sigh of relief.

Walker knew who had fired the cannon too. But he would look right down the barrel of that cannon if need be—perhaps not without fear, but certainly without doubt or misgiving. In that respect, he was that rare breed of man who might be a thorn in the flesh of those around him but who would likely be the one upon whom they would lean when they heard the sound of life's guns. Not unlike him, however, at least in the latter regard, was the instructor whose azure eyes now bore down on him. Walker's latest outburst had torn it for this professor.

"A fool knows not when to keep his tongue," Jackson fumed, walking toward the desks from the front of the room.

Walker leapt to his feet, his ruddy face darkening and the veins in his muscular neck bulging. "And a fool knows whom to accuse, especially in an arena where he has demonstrated such utter and consistent incompetence," he spat out. Jackson, eyes blazing, started to speak, but Walker raised a hand to cut him off. "Either I did make noise, or I did not. When the noise was made, you, sir, accused Mr. Mason of making it. I found it strange—and amusing, actually—that you should accuse Mr. Mason of making noise if you did not think he made it, and stranger still that you should chastise me if you think he did."

Now Walker stabbed a finger in Jackson's direction, as the awe-struck class watched gape-mouthed. "I suppose the amount of the matter is you suspected me, and your accusation was founded on suspicion. I now ask you, sir, if you can qualify me being the author of the noise, and I intend to ask the superintendent if a report made on suspicion can hold good according to his own doctrine at his opening speech before the corps!"

Walker's last sentence echoed off the stone walls of the room. Many of the cadets now stared at their feet. A few, including Patton, turned eagerly to Jackson for his response. Marley's knuckles glowed white from the intensity with which he gripped his wooden desk. He felt it best to hang on to the desk, for he feared what he might do to Walker with those same hands if he let go.

For a moment Jackson and Walker glared at one another, sparks all but popping from their burning eyes. The jaws of both jutted forward, and Marley saw that Jackson's hands were clenched into tight fists. *Brain the scandalous rascal, Jack, for gosh sakes, brain him!* Marley pleaded with his thoughts.

Just when a physical altercation seemed unavoidable, the fire left Jackson's eyes, at least partly, and his body relaxed. A soothing wave at once convicting and freeing came over him. He realized how unlike the manner of Christ his own feelings were toward this obviously unhappy and disturbed young man. The boy needed a response akin to that of what the Lord's would be were He conducting this class. He needed consideration and love, and for his own good, and that of the class, he needed concerned discipline to deter him from the wayward path upon which he seemed determined to embark. When Jackson broke the electrifying silence, he spoke with calm and clarity.

"You may consider yourself under court-martial, Mr. Walker." The image in Walker's eyes turned from rage to shock. "Mr. Marley and Mr. Munford, you will escort Mr. Walker at once to the superintendent's office and have him placed under arrest."

No less shocked than Walker was his cohort Munford. Marley was out of his seat and at Walker's side in an instant, roughly clutching his arm, which Walker jerked away. As Marley and Walker tensed to square off, Jackson spoke again. "Mr. Munford, you will escort Mr. Walker at once to the superintendent's office, or I shall place you under court-martial as well." The words remained even. Something wafted through the words telling Munford he had one good choice, and that was to obey the professor.

As Marley and Munford left the room with Walker, the redhead glared back at Jackson. "You'll find you've pushed it too far this time, you lout," the younger man growled.

If Walker still had sand in him toward Jackson, he was the only one in the class who did. The rest of the period proceeded without incident.

In any event, Irv Cullum had already scrawled his poetic entry for the day.

> *The V.M.I., oh, what a spot,*
> *In winter cold, in summer hot,*
> *Great Lord Al . . . , what a wonder*
> *Major Jackson, Hell & Thunder!*

George Junkin, though a consummate man of thought, letters, and ideals, lived as what few of that sort are—a consummate man of action. He had found himself swimming from one boiling cauldron into another since he could remember. His many and frequent moves had become proverbial among both family and friend. Yet always, wherever he might find himself, he had enjoyed a rich cup of chocolate and a crackling fire before bed, as he did on this snowy late November night. He followed this regimen even in summer when Rush would allow it.

Rush, he thought. *Patient, kind, sturdy, loving Rush.* Bearer, suckler, and raiser of his seven children. How gracious of God to have taken her so soon after the second round of strokes. Broken in mind and body as she was, Junkin had done what he would never have thought he could possibly do—prayed that God would take her to Himself as soon as He was willing. For after all, she had never been of this world anyway, had she? . . . having confessed that "they were strangers and pilgrims on the earth."

Now his work would be alone. *But, oh Lord, why is it that even the fire does not warm me on this evening?* Junkin thought. *Has it truly been six months?* He picked up the framed likeness from the bedstand. *So pretty, so true she was. Wife of my youth. How can I continue my work without you? But I must!* He placed Rush's likeness back on the stand and stared into the fire. *Out of these strange ashes . . . .*

The faint, sweet melody of the pianoforte wafted up the vent from downstairs. A smile creased Junkin's large, lined face. *Yes, that must be . . . Ellie.* The smile grew. *Of all of them, yes, she carries the most of Rush with her. And not just in appearance.* Yet, at times the physical resemblance was so great, when the light caught her face just right, it caused his head to feel light. But even more than that was the sweetness. *Indeed, Rush lives on here as well as there,* he thought. *Indeed.*

"So you'd no idea we have a famed poetess in our midst, Jackson?"

Jackson's ignorance of Maggie Junkin's growing renown as a poetess through Virginia and even some neighboring states astounded Harvey. Jackson, Harvey, Maggie, Ellie, and Anna Morrison sat around the parlor. Sociable chatter, a crackling fireplace, and Ellie's deft fingers on the pianoforte created a warm, jolly atmosphere as the snow blew outside. The sweet fragrance of hot apple cider lent further spice to the ambience.

As usual, identical hairstyles and dresses adorned Ellie and Maggie. Jackson sat bolt-upright in a high-backed maple chair, thumbing through a small hardbound book. Its contents impressed him and his face glowed.

"Five books of poetry published?" he asked, to no one in particular.

Ellie rose from the pianoforte bench and crossed the room to sit closer to the others. She sank into her favorite chair, a plush green velvet Gainsborough. Unspoken understanding had left the chair open for her, as it always was left when she was present. The daughter of a professor at Miami College where Junkin had served as president insisted the chair be given to Ellie after the widowed man died and the contents of his house were disbursed. The daughter took most everything else in the well-fitted home—the family of the professor's deceased wife had been wealthy—into her home. Before he expired, however, the elderly teacher insisted the chair be given to Ellie. She had spent much of one year sitting in it caring for the old man. The professor proved quite crotchety, and it seemed no one other than Ellie, including the daughter, had had much to do with him, even in his last days. That fact had not been lost on the dying, semidelirious man.

Dear Ellie, Maggie had thought at the time with a sniff, *doting on the least deserving, even as the beaus of Miami who pursue her with such vigor are left wanting.*

Pride swelled Ellie's mellifluous voice as she responded to Jackson. "And a novel to be completed and published by summer with a New York house."

Jackson, further impressed, read on.

"Why, you've a true talent, Maggie," he said after a moment, "a gift." Maggie, sitting primly—this demanded great effort—on the front of her chair, looked to the thick rug beneath her. Jackson continued, "I've wanted for some time to write a book myself, concerning the science of optics."

Harvey's broad, open face lit up. "Optics! Why, Jackson, you've told me yourself you hate optics, man."

Jackson's words came patient and even. "The true feat, Colonel, is in mastering that which comes difficult. The sluggard can perform the simple."

"We've heard that you accomplished the difficult in the late war," Ellie said. She glanced at Maggie, her eyes twinkling. "Is it so difficult to attain a normal posture while sitting, Major Jackson?"

"Elinor Junkin!" Maggie was aghast. "That is the second time tonight you've slighted the major."

The gigging did not rattle Jackson. "No trouble, Miss Junkin." Suddenly, he grimaced in sharp pain. "Oww! . . . oh! . . . if you'll please excuse me, I believe I'm having another attack of—"

Jackson leapt from his chair, clutching his abdomen. Ellie and Maggie gasped and looked at one another. Anna lifted the back of one hand over her mouth in shock and Harvey rose from his chair.

Jackson pulled two small vials from an inside coat pocket. He drank from both, sighed deeply, and wiped sweat from his forehead. The others stared at him. The only sound in the room was the sizzling, popping burning of firewood.

"Dyspepsia," Jackson concluded.

Before Harvey could take one step, Ellie and Maggie converged on Jackson. Ellie felt his forehead, and Maggie urged him to sit back down. Anna's hand remained over her mouth.

Jackson held up his hands. "Ladies, please, I'll be fine. The hour is late, however, and I should be taking my leave."

The sound of knocking at the front door echoed through the front foyer and into the parlor.

Maggie was perplexed. "But Major—"

"No, I'll be fine. This condition has proven to be the most difficult of that late war." Jackson turned to Maggie. "You have a marvelous gift, Miss Junkin." Then, to Ellie. "May I call again tomorrow evening?"

"Why, Major," she giggled, "whatever should we do with an evening if you did not call?"

Maggie shot a dart at her as a goofy smile crooked across Jackson's face and he turned to leave.

"Hold your horses, Jackson," Harvey said, "and I'll walk with you. I need to be getting back and checking on Isabella."

Palmer, the poised, distinguished-looking butler, met Jackson and Harvey as they entered the foyer.

"Mr. Jackson, sir," Palmer said, "a man outside name Walker wish to see you, sir." He paused. "He mad, sir."

Jackson and Harvey traded looks. Jackson started for the door. Hill stopped him.

"Let me, Jackson."

"I'll not have another man do my bidding for me."

Ellie, Maggie, and Anna appeared from the parlor, laughing. They sensed the serious air immediately. Jackson and Harvey turned toward them. More knocks, this time pounding, sounded on the closed front door.

"Jackson," Harvey whispered. "Let me. The ladies." A subtle cock of the head toward the women accompanied the last words. Jackson relaxed his body almost imperceptibly. Harvey headed for the front, followed by Palmer.

"Why, whatever on earth is it, Major Jackson?" Ellie asked.

"A problem . . . uh . . . student," Jackson said. He fumbled for more to say. "But nothing that could . . . uh . . . dampen my pleasure at what I have seen or heard here tonight." This pleased them. Jackson was surprised at his own eloquence. *Perhaps those horrid Franklin meetings are beginning to show their benefit.*

James Walker was not interested in Franklin meetings or in talking to Harvey Hill.

"What is it, Walker?" Harvey asked curtly on the portico, tucking the heavy oaken front door shut behind him.

When Walker, sporting his VMI uniform, spoke, a thick aroma of bourbon laced his words.

"I'm expelled, *Mister* Hill, *sir.* Out of the institute. Sent home. Gone."

Harvey knew the matter was before the board of visitors, but was not aware that a decision had been rendered. The number of cadet complaints against Jackson had begun to mount, and Walker had filed countercharges of his own against Jackson. All of these factors served to bring the matter to the attention of the board.

"Why, I'm sorry to hear that, Walker."

"Sorry won't cut it, not now—sir." The last word dripped with bitterness. "I want to see that—man—now. Out here, man to man."

Harvey's face was taut. "This is no time for that, son."

Anger, fatigue, and bourbon had just about unraveled Walker. The ruddy complexion deepened. He looked to the ground and pawed at it with one booted foot, like an untamed stallion. When he looked back up, the steely gray eyes were aflame. He took a step toward Harvey and thrust a finger at him.

"Mexican War or no, I'm telling you one last time, Colonel, or I'll go through you and the door and drag the scoundrel out here myself."

Harvey took stock. He had no doubt he could put the whiskey-soaked Walker on his keister. But the lad was a strapper and full of vinegar in addition to the John Barleycorn, and it might be a messy, and noisy, job to keep him there. Not a tasteful task for the front steps of the college president and minister's home, with his daughters a few feet inside the front door.

"You needn't drag anyone out here, Mr. Walker."

Thank God! Harvey could not suppress a king-sized smile from advancing from one ear to the other.

Jackson, now next to Harvey and shutting the door himself, was not smiling.

Walker stabbed the same finger in Jackson's direction and opened his mouth to speak, the veins in his neck bulging and his blood-red eyes about to pop out of their sockets. But he seemed like a rumbling volcano ready to erupt, and it took a moment for the words to come.

"You, mister," came the growl from somewhere deep and dark. "I have business with you, mister."

Jackson had had his fill of Walker before this evening. If the impudent Williamsburg snob did not know his place before elders and authority, perhaps this setback would help him learn it. *Sad it has to come to this, but the lad will be better off over the long haul learning such lessons now. However, daring to show up on the president's steps looking for trouble, and the president a minister at that, with the man's daughters and another fine lady just inside, and appearing liquored up to boot—well, if Walker wants trouble, he has come to the right place.*

"Any business you have with me will wait until a later date," Jackson said, an edge of danger on his voice at once subtle and yet pronounced enough that it turned Harvey's surprised head toward him.

Walker was undaunted, and sparks flew from his blazing hazel eyes. "No, I intend to settle with you right now, mister."

Jackson leaned ever-so-slightly toward the redhead. "You're drunk, sir." Walker's eyes widened further. "And I'll be pleased to remove you from this portico myself if you do not take the wise course and retreat."

The younger man, venom flowing from his face and spit spewing from his mouth, unbuttoned his coat and slung it to the ground. Jackson stepped toward him.

The front door opened again. This time, Dr. Junkin stepped out, in his robe and slippers.

"What is it, gentlemen? What is going on out here?"

No one said anything. Junkin gazed from Walker to Harvey to Jackson. "Well most assuredly there is some explanation for such clamor on the steps of the president's home at this time of evening. You've succeeded in half-frightening the women inside, two of which are daughters of mine."

Junkin did not know that a third daughter, his youngest, stared bright-eyed out from a second-floor dormer. Her heart raced and butterflies fluttered around in her stomach. *Why, whatever on earth could that wild boy be doing now? Could he be calling on me? No, he seems to be arguing with Major Jackson and—but doesn't he look dashing in his gray coat and all that unruly red hair! He certainly is more impetuous than Joey. . . .*

Back down on the porch, Dr. Junkin sniffed in Walker's direction. "I say, boy, have you been drinking this evening?"

Walker blew out a deep sigh and shook his head. Then he pulled a white cadet dress glove from his pocket and slung it backhanded at Jackson. It popped him on the chest and dropped to the floor of the portico.

"At your service, mister," Walker said through clenched teeth.

Junkin, towering over the others, moved toward Walker. "Young man, you leave this property at once."

Walker glanced at Junkin, then turned and headed down the steps. When he reached the ground, he wheeled back around.

"You let me know when and where tomorrow, Jackson, or I'll tell you." Then he was gone into the night.

The three men on the portico were stunned.

Harvey shook his head, his eyes trailing after Walker. "That boy is bound to die young. I only hope he's sober enough to remember it."

That remark prompted Jackson and Junkin to look at Harvey, then at each other.

When they stepped back inside, the foyer was clogged with people: Ellie, Maggie, Anna, Palmer, Ruthie, and Julia, who was in her nightgown and floor-length robe.

Junkin spoke before anyone else could. "Julia Junkin, you get yourself back to bed."

"But Papa, what did he say—"

"I said back to bed, little lady!"

Julia recognized this as one of those times when her father would be unbudgeable. *Oh well, I'll sweet talk him into telling me what happened in the morning.* She was a happy girl by nature, and she hopped back up the stairs two at a time, robe and all.

"Father, what on earth—"

"Papa, what was that—"

Junkin raised his hands to silence the crowd. "We had a very drunk and very disrespectful young man at our door just now. If ever again you see him on these grounds—" Near the top of the stairs,

Julia stopped and turned back, hurt in her eyes. Junkin swallowed hard. "We had a man who was upset over a matter at the VMI. That is all. Good night."

With that, he headed for the stairs himself. Julia waited for him as he reached the top. Using his hands in a shoveling motion, he shooed her toward her room.

"Tomorrow, my little monkey, tomorrow we shall talk."

He rushed past her, mumbling to himself. When he reached his own door down the hall, he stopped and looked back at the forlorn girl standing by the stairs. He looked down, then walked slowly back toward her. A thin veil glistened over her eyes. Junkin put his arms around her in a long, affectionate hug.

"I think he's got some good stuff to him," Junkin said slowly. "But he has some rough edges, and I have my doubts, as I believe you have, whether he is in any serious fellowship with our Lord." Junkin paused for a moment. "Perhaps it would be best for you not to see—"

Julia stopped him. "I know, Papa, I know." She sniffed back tears and stepped into her room, closing the door behind her.

Junkin liked to have things figured out in life; in fact, he felt he had most things figured out. He did not have time to doubt what he was called upon to preach and proclaim. But one of the first questions he was going to ask when he stared at last into the eyes of his Lord was, "Why the pain, sir? Why all the pain, especially for the young people?" He stood for a moment in the hall, musing about the Lord's methods of bringing His plans to pass. The Lord had blessed him with four good, stouthearted sons. Those were the ones he was to teach. And the Lord had blessed him with the saintly wife of his youth and three wondrous daughters. Those were the ones who were to teach him. A wave of tenderness, feeling, and memory swept over him with such force that he nearly swooned where he stood. Then he looked at Julia's closed door. He stepped toward it and spoke his words softly. "I—I love you, baby Julia."

Shock and sadness pervaded those downstairs. After Harvey offered a brief explanation, Jackson turned again to leave. "Are you coming, Colonel?" The women were hardly in a mood to let him leave yet.

"But Major Jackson," Maggie asked, "what will happen with that boy?"

Ruthie had an opinion, had she been asked for it, as she headed back toward the kitchen. "Ask me, boy ought to have his hide whipped good for smart-mouthing, then some more for back-talking his betters, then some for showing up at the president's house drunk, then some more for threatening . . ." The kitchen door ended her diatribe for anyone who might have been listening in the front foyer.

"I don't know," Jackson said, reaching for the front door. He stopped abruptly, wheeled back around and stood even straighter than usual, to his absolute full height. "Excuse me, please. Miss Ellie? Might I have a brief word with you?"

Maggie and Ellie locked eyes in surprise. Then Ellie turned to Jackson and nodded. She followed him into the small front parlor.

Now Maggie and Harvey shared a quizzical glance. They heard a squeal and turned to see the long-silent Anna happily rubbing her hands together. Her merry eyes danced as she watched Jackson and Ellie exit the room. Then she giggled at Maggie and Harvey, whisked around and sashayed back to the larger sitting room. There, she collected the saucers and dishes the group had used. A chorus of song, alternately sung and hummed, swelled out from her. Maggie and Harvey stared at her as she launched into a lilting romantic ballad.

Harvey spied the concern written across Maggie's pretty face.

"I . . . I think I'll just go ahead and wait outside for the major." Palmer handed Harvey his gloves. "Good night, Maggie."

After he left, Maggie turned toward the front sitting room. She bit her lip. *Surely he's not going to ask her—* She grabbed her hooped skirt, held it up from the floor, and tiptoed toward the muted sound of voices. Other voices outside distracted her. Harvey and her father. *Only one place Papa would be going this time of night.* Maple Tree Hill. Location of the earthly remains of Julia Rush Miller Junkin.

"Well, what is it, Major?" Ellie asked the nervous, rigid-backed man in front of her.

An arm started to shoot up, but Jackson caught it forcefully with his other hand. She almost laughed out loud at that.

The major blushed, bumbled, and stumbled. "I . . . well . . . well, I . . . ," he looked her in the eye, "I'd be obliged if you would accompany me to services in the morning, Miss Junkin—early, if you please—so you can play piano in our young people's Sunday school class." Her eyes widened. "Don't worry, you won't have to hear me teach! Young Willy Preston, Maggie's friend Colonel John Preston's son, will be giving a special message on the importance of reaching the non-English speaking heathen with the gospel."

Ellie stared at him.

"Now, I should add that this invitation is being extended not just as a friend, but . . . well . . . ,"—Maggie listened breathlessly just outside the room—"as someone who in no way merits your favor, but should like to engage your company in perhaps something more than just normal friendship."

Ellie was dumbstruck. Maggie, ashen-faced, pulled the heel of her hand to her mouth. *Oh, God. Oh, God.*

Over her shoulder, across the foyer, Ruthie stood watching the thirty-two-year-old Junkin daughter, dish towel in hand, shaking her head. *Lord have mercy, I knew it, I just knew it, Lord. Lordy have mercy.*

CHAPTER 11

LAURA LAY IN BED, AGAIN, WHEN THE NEW LETTER ARRIVED from her brother. It had the same sure, optimistic tenor his letters usually did, but something more as well.

"My dearest little sister Laura Ann. I have for months back admired Lexington. But now, for the first time, have I truly and fully appreciated it. Of all the places that have come under my observation in the United States, this little village is the most beautiful. Please talk to and love dear, blessed little Tommy and Elizabeth as I would were I with you. Your loving older brother, Thomas."

The next letter, a few weeks later, actually explained why Lexington had shown itself so splendid in Tom's eyes. Though, of course, Laura knew why by reading this one closely—and not even that closely, actually. For she knew Tommy, had always known him, and could most assuredly discern when love for the first time clutched him in its inescapable hand. Just as she knew when it had forsaken her. *Don't trust love, poor Tommy,* she thought but would never dare tell him. *Read your Good Book where it says "Vain is the hope we place in men." Enjoy your moment in the warm, happy sun, but never, never trust it, dear Tommy.*

Indeed, the spring of 1853 was the brightest and most beautiful ever for Tom Jackson. Who was this woman, and what were these feelings sweeping over him? The days after that first awkward invitation last autumn had displayed her for the first time cool and aloof, as though pulling back from his clear designs on a relationship more cordial than friendship. Then, even as the winter set in and the air grew cold, and with it discouragement and doubt about the possibilities of such a pleasant prospect, she began to thaw and blossom anew. And this time more fully and vividly than when just as an acquaintance and friend. This time, he began to catch the first glimmer of the true, boundless beauty of her character and nature. He began to stagger at the enormity of what God had wrought in woman and most especially in this woman, Elinor Junkin.

For Ellie's part, she too, at twenty-eight, felt the advent of feelings never before experienced. Oh, the boys had been at that same Junkin front door where James Walker had raised such a stink, for as long as she could remember. Many had been good, fine boys, and with a couple she had actually been . . . close?—no, not really. Nothing remotely similar to this gloriously earnest, unpretentious, sincere, and kind man.

"Only after having come to know him with the intimacy of hourly converse," she told Maggie one day during a ride through the fields on the high ground east of town, "have I found that much we have attributed to eccentricity is the result of the deepest underlying principle. It compels in me a respect, Sister, that both accompanies new-found affection and that I—we each—had dare not withhold."

Maggie smiled, so happy for her most beloved soulmate, yet so increasingly doubtful regarding Jackson's suitability and qualification for her and so—no, she wasn't hurt; she merely, as all soldiers of the cross, must deny herself, take up her cross daily, and follow Him. No, she most definitely was not hurt. Why, what a preposterous notion! She knew a single woman her age was apt to have silly notions just as a woman of any other age. But God had called her to other duties to this point, more important duties. And if the Almighty intended her to have a man, He was more than capable of providing one. In fact, He alone could know the identity of that proper mate.

In any event, it certainly was not that *major* with his dyspepsia, his embarrassing stiff-backed posture, his heavy side, and his ridiculous flying arm. And besides, was he not an absolute failure in his chosen profession? No, more than that, was he not a pitiable figure of scorn and ridicule, from student and faculty member alike? The more Maggie gnawed on these thoughts as the weeks passed (she was finding it difficult to write much poetry these days), the more convinced she became Jackson was not only someone she herself could never have been matched with—*oh, never in a million lifetimes!*—but neither was he worthy of the apple of both their eyes. In fact, the way that Father and the rest of the family was warming to Major Jackson, it perhaps fell to her alone the duty to break loose any bonds beyond natural affection and sentiment Ellie, herself closer now to thirty every day, may have allowed to creep in through curiosity and the persistent efforts of this ungainly and embarrassing suitor. But she must be careful in such an undertaking, so as never to harm her innocent, guileless sister.

"He is a good, decent, and honest fellow," Maggie said as they walked their winded mounts. "But I feel constrained to worry about such a sinful past, Sister. Why, he has belonged to the church barely more than a year, for goodness' sake. He still has doubts about such foundational truths as predestination and election, and you and I both suspect his lack of regard for the holding to of the Sabbath. And he himself has admitted to you his past bouts with many such evils as drinking, cards, and attending the theater! I just don't understand what you can see in him, dear sister. I just believe you deserving of so much more and—yes—better a man."

Ellie smiled and reached to touch Maggie softly on her arm. Her words were soft and richly seasoned with gentleness. "Yes, I find it hard to believe myself, Sister. He does not seem at all what I would have expected in a man I would—," Maggie's face whipped around toward her, "feel such . . . such regard for."

Maggie's face was pallid. "So you . . . you do have feelings for the major, feelings more than those for a . . . brother?"

Ellie stopped her horse and gazed up at the clear blue winter sky and felt the soothing warmth of the sun's rays against her face as she closed her eyes. Maggie thought it the most beautiful and pure of all the faces ever created by the Master. She detected just a faint glistening of the porcelain skin from the hard ride just completed. *Yes, Ellie deserves the best,* she thought. *And that is not Major Jackson.*

"Yes, I have feelings, beloved sister," Ellie said, her eyes still closed and a happy, dreamy smile spreading across her exquisite countenance. "Feelings like I have never before known. Feelings whose propriety should alarm me were I not so safely and firmly ensconced in the arms and the will of our glorious Savior. For I know that the feelings are of Him and that as long as He remains my Sovereign, He being their source and originator, I shall fear them not."

Her eyes opened and she turned to Maggie, the gorgeous white smile still transfixed. "And I have already discussed the issues you raise with him, for indeed they are important issues."

The look on Maggie's face wordlessly asked, *And?*

"And he said in that sweet, innocent, profound way of his, 'Remember Ellie, I lived, then, up to all the light I had, and therefore I did not then, nor do I now, reproach myself for my past errors.' You see, Sister, the important fact is he has a teachable heart, a heart so soft toward the will and leading of God that he has actually prayed to

God to take him through whatever trial or struggle be necessary to prove and temper that heart. Yes, the major is still fairly young in the ways of our Lord, but I firmly believe him to be one of the most dedicated Christians in these parts and that in time he will prove to be one of the wisest and most mature of all." The memory of these ruminations lit Ellie's face with enchantment and her eyes closed again in sublime joy. "Oh Sister, such a man, committed to holy living as he is, yet with such a deep hold on grace as he has. Oh Sister, I fear that my heart may—"

"No, Sister, no!" Maggie screamed as she turned and gouged her horse into a gallop across the field and back toward town.

Ellie stared after her, a puzzled expression washing away most of the smile. "Oh Sister, dear, dear Sister. Perhaps in time, you too will come to appreciate his qualities."

When Jackson found himself alone with Ellie in the beautiful wooded settings of late winter and early spring, and the harbingers of new life that accompanied them—chirping birds of red, blue, yellow, and brown, and the fantastic arrays of trees coming back to multihued life—the perturbations of optics classes and Walker seemed far away. She was so comfortable, and so comforting. At first, her smile came slower than it had—did she not enjoy being alone with him? But she continued, with occasional exception, to accept his invitations for picnics and rides, and with time the smile increased in quickness and frequency. At first, though he himself talked so much it felt as if someone else were controlling his mouth, and he had nothing whatsoever to do with its operation, she spoke little. Did he direct the conversation toward subjects that bored her? (*A quick remedy for that: continue speaking and moving from subject to subject until something peaks her interest.*) After a time, however, her words flowed freely, and she herself began to direct the conversation where she wanted it, though she continually amazed him with her desire and ability to shepherd the rambling discussions to areas of his interest, without his needing to do so. In fact, she had a curious way of directing their talks along paths of great interest to him, but ones he would not himself have chosen or in some cases did not even realize were there to be explored. He found her helping him to open up stored-away areas of his life and thinking that had seen little or no light.

This phenomenon aided Jackson in a spate of ways, not the least of which was his performance at the Franklin Society. Public speaking was proving more difficult to master than the West Point academic curriculum. But a voice remained with him in times of adversity and dejection. A voice driving him onward. *You may be whatever you resolve to be.* So he practiced evenings in his rented hotel room, forcing himself to speak into a mirror as perspiration dotted his upper lip and dripped from his forehead and his right arm launched itself frequently toward the ceiling. The mirror helped because he had no problem with the physiological mechanics of speaking aloud on a subject with which he was familiar—when alone in a room. However, doing so with an audience continued to present a different challenge. Jackson found projecting to his own visage provided the next best thing to rehearsing before a live crowd. With tenacious, dogged perseverance, despite further humiliations at the Franklin, the professor gradually effected a fair presentation style, then even one of compelling style and skillful articulation and flow of argument.

Classroom success proved even more elusive than public oratory. Walker might be gone, but after two years even Jackson admitted in the quietness of his own heart his lack of talent and inclination in the challenging field of education. Complaints from students and letters from alumni continued finding their way to Superintendent Smith's office, as well as VMI's governing board of visitors. But Jackson's sterling character and exemplary effort, his (barely) acceptable performance, and a dearth of qualified replacement candidates in the subjects he taught combined to secure his continued employment at the school. The lengthy legacy of his war reputation, however, stood as the single strongest, though unspoken, support for Jackson's job security.

In fact, Walker was anything but gone. Absent from the VMI campus perhaps, but, living in the Lexington house of a friend, his initial anger at being expelled had evolved into a furious obsession. Ellie heard through friends that Walker intended an invitation to Jackson for a two-man duel with pistols! Marley caught wind of the same information through the institute's cadet grapevine, and Dr. Junkin's secretary reported to Maggie a similar, though not identical, story circulated to her by a Washington College faculty member. If such rumors concerned Jackson, he did not evidence it, even after Harvey Hill informed him two cadets had seen an official invitation Walker had prepared and was readying to forward to Jackson.

The major preferred directing his thoughts toward the delightful gatherings he shared with Ellie and other friends at the Junkin home, listening to her and her sister Maggie (their hair and dress prepared identically) perform animated duets on the pianoforte. Maggie would surreptitiously steam at the now-hated interloper, pouring her wrath into the keyboard. Ellie would play with joyful abandon and sneak winking little smiles at the man she was coming to love.

Even more enchanting were the idyllic country picnics on which Jackson and Ellie continued to embark. He loved it when she pulled her thick yellow hair back and tied it into a tail, because then he could see all the lovely, sun-kissed contours of her matchless face and enjoy her soft hair bouncing around on her back when she launched into one of her animated stories about Maggie or her father or young Julia and the Kennedy boy who was so smitten over her.

Ellie presented a radically different embodiment of the female species to Jackson than he had ever before witnessed. At times he felt consuming joy; at times, deep perplexion; and at other times awe of her magical radiance simply left him dumb.

A deep, abiding, contented faith constituted a major portion of that radiance. Jackson had long sought the secret to ordering his own heart and life. At times he had been somewhat successful in doing so; at other times, not as successful. The last couple of years especially, the Christianity to which he had increasingly devoted himself had proven quite efficacious for the task. Now, however, he reveled in the close witnessing of one—*and a woman, at that!*—who provided with her life a textbook outworking of all the truths, principles, and ideals embodied in that sublime religious faith. Sometimes it almost overwhelmed him. *How could she be so trusting?* he marveled. *So sure, so calm?* The entire Junkin clan still wondered how, when her mother had died the previous year, Ellie singularly bore the load and buoyed the troops. Her graceful winning smile cheered her brothers, her sweet favors helped pull her father out of his lost funks, and her loving words and consolation kept Maggie from what the spunky older sister herself admitted only to herself to have been the brink of an emotional collapse.

As Jackson learned—from other family members, not Ellie herself—her faith, so natural and certain, was not without great price. The precious, merrily dancing hazel eyes so entrancing to him were gradually, inexorably descending into permanent darkness. And sharp, shooting pain accompanied the descent every step of the way. The extent of notice conveyed to Jackson had been a couple of picnics ended early because Ellie was "fatigued." Yet he remembered as he looked back seeing her stealthily rubbing her eyes and temples on the return rides home.

"Why? Why did you not see fit to tell me?" he pressed her in the Junkin's main sitting room upon learning of the condition from a tearful Julia.

Ellie's immediate response was one of silent embarrassment. She turned from Jackson, but he pulled her to him. Tears streamed from her eyes.

"Does it hurt badly, Ell?" he gasped, pain now creasing his own face.

She gently removed his hands from her arms and placed a soft, cool palm to his cheek, shaking her head.

"Dear Thomas, dear, dear Thomas," she smiled, her voice strong, though the tears continued. When no words were forthcoming, Jackson shifted uncomfortably. She saw in his grieved eyes desperate yearning for some sort of answer. She removed her hand and looked to the floor. She moved to a high-backed wooden chair and sat. Her next words came slowly and with great tenderness.

"My Thomas, I shall tell you because you alone might understand. If not now, then someday." She closed her eyes and looked upward. "'Yet of myself I will not glory, but in mine infirmities. For though I would desire to glory, I shall not be a fool; for I will say the truth: but now I forbear, lest any man should think of me above that which he seeth me to be, or that he heareth of me.'"

Jackson stared, transfixed, as she continued, her eyes remaining shut.

"'And lest I should be exalted above measure through the abundance of the revelations, there was given to me a thorn in the flesh, the messenger of Satan to buffet me, lest I should be exalted above measure. For this thing I besought the Lord thrice, that it might depart from me. And he said unto me, My grace is sufficient for thee: for my strength is made perfect in weakness. Most gladly therefore will I rather glory in my infirmities, that the power of Christ may rest upon me.'"

Now she spoke very softly and quite slowly, careful lest she convey a spirit of pride to this man who had come to mean so much to her it concerned her lest her love for God and His Son be lessened any at all. "'Therefore I take pleasure in infirmities, in reproaches, in necessities, in persecutions, in distresses for Christ's sake: for when I am weak, then am I strong.'" Her eyes opened again and peered at Jackson.

What manner of woman is this? "Have I seen today tears of joy in the midst of great physical pain?" His words were breathless and fragile as the fine English china lining the sideboard along the far wall of the room.

Ellie could not conceal her joy. She nodded, her beautiful ravaged eyes sparkling as they had so often for him. "You have." She was practically giggling.

Jackson had scant referent for this. "I . . . I wish you could have known my mother."

They stared at one another for a long time. Whatever barriers may have remained between the two now melted away into oblivion. They did not touch one another. They did not even speak. But something deathless and unending was given birth in that golden moment married of sorrow and joy. And Jackson became acutely aware of the reality that a plane of human experience existed of which he had never before been aware. Some of it had to do directly with Ellie. And some of it did not.

The lion of ambition held roaring dominance even in the quiet places of Jackson's heart. He admitted it to himself, though to few others. He admitted it to God, but did not at this point know exactly how to dispose of it. Renouncing it and vowing purity from it, unlike with other undesired habits and practices in his life, had not worked. Yet this raw, unbridled, perhaps even mounting ambition held no strains nor even flecks of guile or subterfuge. Jackson merely plopped one foot in front of the other as he stepped through the days of his life. The University of Virginia would reject his application for employment, despite letters of commendation from such men of stature as fellow West Point graduate and Mexican War hero Robert E. Lee of Virginia, but Jackson would nonetheless write the application and speak honestly and openly of it when queried.

Walker's letter arrived the following Thursday. Jackson did not share it with Ellie or any other member of the Junkin family to which he was becoming so close. He went to Harvey Hill.

"The blessed young fool," Harvey grimaced. "Walker threw away his career; now he's trying to do the same with his life."

Jackson did not fear Walker. And though ambition gripped him, it did not own him, and he did not fear what any man could do to affect his goals and plans. They were God's to give out and to take away. And God was a God of order, as Jackson increasingly understood through his discussions with Ellie and the other Junkins, his Presbyterian pastor Dr. William White, and his readings of the Bible and Presbyterian literature such as the Lower and Higher Catechisms and the Westminster Confession of Faith. The concept of the eternal predestination of saved Christian souls for heaven that he once mocked to scorn even made increasing sense to him. And what of the souls God knew would not make it to heaven and His eternal presence and fellowship? Jackson did not yet have that one worked out.

But he trusted and feared God in a way he did no man, certainly the young ingrate Walker. And he knew that trustworthy God of order did not like loose ends or chaos.

The letter challenged Jackson to a duel with pistols, swords, or knives at six o'clock the following Thursday evening on the plateau of the hill commanding Lexington from the north. It was brief, concise, and signed in flowing script by *James A. Walker, Esquire, of South Carolina.*

"I believe I shall have a warrant issued binding Mr. Walker to keep the peace," Jackson said.

This surprised Harvey. He could have found any number of explanations for the surprising statement had the officer and professor sitting erect across his desk from him been someone else. He had come to know that all Jackson did was tied up in duty and honor, or at least Jackson's perceptions of those elusive, and sometimes vastly overrated, commodities. What precisely the antecedent for this announcement might be he hadn't a clue, but he did know that it was a very poorly conceived strategy.

"I believe I should offer a hearty no to that proposal, my friend," Harvey said. "You'll feel the chill winds of contempt and scorn run through you from the cadets should you pursue it."

"They'll brand me as a coward."

"Some inclined against you already probably will."

"Thank you for your advice, my good friend," Jackson said without rancor as he stood.

Jackson did not heed his friend's counsel. Nor did he initiate any attempts at rapprochement with Walker, whom he actually caught glimpses of a couple of times spying upon his movements about town. If Jackson handled the matter with aplomb and failed to tell even one person besides Harvey about the letter, Lexington was abuzz with speculation, gossip, and, especially among the dormitories of Walker's ex-mates in the class of '55, wagers pertaining to the outcome of any potential duel. Walker had informed numerous individuals of the letter and the specific information contained in it. As word spread, people assumed an oversight on Walker's part in the concurrent timing of the face off with the monthly Franklin Society gathering. Then whispers multiplied indicating the expelled cadet's scheduling as intentional in order to assure as large an audience as possible among the area's most respected men.

Twice Marley urged action by his professor and friend to stymie the dark impending event. Jackson said only that his comings and goings were marked by God and he would not succumb to such brutish behavior unless it was forced upon him, and then he would acquit himself as a man should do.

The situation with Ellie proved thornier. The considerable influence and respect her father commanded in Lexington prompted a multiplicity of concerned individuals to come to her with varying versions of the frightening news. So many people visited Ellie and her family, in fact, that a precisely accurate picture of the letter's contents eventually availed itself to her.

The normally winsome woman burned with anger at the young hothead from South Carolina. Eventually, her unhappiness veered toward Jackson.

"Why will he not talk to me of this ridiculous and disgraceful spectacle?" she finally asked Maggie. "I have beseeched him repeatedly, since even before word of this monstrous 'challenge' came to light. He says only that he has sought the magistrate, who has been conveniently absent from his post for most of the past week, and that beyond that he has entrusted his destiny to God."

"Another of the peculiar institutions of our adopted Southern homeland," Maggie said with more than a trace of wryness. "That of the archaic and savage 'duel.' It speaks poorly of the South and worse for Major Jackson, who at least professes an education and a Christian faith."

Maggie grabbed her sister's arm with urgency before the withering undercut of these utterances could sink in. "Oh dear sister, do you not now see how impossibly wrong this well-intentioned but ultimately brutish backwoodsman is for you? Not now nor ever should I desire anything but God's finest for my beloved, but it is impossible to understate the calamity in which you would be engaging should you act other than to terminate this sweet but impossibly flawed courtship at once. To do anything else would . . ." Her voice trailed off and (the intensity of her grip paining Ellie's arm and hand) her eyes looked down.

"Would what, dear sister?"

Maggie paused for effect, inwardly clutching with glee the advantage she knew some foolish young South Carolinian rascal had finally delivered to her. Her blue eyes locked in to the honest, questioning hazel ones she knew and loved so well.

"Would be to take complete leave of your senses."

How much of the tearful tremor resident in those last words was calculated and how much was true concern not even Margaret Junkin herself could know. But it attained its intended objective, and Ellie tearfully determined to postpone furtherance of her courtship with Jackson until an unspecified later date—if ever.

Maggie felt a pang of regret and guilt, for she knew the toll her disciplined and masterfully executed strategy of sabotage had taken on her sister's blossoming relationship with the roughhewn major these past months. *Yes,* she grudgingly admitted even to herself, *he is a good man, and perhaps his desire to know and please God is inordinately sharp even in this town and state of inordinately devout Christian men and women.* But she had no doubts that that same God had used her to interrupt pending catastrophe. Ellie—sweet, fair Ellie—deserved the best this troubled world had to offer. Even if Maggie herself, with her Greek and Latin, her poems and books, and her dark, mysterious cloud, would never deserve any of it. At least, for the first time in a long time, she felt as though God was truly pleased with her. She knew the God she had learned from her father and mother was a powerful one. And they had assured in every way they were able that He was a just and loving one. But it was that shadow, that dark, dark creeping, clawing accuser and mocker that hovered over her that forever taunted the truth Ellie and every single one of her siblings, even young Julia, had so readily embraced. So she would write of how things were, but more especially of how they should be. And she would wait—perhaps for the heaven she did believe awaited even the weak and doubting like herself. Yes, and she would grieve. But she would not grieve over the fracturing of Ellie and the major. No, never would she do that.

"So you can see, Harvey, it's a terrible predicament I'm in," Jackson said sullenly as he again sat across the desk from his friend.

"Yes, I know it is. But you still have time to head this thing off and shake young Walker down before he can do harm to himself. And if he forces action upon you, I know you will conduct yourself with honor."

The steely blue eyes were glassy, and Jackson seemed to have heard nothing of Harvey's comments. "I've never previously been possessed of such a strange feeling and having not the least idea of how to deal with it."

Harvey gawked at his friend. "Fire and tarnation, Jackson, you knew how to deal with that cannonball at Chapultepec, and those people—all of them—heading into the City of Mexico. You've dealt for two full years now with vigorous, energetic cadets needing—depending on the moment—a boot, a bridle, or a fire under their backsides. And I must say, knowing your devotion to duty and God, and your desires for self-betterment, that you have forborne the scoundrel Walker to a degree nothing short of noble. But as to how to deal with this, this challenge . . ." This conversation was making Harvey confused and uncomfortable. He shook his head.

The hollowness of Jackson's eyes confirmed he still resided in his own little world, though this fact was lost on the befuddled Harvey. "I admit to having enjoyed the pleasures of other ladies' company, even in Mexico. And some have ceased social interplay before I would have chosen. But this, this rejection from Ellie is so utterly different, so unexpected. I felt I knew her and the situation better than this."

A smile began to wade across Harvey's countenance. *This man has a duel with a champion marksman in half an hour, and it's the farthest thought from his mind.* Harvey burst into merry laughter. He paused for a moment as Jackson snapped back to alertness and eyed him with bewilderment, then he exploded again into convulsions of high-pitched laughter that, despite Harvey's baritone speaking voice, sounded to Jackson rather like the screams of a hyena.

Harvey stopped long enough to wipe the tears of hilarity off his cheeks and offer, "Why, you're in love, my boy, that's what your problem is!" Then, knowing Elinor Junkin well and suspecting the source of what he believed to be merely a temporary courtship hiatus, he stepped around the desk and slapped the stonefaced Jackson hard on the back. "Relax and enjoy it, my boy. You'd be surprised at how many of us have been struck with the same affliction!"

Tonight Jackson would speak at the Franklin in favor of the proposition that God saves the heathen. But his central thesis took a different tack than that of most others who agreed with him on the general premise. They opined that a loving, and just, God would never consign an uncivilized barbarian who had not the opportunity to hear and believe the saving gospel of Christ to perdition. It would be against His magnanimous and unneedy character. Jackson agreed to this point, but he posited that God would find a way to deliver that gospel to those whom He would prompt to receive it. The others felt the heathen who had not "heard" would be saved by the same God, "using slightly different means." Jackson wrapped the sixth verse of the fourteenth chapter of the New Testament Gospel of John around these men's necks and shook them with it. He took stronger issue with these who agreed with the concept of distant uncivilized pagans being won by God than he did with his ostensible opponents, who agreed with him to the brittleness of the universalistic position, but gave the unreached islanders, desert tribes, and other aboriginals no hope, since they were obviously, by the word of God and by their own heinously brutal and carnal lives, not resident in the chosen rolls of the "Lamb's book of life."

Before holding forth about God and the heathen, Jackson decided to lodge a visit to Lexington magistrate Elkanah Clinton, with whom he would swear out a warrant.

Marching briskly down the steep grade from the VMI to Clinton's office (it had been better than a forty-five-degree angle until a long-term Lexington improvements program had finally put an end to most of the mule- and wagon-strewn calamities resulting from the steep slopes and thick muck caused by the heavier rains), Harvey, like most everyone else, practically had to run to keep up with Jackson.

They caught Clinton just as he himself was leaving for the Franklin convocation. Thus, the harelipped stoop-shouldered man of forty-five was not particularly predisposed to engage in discussion of a warrant, and when he heard for whom it was to be made out, he popped on his warm-weather top hat and asked Jackson and Harvey if they would care to accompany him to the meeting.

"Thank you, Mr. Clinton," Jackson said, "but I should prefer to handle this warrant business before we go."

Clinton stopped and shuffled back around toward Jackson. "I'll tell you honestly, Major Jackson. This is not an off-the-cuff decision. What with the rumors swirling around town and all, I've considered the possibility of somebody coming to me for a warrant. And I've decided that I'll not issue one. At least not for Mr. James Walker I won't. That man is intent on doing grievous bodily harm to somebody, and with his size and from what I hear about his marksmanship and pugilistic abilities, I'm not about to put myself in a position to be on the receiving end of what he's liable to be giving out."

Jackson and Harvey stared at the magistrate, then at one another.

"Are you refusing to serve a warrant on that man?" Harvey asked.

Clinton turned back down the street. "I'm going to the Franklin to hear Mr. Jackson—whose oratorical skills have improved greatly in recent months, greatly—and others hold forth on the gospel and the heathen. I suggest you two gentlemen drop this notion of a warrant and come with me." For just a moment, he returned his gaze to the tall Virginian. "And Major Jackson. Were I you, sir, with your martial skills, I should go to young Walker before he came to me—which I believe he most surely intends to do—and I should go soon."

With that, Clinton waddled off. Harvey was perplexed by the man's behavior. All of Lexington now knew of Walker's announced intention to meet Jackson outside the Franklin meeting to once and for all settle accounts. Of the characteristics Harvey would attribute to Clinton, bravery was not one. Yet, the man had exhibited not only willingness but desire to accompany Jackson in what could prove a death march.

Jackson set off after Clinton while Harvey looked around, as if seeking a higher court to which he could appeal. As none was forthcoming, he muttered, "Ludicrous, absolutely ludicrous!" and took off after the other men.

A bent man with steps less than half the length of Jackson's, Clinton nonetheless matched the major's lumbering stride with the determination and energy usually, but not now, incumbent in his performance as magistrate. Practically running, and spewing forth a running (and vitriolic) verbal estimation of the situation, Harvey still could not catch the comically mismatched pair before they reached the county building.

"Most outlandish, foolhardy, unnecessary display of stupidity I've ever seen," Harvey spouted. "Why, I'll horsewhip the young idiot myself when I see him; he's erased any doubts even his most ardent admirers might have had about the correctness of his expulsion; he's erased any doubts I had because it was a very, very unfortunate decision on Jackson's part to pursue such harsh discipline, and I'm beginning to wonder if Jackson really should be a classroom professor; the complaints and ridicule of the students and alumni truly is tiresome. My lands, the young fool is nowhere to be seen!"

A considerable cluster of would-be spectators, some Franklin members and some not, buzzed with lively conversations all around the steps in front of the building, but Walker was nowhere in sight. The noise stopped cold at Jackson's appearance. The crowd, a moment before rowdy and animated, uttered not a chirp as the major passed through it, his square jaw set like flint and his hard blue eyes set straight ahead. The strange silence lingered for a minute even after Jackson entered the building.

"What manner of man is that, who fairly swoons at a speaker's podium, then stares down death as though it were an uninvited and unwelcome intruder?" one man whispered softly to a nearby friend (as if he were afraid Jackson might leap from the building and confront him for his words).

"The type of man this republic needs mightily when it is threatened, but perhaps has little use for in time of peace and security," his friend replied.

Harvey, meanwhile, had stopped in the street, panting, and watched as Jackson and Clinton marched into the building. He gazed around, then up and down the street. No Walker. *Well, do we have a blowhard on our hands, or just how long is this foolishness going to prevail?* Then he realized his beating heart and sweating brow were not exclusively the result of his spirited walk. And he marveled at the lanky, awkward professor who had just ascended the steps leading to the Franklin convocation. *He knew as well as any of Walker's announced intention to be waiting at those steps. And yet what waits inside that building causes him more fear than what could have been waiting outside it. In fact, I don't believe what could have been waiting outside causes him any fear whatsoever.*

Jackson indeed was not without fear as he stood before the assembled body of the Franklin the next hour. And he indeed failed to secure his warrant that evening. But he did gain the lasting respect and admiration of the Society, whose ranks he never officially joined. Oblivious to threats to his life, aspersions cast on his character for ineptitude at his chosen profession, mistreatment of his former cadet Walker, and cowardice in the face of a challenge of honor, Thomas Jonathan Jackson stood and spoke without notes and without arms springing skyward, and he spoke with power and conviction and authority. He carried the night despite a running internal battle between fleshly fear and godly confidence. And at the end, as the stunned silence lingered following the dying echo of Jackson's final ringing words, it was Judge John W. Brockenbrough who stood and initiated the prolonged ovation. Sitting in his accustomed back row seat, Harvey Hill—well, Harvey Hill actually giggled at his odd friend.

Thus was Thomas Jackson's feeble mouth not opened in power for the sake of a speech.

●◇ ●◇ ●◇

James Walker did intend to meet Jackson as he arrived for the Franklin Society meeting. But he first had to make a stop at the Presbyterian church, where a cadet friend informed him that the arrogant effete snob from New York, Joe Kennedy, had escorted Julia Junkin each of the past several Thursdays to the Women's Missionary Guild meeting.

"He can scarce keep his hands off Julia," the South Carolinian cadet, whose family owned one of the largest plantations with one of the largest contingent of slaves in the state, told Walker.

"Why, how does Julia react to such heathen overtures?" Walker had asked.

"Well, the girls I know tell me she tries to make light of it because somehow she is sort of infatuated with the skunk, but that it truly bothers her and she has actually had to slap his hand several times. I fear if any of the Junkins hear of this, especially young George Jr., there could be trouble."

"They'll not hear of it," Walker boiled, "because it shall not occur again. Lowlife Yankee pagans. Look down their noses at us Southern folk, and they with their pagan, godless ways. They pay their slaves but work them to death. They love nothing but money and treat our fair ladies like dogs. I'll brook no more such insolence from Yankee interlopers."

The South Carolinian chose his words carefully. "Perhaps it is indeed time to send a message to *all* such uninvited scurvy that we don't brook their kind in our fair land."

Walker eyed his friend. "Perhaps if I am efficient I can make time to do so and be in the flush of battle by the time I meet Professor Major Mister Jackson before the steps of the county building."

"And what of Judge Brockenbrough?" He posed the question to solidify an answer, not discover one.

"Judge Brockenbrough's concerns mean less than nothing to me."

All of this pleased the other man immensely, for he felt certain, as did his father and grandfathers, that God took a dim view of Yankees in general, and most especially those who dared bring their evil ways south with them. After all, such ways could be of no benefit to those whose hard work and resourcefulness had built the great plantations that provided, through the sweat of their dutiful Negro slaves, the civilized world with the cotton, rice, tobacco, peanuts, and other staples it had come to demand.

And besides, most of what he had told Walker about Kennedy's actions regarding Julia was true. Well, at least some of it was. *What wasn't would soon be if left untended, right?*

Walker was waiting at the front entrance of the church when Julia and Kennedy arrived. The two men did not like one another for many reasons, chief among them their shared feelings for the budding blond beauty about which both dreamed. But they also could scarcely have been more different. Both were willful, headstrong, and men of their culture. Kennedy had abolitionists in his family, who objected to his choice to travel south for his education. Walker knew that abolitionists, and the industrialists and politicians who supported them for their own mercenary reasons but cared not otherwise about African slaves, intended nothing less than the dismantling of the land and institutions from whose bowels he had sprung. Whether he confronted Joe Kennedy as a jealous lover or a defender of his heritage was a question a more mature Walker would often ask himself in the quietness of his final days.

For confront him he did. After physically removing the violently protesting Julia from harm's way and ordering the other nearby women off the street and into the building, Walker announced to Kennedy that he would no longer tolerate his presence so much as in the same room as Julia Junkin.

"And if I catch you or hear tell of you slighting or insulting any Southern woman at all, I'll break your filthy neck for you on the spot. I don't consider you man enough to call to the field of honor."

"Field of honor," Kennedy scoffed, detestation dripping from the words. "You and your pathetic honor. You haven't a notion of honor, you reckless buffoon. Look at yourself, you ignorant rogue. What do you intend, to fight here on the street, before the very door of the Presbyterian church while your beloved quakes inside wondering what will happen to whom? Why, you impudent selfish fool. No true man would dare choose for her through force of arms with whom perhaps she is to share her entire future. A man of any culture, any learning, any couth, any decency should put forth his best to win her, then leave to her the decision of whom she is to love. A man who cared more for her than himself would do that, don't you think, Mr. Walker?"

Now Kennedy laughed Walker to scorn. "But of course, what are we to expect from a sorry figure who, despite being a champion marksman, horseman, and pugilist, and from a rich and *respected* South Carolina slaver family, is yet disgracefully expelled from a sorry institution that postures as an academy of higher learning. An institution with such laughably pathetic 'instructors' as your favorite professor Jackson, men who could not be accepted as students on any decent campus. But then, I hear you and I are at least in agreement in our disregard for Mr. Jackson, for I understand you intend to proceed from here to kill him as well."

For once in his life, Walker was speechless. This proved unfortunate, since what little restraint his mercurial personality possessed consisted chiefly of the ventilation of frequent violent and hurtful passions through verbal outbursts. Lacking this outlet, Walker was truly one dangerous individual.

"What, no smart response, ex-Cadet Walker?" Kennedy sneered. "No response of any sort? Then leave this church and go to your next fight, you miserable oaf."

The New Yorker walked toward the door of the church. As he grabbed the handle, Walker exploded. "Ahhh!" Kennedy turned to see his foe charging him. He lifted his arms just in time to absorb some of the enormous impact of the strapping Southerner, but not enough to keep himself from being driven hard into the door with such force that, but for the door's oaken constitution, the two would have crashed through it. As it was, the door cracked loudly as the men fell to the paved ground.

They rolled over and over, slugging, grasping, and clawing. Walker possessed a good three-inch height advantage, but Kennedy's aristocratic bearing was offset by a squat but sturdy barrel-chested build, a formidable Irish temper, immense pride, and strong feelings for Julia. He fought back with vigor and force.

The two rolled chaotically into nearby bushes. Walker finally came up on top and began pounding the shorter man about the head and shoulders with wild, frenzied blows.

Inside the church entrance, Julia and the other women and girls heard the ruckus. Julia gasped and tried to shove the door open, but it was split and jammed shut. She ran to another door a few yards away and burst out, screaming and crying. When she saw Walker thrashing Kennedy, she unleashed such an earsplitting shriek that the South Carolinian in all his madness turned toward her. When he did, Kennedy slugged him full in the nose, breaking it and knocking Walker off him and flat onto his back.

Kennedy, bleeding from his own nostrils and mouth, and minus his two front teeth, staggered to his feet. Walker, blood pouring from his flattened nose, struggled to his knees. He grabbed his face and cried in pain. Kennedy cleared his foggy mind with a shake, then lifted his foot and kicked Walker hard, full in the head. The bleeding Southerner groaned and fell back. Again Julia shrieked, near fainting.

Kennedy started for Walker once more, but stopped, a devastating pain slicing through his right side. He grabbed his ribs, then screamed in pain. Walker's attack of him at the door had broken at least one rib and possibly more. He felt sharp stabs of hurt accompanying his heavy breathing and realized with terror that one of his lungs might be punctured. He saw the muscular Walker beginning to rise again and knew he must finish the animal off or himself be finished off. He whipped a knife from his tattered waistcoat and brandished the blade. At this, two or three of the watching women screamed and Julia finally fainted.

Walker turned painfully toward Kennedy, his knees threatening to buckle and his own head a throbbing, bleeding mass of pain. He could barely see through his eyes, which were already swelling up and were welling over with tears.

"I'm going to finish you now, you wicked, lowlife wretch," Kennedy growled as he started for Walker.

Summoning all the force of his enormous will, Walker shook his head, cleared his eyes, ran to Kennedy, grabbed the stout arm that held the knife, broke it, and jammed the long blade deep into the man's heart.

Kennedy collapsed into Walker, who supported him for an instant, then stepped back and let him fall to the ground.

So did James Walker miss his appointment with Major Jackson.

CHAPTER 12

NEWS OF THE BRUTAL KILLING SENT HAPPY, QUIET, CEREBRAL little Lexington into near-shock. Because Kennedy had made more enemies for himself in the town than just Walker and because numerous reliable, and concurrent, witnesses provided an accurate chronicling of the unfortunate incident, surprisingly little ill feeling centered on the ex-cadet. Two other reasons that presented themselves were more surreptitious but also probably even more salient.

For decades, social, economic, and political tension had grown between North and South. Though less acutely than some states further south, Virginia had felt the sharp slap of hostile winds from New England congressmen and their constituents who were frustrated by the political muscle flexed by the South. The South's import was out of proportion to its population and industrial strength because of the savviness of its elected representatives and because of a Senate body that kept the balance of power equal among the sections by allotting every state in the union two members, regardless of population or material advantage.

Nonetheless, events such as renegade Virginia slave Nat Turner's bloody insurrection in 1831, combined with the more inflammatory rhetoric from some Northern leaders, fueled Southerners' suspicions that the North, rather than possessed of consensus opposition to African bondage, actually plotted, using the slavery issue as a flashpoint, the wholesale overturn not only of the Southern economy but the society itself. Men of power in the North, the reasoning went, had come to look upon the South as a competitor and an obstinate, behind-the-times, agrarian thorn in the North's progressive industrial flesh.

The words of abolitionist Senator Charles Sumner of Massachusetts blew like a cold chill through Lexington and the rest of the South. In withering oratory before the Senate body he castigated his fellow senator from South Carolina, the gentle and genial Andrew P. Butler, who was not present at the time. Butler, Sumner boomed, "has chosen a mistress to whom he has made his vows, and who, though ugly to others, is always lovely to him, though polluted in the sight of the world, is chaste in his sight—I mean the harlot, Slavery."

"The doctrine of devils," "outside the five points of hell," boomed other Northern leaders about the practice of one human being owning another.

Joe Kennedy's death, because of his outspoken antislavery views and because he pulled the knife on an already-bloodied Southern boy, was, if unfortunate, understandable. And some whispered it was perhaps not that unfortunate.

Finally, that already-bloodied Southern boy, though cantankerous at times and generally wild with youth and energy, also oozed charm, handsome manliness, and gallantry. (Julia Junkin herself wept to Ellie that she had used Kennedy to spur jealousy in and attention from Walker.) But he oozed these after a controversial and roundly frowned-upon expulsion from the school he loved.

Now, battered and bloody from bravely defending the honor of a Southern woman (five years removed from Ohio and Pennsylvania), and his chosen career lost before it even began, he deserved consolation and even admiration. For here was the embodiment of Southern manhood: fighting back from the dregs of adversity for the woman he loved, and not afraid even to face on principle the formidable Mexican War hero Major Jackson! Not everyone held these feelings, but all the VMI student body, most of the faculty, and many others did, including the majority of the devout Presbyterian women who had witnessed the mortal fight, Julia Junkin among them.

Two Junkin sisters already in the church building who did not learn of the fight until after its conclusion considered Walker a brute and bully—*instigating a killing at the Lord's house, of all places!*—and would not have felt God displeased had the result been reversed, as came close to happening. Ellie and Maggie also endorsed their father's determined forbidding of further contact between Julia and Walker. The Junkin brothers in one accord conveyed their support of this decision to the mending Walker, as well as their readiness to enforce it.

So Jackson continued his teaching and his attempts to win back Ellie. Which exercise seemed more awkward and futile would have been difficult to determine. Walker healed quickly, considered the forced estrangement from Julia tolerable (as other girls in Lexington and both of the Carolinas also filled his eyes), and began to turn his focus back toward the major, whose sorry professoring and hateful recriminations had brought on the whole Kennedy affair in the first place. And the elder Junkin sisters grew in their respective feelings for Jackson, feelings that appeared so different from one another's but after all were quite similar, only differently requited.

To Jackson and other chivalrous young courters over the years, Ellie's winsome, stable sweetness added to the mysterious and desirable aura that spread about her like an intoxicating perfumed net. Jackson was now all tangled up in that net. *"Relax and enjoy it, my boy. You'd be surprised at how many of us have been struck with the same affliction!"*

Try as he might, the frustrated professor could not penetrate Ellie's shell, which, like her overall character, could be firm and determined when she desired. For the first time, he had difficulty even in obtaining an audience with her. When he did, she was polite but guarded. She had erected a silent, invisible, and impenetrable wall far more sturdy than any battleworks he had ever confronted in Mexico or in his Florida service against the Seminoles.

Jackson had suspicioned for some time that Maggie's feelings toward him and his deepening relationship with Ellie were ambivalent. Dare he think the word *gleeful* to describe her current attitude toward the now uncertain courtship? Yes, Maggie appeared as much a mystery as Ellie, but in a secondary way, for it was the younger sister who consumed his thoughts by day and kept him from his usual peaceful slumber at night.

One warm, sticky June midnight he could bear it no longer. Tired and frazzled, Jackson rose from his sweat-soaked bed, dressed, and strode vigorously to Harvey Hill's house three blocks away.

When a groggy Harvey arrived at his darkened door, Jackson stood panting, with his left arm shooting skyward.

"I've got to see Mrs. Hill," the visitor blurted out.

"What?"

"Now, Harvey, I must see her alone."

Harvey tried to clear his head.

"But Jackson, it's the middle of the night. What ails you, boy?"

"I must see Mrs. Hill, Harvey."

Harvey pondered the statement. "Is this about Ellie?"

"Please, Harvey, I must see her, now."

Then occurred an event Harvey had never before witnessed, and never would again. Jackson dropped the one arm and fired the other upward. *Poor fellow is surely in a world of hurt.*

"Listen to me, Jackson," Harvey said, laying a gentle hand on his friend's left shoulder. "Come back at seven, and you can talk to Mrs. Hill."

"I must talk now."

"But you can't talk now!" Harvey caught himself and looked around, then lowered his voice. "Look, Jackson, women are—women are unpredictable. They change, you know? Sometimes greatly, and without any warning. Then they just change back, without any warning again. And sometimes they have to think things over really well. My hunch is, that's what Ellie's doing right now."

"But I thought she . . . she doesn't now seem to . . ." Pain spiked the voice.

"Why that's just the problem, my boy. You don't like seeming. I don't usually, but women, well women are sometimes all about seeming."

"Not Ellie."

"Yes, I'll admit it, Ellie does seem somewhat different about those sorts of things. That's why my advice is for you to take advantage of the summer break and make yourself scarce for awhile. I've a feeling she needs some time to herself to think, but I think you might also."

Jackson sagged.

"But I promise, Isabella will be ready to see you at seven," Harvey added with a consoling smile.

Jackson lowered his arm and extended it to shake Harvey's hand. "Thank you, Harvey. You are indeed a good friend, especially to tolerate me at this late hour."

Harvey accepted the handshake.

As Jackson turned to leave, Harvey called after him.

"They play a desperate game, Jackson, all of them." For once, stone seriousness covered Harvey's countenance. "They play a desperate game."

This comment making no sense to Jackson whatsoever, he merely turned back and resumed his brisk, long striding toward home.

The major kept his seven o'clock appointment, but he had already decided to follow Harvey's advice and leave that very day for a trip across the mountains to see Laura.

On his way on foot to catch the stagecoach out of town, Jackson saw Wayne Marley, sporting a smile on his face and a fishing pole across the bags behind the saddle of his large dapple gray.

"Have you ever gone fishing, Major?" the unshaved younger man smiled, his one eye squinting against the bright June sun.

A slow, curling grin began from deep back on one side of Jackson's face and reached farther and farther across the square-jawed head until his entire blue-eyed countenance was beaming.

"Yes, I have, Mr. Marley, I certainly have."

And from what I have seen of your past catch, Mr. Marley, old Kester and Colonel Talbott back at Jackson's Mill would have thought you a fine fisherman. I hope Reverend White would think as highly of your spiritual commitment.

Marley cocked his head with a queer stare as Jackson strode by him. Then the remembrance of something important flashed across his handsome features.

"Oh, Major, sir, I almost forgot. I meant to come tell you later today." Jackson turned back toward him. "Walker's on the mend, sir, and he told some of the boys he still plans on coming for you, sir. They say even though Judge Brockenbrough let him off with probation for killing his own clerk, he wishes now it had been you he stuck and not Joe Kennedy."

Jackson looked Marley over for a moment before he spoke, as if sizing up whether he was prepared for the message he was about to receive. "'A wise man feareth,' Mr. Marley, 'and departeth from evil, but the fool rageth, and is confident.'"

Just as other disciples in their day did not understand the lessons of their teacher, neither did Wayne Marley understand this one. He shrugged and headed for Rockbridge Creek and that hidden hole he alone had found where the catfish would jump right up onto your hook.

Maggie had never enjoyed her time with Ellie more. And a busy time it was: raising funds and preparing supplies for the Cutters, whose ship left in mid-July for their South Seas missionary destination; accompanying Dr. Trimble with food and medicine in his junkets around the surrounding counties to the poor; and participating in the women's Bible study conferences in Lexington and Staunton, the latter town twenty or so miles down the valley.

And of course, the schedule was full of parties for newly minted graduates of the town's two colleges, as well as various other teas and social functions.

Maggie was pleased that her sister seemed for the most part carefree and content. *Just as I thought, a temporary stage of infatuation of an unmarried woman in her late twenties for the tall, handsome, war hero and his uniform. Or is that selling my beloved too short? Perhaps, but in any event,* Maggie thought, watching the pristine beautiful face closely as it concentrated on knitting together worn socks to be given to some of the local poor and derelicts, *it could never have lasted, and we are fortunate it was cut off before, oh dear Lord, before she committed herself in matrimony.*

Maggie shuddered visibly at the thought, so that Ellie looked at her and asked, "Are you all right, Sister?"

"Oh yes, quite all right."

The one disquieting note in all that had happened was Ellie's complete refusal to discuss Major Jackson or any facet of the courtship with anyone, including Maggie. Never in their lives had either sister kept anything from the other. *And now she has walled me out completely on this matter. Oh well,* Maggie smiled to herself, patching an elbow on an old shirt of her father's that was to be given away, *she is perhaps too overcome with embarrassment and humiliation at having lost herself for a while to discuss the matter. Never before has she done so, and the Christian thing to do is clearly to let her discuss it in her own way in her own time, if she even chooses to do so. Perhaps she now sees her foolishness with the major as such a trifling thing she wishes to forget it ever happened. And now everything can return to normal and we can be together again.*

In her mirth, the thought never occurred to Maggie how for the first time in her life she had kept her own heart from Ellie.

The sad tidings Jackson found at the Arnold homestead evaporated his happiness at seeing Laura again. As he learned was normal, J. L. was not around. Two dirty, runny-nosed children and a haggard, colorless woman of twenty-six were.

As Jackson stared at that woman, his sister, the memories surged into his mind of how she had been. *So sprightly and precocious! With her yellow curls and sparkling blue eyes, her pretty clear skin and honeysuckle-sweet smile. Oh, who was this unsmiling creature with dull uncombed hair, sunken eyes, and stooped shoulders?* Tears filled his eyes as he watched her fire the hearth to warm the small kettle of water hanging over it that would make tea for them. A few feet from the hearth sat his mother's old, scratched rocking chair.

Happily, Tommy and Elizabeth, now nine and seven, seemed outwardly unaware of the sadness and broken dreams surrounding them. They clamored for Jackson's attention, pawing at him and trying to impress him. *How Elizabeth looks like you did, Sister!* Jackson thought as he swept her up and into the air, then around and around. She screamed with joy.

Laura watched, concerned and surprised at the velocity with which her brother was whirling the little girl around in the small cabin. But each time Jackson sought to put her down, she begged him for more. Finally, his aching arms began to shake and he sat down, holding her to him.

"Please swing me some more, Uncle Tom," she pleaded.

Were these the same blue eyes that had pleaded to be taken fishing, hunting, and riding? The ones that had chased after him as Uncle Brake drove the wagon from his mama's, a handful of yellow daisies offered in tiny outstretched hands? They had been just as difficult to deny.

But now they have been denied, he thought as he looked across to his silent sister.

He felt a tug on his trousers. It was Tommy, wonder and uncertainty in his brown eyes. *Yes, he looks like his father.*

"Please, Uncle Tom," the boy stammered, "please, would you tell us about the Mexicans, sir?"

Holding Elizabeth in his lap, he smiled a broad white smile, one rarely bestowed on anyone besides Ellie. *And what a handsome smile it still is*, Laura thought, a flicker of cheer in her tired eyes. *Why, he looks more and more like*—the memory of Warren's winning visage came to her, and the flicker went out of her eyes.

"Why, Tommy, what do you wish to know about the Mexicans?" Jackson asked.

Tommy and Elizabeth giggled at one another. Jackson glanced over his shoulder at Laura, now pouring hot tea.

"Tell us about the big cannonball, Uncle Tom," Elizabeth cooed.

"The what?"

"The big cannonball," she repeated sweetly, "the one that was as tall as you and almost rolled over you."

Jackson's eyes widened and he looked at Tommy. The boy waited on an explanation too. Jackson turned slowly to Laura. She knew her brother and knew his thoughts.

"I never told them nothing, Tom," she said, handing him a steaming, chipped cup and saucer, "only that you fought in the war and you were brave. The McKiddrick boys heard it over in Parkersburg from one of their cousins and told Tommy and Elizabeth."

Jackson looked back at the children. "Well, first of all, I don't know if it was quite as tall as I, but it was big and it came at me so fast, I didn't know if I could get out of the way in time."

"Is that why you picked it up and threw it back at them Mexicans?" Tommy asked.

Jackson turned again to Laura. She shrugged helplessly, her eyes flickering again.

"Well . . ." Jackson coughed.

Eccentric, they call him, Laura thought with scorn as her brother entertained his captive audience. *Why, if he's an eccentric, I'm Martha Washington. It's folks that are fouled up, not Tom. When he's around normal people, children and what not, he's perfectly normal. No, it's folks what are fouled up.*

By the time supper came, wrestling with Tommy and Elizabeth and swinging them through the air had left the children even more full of energy than before, but Jackson on the point of collapse. Laura had shooed them outside while she prepared the meal, and as the children led their stumbling uncle back through the door, he fell into one of the scuffed straight-backed wooden chairs around the dinner table.

Sweating and huffing, he asked Laura for water.

"Ma, can we play some more with Uncle Tom after supper?" Tommy asked.

"Yes, Mother, can we?" Elizabeth contributed.

"We'll see if your Uncle Tom is up to it after he eats. Right now, he looks a little tuckered." Inside, she was cursing her husband. She had grown accustomed to his lengthy, alcohol-soaked absences—and even the beatings that sometimes followed upon his return—but ever since she had received Tom's letter with the news he was coming, she had asked J. L. for once to be around, and just a portion of the time at that. As usual, however, the selfish lout seemed to go out of his way to disappoint her. He seemed most opposed to doing whatever that was most important to her. Perhaps she had made a mistake in even mentioning Tom's visit. Then maybe J. L. would at least have been around some. She knew Tom's straight and disciplined ways, his growing religious commitment, and his modest professional success all put J. L. off. She just hoped that somehow some of it might rub off on her husband, who was proving to be the great disappointment of her life.

As the two children continued to smother Jackson with their affection throughout the meal, he thought of how desperately they must crave their absent father's attention. Laura had never said so, but in occasional small, slight, and mostly unintentional ways, her letters betrayed her bitterness toward J. L. and his lack of husbandly and fatherly virtue. Compassion swelled up in Jackson's chest as he watched the two children wolf down their food. The old pain of loss and rejection panged him anew.

After the meal, Jackson told more stories of adventure and glory, some from his days stationed in the Florida Everglades following his Mexican service. The Florida accounts, Laura realized as she knitted in her mother's old rocking chair, were more adventure than glory. Gladly, she thought, Tom did not allude to his embarrassing and protracted feud with former friend and commanding officer William French. The nasty conflict led to French's transfer to another fort as a subordinate officer, and to her brother's leaving the army to accept his teaching position at VMI.

Tommy and Elizabeth still brimmed with energy when Laura gave the order for them to retire. In unison, they called for Jackson to tuck them in. After their teeth and faces were scrubbed, Jackson carted both still-shouting youngsters on his back through the oilskin canvas that separated their small sleeping area from the rest of the one-room structure. They ignored their mother's commands to quiet down, but when Jackson suggested with a gentle smile that it was time for prayers, both children dove under their covers and prostrated themselves. Jackson wondered how many nights had passed since their father had performed these duties. When he completed his earnest prayer and looked up, he saw Tommy staring at him.

"Why, Tommy, is something wrong?" Jackson asked.

"No sir, it just looks strange seeing a man praying. I thought only women did such work."

"The Good Book is how God talks to us, Tommy. Prayer is how we can talk to Him." He turned to an angle where his gaze could take in Elizabeth too. "Do you all pray?"

The children looked at one another.

"We never have prayed, Uncle Tom," Elizabeth spurted out. "But I'd like to learn how."

"Yeah, me too, Uncle Tom," Tommy nodded.

A pause. Then, in little more than a whisper, "Well, you've got to be very careful." The children's eyes widened and both leaned just a shade toward Tom. "You've got to be quiet, hold your hands together like this, close your eyes, then listen."

"Listen?" they chimed as one.

"Yes, God might have something to say to you first. There's no need for you to start right in on something if He's already got something to say to you about it."

This truly baffled the youngsters.

"But," Tommy stuttered, "but can you hear God speak?"

Still a near-whisper. "Why, sure. Not out-loud noise like you and I talking, but in here, in your heart."

"But if you can't see God and you can't hear Him," Elizabeth said, "how on earth could you know what He is saying to you?"

Jackson smiled. "That's where the Good Book comes in."

"Preacher talk?" Tommy asked.

"God's Word," Jackson said. When this brought more puzzled stares, he rubbed his chin.

"Think of it this way," he continued. "Tommy, you've started writing, haven't you?"

"Yes sir."

"OK. Who's the most special person to you in the whole world?"

"You are."

Jackson started, then smiled again.

"No, I mean regular-like. Normal. Everyday."

"Oh. Ma, for sure."

"Good. Now, let's say you were getting ready to leave this earth forever and go to heaven. You knew you wouldn't see your ma again until she got there, but you had the chance to write everything down on paper to tell her how you felt about her. Are you following me, Tommy?"

"Yes sir."

"Good, son. Well, that's what God did for us with the Good Book. He came to earth for awhile from heaven, then He went back to heaven. But He left us the Good Book to sort of guide us right along until we get to heaven to be with Him again."

"Jesus?" Elizabeth's sky blue eyes were beaming.

"That's right, Elizabeth," Jackson nodded. "God came to earth as Jesus, did good things, then went to heaven to wait for us. But He left us the Good Book. And you all need to be reading it. That way, you know what God wants and likes, so when you pray, you'll know what to pray for and what He'd say to you if He were sitting right here on the bed with you."

This was all a revelation to the children.

"Course, God really is here, we just can't see Him," Jackson added.

Now it was getting truly confusing.

"All right," Jackson smiled, patting both children. "That's enough for now. But you start saying your prayers every night—for your ma and pa and each other and anyone else you can think of." He kissed each child, then stood to leave. "And Tommy, you start reading the Good Book to Elizabeth in the evenings, you hear?"

"Yes sir."

"Start with the New Testament. The Book of Matthew. Your ma'll show you."

Jackson turned and reached for the curtain.

"Uncle Tom, sir?" Tommy asked.

"Yes, Tommy."

"Sir, is God, well, I know He's strong, but is He, you know, good?"

Jackson's eyes twinkled. "Yes, Tommy, He is very, very good. More than you or I shall ever know."

Tommy breathed a sigh of relief. "That's good. I always knew He was strong, but sometimes it's hard to believe He's good." The boy thought about that for a moment. "Is that bad for me to say?"

"No, Tom," Jackson said kindly. "God likes you to be honest with Him."

"Good night, Uncle Tommy!" Elizabeth blurted.

"It ain't Tommy, dummy," her brother scolded, "it's Tom. Right, Tom?"

"Good night, you all," Jackson laughed.

Laura rushed to wipe the tears from her cheeks as Jackson came through the partition. She had heard the entire conversation. With her ears and her heart. *What a horrible mother I must be,* she grieved.

Jackson smiled as he sat down, ramrod-straight as usual, across the scuffed but solid old walnut table that had been their mother's.

"That's quite a pair you have there, all right, little Laura."

She displayed her best forced smile for him. He did not notice it was forced because he was fetching something out of his wallet.

Laura dried her eyes a bit more as he handed her only the second photograph she had ever seen.

"It's young Wirt, the university graduate," Jackson beamed with pride for his half brother, who had been a mere infant when their mother had died.

Laura shook her head in wonder. "He looks just like—"

"Warren," Jackson finished.

She nodded, continuing to marvel at the daguerreotype. "It's so clear. And he's so handsome."

"He finished fourth in his class at Princeton University. Now he's going on to become a medical doctor."

After a moment, she handed the likeness back to Jackson and eyed him. Her own doubts, hurts, and fears had been forgotten for now. *What a fine man my brother has become.*

"You must be awfully proud, Tom."

"Aw," he shook his head, replacing the daguerreotype.

"No, it was you, and only you from the start, I might add, who took an interest in little—well, not so little, now—Wirt." The lad looked to be over six feet tall in the picture. "You who took an interest when even his own worthless father, curse his soul, wouldn't—"

"Laura."

Her words dripped with bitterness and venom.

"It's true, Tom. That wretched oaf was the ruin of Mama, and you and everybody else knows it." The tears were fighting their way back out again as she dropped her head and her voice. "He was the ruin of us all."

They sat in silence for a minute. Outside, a soft spring breeze pushed tree limbs against the house.

Jackson did not want the visit to deteriorate. He had waited a long time and come a long way to see his sister. And she was still unhappy, perpetually ill or on the verge of illness, and married to a man who could be dead or in Canada now for all she knew.

"Yes, Wirt is a fine lad, Laura Ann, a fine lad."

"Only because of you," she sniffed, looking back up. "You paid for him to go to school and learn book reading and the other things. You purchased him land out West—free soil and slave both, just to be safe. You did it all, and you with no money yourself."

He fought the urge to sermonize about the provision of the Lord for His servants.

"I heard what you told the kids about praying and reading the Book," she continued. "That was mighty fine, Tom. They don't much listen to me, and J. L—" She caught herself, not wanting to defame her husband to her own brother.

Jackson leaned across the table and tenderly clasped one of her hands in his. "Don't you see, little Laura, it's not J. L., it's not the kids, it's not being sick or broke or the cold or anything else except what you do with the Lord Jesus."

Laura loved Tom's caring for her spiritually as well as other ways—he who had little, had more than once provided stipends for her, even since her marriage—but these conversations and those in Tom's letters to her always made her somewhat uncomfortable. *Perhaps it is because there is too much truth in what he says for me to be comfortable.*

"You know I am concerned about your hopes in relation to the eternal future, Sister," Jackson continued, his voice gentle and even. "So let's look at it logically. Suppose two persons, one a Christian and the other an infidel, are closing their earthly existences. And suppose the infidel is right, and the Christian wrong; they will then after death be upon equal footing. But suppose the infidel to be wrong, and the Christian right; then will the state of the latter after death be inestimably superior to that of the other."

Her tired, soulful eyes stayed with him, so he plowed ahead.

"And if you will examine the history of mankind, it is plain that Christianity contributes much more to happiness in this life than the way of the infidel. Why, men had no hospitals until Jesus came. Women were mere chattel, in some cases considered of less value than animals. And it was Jesus more than anyone else who stood against the barbarism of human sacrifice and infant abuse and killing."

As he spoke and the blue eyes danced, Laura thought how eloquently he exhibited in his own life the message he doggedly continued to espouse. *Would that more Christians were so; then I might believe.* But she was proud of him, proud of all he had done, and that he still had time for her. In fact, he seemed to be the only person who did.

"So, now having briefly glanced at this subject," he concluded, "to what decision are we forced on the mere ground of expediency? Certainly it is to the adoption of Christianity. And if we select Christianity, the next point is to consider whether we can believe the teachings of the sacred volume; if so, then its adoption should of necessity follow.

"I have examined the subject maturely, Laura Ann, and the evidence is quite conclusive. In fact, if we do not receive the Bible as being authentic and credible, we must reject every other ancient work, as there is no other in favor of which so much evidence can be adduced. And none have more than a fraction of the number of copies of their original manuscripts available as the Good Book—not Virgil, not Josephus, not even Homer.

"Oh Sister, do pray to God for His mercy and eternal life through our Redeemer, Jesus Christ!"

The loudness of the last statement surprised them both as it echoed off the wooden walls. Conviction and confidence sparkled in his eyes. She stared at him.

"Uncle Tom!" shouted Tommy from his corner.

"You shush, Tom Arnold, hear?" Laura called.

Then she smiled, fully and broadly, the first time he had seen her do so since she married J. L. The pearly smile reminded him of a darling girl in a clover patch long ago.

"You know something, brother Tom?" she said. "You are going to make that Miss Junkin a fine, sturdy husband."

This time, he was the one without words. But he blushed deeply, and he had the strongest urge, which he withstood, to shoot his right arm up in the air, as that side of his body was all of a sudden feeling heavier than the other.

Mouth and lips suddenly dry as an August afternoon over in the Shenandoah, he had a sudden craving for a novelty he had recently rediscovered, the delightful citrus fruit called the lemon. He had originally experienced the tangy item in the Mexican War, but not since.

CHAPTER 13

SHE HAD ALWAYS DEVOTED HERSELF TO THE GOOD WORKS she believed Jesus would have pursued had He walked the earth when she did. Others who themselves were counted as devout and committed to the Lord's work marveled at her ceaseless efforts to improve the plight of those less fortunate than herself. In this and in her genial winsome tenacity, she embodied Rush Junkin to such a degree it sometimes took Ellie's father's breath away.

And like Rush, Ellie somehow carried her religion efficaciously with her into her relationships with her own family, friends, and acquaintances. That is to say, Ellie lived that rare splendid Christianity that left its mark on the world around her—a world that confessed the divine faith but often only as an external custom—rather than itself being marked by that world.

Maggie increasingly challenged that world in all-out, no-holds-barred frontal assault, her pen her mighty, slashing, conquering phalanx. Often, no prisoners returned from battle with Margaret Junkin. She was a foot and a half, one hundred forty pounds, twenty-nine-years, and one sex different from her father; but otherwise his image, though not yet possessing the faith of a giant that he had.

Ellie lived her mother's more sanguine but no less powerful faith. Her temperament not outwardly as strong willed as Maggie's, she knew her own mind even better, and she knew she loved Tom Jackson. Cancellation of marital plans after serious courtship with a man she had come to know better than did anyone else reflected no doubts about the major; rather, it had forced her to deal once and for all with long cherished, and secret, desires of going to a far country with the saving gospel of Christ. She had waited for God to provide the man whose heart would be as one with hers in this endeavor. Waited until her life was nearly, perhaps, three-quarters over now.

The man had not come. And she knew now Tom Jackson's course—devout though he was, and called by God as a messenger by word and deed of that saving gospel—to be in this land, not one far away. As sectional tensions in the nation over slavery, states' rights, agrarian economics, the industrial revolution, economic tariffs, religion, and culture in general continued to mount, she had to agree that men like Tom had a special, important place as apostles of reason in a national climate that, even within her own family, had grown sullen, suspicious, and angry.

She loved Tom Jackson, but she could not marry him. *Could* not. Could she? *God, have You not called me to Your service? Have I not always been the one, often the only one, to counsel others to pursue Your known will, Your designs for life, no matter what the cost, always trusting and obeying? And Lord, have You not chosen me out to go where others will not, in order to accomplish Your will? Have You not blessed me with the wonderful rich desire to do Your will above all else? Yes, how blessed I am, for I could never have formed that desire in myself! And is not that will to go where they have not heard? To go where none else will?* She thought of Romans 10:14: *"For how shall they believe in him of whom they have not heard? and how shall they hear without a preacher?"*

So why had God not brought her a man with whom she could go and do such work? Certainly, a seemingly endless stream of them had paraded through the Junkin home through the years of her father's ministry and academic service. She smiled wryly as she thought of the clear-eyed, square-jawed men of God who had pursued her, who had desired her hand. And some of them had gone. To South America, Africa, Asia, the Pacific Islands. To a man, they would have called upon God to share their lives with her had she consented.

But she had not. God had never allowed her to get even close to marriage, not once. It had never even been a consideration. Perhaps He knew how fragile and unsure her feelings really were in the quiet places of her heart. In all else she seemed to understand His plan and design for her life. In love, she had always been unsure, other than the nebulous feeling that someday He would provide the man matched perfectly for her and for the desire He had given her to reach the unreached. *Oh, that I could go by myself! Why must I be accompanied by a husband anyway, my Lord? Could perhaps someday a woman travel abroad with your healing light on her own? I guess that would be unseemly—and unsafe.*

"My thoughts are not your thoughts, neither are your ways my ways." "How unsearchable are his judgements, and his ways past finding out." These verses and others sometimes disquieted her. Had she plans and assumptions not of God? Had she put the Almighty in a shut box of Elinor's making? *Oh, a person could go crazy sometimes trying to figure out the will of the Lord!* She calmed herself and remembered the words of her mother: *"Not if we wait on Him. For if we wait on the Lord, His plans for our life will make themselves clear."* And Rush had added: *"If they are not clear, and we cannot see His hand, we can always trust His heart. 'Wait on the LORD; be of good courage, and he shall strengthen thine heart: wait, I say, on the LORD.'"*

Yes, Tom Jackson would have to wait, perhaps forever, for her hand.

Lylburn Downing was the first person to see Jackson as the professor unlimbered his long legs from the stagecoach. As he usually did, Jackson offered Lylburn a friendly greeting. Not all whites did that, though some did. What struck Lylburn as peculiar about Jackson were his curious habits of nodding respectfully to the older Negro men he passed on the street and stranger still, his practice of bowing in respect for the Negro women, in the same manner other white gentlemen did only before women of their own race.

Many of Lylburn's questions regarding Jackson had been addressed the night Lylburn stood at the door to the Franklin meeting, surreptitiously giving ear to that evening's debate: "What should be done about the Negro?" His appetite had merely been whetted on other matters, and his curiosity peaked about Major Jackson.

The other slaves who had driven their masters in from areas outside Lexington knew to expect the unexpected from Lylburn. So no one was surprised when he tied his buggy's horse to the hitching post, tiptoed to the back door and cracked it open. Lylburn was good for diversions like that, to help keep things interesting. A couple of the slaves would already have told on Lylburn because they thought the teenager uppity and interested in talking and acting like white folks. But he was amusing and, without really trying, he did tweak the white folks' noses. So those potential trouble makers chuckled along with the others as the tall, gangly sixteen-year-old cocked his head and leaned down through the door to listen to the articulate practiced voices echoing forth from within.

"Boy, I'm gonna hold the whip for Marse Russell when he tans your hide."

"Nigger, he'll beat you so hard you'll be leaning like that for good."

But most of it was in good cheer because, despite his uppity ways, Lylburn was somehow an eminently likable fellow who himself had a curious habit of doing helpful things for the other slaves, the sort of thoughtful things normally only a woman would do. But Lylburn was no woman, as the rascal Big Ben and the other slaves had learned on another night, this one outside Colonel Preston's house.

True, Ben's master Sam McDowell was feared by all the slaves as the worst nigger-hater in Rockbridge County. Yet at the same time they feared him, they mocked him to scorn—surreptitiously, of course. For even a slave knew the folly of a man beating up on and damaging his own property. Good healthy slaves were not only increasingly expensive; they had grown gradually more difficult to come by at any cost since the 1808 law outlawing the importation of Africans.

Marse McDowell was the only man the slaves knew of in Rockbridge County who actually physically beat his slaves, though a couple of others were not above other forms of physical, and mental, abuse. Putting aside the feelings of affection and care most masters held for their slaves, it just made no financial sense to mistreat them—for a sane man, anyhow.

But Sam McDowell, whose wife had finally tired of her own beatings and returned north to her family, evidently had little sense (or at least little true wisdom), though his plantation was one of the largest in the county. His slave Ben, being big, strong in body and will, and cur-dog mean, probably by nature, took the brunt of his master's wrath. Oddly, McDowell had been a slave himself—to whiskey—*before* his wife left him. And he had built the bulk of his plantation's size and prosperity *after* she left him. The other Negroes knew well he had built it on the broad shoulders of slaves like Ben.

So Ben vented his rage on other slaves. Mostly, it came through the intimidation of a look or expression. Ben was so big, strong, and mean that he had a difficult time forcing a fight or even a response from any of the other slaves. The numerous swollen ridges crisscrossing his back and shoulders testified to the great physical suffering he had known. Lylburn believed Ben's behavior testified to worse mental suffering, not the least McDowell's use of Ben's mother for his own pleasure, which had occurred shortly before her death and Mrs. McDowell's departure.

So Lylburn, with his unusual, femininelike sense of intuition and discernment, knew Ben had many deep scars of many kinds. And unlike all the other slaves, Lylburn, though several years younger than Ben, had reached out in various ways to help Ben. At first Ben was so confused by such behavior he was unable even to respond. Then, he became suspicious and angry. These feelings crested the night of the gathering at the Preston home when Lylburn detected blood blotches staining the back of Ben's thick shirt from underneath it. Dressing Ben in thick shirts, and never allowing him to go shirtless, fit with McDowell's meticulous practice of concealing his behavior toward his slaves from the other whites in the area. Many whites knew some of his hateful behavior, but he had muted things just enough to escape serious social ostracization.

At first, Lylburn knew better than even to acknowledge Ben's bloodstains. Most of the slaves were more concerned about their own well-being than Ben's because they knew his wrath would not go unsatisfied toward someone, probably before the evening was out. Finally though, seeing the tears filling the mountainous Ben's eyes and his pained, hunched movements around his master's horses, Lylburn was constrained to gently ask the fearsome giant if he would like him to fetch some salve and ointment for his back.

For an instant, relief and thankfulness showed clear in the large black eyes. Then, as quickly, these dissolved to rejection and hatred. Lylburn, having never seen such vitriol, even in Ben, retreated a half step. It was too late. With a guttural grunt from somewhere deep inside, Ben lifted a great hand across his body, then smashed the back of it across Lylburn's smooth brown face.

The blow drove Lylburn into two other black drivers ten feet away, and all three went to the ground like felled timber. Several nearby slaves stared in surprise as Lylburn spit the dust out of his mouth and dared to begin rising to his feet. (When Big Ben struck a slave, the man usually knew to stay down the first time.) However, Ben hauled him up by his freshly cleaned shirt collar, spun him around, and backhanded him with another fierce smashing blow. Lylburn flew into the other two drivers again, just as they were getting back to their feet, and the three went back down in another pile.

Little Jimmy, one of Nathan Carter's slaves, and probably the fastest man—black or white—in Rockbridge County, had by now raced all across the front yard, up the steps, across the portico, and into the house. He did not wish to tell Preston's doorman Gus to fetch Marse McDowell, for these scraps were best kept among the slaves for a variety of reasons. However, when one man's property was in imminent danger of serious damage or even destruction, another, larger, raft of reasons superceded the other considerations. Not the least of these were the financial consequences incumbent on Marse McDowell should Lylburn be seriously injured by Big Ben, and any subsequent consequences meted out by McDowell to Ben. In the end, when such unfortunate events transpired, no pleasant outcome would probably be possible.

Lylburn, bleeding profusely from a smashed nose and a mouth now short two chipped front teeth, was conscious, but his ears rang like the bell tower of the Lexington Presbyterian Church downtown, and even though his large brown eyes were wide open, he could see nothing. From somewhere deep inside himself, this young man who had never experienced the abuse that had so strengthened and toughened his tormentor, found an oaken resolve of his own and began, trembling and unsteady, to rise again. The eyes of the watching slaves grew wide in amazement and respect—*young, silly* Lylburn *of all people to be standing against the bully Ben!* Way in the back of his benumbed mind, Lylburn again felt the two gargantuan, hide-tough hands through his tattered shirt. But this time, the hands released him, and he heard much loud grunting, gasping, and cursing.

By the time McDowell raced onto the scene, three other slaves, their own faces bloody, had Big Ben pinned to the ground and were raining blows down on his head and body.

"Get away, you idiots!" McDowell, himself a brawny man, railed, shoving one black man off Ben and slinging another out of the way. "I said, get away, nigger!" he screamed in the face of the third man, still astraddle Ben. The slave glared back at him for an instant, then got up and moved away. McDowell stared down at the battered Ben, the blood on his large face mingling with tears. McDowell shook his head. "Just can't keep out of the manure, can you, boy? Swear I've never ever seen a harder-headed fool of any color in all my days."

McDowell's steely gray eyes darted around the half circle of uneasy slaves. "You, Jethro, go see if your Marse Jed will loan you to take Ben back to Five Maples in my buggy."

Little Jimmy frowned as he followed a throng of white men out of Preston's house, down the stone steps, and out to the spot between the white picket fence and the street where two servants helped the sobbing Ben to his feet. Jimmy was truly frightened now for Ben because these other white men had heard of the fight and would soon know it was Marse McDowell's boy again who had started the trouble.

And indeed, Ben, with no medical attention to his wounds from the fight, was beaten senseless later that night by McDowell after the owner returned to his plantation from the Preston soiree. But McDowell used the butt end of his quirt rather than the whip because he felt that would draw less blood—on the outside. Then Ben spent three days and nights, still with no treatment for his wounds, chained down in a locked tiny shed out behind the slave cabins.

McDowell had determined to break the rebellious giant or kill him this time because despite the Negro's substantial worth, the master felt he had come to be more of a liability than a benefit. For without the respect of the other white men around Rockbridge County, McDowell would have a very difficult go of continuing the prosperity and expansion of his beloved Five Maples plantation. McDowell knew that that respect had been sorely tested already; the blame he felt certain would attach itself to him for the slave brawl at the Preston party could seal his financial coffin. He already had his credit limit at the bank. And that institution's president, Charles Roark, had a Yankee wife who detested slavery in general and McDowell in particular, the shrew. And the Roarks had been at Colonel Preston's the night of the fight. What would his chances be now of getting financing for the new corn crib and extra stables he desperately needed?

McDowell was tempted to just sell Ben off to his North Carolina cousin who had been after him for two years to do so. But, no, Ben would probably consider that a reward and deliverance, and McDowell was not about to make life any easier on the slave. Rather, he was about to make it much more difficult than it had already been, if the obstinate darkie recovered from his beatings. On second thought, he would bide his time. He would let the boy heal up a bit and let other things settle down. He needed no more controversy or visits from Pastor White from the Presbyterian church or Rector Pendleton from the Episcopal, censuring him for his treatment of his slaves. He needed no more warnings from the town marshal. And he needed his loan from the bank. The cretins at the bank in Staunton twenty-five miles down the road would not deal with him anymore. They considered him "troublesome." He needed his loan, and he needed his respect from the other men at the Franklin Society.

The slaves outside the Franklin Society respected Lylburn Downing. He had healed bravely from his wounds and had kept the same sanguine attitude toward Ben, never speaking a word about him unless it was one of compassion or pity. Some of the slaves felt Lylburn a fool, but all of them respected him. They had started calling him "Preacher" because of how he liked to always quote the Bible and how he would say words over the new babies in the slave quarters and the old folks who passed on. But most of all, Lylburn just seemed to care about folks, black and white, to the consternation of some of the slaves.

"Yep, it's him!" Lylburn said to the other slaves in an excited whisper.

"The Goober," Little Jimmy laughed as Tom Jackson's distinctive voice, just a shade higher than the average, floated out through the door and into the warm summer air.

"The Goober" referred to the man the slaves had noted who throughout the many months he had attended Franklin meetings seemed to have a goober pea (or peanut) lodged in his throat whenever he tried to speak. Many was the week that even Lylburn had looked forward with anticipation toward the Thursday night Franklin meeting, in hopes the Goober would be speaking. If that event terrified Jackson and discomforted his inside audience, those listening outside profited with some of their chief entertainment of the week.

But Lylburn had begun to pray for the Goober, for he had sensed through the long months that, despite the rasping, stumbling, and stammering, Jackson offered insights no one else who spoke did. His thoughts were not fanciful nor eloquent, but they were deep and probing, in a simple sort of way. Or they seemed simple and forthright to Lylburn, until he would be considering one in the quietness of his bed at night, and a new observation would come to mind from one of the Goober's seemingly simple statements of that evening or the evening before or two evenings before. Lylburn would burst at the seams to share his observations and recognitions of implicit and sublime meanings from the Goober's speechifying, but none of the other slaves seemed to care. So he would share them with his dog and his Lord.

And that was it too: the Goober spoke words sometimes that seemed to come not from man but from God. Oh, the preachers and some of the other fine men from around the county spoke as men *of* God, but the fact began to impress itself upon Lylburn that from the start, even when the Goober could barely spit out his words, and the Franklin men could barely stay silent in their discomfort, and all the slaves listening were trying not to disrupt the town around them with their laughter, the Goober was choking out choice pearls of wisdom Lylburn at length realized could only come out of the mouth of a man who had spent much, much time *with* God. Two realizations began to dawn on Lylburn's mind in brilliant invigorating certainty: he wanted to learn to speak beyond himself, with power and courage and conviction (and he knew he could speak much better than the Goober), and he wanted to speak of the things that could come only out of the mouth of a man who had spent much, much time with God.

But on this night, the Goober—who still stammered and sometimes stuttered, but in Lylburn's estimation had gradually become a poor speaker, stylewise, as opposed to a terrible one—spoke about Lylburn. And about fast, laughing Little Jimmy. And about scarred Big Ben, who the slave grapevine said had mostly recovered from his beatings, but was now sullen and withdrawn. For though he did not mention them by name, this night, the Goober spoke about the Negro. While other men spoke of how God had ordained the Negro's place as a servant because of the particular complement of gifts He had given him, some of them sourcing the black's position as having emanated from the "curse of Ham" they saw espoused in the biblical book of Genesis, and others spoke of the need to repatriate all slaves to an African homeland of their own (such as the recently created nation of Liberia), and still others advocated gradual freedom for both black and white from an anachronistic economic system that stymied the crucial process of industrialization, the Goober spoke of how "'There is no difference between the Jew and the Greek: for the same Lord over all is rich unto all that call upon him. For whosoever shall call upon the name of the Lord shall be saved.'" And, "'I am not ashamed of the gospel of Christ: for it is the power of God unto salvation to every one that believeth; to the Jew first, and also to the Greek.'" And, "'There is neither Jew nor Greek, there is neither bond nor free, there is neither male nor female: for ye are all one in Christ Jesus. And if ye be Christ's, then are ye Abraham's seed, and heirs according to the promise.'" *He* saw through the externals to the true issues of the heart and soul—the true issues of life, meaning, and existence.

A fire began to kindle in Lylburn to tell others of these issues, this true message, this true saving message God left men through His Son and His Word. So while some of the other slaves laughed at the Goober and some listened half-attentively because he spoke of their kind, Lylburn stood motionless as a beautiful new day dawned on him in the hot night air of the Lexington where he had spent his entire life. He was a man, yes he was a man, complete and full and important as any other in God's eye. He was a *man!* He needed to tell others that God was for them, and that he was a man. Never again would his life be the same as it had been before this night.

All of this flashed through Lylburn's quick, keen mind as the coachman handed down the Goober's traveling bag to him from the top of the stage. Lylburn had begun to pray to the Lord that he could somehow be around the odd professor more, and learn more of the curious things he had to say. As the lanky man lumbered away, Lylburn offered up another such prayer. Then he remembered why Marse Russell had sent him into town, to pick up some dry goods from the general store, and he hustled off down the street.

Rarely had Ellie been out of Jackson's mind during the entire trip to Laura's. Certainty filled his mind more strongly than ever that God had designed Ellie and him for one another. He simply could not fathom the possibility that it was not to be. Finally, on the stage ride back to Lexington, after much prayer, contemplation, and wrestling of soul, a peace impressed his anxious heart that God was indeed in control and intended either for his love to be reciprocated by Ellie, but at a different time, or for him to learn and profit, apart from her, by the sublime blessing of having experienced so much of her time and radiant wondrous, and magnificently feminine, Christlikeness.

As Jackson strode down the sidewalk toward his apartment, he resolved to work harder than ever for her hand, but trust deeper than ever in God's answer on the matter, whatever answer that might be. He smiled at the joy once again provided him, in the throes of frustration and heartache, by his Lord. *"There be many that say, Who will shew us any good? . . . Thou has put gladness in my heart, more than in the time that their corn and their wine increased."* The noonday summer sun seemed just a bit cooler, and the gentle breeze ferried the remembered pleasing fragrance of corned beef hash and johnnycake into his nostrils from O'Connor's Kitchen half a block up the steep street.

"So what about Mr. Walker, Major Jackson?"

Jackson turned to see Will Russell, who owned a sizable spread out toward the Rock Bridge, stepping out of Wright's Haberdashery, a clutch of sacks under his arm. Jackson knew Russell slightly through the Franklin. The man was aggressive to the point of pugnacity in his defense of slavery, Virginian sovereignty, and the South's agrarian system of life. Jackson could not remember Russell ever before initiating conversation with him on the street.

"Sir?"

Russell stepped down onto the sidewalk. His was not a handsome face, but a sturdy, ruddy one. China blue eyes as arrestingly piercing as Jackson's commanded it, and his hard stocky body advanced with a subtle swagger.

"Why, young Cadet Walker—ex-cadet Walker, that is—has fully recovered from his fracas with the departed Yankee interloper, Mr. Kennedy," Russell said, "and has of late made no great attempt at keeping secret from the community his intent to next dispatch with you."

The statement impressed Jackson as so ridiculous that he could process no immediate response. He did realize, not from Russell's words, but from the irksome manner the man only partially concealed, that he did not like him. The planter did not mean this first public hailing of Jackson as a warning or even the passing of information. Rather, he perhaps was the one who desired information—from Jackson's reaction. *To pass along to his friends?* Jackson wondered. *To James Walker?*

After a long silent moment, the quartet of azure eyes fastened, Russell blinked, then continued, "Odd ideas to be directed toward a West Point man and war hero from a young pup, don't you think, sir?"

"The oddity is not with robust cavalier youth, sir, but with respected men who would be prey, and party to, the dissemination of such unedifying gossip." As he often did, Jackson spoke potent words softly and without rancor.

The ruddy cheeks flushed a deeper crimson.

"Why, I hardly think—"

"Perhaps I shall see you in church tomorrow," Jackson said with a hard stare. Russell hailed from a long line of Scottish Presbyterians. "Good day to you, sir," the major added, politely touching his hat and resuming his stalking stride down the sidewalk.

Russell glowered after Jackson, biting his lip. The sacks encasing his packages crackled as his tensed muscular arm compressed them. *It will indeed be a pleasure to witness Cadet Walker dispatch with your hypocritical hide, sir.* That thought brought the smile back to Russell's face as he called for his slave Lylburn, whom he had received five years earlier from the estate of his wife's deceased father, Philip Downing III.

Fatigue gripped Dr. Junkin like a clever, tenacious foe long crouched nearby in the shadows, who had sprung upon him when, just for an instant, his protective guard had wavered. When Rush was alive, she provided the world's greatest early warning system, discerning even before he when the tides of exhaustion, depression, and cynicism were about to roil over him. Now she was gone, and the neatly written note sat before him on his desk. He had the reputation—some would even say fame—as wise, fearless exemplar and champion of truth and light. Would they ever know just how inadequate and lacking he now felt? How much he had depended on her, needed her? How much he still missed her?

The revelation amazed him. He, who had preached—and lived, he thought—the absolute sufficiency and efficacy of God for one's life. How had she come to be so much a part of him, so vital a part of him? Had he sinned by coming to lean so much on her, though never realizing he had? "He that is unmarried careth for the things that belong to the Lord, how he may please the Lord: But he that is married careth for the things that are of the world, how he may please his wife." Dr. Junkin had long grappled with a spirit of condescension toward the apostle Paul's words in 1 Corinthians 7, toward which he had secretly harbored thoughts as being penned by a man who because of his own lack of marital status, acquired who knows why, had perhaps donned just a bit of a cavalier attitude toward the institution and had maybe even come to fancy himself slightly above it. Junkin did not really believe that, but his old rebellious "sin nature" liked throwing it up in his face. Now that she was gone and the depth of his feeling for and dependence on her had begun to reveal itself, God had brought him into a new period of learning and growth, one he had never anticipated . . . *all praise be to God*. And now, he had the letter.

He did not doubt its validity. Junkin could think of few men in Lexington—or elsewhere, for that matter—more spiritually mature and devoted to God than the letter's author, John Lyle, owner of the local bookstore and elder in the Presbyterian church. Junkin knew also of Lyle's affection and regard for the tall VMI professor who liked to browse through the shop after completion of the day's classes, reading from the classics and the hard-to-gets, and discussing and debating theology. He knew how Tom Jackson relished the spiritual insights and wisdom he soaked in from the mild-mannered, fifty-year-old bachelor. John Lyle enjoyed ruminating with the flesh and blood embodiment of much of what the pages of his grandest books hailed, the noble man of honor who served with equal faith in war and peace.

So the letter most certainly rang with truth, truth of which Junkin had previously heard bits and pieces around the college, the church, and even at his dinner table. But this confirmed it all. James Walker would stand at the corner of Fourth Street and Washington at half past the hour of 9:00 P.M., Thursday, July 22, 1854. He would be armed and would recommend Professor Thomas J. Jackson be as well. It was a matter that demanded satisfaction. It was a matter of honor.

Yes, Junkin felt very tired, in body and soul. Laying next to Lyle's letter on the huge gleaming—and, as always, clear—walnut desktop, was another letter. It was from a congressional friend back in Ohio, one who had sided with Junkin when the final split came on the board of regents and he left Miami University for the second time. The man admitted the chances of Junkin returning to Miami—even if he should desire to do so, which he did not—were next to nothing. However, the congressman urged, that did not preclude him from returning to a college presidency somewhere in the North. He could have his pick of many, including two in particular about which the congressman had taken the liberty to discreetly inquire. One position currently availed itself; the other, well, could, if need be. The leadership of both schools demonstrated eminent—and discreet—interest, even delight, at the prospect of Junkin acceding to the helm of their institution. Both also offered moving expenses, plus approximately 20 percent increase in salary.

Though the congressman valued Junkin's friendship and company, neither of the two schools lay in the legislator's own state. The specter of increased sectional conflict and perhaps even eventual violent conflagration motivated him to urge his old friend's return to his native section.

Junkin smiled in remembrance of his old friend's cigars, wit, and high integrity. He counted the congressman among his best infidel friends. A nominal Romish "faith" would not account for much the day one stood in judgment before Almighty God. Thus, mixed with the business of shepherding an institution of high learning and enjoying one another's company socially, Junkin had long encouraged his good friend's embracing of the redemption found only through true believing faith in the Lord Jesus Christ, should the congressman in fact have been chosen to that elect company by the heavenly Father before the foundation of the world. Thus far, the Ohioan had evidenced no distinct signs of belonging to that blessed community, but he continued to nurture a strong, apparent regard for Junkin, most recently demonstrated by the initiative he had taken in sending his recent correspondence.

There was one conviction the congressman and the theologian-educator shared: a profound, abiding belief in the sanctity of the American Union. They differed profoundly on the issue of slavery—the congressman was an abolitionist, while Junkin, though he thought the peculiar institution an unhappy phenomenon, saw a clear justification of it in the Bible—but both would pour out their life's blood to assure the continuance of the Union. Even here, their motivations differed. The congressman vigorously advocated the idea best expressed by the newly minted phrase *manifest destiny*, and the power, riches, and industrial might attendant to that concept of America's inalienable, God-ordained right of expansion westward across the North American continent to the Pacific Ocean. Junkin argued with equal vehemence his belief that the federal system, whatever geographic annexations might follow, stood as an earthly type of the sacred eschatalogical and celestial reality of God's perfect will.

Yes, sometimes now it all became almost too much to bear, especially without Rush's gentle steadying way. Junkin knew his temper, ever a challenge to him even since his earliest recollections, had reared itself more frequently since his beloved's departure. He felt the whole family had had difficulty not only with the pain of her passing but with their adjustment to it. Perhaps, after all, no one had realized how efficacious had been her role in the nurturing, guiding, and strengthening of the large clan. Perhaps he had not realized it. *Strange the titanic void left for so many with the loss of one person.* The great leonine head bowed. Tears swelled the jet eyes. He had only one place he could go. He wanted to speak, as was his custom for private prayer, but his tightened throat would not allow the words to come. So the words of Psalm 86 poured forth from his heart.

Bow down thine ear, O LORD, hear me: for I am poor and needy. . . .
Be merciful unto me, O Lord: for I cry unto thee daily.
Rejoice the soul of thy servant: for unto thee, O Lord,
do I lift up my soul. For thou, Lord, art good,
and ready to forgive; and plenteous in mercy unto
all them that call upon thee. . . .

Among the gods there is none like unto thee, O Lord;
neither are there any works like unto thy works. . . .
For thou art great, and doest wondrous things:
thou art God alone.

Teach me thy way, O LORD; I will walk in thy truth:
Unite my heart to fear thy name. . . . For great is thy mercy
toward me: and thou hast delivered my soul from the lowest hell.

Thou, O Lord, art a God full of compassion, and gracious,
longsuffering, and plenteous in mercy and truth.
O turn unto me, and have mercy upon me;
give thy strength unto thy servant,
and save the son of thine handmaid.

Shew me a token for good; that they which hate me
may see it, and be ashamed: because thou, LORD,
hast holpen me, and comforted me.

A tide of warmth filled him, and the tears now filling his eyes were tears of joy that the One who had won, kept, and sustained him still did so. Now he would go forth, girded by his Lord, for he knew he would be provided work for the kingdom, and the strength and aid for that work. *How unsearchable and inscrutable such a love that never fails and never ends.*

When he looked back up, his face aglow, he saw Ellie standing in the doorway.

"Come in, princess," he said, the jet eyes kind. Despite the busyness of his schedule and the absence of Rush as his conduit to Junkin family affairs, he had detected the pain stabbing at Ellie that was sourced in her separation from Major Jackson, pain she had worked hard to disguise behind her usual charm and winsomeness. *A father knows his daughter,* he thought, *and this child, though like her blessed mother she ever tries to cover it so as not to burden herself on others, is hurting badly.* For just an instant, he was seeing her again as a scared little towhead standing at another door to another study of his, half afraid to come in, but wanting badly to do so, in order to find out from her father if boys would still like her even though two of her fingers had been chopped off by an axe a few days before in an accident with her younger brother George. Yes, all of his children had needs in different ways, ways a father just came to know. Maggie, for instance, had always endeavored to assert her independence—and in some regards, such as her splendid literary efforts, had. Yet she remained strangely dependent in many ways, both on her younger sister Ellie and her parents, as life seemed one long and vigorous wrestling with God to her, despite her undeniable faith. "Maggie, dear, must you ever kick over the traces?" Rush would ask gently when her eldest child would engage herself in a particularly weighty new complexity of life. In contrast, the road had nearly always seemed to rise and meet Ellie, with her God-given élan and her wonderfully full and confident faith, and through the abundant overflow of that faith, she had always tended to console her father even more than he did her. In all those ways, she was her mother's and not her father's girl. At this moment, that made him love Ellie and Rush all the more.

Junkin saw the pensive little towhead again as Ellie came toward his desk because that indomitable spirit had experienced few situations since the maiming of her hand where help from any source other than God seemed to her to be warranted. As he asked her to sit down, though, it was again Rush of whom he thought, and her example and strength he realized he had been calling upon more often of late, not apart from the Lord, he felt, but as provided by Him. The realization then struck him for the first time that Tom Jackson, still fairly young in the Christian faith, had recently come to gain the same from Ellie in his months with her.

"Papa, are you listening to me?"

The large handsome face reddened.

"Please forgive me, dear," he said, straightening and coming around the massive desk to sit in the chair next to her. *He has rarely come around that desk,* she thought, rehearsing the years in her mind, *but he has never failed to do so when I needed him.* He touched her gently on the knee. "Now you may start again, with my complete and undivided attention."

She squirmed a bit in the chair. *Quite uncharacteristic of her,* he thought, *even in a difficult situation. She really likes him. I think I do too. He's not what I would have expected for her, or maybe even would have chosen—but then again, maybe he is.*

"I was going to talk to Maggie, but she . . . she is not an objective source on this subject. Neither is Isabella, nor Ashley, nor Jennie Sue, all for different reasons. And Mother—"

She saw his slight wince.

"Papa," she finally blurted—that was uncharacteristic too—"I am troubled and distressed by Major Jackson."

"Oh?"

"He has become quite a nuisance to me, Papa."

Junkin smiled. "But the boy hasn't been here since you sent him away two months ago. Did he write to you?"

"No, Papa, he . . . he is really irritating me, Papa."

The wide, shimmering eyes searched his face for answers—*no,* he smiled to himself, *for confirmation.*

"Are you telling or asking, Muffin?"

"Why, Papa, you haven't called me that in a long while."

And you have never been in love like this. It pained him for just an instant. But then a glad, thankful feeling swept over him.

She spied the twinkling eyes in his otherwise deadpan face.

"Papa, why are you laughing at a time like this?"

He reached over and unlimbered his long arms around her, pulling her to him and patting her firm, rounded back with a big strong hand. His chest and shoulders offered an enormous cavern of shelter and safety, and the same slight fragrance of manly toilet water flavored her nostrils as had done so when she long ago cried in his arms about her chopped fingers. *Many things in this world change,* she thought, *but very little about Papa does.*

After a moment: "Papa?"

"I'm not laughing, Muffin, I'm rejoicing."

She pushed him back a bit.

Still, the dark eyes danced with acceptance. *He can be a difficult man,* she thought, *but when I need him, he is always on my side.* Another thought pricked her sanguinity. *Poor Thomas never knew such support from mother or father. . . .*

Then she and her father were laughing—no, giggling—as though they had together discovered the secret to some long hidden treasure trove, one sought after by a multitude who had either failed in the quest or succeeded for a moment, then lost the great pearl of their pursuit. But she and he had found it. They both had it. And indeed it was a precious gift.

She had all her answers now. Much was spoken between father and daughter, but no words. He had, as he always had, shown her the whole world and more. And he had done it, as he sometimes had, with no oratory. Sometimes he indeed was difficult, as was Thomas. But she loved them both, and she would marry Thomas, if he would still have her.

A couple of oddities had impressed Anna Morrison on this latest summer trip from North Carolina to visit her sister and friends in Lexington. For one, Maggie Junkin, usually a gracious and intelligent but rather melancholy woman, had been swishing her hooped skirts around in a swirl of gay cheer ever since Anna arrived in town. At the same time Ellie Junkin, by nature the warmer and more affable of the sisters, had seemed aloof and distracted. It was not Ellie who normally immersed herself in the production of flowing lyrical sonnets of beauty and power, while standing a bit apart from the world passing around her; the younger sister, until now, had rather kept her considerable energies and will affixed to the people and needs facing her in her daily comings and goings, in a more Christlike manner than perhaps anyone the North Carolina preacher's daughter knew.

Cherub-faced and just slightly, if pleasingly, plump, Anna rarely gave herself to the practice of deep reflective thought and contemplation, so she did not dwell on this odd reversal of normal behavior and attitude in her friends the Junkins. She did take note, however, and wondered how much of Ellie's behavior, at least, stemmed from her breaking off courting relations with Major Thomas Jackson. Anna's sister Isabella had of course told her of this surprising development earlier, but neither Ellie nor Maggie had mentioned it, and Anna would not have dreamed of herself broaching such a potentially tender subject. In the meantime, she enjoyed as always the opportunity to share tea and conversation with Isabella and the Junkins, as well as sport for them the beautiful, new, lime silk taffeta dress she had bought in Charlotte on the journey up from home. Yes, it and her other new purchases had necessitated the half dozen suitcases and portmanteaus she brought, and very nearly a second traveling servant, but she only visited Lexington once a year, so was not a bit of extra effort a small price to pay for such an occasion?

Oh, this heat is infernal, Anna frowned with a sigh, fanning herself. She should have followed her own instincts and either made her visit before the summer heat hit, while en route to see her cousins in New England, or later, after it had broken, on the way back south. But Isabella had been insistent that this July sojourn occur simultaneously with the handsome Major Jackson's return from his sister's west Virginia abode.

It was true that many felt the VMI professor quite eccentric. Yet she had never felt so the times she had been around him. Nor did Ellie or Maggie. In fact, it seemed the better people knew the major, the less likely they were to consider him odd or eccentric and the more inclined they were to count him quite uncommon, perhaps, but in a fine and noble way.

Anna was frowning again at the inconvenience of mesh gloves on such a hot and humid day when Ellie stood up.

Maggie, though trying not to, noticed the tinge of sadness betrayed in her sister's dulled eyes. Vim had so filled those beautiful eyes last night, after Ellie's talk with her father about *him*. (Maggie could scarcely now bring herself to say or even think his name.) Her beloved sister had seemed more like her true self than she had in months. Today, though, Maggie knew her sibling feared she had squandered a grand provision of God for her. *Oh, I don't know what to think anymore! Her happiness is my chief desire in life, yet that happiness seems, for once, to be tied to her relationship with another individual, rather than just God, and an individual who would be the last on earth I should expect her to fancy.*

Ellie spoke during a brief break in the other women's giggling about some of the new fashions appearing in the latest issue of *Leslie's* from up North that they were passing around.

"I'm sorry, ladies, but I'm due at the hospital in half an hour," Ellie smiled.

Maggie eyed her sister. *Always helping someone, even through her torment.* The realization at once conjured feelings of pride, admiration, and irritation in the elder sister. And maybe a twinge of guilt. Maggie drank tea for which she was not thirsty. Ellie smiled again as she turned away. *He is not right for her,* Maggie grimaced, *he is not. And yet, I can so understand why he, yes, being a good man—all right, there it is, he is a good man—should find her so desirable. But how can he seem to have such a profound effect on her? He is, truth be known, a rather uncommonly good and decent man, yes, and learned too. And kind, pious, thoughtful, trustworthy, forbearing of those—I— who abuse him. Perhaps he is even fun, in his unique way, to be around. But does any of that explain why she should apparently have so fallen for him? Why, is there any explanation for it at all? Well, if naught else, it furnishes fascinating possibilities for my novel—*

And then there was a knock at the front door. Before Ellie could even exit the room, the servant had placed a card in her hand. Somehow, somehow, Maggie knew whose it was and for whom it was intended.

For the first moment or so, everyone watched Ellie expectantly. When she continued, motionless, to stare at the card, the ladies began to exchange quizzical glances. Finally, Isabella spoke.

"Why, whatever on earth is it, dear?"

Ellie turned slowly toward them, her upturned palm still clutching the card. A confused look draped her countenance. When she did not immediately speak, Maggie stood, crossed to her, and took the card. Her ruddy complexion washed darker as she, too, stared at the card.

Isabella raised her eyebrows to a couple of the other ladies sitting in the parlor gathering.

"It does seem as though the devil himself has left us his salutation this afternoon, darlings," she said. "Would someone kindly share the heartstopping news before the suspense kills us?"

Maggie spoke, but only to Ellie. "But why, what should bring him calling on you now, Sister? A gentleman courter who has been politely but firmly rejected knows better than to—"

Ellie did not hear, not any of it, nor any of them. For, upon learning the identity of the man who waited outside, all in the small clutch had an opinion, some several. For Major Jackson was many things to many people, usually, as Maggie had learned, depending upon how well they knew him.

What he was to twenty-eight-year-old Elinor Junkin was immensely—and amazingly—welcome.

What manner of man is this? Ellie pondered. *So quiet, so gentle, even so awkward in his own precious way. Oh, of all of them who have been sent away, that he should be the one to return; the one who will not be denied, who will not go away. But in the end, were not all the others, polished and scrubbed and refined as they were, mere boys? Here, here have I found—have You found for me, Lord—a man. Whatever else he is or is not, he is a man. And a gentleman. And on the very day when I thought my heart should finally break for loneliness and sorrow. Perhaps now it should burst instead—with joy!*

And so it was settled. But of course, it had already been settled. "*'There be three things which are too wonderful for me, yea, four which I know not . . . the way of a man with a maid.'*" Ellie looked up at Maggie, the lustrous eyes again full and alive, reflecting the crystal light above her, the magnificent ivory smile painted across her features like the emerald green the Lord painted across lovely Shenandoah bottomland in spring.

Maggie stared speechlessly after her sister as Ellie rushed from the room, crinoline skirts rustling.

Isabella smiled from where she remained sitting. "Why I do believe only one man on the face of this woeful globe could have such an effect on our friend." She sipped more tea, the corners of her mouth curled upward in glee even as the exquisite china pressed against her full lips.

Anna giggled and squirmed happily in her chair. *Oh, how absolutely perfect!* she thought to herself. "Maggie, aren't you excited for your sister? When do you think the wedding will take place?"

Maggie stood staring at the doorway, as transfixed as General Washington's statue over at his namesake school, as the chopped, slightly high-pitched voice of Thomas Jonathan Jackson sounded from the front foyer. Somewhere in the deep recesses of her stunned mind, she heard the women around her chattering and laughing with happiness at a union each, even Isabella, had finally come to know was knit together by the inscrutable, unsearchable hand of Almighty God. Numbness claimed all of Maggie's bodily members. From her strange doleful haze came Psalm 6:6. The verse had run through her mind for months and months, though less so in those recent ones since Ellie had sent Jackson away: "*I am weary with my groaning; all the night make I my bed to swim; I water my couch with my tears.*"

CHAPTER 14

AS JACKSON'S RELATIONSHIP WITH HIS GOD DEEPENED, HE grew increasingly able to depend on Him through even the most worrisome of situations. Yet, the professor also grew in his understanding that those situations would continue to arise until glorious transformation into the presence of Almighty God ended them. Such would be one of the countless dividends of having persevered in His power through life's travails, knowing that "our light affliction, which is but for a moment, worketh for us a far more exceeding and eternal weight of glory."

And the desire to hear "well done, good and faithful servant" became a driving urge in Jackson as he pursued his daily duties and activities.

Yet, he knew worrisome situations would present themselves. So the visit from Ellie's physician brother John with additional, and pointed, information about Walker's sanguinary intentions did not shake him.

"He has made it plain to several that he will be waiting for you at the crossing of Washington and Fourth Streets following tomorrow evening's Franklin Society meeting," John said.

After thanking John for his concern, Jackson resumed staring out the window of his boarding house drawing room, his countenance blank and his straight-backed carriage erect. He must continue committing the next day's optics lesson to heart.

It's just as brother Ebenezer said, John thought. *The man looks to be in a trance.*

John and Jackson had always gotten along well. Devout faith, a love for literary classics, and an enjoyment of the Spanish language were among their shared pleasures. But now John shifted uncomfortably. He eyed the door, then the immobile professor.

"My sister," he stammered, "my sister is frightfully worried about you." For a moment, the glacial countenance thawed and Jackson glanced at John. "She would prefer you to leave Lexington for as long as necessary rather than risk getting yourself seriously injured or even—," Jackson looked away, "rather than risking yourself against this young hotspur." *Of course,* John mused, *the rest of the town is questioning your courage for not already having faced Walker down.*

That hurt. Jackson seethed inside. The impudent young rascal Walker had brought things to such a boil that Ellie was not only fretting, but actually wishing Jackson would tuck tail and run for his own safety! Insults and threats directed toward Jackson himself did not faze him. But when it began to make his true love "frightfully worried" . . . . His exterior returned to granite, but his insides were churning. Two competing currents swirled within him. One, to go and be done with young Walker at once. Swordsman, horseman, crack shot, or whatever else the carrot-topped Carolina cavalier was or fancied himself to be, Jackson had been through the Point, duty in Florida and New York, and had seen the best and worst men could be in Mexico. The thought never entered his mind that he would not wipe Walker from the face of the living earth as easily as Almighty God had often turned the obstinate Old Testament Jewish nation upside down and wiped it clean like a dish.

Which led to the second stream of thought. That centering around the gentle Shepherd, exhorting and being an example to the flock. *Christ would not go and slay a wayward sinner, would He? He would give him a second chance, and a third, and as many as he needed— wouldn't He? But young Walker is pushing me into a corner. Even Superintendent Smith wonders why I have not taken action. Now my career opportunities may be getting affected—yet, "If any man will come after me, let him deny himself, and take up his cross, and follow me." God's way or man's: the eternal struggle.*

John started to press his point further, but knew better. Jackson would already have absorbed the message. The mild-mannered physician walked to the door, opened it to leave, then turned back to his friend.

"I have on good word that Mr. Kennedy was not Cadet Walker's first killing," he said, his soft voice tinged with raspiness. "There was another man, in South Carolina, just before Walker came to Lexington. It was with pistols that time, and the other man was an officer in Mexico. Walker shot him through the heart."

As John stepped through the door, he turned back. "But it was a fair and honorable killing."

Jackson's visit that evening with Ellie in the Junkin parlor proved a short one. She had developed a nasty summer cold. And the nature of their current discourse did not aid her condition.

"But I know Cadet Walker is a crack shot and an accomplished swordsman, and has already killed at least one man in a duel just such as this one," she said, sniffling, a lacy white kerchief in one hand. "And Isabella says the rumor has it he shot another man from North Carolina, though he didn't kill that man."

Jackson sat across from her with his customary rigid posture, his face stony. It seemed to him Ellie and he had gotten on splendidly since his return. Internal barriers of hers—of what sort, he did not know—seemed to have come down. But this—this issue was difficult for all.

"I would rather you leave again, Thomas," she continued, now looking him straight in the eye, "than face a futile, meaningless, and perhaps even shameful death at the hand of this mean-spirited hotspur."

Jackson's face flushed. He stood.

"I shall go now," he said quietly. He started to turn, then, brow furrowed, spoke again, still in soft tones.

"I have not sought this fight, Ellie. I have done everything to avoid it, and shall continue to do so. However, if duty so dictates the course of events that peace without honor is impossible, then I shall determine to remember that a man's good name is preferable to a lifetime of safety, peace, and—," he glanced at the floor before looking back at her, "even a lifetime of happiness with the woman he loves."

Surprise filled her luminous eyes. He had never spoken the word before. *And now, to use it in* this *context!* Her eyes flashed with a fire he rarely saw, and had not seen at all since his return from Laura's.

"Tom Jackson, you know your Scripture tells you that he who lives by the sword shall perish by it."

Jackson stood for a long while, staring at the floor. He knew her words to be true. He knew also that God had not allowed King David to build the holy temple because he was a man of blood, and the Lord desired a man of peace for that important task. Yet, God had used David in other ways. Those ways included righteous war to defend the Almighty's chosen people. When Jackson spoke again, his words were not more than a whisper.

"If a man has not his name he has nothing."

Ellie looked downward as if struck. "I think you had better leave now."

Jackson started to speak, then turned and left.

Elkanah Clinton snapped the shade down, but he was an instant slow. Jackson caught the oilskin's final unfurling and knew Clinton had not yet left for the Franklin. It took a couple of minutes of rapping, then pounding, on the door, but the stoop-shouldered magistrate finally emerged.

"Why Jackson," the older man exclaimed, donning his trademark top hat, "didn't know you were out here."

Jackson ignored the lie.

"I've come again to ask you to swear out a warrant for—"

"I know, I know," Clinton waved, turning and heading up the wooden sidewalk. "Ex-cadet James Walker." The emphasis Clinton placed on *ex* suggested to Jackson that the topic was by no means a new one for the nervous magistrate. Jackson thought he detected a slight twitching of the harelip.

"I must insist," the professor said, his own long stride barely keeping pace with the hunched man's furiously shuffling little legs, "that you acquit yourself of the duties authorized you by our sovereign state—"

"And I must insist," Clinton blurted, stopping and wheeling to face Jackson, "that you desist in your protestations and go about doing what everyone in this town wishes and expects you to do: face up to young Walker's challenge and be done with it. I shall see you at the Franklin, sir!"

The words of the riposte echoed off the street's sturdy brick buildings as Jackson, speechless, stood and watched the little man waddle off. Ellie's visage, at once frightened and embarrassed for him, filled his mind's eye.

Perhaps honor dictates a different course than I myself should have chosen, Jackson sighed to himself. He straightened himself, flung his left arm straight up into the air, and marched toward the courthouse.

Judge Brockenbrough's anger toward Jackson flared for a different reason than most of those at the Franklin. A number had become openly scornful of the tall, enigmatic professor's reticence to satisfy Walker. Some were merely disappointed at a thus far squandered opportunity to break the monotony of mundane Rockbridge County life. Another group was contemptuous of the entire business, and respected Jackson all the more for his attempt to evade a martial confrontation. The latter group was not necessarily comprised of Jackson's closer associates and friends. Taken on the whole, the respected men of the Franklin Society were an inordinately Christian group with an inordinate ambiguity in the working out of their religious beliefs regarding this particular matter.

Brockenbrough still seethed from the loss of young Joseph Kennedy. True, Kennedy had been somewhat high-spirited, as most from Irish stock tended to be. But he had also evidenced brilliance, shrewdness, and a disciplined mind, which most tended not to do. Brockenbrough had always felt Proverbs 23:12, "Apply thine heart to instruction and thine ears to the words of knowledge," had fit Kennedy like a well-worn pair of doeskin gloves.

And now he was gone. This powerhouse of willful young intellect and articulation. This son of lifelong friends. *Yes,* Brockenbrough fretted again, as he had a hundred times before, *the boy could have been one of the great advocates, could have been . . . my successor?* Then, sweltering in his front-row chair in the courthouse, large, lazy ceiling fans notwithstanding, the judge physically shook his head. *No, somewhere, sometime the wineskin would have burst.* Young Kennedy was no abolitionist—few of the Irish north or south were—but Brockenbrough had watched as the young man's antisecession and antislavery views had crystallized in the two years he had been immersed in the Southern culture, just as those of the Virginians who were Kennedy's regular verbal sparring partners had, but in the opposite direction.

As the men on either side of Brockenbrough eyed the judge with concern, then one another, he heaved a great sigh. *No, the boy would have returned North before he could have long attained to the stature here of which he was eminently capable. Or he would have been—* Brockenbrough lowered his head and shook it slowly. *What a waste, what a pitiable waste of goodness and God-given talent and ability.* A shiver then rippled through him and his head shot back up, staring ahead but seeing only darkness. Was it a harbinger? One small earnest on some great debt yet to be paid by America? Only then, as he gazed around, tugging at his suddenly tight collar and pondering the feasibility of stealing out for a quick touch from the well-worn leather-encased flask tucked in his breast pocket, did he see the concerned expressions furrowing the faces of first one, then the other of the men seated next to him.

The gas mantles already shone around the perimeter walls of the courthouse meeting room even though more than an hour of hot summer light remained outside. As Jackson entered, he sensed heads turning toward him and voices hushing, as had happened the last time he entered a Franklin meeting with the martial specter of Walker looming somewhere outside. This time, however, all noise shrank from the cavernous room, save the fans' soft whirring.

Never before had Jackson heard the sound of his own boot heels thumping off the wood floor and echoing around the room. He reached his usual row and turned to enter. His usual chair was tipped forward, the top of it leaning against the chair in front of it. Jackson stopped and glanced around at the men near him. No one met his gaze. He stepped for the chair. A knee-booted leg stretched forward and blocked his way. *Will Russell.* This tough planter was looking at Jackson—squarely in the eyes.

"Don't you have an engagement elsewhere at this hour, laddie?" Ill-concealed joy swam in Russell's china blue eyes.

"I do not, and I would appreciate the removal of your leg, sir," Jackson replied evenly.

"Well now, some of us would appreciate the removal of your lard hide from this building until you dispose of your outstanding business honorably," Russell said, the eyes narrowing. No one nearby moved or looked in Jackson's direction.

"Hey, what's going on over there?" came a voice from a few rows over.

Steel girded Jackson's own eyes as his trim hard body went taut.

"Gentlemen, is there a problem back there?" asked Mayor John Letcher, from the front.

"You and your high and mighty West Point," Russell growled. "You ain't nothing more than a bunch of spoiled rich college boys thinking you're above us commoners. And you with guns no less." Danger now filled the planter's eyes as he lowered his leg and stood, jabbing a stubby brown finger at Jackson. "Well let me tell you something, mister, captain, professor, or whatever in Hades your current title is—"

"That's quite enough, Mr. Russell."

Jackson and Russell turned to see Dr. White, their pastor at the Lexington Presbyterian Church, standing in the aisle. A gas mantle on the wall behind him highlighted the silver streaks in his bush of dark hair. Stealing up behind White to stand in support was lanky bachelor John Lyle, Jackson's friend and bookstore owner.

"If anyone is to leave, Mr. Russell," White continued, "it shall be you."

The words were courteous, but freighted with authority. Russell's chin dropped just a bit as his face blanched in defeat and embarrassment. He turned back to Jackson for an instant. The taller man's gaze was steady. Then Russell looked away and sat in his own chair.

Jackson turned to White. "Thank you, Pastor. I apologize for the inconvenience to you, sir."

A friendly smile returned to White's normally jolly face. "Not at all, Tom." He included the men all around him in his next comment. "Now, shall we all enjoy an evening of spirited discourse?"

Jackson did not speak from the Franklin podium that evening. For the most part, he was quite attentive toward those who did. But the written message from Dr. Junkin that resided in the stiff-backed professor's inside coat pocket vied for his mental attention throughout the meeting.

Junkin, before leaving down the Shenandoah Valley for a week of preaching, had sent the message to Jackson. It explained with respect and deference the toll that Jackson's festering problem with Walker was taking on the normally vivacious Ellie. And it offered prayer and any counsel that might be desired.

Again, turmoil. Love or hate. Christ or death. Did he even have a choice, or must the two exist together in his life? Just as troubling loomed an insidious invader who had often wormed itself into Jackson's thoughts. In fact, as his bonds with Christ had grown stronger the last several years, the invader had strangely grown in strength as well. Why? Why should his ambition grow stronger and deeper when it would seem that growth in Christ would lessen and eventually eradicate it? It did not make sense, for he honestly believed his Christian commitment and devotion had grown. Why, then, the tenacious—and increasing—challenge with ambition? The near desperation with which he had pursued the teaching position at the University of Virginia last year, and the initial funk into which he had descended upon not attaining it, had concerned him. Whatever teaching position God willed for him should have been satisfactory to him. But it very nearly was not. And now the black talons of ambition curled around him even as he deliberated how to deal with the Walker situation.

As Major John Preston—the thought crossed Jackson's mind how much he had come to like the hearty, multitalented man whose monumental vision and energy in the conversion of the state arsenal to VMI had assured his and its lasting mark on Lexington and Virginia—coated the building with his rich, literate baritone pronouncements about God's designs for unreached aboriginal heathen, Jackson resolved to satisfy young Walker tonight. With mercy and forbearance, he hoped, but one way or another in finality. His color rose as he thought of dear Ellie fretting herself in her chambers. War was one thing; in war, a soldier's bride simply had to live with parting, loneliness, and fear. It was, sadly, her portion of the load to bear. But this fool's errand of Walker's must be stopped. Jackson determined that if Walker for some reason missed tonight's announced engagement at Washington and Fourth, he would go find the man—*yes, he was a man; he had shown himself that and must be treated purely as such*—if he had to take Lexington apart piece by bloody piece in finding him. When innocents were affected—as in this case, Ellie—the Scriptures were plain spoken that worse than an infidel was he who failed to protect their heart and virtue.

After Preston received a standing ovation for his deliverance, even from those who voted against his position that a sovereign God would indeed convey His saving Word efficaciously to those in distant lands, and bring those to Himself whom He had foreordained as His, Jackson stood and left. He never saw the brooding Russell, who had sat next to him in discomfort throughout the meeting, nor the other eyes that followed him, most with curiosity, a few with contempt.

Pastor White, John Lyle, Harvey Hill, Jackson's banker friend John Carlisle, and his attorney friend Elisha "Bull" Paxton all wanted to talk with him, but he had left the building almost before they were out of their seats. A couple of men caught sight of the professor striding out the door and wheeled to follow him, urging along others.

Outside, they learned from other men who awaited Jackson's emergence that Walker indeed stood waiting at the corner of Washington and Fourth. And he stood armed with pistol, sword, and bowie knife.

Jackson had suspected it would come to this. Last night he had walked to the empty Presbyterian church long after Wednesday prayer meeting and knelt for a long while at the altar. He prayed for wisdom and guidance, asking the Lord to reveal to him the specific sins of his own heart. And he asked God's blessing on the soul of the troubled young South Carolina hotspur.

He did not see nor hear the growing crowd behind him as he marched toward Washington and Fourth. Most of them were nearly running to keep pace with his long swift strides. The whole town knew what this was about.

Ten-year-old Willy Preston, the VMI founder's son and winner five years running of his Sunday school class's Scripture memory contest, joined the throng that now approached a hundred as it poured down the lamplit hill toward Fourth Street. He glanced around nervously for his father, but did not see him. Then Willy heard rushing footsteps from behind. In the lamplight, he saw more people and two buggies clattering into view. The first of them was driven by Lylburn Downing. Will Russell sat next to him, his face aglow in the dim light. Lylburn's and Willy's eyes met for an instant and the friends traded a surreptitious smile and nod as Russell's buggy passed.

Ahead, Jackson's attention was fixed on the job at hand, whatever that might be. As fear touched the professor, Charles Wesley's "Jesus, Lover of My Soul" seemed appropriate, both for himself and for Walker. Long arms swinging by his sides, back erect and boots thunking on the sidewalk, Jackson softly mouthed the words.

> *Other refuge have I none,*
> *Hangs my helpless soul on Thee;*
> *Leave, O leave me not alone,*
> *Still support and comfort me.*

The words and his own off-key notes began to soothe him.

> *All my trust on Thee is stayed,*
> *All my help from Thee I bring;*
> *Cover my defenseless head*
> *With the shadow of Thy wing.*

He began to smile and his head turned upward. He did not see the sparkling, starry summer sky, nor hear the crowd behind him that was now two hundred, but he felt the strong, sure arms of his God. He prayed that God would measure justice and mercy both to himself and to James Walker, and knew that He would.

When Jackson again looked forward, he saw the big Carolinian standing twenty feet straight ahead, his bright red hair bared, his legs spread apart, and his hands on his hips. He wore his VMI coat and trousers, crisp and clean. And he wore two pistols and a sword that hung to his side.

Hot fire danced in Walker's hazel eyes. He started to speak, but Jackson, sturdy and stiff-backed, kept coming.

Way back in the crowd, Willy jumped up and down to see the action, then slipped through the now-hushed group and around toward its side. Just as he came out, atop the entrance stoop to John Lyle's bookstore, he saw Major Jackson step to within a foot of Walker.

Funny, Willy thought, *I always thought Walker was several inches taller than the major.* And indeed he was three-and-a-half inches taller. Yet somehow, the straight-backed Jackson, nearly nose to nose with Walker, seemed to be looking straight into the younger man's eye. *Was Walker slumping a bit?*

Again, the South Carolinian began to speak. But the grim visage inches away from him gave him pause. *Those eyes,* Walker thought. *They said his eyes got that way in Mexico when the fire was hot and death was in the air.*

Walker wanted to kill Jackson, but it was discomforting, and disconcerting, being so close to the fanatic as to smell the garlic on his breath from supper—or could it have been lunch?

Without thinking, Walker took a half step back. He didn't trust letting Tom Fool this close to him.

Jackson's face betrayed no expression. But his eyes seemed to Walker to have taken on a life of their own. Their normal steely blue-gray seemed to have boiled into twin white-hot anthracite flames.

A rustle went through the crowd as two muscular VMI cadets shouldered their way to the front row. Stocky Johnny Patton and rangy Tom Munford, tense with excited anticipation, smiled at one another, then turned their eyes to the drama playing out before them.

Walker swallowed as Jackson covered the backward step the red-head had taken a moment before. Again, the two men stood nearly nose to nose.

I'm going to kill that—Walker thought to himself as he again stepped back. But again, Jackson covered the ground an instant later.

Patton and Munford glanced at one another. *What is this?* Patton thought. *A duel of honor or a bizarre two-step?*

His broad, hard shoulders tense, Walker started to shove Jackson away from him. But the eyes stopped him cold. What was it with those eyes?

For the first time, Walker glanced around at the crowd, biting his lip. He saw Patton and Munford and a few other cadets who had stayed in Lexington for the summer. And he saw others—

Now Jackson stepped forward, the toes of his gargantuan boots touching Walker's brightly polished, black cadet boots.

Uncertainly, Walker reached for one of his pistols. His hand froze on it. *Those eyes are going to burn a hole right through me,* he thought, perspiration running down his cheeks and neck. He took a couple more steps back, quickly. When Jackson came on, Walker stuck a beefy right arm straight out to forestall him. Jackson, his own arms never leaving his sides, walked right through Walker's arm until the men again stood toe to toe.

Walker, his face ashen, gnawed on his lip. Then, for the first time, he returned Jackson's stare with force. Gazing into the Virginian's blazing white eyes, Walker saw—*hell.*

Walker's own eyes widened in shock, and he began to step back again. Once, twice, three times, his face bereft of all color.

Patton and Munford grimaced at one another. In his buggy, Russell squeezed his legs until his knuckles turned waxy white. Lylburn and Willy, across the crowd from one another, stared in gape-eyed amazement.

Jackson, eyes still ablaze, stood his ground, but did not advance. Walker, glancing once more around the crowd, then back at the mute specter before him, his eyes threatening to pop out of their sockets in horror, wheeled around and strode, half running and half walking, into the darkness. As he did, he nearly ran over a bear of a sixty-two-year-old Presbyterian preacher and college president who had come to break up another of those disgusting matters of Southern honor for which he had little understanding and less tolerance.

Jackson watched Walker's retreat, his eyes landing on Dr. Junkin as the man stepped into the intersection of Washington and Fourth Streets. The professor's eyes softened to their normal hue and his countenance loosened.

"Dr. Junkin, sir," he bowed in deference. "A pleasure to see you tonight, sir."

Junkin walked toward Jackson, gazing around at the stunned crowd.

For a moment he said nothing. Then, his face sad and old, he touched Jackson's shoulder softly, bowed his head, and turned to leave. Only Jackson and a couple of others at the front of the crowd heard his one-word lament. "Christians."

Then, as Jackson started to follow Junkin, the crowd awoke, many of them converging upon the strange professor with congratulations, slaps on the back, and laudatory handshakes.

Patton and Munford stared at one another as men rushed by them.

"Well, I can't think of much good that came out of that," Patton sighed.

"I can," Munford grinned. "You owe me a five spot."

"Why, the heck—"

"Jackson still standing," Munford said, raising his hand to silence his reddening friend, "that was my statement. Well—there he is, still standing."

Patton frowned, then pulled paper money from a pocket and slung it at Munford.

"What in the world got into Jim Walker," Patton growled, "I'll never know."

"More like what went out of him, partner," Munford chuckled.

"Guess maybe he wasn't institute material after all."

Patton's eyes searched Munford's for confirmation of the statement. Munford's raised-eyebrow silence spoke what both men were thinking: whether or not James Walker was Virginia Military Institute material had exactly nothing to do with whatever they had just witnessed.

Jackson brushed his newfound admirers aside and headed for his apartment.

Halfway down the street, Willy caught him, just as Lylburn brought Russell's buggy to a halt a few feet away.

"That was quite a show back there, Major," Russell smirked, contempt dripping from each word. "But there was a matter of honor that was not satisfied. And next time, it may not be some loud-mouthed greenhorn facing off with you."

Jackson squared himself toward Russell.

"You watch yourself, Major Jackson," Russell said, his growl lower and more dangerous. "You may have railroaded that cadet, but you try shading me, mister—ever—and I'll not need no highfalutin fancy pistols or swords. I'll do the job with me bare hands. These hands, mister, that have worked the land a long time afore you showed your high and holy college boy's face around here."

Jackson stared at him, his eyes normal.

"Move it, boy," Russell shouted at Lylburn, who looked for an instant at Willy, then drove the buggy on.

Jackson watched the vehicle for a few seconds, then turned toward Willy. The youngster stared up in awe as if viewing the incarnation of one of the Homeric heroes he had long adored.

"Willy, does your Ma know where you are?"

The boy blushed. "No sir, Major."

"Then come," he said, placing his arm around his young admirer, "I'll walk with you."

For a moment, neither said anything.

"Were you scared?" Willy finally spoke.

"At first."

Another long pause. A man on horseback galloped by and shouted, "Attaway to show him, Major!"

"Why did he want to kill you, Major?"

Jackson pondered that. Conviction pressed in on his own soul.

"Because men's hearts are evil, son. Indeed, they are dark and they are evil."

CHAPTER 15

MAGGIE KNEW SOMETHING HAD OCCURRED THIS EVENING, something that involved Major Jackson. And she knew something else involving him was about to occur.

Sitting in her upstairs bedroom at her desk, she dipped ink from the well. Next to her lay an open copy of the *Atlantic*. It had long been one of her favorites. Like other publications from the North, it devoted increasing portions of its pages to the array of issues and conflicts that all pointed in one direction: growing sectional conflict. And like other publications with nationwide distributions, it found great difficulty in knowing just how to approach the stories. Yet Maggie had detected a gradually increasing inclination toward the propagation of ideas and practices Northern and the questioning of certain things Southern.

Just now, though, it was coming. Her heart was heavy and she was on a tear. The words written in her flowing hand at the top of the page read, "To My Sister." The lines below had rushed forth from that deep, hidden reservoir somewhere within that she had come to know was a special and personal gift from God. She knew He had given her this and much more besides; she as yet knew less how to reconcile her anger toward Him for the many pains, tribulations, and unanswered questions that abounded in life.

She paused and read the words that had tumbled out so rapidly that she had had no time to think of them herself. The speed with which she had written them had indeed been limited only by the physical limitations of her hand putting them onto the page. She knew that for whatever reason, she was now, as she had often been before, merely a courier for someone else's messages.

> *A cloud is on my heart, Ellie,*
> *A shade is on my brow,*

And the still current of my thought
Glides often sadly now.

The careless smile comes seldomer
Than once it used to come,
And when the playful jest goes round
My lips are strangely dumb . . .

She heard Ellie's precious sweet laughter from downstairs. *It was him—that coarse, odd mountain man who made her laugh like that.* Tears filled the limpid eyes. Then a surge of anger rushed through her and she snapped the quill in half.

"Good-bye, my beloved," she rasped.

"But I don't understand why you had to go face up to him like that," Ellie said, her voice fraught with emotion. "You—or he—or both of you could have been killed. I—I just don't understand it."

Jackson had been excited when he arrived at the Junkins' a few moments ago. After leaving Willy with his bedridden mother and his father, who had somehow heard nothing of the showdown with Walker, though half the Franklin Society attended it, the professor, his "Irish" up as well as his blood, had turned and headed toward the Junkins.

He had, in fact, been so excited, and felt such a burden lifted from his shoulders, that he had marched to Ellie's doorstep, a fistful of freshly-picked magnolias in hand, with the intent of proposing marriage to her one last time. Surely, with most of the summer to contemplate the decision, she would have come to the same decision he had: God intended the two of them to spend the remainder of their mortal lives together.

Now he was beginning to wonder if the current conversation could be completed with his and Ellie's *friendship* intact, much less a marriage proposal offered and accepted.

"It—it seems so foolish and selfish," Ellie continued, rising from the green velvet Gainsborough chair. She plucked a thin, slightly frayed three-cornered stole of Mechlin lace (that had been given her mother back in Philadelphia) from a nearby end table and draped her shoulders with it.

Odd, Jackson thought, *it is quite warm outside as well as in this house.*

"Yes," Ellie continued, pacing, "I just don't see how I could ever consent to spend my—that is, I don't, I just still don't understand a man who would—"

Such strange behavior for Ellie, Jackson thought. Rather than feeling a chill, he felt quite warm. He even did something unusual for him. He stuck his finger inside his tight collar and pushed it out a bit. Dampness permeated the collar.

Now Ellie circled the room, eyes fixed on the rugged floor as she spoke.

"I just don't understand you, no, not at all," she muttered. "It's just like Maggie says, you're a good man, but you're not the least bit conventional, you don't concern yourself with the things that concern other men, you care not one wit for what others think as long as you believe yourself to be in God's will, and—"

Then he was standing in her path and gazing down into her eyes. Gently, he took her hand and held it as carefully as though it were a piece of the fine Old Country china that lined the walnut sideboard against the wall behind him.

"I know I don't have what some men have. I sure don't have money and fame—though I am thrifty, and I intend someday to restore the good Jackson name so that my grand forefathers would be proud."

She looked up at him, the hazel eyes melting into his strength.

"But I am a man who loves you. And whatever I have now, or ever, shall be yours. Most of all, you can trust that I shall love you with all there is in me for as long as I live. I shall never do less than the Lord would have me to do after entrusting you to me for these few short, passing years here on earth."

His face, set and strong-jawed, contorted slightly.

"I . . . I . . . ."

She stared, her pretty, full lips parted, wondering what was next, not sure if she was standing or sitting.

He shook his head, then exclaimed, "I have the greatest urge just now to shoot an arm into the air!"

She burst into laughter, and her old élan was back. "Why Thomas Jackson, can you not think of something better to do with that silly arm than shoot it into the air!"

He looked deeply into her eyes, then reared his head back in great, sweeping—silent—laughter, as was his way. Then he held her desperately and kissed her with all the love that the years of waiting and wondering and hoping had brought him.

He knew that God was in heaven, and He had given her to him. He knew it with all his heart. And somehow, in this most sublime moment of his life, he vowed anew to that God that regarding his love and care for Ellie, as with all things in his life—only this ever more so—*Whatsoever my hand findeth to do, I shall do it with my might.*

CHAPTER 16

THE YELL—SHRILL AND HIGH-PITCHED THOUGH IT WAS— should not have surprised Maggie. And in a way, it did not. Yet anger cascaded in among the hurt as, despite her most vigorous efforts to the contrary, she felt the earsplitting shriek, though not unexpected, cut like a painful cold dagger deep within her bowels. For just a moment, the enormity of it bowed her head down toward the paper upon which she wrote. *Him,* she thought, almost in a curse. *She's leaving me because of* him! Sparks danced in the blue eyes.

She walked to the dormer and looked down. She saw only Jackson's back, quickly disappearing down the spruce- and oak-dappled hill toward town. The shout continued unabated. *There he goes, like some common miner or field hand, acting as if it took him a few shots of liquid courage even to get up the nerve to ask her.* Color flooded her pale visage. *Nothing could stop that man,* she thought, remembering how she had once actually refused him entry to the house just prior to his leaving for his sister's.

And that's the place to where he should return, she told herself with a frown, *back to his backward mountain people.*

"Oh-h!" she exclaimed, grabbing the thick fiery red hair she had recently taken to parting down the middle in the fashion of the day. Her blood boiled within her. For a moment, so much blood rushed through her benumbed brain she thought she might pass out. Finally she caught hold of herself.

Oh, the very detestable thought of collapsing because of him! She would turn it, as always she did when the events of the world swung against her, to something good, something of worth. She would turn all her considerable, and as yet unfulfilled, energy and passion to the sheet of paper still staring up at her from the oaken desk.

As Jackson's pealing faded into town, the heartbreak gave birth to the words that poured forth again.

> *Forgive these saddened strains Ellie*
> *Forgive these eyes so dim!*
> *I must—must love whom you have loved*
> *So I must turn to him—*
> *And clasping with a silent touch,*
> *Whose tenderness endears,*
> *Your hand and his between my own,*
> *I bless them with my tears.*

Ellie's wedding day. Ruthie's step evidenced even more spring than usual, despite the August 4 warmth. And it could have evidenced even more had not that same troubling subject again been passed abroad through the oral transmission of the county's Negro grapevine.

Ruthie still felt things were the way they were and that meant white folks on top. She was not about to jeopardize her exalted position with an exalted clan by supposing things could or even should be the slightest bit different in this old world. This was not her world anyway. "For we are strangers before thee, and sojourners, as were all our fathers: our days on the earth are as a shadow, and there is none abiding."

Yet, some she respected had begun to pass on tales of the great "railroad" through which slaves were increasingly passing northward to Canada, through the aid of abolitionist white folks. And of the writings and speakings of a man named Frederick Douglass. Bits of speeches in the North—*public speeches, no less*—had drifted down the grapevine to Rockbridge County. She had heard power and inspiration in Douglass's words. She had also heard he was not a believer, and had said awful things about the church, especially the Southern white folks' church. She had mixed feelings about this, though she remembered how God had used the infidel Chaldeans to chasten hard His wayward Jewish people.

But Ruthie was not sure she wanted black folks freed up, at least in large numbers, anyhow. She felt many of them, especially among the young men, needed a strong hand to keep them out of trouble. And besides, they were likely to be less respectful and compliant toward her, a free niggra.

Still, since that white woman's book *Uncle Tom's Cabin* had come out last year, there was more talk around the grapevine than in previous seasons, and more white folks than before, not just in the North, but along the slaveholding "border" states and even in the South, were evidently, even if often behind closed doors, questioning the continued economic and moral viability of what her free friends in Pennsylvania called "that peculiar institution." She also perceived that the stance of many in the border states and the South was hardening as a response to the pressure they perceived increasing against them.

Uncle Tom's Cabin had been a lively topic around the Junkin table. Most of the family did not stand against the rights of slaveholders, if they acted in a humane, Christian manner. In a perfect world, of course, the practice would not exist, but it was not a perfect world, and many white folks, frenzied abolitionist rhetoric notwithstanding, felt the release of their slaves to freedom would be a criminal act, dooming the Africans to destitution and starvation in a land where they were incapable of fending for themselves. The Junkins saw *Uncle Tom's Cabin* as a polemic riddled with flaws, not the least of which was author Harriet Beecher Stowe's failure to have ever even set foot in a slaveholding state.

Yet, Ruthie had the impression, what with her uncanny knack for garnering information from people on all corners of her life, that the vivid storytelling of the book had caused many white folks to reconsider—or perhaps consider for the first time—their thoughts regarding the practice of slavery. She had heard John Junkin, when he visited his father's Washington College home one evening for supper, read from a Northern religious publication the cries of the famed white evangelist Charles Finney against slavery as "a great national sin. . . . It is the church that mainly supports this sin. . . . Let Christians of all denominations . . . write on the head and front of this great abomination *Sin!* and in three years, a public sentiment would be formed that would carry all before it."

All in all, the issue rather irritated Ruthie, and, truth be known, she would rather have preferred it to disappear one way or another, leaving her alone to the successful operation of the president's house, whose inhabitants, though she had no illusions they realized it, could scarcely have gotten along without her.

Oh, she be beautiful, Ruthie thought, as she led Ellie down the broad carpeted winding staircase from her room to the large sitting room where Dr. Junkin would shortly conduct the wedding ceremony.

Anna caught her breath when Ellie passed, stunned by the radiant beauty and joy emanating from her happy friend that seemed to fill the room. Herself a content, sanguine person by nature, a quick thought nonetheless lanced through Anna's mind: *Oh, Lord, to have such a love for such a man, and have it requited!* Then she noticed Isabella attempting to catch her attention. Anna's eyes twinkled as they made contact with her sister's. *Yes, I know, he was standing, arm thrust into the air, as we entertained him at the pianoforte only last evening, never so much as breathing a word that he had proposed to Ellie the night before and was to be married today! Thank Providence for brother Harvey's dawn announcement today, for he himself, the best man, had just learned the news! What manner of man is this?*

And indeed, Ellie looked divine. She wore the same dazzling cream dress and flowing train her grandfather had had made for her mother nearly forty years before by the finest dressmaker in Philadelphia. Her porcelain skin glowed, her eyes glittered, and her trim, comely body filled out the dress in the manner that young womanhood should. When she descended those steps onto the main floor, one-eyed Wayne Marley and even debonair Harvey Hill could only shake their heads in wonderment. And her brothers knew this was not only their devoted, loving, charmed sister; this was the most beautiful girl in Rockbridge County.

Maggie was a wreck. Tears streamed down her face. She had never seen Ellie so beautiful and happy. And yet it was the very day she was losing her. *Oh, this just can't be happening!* her brain cried to her as her father began the ceremony, his voice sure and strong, but his eyes misty.

She glanced over to Jackson, stiff and erect and bedecked in a uniform so clean and fresh she assumed it must have been borrowed. *If one of those arms so much as lifts above his waist, I swear I'll grab it and wrench it off!*

Poor girl, and don't no one else even know, Ruthie sighed to herself as the vows began and she saw teary, taut-faced Maggie standing as though she were a pine tree awaiting one last thunk of the axe before toppling. *And now she be plum scared of the future, thinking she won't have Ellie no more, but still somehow thinking she will. But she can't. That's just the way things be in this wicked old world. That's right, "a man and his maid" . . . She be better maybe when it all over.*

Jackson thought he had never loved anything in God's creation as he loved the radiant woman who now stood before him. A hurtful thought panged him that perhaps he loved her too much. He quickly confessed that, then he was staring into the wide sparkling eyes of his future. The wife of his youth, the children who would be the sister and brother he had lost and for whom he would be the father he had lost. The wife who would help fill what had been lost long ago with his mother's passing, and who would fill so much more. The family that had been taken from him. The belonging, the loving. He could be safe again. *Ah, dear God, I can be safe again.*

And then he was kissing her rich, full soft lips. He had kissed her only the one time before, on the night she accepted his proposal, because she was a treasure of the Lord's and not to be trifled with or endangered in any way. But now, *Oh,* he pulled back finally because he thought he might fall, and for a moment, though he heard the rich baritone voice proclaiming, "And what God hath put together, let no man lay asunder . . . ," he saw nothing but black, and that black seemed to be moving and spinning. And then, gradually, all returned to focus and it was her smiling face, the face of an angel, that he saw first.

A bit later, it was time to go. The modest gathering of family and friends had reveled in the joyful experience. After initial responses comprised of varying degrees of shock and amazement, almost all of them had come to see the union as a strange, unique, yet ultimately natural and ingenious—if unexpected—one. The more religious among the group might even have considered it a match made in heaven.

Jackson drew deeply of the fresh bracing aroma of pine, maple, and spruce as he and Ellie stepped out the front entrance onto the shaded portico. Actually, it was not hot for an August day. *The Lord has seen even to that detail on this day of days,* he thought. He saw the gathered throng beyond the white colonnades. The group had enlarged to include a number of people who had not been invited to the smallish wedding. Beyond the people, the lush green hill sloped gently down toward town.

The Jacksons descended the front steps of the president's home, ducking volleys of rice hurled by the now-sizable throng.

At the foot of the steps, Jackson saw beaming, young Willy Preston. Another boy, perhaps slightly younger, his mouth wide open, stood next to Willy.

"You—you're the man who stared down the cannonball," the awed youngster stuttered.

Jackson stopped. For an instant, he was looking up at his own smiling father. Jonathan winked at young Tom and tousled his hair.

The vision passing, Jackson swallowed, then smiled and rustled Willy's friend's mop of yellow hair.

Back in the wide, open entrance to the Georgian style home, Maggie stood alone, looking out over the gay scene. *"This world passeth away,"* she thought. She watched as Jackson and Ellie stepped into a waiting buggy. Her face wet, she gnawed her tight lower lip and bowed her head, her body swaying, almost imperceptibly.

Something wrapped itself around her shoulders. When the contact registered with her dulled mind, she looked up. Her father smiled down at her, with great tenderness. She started to shake her head as if to protest whatever it was he was thinking, as she had done so often in her adult life, but her magnificent strong will was gone and all that was left to do was burst into tears and bury her head in his great chest.

Quebec's high Plains of Abraham stretched serene and beautiful toward the golden setting sun low in the west. Its lingering amber rays reached across the field to embrace the honeymooning couple—and Maggie—as they walked across the silent plateau, Ellie and Jackson arm-in-arm.

The echo of Jackson's steady baritone voice broke the quiet.

"Ever since Dr. Barney prescribed buttermilk for me when we were in New York, my health has been much the better for it."

Maggie, whose heart had leapt for joy when Ellie invited her on the trip—their own mother's sister had accompanied her on her wedding trip—peered at Jackson. Her newly minted brother-in-law's rugged physical regimen did his health no harm either, Maggie thought. Last evening, while borrowing some medicine from Ellie for her eyes, which had grown weary and sore in recent months, Maggie had caught a glimpse of a shirtless Jackson. His hard, defined muscular physique had taken her breath away. The efficacy of his vigorous early morning walks and his jumping and leaping exercises, arms flailing all the while with his heavy little steel handweights, now made sense to her. So did Jackson's spartan diet, which varied, depending on the season and his menu of the moment, from cornbread, plainly dressed meat, and milk to water and stale bread.

For just an instant, her mind wondered as her gaze lingered on the tall, erect Virginian. *How must those arms feel around a woman?* Then she shook her head, remembering the Scriptures upon which she had lately been ruminating. *"You are a foreigner and alien in this world . . . set your sights on things above, not things below . . . abstain from fleshly lusts, which war against the soul."* Her eyes darted to Ellie. Thankfully, she had not, nor had Jackson, spied the searching blue eyes.

Maggie's cheeks felt flushed as she walked. The color was not at first precipitated by anger, but after a moment it was. When Jackson's free arm flared skyward and stayed there, Maggie tossed her red hair.

"Thomas Jackson, I recognize that you have ailments," she said. "However, I sense that you are perhaps just a bit preoccupied with them?" Ignoring Ellie's surprised stare, she plowed on. "Your arm, your doctors, your medicines, your foolish diets of stale bread and warm milk. Major, I just—"

"Why, Maggie dear," Ellie cut in, "whatever in the world has gotten into you? You've been cross with Tom the entire honeymoon. He's liable to wish you hadn't come along!"

"No, that's all right," Jackson said mildly. "She has had to suffer it through Philadelphia, West Point, the St. Lawrence, Montreal, and now here. I must indeed seem a bore with my many ailments and medicinal pursuits."

"No, dear, you've good reason to be concerned," Ellie said. Suddenly, she yanked Maggie around by the forearm—hard. "Now, you listen to me, Sister. I still love you as much as ever. And because of the housing shortage in Lexington, we're going to be living just down the hall from you. So from now on, I want you to treat my husband with respect."

The sisters stood nose to nose, their eyes blazing. Jackson, his face pallid and his mouth wide open, was speechless. Finally, Maggie jerked her arm away.

"It might even make it a bit easier to feel some love for him," Ellie added, tears welling in her eyes.

Maggie winced at the last statement as if struck.

Jackson, looking for a hole into which he could crawl, instead spotted something of interest up ahead. His arm dropped and his dark blue eyes lit up.

"Come on, ladies, there's General Wolfe's statue."

Ellie, a rare anger enveloping her, lanced her sister with one more glaring look, then accepted Jackson's outstretched arm, ready to go. But he offered his other arm to Maggie, his eyes kind.

Maggie spoke quietly, refusing to look him in the eye. "I can walk alone. You just go ahead."

Ellie seethed again, but Maggie stuck her tongue out at her after Jackson had turned away.

General James Wolfe had led the British to glorious victory over France for possession of Canada. A large, bronze monument, haunting in the fading gold light, commemorated his brave, martyred service.

Jackson doffed his kepi cap and stepped gingerly toward the statue as if entering into the presence of the Almighty Himself.

His words were hushed and reverential. "Here, General Wolfe led his men in the final decisive battle that won Canada from France for England."

Suddenly, he whirled around and pointed. "*There*, Wolfe fell!" He whirled again. "*There*, his inspired men rallied from their retreat, pivoted, and drove the French from the field!"

He turned and faced the sisters, Maggie having just caught up, his eyes now blazing. "Canada has been the Crown's since that fateful day."

The women stood dumbstruck by the uncharacteristic outburst. They looked at one another. Ellie started to speak, but Jackson, not noticing her intention, swept his arm around the plain and thundered.

"'I die content!' Wolfe's dying words. I die content!" He turned toward the sisters, his eyes white-hot. "To die as he died, who would *not* die content!"

Ellie and Maggie stood, not quite comprehending, as Jackson's words echoed across the dim ghostly plain.

Ellie, bothered by a facial problem that had imparted occasional and partial paralysis, remained at the inn to rest one afternoon a week later while Maggie and Jackson took a canoe ride with a boatman down the beautiful and apparently benign nearby Niagara River. Ruggedly gorgeous and fed by the upriver falls of the same name, the Niagara moved along at a moderately brisk clip, but the boatman assured his passengers this was its norm.

As Jackson drank in the picturesque scene, the bright summer sun bathed the river, which lay against verdant hills that rolled away on either side of it. Maggie sat more straight-backed than Jackson, her arms folded and her chin set as the water swirled outside the canoe.

"Beautiful, isn't it?" Jackson said. When no response came, he asked, "What's wrong, Maggie?"

"I should never have let you bring me out on this river. We're too close to the Niagara Falls, and anything could happen." Curt tone, clipped words.

"But Maggie, you were the one who wanted to come," Jackson replied softly.

A sudden pitch in the canoe threw Maggie off balance. She turned to the boatman.

"My lands, sir, do you not know your job?"

"Maggie!" Jackson exclaimed. This excursion, like much before it on the trip, was laced with an undercurrent of tension, the source of which Jackson could not quite identify.

She cut him off by again folding her arms and looking away, her eyes now twin piercing blue rays. A moment later, the canoe pitched anew.

"That's it!" Maggie shouted, attempting to stand. "Turn this canoe around, boatman, we're going—"

Then a stronger surge of current rocked the sturdy canoe in the opposite direction, throwing Maggie across the craft and half over its side. Her face landed inches from the churning river. She choked and gagged on the cold water as it spewed up into her eyes and nose.

Jackson leapt across the canoe as the boatman struggled to control it, just as another violent pitch tossed Maggie's legs and lower body up and toward the water. The Virginian's lunge corralled the airborne woman as she went over the side.

He slammed her down against the side of the canoe. Astride her, his eyes burned an electric blue just as they had at the Wolfe monument. The two dripping faces glared at one another, mere inches separating them. Maggie squealed and struggled to break free. "You," she gasped, "you didn't even tell your own sister about the marriage!"

Jackson cocked his head, a quizzical look on his soaked face.

Maggie strained against him, but he had her wrists pinioned. She relented.

The two breathed in great heaves from their exertion. Then they stared into one another's eyes for a long moment.

"Oh," she uttered softly, going limp.

"Now Maggie, I want you to sit still and trust this man, as I do, to get us back in." Jackson's words were kind but firm. He turned to the shaken boatman, who nodded and sped up his already furious rowing tempo.

Maggie stared at Jackson, her breath still coming in gusts and her chest heaving. But now it was not from anger. Her eyes softened and her lips parted.

"Yes, Tom."

The confused thought that she had never before called him by his Christian name flickered through his mind as he helped his new sister-in-law up to a sitting position.

The sanctuary and gallery of the beautiful Lexington Presbyterian Church were filling to capacity, as invariably they were for Dr. White's Sunday sermons. White, an adequate preacher, was a profound Christian thinker and a widely respected theologian. He stayed in Lexington despite offers from larger churches in larger cities because he believed strongly God had called him to this lovely Shenandoah burg. And like his colleague Junkin, an environment rife with the eager young minds of the college campus provided a particularly stimulating opportunity to impact his world with the truths and power of the Christian gospel.

Unlike many of his peers, offers of larger congregations and salaries did not in and of themselves constitute "God's leading" to greater challenges for White.

Jackson led Ellie, and Maggie, to his customary fourth row aisle position. The major had read how Unitarianism and the Armenian theology that elevated the goodness of the race of man and the efficacy of his efforts in his own salvation and his ongoing sanctification, while lowering the high Calvinistic view of the sufficiency and totality of God in these works, had gripped the North. He believed the Second Great Awakening of Timothy Dwight and others to have been a mere shadow, and a corrupted one at that, of the First Great Awakening of Jonathan Edwards, George Whitefield, *et al.*

As he bellowed out, several keys off, the great hymns of the faith, then settled in to listen to White's God-centered preaching, it struck Jackson that while politics, economics, slavery, and a host of other issues dominated discussions related to the mounting sectional disputes, the divisions were at heart theological differences. The North, founded by Puritans upon the purest biblical—Calvinistic—precepts, had gradually, despite the Great Awakenings, drifted toward a much more pluralistic, man-centered, national religious landscape. He knew the Roman church had made great inroads in the North because of the huge numbers of Germans and Irish who had immigrated to America over the last twenty years. Unlike some of his Protestant peers, Jackson did not disdain the Catholics, for, partly because of his experiences in Mexico, he felt their religion included much good. Nonetheless, it and the rainbow of other religious stripes inculcating the North had created, in Jackson's view, a corporate national view of reality very different from that in the South.

The South, primally dependent as it was on the fruits brought forth from the soil, must fall upon the mercy and provision of God all the day long just for its sustenance. If God did not bring forth the bounty of His green earth, the South would perish. Jackson admitted to himself that some in the South were also dependent upon God to keep their lessers in the proper place. He knew that a society founded upon good, clear Christian order—where masters were kind to their slaves, "crackers," and others, and those groups knew to accept graciously the kindness as they stayed in their place—was a society for some that was eminently desirable to keep in place.

The North, meanwhile, found itself in the throws of an industrial revolution that was largely eluding the South. Most whites in the South, regardless of their social strata, were relatively content with their station in life and the possessions the Lord had allotted to them. This, because most Southerners, even backsliders and the unconverted, were steeped in the reality of the Almighty God of the Bible as central to all things, both in this life and in whatever life was to follow. In the North, however, fantastic material production and possession were developing as the upshot of the new steel machines and factories. Not only were the people there raised in different countries, with a dissimilar God(s?), but they were making new gods for themselves as they went.

The European higher critical school of theology had also made much greater inroads into the New England colleges and seminaries than it had in the South, which helped nourish the notions of man's capabilities as captain of his own ship. In summary, from what Jackson had read, seen with his own eyes, and heard from his Northern friends, there was no longer any sort of theological consensus in the North. And that worried him greatly. In fact, the contemplation of it actually kept him awake a couple of moments farther into White's sermon than usual. He heard nearly ten minutes of preaching on this pleasant late October morning in 1853 before his chin found its permanent resting place against his chest.

"There he goes, Munford," Johnny Patton whispered with glee as he leaned over the balcony railing from his front row seat, his eagle eyes honed in on the now slumbering Jackson. "Right on cue."

Now Munford, next to Patton amidst the throng of VMI cadets, surreptitiously craned his head over the railing, a spark of mischief in his eyes.

Patton, his thick, tousled hair only partly corralled by an earlier wet combing, could barely harness his voice to an intense whisper.

"Go ahead, Muns, do it!"

Now White had interrupted his sermon from the fifth chapter of Matthew to lead the congregation in the Lord's Prayer, or the Disciple's Prayer, as he referred to it.

"Our Father, who art in heaven," White intoned, his head bowed.

On the fourth row, Jackson sucked in a loud, long lungful of air, garnering the attention of his wife, her sister, and several other nearby parishioners.

Upstairs, Munford deftly brought a pea shooter to his lips, then blew a tiny missile down toward the floor.

"Give us this day, our daily bread," White and the congregation continued.

Munford's projectile thwacked into the back of Jackson's head just as the major unleashed a vibrato from between his lips. These two occurrences resulted in an explosive gasp from Jackson's mouth.

"What!" Jackson shouted over the prayer as he came suddenly to his senses.

Patton, Munford, and their fellow cadets in the gallery erupted in an involuntary burst of laughter.

The good folks around Jackson were not amused.

Dr. Junkin and Julia, seated on the second row, turned back toward the commotion.

White looked up in bewilderment.

"And, . . . er," he sputtered, before looking back down. "Uh, forgive us our debts."

Ellie's eyes nearly popped out of their sockets. "Shh, dear," she urged.

Maggie, on the other side of Ellie, peered up at the clamor in the gallery, then looked at Jackson. Sadness etched her face.

Across the center aisle and back a couple of rows, Russell leered at Jackson. For the stocky planter, prayer time in church was merely a good opportunity to mull over property and business considerations that he often found himself too distracted in the course of a normal working day to consider with focus and clarity. Russell appreciated God's kindness in allowing him this private, uninterrupted time of planning.

Watching Jackson make a fool of himself anew brought to Russell's mind Willy Preston, young son of the arrogant, holier-than-thou VMI founder, which brought to mind Lylburn Downing. And the sudden realization that Russell had seen his best servant boy in the company of young Preston numerous times in recent weeks. Was it

Russell's imagination that the two boys had exchanged a sly, knowing glance at John Carlisle's fete last Saturday night?

Lylburn is a good boy, Russell thought, but he would have to nip in the bud any developing social relationship between the two youths. A cousin of Russell's had lived just one farm over from a spread where the murderous renegade slave Nat Turner had butchered an entire family of white Virginians during his infamous 1831 rampage. That and other incidents had impregnated Southerners with a fear of servile insurrection they had not previously known. And it had left some of them, like Russell, with a secret loathing of the African transplants, and given them leave to take measures, however extreme, to keep their slaves in tow.

As Jackson, crimson-faced, gazed around in confusion, Russell contemplated how he could parlay this ridiculous—and regularly-occurring—incident, and others, into action to Jackson's detriment. *Look at that self-righteous hypocrite,* Russell seethed, *talks all about Jesus, carries his Bible where he goes, looks down on everything from dancing to tobacco to cursing to drinking wine, and truth be known, he has so little interest in the things of God, he snores through every sermon, right there in the same seat on the aisle, on the fourth row!*

Russell had a sudden, overwhelming urge to stand and shout directly at Jackson to leave the church and not come back until he could at least have the courtesy to those around him to stay awake during Dr. White's sermon. This strong feeling ended when he remembered his friend on the VMI faculty who detested Jackson's poor classroom manner and had long wished for the major's departure from the institution. True, the professor in question was an Episcopalian, and rather a lapsed one at that, *but at least he makes no pretenses toward holiness when he does not himself possess it,* Russell thought.

His scowl transformed gradually to a smile as he further remembered the two young cadets, one recently graduated and now running his family's considerable plantation in North Carolina, who could certainly be counted on to bring forth supporters from their quarters in any move to oust Jackson from his beloved and misbegotten teaching position.

As White finished the prayer and resumed preaching, Russell continued watching Jackson, who was already beginning to nod again. *Perhaps, Major Jackson,* the squat, tough landowner thought with derision, *that choice fourth row aisle seat shall soon find itself in need of a new occupant.*

Wizened old Mrs. Coulling, sitting directly behind Ellie, had other ideas filling her mind. She tapped Ellie on the shoulder.

"Would you like to borrow my hat pin again like last week, dearie?" she asked with ancient, earnest eyes.

Ellie had always loved the pealing of church bells. To her, they were pure, clarion proclaimers of good news for this difficult life and the promise of entry into a next life of eternal bliss, contentment, and joy. These feelings had been strengthened as her mother died last year on a Sunday, against the backdrop of the same bells Ellie now heard ringing sweetly from the Lexington Presbyterian belfry.

Maggie's words regarding her mother had said it best, Ellie thought: "Her death was no leaping into the dark. She died in the bright hope of an unending immortality of happiness."

Ellie looked up at the tall, handsome man who held her left arm in his right as they strolled along the sidewalk, away from the church and toward home. He remained, as always he had been, a mystery to her in so many ways. At first she had thought her inability to decipher what he was about was a chief item setting him above the many other fine young men who had sought her affections. Eventually, however, she realized that just the opposite was true: she had come to love this man largely because he was so singularly straightforward and trustworthy. If he was possessed of a speck of guile, she had yet to discern it. She felt so safe with him.

Yet, there were incongruities. They were discussing one of them just now.

"But darling," she said, her voice steady and sweet as it almost always was. "Could you not at least slump down in your seat? Perhaps that way, it would not be as hurtful for you."

As usual, he had thought through the issue and his position.

"I'll do nothing to make sleep come easier than it already seems to do each week. But if indeed I do sleep, I deserve all the humiliation I receive."

To this, she merely offered a sweet, compassionate smile and pressed her head to his shoulder. They had, after all, only been married three and a half months.

"Hello, Jacksons!"

The Jacksons both knew before looking across the street that it was the golden baritone voice of Colonel John Preston, a singing voice that was everything Jackson's was not.

"And hello to you, Prestons," Jackson returned with a rare smile. He really liked big, strapping Preston. So did most of the rest of Lexington. The consensus of thought held that the VMI stalwart's striking chiseled, square-jawed handsomeness seemed at variance with a heart that was one of the humblest and biggest in Rockbridge County.

Something else was not quite as commonly known, despite Preston's key role in the founding of VMI and his evident material success. Jackson had heard both Lyle and Carlisle, on separate occasions, refer to Preston's mind as one of the keenest and shrewdest in the Shenandoah Valley. Over the past year, such proclamations had twice prompted the major to accept invitations from the older man to participate in business investments with him. Jackson assumed other such opportunities would present themselves in the future, and he would accept them as well.

All things considered, Colonel John Preston seemed the most blessed and fortunate of men.

"Are you coming to sing for our Sunday school again next week, Willy boy?" Jackson called.

"Why, yes sir, Major Jackson!" young Willy Preston shouted. "Glad to, sir!"

The Prestons waved as they turned down a different street to head north, while the Jacksons continued east toward their Washington College abode.

"Fine boy, that Willy, finest around," Jackson said.

"I think he looks just like his father," Ellie said.

"I think he looks just like Preston," Jackson said. "But not only on the outside, on the inside too."

Ellie glanced up at her husband. "Having problems with your ear again?" He nodded. "But I thought it was the left one which was bad."

"It was, last time," he said. "Now I'm having problems hearing out of the right one."

A handsome elderly black man approached the Jacksons from the other direction, supported by his sturdy old walnut cane. Known only as Mr. Jefferson and dressed in a worn but neat black frock coat, he had belonged to the Callaghan clan for more than fifty years until the last of them died out four years before. Then, with everyone around Lexington knowing and liking and respecting him, the thoughtful old gentleman had just sort of drifted into freedom.

As he always did toward older citizens both colored and white, Jackson doffed his kepi cap and bowed respectfully to Jefferson, who flashed a brilliant ivory smile and bowed in return.

For a long time after Jackson's arrival in Lexington, the blacks in the community had been suspicious of his bowing habit. In time, however, Jefferson and others began to pass the word that, indeed, the action seemed an authentic outworking of an authentic Christianity that saw all mankind as created in the image of God and therefore meritorious of dignity, respect, and honor. These and other actions of Jackson's, such as his frequent aid to blacks in need of medical attention, prompted those in the African-descended Lexington community to take notice, then, secretly, to hold him in high regard.

"How sad it is, dear, what some—even some of your friends— think of your habit of showing the old Negroes your respect," Ellie said.

Jackson sighed. His thoughts turned toward the enmity held by a vocal minority of Northerners toward Southerners regarding their "peculiar" institution and how it had increasingly perplexed him and caused him to evaluate his views on the issue. Of course, he attempted to follow this practice on all substantive matters in his life. Some things in life he just did not understand.

"Slavery is a troublesome institution," Jackson said quietly, "and I wish all the Negroes were free." He glanced back over his shoulder at Jefferson, moving off down the street.

"Yet have I searched the Scriptures in vain for sanction against it, and found none. I still see it not as a desirable thing." He paused for a moment. Not far away, a whippoorwill sang. "I can only trust Providence to have implemented laws for the bound and the free, and allowed such a thing for ends that it is not my business to determine."

Just then, a shadow fell across the Jacksons. They turned to see Wayne Marley coming up beside them, astride his horse, rifle strapped over one shoulder. The cross atop the Presbyterian church down the street stood over the same shoulder.

"Good morning, Professor," Marley said with a smile. He tipped his hat. "Mrs. Jackson."

"And to you, Wayne," Jackson said. "Still finding other ways to spend the Sabbath, are you?"

"Ah, Prof, you know how good the squirrel hunting is around here this time of year." He spoke without affection, as if the exchange were a familiar one.

"Hunting squirrels will stand you in no good stead when you stand before your Maker, Wayne."

This was a bit more direct approach than normal, and Marley did not know what to say.

"Will you be back in time to sup with us this evening, Wayne?" Ellie interjected.

"Why, yes ma'am," Wayne said quickly.

Jackson glanced at his wife. She cocked her head at him.

"Very well, Wayne," Jackson said with a nod. "5:30." Marley smiled as if being granted a reprieve. "But you think about what I said while you're out shooting squirrels on the Lord's Sabbath."

"Yes sir, Prof," Wayne said, again tipping his hat to Ellie, then riding off.

"Probably got a bottle and a deck of cards with him, too," Jackson said, shaking his head in discouragement and looking down at the ground as he spoke. "Cannot find a job to rescue me from that band of irreverent fools to save my life, and the best young man I ever taught shows no sign of being any closer to finding Christ than he did whilst courting señoritas and tequila in Mexico. My career amounts to exactly nothing."

This unusual outpouring caught Ellie by surprise. *What is going on here?* she thought as Jackson tensely continued walking, head down. She chose her words carefully.

"Major Jackson, I love you and I'm so very proud of you. I know you'll be faithful to please Him by working on the two *A*'s."

"I know, I know," Jackson nodded, exhaling. "Ambition and anger."

"The one does prompt the other," she said gently, turning him to her. "And you are so much better than the both of them."

Jackson's throat tightened.

"You are so many things to me, I don't know where to begin," he said finally.

"Begin by loving those boys where they are," Ellie said, clutching his arm more tightly. "You've no way of knowing how the Lord desires to use you."

This time Jackson clutched her and kissed her, right there on the street, with all his heart, in front of Will Russell and everybody.

"But hardly anyone I know supports leaving the Union, Father," said George Jr. The youngster had accepted the formidable challenge of contending with his father in intellectual debate as they and Maggie, Julia, Ellie, and Jackson sat supping around the table.

"There are powerful forces in both North and South that do wish such a scenario, however," said Dr. Junkin, spearing a renegade pea.

"But who?" George Jr. asked.

"Mostly, the aristocratic planter class in the South, and other landed gentry," his father replied, noticing that Maggie had not touched her food. Rather, she had stared at her plate, motionless, the entire meal, her hands folded neatly in her lap. This was not the first time of late he had noticed her doing so.

Junkin cleared his throat and returned his gaze to George Jr. "No more than 15 percent of Southerners own even one slave," the older man continued. "But those who do feel ineffably yoked economically to the institution. And in the North, there are those for whom slavery is less an evil than having an economic system next door that cannot be brought under heel."

George Jr. shot a confused look across the table at Julia, who shrugged.

"Father, you have been forced out of the last three university presidencies you have held," Ellie said, her eyes dancing. "If you continue as you are, you'll surely make it four."

Junkin's eyes flashed. "This glorious temple of liberty shall not be hurled down and torn to atoms." His fork-clenching fist thumped lightly against the table to accentuate his words. "No! The Union must be preserved. It is God's will. And God will move heaven and earth to accomplish that will, even unto the utter destruction of those who stand in its way, regardless of their motivation!"

Those in the room were dumb with silence. They had heard the grand old patriarch hold forth many times on the necessity for preserving the Union, had even seen the ancient old Celtic fury flare in his face and voice. Never, however, had they witnessed the man as intractable and volatile as he was tonight.

A sick feeling settled in the pit of Jackson's stomach as he realized that when good men like Junkin became so emotional, almost irrational, on issues for which clean, neat solutions might not exist, frightening days might lay ahead.

As the family, heads down, rushed to resume their meal, Junkin, a bit self-consciously, turned to Jackson.

"And what about you, my dear son," he said, his voice again soft and pastoral, "where do you stand on the issue?"

"I am a Union man first and last, sir," Jackson replied without hesitation.

Suddenly the kitchen door flew opened and Ruthie rambled in, coffeepot in hand.

"Somebody got some news to tell," she blurted. Silence again beset the room, except for the pouring of coffee and the swishing of her dress as she moved deftly from one person to the next. "Well, better spill it honey, or I'm a-gonna."

Ruthie stared straight at Ellie, who looked down at her lap. Jackson turned to her.

"Ellie, what is it?" he asked.

She looked up at him, her beautifully sculpted chin quivering and her hazel eyes welling over.

"Something for which you've waited a very long time. Something very special."

Jackson's face was blank. He looked across the table to Maggie. She had at last looked up, and tears streaked her face—a very sad face. As she rose quickly from her chair and left the room, Jackson turned back to Ellie, his eyes widening and his mouth opening.

"I'm going to have a son!"

"No, you big lummox," Ruthie scolded, halting her pouring and shaking her head, "your wife's going to have a baby."

For just a moment, the disciplined, courageous, and controlled Thomas Jonathan Jackson thought he might faint.

CHAPTER 17

THE REVEREND DR. JUNKIN HAD ALWAYS BEEN A BUSY MAN, far busier than most men of his day. And he readily admitted that his beloved Rush had exerted a far more profound influence on the development of their children than he had. But, he was also a far more persistent and observant student of his children than most of his time. For a man who often did not brook dissent with his own strongly held opinions, he possessed an unusually sensitive spirit toward the feelings of his own children. If one of them were even in the same house with him, he knew if strong feelings or emotions, of any sort, gripped them.

And yet even the most obtuse father could have seen that something troubled Maggie tonight at the supper table. That something had troubled her since—well, for a long time.

Now, even this great, good man who had seen most of what Adam's fallen race was capable of in his more than sixty years sat ashen faced on the corner of his eldest child's bed as a volcano of emotions ruptured forth from her.

"I am thirty-four years old," she screamed, alternating between tears and a deep defiant, bitter vitriol Junkin had never before witnessed from her. "Thirty-four years old! And I cannot—cannot!—tell you how I have felt since Ellie's marriage. Humbug," she choked, shaking her head as if she were a sick child ingesting a bitter elixir. "Indeed I almost shrink from allowing the word to cross my lips!"

Suddenly she sprang up from the bed and stalked from one end of the room to the other. "And as to her changed name! It jars my ear even to hear it." Junkin jerked as she slammed a slender small fist onto her writing desk, then swept a stack of papers from it. They fluttered to the floor like the quiet golden maple leaves did in autumn outside the house. "It took from me my only bosom companion, the only one I shall perhaps ever have, and put between us a—a stranger." The venom and reproach dripping from the last word were so thick that Junkin blushed in embarrassment and looked down at the floor. Even Maggie halted her exceptional outburst and furious marching. Her shoulders sagging, she let loose a long resigned sigh. "Well, it's all done now. And I know I mustn't rebel, though I'm afraid I have done so too long."

Junkin felt a sharp prick in his heart as she looked him in the face for the first time in days. He ached for her as he saw the tears filling her lovely blue eyes. "I know I must be content, Papa, to be left like the last leaf on the tree."

She stood in the middle of the room, looking to him very small and frail. She had in fact lost more than ten pounds from her already diminutive figure. Even as a little girl, she had rarely let anyone see through to her soul. From somewhere, she had sustained a deep and ancient wound. A wound that had dearly damaged her. And had made her a great poetess. The big man stood, crossed the floor, and took her in his arms. Her soft cries were barely audible against his fine woolen coat.

Returning to the Blue Ridge Mountains always brought a settled feeling over Jackson. But deeper than that, it just brought *feeling* over him. Feeling that could not be described in words. Feeling from memory and love and loss and life. Feeling that, unbeknownst to him, was beginning to creep into his heart about the Lexington and Shenandoah Valley where he had now, as the autumn of 1854 began, lived for more than three years.

Magnificent and serene, the Blue Ridge stood like lonely, timeless sentinels over the land of Jackson's earthly birth. As he gazed out the stagecoach at them, he remembered anew how Almighty God's presence presided over all things, and remained vigilant no matter what perturbations of life might befall him. *"O Lord, how manifold are thy works! In wisdom hast thou made them all: the earth is full of thy riches."*

The ride over the rough, dusty mountain roads had been difficult. Had he known how difficult, and the toll it would take on seven-months pregnant Ellie, he would not have come. Yet, Laura's place lay only a few miles ahead, and he felt this perhaps the most important visit he had ever made to her.

Laura had not written to him until he had been married for six months. He did not mean to slight his beloved little sister with his quick marriage to Ellie. Yet, spiritual, mental, and physical reasons—good reasons, not sinful ones—had manifested themselves into such sudden matrimony that many even in Lexington had not known of its occurrence until they read of it in the town newspaper.

Nonetheless, Laura, already sensitive and prone to take offense at any perceived slight due to her unhappy marriage and spiritual sadness, felt deeply wounded at not having been even notified about her brother's matrimony until receiving a letter from him while he honeymooned. She had, for the first time in her life, ignored Jackson's missives and entreaties. For months, they went unacknowledged.

Finally, on one snowy February day, his heart leapt for joy as a letter came from her. It contained a lock of her hair, in return for locks he had sent to her of his and Ellie's. Other letters had since come, slowly at first, then returning to a more normal and regular routine. Now he felt all would be OK again. Still, the lamentable condition of Laura's spiritual lostness persisted. He hoped that meeting the winsome and mature Ellie might influence his little sister in that regard.

But now, as the stagecoach bounced dustily along the high mountain road, his thoughts and concerns were directed toward Ellie and the baby. Could he have counted the number of times he, the orphan, had dreamed of, thought about, and planned for, his own new little person? Over and over, he had placed these considerations, and his fears and doubts, back in the Lord's lap. His stomach churned as he saw Ellie, very large now, wince at a particularly sharp bump. He had known many folks whose babies were born dead, or who died shortly after birth, or at a very young age. What would he do if that happened to his and Ellie's little precious one? He must trust in God for it, or it would drive him crazy. He thought of his ready response to John Junkin one recent night at the supper table when John was visiting from Trenton and challenged him on his, Jackson's, confident assertion that he, as a follower of Christ, could suffer any combination of misfortunes, and with good cheer, if he knew they were the will of God.

Yes, he had said, in regard to blindness. Yes, to spending the rest of his earthly life on a bed of searing pain. And yes to accepting "grudging charity from those on whom you had no claim."

"If it was God's will, I think I could lie there content a hundred years!" he had said with conviction.

But as he watched his precious Ellie, tired and trying to sleep amidst the bumping and dust, the merest trace of doubt flickered across his mind. *Could I, if the worst* . . . . Then he remembered other words spoken to him by John Junkin, many months ago.

"Whilst the rest of the family, even to some extent my father," John said, "struggled to live out the next day, much less make sense of the pain and loss, Ellie, who was closest to Mother of all the children, accepted her death in Mother's own Christian spirit.

"She was the only one," John whispered, "who unyieldingly believed and asserted—in her deeds more even than her words, which is the far more difficult thing—that not only God's will, but His timing was perfect. She believed that we should rejoice for Mother that she was brought home to the loving arms of the Father at the perfect point in time, and rested in the security that only then would any of us be called back to Him.

"She was a tower of strength for all those trying months," John said, the awe clear in his voice, "and each and all of us, even Father, leaned mightily against her."

What manner of woman is this? Jackson wondered as he watched her. As had happened several times of late, his throat tightened on him as he considered this wife of his youth with whom God had bestowed him.

"She 'staggered not at the promise of God through unbelief,'" Jackson had heard Maggie tell young Julia of Ellie, quoting the apostle Paul from the Book of Romans, even while confessing her own failure in the same regard, "but was strong in faith, giving glory to God.'"

Jackson sat amazed as he realized how the people who had truly influenced his life for the better, who had helped mold his inner man, his character, were all women. His own mother. "Granny Nancy" Robinson. His wife. For it was Ellie's example of natural kindness toward others, especially those who were without, that was teaching him to temper his duty with charity. She alone had spotted the terrific earthly ambition ever crouching at the doorway to his soul. And she stood when he felt faint or faltering, disillusioned with his life and station.

"'Man's heart deviseth his way,' Thomas," she said, uttering words from the yellowed, dog-eared pages of her Bible as naturally as she took her next breath, "'but the LORD directeth his steps.'"

Yes, the God he saw shining through Ellie was indeed a God worthy of his worship and service! A sturdy God, immovable, unshakable, capable of his trust, even in the face of ancient wounds that bade him turn toward fear, hopelessness, and distrust.

Then Jackson felt eyes upon him. It was the dandified man with the checkered coat and tall hat who looked immaculately groomed, but, oddly, smelled as though he had not had a bath in weeks. Jackson guessed him as a peddler. The soldier-professor noticed the man's bewildered eyes on his, Jackson's, upraised left arm. Two other passengers slept, despite the turbulent travel.

"I still think of her as she was when we were young, all curls and ribbons," Jackson said to Ellie, who had given up all attempts at sleeping. "It breaks my heart to see her continuing in almost constant illness and in spiritual darkness."

"From her letters, she sounds quite the adoring little sister," Ellie said with a smile.

Jackson blushed just as the stagecoach bounced over a particularly rough bump, which threw Ellie into his lap. As he helped her, with both arms, to sit back up, he saw pain etched across her face, which in the mysterious way of a woman great with child, was more beautiful than ever before.

"Are you all right, Ell?" he asked.

"Oh, it's fine," she said, closing her eyes. "I've just had some slight nausea today. It's probably more of my afternoon morning sickness."

Jackson smiled, then, resuming his rigid-backed, extended-arm posture, peered at the other passengers. All eyes were closed. He turned back to Ellie and patted her stomach, gentle as could be. Awe enveloped his face. He glanced around once more to make sure all were sleeping, then lowered his head to her midsection to listen. The peddler's eyes opened to just a slit. *Such a shameful public display and disregard for decorum!* he thought, staring at Jackson as though he were a carnival freak.

After a moment, Jackson's head shot up, his face beaming.

"I felt it! I felt the little tiger kick me," he shouted, "right here, in the ear!"

She looks older than twenty-seven years, Tom thought as the worn wooden door opened to reveal the weary face of Laura Ann Jackson Arnold. He could not miss the pallid complexion and yellowish eyes. But Laura's eyes lit up at the sight of brother Tom and his pretty wife Ellie.

"Tommy!" she shouted. She fell into his arms, the effort belying her withered appearance, hugging him and fighting back tears.

"Oh Tommy," Laura continued, "it's been too long, way too long."

She gazed up at him, her eyes full of love. Then she turned toward Ellie. Suddenly, Laura was aware of herself. She flicked nervously at the worn, dirty dress, wiped her eyes, and patted her hair.

"Oh," she tittered, "you must think me a fright, come all this way and see somebody looks like me that's Tommy's sister, must be a terrible disappointment to you."

"I'm proud to meet you, Miss Laura," Ellie said. The conviction in her voice stirred Jackson. Ellie embraced Laura.

"Uncle Tommy! Uncle Tommy!"

Ten-year-old Tommy Arnold and eight-year-old Elizabeth Arnold rushed screaming across the room and leapt toward Jackson. He tumbled to the dusty wood floor with them, the three of them rolling, wrestling, and squealing.

Laura noticed the grin spreading across Ellie's face as the horseplay continued. "I see you've noted Tommy's unique way of communicating with children," she said with a smile.

Later, after the sun had set glowingly down behind the western reaches of the Alleghenies off to the west, Ellie and Jackson sipped tea at the old dinner table. Laura emerged from another room and shut the door behind her, but not before her son's voice rang out from within the room.

"But I want to play some more with Uncle Tommy!"

Laura trudged to the table and dropped into a chair.

"They adore Tommy more than their own father," she said in her typically direct way. "Maybe 'cause they see him more often."

Ellie and Jackson traded a quick glance.

"Where is Johnny?" Jackson asked.

Laura sighed. "He prefers the company of the ruffians down at the social club." Weary, she looked down at the floor. "Course, with the way I feel and look, who could blame him for drinking his problems away?"

A long pause followed before Jackson spoke.

"Sister, we've discussed it many times." He clasped her hand with his own. "Do turn to God and cast all your care on Jesus."

Tears began to run down Laura's face.

"I *am* afraid to die, Tommy," she said. "But anymore, I'm just as afraid to live."

"If you do not believe the teachings of the Bible, Laura, at least obey its doctrines, and I believe that *God* will give you faith." Now Laura wept. Ellie's perfect chin started to quiver. "Make but the effort, Sister, and death will be disrobed of its terrors. Will you not have some faith in the prayers offered for you by our dear dying mother and brother Warren?"

Laura held her hand to her mouth. Ellie stood, rounded the table, and bent over to hold her husband's sister. Laura sobbed against Ellie's shoulder. Jackson's eyes misted over.

"It hurts so badly," Laura sobbed, "it just hurts so badly. I need someone to love me." She looked up at Jackson through her tears. "I know you've always been the same way, Tommy. Both of us have."

Jackson stared stoically at her.

Autumn color splashed everything surrounding the Arnolds' log home in the dawn's early light as Ellie and Jackson loaded their luggage onto a buckboard in front of the cabin, which sat at the base of a tree-dappled hill.

It was time to return to Lexington. The visit had been good. It had melted away any remaining vestige of tension between brother and sister from the missed wedding invitation. Friendship had blossomed between sisters-in-law. For a few precious days, Laura's troubles receded. Even J. L. proved amiable, though he continued not to buy Jackson's religious persuasions. And the visit knit the Jacksons together more tightly as they experienced the unifying bond of ministering to the deeply wounded Laura.

J. L. was again away, fishing, as Ellie and Jackson each in turn embraced Laura.

"You're so," Laura stammered to Ellie, "you're so pretty, so sweet—so perfect." She looked adoringly toward her brother. "You're all I would want for Tommy." Ellie returned this high compliment with another hard hug, her baby blue traveling clothes rustling against Laura's frayed old work dress.

Laura stared at Jackson. Her face brimmed over with emotion. She started to speak, but couldn't, then started again, before noticing her children had surreptitiously edged their way to their uncle and were now tugging on his pant legs. He swept them up into the air, one in each strong arm, and swung them around, kissing them as they squealed and shouted. Then he placed them back on the ground and helped Ellie up into the wagon. His wife moved stiffly, and rubbed her stomach as she sat.

"Are you all right, dear?" Jackson asked, noticing the slight glistening on her upper lip and forehead, so early in the day. She did not answer, but gave him her dreamy white smile and patted his arm.

As they drove off, Jackson looked back over his shoulder. Laura and the children smiled and waved. He thought how much better his life was than it had been on that other day of parting. But this time, his little sister did not chase after him.

October 22, 1854, dawned crisp and clear in Lexington. The stately oaks, maples, and spruces standing sentinel around the president's home at Washington College sang with the bright orange, yellow, and red splashes of the Master's palette.

Inside, likenesses of the Junkins' middle daughter adorned a walnut sideboard near the dying parlor fire. A pencil sketch depicted a precocious, bright-eyed baby girl. A painted, color portrait showed a blossoming, sweetly-smiling teenager with flashing hazel eyes. And a framed photograph revealed the embodiment of beautiful American womanhood, her yellow hair piled atop her head in the style of the day, all the better to reveal the exquisite sun-kissed face that had stopped so many hearts.

Jackson started at the sound. He had heard nothing for an hour as he sat ramrod-straight in a wooden chair in the upstairs hallway. Now Dr. Ryan emerged from the Jacksons' bedroom, medical case in hand and crinkled frock coat folded over his arm. A stethoscope hung unevenly around his neck. Jackson had been up all night; Ryan looked worse than that, his normally manicured white hair frizzy and in his eyes, and his handsome fifty-year-old face creased with heaviness.

The physician stood for a moment, his glazed eyes fixed on the floor. Then, noticing Jackson, he opened his parched mouth to speak. When no words came, he pursed his lips and shook his head slowly and with much sadness.

Jackson stared at Ryan, blood rushing to his head and his eyes dilating. For a moment, he leaned in the chair. Then he stiffened, but it was all more than he could comprehend. He just sat there for quite a while longer, neither seeing the anguished faces of Ellie's brothers, sisters, and father as they left the room, nor hearing the sobs none of them could contain for their beloved deceased sister and daughter and her dead baby.

CHAPTER 18

LUMINOUS AUTUMNAL SUNSHINE BATHED THE LUSH SHENAN-
doah Valley foliage surrounding the Lexington Presbyterian cemetery.
Dr. White, the sun illuminating his clean white hair, began the graveside rites, his own grief fighting for possession of his countenance.

Maggie had always liked the fall best; she remembered how Ellie
had favored spring. Though the sisters dressed identically, Maggie preferred dark, muted colors; Ellie liked fresh, bright pastels. As the whole
of her one hundred pounds, covered in black, her face shrouded by a
veil, trembled, she knew too that while she wrestled incessantly with
the shadows of darkness—why she did not know—Ellie had been an
angel of the light. *Yes, she was sent here for a brief season to be a reflection of Christ for all to see as an example,* Maggie thought, *as a lantern
in the dark—oh, it is so dark!—as a pointer of the Way.*

The Junkins formed the front of the throng. John, Ebenezer, William, and their wives, George Jr., Julia, Maggie, and the Reverend Doctor, his great lion's head garnished with tears. Ruthie and Moses stood
nearby. After a few moments, Ruthie, through gobs of jumbo-sized
tears, happened to notice that the entire cemetery, and beyond, was
filled with people, black and white. *I didn't know they was this many
folks in all of Rockbridge County,* she thought with a gasp. But she
nodded her head as Matthew 10:26 came to her: *"For there is nothing
covered, that shall not be revealed; and hid, that shall not be known."*

For once, Ruthie thought, here was a person whose many *wonderful* deeds, most often done in private or even anonymously, were
being revealed to the world through the size of the crowd. Ruthie's
large amber eyes surreptitiously scanned the multitude. *Land sakes,*
she thought, *hundreds and hundreds. I been around these parts
nearly my whole life and I never seen more folks show, for a wedding*

or a funeral. And it ain't because she's the Reverend Doctor Junkin's daughter, neither. It's because—then a remembrance struck Ruthie.

When her beloved son Matthew had taken ill with scarlet fever several years before, it was Ellie Junkin who had risked her own life to go every day for weeks, until the boy died, to tend to him, night and day, whenever Ruthie herself needed to go to work or to sleep. Ellie did not catch the fever, but her own health so deteriorated because of the strain and exhaustion that Dr. Ryan confined her to her own bed for a month after Matthew's passing.

But even that was not what shone brightly through the years to Ruthie. What she still could not comprehend was why a white woman—and a high-class white woman at that, and the most beautiful girl in the entire county—would give up a summer trip to Europe for which everyone who knew her knew she had dreamed since she was a child and for which she had saved for five years, in order to care for a doomed Negro child. The only reason Ruthie even knew the considerable amount of money Ellie had saved for the trip was that she had "overheard" the Reverend Doctor and his wife discussing it through the wall. (Or to be exact, through that upstairs stove vent that had a way of coming open, usually when important conversations were taking place in the downstairs parlor directly below—which also featured a stove whose vent plate seemed always to be coming off.)

But even the elder Junkins did not know that an identical amount of money as Ellie had saved had mysteriously, and anonymously, appeared one day in an envelope on Ruthie's kitchen table. As far as Ruthie knew, Ellie went to her own grave without having ever told anyone, including Ruthie, where her Europe money had gone. And without ever breathing one note of disappointment that she never made it to the land whose photographs and daguerreotypes filled three volumes of picture books in her room.

Ruthie glanced around the assembly again. *If that happened to us colored folks,* she thought, *how many other folks at this meeting could tell such stories? "Of whom the world was not worthy." That be the kind of Christian I needs to be. I'm all selfish and scheming and the like.* Only then did Ruthie remember other, little, things Ellie had done for her through the years, expecting nothing in return and with no one else knowing. She hung her head and began to weep great huge tears, which spattered the ground at her feet.

As White proceeded, his manner changed. As it had only a couple of years before with Ellie's own mother, his focus gradually changed from the seen to the unseen, from the earthly to the heavenly, from the sorrowful past to the glorious future. Maggie wanted to believe it, wanted to believe it all, but she was tired, tired of the promises, the waiting, the denial, the deferment of all that seemed good and kind and sensible. Oh, she was tired of death and separation, and she was so mad at God she actually looked up toward the sky and clenched a fist, but caught herself before she raised it.

As the cool breeze kissed the veil against her flushed face, the sweet scents of wild mint and clover reached her. Feeling guilty, she turned her glare from God toward the second object of Ellie's love—*Yes, he had become second, curse his righteous, upstanding soul!*—the grieving husband of her beloved sister. He stood tall and rigid, cap in hand, and dry-eyed, though his pale face looked as though it might melt right off his head and down onto his blue uniform at any second. *Oh, I hope you're satisfied,* she thought as her burning gaze remained fixed on him, her heart pounding. *The final, best years of her life, and you take them, then you use her to assuage your rightfully guilty conscience with your own sister. Then you* kill *her, oh, you selfish, you—*

Then Maggie saw that it was her brother John's arms steadying her so she would not fall.

"Should you sit, Sister?" he asked. She shook and her knees felt near buckling. But she would not let *him* or *Him* beat her. She jerked her arm away from John and looked back toward White. There was no reason to hide her true feelings anymore. *Yes, Ellie has gone on to a better place, and for that I am thankful. But meanwhile, I am stuck here on this same horrid planet, and now without her!* She knew then she would have to take a trip, and a long one, for the sake of the rest of her grieving family, if nothing else.

Jackson's thinking processes, meanwhile, were returning to him, despite the pain blasting his mind. It was as though the Lord had anesthetized him for a couple of days after the surgery itself. Now the long, agonizing healing process would begin.

I can hardly realize yet that my dear Ellie is no more, he grieved, deep in his soul. *That she will never again welcome my return—no more soothe my troubled spirit by her ever-kind, sympathizing heart, words, and love.*

Jackson heard no more of his pastor's words. Nor did the touches and pats of loved ones register. He stood where he stood for a long time, until the shadows of the day were very long, the wind rustled through the crisping leaves, and the sky turned a threatening blue-black.

The crowd had long since departed. Only Junkin, Julia, Ruthie, and Moses remained. The latter three sat in a buckboard. Junkin started to climb into the driver's seat, but turned back toward Ellie's grave. He saw the back of his only son-in-law, as Jackson knelt over the freshly placed earth.

The older man walked slowly to the younger and placed a giant, gentle hand on his shoulder. Jackson did not move. His steely gaze remained directed on the grave.

Junkin, his imposing carriage sturdy and erect, felt a long dull ache cutting deeply through his weary bones. His doleful brown eyes focused on his daughter's final earthly resting place. Then they moved to a smaller plot beside hers. *My first granddaughter.* His eyes misted over. He had seen so much death, much of it very close. *The wife of my youth and three of my children now, Lord.*

And he would see so very much more before the book of his days was closed.

Junkin patted Jackson's stiff shoulder softly, then turned away in sadness.

Jackson's mind, long numb, now raced. *Oh, what manner of woman was this!* Only could he think of Socrates' Aspasia. *"She was not only the most beautiful of women but a woman of mind and character and charm and tenderness, and the women of Athens owe much to her."*

Jackson sighed deeply. *She has left me such monuments of her love to God,* he thought, *and deep dependence upon her Savior's merits, that were I not to believe in her happiness, neither would I believe, though one were to rise from the dead and declare it. God's promises change not. She was a child of God, and as such she is enjoying Him forever.*

He could not know that Maggie, still in black was at that moment being helped into a horse-drawn carriage in front of the president's house by a driver in bright blue livery. Her face remained veiled as the carriage pulled away.

If she retains her pure, human affections in heaven, Jackson's thoughts continued, *I feel that she will derive pleasure from the acquaintance of anyone who in this world loves me, or whom I love.*

Now the cemetery was dark and foreboding. The chill wind roared, sweeping crackling leaves and even some branches across the lonesome graveyard. Lightning flashed and thunder cracked.

Still, Jackson remained at his wife's grave. Now, however, he leaned bodily across it, face down. Rain began to pour as he writhed in the dirt, clawing at it, his agonized soul in battle with itself and with forces much larger than himself.

For he had been here before.

The rain lashed him and the thunder, lightning, and wind created a hellish dreamscape and deafening cacophony as he struggled to his knees and looked into heaven, his coat and face smeared with mud, his body soaked. He raised his right arm toward the sky, his face contorted and his blue eyes electric.

His body began to tremble, then shake, the veins in his neck and forehead bulging. His frenetic mind raced onward. *The dearest of earth's spots, the grave of her who was so pure and lovely—but* she *is not there. Even so, I fight viciously an urge to dig up her coffin and take one last look at Ellie's dear ashes!*

Jackson's body began to sway and his head to loll back and forth, the right arm still extended, the rest of his body continuing to shake and his eyes rolling back into his head. He seemed about to explode. Suddenly, his body went stiff. Then it relaxed. His arm came slowly down and his eyes closed. The slightest of smiles crept across his face as the rain cleansed the mud from it. He remained stationary, the faint smile painted on. The thunder, the lightning, the wind, and the rain all ceased.

"But religion is all that I desire it to be, Maggie," he would later write, while not void of his own pain and sorrow, to his grief-racked sister-in-law as she traversed Europe. "I am reconciled for my loss and have joy and hope of a future reunion, that you and I will soon join her, and that she will escort us to that heaven of which Melville speaks so beautifully."

CHAPTER 19

SHE CAME TO HIM WHEN HE LEAST EXPECTED HER, USUALLY. Sometimes it was in the dark quiet of midnight. Sometimes in broad daylight surrounded by people, even at the front of his full VMI classroom.

Usually he was glad to see her. If he was alone, he would talk to her, for many minutes sometimes. Sometimes, though, her visage and remembrance were too painful and he wanted to flee from them. But mostly, Jackson joyed in the queer seeming of Ellie's being near. After all, she had been his wife, his best friend, his lover, his partner, and in many ways his spiritual and personal mentor.

One frigid early morning in the deepest darkness of early February, Dr. Junkin was himself awake. He laid a log on the fire in his room and put some thoughts to writing for an upcoming sermon he would give in Richmond. And he prayed for humility and deliverance from his wrathful attitude toward the Episcopal Superintendent Smith at the VMI. And for his repeating the old joke to Major John Preston that the Anglicans' only advantage over the Papists was that they could read. *But oh, the Genuflecters can be infuriating! The most infuriating thing about them,* Junkin thought with a smile, taking a photograph of Rush in his hands, *is that they cannot be persuaded to agree with me on some things. (Most things, yes, certainly the most important things.) So you always said, dear heart, with love and kindness, of course. And so you were, of course, correct. But—ah, my darling,* he smiled at Rush, *as you said, the heart doth have its reasons. And my heart has so far to go. I am not a humble man, not a forgiving man, not a kind man.*

Just then, Junkin heard a noise outside. He peered out the curtains. Down below, in the snow, a tall figure walked briskly from the front of the president's house toward the street. "Why, it's Thomas,"

Junkin exclaimed. Thinking Jackson might be out for his usual early morning sojourn, he turned to the brass clock that sat on his desk. "Surely it's not already—no, only two o'clock."

Now Jackson was sprinting headlong down the street. Junkin noticed his son-in-law wore nothing but his flannel pajamas! "Oh, my son, my dear, dear son," Junkin said, closing the curtains.

Jackson's frantic, tearful rush through the streets of north Lexington left his stockinged feet scraped and nearly frozen. But it had been brewing for weeks. The emotions and the pain within him had swelled to where he literally burst into this run, with no forethought or planning. And it succeeded in helping clear his head. For months Jackson had been in a sort of mental fog. His faith had sustained him, and his duties at the VMI and elsewhere had not seriously suffered. But he had been at a loss to resume what he thought of as "forward" thinking and planning. He merely accomplished his assigned tasks, though he did have an uncommon sense of closeness to God. In fact, he felt God had been revealing truths to him that he normally would not have been open to hearing.

And perhaps, he thought, as he huffed to a halt near Lyle's bookstore downtown, *God has constrained me from attempting to move ahead too quickly on my own, while at the same time supplying me with sufficient grace to sustain me through this difficult time and to prepare me for the work that lies ahead.*

Then he thought he heard something on the vacant street behind him. He whirled around. Nothing. Then, something else, strange. What? Someone was nearby, evidently in the shadows. "Who's there?" Jackson called. No one. Then a series of words came to him he had not heard in a quarter of a century. And of which he had no recollection having ever heard.

"But first, the Lord has some things that He wants you to do here. Some good and exciting and wonderful things. Then, when He brings you to be with us, we'll all be able to celebrate all of the fine things you did on earth. Does that make sense to you, Son?"

"Mama?" He uttered the word for the first time in years as he whirled around again. "Is that you?" The only sound was John Lyle's shingle creaking against the building in the winter wind. But he was sure she was nearby. And so she was.

Maggie Junkin left an ocean of tears in Europe. Night after night she cried until she could cry no more. More than once, concerned boarders in nearby rooms inquired as to her well-being. Through her grief, she began to sense that the God toward whom she had so often been condescending, arrogant, and unbelieving, was perhaps moving in her life. As the days passed, her soul still aching and her body in literal physical pain due to a worsening eye affliction, she began to eschew her previously planned trips and sight-seeing and again write in her journal. After a while, she began again to write poetry. Much of it was not her best work, and she found herself discarding a lot of it. But the realization grew on her that *yes, God is here at work*. And for some reason, He wanted her writing, but not, proximately, for the many who had come to know and love her poetry. For this season, she was writing—no, *He* was writing through her—to herself.

The words poured forth and became their own new ocean. One time she wrote, without stopping, pen to paper, for twelve straight hours. Then slept for twenty-six hours.

"You have called me out, O Lord," Maggie wrote, "called me aside, like Ezekiel to the brook and John the Baptizer to the desert and Paul to the wilderness, because You have things to show me and tell to me. But what, Heavenly Father, for I, who am slain of spirit and soul and laid prostrate in my grief and suffering? I, who 'am weary with my groaning; all the night make I my bed to swim; I water my couch with my tears.'

"My heart? Yes, 'the LORD looketh on the heart.' I know I am selfish and proud and unloving. But my God and King, Lord of my heart, what is holding me back? What is—has—kept me from Your purposes? Fear? Anger? Lack of faith? Oh, show me where You wish me to start!"

Sweating and faint with exhaustion that balmy March day of 1855 in Paris, she collapsed in tears onto the small hard bed in the tiny room she had rented. Had she the strength, she would have pounded the bed with her fists, as she had so often done her own bed in Lexington, and the other places before that. Her exhaustion was so complete she could no longer even cry. She could, in fact, utter no sound whatsoever. And because she could not, she heard for the first time, faintly and carried by a brisk wind directly toward her rooming house, the pealing of church bells.

Many thoughts now raced through her mind. She thought of her mother, her father, Ellie. For some reason, she thought of the free black servant Ruthie and the boy Moses that Ruthie had brought with her one day to the president's house. She had thought recurrently of them ever since leaving America on the steamer.

Then Maggie realized that church bells had been there for her since the beginning. She could remember her father lifting her high into the air atop his strong broad shoulders so she could reach the clanging "chells" as she called them at four years of age. Tears began to fill her eyes as she realized that somewhere along the way she had stopped reaching for the chells. Oh, how she of all people had been so blessed and so nurtured, and how her heart had grown so cold in all its knowledge of Greek and Latin and Hebrew! She wanted at that moment to run all the way home to her father and Lexington and the church bells there and get on her knees and pray for forgiveness and a new, clean heart.

"Oh, I have been dirty for so long!" she cried out the window. The old Gaelic woman next door had heard it all before, much of it from this strange little scarlet-haired *Ami*, and she cackled aloud as she snapped the neck of the scrawny chicken that was to be that night's supper.

Maggie could not run home to Lexington, but she could run to the sound of the church bells. And this she did, unseemly as it was for a woman of the South to rush hoop-skirted through the crowded day-time streets of gay Paris, and alone at that, her thick, uncombed trusses streaming behind her in the biting breeze. All she knew was she had to get to the church bells.

She had no problem moving to their sound, though it took a long time to get there. In fact, she ran over hard, mostly cobbled streets for five miles before she saw the great stone cathedral from which the bells tolled.

"Oh, it's Catholic," she frowned. *No, it's God.* And she raced up many stone steps and through two huge oaken doors that had inexplicably been left wide open. The cavernous, darkly beautiful sanctuary was the largest she had ever seen. Its ceiling appeared to arch at least five stories high. But she paused for only an instant before swishing on toward the altar at the far end of the enormous building. When finally she reached it, she threw herself down on her face and began to weep.

After five minutes, she felt a gentle hand on her shoulder. She jerked up to see an ancient, kind-faced priest. She understood his French, but struggled to speak it herself. It had been too long. They both switched to English.

"You are sad, my child."

Maggie tried to speak, but burst again into tears.

The old priest took one of her hands and held it, again gently.

The sound of another woman's voice interrupted. From several feet away, toward one side of the sanctuary, she directed a couple of brief sentences in hushed French tones toward the priest. She was very young and very pretty, and she smiled and waved in a callow sort of fashion toward the cleric as she moved quickly away and out of the room.

Maggie took a kerchief out and dabbed at her nose, then smiled at the patient, quiet man. "Has the young lady been crying as well?" she asked.

The priest's friendly crinkled face broke into its own warm smile as he motioned for Maggie to follow him to a nearby pew. After they sat down, he spoke. "It is a very sad story, mademoiselle, though not one without hope."

"May I ask what happened with the young lady?" Maggie said. "Can you, I mean, are you allowed—"

The priest chuckled. "Don't worry, my Protestant—yes? yes—friend. It was not a confession box matter, I believe you call it? Much of the town knows of the fine Richard Chevalier family. Sad to say, the wife of the young scion of the family recently perished in a tragic accident. She was—" At this, the priest averted his gaze to the floor. "She was a remarkable young woman, with all the earthly gifting one could ever hope to find in a young woman." Then he looked up again. "Most of all, she was a fine Christian.

"Sad to say," the priest continued, "young Chevalier, normally a prince of a fellow and himself devout, has been stricken almost to incapacity by the tragedy. He badly wanted a son by the girl, and that had not yet happened either. I do not know if the boy has eaten—how do you say?—as much as a biteful of food since the girl died." Again, the priest lowered his head. "And now the wickedness of alcoholic spirit has overcome him. The girl you saw is the sister of the dead woman. Sad to say, she, riddled with guilt, now bewails the jealousy and contempt she held for young Chevalier."

The priest looked back up. "Her words of condemnation toward the boy, as he knelt in penance by that very altar some days after his wife's death, were the final action that led to his descent into drunken stupor." The priest sighed, now even his bald pink pate crinkling. "Thus we have two damaged people, and many other sorrowful family members and friends."

"But why?" Maggie gasped. "How could she treat him so?"

The priest shook his head. When he spoke, Maggie felt as though the sturdy old cathedral itself was elucidating the truths and wisdom of the ages. "She felt he came between her sister and her. She tried to punish him with contempt while her sister lived. After she died, she blamed young Chevalier for taking her sister from her, and her hatred grew beyond reason. Sad to say, she did not understand how deeply the wound of his wife's loss had pierced the fine young man."

The old Frenchman sighed again and rubbed his head. "If there is any hope in the tragic matter, it is that the girl you saw has begun to realize her error. She has begun to feel compassion toward the young man instead of spite and hatred. And in it may be her own salvation." He shook his head and gazed up at a huge, gleaming gold cross mounted over the altar. "Sad to say, I feel it is perhaps too late for young Chevalier. Though," he said, turning back to Maggie, "we have an all-kind, all-knowing God with whom all things are indeed possible. We must never lose hope nor stop praying. Now tell me why this fine young American woman is weeping today at our altar?"

Maggie was thunderstruck. *How I have damned him!* she thought with horror. *How I have cast him into outer, outer darkness! How I have cursed his soul to fire and damnation! What have I done?*

Her vacant expression and glazed eyes disturbed the priest. "Is *mademoiselle* feeling well?" he asked.

After another moment, she snapped to. She blushed with embarrassment upon realizing the Frenchman had fixed his concerned gaze on her. Then, to her own astonishment, her ruddy face broke into its first smile since before Ellie's death, and the dull blue eyes emitted a bit of their old spark.

"Sir," she said after another moment's pause, bowing, then extending her hand, which the priest gently clasped, "I believe I may indeed yet be well. Thank you, kind sir, thank you."

She stood and turned to leave, some of the old bounce returning to her diminutive step. She still did not care for Thomas Jackson, the husband of her beloved dead sister. But God could not have been plainer if He had painted the words with His finger across the sky. He wanted her to at least begin *trying* to love her brother-in-law. Her spiritual salvation, she knew, was not in doubt. But the salvation of a meaningful and loving earthly life for her might be gained with this beginning.

Actually, she did not suspect the half of it.

I shall do it for God, she thought, her fine chin set. *I shall do it for Ellie.*

CHAPTER 20

JACKSON DID NOT KNOW THE BELLWETHER EVENTS OF MAG-gie's European sojourn. On his own, he had felt compelled to write to his often antagonistic and spiteful sister-in-law. Oddly, she seemed the only person to whom he could fully devolve himself of his deepest feelings regarding his dear departed Ellie.

Maggie received the first letter the morning after her trip to the Catholic cathedral.

"Those days of sweet communion with Ellie are gone to me," Jackson wrote, "yet I rejoice in the thought that naught disturbs her unalloyed felicity; her spirit now, and for ever, will continue to bask in the sunshine of *God's* favor."

Further did these heartfelt words from Jackson soften Maggie's heart toward him. Now, though she still stung at his "hijacking" of Ellie from her, Maggie for the first time, since the evening in the Junkin foyer when she overheard him announce his romantic inclinations toward Ellie, began to see Jackson for Jackson and not through the all-encompassing lens of her feelings for Ellie.

She began to feel true pity for Jackson and not just for herself when a subsequent letter arrived a few days later.

"I do not see the purpose of God in this," he wrote, "the most bitter, trying affliction of my life, but I will try to be submissive though it break my heart."

Her eyes widened and the emotions in her heart swirled as she read on.

"My heart yearns to see you, Maggie; and yet it may be best that we should not so soon meet; for my tears have not ceased to flow, my heart to bleed. I cannot realize that Ellie is gone; that my wife will no more cheer the rugged and dark way of life. The thought rushes in upon me that it is insupportable—insupportable!"

At this, Maggie's head dropped and she began to weep anew. "Poor boy," she sobbed, "what have I done to you, my poor, poor boy?"

Only was she comforted when she returned to the final lines of Jackson's letter. "But one upward glance of the eye of faith gives a return that all is well, and that 'I can do all things through Christ which strengtheneth me.'"

As Maggie dabbed at her wet cheeks with a kerchief, she whispered, "I begin to think I may have greatly misjudged you, Thomas Jackson."

Pity (and, Maggie blushed, a slight flutter of the heart) turned to worry at another letter, just a couple of days later.

"From my heart I thank God that though He has left me to mourn in human desolation, He has taken dear Ellie to Himself," Jackson wrote. "Her companions are of the Glorified Host, and I look forward with delight to the day I shall join her. Pure and lovely companion of my happier days, I feel that she entered upon the blissful enjoyment of which the human mind cannot have any conception.

"Ere many long years roll by I hope to be with her," the letter continued, "where there will be no separation. We loved each other on earth; and shall that love be diminished in eternity? Had I but one request on earth to ask in accordance with my own feelings and apart from duty, it would be that I might join her before the close of another day after this."

For hours, Maggie stared at the letter, reading and rereading it until it lay soft and worn in her small strong hands. Then she grabbed her own quill and ink jar and began for the first time to write to her brother-in-law. Purposely few were the lines, and limited to her concerns for Jackson's well-being.

A few weeks later, on the very day she completed her packing to return to America, a response arrived from Lexington.

"I regret dear sister that I should have pained you by anything in my letter, and take this earliest moment to explain myself," Jackson wrote. "I had reference to that change, which of all connected with earth, is to me, most desirable; from a world of sorrow, to one of joy. But you must not understand me here, as being anxious, for I know that in due time if I faint not, all my hopes will be realized. I have many thoughts about the future, and sometimes think that I am about entering upon its fruition; but this is human judgment; which with God, we know is foolishness."

Maggie, though in Europe, began to see what others of Jackson's friends did not. The Virginian was not giving up. Rather, he was resolving to reconsecrate himself to Christ. A letter that did not reach Maggie until after she had returned to Lexington confessed to her how only the loss of Ellie could have shone light on Jackson's own continued shortcomings and sins! And he did not leave to the surviving sister's imagination the uncovering of them.

"*Ambition,*" his pen shouted, "how often did she who is no more on this earth encourage me in her singular loving way against it? Also resentment, and to work for humility in all I do.

"If you desire to be more heavenly minded, Maggie, think more of the things of heaven, and less of the things of earth," he wrote.

Conviction of how much this man still relatively young in the Christian way had grown in his spiritual nature and how stunted through stubbornness, selfishness, and self-will had been she who had lived in it since the cradle, mingled with such a stirring in her heart that she sat on her bed so as not to become lightheaded.

As Lylburn Downing's earthly life grew more difficult, his spiritual one grew stronger. So, he guessed, was it so for most of those great men of faith of whom he had learned in the Bible's Book of Hebrews. Lylburn, like almost all of the other slaves he knew around Rockbridge County, had been treated well by his master. Oh, Lylburn knew Will Russell's brooding temper, but the teenager had long since learned when to "skedaddle" in order to escape the planter's occasional rages against the world.

But the world was changing and so, evidently, was Marse Russell. From what Lylburn knew, the man had not touched alcoholic spirits since he married his wife, who died delivering the couple's stillborn third son in 1845. Not touched them until recently. Lylburn, as Russell's driver, had heard the talk. Russell and many of his friends grew increasingly angry at what they perceived as economic, social, and political—*was the word "condensention"?* They seemed upset at what folks up North, whom Lylburn did not think had slaves, were doing in a city called Washington, which Lylburn assumed was named after George Washington.

And here the red-faced planter, his face nearly glowing in the dark with rage, went again, to John Carlisle, as Lylburn drove the two men home in Russell's carriage after a board meeting at the bank.

"The North continues to fatten himself and grow rich upon the South," Russell railed. "We depend upon it for our entire supplies. We purchase all our luxuries and necessaries from the North, yet the Northerners abuse and denounce slavery and slaveholders, then get rich clothing our slaves with their manufactured goods, their hats, and shoes. You know it's true, John.

"Our slaves work with Northern hoes, ploughs, and other implements," Russell blew on. "The slaveholder dresses in Northern goods, rides in a Northern saddle, sports his Northern carriage, patronizes Northern newspapers, drinks Northern liquors, reads Northern books."

Russell broke into a racking cough. Carlisle glanced at him, remembering the stories he had heard of the man's return to the bottle. *Is that a trace of brandy I smell just now?* In any event, Carlisle did not like Russell and did not like his rantings, whatever the subject, and felt a fool to have accepted this ride. It did pain him to recognize the truth in much of Russell's present tirade.

The planter continued undaunted. "In Northern vessels," he said, "our products are carried to market. Our cotton is ginned with Northern gins, our sugar crushed and preserved by Northern machinery. Our rivers are navigated by Northern steamboats, our mail is carried in Northern states, and our Negroes fed with Northern bacon, beef, flour, and corn.

"You are perhaps a more even-tempered man than myself, Carlisle," Russell finished, out of breath, "but can you deny that any of that is true?"

Carlisle shook his head in the negative.

"Then we must—"

"What, Russell?" Carlisle interrupted sharply, for the first time. "We must what, man? Leave the Union? Establish our own country?"

This is one of the better ones I have heard in a while, Lylburn mused to himself. But as he listened, he heard faint laughter—*could that be coming all the way over from the Washington College president's house? Yes, from the open window on the second floor. It must be that crazy army professor and his dead wife's sister again. How can the two of them, of all folks, with his wife and her sister only dead six or seven months, always be talking so loud together or laughing when I brings this carriage by here at this time of evening?* Then Lylburn heard what sounded like a shout from the professor—the youngster had heard it before—followed by a pause, then familiar squealing laughter from the woman. He shook his head with a smile and thought, *And white folks rules this here world.*

Later, as Lylburn was currying the sleek black horse back at the barn, he thought of how white folks in general and Marse Russell in particular seemed to be fussing more and more. Lylburn, of course, was always thinking. He couldn't stop his mind if he tried. It bothered him that Marse Russell had shoved him, hard, into that there barn door the other night. Lylburn still had a bruise on his cheek from it. Sure, Lylburn had messed up, but never before had Marse Russell grabbed him by the neck and slammed him, face first, into a door. Of course, the pungent smell of spirits on the man's breath pricked Lylburn's nose when it happened. But Lylburn also sensed Marse Russell was *scared.*

Lylburn knew that colored folks reading and meeting in public with white folks used to be allowed. Some of the older slaves' masters and mistresses had personally taught them to read. And they had met out in public with each other and white folks for all sorts of things. One old black man had learned to read because he wanted to be able to study the Scriptures so he could better preach them to the other Negroes. And his master was the one who suggested he learn, and who paid for a fancy teacher to come in almost every day and learn him to read.

But then Nat Turner had led his uprising back in 1831 or so. The renegade slave and his henchman had slaughtered more than sixty white men, women, and children as he rampaged through Virginia. That was bad enough. But when whites in Virginia found out the abolitionists up North were glad about the killing and supported however much more it took to free up the slaves, a darkness descended on the state. From what Lylburn could figure, the darkies' dreams went out across Virginia like a doused kerosene lantern after Nat Turner cut his swath.

Sometimes Lylburn thought it would be great if things went just like the abolitionists wanted, and he and all the other slaves got loosed up to whatever they wanted. But then when he would think more about it, he would get perplexed and a little frightened. He was afraid some of his friends might hurt some white folks bad. Then he would realize that the white folks would still have all the money and property, and they would still have all the learning and guns. Course, maybe the darkies could buy guns and land. But which white folks would sell it to them? Seemed the white folks might be more contrary if they were forced to do things than if they decided to do them on their own. Leastwise, that was how Lylburn himself was. He had heard a lot of good men, around Rockbridge County, agreeing that the slaves should be set free. But since those men had invested their moneys in the darkies, if they didn't get paid for them, many of them would be busted if they turned them loose. And, like Lylburn, those white men kept asking the question: how could the darkies make it on their own? One day he heard Major Preston tell Father Pendleton of the Episcopal church that he was afraid God would judge him for whatever happened to his slaves if he turned them loose.

And, he knew many of the men felt the abolitionists and factory folks in the North, some of whom seemed to hate the fact there even was a South and looked at it like a competing nation, were just using the slave issue to put the South in its place regarding money and power. It sounded as though they must be having some success at doing this too. Thus perhaps was Marse Russell frightened. Yeah, folks would have been mighty surprised to learn what all Lylburn Downing took in and thought about.

After a while, though, Lylburn's head would always start to hurt if he kept thinking on these matters, and he would pray to God to work them out just the way they should be. *Like over there in England, Lawdy. I heared the white folks over there worked things out and they all give up they slaves on they own, and things went right smooth. Black folks, white folks, everybody fine, no fighting or fussing.* Then he would think about preaching God's Word. Standing right up there in that pulpit and preaching the gospel message of salvation through Jesus Christ. He knew folks needed to hear it, especially colored folks. Then he would go back to work for Marse Russell.

Until these nightly "Spanish lessons," which had largely evolved into joke telling and socializing, Maggie had no idea Jackson even possessed a sense of humor. But as she doubled over again in the rocking chair that had belonged to her enigmatic brother-in-law's mother and her mother before her, she, through her wailing laughter, began to suspect that she had grievously misjudged this man, even though she had now, in the fall of 1855, known him for years and had lived under the same roof as him for two and a half years.

"*Mi amor, mi corazon!*" Jackson thundered in his booming baritone, with a great sweep of his long arm. The peculiar sight of this peculiar shy man bursting into theatrics was greatly more amusing than the silly story he was recounting from his days of courting *señoritas* in Mexico. "*Vaya con dios, mi amor!*" Frighteningly, he sang this line.

"No, Major, please, please, stop," Maggie gasped as Jackson wound up for another gust. "No, I mean it, please, I'm hurting."

He relented. She bent over in laughter, grabbing her ribs. For the first time, Jackson's serious facade softened and his blue eyes twinkled. *Perhaps she is finally beginning to at least tolerate me,* he thought.

She fought for air. "I haven't laughed this hard since—" Her expression stiffened and her eyes shot toward Jackson. His thin lips parted as his eyes, dulling, met hers. He glanced away. She looked down. Both were quiet for a moment. Somewhere outside a dog howled. Then Jackson peeked back at her. Her eyes met his and they both broke into laughter.

"My dear major," Maggie said after another moment, "I certainly now understand why you melted all of those dear *señoritas'* hearts in Mexico. But please, my nightly Spanish lessons are developing into far too enjoyable an event." Then the blue eyes dazzled with the old mischief. "Your cadets don't enjoy you like this, do they?"

It was a full moment before he caught her glint and the twinkle returned to his own eyes. And he was laughing with her again. This time Jackson was the one whose laughter forced him to a chair, where he sat, holding his side. After a moment, the laughter subsided, and the two sat in silence, staring in different directions.

"So what did you think of my idea?" Maggie said.

"A fine idea," Jackson said. "I talked to Pastor White and learned that he did indeed initiate several attempts in years past. So have some of the other churches, here and around the South, notably in Texas. Unfortunately, at least regarding our church, they were used to a more boisterous sort of meeting and did not relish our calmer, quieter proceedings."

She sat up on the edge of the rocker and faced him, her green satin dress rustling. The sight of her shapely, diminutive body and its perfect posture unexpectedly filled his eyes and flushed his face. He squeezed the arms of his chair.

"I know you can do it," she said. "I don't believe anyone else can, but you can."

They stared at one another.

Ruthie did not know for sure if she had ever heard a more terrifying singing voice than Major Thomas Jackson's, but she suspected she had not. She winced as he bellowed out "Amazing Grace," loudly and off key. *Maybe some lessons from his friend Mister Lyle, the church*

choir leader, would help the poor soul, she thought. *Well,* she thought with a smile, *You gifts us each one different, Lawdy. And Major Jackson, well he just plum missed out on the singing gift.*

If the eighty black children and teenagers packed into the Lexington Presbyterian Church's Christian education hall with Jackson for his new colored Sunday school class noted the major's lack of musical acumen, they did not let it affect their own splendid, soulful, swaying choruses of joy.

"How sweet the sound!" Jackson crowed.

"That saved a wretch like me," sang the crowd, "I once was lost, but now I'm found."

"Was blind," Jackson continued, "but now I see!"

What wonderful worship, Jackson thought, letting slip a rare smile as he glanced around at Maggie, who accompanied the singing on a nearby piano. Her whole face lit up as she caught his smile. *My, I never noticed how attractive she looks in white,* he realized. *She is why we are here. Her idea and her belief in—me.* Jackson's throat tightened a notch. Then he heard a vigorous knock at the locked rear door of the room, the largest other than the sanctuary in the entire church. The assembly turned as one toward the knocking. Jackson cocked his head to one side and thought, *I swear, the angels will have to hunt that boy down, else he'll be late for his own trip to glory.*

Jackson cleared his throat and the smile evaporated from his again stern countenance. "Very well, let us break up into our groups."

Jackson glanced over to the wall where John Preston—widowed five months previously—John Lyle, and several other white men and women stood. Then he looked again at Maggie, who rose with an effulgent smile from the piano. *She has been much more civil to me since she returned from Europe,* he thought. *She is actually quite lovely.* The knocking at the door resumed, quicker and louder, now echoing off the walls. Jackson shook his head as if clearing the early morning grogginess. *Losing a man's wife, even a year ago,* he thought, *causes him to think strange things sometimes.* A confused stir rippled through the young people.

"Now friends," Jackson said, "Do we usually stop class when Lylburn is late?"

A smattering of giggles swept the children, then Ruthie called out, "Well, let's don't be keeping the Lord waiting. You need Him, He don't need you." As she began to shoo along the children around her, they split into several groups, some staying in the education hall and others moving to nearby rooms.

Thank You, Lord, for Ruthie, Jackson thought. He had received enthusiastic responses from nearly all the slave owners upon whom he had called and asked to send their young blacks to his now month-old Sunday school class. Still, he felt certain that some of those youngsters who were allowed the choice of coming, as well as some of the free ones, would not have attended if not for Ruthie's active participation in the new ministry. And even those who had been told to attend would not be behaving as responsively as they had these several weeks if not for her considerable presence. He had begun to realize, just by how the young black children responded to her, that she was possessed of a powerful respect in the Negro community. All Maggie had told him when she brought Ruthie was, "She wants to do it for Ellie."

Even Ruthie, however, seemed helpless to engender any sense of punctuality in the young man who stood outside beating on the front door.

Preston, himself eyeing Maggie, moved toward her and whispered, with some humor, "The poor kid's less than three minutes late."

Maggie's only response was a knowing grin.

As Preston watched her bustle off toward the class she helped teach, and eyed the throng of happy laughing youngsters moving toward the classes designed for their love and care, he wondered at his strange, hard, kind friend Tom Jackson. Thomas Carlyle's words came to him: *"The work an unknown good man has done is like a vein of water flowing hidden underground, secretly making the ground green."*

Outside, seventeen-year-old Lylburn Downing, perspiring, but not from the sixty-degree late November afternoon, heaved a sigh and swatted at the doorknob.

"Blast it all," he murmured.

Anger had become such a constant in Will Russell's life that he would likely not have been comfortable without it as the new year of 1856 dawned over the Shenandoah Valley. The tariffs Northern congressmen were passing on the products of Southern states, the condescension of Northern churches toward Southern ones related to slave ownership (Why, the Methodists and Baptists, theologically ignorant and wrong as they were, had already split into Northern and Southern wings), the self-righteous arrogance of that Jackson and his egghead school crowd—Russell felt his world closing in on him and thanked Providence for the elixir of alcohol.

Soon, however, he felt he would have plenty of cause to smile. Alcohol or no alcohol, he would begin to take back charge of his world, or at least what significant parts he could.

"See, there it is," Sam McDowell exclaimed as he and Russell stood examining a thick old book at the foot of the steps leading out the front entrance of the Lexington Presbyterian Church. "I'm telling you, it's illegal."

A warm glow filled Russell's breast as he took the old volume titled *The Virginia Code* from his friend. Russell's blue eyes lit up when he spotted the precious passage. Before he could say anything, Jackson and Maggie emerged from the church as the shadows of Sunday afternoon's late amber glow lengthened. The colored Sunday school, still growing in size almost every week and now over one hundred young people in attendance, had met earlier. Russell and McDowell exchanged smiles as Maggie gave Jackson a perplexed look.

"Hello, gentlemen," Jackson said as he and Maggie reached the bottom of the steps.

"Afternoon, Major. Miss Junkin," McDowell said, tipping his hat. "Major, would you be so kind as to allow us a word?"

Jackson turned to Maggie. "It's all right," she said. Then, giving the tall professor a fetching smile, she added, "I'll see you at home."

The men each nodded in deference to Maggie as she left.

"What may I do for you men?" Jackson asked, his posture rigidly erect. He noticed McDowell's huge driver, Ben, standing nearby in the street with McDowell's buggy.

McDowell jumped in. "Major Jackson, were you aware, sir, that a statute exists in *The Virginia Code* that disallows the public assembling of Negroes for such gatherings as your Sunday school?"

Jackson felt his face begin to boil. From the corner of his eye, he thought he spied the slightest trace of a smirk coil up on one end of Russell's mouth.

"Now I have examined the statute myself," McDowell continued, "and I have conferred with the attorney of the commonwealth. And there can be no doubt that your assembly is an unlawful one."

Sparks began dancing in Jackson's eyes. He shifted his head slightly toward Russell. "Do you go along with this pap, Will Russell?"

"It's in the book, sir," Russell said, his chin thrust out like an accusing finger.

Across the street, towering attorney-at-law J. D. Davidson, lumbering along with hulking strides, spotted the gathering. "Uh-oh," he mumbled, hustling toward the church.

"Well, it doesn't much matter what you or God thinks, does it, Major Jackson?" McDowell crowed. "What matters is that *The Virginia Code* thinks you're out of line with your niggra Sunday school class."

Jackson could see Ben just over McDowell's shoulder. The strapping slave had dull lifeless eyes. He did not even seem aware that a conversation was occurring mere feet from him. Before Jackson's anger could spill into a response, a panting Davidson intervened.

"My good men," the huge man puffed, "to what do we owe the honor for this spirited gathering?"

"Sir," Jackson replied without pause, "we have men here who seem not to concern themselves with the lost plight of the heathen if they be black-skinned."

"Not if saving them means bringing them under the same church roof as our women and children!" McDowell blurted.

"Nor any other roof, I suppose, Mr. McDowell," Jackson said. "Or didn't you know that our fair town has yet to offer any formal group education—writing, mathematics, religion, or otherwise—to the colored folk who comprise one-fourth of it?"

Davidson raised his basketlike hands. "Gentlemen, please," he pleaded, "let's discuss this as friends. We do need to be compassionate to those less fortunate than ourselves, Sam." Then he turned to Jackson. "But Major, whilst I lament that we have such a statute on our code—through the fault, I might remind you, of abolitionist Yankees and the murderous renegade slave Nat Turner—I am satisfied that your Sunday school is an 'unlawful assembly,' and probably the grand jury will take it up and test it."

Jackson could not believe his ears—Russell, a Presbyterian like himself and Davidson and McDowell, Episcopalians. "J. D. Davidson, sir, if you were, as you should be, a Christian gentleman, you would not think it or say it!"

Davidson's huge jowly face flushed. "Well, now, hold on just a minute, my good fellow. I don't take such treatment from any man."

"Sir," Jackson said evenly, "should you think your inordinate size a distraction to me, I would bid you think otherwise."

Words and normal men, in courtrooms and elsewhere, Davidson might parry with ease. But the white-hot glow emanating from Jackson's electric blue eyes unnerved the counselor. The big man hesitated.

"Good evening, gentlemen," Jackson finished, wheeling and loping down the sidewalk in the direction taken by Maggie. For a moment, the other three men stood speechless.

Finally, as Russell, not quite sure, bit his lip, McDowell spoke. "That there is one strange nigger-lover."

Davidson turned to him. "Mr. McDowell, you, sir, are a considerable property owner, and a fellow Episcopalian, though from your infrequent attendance at Father Pendleton's parish, perhaps not a devout one. But you have never shown yourself a kind or compassionate man. Shut your sad mouth."

Jackson stormed down the street. His eyes flashed, but he calmed in time to nod with respect to a middle-aged white couple he passed. Then he charged on in a lather. He had a sudden craving for a lemon.

Part of what galled Jackson was a fear gnawing at him for not the first time: *Are the other men right?* Oh, McDowell and Russell were mean-spirited infidels, church membership notwithstanding, but Davidson was a good, God-fearing man. Jackson knew there were others like him who held similar views regarding the Negro as well as mixed race assemblies. And he knew the substantive reasons the laws had been placed on the books in the first place. Nobody had liked doing it, at least no decent humane person. But the growing pressure of Northern abolitionists and industrialists—directly against Southern whites and indirectly in attempting to undermine black Southern slaves—had rendered the measures, in the opinion of Jackson and most other Southerners, necessary for the public safety and peace of mind. *Am I right in doing what I am doing, or should I allow God in His omnipotence to reach the many slaves still heathen through less divisive and legally questionable means?* he wondered. Jackson's frustration and anger mounted with his confusion. A moment later he noticed through his foggy funk an elderly black woman, just as she passed him. She seemed vaguely familiar. Just in time, he tipped his hat and nodded a respectful greeting to her.

After the woman passed, Jackson stopped and looked back toward her. He took a deep breath and asked the Lord to cool his volcanic temper and provide him much-needed wisdom. He felt a mild pacific wave pass through him that not only melted his anger, but brought before him a scene that had occurred when he was seventeen years old, one he had not thought of in years.

On that long ago gray, late autumn day, Tom and his friend Thaddeus Moore rode through the Virginia countryside. They saw a group of funeral pallbearers, some white and some Negro, carrying a handsome black coffin across a road from a cabin to where a fresh grave lay dug in a brown field. Fifteen or twenty black men, women, and children followed the pallbearers.

"Coffin's nice, and a fine, deep grave, too," Thad said in his soft western Virginia drawl.

"Well, I'm sorry for them, I am," Tom said in a low voice, shaking his head. "I think they should be free and have a chance."

Thad stared at him.

"It would probably be better not to make known such views, Tom Jackson," Tom's riding mate warned.

"Joe Lightburn said they should be taught to read so they can read the Bible, and my brother Warren said the same before he died last year, and I think so, too," Tom said, gripping his saddle horn hard in conviction.

Thad pondered that for a minute before he spoke. "Well, if it were carried out, we'd have to black our own boots, Tom."

The men lowered the casket into the hole. One of the white men stood to the side, observing. He held a large book that looked to Tom to be a Bible. Tom reigned his big bay around to resume the ride. "With me," he replied, "that would be only on Sunday and not even in the winter."

Thad stared after his friend as he left, then smiled and followed him.

Next, Jackson saw, clear as if it was the day he first saw it, the kindly visage of Uncle Robinson smiling down at him as he led Tom and Laura in to their mother's deathbed.

Then, like it was today, Granny Nancy was waving to him with great energy to come across the farm pond for Bible reading.

"My dear son, you look a bit flushed."

The soothing deep voice of Dr. Junkin brought Jackson back to the present. His father-in-law stood next to him, near the entrance to the Washington College president's home.

"Dyspepsia acting up again?" Junkin continued.

Jackson nodded wearily, rubbing his forehead with his hand. "And my left eye."

"Oh, the left one this time?" Junkin asked. Jackson nodded. Junkin stared at the younger man for a moment, then spoke again. "Walk with me a bit? This handsome gold cane you gave me last Christmas makes my trips to the office and house calls much more tolerable, but good company is even better."

Jackson let out a gust of relaxed breath and began to walk with him. "Ellie had long wanted the cane for you, sir. So, you see, even though she was with Jesus, you can consider that it came from both of us."

From her second-floor bedroom's dormer window, her hands gripped together in front of her, Maggie watched the two men walk away. She took a deep breath, then let it out. Keeping her hands together, she turned and crossed to her bed, kneeling beside it rather than falling upon it as was her norm. She bowed her head and prayed with great fervor, the knuckles on her smooth small hands turning waxy white with the pressure of their mutual grip.

Junkin and Jackson strolled all through the heart of Lexington. As they—as Junkin—talked, Jackson greeted Carlisle as he stepped out of his factor's office with a coat he had earlier forgotten to take home. A few moments later, Jackson waved at the bachelor Lyle through the window of his book shop. Seeing these familiar places and friends and listening to Ellie's wise old father, the professor felt his spirits lifting. As had happened so often, it seemed as though God knew just when to reach into Jackson's heart and touch the Virginian's weak, weary vessel of life with the same finger that had written with fire on the stone tablets at Mount Sinai. *Who, indeed,* he thought, *was right and who wrong about the colored Sunday school and reaching the Negroes with the saving gospel of life!*

"So a man without God in his life," Junkin said, placing his arm around Jackson's shoulders and happy as ever to have a pulpit and an audience, "is a man without the wisdom of the ages, and like unto they who wandered forty years in a literal desert without remedy for their hardness of heart."

A bright tide of joy washed across Jackson's face and his rigid features relaxed, his eyes even beginning to twinkle as he remembered King David's ancient words in Psalm 40:2: *"He brought me up also out of an horrible pit, out of the miry clay, and set my feet upon a rock, and established my goings."*

"Major Jackson—I was just coming to see you." Jackson looked ahead to the sound of J. D. Davidson's voice. The giant had emerged from his own office, just yards ahead of Jackson and his father-in-law, waving a sheet of paper held in his hand.

Jackson's face brightened further. "And I you, sir," he said.

Davidson blanched at this and stopped in his tracks.

"To apologize to you, sir," Jackson added.

A wave of relief covered Davidson's face and he came on. Junkin lifted his cane and turned to leave, a warm sparkle in his own eyes.

"If you gentlemen will excuse me, I'm off to visit a sick student," Junkin said, smiling at his son-in-law.

"Good day, Father," Jackson said. Then he turned to the other man. "Mr. Davidson, I am afraid I wounded your feelings earlier. I have come to ask your forgiveness of my unchristian words and tone."

Davidson's jaw dropped. "Really?" he asked.

"Yes, sir," Jackson said. "Honest Christian men should certainly dispose of honest differences in a Christian manner. I was discourteous to you, sir, and allowed my flesh to get the better of me."

"Why, no, Major," Davidson drawled, shaking his head, which appeared much too small for his gargantuan body. "I must insist on accepting the blame. I've written it all down here." He motioned to the paper. "Sometimes I find that even as a counselor of the law, I am best equipped to convey my thoughts on troublesome subjects with the pen. Come into my office and let's visit over some tea, Major."

Jackson nodded and followed Davidson down the sidewalk toward his offices. The men stepped through the high, wide oaken doors, which had been custom fitted at great expense for the proprietor of the establishment.

"My constitution will not allow for tea or coffee, Mr. Davidson," Jackson said once inside the finely appointed offices, refusing with a gentle wave of his hand the other man's offer of a seat, "but I'll gladly accept water. I've been moving briskly for some time now."

"Surely, Major, surely," Davidson said, reaching for a jar of water and a stone cup. "And though you and I are both aware of the strong feeling on the part of some against your Negro Sunday school, I am now inclined to believe that the healthy Christian sentiment in the community can sustain it, and I for one am determined to see that it does."

"Why, thank you, Mr. Davidson," Jackson said, his strong back rigid as a board and his clean shaven face thrown back high in the air, but not in a proud way.

"I am afraid I am not the one who merits any thanks," Davidson said, handing Jackson his water.

A couple of blocks away, the Lexington Presbyterian Church stood in stately solitude. The faint late rays of sun took the stained glass windows along the side of the building and birthed from them fantastic cornucopias of color and light against the shadowed interior of the quiet sanctuary.

Surreptitiously, two slender black arms pushed up a small plain window on the dark side of the building. Then the head of Lylburn Downing appeared in the window from below, his furtive eyes darting first one direction then another.

With cat-quick suddenness, Lylburn lunged through the open window and landed with a thump on the hardwood floor of, he realized, *Dr. White's office!* Up in a flash, his heart pounding against his flannel long johns, he closed the window. Then he stared around him at the dim pastor's study.

"Sweet Lord Jesus," he whispered, struck with awe. "Look at all them books. And they be the Lord's books too." Books lined three walls, from one end of the room to the other. They stretched from floor to ceiling. Thick books, thin books. New, brightly covered books, and old, tattered volumes. Never had Lylburn seen so many books together in the same place in his entire eighteen years.

He stepped gingerly to one long shelf. His bright eyes darted to the window, then the room's closed door. Slowly, delicately, his right hand moved toward a particularly thick and venerable looking offering. He uncoiled his index finger to touch the revered volume. Just before he made contact, his hand jerked back as if touching a hot coal. Not only was this holy material, it was *forbidden* holy material. He was not to read it. He was not to even be in this building without permission.

But inside the covers of that sacred text, Lylburn knew, lay the secrets to this present life. Therein stretched the road to happiness, contentment, wisdom, and peace, such as they were available in this temporal darkness. He stretched forth his finger again, and—*thwack!*

"Ah!" he screamed, spinning toward the window. A huge blackbird fluttered away after having crashed against the glass. For a moment, Lylburn crouched and listened. *Nothing.* His rich honey eyes wide, he turned and reached for the doorknob and pulled the door open.

Darkness filled the hallway, but he could see odd bright streams of light flowing from the sanctuary at the far end of the corridor. With the stealth and quick light feet of a savvy Cherokee, which he often imagined himself being, he crept toward the light. No small sound betrayed his movement.

Then Lylburn found himself in the sanctuary. A strange brilliant rainbow glow filled the room as the sinking sun sent its farewell beams of light and life through the thick stained glass that etched the images of prophets, gospels, apostles, epistles, and the revelation of the Lamb Himself.

At first Lylburn just stared in awe around the large quiet room. He blinked his eyes as the colorful rays that shot past him seemed to come alive, dancing and flashing across the sanctuary. He noticed that, though the sunbeams were shooting in toward the center and rear of the room, the quirky reflection of a multihued prism had pooled against the polished walnut pulpit.

As the Scriptures had increasingly occupied Lylburn's mind, especially since the Goober—er, Major Jackson's—colored Sunday school had begun, a verse now leapt into his mind at the fantastic sight of the color-splashed pulpit. *"And there appeared unto them cloven tongues as of fire, and it sat upon each of them."*

Was this what it was like for the apostle Peter and the others, Lylburn wondered, *on that day when God sent His Holy Ghost?* And then he was dancing in the light and radiance of God's love and power, as they had done. Lylburn whirled around and around as he made his way down the center aisle toward the pulpit. He laughed freely and without care, as he had not laughed since he was a small child with his dear sainted mother, before she had gone to be with Jesus. He had almost forgotten about his mama for a good long time, until lately, since he had really been learning a lot about God. He had for some reason begun remembering her much more often. She was the first one he ever remembered telling him about Jesus. Maybe that was why he was thinking about her more often now, because he was thinking more about Jesus again, like he used to do.

Some moments later, Lylburn found himself standing behind the pulpit. A splotch of rainbow light bathed his face, and he began to feel power surging through his body and mind. *Was this how Peter felt,* he wondered—Peter, the big-mouthed coward who had bragged and bragged, then betrayed Jesus—*when God filled him up with power and strength on the day of Pentecost? He knew he had to preach and now I know I have to preach.* And there it was, as simple and true as the breath he drew. God had placed him here to preach His gospel. Why hadn't he seen it before? Had God not been ready for him? *No, I've not been ready for God.*

And then Lylburn Downing began to preach the Word.

"For those of you who's smart enough to be here on time today," Lylburn bellowed, "here's today's lesson from the Holy Word of God."

Lylburn bounded down the couple of steps fronting the pulpit and snatched a Bible from a pew. Stepping back behind the pulpit, he thumbed to the appropriate page, kept the book in one hand, and raised his other arm into the air for emphasis.

"I say, brothers and sisters," he boomed, "we is a wicked and perversive generations! All of us has gone to stray and other messages of sins and we has lost our ways, dear child!" He looked down to read from the Bible. "Like the man say in Isayer, woe be to them that calls good evil, and to thems what calls evil good!"

He laid the Bible down and strutted to one side of the altar.

"And woe be to Billy Randolph for showing late again! I hear you knocking out there, Brother Billy. But the door be shut, and you out there with the devil for another week, brother. Amen!" Lylburn glanced to the side without turning his head and spoke out of one corner of his mouth, as if to a front-row parishioner, "Gonna have to sneak in the window again." Then he swept his arm across the sanctuary, his strong full voice echoing off the walls. "Now I say turn, my beloveds, to the Book of the Psalms, chapter 72, for this afternoon's reading from the Holy Scriptures of our Lord."

His eyes focused on the Bible; he continued to speak, with deep passion.

"'For he shall deliver the needy when he crieth; the poor also, and him that hath no helper. He shall spare the poor and needy, and shall save the souls of the needy. He shall redeem their soul from deceit and violence: and precious shall their blood be in his sight.'

"Amen. Now let us pray, dear brothers and sisters," Lylburn concluded. "Then we shall breaks up into our onliest groups."

The fact that Lylburn Downing could never have read verses of Isaiah from the Book of Ezekiel, to which his Bible was opened, and upside down at that—the fact that Lylburn Downing could not read at all—did not diminish the effect of the ringing new noise on the walls of the church.

CHAPTER 21

IT WAS NOT THE SAME AS RIDING WITH ELLIE, BUT MAGGIE could not deny that the rollicking equestrian excursions with her brother-in-law had become the highlight of, well, of her week, at least.

Once again, her strapping chestnut Odysseus nudged out Jackson's nondescript gray as they crossed under the huge ancient oak that served as the finish line for their frequent sprints.

As they guided the lathered mounts toward the familiar ridge that overlooked Lexington, nestled amidst the splendid visage of a Shenandoah spring, Maggie peered at her brother-in-law. "Sturdy" she thought of him in the saddle. Long, angular, and awkward in the day to day, neither did he shine splendid and acrobatic astride his mount like many of Virginia's boys and young men. *Were these folk* born *atop the bare backs of their sleek thoroughbreds?* she often wondered. Nonetheless, whether at the cantor or the gallop, and she had seen him often at both, he sat his mount as her father stood in a pulpit or her brother John, returned to Trenton, handled a scalpel. Competent, not spectacular.

Jackson offered a high, quick, gleeful utterance Maggie could only describe as a giggle. Rarely had she heard the sound before—until these last months of fellowship with her brother-in-law.

"I do not believe that I have won a horse race since ole Uncle Cummins used to put me atop his big gelding and race me around the fields of western Virginia for his whiskey and tax money," Jackson said, his face betraying a trace of a smile, but his voice rich with mirth.

"Well you are doing the Lord's work, here, Thomas," Maggie said, stroking Odysseus's mane. When Jackson stared at her, she said, "Helping an old maid accustomed only to thick dusty volumes, foreign tongues, modern publications, and the quill and scroll come out of her hiding into the open."

Jackson's eyes betrayed him for an instant at the sight of her fine womanly form, her breathing revealing a slightly more rapid cadence than normal from the ride. "Sister, that is not the description I should offer of you."

"Oh? And what might your description offer?"

Jackson reddened and he shook his head. "No, no, I stand convicted, my tongue once again, like a ravening beast—"

Before he could conclude, she shouted, "Down the hill," and was off like a streak down the rich green carpet.

The sweet singsong of orioles and whippoorwills charmed Maggie's and Jackson's ears as they walked their winded mounts back toward town, and their nostrils and heads drew in the intoxicating elixir of full spring in the emerald Shenandoah like eager sponges sucking water.

As Jackson, rigid in the saddle, allowed himself to glance around and take in nature's festive community, the realization began to dawn on him that, after a trying season of darkness, his affection for Lexington and the Valley had deepened. He thought of all that now held meaning for him in the lush country. He shot a sideways look at the woman on the horse a few feet away from him. In so many ways, Ellie still lived through her. At times, despite the differences in coloring and size, when he looked at Maggie, before his eyes trained on her, a jolt would coarse through him, as though he were back in the presence of she who had so opened life's gate to him.

In other ways, Maggie could never be mistaken for her sister. Jackson remembered the confused, involuntary stirring of his soul when love for Ellie overtook him. What was it that now sometimes caused blood to rush to his head, his heart to pulsate, and his stomach to lift toward his throat when Maggie would flash those fiery eyes just so, or tweak him with her razor-sharp, but richly feminine wit? He did not know, and he determined he should not know.

"Thomas Jackson, your colored Sunday school is nothing but a smashing success," Maggie said. "I was leaving some yarn with Reverend Pendleton at the Grace Episcopal rectory the other day, and he told me your school is stronger than St. John's in Richmond's ever was."

Crimson flooded Jackson's clean-shaven, sun-burnished face. St. John's was one of the largest churches in the state, and a fine, gospel-preaching one too.

"I believe my heavenly Father has drawn me closer to Himself through my trial," Jackson said. The thought struck Maggie that she had never once heard him speak of his "trial" to anyone besides herself. In fact, her father had once commented his amazement at that fact, and his concern that Jackson would be damaged by keeping his feelings "all bottled up like a poison that needs lancing."

Jackson turned toward Maggie and stared for nearly a full minute, chewing his wafer thin lower lip. She felt it, but kept her gaze ahead. He saw in her a vibrant woman, in recent months, he believed, a woman growing in her faith. But also a woman pierced with a deep abiding melancholy. The kind of remorse and sorrow sometimes inexplicable, which only the full washing of God's grace could cleanse.

Finally he announced, "Maggie, I should wish for you to come to me with your every joy, and every sorrow, and let me share them with you."

The declaration so struck her that she could neither deflect nor absorb it. She reined up and stared at him. The blue orbs gleamed, then watered. Then she turned Odysseus back toward home. They rode on, the quiet punctuated by the soft crunching of hooves on the clay path beneath them.

After five minutes, Maggie broke the silence. "It is frustrating to write well and yet be judged not for my abilities, but because I am a woman."

Jackson listened as they rode.

"I have not written well since Ellie—and mother—" She paused, then looked at him, a wry smile creasing her pretty face. "I have sometimes wondered if I would receive a different response if I were to submit my work under a male pseudograph."

"But you are the most respected poetess in all the South," Jackson said, waving one hand for emphasis. "And when I have been North, many know you as well."

Maggie did not respond or look his way.

Jackson shook his head. "Perhaps *Silverwood* will force them to respect you."

The name swung Maggie's head toward him. Lightning flashed across her face. She could not at first find the words, and directed her gaze back to the road. He let her think as a couple of bluebirds chirped their courtship in a nearby elm tree.

"I pray so," Maggie said at length. *Silverwood.* Her secret storehouse of memory, her treasure trove of hopes and dreams. Halls echoing with lost sweet voices and dear pattering stockinged feet.

I would be patient, I would find
How much the thought can reconcile—

Can lift me up, and make me glad,
That only for a little while
Shall I be left behind!

She cocked her head toward him, the shining scarlet trusses parted down the middle in the style of the day. "And someday I shall share with you the true meaning of the word." Then, the eyes to her soul opening to him like the blooming spring petals of a rose, as he had never seen them: "You will be the only one I ever tell."

Russell could not remember feeling happier while sober in years. But, yes, the occasion did call for a snifter of brandy in toast. Rather than calling one of the house servants, he poured it himself and kicked his short, powerful booted legs up on a cushioned ottoman in the first-floor office of his main house.

He had never liked the VMI, nor its arrogant eggheaded men and boys, who felt themselves, landed or not, superior to those in Rockbridge County who were possessed of true substance and ability. But Russell knew he had not enlarged his plantation, nor built his ancillary business interests without such gifting—and without a certain dogged tenacity that had first won his ancestors their prized low country land and herds from the demon Campbells; later parlayed those sweet triumphs into grander success on one wild and very un-Scotslike turn of pitch and toss in coming to the New World; and finally wrested the land from the same detestable Anglican patricians they had despised in the Old, as well as the occasional red brute who had to be shoved farther back into the trackless wilds not yet fit for the white man.

Now that tenacity had paid off for him in the matter of Major Thomas J. Jackson of the Virginia Military Institute. Despite the sputtering European cotton markets that were muzzling profits from the cotton fields he owned further south, for the past two years, Russell had channeled a consistent flow of funds into the VMI. His twin goals: influence and the unhorsing of Jackson as a VMI faculty member.

"Square Box," Russell shouted to the lengthening sun rays as eventide approached. He could not restrain his laughter. The fields were planted, the rain had been just right, and he had bought himself influence on the VMI Board of Visitors through Mr. Charles Mason. "Aye, I do not know if I can stand to wait until Sunday worship to call the man Square Box." This latest sobriquet had accrued from a Maryland cadet's observation of Jackson's size 14 shoes, which the cadet first coined as "boats" then as "square boxes." The laughter bubbling up from Russell's throat collided with the quaff of hot brandy racing down it and he nearly spit the spirit up. A portion of it, in fact, snuck into his nose, which Russell had noticed of late was increasingly maroon in color. He had determined that spending more time in the sun was preferable to and more probable than spending less time in the cups.

Aye, but it's nice to sip in triumph, he smiled to himself.

Charles Mason had lodged the first complaint ever submitted against a VMI professor. The man had registered a complaint made by his cadet son, beefy Jimmy, that Jackson had a "rigid aversion towards me in my recitations." That was four years ago, in 1852. At that point, Mason had been cordial and patient in his protest, due partly to his recognition of Jackson's towering Mexican War reputation, which had grown larger under its own energy as the years lengthened since the conflict. Still, no complaint, cordial or otherwise, had ever been received against a VMI faculty member, and though no action was taken or even considered against Jackson, a stir ensued, limited not just to the faculty, but to the students and some of the townspeople.

Russell remembered all this when by chance a year ago he happened into partnership with Mason, a Tidewater Virginian, in the purchase of a packet for cotton shipment to Europe. Though Mason had not taken further action against Jackson, he felt his son's subsequent quitting of the institute and general ne'er-do-well activities since could largely be laid at the feet of Jackson, whom Mason believed had "broken the boy's spirit." He failed to consider the consequences of an indulgent, mercenary mother, his own long absences from the boy as he grew up, and the hard reality that James Charles Mason never wished to attend VMI and hated every day he did.

As these events were revisited under the balming influence of the fine brandy offered by Mason's new business partner—a business partner he had grown in desperate need of, being himself almost totally dependent on his flagging European cotton sales—a plan emerged in Russell's mind. He had heard of other disgruntlement with Jackson from VMI cadets during the Virginian's five years of professoring. Now he had met not only the father of one of the most disgruntled cadets, but a man whose best friend, Morgan Frost, stood on the school's governing board of visitors. That man's influence had led to Mason sending his indifferent son to the institute in the first place.

Indeed, the plan had worked to everyone's benefit. Mason obtained the business partner he needed, and Frost had a new friend, Russell, who had become a healthy donor to the school, which itself seemed greatly to be benefiting from the arrangement. To Frost's mind, and all others except Russell and Mason, the fiery landowner had become a veritable diamond in the rough both for the institution, which happily plowed the planter's liberal funding into capital expansion, and for Frost, who not even himself was aware that Mason had purposely orchestrated both Russell's fresh new relationship with the school and his growing social relationship with Frost, who resided thirty miles down the Shenandoah Valley in Staunton.

Russell also took great pains in the reconnaissance of information related to ongoing complaints about Jackson at the VMI. He rewarded a certain cadet, later drummed out of the corps for other indiscretions, for information about classroom incidents and cadets who disliked Jackson. He assimilated information gleaned from businessmen around Lexington. He even had Lylburn Downing and other slaves serving as "ears" for him in their comings and goings around the town.

When the time came that the number of complaints against Jackson, who had now come to be seen in most quarters as a fine man, a competent artillery instructor, and a sorry professor, prompted the Society of the Alumni to bring the issue to the board at its summer meeting, Russell made his move. Knowing full well of the alumni organization's plans, he feigned ignorance of them and, sober and remorseful, paid a midnight call to his "friend" Frost.

Rarely had Russell ever enjoyed himself as he did in reciting to Frost a litany of unfortunate events that had reached his ears about a "certain Major Jackson at the VMI who, it pains me to say, attends my own splendid church." He proceeded to explain to the attentive Frost that he had for years ignored stories critical of Jackson's teaching— "not Jackson the man, I tell you, for I can vouch there is no more upstanding a Christian man than you can find in Lexington town, nor I would venture, all of Rockbridge County—" because of his aversion to hurting a brother in his church.

"What tore it, however," Russell had said hoarsely, his head drooping, "was when a group of town fathers, respected and successful businessmen all, came to me and asked, knowing full well my love and affection for the institution, 'What are we to do about this fine man, whose tutorial inefficacies are bringing a blight upon it?'"

Through crocodile tears, Russell had raised the china blue eyes to Frost and whispered, "I knew not what to do, sir, other than to come to my dear good friend, whose love for the institute supersedes even mine, on this midnight, and lay my heart's troubles at your feet."

Russell had gone on to explain that of course he could not divulge the names of the "town fathers," for they never dreamed he, such a friend and supporter of the major's, would take their concerns to Frost, and would have been mortified had they known so.

So now the eve of the board's meeting had arrived. And as Russell drained another tumbler of his expensive amber elixir, Lylburn could hear the man's roaring laughter from his own small cabin two hundred yards away. It brightened him to hear the sad man laugh again, but the reason he suspicioned for it did not. He knew his master had been plotting against the Goober for a long time now, and he did not like that one bit. He felt certain the Lord did not either, and *Marse Russell, he be a church-going man too. Leastways somes of the time. Must be his woman dying and the demon rum got him by the collar,* Lylburn thought.

All Lylburn knew was to get back down on the dirt floor of his shack, where he had worn more than one set of holes through the knees of his pants, holes over which he himself had sewn patches, and take his concerns to the Almighty, who *"will hear when I call unto him."*

Russell, meanwhile, allowed himself the luxury of rehearsing in his mind a medley of the best "Square Box" stories that had circulated to him. It seemed too good to be true, all the antics he had heard regarding Jackson's classroom. Among the planter's personal favorites were the reports, repeated and voluminous, of the myriad animal sounds that had visited (and evidently continued to visit) themselves upon the sometimes hearing impaired professor from the ranks of the cadets sitting in his own classroom. Russell had heard first- or reliable second-hand accounts of birds (crows, parakeets, canaries, and macaws) chirping, cats meowing, dogs barking, hyenas howling, horses neighing, cows mooing, pigs oinking, and monkeys and chimpanzees—sometimes in groups—making their distinctive presence known, more than once accompanied by the separate flights across Jackson's section room of both banana and peel.

He also enjoyed the tales of a cadet named Massenburg spitting tobacco in the classroom, and of "paper pellets" zinging past the major's head inside his classroom and bricks zinging past it outside. And the intriguing questions that tended to present themselves to Jackson alone among the VMI faculty, such as that of one cadet Davidson Penn, who solemnly inquired, "Major, can a cannon be so bent as to make it shoot around a corner?" Russell enjoyed the reported response of Jackson almost as well. The professor paused for a long moment of silent consideration, then pronounced his answer: "Mr. Penn, I reckon hardly."

Accounts of gargantuan feet being drawn on the chalkboard of Jackson's section room abounded. Also, the sizable corpus of cadet poetry that had blossomed regarding the major's professorial acumen, including the one whose final line referred to him as a "h——— of a fool."

In one celebrated instance, a plebe was strapped into a chair by upperclassmen. The plotters set a trash can full of water and various other substances, some of them better suited for cadet chamber pots, atop the helpless "rat's" lap. The upperclassmen then tilted the gagged and blindfolded plebe, the trash can, and the chair against the door to Jackson's room. The sight that ensued when he opened it was not a pretty one. After cleaning up the mess, including the unfortunate uniform Jackson wore at the time, the perpetrators were court-martialed out of the institute, a fate not unusual for those who drew Jackson's ire, though it did take extreme accomplishments, particularly in the section room, to achieve that distinction.

Some of the parade ground artillery drill stories held their own charm for Russell, including the one where a group of cadets Jackson commissioned to serve as horses pulling cannon suddenly "bolted" toward him, prompting him to draw his sword until they veered away. One cadet, whom Jackson put on report for failing to trot during his duties as a horse, defended himself to the investigating committee by saying, "I am a natural pacer."

One choice incident came directly to Russell from McDowell. That rough-hewn planter stood among a startled crowd of observers one day on the VMI parade ground who witnessed a group of cadets-cum-horses pulling a full caisson tear out in mock fright of the stern countenanced Jackson. The "horses" scattered the startled crowd of dignified men and elegant ladies, Jackson all the while yelling himself hoarse in vain endeavor to recall them.

Even VMI Superintendent Smith, a close Episcopalian friend of Rev. Pendleton and from the start a strong supporter of Jackson, finally admitted in writing that the tall professor with the taller shadow of war renown is "a brave man, a conscientious man, and a good man, but he is no professor."

Russell, in his cups, had quite convinced himself he would be doing the institute and its cadets one gigantic favor by helping unseat Jackson when some of the other stories began floating through his alcohol-soaked mind. The stories of a stiff-backed professor trudging two miles through snow at three in the morning to confess to a shocked cadet his own error in reprimanding the lad for what proved to be a correct answer the day before in class. Or of that same professor on another frigid winter night bringing soup to a sick cadet. Or of the professor secretly paying out of his own modest salary tuition dollars needed for a dirt-poor Valley plebe, even a middling student only because of Herculean tenacity and heart, to return to the VMI for his second year.

These stories the planter tossed off, as he stumbled in the darkness and grabbed the sweet desired decanter. *Ah—empty!* Rage more than disappointment filled him, for he did not wish to leave the room to retrieve more brandy. He grabbed the cut-glass container with a thick tanned hand and hurled it with such force that he heard it dashed into a hundred pieces in the blackness. *Blackness, at length* all *is blackness,* he thought. "More brandy!" he screamed to Lije, the house servant. Russell had not always treated his slaves as he had been treating them. He had not always plotted against Jackson. And he had not always been ruled by alcoholic spirits. But the markets, it was the markets in Europe that continued to pinch him. And the Northerners, those cursed Northerners with their industrial schemes, their sweatshop factories, and their political, economic, and moral squeeze against him and other good, self-supporting Southern landowners.

Yet now even more of the respected men in Virginia were openly voicing their disgruntlement with the slave practice. Why, he had heard that the famed soldier Robert Lee, perhaps the greatest of the Mexican War heroes, of Arlington plantation, facing Washington City from the Virginia side of the Potomac, whose wife Mary Custis Lee descended directly from the line of Martha Custis—Mrs. George Washington—actually planned manumission of all his own slaves. *Easy for him to do, stationed away off in Texas as a career soldier,* Russell grimaced. *It hardly pays to be a white man and a landowner in this country anymore.*

The only thought that could cheer him, and the last thought that fired his imagination before he sank into a night-long stupor, was the specter of Major Thomas Jackson packing his meager belongings and departing forever from Lexington, Rockbridge County, and perhaps even Virginia herself.

The news of John Brown, the latest chapter of "Bleeding Kansas," tore through Virginia like a cold scythe. Mothers feared for their children; fathers, for their families and homes. Jackson felt his wisdom ratified in not encouraging his half brother Wirt Woodson to purchase further land in free-soil territory. Jackson had kept in loose communication with the young man, now twenty-five years old, ever since that unforgettable day little infant Wirt nursed atop his dying mother's breast. Now Wirt, living near Parkersburg in western Virginia, shared Jackson's interest in land purchase out in America's spreading frontier.

Jackson had long passed stipends of cash to sister Laura to help in the support of young Elizabeth and Tom Arnold. And he had supported Wirt's education and bought him land in both free and slave-holding areas. Now land speculation, and perhaps a move West, drew Wirt like a siren's song. Complicating the matter was Wirt's desire to locate more land in free-soil territory.

"If I help Wirt secure any more free-soil land," Jackson wrote Laura, "he would probably become an abolitionist; and then in the event of trouble between North and South he would stand on one side, and we on the opposite."

The concern panged Jackson for just an instant that Laura herself might be facing a decision as to what side she would stand on should "trouble" come. The visit with Ellie to see his sister two years ago had healed the sibling relationship. In fact, he had commented to Maggie during one of their nightly Spanish lessons that that trip had probably cost him a wife and child, but it had at least returned to him a sister. However, the letters he received from Laura revealed an increasingly bitter spirit, one that seemed to find a wide variety of objects upon which to visit that poisoned wrath—most sadly, God, but also the institutions of marriage and family, her womanhood, her age, her neighbors, various of her local government officials, and the South. Why the latter had crept into view as a target of her venom Jackson could not figure. Was it submerged resentment for the sublime pleasures he had found among wife, family, and friends in Lexington? He trusted that the geography of the heart would ultimately win out over that of the sections.

When news arrived of the fanatical abolitionist Brown's rampage that killed first a black freedman, then butchered several proslavery white Kansans with broadswords in front of their families, Jackson began to wonder about the wisdom of purchasing land in an increasingly unstable West. His career and financial mentors, Bennett and Carlisle, finally convinced him to abort such plans. Having prudently invested his earnings in stocks, and with a directorship of the Lexington Bank looming—the professor's disciplined life and the financial canniness emanating from his Scots side had marked him with favor in the eyes of the other board members, Carlisle, and several older town fathers, including (in a sharp reversal of earlier feelings) Judge Brockenbrough—Jackson determined to aid Wirt through other means. He would not forsake the son of his own sainted mother. Nor would he forsake the continued support of his beloved, benighted sister and her offspring.

Another riddle sifted its way in and out of the backwaters of Jackson's consciousness: why did the murderous actions of Brown, whose reported calls for servile insurrection had previously struck terror in the hearts of Southerners who remembered Nat Turner's carnage of men, women, and children, bring applause from some quarters in the North? Admittedly, they were small, vocal factions; but more disturbing, why did the more reasonable mainstream of Northern citizenry not react vociferously against the Browns of the world—and the industrialists who bankrolled them?

Standing to leave his room down the hall from Maggie's in the Junkin home, Jackson decided to depart for his daily afternoon journey to the twenty-acre spread he had purchased a couple of miles east of town. He had begun several small gardens on the spread after Ellie's death. His erstwhile companions the cabbages, tomatoes, squash, zucchinis, turnips, cucumbers, and okra had become some of his best and most loyal friends. Each day they were there, ready to be tended, nurtured, and loved. Jackson did not even realize that his love and devotion to them grew partly because, unlike people, they would be there for him each day. They would not leave him. He could count on his green friends, and he loved them and took care of them. He had no one else now to love and take care of.

Kneeling amongst them and drinking deep of the serene rich fragrances of the Shenandoah brought him the same sublime sanctity of soul as the mountains to the west had brought him early in life. Craftily, this lush valley had snuck its way around the soft places of his soul. Edgar A. Guest had not yet penned the words, but already the sentiment was in Jackson's heart:

> *Fer these are scenes that grip the heart, an' when yer tears are dried,*
> *Ye find the home is dearer than it was, an' sanctified;*
> *An' tuggin' at ye always are the pleasant memories*
> *O' her that was an' is no more—ye can't escape from these.*

More and more, Jackson felt the adopted earthly child of the Valley, just as he increasingly felt the adopted heavenly child of God the Father. He would, betimes, stand with fierce might against those who would attempt to desecrate both.

◆◇ ◆◇ ◆◇

Since her return from Europe the year before, Maggie had gradually taken to herself the formidable duties Ellie had for years been performing through her de facto leadership of the Presbyterian church's Poor and Colored People's Benevolences Ministry. Rather, they had strangely taken themselves to her, through her chance meeting with one of the children at the church, who asked her if she would come see the child's twelve siblings, and through the overflowing graciousness of the people's response to Maggie.

Though rigorous and not complimentary of Maggie's inclinations nor natural aptitudes, she found the work, to her surprise, a salve to her soul. In fact, though awkward, ignorant, and often misguided in her aid to the unfortunate folk, black and white, to whom she ministered, she found that the humility and grace it bestowed upon her quickened her spirit. Happily, this restored the richness and strength to her long-dulled pen.

So did Longfellow, whose epic lines seemed dipped from the precious deep pools of her own life's tears:

> *Only those are crowned and sainted,*
> *who with grief have been acquainted.*

And, from *Holidays:*

> *The holiest of all holidays are those*
> *Kept by ourselves in silence and apart;*
> *The secret anniversaries of the heart.*

Now flowed forth the dreams, hopes, tears, joys, and feelings from the deep-running waters of Maggie's own secret still places. Now flowed forth *Silverwood.* Maggie's reputation had indeed grown as a poetess—north, south, and west. Still, however, loomed the fortress of male hegemony around the exalted positions of American poetry. *Silverwood,* a novel, would finally place Margaret Junkin Preston inside that jealous high ring. And *Silverwood* would extinguish ghosts and pay homage to dear departed sisters and brothers and mothers and lost sweet loves.

Silverwood would be Maggie's belated paean to those to whom she, with her high fine flowing lines of script and verse, could never speak her true heart. And it would be her passport into the literary immortality God must have deigned for her (why else the sensitive, haunted, oft-tortured road she traveled?). Both, at the same time. And how the words now streamed forth from her again-potent quill. *Sil-verwood*.

In time, she would tell its secret. But only to him. And yes, *Silver-wood* would be *of* him as well. Him, him.

Only then did the telltale truth of her aching wounded heart swell over her, in the same manner that her word spread across the pages as a tidal wave—unexpected, unwanted, irresistible, irrevocable. She had loved Ellie *and* she had loved *him*. She still loved Ellie and now she loved him again. She did not wish it, but it was so. *Oh, God save me!* she uttered, her head falling nearly to her lap.

The open frayed letter on the writing desk in front of her caught her eye. She knew the words without reading them, for she had read them dozens—*hundreds?*—of times. Written to her from the major during her two-month winter visit to her cousins in Philadelphia earlier in the year: "Only the necessity of your regaining your health could warrant the pain of my being deprived of your precious company. . . . I want to see you very much. . . . Good-bye my dearly loved sister. Your very loving brother. Thomas."

Surely he had no surmisal that her flight north was due to the smoldering emotions that threatened even those months ago to boil over if she spent one more evening's worth of "Spanish lessons" with him?

"No, no!" she cried out, causing Ruthie downstairs to look up from her preparation of dinner. Again she dipped the quill into the eager waiting ink tank. *I shall not stop,* she purposed. *Somehow, it shall all be used.* Then she wrote more.

"My heart could not hide from me," *Silverwood's* autobiographical author-heroine Edith wrote of the handsome, pious young man— whose heart had been captured by Edith's wise, beautiful, devout, and simple-hearted sister Zilpha—for whom she pined, "that for *his* sake, I was striving to develop to the utmost, whatever native powers I possessed—for *his* sake I persisted in studies such as *she* thought too much out of a woman's line—that it was his tastes, rather than my own, I was seeking to please—*his* stand-point I loved to assume—*his* sympathies to which I was fitting the key, which, nevertheless, wound readily through the same wards, and unlocked kindred feelings in the depths of my own nature."

She stared into a nearby mirror. *Is it I?* Then, as the remembrance of her and the major's shared loss, their streaking gallops across the Valley, their months and months of "Spanish lessons," even their first long-ago meeting in her own home pulsated across the tableau of her vivid evocative mind, the quill raced as if possessed with a soul of its own to drink again from the dark blue jar.

"His sympathies, so unutterably satisfying; his words of precious consolation; his beautiful prayers; his sweet helpfulness in teaching me the uses of my sufferings; the touch of his hand; his arm wound so frankly about me, as it might have been about Eunice or Sepha [Zilpha's sisters]—ah! they were all too soothing, too strengthening, too beguiling!" *Yes, it is coming!* she thought. *They are all coming to me as before, when Ellie was still*—"I felt the fainter when the arm was withdrawn, for it *was* withdrawn, and I sank down weaker, wearier, lonelier than before. Shame, shame poor heart! that when thou hast God to lean upon, thou shouldst yet cling with such a fond conviction to the belief that the love of human heart like thine own, could endue thee with a mysterious strength to do and to bear all things!"

Finally she laid her throbbing aching head down on the desk in front of her. She knew the pain emanated from her eyes. For a long while they had posed minor irritation to her. Dr. Cartwright, the eye doctor in Richmond, had pronounced her vision fine. He and others had found no physiological problems at all. Yet the pain, slight at first, had grown ever more bold in its assertiveness. It presented itself most often during periods of intense concentration of mind. When she wrote. When she wrote her most challenging and her most brilliant. Now, for the first time, however, an episode proved so painful as to disallow her to continue writing. This, even after rehearsing in her mind various of the Scriptures, as Ellie used to do and as the major now did and encouraged her to do.

She managed to call out her door for Ruthie's assistance with a cold pack for her eyes before she collapsed onto her bed, on her back, not her face this time.

"Sweet potatoes, I should be planting sweet potatoes," Jackson said aloud the next afternoon to his friends the cabbages, the squash, and the zucchinis. "I have never enjoyed the sweet potatoes we have at the president's home."

Then he heard the nickering of a horse. It was not his. Down the road, back toward town, came a buggy. He recognized it as Judge Brockenbrough's. As it thumped closer, through the luminous Valley afternoon, he saw Maggie in the front seat, next to the judge's servant Jeff, who drove. Crowded in the back were the judge, John Preston, and Carlisle.

Jackson stood and walked to the group as Jeff pulled the judge's great grey up. Jackson could tell from the expressions of the group they had not come to pay a social visit.

"It's that ornery son of Scots, Will Russell," Carlisle, dapper as ever in a white linen suit, said a moment later. "And I say that as a son of Scots."

"We've learned he desires your ouster from the VMI," Brockenbrough said.

Jackson noticed the resplendence of Maggie in canary yellow, with matching fingerless gloves, bonnet, and parasol. But pain etched her face.

"I've suspicioned ill intent toward you for some time on his part," Carlisle said. "As you may know, he has lately taken to drink in a way unlike before." Jackson knew, and everyone knew. Lexington was not a large town. "I've learned quite a bit about the man as I've asked, discreetly, around. For instance, John Lyle allowed to me in the book shop the other day that a couple of years ago, Russell attempted with money and influence to garner a seat as an elder for himself on your church's ruling session."

Jackson had heard the like. Pastor White squelched the snaky attempt. Then the good sixty-year-old Reverend Dr. Junkin, all six and a half feet, 245 pounds of him, had threatened to physically remove Russell from a church finance meeting to which the planter was not invited.

"I have friends that serve on the VMI's board of visitors with Mr. Carlisle here who know that a fast—and relatively new—friend of Russell's, Charles Mason, whose son you rightfully helped send packing as a cadet not many years past, has attempted to parley certain alumni complaints with you into your removal," Brockenbrough sniffed. "Russell has done nothing directly himself, other than provide 'valuable' and 'regrettable' information about you to Mason, who has an old friend on the board who has never liked you. They shall attempt to engineer your ouster at the board's annual meeting this weekend."

Jackson's face flushed red and his eyes burned white hot. Carlisle recognized these rare, potentially fearsome signs.

"Tom, we believe we have the votes on that board to put down this move, or at least forestall it until a bit of the fire dies down and it is forgotten," Carlisle said, his lawyer's words coming rapid-fire. "But the word has slipped out in certain quarters around town, and we felt it best that you were at least aware."

Jackson remembered now a comment of Harvey Hill's before that good friend returned a few months ago to North Carolina and a teaching post at Davidson College, where his father-in-law, another Presbyterian minister, served as president. Harvey had told Jackson of rebuking Russell to his face for his incessant gossip and backbiting. When Russell had bit back, Harvey had offered him the opportunity of martial satisfaction.

"But the pompous cretin knew the roads I had traveled in Mexico," Harvey had said, looking Jackson full in the face, "just as he knew the roads you had." At the time, Jackson had wondered if Harvey's words carried more import than was apparent on the surface. He had almost asked him such, but had let the comment go. Now he wondered anew.

"I myself don't fancy him or his friend Sam McDowell," Brockenbrough said. "It has been my witness that neither are to be trusted over the long haul to be square in a business transaction. At least, not always, they are not."

Then why is McDowell on the board of the bank and virtually every other major institution in town? Jackson thought. But he knew the answer to that. A sprawling tobacco plantation, which required the labor of over sixty slaves, including the surly, strapping Ben, who, Jackson had heard, had caused some disturbances among other slaves.

Jackson glanced at Preston, who stood quietly. The whole business obviously embarrassed the latter. He looked as if he would rather be just about anywhere else. Still, he stood there on this quiet country road, a widower himself now for nearly a year—after a quarter-century of marriage—painful as it was for him to witness the inevitable embarrassment of a friend, teaching colleague, and business partner. *What a grand friend you are, John Preston,* Jackson thought to himself as he eyed the great, handsome, broad-shouldered man who had been the single greatest force behind the founding of the VMI. *You are a man, sir, who* loves *the institute.*

Maggie saw first the anger boiling in Jackson. When his right—*no, it's the left*—arm, shot straight up, she knew trouble was afoot. So did Carlisle.

"Now Tom," Carlisle began.

Jackson fixed his gaze on the attorney.

"Is this merely the skulduggery of that drunken planter?" he inquired. The chill of the words caused Maggie to flinch.

Carlisle shifted his feet and turned to Brockenbrough for help. Even the stately, respected judge did not relish tackling this one.

"You do have opposition in certain other quarters," Brockenbrough said at length. "Certain, er, respectable quarters."

Jackson's gaze remained trained on Carlisle, who Maggie feared might melt under the heat.

Finally, the lawyer sprang into action. "Look, Tom," he said, employing his hands to plead his case. "Certain of the alums—"

"Which alums?" Jackson asked.

"Well, certain—"

"I would like to know names—"

"*Certain* ones, confound you!" Carlisle shouted, his crimson neck contrasting with the soft white linen of his coat. "Tom, surely you must know that certain cadets through these past years have not appreciated your professorial acumen. Now certain of the alumni have asked John Strange to take their complaints to the board."

This struck Jackson like a thunderbolt. Professor John Strange, a colleague of his on the VMI faculty, had always seemed an earnest, guileless friend.

"Professor Strange holds nothing against you personally," Brockenbrough chimed in. "But he feels the issue has become divisive enough among the students and alumni that, whatever its resolution, it needs to be addressed by the board."

Divisive . . . among the students and the alumni. Jackson's head swam. And he did something Maggie had never before seen him do. He dropped his raised arm and lifted the other in its place.

For a moment, only the chirping of a nearby oriole invaded the silent rustic sanctum.

"The complaints are poor discipline in your section room, difficult subjects becoming more so under your tutelage, and some hold you to be 'a h—— of a fool.'" Perhaps "Big John" T. L. Preston was the only man alive who could and would have said those true words. Carlisle and Brockenbrough stared in shock at the towering, broad-shouldered man with his handsome granite-jawed face and thick lustrous jet hair.

Maggie stared, too, but her shock metamorphosed into an appreciation and respect for the man she had not before held. For she alone among the unhappy party recognized Preston's wise, gentle, and true words as the best of all approaches to take with his besieged friend.

Sure enough, Jackson nodded his acknowledgment, his eyes meeting Preston's, who remained level. "Yes, I have heard all those accusations."

"Now the board meets this weekend," Carlisle repeated, perspiration now swelling on both his brow and upper lip. "My heavens, Tom, we did not wish to create a scene here, we just thought it proper for you to be aware, since numerous others are, of the events that are transpiring."

Now it was Preston who grew uneasy with Jackson's countenance. "What think you, Tom?" the big man asked.

Jackson looked at his colleague. *Oh-oh,* Preston thought. *The eyes are hot again.*

"Thank you, John," Jackson said, "and you gentlemen. And you, ma'am." That form of address unsettled Maggie. "I shall now undertake my own request to the board."

"What do you mean, son?" Brockenbrough asked.

"I shall call for institution of a formal investigation of their charges of me."

The others stood dumbstruck. Finally, Carlisle, loosening his starched collar, spoke.

"Uh, Tom, my friend, please, that would do no good, I promise you. The board will do what it will do. I don't think, despite Russell's antics, that anything untoward is taking place here."

"No?" Jackson's electric eyes bore coldly in on Carlisle.

"John is right," Brockenbrough said. "With or without Russell's subterfuge, I believe these proceedings, distasteful as they are, would be working their way through the system. And I also believe, with or without Russell, your name will be exonerated."

Those proved the wrong choice of words.

"My name?" Jackson said, clenching the fist on his upraised arm and stepping toward the group. "My name—the name of Jackson—is a fine, proud name, Judge. Should I soil it, it should deserve whatever infamy besmirches it. But this I have not done. No!" Maggie shook as the word echoed across the low rolling hills. "I shall fight this, and I shall fight those who should seek to bring ignominy on my good name."

Now he was within three feet of the others. "Gentlemen, a name is what a man is, under Christ," he said. "Take away a man's name and you have left him desolate and his service for our Lord devastated."

"But Tom," Preston said in his gentle way, "our Lord Himself told us that if we did His work as we should, we would suffer reproach, slander, and even persecution. He warned us that we had better receive them or something was wrong."

"But not against my name!" Jackson thundered, bringing the upraised arm down and turning it into a fist that shook in the face of Preston himself. "I shall bring down any who come against the good and righteous name of my mo—of Jackson."

Now the others, even Preston, stood ashen-faced. *His eyes,* Maggie shuddered, *his eyes look* white *with fury.* Slowly, Jackson lowered his trembling angry fist.

"Never," he whispered, his low voice powered as with the sound of rushing waters, "never shall the good name of Jackson be sullied without challenge." Slowly, as his stare moved from Preston across the row of shocked faces, Jackson's eyes cooled to a glint.

There seemed nothing left to say, so after a long awkward moment, the group, except for Maggie, turned as one to leave.

"Now we shall commit all to prayer," Jackson said

The others turned back to him, in various stages of stupor. Brockenbrough cleared his throat. "Uh, I say my prayers like the next man, Major. I can remember saying a few for you those first times you stood before the Franklin. But with men like Russell, action, not thought or contemplation, is necessary.

"I trust the judgment of the board regarding the legitimate concerns of students and alumni," the judge continued, "but if I offer any prayers, they shall be prayers for the quick dispatching to perdition of these other mountebanks for whom I have so long had to forbear."

Carlisle, a good man but not a believing man, cocked his bewildered head at his old friend.

"I'm afraid that sometimes men do not fear God, my devout comrade," he said with a languid smile. "And these men who do not fear God, do fear lawyers."

Jackson stood, his gloved hands clasping clods of black Virginia earth. "Why, I could know no other course than prayer, good friends," he said. "I have so fixed the habit of prayer in my own mind, that I never raise a glass of water to my lips without a moment's asking of God's blessing. I never seal a letter without putting a word of prayer under the seal. I never take a letter from the post without a brief sending of my thoughts heavenward. I never change my classes in the section room without a minute's petition on the cadets who go out and those who come in."

All stood staring for a moment at Jackson, wondering—but knowing better, really, since by now each was greatly acquainted with him—if mitigating or qualifying words were yet to come. *This man,* Preston knew, *means nothing more by his words than they themselves. And this man, imperfect as he is, practices them.*

"You really do all that, Tom?" Carlisle asked. "Don't you sometimes forget?"

Jackson stared down intently at his cabbages and squash, as though one of them would break out into verse and give him an answer to the preceding question. After some seconds, he looked up and said, "I think I scarcely can say that I do; the habit has become as fixed almost as breathing."

When Preston, Brockenbrough, and Carlisle offered more wan smiles—they knew by now to receive Jackson absolutely, even painfully, at his word, even if that word made no sense—and turned to leave, Maggie continued to stare, her blue orbs radiant. She who at thirty-six years of age had never known a man in the biblical way felt competing urges to cross to the major, put her arms around him, and hug him like she had hugged no other man, and to flee from him and never look back. Did she know him as she had thought she did? She remembered something he had said to her a long time ago during one of their normally light-hearted evening sessions: "Nobody knows anybody, Maggie, not really."

Not perceiving any of this, Jackson smiled at her, and at Preston, who had stopped when noticing Maggie's failure to move, then knelt back to his garden.

Oblivious to Preston as he walked to her side, the one urge won out over the other (of course it had to, as the sea had to rush upon the shore) and Maggie asked Jackson, in the most unintentional girlish fashion, "See you home for supper?"

He looked up from the tomatoes back into which he had already plowed. A smile—*rare*, thought Preston, *to see Jackson smile twice in the same setting, especially after such an exceptional outburst, though he be a happy man even without smiling*—spread across his tanned earnest face, his teeth white and strong. "Yes," Jackson replied, "yes, and Spanish poetry after."

Her whole face flowered as a field of lilies of the valley in new spring, and she grabbed her skirts, turned and whisked right past Preston, never seeing him, spring in her step on the chunky soil. Preston's large eyes followed her, a confused silly grin now crossing his own features. Then he looked back to his friend, fellow professor, and business partner Jackson and haltingly bid him a good day, before returning to the buggy and departing with the others.

Jackson drank in the familiar sweet Shenandoah aroma. He would deal with Russell and the other miscreants. But later. Not much later, but later. For now, he would not allow them to spoil the lullaby of the birds on this pastoral healing acreage of his mind. Yes, his feathered friends sang just loudly enough to please, but not so loud as to intrude.

Refreshed again, content, and, though it would surprise most of his dear friends and family, truly happy, he looked back to his friends the turnips, the snap beans, and the okra and smiled a third time, a doting, tenderhearted smile, thoughts of miscreants and plotting planters suddenly as far from his mind as the distant guns of Mexico. *Ah, good mates you are, every manjack of you,* he thought, touching them as though they were newborn human babies. *But somehow, something is missing.* He wiped his damp brow with the heel of a gloved hand, then sat staring, not seeing the onion before him. Old remembered words from Genesis 2:18 came to him: *"It is not good that the man should be alone."* Then the bright proud coat of a streaking blue jay caught his eye, and he followed its path into a lush peach orchard not far away. *Someday,* he thought, *I should build a home out here for*—for whom? He sat up and looked around. *For Maggie and me?* All of a sudden the possibility filled his mind, and with it feeling for her such as he had never had. He stood right up on his big booted feet, squishing a squash beneath them.

He looked heavenward. *What?* Then he began to stalk around the neatly laned garden. *Maggie. Oh my, my, my.* Then all he could see was her crafted spare body, not even her pretty delicate face and fiery tresses, with its auspiciously swelling femininity in the most surprising yet appropriate places. But he was not really seeing her as much as he was feeling her, in his breathless soul. Then came bolting into his mind one—no, two—scenes of which he had taken scarce note when he witnessed them but which now threatened to knock him physically to the rich ground beneath him. Twice in recent weeks he had caught full views of Maggie's slender perfect feminine ankles beneath the layers of long hoops. Once in the dining room, when he did not allow his gaze to linger, and once outside as she stepped into a buggy, when he did. *Nearly two years it has been,* he realized. His view darted upward again, but this time to the warming yellow ball. *It's not that hot today is it?* he thought with a squint, wondering and amazed at the source of this sudden insanity. He had not felt such enthralling passion even when he fell for—Ellie.

Oh God forgive me, my darling Ellie, he thought. *From whence these overpowering thoughts, when the Southern Presbyterian Church in its teachings and its practices clearly forbid the coming together of a man with a sister of his deceased spouse?*

CHAPTER 22

NOW THE BOARD OF VISITORS OF THE VIRGINIA MILITARY Institute met for its annual session in Lexington. The slow whirring of the academic building's high ceiling fans served as the only mitigation against the sweltering Virginia July that hung on the tense assembled men, most of whom would rather have been in discussion of nearly anything other than the supposed mismanagement of the school's Department of Natural and Experimental Philosophy, and Major Thomas J. Jackson's continued academic career.

John Strange made the case against Jackson before the board on behalf of the disgruntled alumni. Morgan Frost made it for the current cadets and Lexington. Superintendent Smith, the sweat streaming down his face not sourced merely in the oppressive heat, could only stand up for Jackson's "bravery, conscientiousness, and goodness as a man"—but, in earnestness, not his professorial success.

After fourteen straight hours, when all had said, or shouted, their piece and the last faint rays of the day's heat ball melted into the shadows of the campus's well-manicured lawns, and with nearly as many opinions still abroad about Jackson as were men assembled in the room, board member and Virginia adjutant general William "Old Frederick" Richardson, who had said nothing all day, rose to his feet.

His considerable jowls drooping and the years of his life cut deep into his face like a hard chisel into granite, Richardson nonetheless maintained the ruddy complexion and barrel chest that had accompanied him through land and flaming sea in the War of 1812 against the British, a partial scalping in the Blackhawk Indian Wars, and malaria and a shoulderful of Santa Anna's shell in the Mexican War.

"Gentlemen," he said simply, "I propose we table the matter of Major Jackson and his department for further consideration."

At that, even one of the ceiling fans joined the silence by ceasing its motion in midwhir. But the one man who would most certainly have objected to laying the matter on the table, Frost, had been taken suddenly ill with a withering attack of diarrhea only moments before and was already being spirited home in Dr. Ryan's buckboard. Though doubled over in pain as he left the institute, by the time Frost arrived home, the only evidence remaining of his sickness was an unfortunate pair of dress gray trousers that Mrs. Frost, in true feminine intuitiveness, had been after Morgy to get rid of anyway.

Frost raced back to the VMI, only to arrive as the last board members filed from the darkened academic building.

The board of visitors may have been too sapped and worn to object to Jackson's reprieve, but Russell was ready to take the low road again, as his forebears might have against the nefarious Campbell clan, when Frost brought the news to McDowell's sumptuous walnut paneled office in town.

It looked surely to Frost, McDowell, and Charles Mason as if the thick green veins in Russell's bull neck would finally burst free from their moorings, as they had long threatened. The planter stormed from one of McDowell's rooms to the other.

"Aye, were this me rooms, Sam McDowell, I'd surely be about rending them asunder even now," Russell shouted.

"But I don't understand why no one raised an objection," McDowell said to Frost, "why you did not."

Perhaps the six eyes burning into him were more to account for the sudden crimson wave over Morgan Frost's shamed features, or perhaps it was his own embarrassment at the recollection of his sudden, quite temporary, indisposed condition, or perhaps it was a combination of both. But he thought he felt his discomfort returning when Russell stormed from the room, barking over his shoulder, "Aye, that fountain of wild looney confusion, that inmate-run asylum up on the hill has certainly seen its last penny from Will Russell."

Lylburn, waiting outside with the surly Ben by the buggies, heard his master coming.

"Lawdy he sound mad this time," Lylburn said with a frown. "Way Mister Frost looked when he got here, the Goober must have done all right today."

"Hmmph," Ben grunted.

Then Russell was with them, slugging from his metal flask, Lylburn noted with disappointment and, for perhaps the first time, actual fear. The planter, his lips wet, stared at the two slaves. Both averted their gazes. But Russell needed them not to. He needed something or somebody upon which to vent this most urgent and startled anger. When he was younger, he beat on men sometimes when his blood rose. In recent years, in secret whenever possible, he sometimes beat certain of his horses or kicked specific mangy dogs that lounged around his land. He had never beaten his slaves, partly out of remembrance of and respect for his beloved departed wife and partly because of the hard practical truth that the considerable and growing financial investment in human property militated against him and other owners physically harming the slave. An industrial city factory could merely dredge up more immigrant, colored, or child labor, in which it had virtually no investment, to replace that which it used up. A slaveowner had his entire fortune wrapped up in his property: human, animal, and land. Rarely was the slaveowner foolish and irresponsible enough to physically harm his blacks.

But Will Russell, sans the rudder of his life for the nine years since his wife's death, felt it all pressing in on him. He wanted to grab Lylburn by his collar and sling him against the buggy, then grab him around the neck with one tough hand and shake him up and down.

"You're scum, they're all scum," Russell snarled, his spit sprinkling Lylburn's contorted black face like a garnish of cottage cheese.

Just as he raised his hand to strike Lylburn, he saw Ben charging around the buggy to stop him. Russell dropped his hand, jerked his Colt's revolver from its holster—he had begun packing the pistol wherever he went ever since the news hit about John Brown—and got it aimed just as one of Ben's cheekbones bumped into it. The strapping slave froze, his eyes growing wide in horror. Keeping his other hand on Lylburn's neck, Russell cocked the hammer back and stared up at the hulking Ben. A sly grin started from somewhere off in the corners of his mouth like the first tiny shoots of the spring crops emerging from the black rich Virginia earth.

For a long moment, Ben's gaze fixed on the long barrel of the .44, and Russell's fixed on those huge white eyes of Ben's.

Lylburn was too terrified even to pray, but the Lord heard the groanings of his spirit and the entire situation suddenly struck Russell as extraordinarily humorous. He reared back his thick head and laughed, then let the hammer return to its normal resting place and pulled back the gun.

Ben needed no further cue. He turned and ran on foot until he reached the freedman's house miles down the valley near Staunton where he had been told he could begin a long trek north until he reached a place called "Kanadee." There, he could not by law be fetched back to Sam McDowell as he could if caught by lawmen or bounty hunters in the Northern states. For only months later the Supreme Court of the United States would affirm in its famed *Dred Scott vs. Sandford* decision that residence, even of a prolonged nature, in a free state did not automatically free a slave.

Russell turned to Lylburn, saw the fear that racked the boy's eyes, and remembered a similar fear of his own long ago as a small boy when once a renegade Indian had him by the throat and would have finished him were it not for the axe of his cousin Iain that split the man's spine. Then an awesome thought pierced the Scot's mind, a thought that had long ago been accepted by most every other land-owner in Rockbridge County. *Why, this African boy is truly as human as I,* he thought, a dawn waking something in him long dead.

Taking his hand off the frightened youth and gently patting the boy's shoulder, Russell said, "Come on, lad. Let's go home." Then, thinking of the wife and two children who had perished there, he added, "Such as home is."

And he did not again lay a hand on one of his slaves, though he was not bereft of other questionable deeds against slave and free, nor did any other slave owner in all of Rockbridge County, save Sam McDowell.

Late the next day, after Maggie had rocked for a long while in Jackson's chair, she heard her father enter the home downstairs. Only then did she notice that the remaining rays of the day's light had grown long and pale through the side window of her bedroom, next to which she rocked. *I must have dozed off; it's nearly time for supper,* she thought with a start. Her eyes felt better, though. The dull aching pain they occasionally thrust upon her, pain that infrequently expanded into sharp, stabbing hurt, was most easily assuaged by clos-ing them for an hour or two. The energy expenditure engendered by the pain then provided easy entry into sleep. Dr. Cartwright in Rich-mond had recommended her visitation to a colleague of his in Bos-ton. She could not as yet clear her crowded mind to focus on such a trip, which would take her away from Lexington for some weeks.

Her single concern now lay in discovering just what the Presbyte-rian Book of Church Order said regarding the marriage of a person to their dead spouse's sibling. She heard the familiar heavy steps of her father clacking up the hard dark wooden staircase. No, she didn't think after all she could wait through supper to ask him. She would speak with him now.

She found him in his room, sitting at his desk and flipping through some mail. Outside the window behind him she saw the white fluffy blossoms of dogwood, aglow with the splendid closing sheen of eventide.

"Hello, my Maggie," came the sure deep voice that grew strangely high when he delivered his greatest preaching. The sunstreaks slicing through the dogwoods lent his fluffy white beard the same aura as that possessed by those trees.

Were the subject Homer, Virgil, Keats, Hawthorne, Bach, Handel, Michelangelo, the Founding Fathers, or even the Lexington Presbyterian Poor and Colored People's Benevolence Ministry, she could have picked, charted, and commanded the conversation. But the Presbyterian Book of Church Order and its application to her most intimate thoughts and personal dreams—well, it seemed supper time had arrived after all.

Again she could not eat, so the tea tasted better than usual that evening as she sat reading *Shakespeare's Sonnets* in her favorite armchair in the sitting room. Her gaze lifted upward as the faint sweet melody of the ancient wooden music box her father's Scots-Irish ancestors had brought from the Old Country wafted down from his room. Strauss' *The Emperor's Waltz*. How her mother had loved it. What kept that little contraption in one piece the way her father played it, especially since Rush had died, she could not figure.

Junkin's sudden appearance in the doorway startled her. She had not heard him descend the stairs. Perhaps he came down the back stairway.

"Hello, Father," she said.

He wore the beautiful burgundy satin robe Rush had given him just before her condition nosedived. Its gold piping still gleamed. Beneath it he wore his pajamas and his lightweight summer slippers. But he carried no book, an unusual occurrence, especially when no one other than family was in the house. Jackson was away at the Franklin meeting.

"Hello, my Maggie." He sat in the straight-backed antique walnut chair across from her. He seemed a shade nervous, also unusual for him who was usually so sure and certain of himself, his beliefs, and his place in the world. "How is *Silverwood* coming?" he asked after a moment.

"Fine," she replied.

"Good."

They both sat staring at the other, then away at other things such as the piano, the empty fireplace, and the thick Oriental rug Washington College graduate Jonathan Bennett had brought back the year before from a trip to the Far East.

"So when do you think you'll be ready to submit it?" Junkin asked.

"Soon." Her face was flushed.

When the old Junkin family grandfather clock against the far wall chimed the eight o'clock hour, father and daughter both nearly jumped out of their seats.

After a moment, Maggie sighed and slammed her book shut.

"My little redhead has something on her keen mind besides *Silverwood,*" Junkin said.

She tried to speak, but could not. Never in her life had she ever spoken to her father about anything remotely as difficult as this.

But he was her father. "How is our dear Thomas these days?" he asked. "I have not chanced to visit much with him since I have returned from the presidents' meetings up North."

Her face burned so hotly she looked away in hopes he would not see.

"You and Thomas have been blessed with a deep friendship, have you not?" Junkin's words grew more probing yet more gentle.

She looked down at the worn leather volume of Shakespeare and nodded.

"I would consider him one of the few young men I have known that I consider worthy of the hand of either Ellie or you."

Her heart pounded through her bosom.

He paused a long moment to give her opportunity. She remained silent and motionless.

"And I have always thought you and he had more in common than any young man you have known." He eyed her. "Much more so than he and Ellie had."

Her head shot up. "Father, such a thing to say."

"We loved our dear Ellie. Still do. And yet I have heard the two of you for hours laughing and rejoicing together in his room—in English, Spanish, and Latin. He has always been careful to leave the door slightly open."

Maggie's head swam, but her gaze remained fixed on her father.

"For either of you to have the affection of the other would bring honor to both," he said. That was it.

"But why, Father, why that rule?"

"Yes, *that* rule," he said, his brow furrowing as he leaned back, stretched and crossed his legs, and sighed. "That old confusing detested rule."

"It just is not sensible," she said, "not in our enlightened day. Not in our enlightened church, Father. Our church of all churches that should know better, with our proper high view of God, His majesty, and His glorious Son."

Junkin puffed his craggy cheeks and beard and blew out as though releasing pent-up steam.

"It shan't be a rule much longer, I suspect," he said.

"Does it not seem to you such an archaic precept, Father?"

"Yes, it probably does, my dear." He did not look her in the eye.

"Does the Northern church still have it?"

Now he looked at her. "I believe you will see it pass from them at the next annual meeting."

Her countenance reached plaintively across to him, but she said nothing for a couple of minutes. The grandfather clock clicked and clicked and clicked.

"Yes, it does seem so archaic," she finally said, looking down.

The silence after this lasted so long that the clock chimed for the quarter hour, then kept ticking.

Junkin sat up in his chair and scratched his beard. "Delightful that the major received back his mother's rocking chair," he said.

"His grandmother's, Father," she snapped. "And he received it back nearly six months ago."

"Oh, I—I guess I didn't . . ." Junkin muttered as he slumped back into his chair. After another moment of silence, his brown eyes brightened and he said, "Nice to see Major Preston coming around."

Maggie just stared at him.

Junkin paused, then went on. "Fine man, that, and well able to support—"

"A large family, Father!" she shot. "Seven children—a very large family, indeed!"

Junkin's mouth hung open at an odd angle and he watched her. He knew the volcano capable of emerging from his smallest and eldest. It witnessed the quiet deep reservoir of fury his own soul, rarely now, could evince. Or more accurately, that of his mother and her Celtic forebears.

Now Maggie tossed Shakespeare to Jonathan Bennett's Oriental rug and leapt from her chair. Junkin knew the lava was coming.

"If I ever marry a widower, and especially a widower with children, you may put me in a straitjacket and escort me to the mental sanitarium, Father!" she shouted, a tiny finger thrust at him.

Junkin said nothing as she began to pace the floor.

"It is undoubtedly the silliest, most unnatural, and ungodly law put on the books since the Pharisees and their detestable Talmud!" she barked. She continued to pace, her hands now on her slender hips. "Forbidding a man to marry his dead wife's sister because in God's eyes they're forever brother and sister." She turned and poked the same finger at her father. "The Presbyterian Book of Church Order. Phooey—it reeks of popery, if you ask me!"

"Well now, my dear, I don't recall that anyone did ask you, but I do believe that this controversial prohibition shall eventually be expunged from the Book of Church Order here in the Southern church as well," he said with equal parts kindness, confusion, and regret.

Maggie's shoulders drooped just a bit and turned toward the empty fireplace. After a moment, she spoke, in barely more than a whisper, "Eventually."

Russell, Frost, Mason, and McDowell were not alone in their chagrin at the decision of Richardson and the VMI Board of Visitors regarding Jackson's continued employment. However, the Society of the Alumni, though not thrilled, did feel satisfied that its concerns had been addressed and would now be monitored. If improvement did not evidence itself, the alums now felt confident that the board, under pressure, would deal more severely with Jackson. And after all, most of the alums preferred an improved Jackson and department to a disgraced, departed, not improved Jackson.

The person angriest about the entire affair—and its resolution—was Jackson himself. *Why were the perpetrators of this perfidy not dealt with?* he asked himself as he rode up and down the steep hills that comprised Lexington's network of streets, toward Superintendent Smith's office at the VMI. Until 1850, just before Jackson's arrival in Lexington, the grade of the town's dirt roads was so steep that after heavy rain, some of them were literally impassable. The fatal slide of a mule team and wagon down Washington Street and into a mother and her four children, two of whom were crushed to death, belatedly raised the necessary furor to force the expenditure of funds to soften the grade of several of the most heavily traveled streets. Still, the steepness of some remained severe.

Just past 7:00 A.M., the early August morning already hung over Jackson like an oppressive canopy. *No wonder most of the immigrants remain in the North,* the professor thought to himself. *Prolonged seasons of such heat and humidity enchant very few, especially those accustomed to the green fields of Eire or the mountains of Bavaria.* Then for a fleeting instant, the thought flickered through his mind that should the unthinkable—war amongst the nation itself—occur, the verities of weather should prove of great advantage to the free state sections to the north and west, with their burgeoning populations, not to mention their factories and industry.

Jackson stepped down from his horse, tied it at the hitching rail outside the school's administrative building, where his academic fate had been determined a few weeks before, and headed for F. A. Smith's office.

"I can understand your feelings, Tom," the decent erudite urbane Episcopalian said a few moments later to his erect-backed professor. "But my recommendation is to let this one go. The actions of General Richardson and the board effectively place you beyond the scope of further scrutiny unless something disastrous were to occur, which I do not fear happening. In fact, your position is now stronger than before with all but your few intractable detractors, not just because the board has spoken, but because the process has allowed the complainants a release for their emotions, which often is more important than an acquiescence to their actual stated desires."

Jackson's firm countenance did not betray the anger boiling inside him. Inflammation of the tube leading to his right ear, chronic inflammation of his throat, and a persistent dull ache behind his left eye did not help his demeanor. The board's deflection of the attacks against him brought no more joy to him than would his students' not shooting him in his section room. Why be happy at the absence of commission of an act that should never have been contemplated in the first place? The fact that his name had been sullied by those who should have known better made the issue now the proper dealing with of those miscreants.

"I respectfully request initiation of a formal investigation into the charges brought against me, and of those making them," Jackson repeated.

Smith knew, liked, and respected Jackson. He also knew the major was fortunate to still be in the employ of the school. Going after those whose concerns had been legitimate and widespread would be a fool's errand. The superintendent's eyes brightened as he remembered a piece of news he hoped would mollify Jackson.

"Let me offer you some encouraging news, Tom," Smith said with a broad smile. "We both know the obstacles you have faced in attempting to demonstrate the scientific truths taught in your classroom without benefit of even a basic laboratory." How Jackson did know that, and how the memories of gales and years of scornful cadet laughter were burned into his remembrance. How many times had an experiment put tediously together by him collapsed into broken, smoking disaster at just the instant its objective was to be accomplished?

"Well I have happy news for you, Tom," Smith continued. "The board of visitors has taken notice of the restraints under which you have worked, and in support of you has given authorization for the purchase of a laboratory for your use in the section room." Jackson's blue eyes widened and for a heartbeat a smile threatened to part his sun-burnished face. This was fine news indeed. But then he remembered the purpose of his errand—*no fool's errand this!*—and his grim countenance returned. With this, Smith knew he had lost.

"I am pleased to hear the department shall now possess a laboratory," Jackson said, wincing as a spear of pain shot through his inner ear. "It shall allow enhanced performance of the required experiments." Then Jackson's eye twitched and for a bare instant his carriage leaned forward, almost imperceptibly, before shooting back to its original, and usual, straight-backed posture. Smith's trained eye observed this, as well as a freshly minted bead of perspiration on Jackson's brow.

"Still I am compelled to respectfully request initiation of a formal investigation into the charges brought against me, and of those making them," Jackson repeated again, as if he were regurgitating for the second, third, or fourth time the answer to a question in his classroom that, no matter how many times he recited in identical fashion, memorized to the letter the day before in his room at home, no one could understand.

Smith eyed his subordinate. Of all the unlikely scenarios he had ever witnessed in his years at the VMI. *You are probably the worst professor this institution has endured in its nearly twenty years of operation,* Smith thought, sitting comfortably in his chair with his legs crossed. *Students attempt to brain you with everything from spit wads to bricks. Faculty colleagues roll their eyes when the subject of your tutorial acumen is broached in their presence. Alumni who have sat under you clamor for your dismissal. Townspeople produce jokes about you and your section room, jokes often more lighthearted and merciful than the reality of those benighted classes. Yet here you sit, preparing to assault all of these, most of whom are perfectly correct in their concerns about you.*

But Smith had to admit that he would also trust his life to this man who sat indignantly before him. The superintendent too had heard the stories through the years of Jackson's apologies to and aiding of various cadets and others, including Lexington blacks, whom he felt he had wronged or whom he felt needed assistance. The man, beset with flawed humanness, also walked in honor and upright steadfast integrity in a day when many still talked of such notions but fewer and fewer seemed truly to practice them.

Were I to suffer insult or hurt, here is the man I should want to take up my cause, Smith thought to himself, *for I suspect he should defend it, if needs be, even unto death.* The old psalm of another warrior, King David, called out to him: *"I have pursued mine enemies and overtaken them: neither did I turn again till they were consumed."*

Wiping a bullet of sweat from his own brow, Smith sighed and instructed Jackson, "Use these sheets of paper and articulate your reasons for requesting this investigation."

CHAPTER 23

"WHY, THANKS MIZ JUNKIN," WILLY PRESTON SAID, BEAMING from one freckle-sided end of his beautiful face to the other as he stood at the front entrance to the president's home. Never had he seen such a large pie. And it was still steaming from the oven!

Maggie tousled the thirteen-year-old's thick mop of auburn hair. *And never,* she thought, *have I baked a pie—large or otherwise.* Without Ruthie's help, this one would not have been baked.

An expression of heavenly satisfaction displaced Willy's smile as he allowed the steaming sweet tangy aroma of gooseberry to curl up into his nostrils.

Maggie giggled, in a way Ellie used to do, but she herself rarely did. Children still irritated her to distraction, and even this bright wonderful young boy from such sturdy stock bothered her by the sheer number of his visits. Yet Willy seemed to free her to giggle and laugh and do other things, like bake gooseberry pies.

"You deserve it, young Willy," Maggie said. "The major's colored Sunday school could never have made it the way it has without the way you have been helping with the young people. It is still growing, you know. We had over 150 for the first time ever last Sunday. I don't know what is more valuable, your teaching, your singing and piano playing, or just the way you love and minister to those boys and girls, Willy. It's quite uncommon for a boy of your age, you know."

Now Willy's face grew hotter than the heavy pie he stood holding. Blood rushed across his chin, cheeks, and forehead, and he shifted in embarrassment from one foot to the other, gazing down at the pie.

"Well, you'd best run along now, Willy," she said. "You don't want to keep Major Preston waiting on you for supper."

When he looked up, his honey-colored eyes radiant, Maggie thought, *And beyond all else, this boy's face is prettier than any girl's his age in town. But he has many other admirable qualities that super-sede that, which anyway is a work of God and his parentage and not of himself.*

"Miz Junkin, can you keep a secret—from anyone—if I tell you one?" the boy asked, his face full and vulnerable.

She smiled, thinking, *What a precious boy,* and remembering her own long-ago season of carefree girlhood. "Why, certainly, Willy. What is it you wish to tell me?"

Again, the nervous shifting of feet. A blue jay called from a nearby elm. "Well, Father, you know, has been alone since Mother died almost a year ago." Willy looked up at Maggie, his face at once hesitant and hopeful. "And—" Now the rich honey eyes filmed over and the boy's square sturdy jaw—*like that of his father's, that fine, dear, though increasingly bothersome, widower,* Maggie thought—went slack and he looked back down at the pie.

"And what, Willy?" she asked, wondering if Major Preston needed help in choosing new curtains or in dealing with a particularly trying problem with one of his children.

Willy looked back up. "You wouldn't ever want to be a mother to seven children, would you, Miz Junkin?"

The words so stunned Maggie that she could only utter, "What?" as her mind went cloudy.

"You know," Willy proceeded, a bit braver now that the actual pro-nouncement had squirmed out into daylight. "Marry my pa and come live with us and—" The thought of tender loving motherly arms chopped Willy's words in midsentence. He, the bravest of the seven, had never parted with so much as one tear since Sallie Preston had cou-rageously parted with earthly life eleven months before—the same Sallie Preston who had always said, half in humor, half in earnest, that should she depart betimes from the earth, Maggie Junkin was who she wanted for her children's stepmother. Now something large and sharp seemed to be snagged in Willy's throat. Again his eyes fixed on the pie. This time, though, a large dewy tear plopped onto the crisp brown crust.

Maggie's mouth opened in amazement. From somewhere came feelings she had never before experienced, and she wanted to hold this boy and squeeze him until all the hurts she suddenly realized dwelt within him went away. For how well she knew the piercing grief of loss. Yes, how well, her own mother just a few years before, and of course—

Suddenly gooseberry pies and Sunday school classes and pretty freckled faces were forgotten, and she was holding him and he was weeping into her soft and safe bosom long wrenching tears of lost-ness and left-behindness. And of course, despite her awkwardness and reluctance in dealing with a sobbing child, she knew those feel-ings. She had written poems about them.

After he had left, his sumptuous bounty seasoned with the cleans-ing rain of the beginnings of growing up in an uncertain world that made heaven all the more certain and all the more needed, Maggie felt the strongest urge to rush upstairs and write. But first she would have to go to Major Jackson's scuffed scarred old chair and rock as she often did when he was gone and she had to think. For now she began to rehearse in her mind that Jackson's close friend, teaching colleague, and business partner Major John Preston must have been entertaining similar thoughts to his own son's. For indeed, that fine, honorable, handsome man of integrity had so strongly pursued her in recent months—mostly in the course of spiritually sanctified activities at the church, of course—that she wondered at her own blindness in not recognizing the man's feelings and intent until now.

Back in the kitchen peeling onions (Moses was home sick with the croup), Ruthie pondered the heartrending scene she had surrepti-tiously witnessed moments before at the front doorway to the presi-dent's home. She had long since learned where every board and stair that creaked lay in the house, as well as which ones kept secret her oft-stealthy whereabouts. After all, how could the person entrusted with the operation and well-being of an entire household properly acquit herself of those duties if she did not have at least a working knowledge of the issues, fears, and concerns occupying the minds of those under her charge?

It pleased Ruthie to see the friendship deepening between Maggie and the boy, Willy. And yes, what a fine boy he was. From a fine fam-ily. And a fine father. And Ruthie had for quite some time seen that about which Maggie in her reclusive bookishness and learning hadn't probably a clue: John Preston was desperately smitten with the little redhead.

This all caused Ruthie, despite herself, to smile. *Lawdy,* she thought, a wide grin flashing across her face, *got two men now, near best friends, down serious with the love disease for the same girl. And she live under my roof. Lawdy.* Ruthie felt as though she could pin-point the exact date Major Jackson had consciously fallen for his departed wife's sister—and it was a good spell after she, Ruthie, knew he had fallen. As she thought of the two tall, handsome soldier-educators, she sucked in a deep breath, then blew it out. *Lord, I don't know if the girl can handle all this sudden prosperity at once,* she thought. *Maybe I'll have to help set her straight on some things. 'Course, the heart has its own reasons. And I know the girl, and I know which man she love. And sure enough it's the one she shouldn't.*

Then her thoughts turned to the disquieting appearance earlier in the day of the handsome black freedman Mr. Stokes. Ostensibly coming to the president's home with a new shipment of books from somewhere up North, he had finessed a private conversation with Ruthie in the library about the overland railroad or underground pipeline or whatever it was called.

Ruthie had long heard tales of the effort. She knew Big Ben McDowell had made it, if not yet to total freedom, at least to the harbor of white abolitionists in Pennsylvania, en route to Canada. What had jolted her like the kick of a stubborn mule was the smiling Stokes' soft-spoken statement: "You are the person folks say we need helping us in Rockbridge County."

Of course, she had threatened Stokes with exposure and thrown him out. Did he know the charges possible against him for such utterances anywhere in the American states, especially in the South? She had so many reasons to reject his invitation she could not count them. Not the least of them was love for and loyalty to the Junkins and others. Aiding in what amounted to the theft of expensive "property" (of course, her fellow coloreds were more than property, but the fact was white folks owned them, had since their European forebears had founded the nation, and had wrapped up their fortunes in the purchase of and providing for them) and betraying those owners who had always been kind to her was beyond her comprehension, even if she possessed the desire and courage to do it. She possessed neither. Nonetheless, news of Ben cheered her. He had been the miserable brunt of a miserable man's bullying.

Maggie rose the next day rested and vigorous. Nearly always her small energized frame charged from early rising until laying down in the evening, even if the charging was sometimes more mental than physical. But shadows had often enveloped both mind and soul, though since the Catholic church experience in France, a freshness and new hope of heart had illumined her, evidencing itself in a larger concern for the feelings and welfare of those outside herself.

Still, though, she battled the encroachments of her own peculiar strain of the intellect's skepticism. Though humbled, broken, and thus more kindly to others, she still wondered before God as to why He allowed so much suffering in the world. Oh, why could she not have dear Ellie's blissful trusting faith and acceptance that God's sovereign will was working itself out perfectly in the world, despite the evils that abounded? And she wondered if He truly had charted for her, if not a happy course, at least a good course, and one relatively free of continual heart-wrenching suffering, pain, and loss.

Oh, God, she asked Him, not crying out as much as asking a question of a humane, powerful, intimate relation, *am I truly in Your sight? Are my day-to-day, even minute-to-minute, concerns truly concerns of Yours? Are You, Heavenly Father, truly working for my best?*

That reminded her of Jackson's favorite verses of Scripture, Romans 8:28–30, the ones by which for some years now he had truly seemed to live: "And we know that all things work together for good to them that love God, to them who are the called according to his purpose . . . whom he . . . did predestinate . . . called . . . justified . . . and . . . glorified."

And the verse that followed: "What shall we then say to these things? If God be for us, who can be against us?"

These thoughts cheered Maggie, increasingly as the day went on. Cheered her that God did take notice of her, and was for her and did work on behalf of her. Her heart swelled and her pen flowed on what she now knew would be not only her personal purging and catharsis, but her mightiest work of literature: "He doth use the broken reed to stablish the mighty forest."

The prospect of Thomas Jackson's strong arms around her for all of life's years as they had once long ago so briefly been midst the swirling current of the Niagara River cheered her most of all, and her heart, which she herself knew to be "deceitful above all things, and desperately wicked: who can know it?" had in stealth even from herself, convinced her that Clause XXIV:4 was not only archaic and wrong, but soon, very soon, to be turned out as it should have been long ago. *Actually,* she thought in derisive condescension, *dour, evil men, prey to Anglican writ and thus that of the Papacy, should never have written it in the first place.*

Oh, yes, she thought, her heart aflutter like a newly winged monarch, *did not the godly bookseller and elder John Lyle—bless his heart, so ill now—himself say not long ago that he expected expunging of the rule at the next general convention of the Southern Presbytery?*

Even as she wrote of human loss and sorrow, even as she birthed *Silverwood,* her mind raced simultaneously along on a separate track, as she had trained it to do, marveling at the prospect of life not alone, but with him! His merry eyes, his precious silent laugh, his rigid straight-backed righteousness. And other, unthinkable, thoughts that forced her to rise and walk among the morning glories and jonquils that wrapped the president's home in their loving bright care.

She could not keep the smile from her face, which had so often and so long frowned that thin sad creases descended downward at oblique angles from the corners of her fragile pretty mouth. Surely now, they would make it. Their bond, forged in the furnace of mutual tragedy and despair, would outlast the silly contrived machinations of small minded busybodied little men. He and she would not break the rule; they would outlive it.

It could not be clearer. Right there in Clause XXIV:4 of the Book of Church Order. "A man shall not marry his deceased wife's sister." In the eyes of the Presbyterian Church, Thomas Jonathan Jackson and Margaret Junkin Preston were forever brother and sister. Any other kind of relationship was out of the question.

Jackson looked heavenward. *Thank You, Heavenly Father, as always, for Your kind, merciful, and clear instruction, he thought. "Thy word is a lamp unto my feet and a light unto my path." But why do I have these feelings, O Lord? Are they of You? If not, then whom?*

Then Jackson did something unusual for him. He rose from his knees before the completion of his prayers and walked to the window of his room. Looking out, he saw the verdant green surroundings of General George Washington's namesake school. And beyond, just a few hundred yards away, the wide flat expanse of the VMI parade ground. A boy had asked him questions about Christ just the other day on those grounds, after drills concluded. Jackson was able to share the unsearchable and ineffable riches of Him. How much easier and more natural it was to speak of the Savior than of worldly matters! He did not have to memorize or prepare or practice that presentation. *Of course,* he mused, *I guess in a way I do rehearse every day of my life in my private times with You, Lord, and many times during each day.*

Jackson smiled as he thought of the Lexington Presbytery's progressively greater support over the past year of the Negro Sunday school. After its somewhat controversial genesis, the classes had quadrupled in size and now possessed the official endorsement of the church's ruling body for the county.

But ruling bodies and Sunday school classes were not what now claimed Jackson's attentions. As he felt the balmy early evening breeze waft in through the open window, with not as many mosquitoes as usual, he could think only of scarlet tresses sometimes neatly bound in place but more often escaped to roam free and untamed as she whose now-cherished crown they adorned.

Jackson chased away the encroaching impermissible thoughts of those scarlet tresses with a fevered shake of his head. Then a nightingale called and the first sweet scent of the valley of Virginia at eventide beckoned to him. Out there? Was God summoning him to come out into the high hills that encased Lexington? *"He went up into a mountain apart to pray: and when the evening was come, he was there alone."*

Jackson felt a strange compulsion, in midprayer, to walk right through the door of his room, out of the house, and to the stable to get his mount. Then, to the hills . . . *But Maggie will be here any time—no, she is passing out food at the church with the benevolence ministry tonight,* he thought.

Even as he looked out the window to the sky and voiced the words, "Is this what You want, Sir?" the answer was imprinted on his heart. Thirty seconds later Jackson was marching down the sidewalk to get his horse.

He reached a small clearing perfumed with lilacs and cedars after the sun had dipped into the western horizon. Behind him, he could just discern the ghostly peaks of the Blue Ridge, purple in day but now blackest black against the star-strewn, navy blue, summer Virginia sky. Ahead, a vibrant fiery belt of dying coral heaven blazed above the distant long line of the Alleghenies. Beyond them, the West.

Jackson tied his chestnut mount to a maple tree and found a seat on the grassy floor. Ever had God's creation beckoned him forth when he needed healing and balm for the soul.

What did not make sense in the rooms of town homes flowed easily into his understanding, for instance, when he knelt with grimy hands among the squashes, beans, and onions. He thought of others who had come aside with the weight of the world on their shoulders. Closer to his heart, he thought of those who had come aside to reckon with loss. With sacrifice. With offering. As the still air cooled and sweetened, he thought of Abraham upon Mount Moriah with his only son Isaac, by the literal timeline of the biblical account not a boy but a full grown man of at least forty years of age. And Jackson thought of Him who "was wounded for our transgressions."

A hawk soared calling across the dying crimson celestial embers. What had happened? From whence this tempest in his heart? And of all people, Ellie's sister. Shame and excitement at once pulsed through his body. Only his left eye ached a bit tonight, though the hearing seemed stymied in his right ear. He thought of dear Maggie and the increasing difficulties posed by her eyes. Oh, how those enticing azure eyes danced. How they called, convicted, and unsettled! On the point of questioning God that He would allow such a tidal wave of feeling and, yes, passion to overtake him about something that was forever to be denied, at least until the church revoked Clause XXIV:4, Jackson remembered the Scriptures he held in his raw strong hand. He could not now see the thick veined topography of that hand, nor the holy decrees that sanctified the soft worn pages of his testament. But its blessed writ lay engraved on his troubled heart: "God's judgments are altogether good and right and helpful to the soul." Yet, was Clause XXIV:4 the judgment of God? Or flawed human heresy? Sin, as the Bible indicated that which missed the mark of God? How in fact did it, did any of the church's edicts differ from the often despised volumes of Papist dogma?

"Oh Lord," he shouted aloud to the silent heavens, "have you called me out here for a purpose other than what I have thought? Am I to take my stand as Luther, Cranmer, Knox, and so many others have, even back to Paul, Peter, and the other sainted apostles—every one of them murdered for his faith, save John who saw the apocalyptic vision then was dropped into a vat of scalding oil? Even as *He* did?"

Jackson stood and paced across the clearing, crunching flowers beneath his boots. His left arm shot into the sky. As the Scriptures spoke to him, his trouble mounted. He was to be under the authority of God, first and always. But God had said, "Obey your leaders, and pray for them." And part of what his spiritual leaders had ordered of him was to obey Clause XXIV:4, was it not? Or did they say, "Obey all we and the Scriptures say, except Clause XXIV:4"? Or did they say, "Henceforth, do not obey Clause XXIV:4; it is an archaic and needless little cuss of a rule, and will eventually be overturned anyhow"?

Had not, after all, God ever directed him along the course that was best for him? And if the preference of that course was not immediately, or ever, apparent, had God not first stated, "Trust in the LORD with all thine heart; and lean not unto thine own understanding. In all thy ways acknowledge him, and he shall direct thy paths"? And, "If ye love me, keep my commandments"?

Somewhere deep inside pulsed another truth Jackson had tried to ignore but could no longer. Having been a pure man who only at age thirty had drunk with deep rapture the bliss of the marriage bed, then having suddenly lost that blessing—for nearly two years—he knew well now the truths of the sainted apostle Paul's words, "It is better to marry than to burn."

Only could he continue in close proximity to Margaret Junkin by marrying her. If he could not do that, he must soon dishonor her, God, and himself.

"But I love her, Father!" he screamed upward. "I want her—I need her!"

His words echoed off adjacent hills and came back to him, not as a rebuke but as a gentle reminder of his smallness, his silliness, his dullness. And again he remembered Abraham, who had early saddled his ass and ridden to a high place, tied his son, and, tears streaming down his face, lifted the knife to slay him, only because God had asked him to do so. Then Jackson remembered that God in His kindness and mercy had said to Abraham those words so unreachable and unfathomable by the frail human mind: "'Lay not thine hand upon the lad, neither do thou any thing unto him: for now I know that thou fearest God, seeing thou hast not withheld thy son, thine only son from me.'"

And Jackson knew that millennia later, another of God's chosen who would eventually offer his own life up as a sacrifice had recalled that Abraham "staggered not at the promise of God through unbelief; but was strong in faith, giving glory to God."

And so did God then use Abraham greatly. Jackson hung his head. *Yes, Lord, it is necessary, to restore the fair Jackson name.* Then he shook that handsome head with violence, looked upward again, and called out against his ancient enemies, to let God know he agreed with Him that ambition and human glory were indeed repugnant interlopers and detestable surrogates in the working out of God's glory. "No, no, no, for Your name Lord, not mine, for Your sake." And then he hung his head again and he began to weep many heartfelt tears. They were tears of joy and love that he, an earthly orphan, had a heavenly Father who so loved him as to provide only His best for him, and protect Jackson from danger and unforeseen harm. And they were tears of sadness that the treasure of his heart, for whom he felt a firestorm of desire beyond any he had ever known, must be placed on that same altar where Abraham had placed the apple of his own world-weary eye.

How had Maggie's eyes seemed to come finally open about Tom Jackson just as she began to fear God might be intending to close them from the rest of the world! And yes, he had assuredly developed feelings for her, too, of this she felt certain. He had evidenced toward her the same earnest but sometimes stumbling manner he had toward dear Ellie when smitten by her.

Now as she waited on the settee in the sitting room for Jackson's return from taking soup and crackers to a sick VMI cadet, ladylike as she could muster, she felt a pang of remorse at the oceans of resentment she had spent on both Tom and Ellie and what they had together. For an instant, her head drooped and the guilt of it—*so little time they had, after all*—nearly overcame her. But no, she would not allow this long awaited happiness, this sublime opportunity for a new and fulfilling life to be tarnished in the least by the remembrance of emotions that, while regrettable and unchristian, were natural and quite involuntary.

Ruthie had scolded her: "A lady in the South stepping out on a night during the week with a man she is not even courting, alone, after dark—why, you sure showing your Pennsylvany through clear this time, child." Her father was at the school chairing a budget meeting with the regents. Julia was at home, but immersed in preparations for and dreams about her own upcoming wedding with a fine young Lexingtonian named Junius Fishburne who had succeeded the departed Joe Kennedy as a law clerk for Judge Brockenbrough. So, other than Ruthie and Jackson, no one knew of her impending stroll through town. And that was just fine with her. It was no one else's business, Clause XXIV:4 or no.

She tossed back her head and stared at the ceiling, sparks of light dancing off her sumptuous eyes like leaping fiery phantoms. She closed her lids and saw a new, better world, one that now seemed eminently possible to her.

It was a world of children—hers with Tom. Of love—hers and his. Of life—long and sure and made better and more meaningful by walking through it with him. Her heart leapt in her chest and her head and body swung forward, her eyes opening.

"Whee!" she fairly shouted, her happiness resounding off the far wall, before which stood the piano Ellie had played so well.

Then the large oaken door swung open and Jackson marched in.

She rose to greet him, then remembered better and sat, waiting for him.

What a handsome and honest face, she thought as he stepped into the sitting room. *And serious tonight, too—more serious than usual.* And no card either, though he expressed no less graciousness to her than normal.

"Has it been a difficult day for you, Major Jackson?" were her first words.

He straightened and looked her in the eye. "Yes it has, Maggie."

But she had other things on her mind and purposed to turn the day to the better for him. Not waiting for his usual proffered arm, she ran hers through his and led the way outside, her excitement and anticipation bracing her against the expected wind and chill. Instead, the night had stilled. So still was it in fact that she slowed her rapid gait.

"What is it?" Jackson asked.

"Why, where went the breeze?" she asked.

"I don't know," he replied, looking up at the sky that was suddenly bereft of any clouds at all. A full milky moon, curtained behind the puffy silver banks moments before, now beamed down from high above the Blue Ridge.

"Strange everything cleared off, isn't it?" she asked, curious and happy.

"Yes," Jackson whispered. Then he gathered himself, squeezed her arm, and led across the lawn toward town.

Mostly, she spoke. Some about Northern anger with the Southern-European trading axis. Some about the heated congressional battles over tariffs. And some about the Crimean War situation. A certain already famed, English light cavalry brigade had launched an ill-conceived but heroic charge into the teeth of an overwhelming Russian position. Horse against cannon and grossly outnumbered. All of it, according to early accounts, due to bureaucratic bungling. And yet already was it capturing the imagination of the Western world.

Jackson had heard the story as well, from Preston, after a business meeting in which they consummated a partnership with two other townsmen to purchase a tannery. He and the VMI founder had also begun to discuss the mutual purchase of some timber lands down in North Carolina. The more Jackson saw of Preston, the more impressed was he with the squire, who had recently been elected an elder at the Presbyterian church at the same time Jackson was elected deacon.

Preston's patient and pacific example during the grief of losing a woman who had born him nine children, two of them already with their Maker, proved not the least impressive of his attributes in Jackson's eyes.

"My, that John Preston can play the piano almost as well as Ellie could," Jackson blurted suddenly. "And he speaks seven languages. I barely know Spanish."

"Nonsense, Major," Maggie replied in an instant. "You've written me entire letters in the Spanish hand. And you've qualities Major Preston could not hope to have."

"Well, he is certainly a man of no mean estate," Jackson said.

"Most of it inherited, no doubt," she said, the harsh tone turning Jackson's head briefly toward her. Her delicate narrow chin jutted out as defiant as the battle flag of a John Paul Jones' warship. Jackson gnawed at his thin lower lip and glanced around. He spotted a bench across the hard-packed dirt street. Its back leaned against the iron retaining wall in front of the Presbyterian church, whose sturdy, lunar-radiant steeple rose into the sky as strong and sure as the theology of one of John Calvin's twenty-two *Institutes*. *It will do as well as any,* Jackson thought.

"Maggie, would you care to sit a spell over by the church?" he asked.

Her face glowed as she turned toward him, only partly because of the moon that bathed it. He had never thought her a beautiful woman until that moment. His chin dropped just a notch and his gait slowed. He cleared his throat and led the way off the sidewalk into the street. The sad specter of drunken, one-eyed Wayne Marley charging his steed down the same street a few nights before returned to Jackson. *What a waste,* Jackson thought as he assayed the diminishing possibilities for the young man Jackson had once thought so promising but who now seemed bent on his own self-destruction through alcohol, gambling, and, town gossip had it, several different women of ill repute in the poor white trash shanty section across the Maury River.

Then he and Maggie were together on the bench, her crinoline skirts pressed closer to him than ever before. The intoxicating fragrance of verbona sachet, which he had never before smelled on Maggie, wafted up through his nostrils and so filled his already light head that he thought he might faint.

At this last, in artful feminine collusion with the rest, he almost did not say what he had planned to say. And that would have been most unlike Major Tom Jackson, for when he set his face to do something, it was set like flint.

The church bell tower rang once, signaling the half hour. He half shook his head, his eyes darting upward. *Could it be I was wrong about what You want?* Other men might wonder the length of their earthly days, but Tom Jackson knew God had ordained all things from before the foundation of the world; so while he might regret what he was about to say, he would never again doubt it.

He started abruptly to speak because he knew if he waited even one more instant his fainting heart would bid him propose a different destiny for the both of them than he yet intended.

"I shall leave in the morn for Europe."

He could not turn before then, but now he did, in time to see the pretty jaw drop open.

"Well, Thomas, er, Major, I had no idea."

"I know you didn't, dear sister," he said with all the tenderness of the Gentle Shepherd who was the only one for whom he could commit such an overwhelming act. "And we both know you need to stay—my sister."

She stared at him, then they both looked away. A dog barked somewhere, but she said nothing. He began to fidget. "Please, Maggie, I must solicit your aid in this most difficult matter. For I fear my resolve is not as it normally is. I fear that I have allowed my feelings to take hold against my known understanding of the church's will."

Her head dropped slowly down, her chin touching her mother's favorite old gold broach of Revolutionary War Philadelphia, the broach Maggie had worn for the first time and specially for tonight. Out of the corner of his eye, Jackson saw her small feminine hands clamped together in her lap so tightly that her knuckles glowed white even in the moonlight.

"I just wish . . ." he started.

Then, another long pause. He heard the high song of a mocker from somewhere above and behind on the church.

"That—Ellie never died?" Each one of the soft words marched out alone, under its own power, like rigid pallbearers carrying her earthly future down into the cold gloomy gray yard of the dead.

"Yes." More silence, then a thought struck him and he looked up, his eyes wide and hopeful. "Perhaps we could get a clarification from Father on the intent of the prohibition. Perhaps in some cases they might even—"

She looked him square in the face, tears streaking her smooth cheeks but her eyes strong and clear. "No," she said. "I trust that we are both aware of the intent of the rule. And to reject the authority that God has placed over us is to reject Himself. He who has given us—," on this her eyes filled, then brimmed over, and she began to choke, then bowed her head again, the tears plopping against and caught by her crinoline skirts—"everything."

Only then did Jackson realize what a magnificent work God had done in this sweet dear woman, this woman of honor and elegance and substance. This woman through whom Jackson knew God would now do mighty works. Jackson's own eyes welled over and his granite jaw began to quake. He gnawed again at his lips and wished her for himself so badly that his head began to ring.

She raised her face again, and they stared at one another for a moment with sweet plaintive longing. Then a shadow fell between them. They both looked down. Maggie gasped. Jackson's eyes shot up in the direction of the persistent mockingbird, to the cross that stood high atop the church. The inordinate brilliance of the moon, early so high, held the cross in eclipse. So blinding was the glare that Jackson had to shield his eyes from it.

"Look," said Maggie.

Jackson turned his squinting gaze back to the ground, where the shadow cast by the church cross fell between Maggie and himself. One side of the shadow reached to touch him and the other to touch her, connecting them with its outstretched arms.

Jackson stared at the cross, then at Margaret Junkin's sublime wonder-laden face. He knew then that she would be all right, that he served a high, holy, and unmatchable God, and that though he would tell no living soul, he would love her to his dying day.

CHAPTER 24

HE DID NOT UNDERSTAND WHAT PLACE IN HIS LIFE THE LORD intended for Maggie. But prayer and the daily searching of the Scriptures, like the Bereans, provided sufficient strength, leading, and solace for Jackson—even as the pain of guilt and loss wracked him—without his gathering the input of other men. More and more he found himself keeping his own counsel in the important matters of life. He had found Christian men—not new converts, but those men who had long known the Lord—who too casually sought after the advice of their peers on important matters, either had not studied "to shew thyself approved unto God, a workman that needeth not to be ashamed, rightly dividing the word of truth" or were not particularly desirous of following that revealed will when it inconvenienced them. Therefore they merely looked for escape avenues through other men's counsel.

Now, as the North Atlantic summer sun bronzed his face and the soft sea breeze misted against it, he considered anew the excellencies of her whom he could never have. A deep abiding feeling had impressed him these last many weeks in Europe and in transit to and fro that she would forever reside in a most special of secret places in his heart. For whom could he tell, even if he wanted? He would hold her incomparable treasures and delights—those that God had in His kindness allowed him—for safekeeping in their own cherished compartment. Just as those different ones of her sister resided in an adjacent revered place.

He felt a strange sense of incompleteness, of something that had once been there being now gone, oddly similar to what he had experienced at the loss of Ellie two years before and not unlike the feelings he had heard expressed by men who had lost arms or legs in battle.

Yet at the same time a growing sense of purpose and anticipation pulsed through him. For he was not unaware that sacrifice and a painful turning away from the unlawful were not practiced in a godless vacuum. No, the Almighty delighted in them, honored Himself through them, and rewarded those who practiced their painful disciplines with joys beyond those available through the earthly ways.

Jackson marked the apostle Paul's words of encouragement directed "to them who by patient continuance in well doing seek for glory and honour and immortality, eternal life."

And so had the Lord brought into near-constant remembrance to him these past weeks the assuring words of Hebrews 12:11: "Now no chastening for the present seemeth to be joyous, but grievous: nevertheless, afterward it yieldeth the peaceable fruit of righteousness unto them which are exercised thereby."

These words, in fact, he had just completed penning in the letter to Laura that lay before him. *Oh, Laura, my sorrowful and long-suffering dear—if you would but turn to the Savior!*

He reviewed his words: "My dearest sister, with tears in my eyes, and a heart devoted to my God, I look into the future beyond the limits of this transient life of care; and see the dark gloom that is to exist throughout infinite duration. That whilst I am to shine like a star in the firmament forever, you are to be assigned to unending misery."

He paused, laying the pen down and looking to the sky. *I still cannot fathom, Lord, why You deign to quicken the heart of one and not the other,* he thought. The specter of a precocious little girl with bright eyes and long flapping yellow pigtails leading him on a merry chase through green clover caused Jackson to swallow hard. Such issues were hard because they were not just musty doctrines on yellowed pages, but human, immortal souls. And, in this case, his baby sister, whose most recent correspondence revealed a barely existent marriage of continued strife, and a life of increasing despair, hopelessness, and now, Jackson winced, bitterness.

Yet, through love and loss and the leading of the Gentle Shepherd in his life, he believed he had now come to accept absolutely and unshakeably the words of Holy Writ, even when it spoke to ideas far beyond him, such as God's sovereign election of one soul and not another. Thankfully, Jackson possessed the words of both Dr. Junkin and Dr. White of the Lexington Presbyterian Church: "Ours is not to wonder why Holy and Almighty God would pull one from the fires of perdition and leave another, but rather to marvel that He should rescue *any*, being unworthy and rebellious all." And of course, Paul's towering and precious verses addressing the subject in the first chapter of the epistle to the Ephesians.

"My sister," the letter continued, "do reflect upon my course of life . . . and then consider how I could ever have been satisfied of the truth of the gospel; unless it is true."

As he descended the gangplank from the ship at New York's teeming port, Jackson thought to himself in that sort of half prayer, half thought not uncommon to the man of God whose soul is wrestling with an issue of great import, *If you wish me to follow Your perfect and revealed will, I must call upon Your wisdom, understanding, and strength in that matter.* It was Maggie. And a Maggie he would soon be seeing again (How his heart, against his will, leapt at the prospect!) and with whom he would be sharing the same roof.

Oh Lord, he cried in his heart, looking toward heaven, not even noticing as the New York crowd pushed and shoved him in a manner quite unknown in Virginia, *since knowing Ellie, I have such—needs—now.* At once a great compassion swept him for that great company of souls whose strongest physical yearnings could not within God's law, and love, be met. Yet did he acknowledge at once that such trials could be yet one more means by which his loving heavenly Father tempered him into an unshakable and immovable man of God. *"There hath no temptation taken you . . . but God is faithful, who will not suffer you to be tempted above that ye are able; but will . . . make a way to escape, that ye may be able to bear it."*

Jackson sucked in a great gust of breath and thought how much more potent were these urges, especially in one who for a season had experienced their rapturous sating, than most others with which he had dealt: his tongue, his pursuit of the material, his diet, and earlier, his draw to the pleasures of alcoholic spirits.

Approaching the baggage area, he became aware of the persistent whistling of a familiar tune. He turned to find the originator of the sound but could not. On, the airy melody continued, with no source in sight. Then as the surrounding roar of impatient humanity continued, the song came to him. "Anna My Ageless Love." *Yes, that is it! The old Celtic song of the mountains. Mama used to sing it and Uncle Cummins—dead in the California gold rush of '49, God rest his restless soul—played it on his fiddle.*

This, plus the dropping of a large trunk on Jackson's booted huge foot when the significance of the ditty struck home, pointed him toward God's abundant provision for the remainder of his earthly days: yet another saintly spinster and daughter of a Presbyterian minister and college president.

"I must contact Harvey Hill," he rehearsed aloud, drawing a cocked brow from the salty old Yankee baggage checker. "Yes, I must contact old Harvey." Then, heaving the enormous trunk over his shoulder and onto his back, which cocked the checker's other brow: "No, I must contact her directly. I must go to her. I shall see Harvey when I arrive there."

"If this be of God," Jackson continued, beginning nearly to lope with long ambling strides despite his heavy cargo (he would have shot an arm upward were it not for the trunk), and drawing mere glances now from New Yorkers on the street, who considered him merely one more oddity in a world full of them, "He shall have her awaiting me upon my arrival. He shall, in fact, have had her waiting, preparing her through life and the teachings of His heart as He has prepared me."

Jackson's destination: Davidson College in North Carolina. Since the previous autumn, Harvey Hill had served on Davidson's faculty under the institution's president, his father-in-law. "Her" was Mary Anna Morrison, who once had cleaned up the sitting room after Jackson and the Junkin sisters.

She wrote in her flowing lyrical hand even as the stagecoach bounded toward Richmond and the long train ride north to Philadelphia. *Silverwood*. Chronicle of her soul. Her heart poured out through God's blessed watercourse of release directly onto the page:

> The union of the two forms one perfect soul: and she will wholly satisfy him, for love will stand and hold the torch by which they will study together all of life's beautiful and mysterious lessons. And I; shall I sullenly shut my page, because for me, this torch is an inverted one now? Shall all my book of the future be blotted, or its record of blight be written only with bitter tears? This is what a thwarted heart would dictate; but what right have I to let a fellow mortal shadow from me all brightness? There are other torches than that of love. Fame holds a flaming one. Shall I let the dormant power I am sometimes half conscious of, flash forth to meet it? Yes, if I would find, in the end, that from which my woman's

nature would turn, misled and unsolaced—that which would go out, and leave me in pitiless gloom.

Maggie looked out at the green happy Shenandoah vista. *Ah, the blessedness of knowing God better now and loving Him more, and, yes, having come to love these gentle precious acres breathed out by Him in some of His greatest inspiration.* The thought struck her for the first time, easy and natural, that she, much-traveled, would likely never leave the Shenandoah. The only man she had ever loved had just abandoned the stage of her life's future like a departing thunderbolt, yet in that she clung more firmly than ever to her home of nearly a decade. Their kindly, gentle ways; their quaint Old World courtliness, courtesies, and considerations; even their aristocratic conceits and veiled violence. Yes, these last mars of imperfection further endeared Virginia to her, hallowed its people in some inexplicable way, allowed her in her own flawed perfection to feel more their peer.

She empathized with the slaves' yearning for freedom, and considered slavery a tragic stain on the nation. Yet the blacks of Rockbridge County whom she had met seemed for the most part happy and content, at least as much so as their white masters. (She had never been to the McDowell plantation.) And many of the good men of Lexington professed their belief and desire that the institution was on a gradual decline that would end either in its natural dissolution or in some sort of economic settlement from the larger Union. Yes, the South, and other sections of the nation, possessed more slaves now than twenty or thirty years before; but for most planters the profit margins were narrowing, and the business of owning and caring for slave labor financially was proving an increasingly problematic one.

And more Southerners now tended to question slavery from a moral standpoint, despite the Bible's evident support of it and clear lack of prohibition against it. That had long disturbed her. Why did God not speak against so disturbing and divisive a subject? Northern preachers claimed the larger doctrines and sweep of Scripture could never lead to any but one conclusion: that ownership and possession of one's fellow man was inhuman and evil. Yet some of the men she most respected in Lexington—Pastor White, John Carlisle, Thomas Jackson, *oh, all right, and John Preston*—though not happy with the Negro's earthly plight, presented a powerful, persuasive, and systematic case from Scripture for the sanctioning of slavery. Most of them believed it to be, even putting aside financial considerations, the reluctant duty of the white as his needy "brother's keeper." Less than

25 percent of Southerners owned slaves, and they had inherited the practice from the English, who had forced it on early American colonists. Why, even her own Yankee father believed the Bible sanctioned a humane practice of slavery. She agreed with him, and many others North and South, that blacks should be repatriated to the African colony of Liberia purchased by Thomas Jefferson and others for that purpose, so that they might not be forced to compete with the white man. She had done work supportive of that end. Still, no immediate solution loomed for the vile predicament.

Further, the growing surliness of her Northern cousins toward the South's peculiar institution and, yes, the South, had raised her "Irish" and pushed her more toward sympathy with the Southron who had from the start welcomed her whole clan with love and acceptance. It had also left with her an increasing distaste for the generally more acquisitive and mercenary nature of the Northerners she knew.

But it was Thomas Jackson who claimed her thoughts. *Thomas, Thomas, Thomas. He loves someone else, he must,* she thought. *Could it still be Ellie? Yes, but not in that way. Or is it just that he must love someone else but does not as yet?* In any event, after years of living just down the hall from him, she knew Thomas Jackson. And she knew he was lost to her.

Her eyes fogging over, she looked back to the paper before her. Then it was as if God directed the pen to the navy pool, and wrote the words for her:

> There are others to be loved and lived for. To be happy was not God's first object in creating us, but to be holy, to do, and to bear, that happiness may follow. How often have I pleaded the theory of necessary discipline; and now, when it comes, to teach me to grow stronger, and better, and more unselfish, I faint over the lesson, I murmur—so inconsistent, and so like *me!* Part, "fine gold"; part, "miry clay!"
>
> But a dearer than he puts it, even one who, above all others, can be "touched with the feeling of our infirmities," earthly and human as they are; one who will not turn from me, though my heart be as an empty sepulchre, if, with the weeping Mary's glad faith, I can fall at his feet, exclaiming—"Rabboni!"

CHAPTER 25

WE'VE GOT THEM WHERE WE WANT THEM NOW, UNITED States Cavalry Lieutenant James Ewell Brown ("Jeb") Stuart thought, allowing himself a slight smile.

Stuart and his men already had their single shot carbines pulled out to fire into the three hundred Cheyenne facing them one hundred yards ahead. Now the full six-company cavalry force advanced on the warriors. Following the jarring carbine introduction, Stuart would have his men draw their pistols and charge. Perhaps he had developed a reputation in some quarters for reckless cocksureness, but those who knew Stuart also knew he had learned well his military theory at West Point and had learned even more these last three years on the Western plains.

"Draw sabers! Charge!" another's command rang out.

Sumner, Stuart realized.

At first the barrel-chested Virginian thought his keen ears had betrayed him. *That fool,* he thought. *We could have dealt with these Cheyenne swift and sure if he'd kept his mouth shut.*

But Stuart had little time for reflection now. The Cheyenne, mounted on their fresh ponies, had bolted at Sumner's loud cry for a saber charge. Now the soldiers had lost the initiative, and it would be the devil to catch the braves.

Stuart knew his removal as company quartermaster had not merely been due to his clash with Sumner over accountability. Nor had Sumner just disagreed with Stuart's views on "the practice of virtue." They threatened him. "Virtue" in the mind of Jeb Stuart, who toted his beaten little Episcopal *Book of Common Prayer* with him, whether through swollen streams or windswept prairie, stood in contrast to "the elegant vices of city life." He lost no love for the latter and the "new-made city friends" to which he felt a couple of his southwest Virginia boyhood friends had succumbed.

Neither Sumner nor most of Stuart's peers understood how the wildest, best-riding, most brash and fearless, and arguably most formidable physical specimen among them could also desist from everything from alcoholic spirits to tobacco to cards and every form of wagering. But, aside from Sumner, most all the others liked and respected "Beauty" Jeb Stuart (the Virginian's recently acquired beard had done great justice to the high-cheeked, weak-chinned facial features that had garnered his sobriquet at West Point) even if they did not understand him.

Tom Munford, one of many who had bedeviled Major Thomas Jackson in his VMI section room and who now rode with Stuart, had asked Stuart about his disciplined practices around a lonely Nebraska campfire one summer night.

"Some thought I had renounced the cross when I went to West Point, a place usually considered at great variance with religion," Stuart told him. "But I rejoice to say I still have evidence of a Savior's pardoning love."

When Munford pressed him on how he could forego the few mean worldly pleasures available during the long trackless months of frontier soldiering, Stuart replied, "When I entered West Point I knew many and strong temptations would beset my path, but I relied on 'Him whom to know is life everlasting' to deliver me from temptation, and prayed God to guide me in the right way and teach me to walk as a Christian should; I have never for a moment hesitated to persevere; indeed, since coming to this far land I have been more than ever satisfied of the absolute importance of an acquaintance with Jesus our Lord."

Munford did not at that point understand Stuart any more than he had understood Major Jackson, but Stuart was certainly more fun than Jackson, though the latter had provided his own unique, if unwitting, brand of enjoyment.

Until the recent order to suppress the Cheyenne, frontier soldiering had proved boring and lonely for Stuart as well as most of his *compadres*. Hot in the summer and harshly frigid in the winter, the one constant about the American plains was their sweeping wind. Occasional incidents punctuated the long periods of drudgery. One such episode for Stuart was a face-to-face confrontation with John Brown when he, Sumner, and a detachment of troopers were sent to disperse armed groups in the smoldering Kansas slavery conflict. Brown had in tow several Missouri militiamen he had captured during the "Battle of Black Jack" a few days earlier. The radical abolitionist reluctantly released the Missourians, but shortly afterward Stuart heard news of Brown's butchery of several supposed proslavery men with broadswords. The victims included a black freedman.

Stuart possessed two main consolations on the frontier (aside from his God and his practical jokes at the expense of fellow troopers): his wife and his brand new baby girl, both named Flora. He pined for the day of his return to Fort Leavenworth and the two Floras. He had not yet laid eyes on the younger one. He had always wanted daughters and now one awaited him!

But the Cheyenne were escaping. Because of Sumner's misguided charge, the warriors had scattered in both directions down the Solomon Fork of northwest Kansas's Smoky Hill River. Stuart whistled for a cluster of his men to follow, and they pursued one contingent away from the river and across some soft rolling hills. Several of the soldiers' mounts played out pursuing the fresher Indian ponies. Finally Stuart's big charger, Dan, lather blowing back into the Virginian's determined face, gave out with a groan.

Stuart leapt from the heaving, barely standing animal, his strapping body landing nimbly on both booted feet. Along came a Tennessee private, astride a fresher horse, and the lieutenant waved him over.

"I'm commandeering your horse, soldier," Stuart said.

"Sir?"

"I'm taking your horse to resume the pursuit. You can follow when mine's rested."

The private did not like it, but he had no choice. In a flash, the big Virginian sprang up into the saddle, reined the animal around, and lit out again.

Another mile or so and he saw a Cheyenne brave on foot, cornered by a couple of soldiers. As Stuart galloped up to the group, he saw the Indian pull a revolver and point it at a nearby mounted sergeant, whose Colt was holstered. Stuart, Colt in hand, charged the Indian. The Cheyenne, at the point of pulling the trigger, turned toward Stuart and swung the pistol around at him. As Stuart thundered past the man, he aimed and the two fired almost as one. But the Virginian's shot was a shade quicker and the Cheyenne fell, hit in the thigh.

"Wait! I'll fetch him," shouted redheaded Private Simpson, always an impulsive sort. He jumped from his horse and scrambled toward the Indian. But the youngster tried to do too much too quickly and he stumbled, accidentally squeezing off his final round into the dusty hard ground. Simpson stood blank-faced, his mouth hanging open a few feet from the wounded warrior. As Stuart reined his horse back around for another pass and before the other two troopers present could draw down on the Cheyenne, the wounded man got to his feet and leveled the revolver at Simpson.

Again, Stuart exploded into action. He fired at the Indian from where he was, but the hammer clicked empty. As the warrior again turned toward him, aiming the pistol, Stuart slung his own Colt away, jerked out his saber, and spurred his mount.

Got to get there, got to get there, ran the chorus through Stuart's mind in the eternity of an instant it took him to close on the Indian, whose grim eyes showed he intended to dispose of this blue-jacketed nemesis once and for all. Then Stuart was upon him, raising the heavy sabre and crashing it deep into the warrior's yielding skull—and feeling the foe's bullet cut a burning swath deep into his own strong unprotected chest.

Jackson remembered her as sweet, gentle, intelligent, pretty, and devout. She remained all of these. Indeed, it must be considered one of the most successful campaigns upon which he would ever embark.

Harvey Hill and his wife, Isabella, laughed heartily—but happily—when the polite, gentlemanly letters began arriving at the North Carolina home of the latter's sister, Mary Anna Morrison.

"I'd not be surprised soon to see him on her doorstep," Isabella smiled in private to Harvey.

"If so," Jackson's old comrade said with a broad grin, forgetting for a moment the back pain that had become chronic and for which the doctors could do nothing, "our lives shall soon be the livelier for it." Harvey had seen Jackson in action in the courting arena.

A strange sensation had come over Jackson. It was at once the realization of immense affection for and interest in Anna Morrison, the submerging of affections past, and the determination to move upon his convictions. It, gently, redirected his course of life. The sensation was near-palpable and seemed almost like a spell, though he hesitated to think of it in such sorcerylike terms. He had never heard of such a thing, at least among Christians. But he also knew that "the king's heart is in the hand of the LORD, as the rivers of water: he turneth it whithersoever he will." So when Jackson considered his desires, his needs, the written revelation—and Anna—his course seemed simple, as normally it did as he walked through life's pilgrimage with his Savior.

As he had in Mexico and Virginia, Harvey Hill laughed in delight at his old chum on that cold clear December day in 1856 when Jackson, ramrod straight and bedecked in blue uniform and brass buttons, marched up the walk to the Davidson College president's home. Davidson faculty member Hill lived at the residence with Isabella, the president's eldest daughter.

At thirty-two, Jackson knew well that he courted an entire family, not just a prospective wife. And what a family. Anna had not only a father who was president of a college, but a grandfather who was a general in the army and an uncle who served successively as governor of North Carolina, United States senator, and secretary of the navy under President Millard Fillmore. Within two weeks, however, the family—including prospective wife—were won, and the tall, faintly odd major had returned to Virginia.

Then began the true courtship and wooing. For months, Jackson sent over the Carolina mountains to Anna tender melodious letters, seasoned with Christian affection.

"As my mind dwells on you, I love to give it a devotional turn, by thinking of you as a gift from our heavenly Father," he wrote. "How delightful it is thus to associate every pleasure and enjoyment with God the Giver!"

And in another letter, "When in prayer for you last Sabbath, the tears came to my eyes, and I realized an unusual degree of emotional tenderness. I have not yet fully analyzed my feelings to my satisfaction, so as to arrive at the cause of such emotions; but I am disposed to think that it consisted in the idea of the intimate relation existing between you, as the object of my tender affection, and God, to whom I looked up as my heavenly Father."

Had God used the relationship with Maggie as a necessary bridge over the swirling currents of Jackson's lifeworn emotions and scars to this balming new union? If so, He had mixed it liberally with the strange sensation that the major *should* still be in love with Maggie, but now desired Mary Anna Morrison above all earthly things—and how sudden had come the turnabout! Merely the outworking of God in the lives of those frail flawed creatures who by grace through His Spirit had come the long road to ask His utter will in their lives? *"Whithersoever He will . . . "*

After Jackson moved himself out of the Washington College president's home, his partner and friend Preston made evident his intentions to move Maggie Junkin out as well—into his own large home out on the north edge of town on the road to Staunton.

Maggie seethed, however. It was as though Preston's considerable attributes of character, scholarship, ability, wealth, kindness, physical attributes . . . *(the list really did just go on and on,* she thought with a reluctant grimace) caused her to detest him all the more. Perhaps because each pointed another accusing finger at her? ("Honey, here in the South," she could *feel* the townfolk saying, "a woman of your age, with a prince and Virginia nobleman like J. T. L. Preston comin' a callin' . . . well no more sense than God gave a cabbage should tell you that this is His provision for your *deliverance!*")

Had it been Mrs. Preston who survived, she would have been required to observe the customary year of mourning and black. But being as it was Mr. Preston, a wife and mother for five children still in the home was required—and fast.

But Maggie also cried. It hurt, and hurt deeply. Only Ruthie knew the many nights through the winter and spring of 1857 that Maggie cried herself to sleep over her crushed dreams. *But were they yet crushed?* Maggie asked herself—and Ruthie, in a rare and new sharing of her heart with someone other than Ellie. *No, they can't be,* she herself answered. *But what of the whisperings of doings with Anna Morrison in North Carolina,* Maggie fretted, *and secret letters to and fro?*

She truly believed she trusted God's judgment. Yet, "the heart, who can know it?" How could she have been so certain Jackson and she were meant to be together? Were her will and the Lord's that far apart? Her whole body ached as though she had been beaten. She wondered at her mind's capacity to absorb such overwhelming pain and remain lucid.

And she wrote. *Silverwood.* "My own blind heart alone is to blame for the throbbing pain that aches through it, and it shall bear its own punishment," she wrote. "Many and many are the unrecognized martyrs that have walked smiling over this earth, while the fiery cross to which they have been bound, burned, and the ashes of blight smouldered above their dead affections. If it is appointed me to join their train, have I any right to murmur?"

But then came the day that *Silverwood* was complete, or at least as complete as Maggie could make it. And came another day when Derby and Jackson published it, in New York. And more days, when to Maggie's growing shock, the literary critics ridiculed it and the public ignored it. Missing from it, said the critics, were the pithy potent urgency and unsentimental power and poignancy of her poetry. *Silverwood* merely bored the public, the few who read it.

"No, no; very slowly, very beautifully, has the belief of what I now realize, grown upon me; but too slowly to keep pace with my own strengthening love," spoke the devout upright hero of *Silverwood* at the book's close, as he finally requited the lonely heroine's love, after having first loved her sister.

But books are not life, and Maggie's pain grew as even her book proved a disappointment. In a rage before God one black midnight she cried out, "Oh I know, I know, I have made yet another idol and You are a jealous God and want no pretenders to Your throne, whether sisters, husbands, or literary pursuits. Must You insist on my being worth all the pain I cause us both?"

Still, she swore, only one person would ever learn the secret of *Silverwood*.

Another of Jackson's series of strange sensations was the urge to stop Preston and his courting of Maggie. *Why?* he thought to himself one night after he had parted company from Carlisle en route home from a Franklin debate. *I don't want her seeing another,* he answered himself honestly. *But God has brought you Anna Morrison, has He not? Then let Maggie go. But,* he argued with himself, *she has ridiculed Preston for months, at least behind his back, and virtually to his face of late. . . . The Lord God Almighty can be trusted not to err in placing together two Spirit-led Christians.*

With a vigorous jerk of his head, his jaw set, Jackson sped up to the quick step, his left arm springing skyward. *I must be home and writing Anna the good news of thirteen-year-old nephew Tommy's coming next year to stay with us.* Laura's Tommy and Elizabeth and Julia's Wirt—though rarely seeing them, Jackson poured forth generous kindness to them all, and all of them loved him.

Dr. Junkin took a full heart one spring morning to visit Rush at the quiet verdant cemetery out past the northwest edge of town.

The country morning smelled like God had let loose another of His elixirs of Eden *peculiar,* Junkin swore, *to this sublime valley.* Junkin drank deeply of it through the nostrils of his strong Roman nose. Early violets sprouting brightly around his wife's marker prompted him, doffing his black wide brim and holding it in his hands, first to talk to her of Maggie. Grieving, silent Maggie.

"The eldest," he said, more slowly and respectfully than ever he spoke to anyone else in his life. "Pray for our eldest." That was all he need say. Rush would know the rest.

"Received a postal from John just Tuesday last," he said. "All is well in his medical practice in Trenton and with George and his law practice in Philadelphia. Ebenezer and William are fine, too, with their splendid Southern wives. William is just nine miles down the road at Falling Waters, as you know.

"And Julia is love-smitten again with that nice Fishburne boy," he said, shifting his feet as before a throne of royalty. "First time I've seen brightness in her eyes since, well since the unfortunate incident with . . . er, uh . . . that cadet, ex-cadet, anyway.

"And I guess you and Ell are joyfully sharing company before the King. Soon maybe I'll be joining you. For some reason the Lord keeps seeing fit to stick my feet into more things it doesn't seem feet should go into." He paused and looked down at a strapping red ant carting off a small black spider as trophy and breakfast. "Ellie was our best," he concluded with a sigh, "but Maggie may yet be our greatest."

He turned to leave the shaded garden, savored the sweet rhapsody of nearby white- and pink-flowered arbutus, then remembered one last thing. "Oh, keep praying that these fools won't rend this nation asunder. If they could hear my inaugural address this year, 'Christianity, the Patron of Literature and Science,' about how a college is a religious not a civil institution and that the God-fearing need to be directly involved in education, they might learn something.

"Some of these Southern Democrats seem happy enough to dissolve the Union to keep their slaves," he continued, shaking his great woolly head. "And this new Republican gang—well, they seem happy enough to dissolve it to get rid of the slaveholders. God save us from them all, my dear. And God help us."

With that, he let himself out the squeaking iron gate, as he had every morning for four years.

As he had with Ellie, Jackson attempted to keep his engagement to Anna secret from as many people as possible for as long as possible. In this he succeeded remarkably well. One person with whom he had lived under the same roof for several years learned not of the pending matrimony until a late date indeed.

Early one bright June morning Maggie sat on the back veranda of the president's home sipping the zesty Southern potion known as ginger ale, in which she had come to delight, and reading from the "majesty" she considered as Milton's.

"Ma'am?" came a halting call from the corner of the house.

Maggie looked up to see Willy, his squirrel rifle slung over his back, hat in one hand, and a wad of jonquils bursting with yellow splendor in the other. Her face lit up nearly as the flowers in Willy's hand. *Such a sweet fine boy,* she thought. *If ever I take a liking to a child, it will be him.*

"Why hello, Willy," she said with a smile. "Do please come over." Blushing, he did, stumbling and almost falling over a thick tree root that snaked defiantly across the otherwise smoothly trimmed green lawn. "What have you there?"

"Brought you some flowers from down by the river, Miss Maggie," he said, ducking as he handed them to her, his blush growing scarlet. "Grabbed them up whilst Wayne Marley and I were hunting."

She sat staring at them. Warmth flooded the heart that had tried so to stay thawed in the difficult months since Clause XXIV:4 had burst her world apart the previous summer. She had known it was for the best; deep in her heart she had known—thought—it was for the best. After all, it was God's divinely decreed will through His appointed undershepherds, was it not? And since Paris, she had felt the Lord's hand strong and sure with purpose on her life. Still, she now knew she could not, try as she may through reading, writing, and even love, escape the pilgrim way that the grand old Scot Rutherford had said "costs Christ and all His followers sharp showers and hot sweats ere they win to the top of the mountain."

She looked up at Willy. *A fifteen-year-old schoolboy with a crush—on me,* she thought giggling to herself. *How dear.*

Willy wanted desperately to run off, yet more desperately to stay and while the day away with this mysterious and electric scarlet-haired woman with the shimmering blue eyes.

"Well sit down, Willy," Maggie said with a wave, pouring him a glass of ginger ale from the silver decanter.

She sat staring at him, her eyes twinkling and her diminutive hands in her lap. She actually did not know what to say next. She had never known what to say to children, though she believed she liked this young man more than any she had ever known. His words saved her the effort.

"Great news about Tom Jackson and the lady from North Carolina," he burst forth, at once feeling exposed as a foolish child and established as a sage herald.

"Oh?" Maggie replied calmly, even as her heart began to pound.

"Yes, he's heading down there in two weeks to marry."

Then, to her everlasting surprise, Maggie's earthly destiny laid itself before her with such clarity that she would never once doubt it, though often she would wonder how it might have been different if not for Clause XXIV:4. *This precious boy, with his flowers and other little gifts and his repeated clumsy visits, is God's tool to birth in me love and affection for children, even someone else's children, even lots of children, Lord help me,* she now saw. *And John T. L. Preston, that magnificent figure of a man, who worships the ground upon which I—I!—walk, he is God's bountiful provision to me for love and companionship.*

And now I shall take my place in—can I be saying this?—that rarefied Old South order where I may glory not in my own position, but be better used of the Everlasting King to champion His liberating gospel, moreso than ever I could, or would have if merely cloistered behind my books and poems, good friends though demanding ones they be!

A fine, blessed feeling of love, respect, and affection then flooded over her for John Preston, a proud and lonely man who for months had pursued her in an increasingly less subtle manner. As God had given Tom Jackson His brand of love for Mary Anna Morrison, and before that, Ellie Junkin, so did He now give it to Margaret Junkin for John Preston.

That was when she knew the answer to Willy's next remark—"Are you ever going to marry my pa?"—would be yes. And that is when she believed finally and fully, amidst pain, doubt, and fear, the truth of the Scripture, "For the eyes of the LORD run to and fro throughout the whole earth, to shew himself strong in the behalf of them whose heart is perfect toward him."

Her tears, this time, were tears of marveling and joy.

CHAPTER 26

ANNA AND JACKSON MARRIED JULY 16, 1857. MAGGIE AND Preston married seventeen days later. Dr. Junkin married them, proud of his daughter for honoring God through her obedience to Clause XXIV:4 and her cheerful acceptance, finally, of Preston's bidding. It was, he told those gathered, "the very finger of God."

Willy stood as his father's best man. Maggie loved Preston, but the prospect of Willy as a stepson and companion moved her as much as being with her new husband. Jackson had, for now, receded almost completely from mind.

The Jacksons set off on a lengthy trip North, retracing much of the trail of his first honeymoon. They spent several days with Dr. Roland Houghton, whom Jackson had consulted periodically for years regarding his various health infirmities. (Houghton and his wife, a published author, had been friends of the late Edgar Allan Poe, who dedicated two poems to Mrs. Houghton and wrote *The Bells* while staying in the Houghtons' home.)

But on this trip Jackson's health began to deteriorate. Though pleased upon his return to Virginia with the home he and Anna had purchased on Washington Street, his physical condition worsened through the fall and winter. No amount of 6:00 A.M. baths, brisk walks pumping metal hand weights with his arms, parade ground drill, gardening, diets of cornbread or stale bread, or even matrimonial gymnastics could alleviate the dilemma.

By February 1858, Jackson's throat was inflamed, one ear virtually deaf and the other affected, and his throat had to be cauterized twice a week. By April, his eyes, beset with blurring and pain, had joined the growing chorus of complainants.

Even his nose was "internally affected," he wrote Laura.

And legions of latter-day Johnny Pattons had sprung up in Jackson's VMI section room and out on the drill field, part of their torment toward him undetected because he could not hear it, or in some cases, see it.

Anna knew the discomfort and dysfunction to be great when she observed Jackson's usual buoyancy flagging. He even began to snap at her and their slaves—all of whom had in some manner requested that Jackson purchase them—during morning prayers and Bible reading.

"It is the closest I have come to despairing," Jackson whispered to her one agonizing night in bed. This shook her. "Except for—," he said, patting her gently on her rounded tummy. His blue eyes twinkled in the milky moonlight that cascaded into the room through the fluttering white lace curtains.

"You're still so sure it's a she?" Anna purred.

"A Mary Graham Jackson it is," he said, forgetting his pain, as often he did when considering the miracle forming in his wife's abdomen. A miracle for which he had hoped since first laying eyes on Laura's Tommy and Elizabeth. The miracle of being able to give as a father what had been torn from his life.

Then he lay his head against her stomach, as often he did.

Anna stroked his long thick mane. "We should name her after your mother, not mine," she said.

He lifted his head and turned it toward her. The angelic glow of a pregnant and serenely happy woman enveloped her. He smiled. With Anna and Mary Graham, the hurt all seemed to go away, though the pain did not. *"And we know that all things work together for good to them that love God, to them who are the called according to his purpose,"* he thought, reciting Romans 8:28, his favorite verse from the Bible.

"My *esposita*," he said, recalling the Spanish term of endearment he had learned in the Mexican War, and kissing her softly on the cheek, then the lips.

She responded with abandon to his advances, and had it not been for little Mary Graham, another Jackson might well have been conceived that quiet balmy April night.

"A house with golden hinges, that's what it is," Jackson said, "with a place for everything and everything in its place." Then he stared for a moment, not seeing Anna, her enormous tummy, nor her sewing. She barely heard his next words. "So unlike the world outside."

"Do you have to go, darling?" she asked, laying aside the knitting. She didn't like to sew anyhow. And she had never really had to learn. She had, in fact, never really had to do anything she did not want to do, as long as she acted and spoke as a proper Southern Christian lady. But her lack of interest in the sewing art had disappointed her mother.

"Stay and I'll have Hetty make us some tea and I'll read some *Shorter Catechism* to you," she said. Hetty had begged to come north with Anna, whom she had wet-nursed from the womb, when the new Mrs. Jackson had moved to Virginia (with her forty-one trunks of clothes and belongings). The kindhearted Dr. Morrison had consented, and had further granted the desires of Hetty's twelve- and sixteen-year-old sons to accompany her, though this move proved a serious financial hardship to him. Like most Southern slaveholders, rare was the day when he split up a slave family who did not want to be split, regardless of the financial hardship involved in such considerations. Slaveholding whites felt it part of their God-given responsibility in the nurture, protection, and gospel proclamation to the benighted Negro race.

"Darling *esposita*," he smiled, snapping from his stare and buckling on his gleaming steel sword, "you know I must go."

"But certainly it is a hoax," she said. "Few are the blacks who would countenance such vile treachery, and fewer still those capable of it."

"Agreed by all," Jackson nodded, pulling on his blue jacket, "but no one expected the savagery of Nat Turner, either—and he a professing believer."

Then he kissed her and felt her soft largeness against him. It gave him pause, and he looked into her round doe eyes, which reflected the amber light of the lamp by which they read each evening— always she to him, as he refused to read but by natural light. A memory flashed across his mind, emerging from a dusty closet of someplace long, long ago. *Dare I?* he wondered. He stood transfixed for a moment, rigid as a board, his eyes dilating. Then he remembered that what was past was past, and he slowly bent down to her protruding abdomen and leaned an ear against it. *Yes!* The thump of another live being—*My child!* Only then did he remember how desperately he wanted a child. As time had passed when he was a bachelor, his yearning for a child had blossomed to an equal passion as that for a wife. Then with the coming of Ellie's baby, he had been beside himself with eager anticipation. Now he felt—giddiness. *Oh Lord God,* he prayed silently, closing his eyes and lowering his head, *I beseech Thee in Thy mercy to protect this woman and her child. But if—*

"Darling? Are you all right?"

He looked up at her lovely kind face, aglow in the lamplight of eventide. *Heavenly Father, You have indeed been gracious and compassionate to provide to me, once again, such a sweet soul as a companion, as a wife and a mother to my children.* He rehearsed the baby's room in his mind, the innocent roses on the wallpaper, the tiny socks and bonnets, and realized for the first time how much he hoped for a future awash in this house with golden hinges, his garden, rocky though it may be, and that he "may lead a quiet and peaceable life in all godliness and honesty," as the apostle Paul put it.

And then he was out the door and marching through the darkness to the institute. For he was the one man that cadet, faculty member, and president alike, all having scorned him at one time or another, needed in their midst in case the note found that afternoon just outside town on the road north to Staunton were true. The note containing plans for three hundred slaves to attack the Virginia Military Institute's state arsenal, kill all whites in the vicinity, and depart with the enormous cache of arms and ammunition.

Jackson did not at first recognize the greasy, bearded ragamuffin who staggered into his path as he rode toward the VMI. The wind had suddenly kicked up, the night growing cool, and the man on foot's long shaggy hair blew into the face of his bare head. But Jackson knew only one man in Lexington who wore an eye patch and, sure enough, the scarecrow's customary aroma of alcoholic spirits soon wafted up to the professor.

"Is that you, Wayne Marley?" Jackson called over the growing din of the wind.

The man stopped and looked up.

"Major Jackson?"

"What are you doing out here, Wayne? Weather is coming."

Marley stared at Jackson, then looked down, his shoulders sagging. He said nothing.

Jackson's horse snorted and pawed at the ground. A storm was coming, Superintendent Smith was waiting for him, and big trouble could be afoot tonight. He needed to go. Yet, his heart panged as he remembered how far this once promising young man had fallen.

"Why don't you go to the house and have Anna scare up a meal and a bath for you, Wayne," Jackson said.

Marley looked up. "Anna?"

Jackson stared at him. "My wife, Wayne."

Recognition and shame merged, flickering in Marley's good eye. Then he lowered his head again, mumbling, "You mean your slaves, not Anna, don't you?"

"What's that?" Jackson asked.

Marley shook his head, not looking up.

Jackson leaned with his hands against his saddle horn and twisted in his saddle, its polished leather creaking. "Wayne, you've become a drunkard, a whoremonger, and a general ne'er-do-well. Why?"

Marley's head shot up again and he started to blurt something out, his eye flashing now. Then he relented. Only Tom Jackson commanded the respect with him to say such a thing. Marley had stuck his knife in the side of the last man who had insulted him. But that was in the alley behind Gore's Tavern across the river. And the other man had been drunker than Marley. Jackson sat cold sober on his horse.

"You disappoint me, Wayne," Jackson said at length. "What is more, you disappoint your Maker."

The latter did not matter in the least to Marley, but the former did greatly. Again, he hung his head.

"Go back to your gutter, Wayne Marley, or wherever your father Satan should take you," Jackson said, snapping the reins to urge on his horse. The professor never knew that those words that so chilled and sobered Wayne at the time would in time turn him from one destiny to another.

"There you are, Tom," Smith said, hustling across his office to shake Jackson's hand. The younger man could not recall the older greeting him with such enthusiasm in the seven years he had served under him. The kerosene lamp on Smith's desk flickered as he rushed past it. Otherwise, muggy darkness enveloped the room. The burgeoning wind swept in through an open window and tossed Smith's curtains around like ghostly veils. A hint of rain now rode on the contentious breeze.

The normally reserved Smith whipped back around to his desk and retrieved a sheet of paper. "This is it," he said, handing the paper to Jackson.

"I prefer not to read in such unnatural light," Jackson said, handing the paper back to Smith. "Your appraisal of the letter?"

"Oh, yes," Smith mumbled. "Well, my appraisal—and I have apprised General Richardson—is that I don't presume to say whether or not it is a hoax. It may not be, but my confidence is not excessive in the ability of the colored population here to bring off something such as this. Nonetheless, folks over in Buchanan are spooked too. Rumors have run rampant around there for weeks. So I've sent a detachment over to them as well."

Twenty-five miles to Buchanan, Jackson thought. *In the dark and in this weather. These people are indeed spooked.*

"Now, I've issued ball cartridges to the guard here and stationed half of them in the guard room and the other half in your section room," Smith spit out, pacing the floor and occasionally glancing out the window into the eerie darkness. He turned to Jackson, who stood ramrod-straight. "You may blame Major Gilham for suggesting you come back on duty, Tom."

One of Jackson's eyebrows arched a shade. Smith sighed, rubbing his perspiring forehead with a kerchief. "You know some of the students—yes, and some of the faculty—don't appreciate your scholarship, Tom."

And some of the administration and some of the board of visitors, Jackson remembered.

Then Smith placed a hand on the strong shoulder of his subordinate and looked him in the eye, as if searching for something he had lost. "But all of them know you as the hero of Contreras and Chapultepec, even if they never mention it."

Jackson did not flinch or speak.

Smith removed his hand and returned slowly to his desk. "Go to your section room and supervise them," he said over his shoulder. "Stay there until dawn."

"Yes sir," Jackson said, saluting and leaving.

Smith leaned back in the leather swivel chair and stared again out the window into the dark tumult, drying his neck and forehead. "Not on my watch will an insurrection begin," he whispered. "Not on mine and Tom Jackson's, by d———."

"Sure enough he's scared," Bubba whispered in the dark to the others in the single slaves' cabin down the hill from Will Russell's big house. Bubba himself, truth be known, felt fear at this moment, what with the wind swirling and lightning flashing outside. A storm coming, plus all these rumors of slaves ready to revolt or fly north—no one could ever seem to find one who really was—and worry that Marse Russell might catch wind and, to be safe, put the fear of the Lord into somebody.

"We just better hope Marse Russell don't hear tell like Marse McDowell, else they be Hades to pay 'round here," Bubba exclaimed.

"You fool nigger," came Big Sam's bass voice from across the room. "You think Marse McDowell know and Marse Russell don't?" A heavy boot followed his words, thumping Bubba in the forehead and knocking him flat back onto his cot. Big Sam's aim seemed as good in the dark as at noonday.

"They be the Goober again, readin' the Good Book," said Shorty.

A dozen sets of copper eyes shifted to the cot in the far corner of the quarters. Sure enough, each could see the faint gold flicker of light under the oilskin blanket.

"White man's law and black man's brain, won't neither let the Goober read, but he don't know it," said Jethro.

The group laughed deeply as one, but no boots were thrown.

Big Sam spoke instead. "Say, Goob, how you 'spect white folks ever to lets you talk preacher talk if'n they don't let you read the words in the Book you talkin' from?"

"Yeah, Goob, you ain't 'posed to have no light on after dark, neither," said Elijah.

After a moment, as rain begin to pound against the wood cabin, the oilskin came slowly down, revealing the quivering candle, a pocket Testament, and the dark face of Lylburn Downing. His frequent favorable references to Tom Jackson, "the Goober," had earned him the same sobriquet from his comrades.

"You gemp'mans want to hear somethin'?" Lylburn asked, his serious tone barely discernible over the din outside.

"What that be, Goober?" Shorty asked.

Lylburn swung his slender body up, his bare feet touching the hard dirt floor. He held the Testament in his hands, close to the candlelight. He cleared his throat. "And this ain't from no memories, gemp'mans," he said. "This be as I read it with mine own eyes." He peered down at the Book, now holding it with one hand and using the index finger of the other to mark his spot.

When he spoke, he spoke slowly, and at first waveringly. "But . . . know . . . that . . . the Lawd . . . hath . . . set . . . apart . . . him . . . that is . . . godly . . . for . . . himself: . . . the Lawd . . . will . . . hear when . . . I call . . . unto him." As he went on, his words became more certain, more clear, more confident. "There be many that says, who will show us any good? Lord, lift thou up the light of thy cow . . . can . . . cout-enance upon us."

Then Lylburn grabbed the candle and stood to his bare feet, looking up toward the heavens as if to still their loud fury as rain lashed the battered shake roof and thumped through it into the same strategically placed buckets that always caught the leakage. "Thou has put gladness in my heart," he shouted upward, no longer reading, "more than in the time that they corn and they wine increased."

Now the rain slowed and Lylburn lowered his head, sweeping his gaze around the small dark room where a dozen sets of wide eyes fixed on him. He felt the strength of the Lord pulsing through him. "Now I will both lay me down in peace, and sleep," he said. "For thou, Lord, only, makest me dwell in safety."

Then he closed the Bible and stood there for a moment. No one spoke. Outside, the storm had stilled and the beaming radiance of a full moon now lit the room through the one open spot in the walls. Only the breathing of the sweaty men in the cabin could be heard. Lylburn started to sit, then remembered something. "Oh, that last part," he said, "that weren't readin', that be from my memories."

Big Sam and Elijah both stayed awake for some minutes thinking, which was much longer than usual, though no one knew. More than once, as tonight, Lylburn's words had given them hope beyond the boring, mundane routine of their daily work. That Lylburn, he had a way with words.

VMI cadets and faculty alike joyed in the appearance of Tom Jackson in his section room that spooky night. More than one man and boy, as all wordlessly tendered leadership of the tense situation to Jackson, experienced shame at recollections of actions, attitudes or words that had mocked the awkward, earnest professor of natural and experimental philosophy. But none mocked him this night as he rattled off instructions and assigned postings. Nor would they, for a few weeks. By the end of the spring term, of course, their more immediate memories of fear and concern from the baseless insurrection rumor would pass, and the war hero would once more become Tom Fool.

The frightening night and the storm passed without sign of servile revolt. Jackson had doubted any would occur, but never would he shirk duty. Now, as he strode home, red veins streaked his eyes and he relished the prospect of his daily early morning bath. He thought that he would not walk again after his bath as he normally did. He would sleep, at least for a few hours, as morning classes at the VMI had been cancelled due to most of the cadets and faculty having been up all night.

His poor ears, at least one of them, heard his servant Albert's cries before his poor eyes saw the wiry, handsome young man racing toward him on foot across the rich rolling Washington College grounds. Even in Jackson's fatigued condition, he thought it unusual for the placid Albert to be so excited. The young man's drive, intelligence, and integrity impressed Jackson and had ever since, at Albert's beseeching, he had purchased him from an upcounty farmer dying without an heir. Albert had likewise determined the quality of Jackson's character through other blacks and, in urging the professor to purchase him, had boldly challenged the older man to allow him to purchase his own freedom by working as a waiter at the Lexington Hotel. To this Jackson had agreed, and Albert now worked toward freedman's status at the rate of fifteen dollars per month. Albert also did a full complement of duties for the Jackson family and, with Jackson's silent knowledge, taught himself to cipher and read each night by candlelight in the attic quarters he had requested. Albert had plans for himself far beyond being a house slave.

But just now he sprinted to Jackson and sputtered, "Miz Anna, sir, it's . . . well, sir, it's *that* time."

Jackson's eyes widened. *"That* time?"

Albert shook his head up and down. Then, without another word, the two of them bolted as one toward home.

Jackson took the eight front steps in two bounding leaps and charged down the wood floored front hall toward the front bedroom. *Please, Lord, oh please, this time, Sir, please,* he pleaded.

Then he heard tiny squawks and he was pushing himself past Hetty, through the bedroom door, and to the bedside of the barely conscious Anna. This time he would not be kept outside. And this time Dr. Ryan smiled. As the physician packed his stethoscope and other utensils into his worn leather medical bag, he touched his hand gently to Jackson's shoulder and said, "You have a wife and a child, Tom."

Jackson's eyes grew until, like the heart he felt pounding within his breast, he thought they would pop out of him. He turned to Anna, *dear, sweet, darling Anna,* and a love beyond any he had ever felt for her surged through him, as she smiled weakly at him, her face wan and her hair matted to her forehead and ears with perspiration. As though handling the most delicate china, he took her soft white hand and kissed it, then bent to kiss with great love her cheek.

Then he heard it again, the tittering, spluttering sounds of new life. He turned to Amy—the young slave who, like Albert, had petitioned Jackson to purchase her—who held a tiny bundle of pink-headed joy in her husky arms. If Jackson's feet and even his legs were connected to the floor he could not tell it as he moved toward the wondrous creation.

He stood dumbly staring at Mary Graham Jackson, who coughed and cried, then—all in the room agreed—grabbed for Jackson with a tiny pink hand. Jackson had no words, only a heart that overflowed with love and praise for a loving heavenly Father who would so bless him, an unworthy sinner who had so needed and wanted his own parents after they had left him.

Amy offered little Mary to Jackson, but the gawking father shook his head and leaned away. "No, no . . . I don't . . . I can't. You hold her. I shall have time when she's less . . ."

"Fragile?" Dr. Ryan chuckled. "Yes, my friend, there should be plenty of time for you to hold her, especially after you, like the many who have gone before you, have realized she shan't break in your arms." With that, the good doctor patted Jackson's shoulder again. Then his red old Irish face crinkled a bit. "She does appear to possess a slight case of jaundice, Tom, that I shall keep a close watch upon. And she is tiny, only four and a half pounds. But she appears quite game."

Jackson looked down into the innocent blue eyes and saw himself, saw love, saw eternity. *Mine,* he thought with praise overflowing, *flesh of my blessed flesh. "Blessed be the* LORD: *for he hath shewed me his marvellous kindness."*

Jackson indeed learned quickly to hold, hug, and kiss little Mary Graham. And to lift her above his head, speak baby talk to her—in Spanish—and tickle her behind her ears where, like her mother, she seemed exquisitely sensitive. He especially loved to elicit little cackling coos of joy from her. She would stare at him like she did at no one else, with the same luminous blue eyes he had. But when she slept he would stare at her until Amy or Anna would need to lead him by the hand out of the room. He would stare at her sweet tiny hands and fingers, her pink feet and toes, her little ears, and her button nose. And he would marvel at the wisdom of King David the psalmist's words, "The fool hath said in his heart, There is no God."

His and Anna's health even improved a bit, though after two weeks of the most devoted and loving attention, little Mary's had declined slightly due to her pesky jaundice.

Strange, Maggie thought, *that of all the houses in town, it should be the one in which John Preston was born in 1811 that the Jacksons would buy.* Maggie did not accompany her husband when he first showed the structure to them, and she did not accompany him to visit when they moved in.

Now, however, it seemed time. But for some reason she did not particularly want Preston with her when she called. For one thing, she still smarted from the realization that her proud, accomplished husband, in his heart of hearts, resented his wife's "giving any part of herself to the public, even in verse." He had not been accustomed to such with Sally as she bore him nine children and captained one of the Valley's most respected family households. Tom Jackson, Maggie remembered with a twang, only encouraged her forward in her literary pursuits, poetic and prosaic. Never was he threatened by them. He had even sent her a warm note of encouragement upon the disappointment of *Silverwood,* urging her onward with her pen, even though she had failed as yet to divulge to him as promised the novel's vaunted secret.

As she ascended the steps to the streetfront brick house, a canary yellow parasol shielding her from the penetrating sun and matching the bright spring hues of her best dress, a Chinese silk with high Empire waist—yes, it was outrageous for her to go visiting in it, during the day no less, but she simply had to!—Maggie realized that only a glimmer of the immensity of Jackson's contribution to her life had even begun to strike her. He it was who had most brought her out of her lifelong reclusivity. Indeed, Dr. Junkin's sometimes harsh Covenanter ways, learned as they were and as they inspired learning in Maggie, had early helped push her behind books rather than bring her out front of them.

The commercial and critical failure of *Silverwood* would have devastated her in past years. But as it was, after laughing years of evening "Spanish lessons," she mainly giggled at her good "fortune" (she could not claim wisdom, for she had expected great success for the book) for not allowing the publishers to assign her name to it prior to its release, despite their most fervent protestations.

An anonymous 425-page goose! she giggled to herself as she arrived at the Jacksons' front door. *Back to poetry I go.* Just as she began to knock, something caught her eye. Gazing around the empty Saturday afternoon street for witnesses and despite herself, she peered through the nearby open window, whose shutters had been closed, but not quite completely. Inside the rustic home unfolded a scene that created in her a swirl of emotions it would take her weeks to sort through.

A tousle-haired Anna crept through the front room, Jackson's study. Despite her floor-length petticoats and skirt, Maggie saw the woman's feet were totally bare—and her ankles, too, visible as the dresses swished about them!

Maggie held a fingerless lace-gloved hand to her mouth, her face blushing and her heart fluttering. *And she,* Maggie thought with just a trace of a sneer, *Lexington's newest and most notorious clotheshorse.* Before the redhead could feel guilty for her thoughts or snoopiness, she heard Anna's soft lilting voice. "Tommy, oh, Tommy."

Tommy? Maggie thought. *I never called him that.*

"Where are you, Tommy?" From within, nearing the front hallway from the sound of it. *The baby—poor sick darling—must be asleep,* Maggie thought. "You can't hide from me, Tommy."

Amazed at her own voyeurism, Maggie squinted with great energy through an opening in the curtain of the front door. Yes, there came Anna—then suddenly, leaping from behind the stairwell, flew Jackson, waving his long sword high over his head like an executioner, and bringing it down—"No!"

Maggie's cry fell unheard inside the Jackson home, eclipsed by Anna's piercing shriek. At the last second, Jackson had veered the sword away from Anna's head, not decapitating her as he had feigned.

Maggie's breath caught in her narrowed throat. "What?"

Then Anna was lunging, half-angry, at him, and he, laughing, was intercepting her arms and whirling her into a choppy polka—his feet were bare too!

Why, they're dancing, Maggie pouted to herself. *He never danced with me. He never danced with anybody!*

Up and down the front hallway she saw their forms spinning, heard their laughter echoing, felt their floor shaking. Maggie did not know whether to laugh or cry. *He never once even* suggested *dancing with me, the old bluestocking.* Then her pretty painted mouth thinned at the remembrance of Anna's gay, slightly spoiled ways. *But of course, I'm no Su-thun belle.* And she turned, parasol, lace gloves, Chinese silk dress—*such dresses are not for me anyhow*—and all, and left.

Has he truly so soon forgotten me? she thought with a grimace as she walked toward her own home. Then she shamed herself for such a covetous, self-centered thought. *I must be about supervising the servants for the family's dinner.* For that family consisted of seven, and in three months, eight, children. Maggie patted her still only moderately rounded tummy and smiled, then glanced upward, shaking her parasol-shaded head. *I know, Sir. All things . . . all things work together . . . I know—he believed it and so do I, Sir.*

The Jacksons' season of rapturous afternoon abandonment ended only when little Mary fell into another fit of gagging and coughing. Jackson, a knifing cold dread driving the breath from his lungs, shot out of the bed, threw on shirt and pants, and ran down the hall to the baby's room. Hetty, spending the afternoon in the room, already had Mary in her arms.

"Better fetch Dr. Ryan this time, Major," she said, her round chocolate face etched in fear. Little Mary, whose worsening jaundice had rendered her skin increasingly yellow as she neared her one month birthday, now looked scarlet, so terrific were the spasms that racked her.

"Doctor! Doctor Ryan!" Jackson screamed, running toward the front of the house.

"Sir," Hetty's normally lazy and vaguely troublesome sixteen-year-old son, George, said, intercepting Jackson just as the frantic father reached the front door, "I'll go for Doc Ryan, sir."

It took a moment for the words to register and Jackson stared at George. "I'm going, sir," George nodded. He turned and exploded out the door and down the steps.

An instant later his twelve-year-old brother, Cyrus, flew after him, pausing only to say to Jackson, "I'm going too, sir, and I knows this Doctor Ryan and he gonna fix you little girl right up, sir—the Lord told me in mornin' prayer time you had for us today, sir." Then he, too, raced out, the front door banging open behind him.

Dazed, Jackson turned and gazed back down the hall. It seemed a long way to Mary's room. From somewhere he heard a shrieking wail he thought sounded oddly like his wife's voice. Then he found himself standing before her as she, wearing only a crinkled basque and petticoat, sobbed with deep, racking, guttural moans, her fat teardrops plopping against the face of the still, tiny child she cradled in her arms. . . . *They all leave, they all go away from me, every one of them. . . .*

CHAPTER 27

ANNA NOTICED THAT IN THE MONTHS FOLLOWING LITTLE Mary's death, he who had loved children began to treasure them each as priceless irreplaceable gems whose souls might be immortal but whose earthly days could prove as fleeting as the bloom of new-grown laurel.

The children of the village had always delighted in evening excursions with their parents to visit their 175-pound playmate; now they squealed with delight at such opportunities. And now, too, various mothers came to visit with, and at the request of, their children, afternoons before Jackson made his daily pilgrimage to the farm.

Anna stood watching out a back window of her home as he pruned the sumptuous new blooming of chrysanthemums, some red and some white. His nephew, Tommy, now a lanky thirteen-year-old, stood with him.

Sitting on a sofa a few feet away from Anna was Laura. She had returned from her western Virginia home of Beverly with Elizabeth to retrieve Tommy. On this bright May morning in 1859, the boy had completed a ten-month stay in Lexington with his favorite uncle and aunt. If Tommy had a hero in the world now, it was the uncle for whom he was namesaked.

"It is as though God took from him another little one and recompensed him with an entire village of little ones, all clamoring for 'sky-rides' above his head, wrestling with him on the floor, and seeing who can pick the last petal off the daisy," Anna said softly, her back to Laura.

"He," Anna started again, her voice heavy and cracking, "he at once fills me with pride and shames me. I, the daughter of a Presbyterian minister, yet so—so sheltered, so—spoilt." She looked back out the window. Jackson and Tommy were turning to come back to the house. "All I have thought of since Mary—" Her voice cracked again and she lowered her head once more. "All I've been able to see is my own suffering and emptiness, and even that with Hetty, her boys, and Amy swarming to meet my every whim.

"And he—he, though his eyes, throat, and nasal tubes have given him so much pain and discomfort that we must soon go again to the Northern doctors, he who has grieved to the extent his heart capable, seems only to grow a larger heart filled with more compassion and sweetness that must be released to others or that very heart which berths them will surely burst."

Laura, a hard and sad thirty-two years of age now fixed in her face, stared dully out the window. *Why should this rich belle consider her suffering any worse than the legions of other mothers in this nation who have lost children,* she thought with distaste. *And few of those mothers had a stable of slaves, a half-room full of wardrobe, way too many airs, and a—a husband who loved them with which to console themselves.*

"I am astounded to learn how he has given of himself," Anna continued, unaware of the thin frown and lack of empathy emblazoned on Laura's tanned, none-too-subtle face. "Not even considering his contributions to the bright futures of year after year of young men through a job I know he detests, though he would never admit it. His founding of the colored Sunday school—my Hetty tells me she learned he actually gave a young Negro boy named Lyle or Luther or whatnot, a pocket Testament, knowing full well the boy is teaching himself to read in private.

"Why, Pastor White at the church says Tom's the most dedicated deacon he has, the way he works with the older folks, the widows, and the benevolence ministry. He saw to it that both the Franklin Debating Society and the Lexington Bank (on whose board he sits) gave to some desperately needy Presbyterian missionaries last year. He still helps out that unfortunate half brother of his, Wirt, though he has cost him a small fortune," she continued, as Laura, who already knew it all, rolled her eyes in irritation.

"And the education he, John Preston, and various other tutors around Lexington have provided Tommy—well, Margaret Preston told me few institutions of higher learning would surpass it." *Better Maggie Junkin than you married him,* Laura thought with venom. *She's high and uppity, too, but she has fewer airs and it's she he truly loves.* The last thought brought a half smile to Laura's face.

Anna lowered her head and paused so long that Laura started to inquire what time she could be leaving for Beverly with the children.

Then Anna, her back still to Laura, began to weep softly.

"He even thought of your Elizabeth in writing the letter about Mary to her and not you," she said. "He always thinks first of the children. That's why they all love him so much."

The mention of the letter felt to Laura like a dart piercing her heart. Only two things on earth could still grip her desolate remaining emotions—Tommy and Elizabeth. What hurt one of them hurt her thrice over. For months Elizabeth had carried on a correspondence with Jackson, in eager anticipation of her new little cousin. Elizabeth thrilled even more when the newborn proved to be a girl. Then Mary died.

Laura had practically memorized Jackson's tender letter to Elizabeth, had worn it to a crumpled, faded yellow. Its words had drawn her with some mysterious pull that she could not have identified had she been asked what it was. She had read them over and over, unlike most of the religion-tinged missives he sent to Laura herself.

At this moment, the crinkled letter resided in the small purse Laura carried with her and held in her hand on the sofa.

"Your sweet little cousin and my daughter," Jackson had written, "was called from this world of sin to enjoy the heavenly happiness of Paradise. . . . Whilst your Aunt Anna and myself feel our loss, yet we know that God has taken her away in love."

"Jesus said," the letter continued, "'Suffer little children and forbid them not, to come unto me: for of such is the kingdom of heaven.' Did you ever think, my dear Elizabeth, that the most persons who have died and gone to heaven are little children?"

Anna and Laura each knew what resided in the letter. There seemed nothing more to say, so they sat in silence until Jackson and Tommy came in.

After George and Cyrus had loaded the Arnolds' bags onto the back of the buggy that would transport them to the Lexington stagecoach depot, Laura cast an odd glance at Jackson in the front hallway.

"Brother," she said, "what will you do if the state secedes?"

The question puzzled him. "Why, I don't know, sister," he said. "I suppose I should remain loyal to the dear Union for which I bled, as always I have. I can think of no conceivable scenario in which I—or indeed, most all of Lexington and Virginia—would turn against our flag, short of a groundless, outright assault upon Virginia. And I cannot imagine that ever happening."

Laura, dark rings still under her eyes even after a lazy week in Lexington, decided to plunge on. "But secessionist fever grows all across the South."

"But do you consider Virginia a part of the Deep South?" Jackson replied. "I do not. Certainly not a part of the Cotton Belt South. Like Delaware, Maryland, Kentucky, Tennessee, and others, she is a border state."

"Still, though, the fever grows here too," she persisted, "at least in that portion of the state east of the Alleghenies. With few slavers in western Virginia, the fever is less common."

Anna's eyebrows arched upward as she glanced at her husband. This confusing dialogue discomforted her.

"But I do not equate a country's incidence of slaveholding with its degree of secessionist fervor," Jackson said evenly. "Other constitutional abuses by the North have Southerners more alarmed than those regarding slavery. Only the fire-eaters are energized on the slavery issue."

Laura's eyes blazed. They did not see Tommy and Elizabeth enter the room from downstairs with Amy. "Fire-eaters, phooey, Tommy," she said, "look around you. This whole section is lazy, arrogant, uneducated, and built on the sweat of ignorant Africans. Oh you—I mean them—and their calm, sweet, smiling *Jesus*. Why it makes me want to wretch."

Anna gasped.

"Why are you yelling, Mama?" Elizabeth asked in fear, going to her mother and hugging her.

Jackson walked to Laura and wrapped her and Elizabeth in his long muscular arms. Laura's head lay against his chest. For a moment, all was quiet except for a wagon passing on the hard dirt road down below. Then Jackson leaned down and whispered so softly in his sister's ear that no one else could hear what he said.

"I am so very, very sorry you have been hurt, dear sister." He paused. "Please don't condemn the many wonderful people of our town and country who would love nothing more than to have you live among them."

Her head flew up and she pushed him away. Her voice dripped poison and rage. "Not *my* people, Tom Jackson, never will these churchgoing hypocrites be my people!" She pushed away Elizabeth's proffered arm. "My people—and yours, Tom, truth be known—are mountain people, simple people, without airs." Her eyes shot a fiery dart at Anna, whose mouth dropped open and face blushed scarlet.

"And that's where I'm a-going back. Out the door, Tommy and Elizabeth."

Tommy, as shocked as everyone else, hesitated. "But Ma—"

"I said out, d—— you, Son!" Laura screamed, her chin distended and the veins of her reddened neck jutting out over the worn collar of her calico dress.

At this profanity, all in the room gasped. Laura belatedly discerned the impression she had left.

Jackson knew the years of neglect and ridicule absorbed from her husband, and her own rejection of the Lord's salving gospel, had formed a bitter shell around Laura. Until now he did not realize how fearful that shell had become.

Jackson shook Tommy's hand and hugged him. "Be disciplined about your Latin, Tommy," the professor said, "and it shall unlock for you any language you choose to explore."

Then he picked up ten-year-old Elizabeth, hugged her, and kissed her. She spotted something hanging conspicuously out of his jacket pocket. "Why, Uncle Tom," she squealed, "you got me a new dolly!"

"Why, I don't know," he feigned as she jerked the little pink stuffed character from his pocket and squirmed out of his arms to the floor. She clutched it with all her might and smiled brilliant blue-eyed mirth up at him. "I'm going to love it more than any of the others," of which there was only one, "because you gave her to me."

With that, she bounded out the door, pigtails flopping. Tommy, Anna, and Amy followed her.

Brother and sister stood alone, her head bowed. He pulled her to him and hugged her again, for a long time and with much love. She felt his love and felt love toward him. Her tears stained his blue VMI coat and she cursed life and its unremitting darkness. Then she pulled away and left without another word.

Lieutenant Colonel Robert E. Lee remembered the name John Brown from the "Bleeding Kansas" reports of three years before. A nervous, high-strung religious fanatic whose mother had insanity in her family. A bankrupt, often in court, and often accused of dishonesty. A man who believed God had commissioned him to abolish slavery—violently.

Lee remembered how Brown had begun that process in Kansas by butchering five defenseless settlers, including one free black. And now the old boot, nearly sixty years old, was holed up fifty yards from

Lee in the small brick firehouse of the United States military arsenal at Harper's Ferry, on Virginia's northernmost point, just across the Potomac River from Maryland.

The night before, October 16, 1859, Brown had led an assault on the arsenal, which had a single guard, and captured it. The only casualty was a free black railroad employee killed by an errant shot. Brown intended, as Lee understood it, to use the weapons and ammunition to engineer a slave revolt and establish a sovereign new nation in western Virginia, composed of white abolitionists, freed slaves, and Brown himself as commander in chief.

Lee bit his lower lip as a fellow Virginian, strapping young Lieutenant J. E. B. "Jeb" Stuart—Lee's favorite cadet when he served as superintendent at West Point—scurried toward the barricaded firehouse door with the stealth and speed of the Plains Indians Lee and Stuart had both been fighting until the past few weeks when each, separately, had been recalled to Washington for new assignments.

How had such madness been born? Lee wondered. Now it would be even harder for men of moderation like himself to talk down the Southern fire-eaters who so spoiled for disunion and, in some cases, war. Ever since the 1831 rampage of another "religious" fanatic, the demonized Nat Turner, murdered sixty-one Virginians, most of them women and children, the Old Dominion had endured rumors of servile insurrection, repressive laws of assembly between black and white, and the increasing scorn and ridicule of Northern abolitionists, many of them living off the comfortable fruit of slave-wage factory serfs.

The nation's largest churches, the Methodist, Baptist, and Presbyterian, had split into Northern and Southern branches. Thankfully, Lee thought, his beloved Episcopal denomination had not. But even as he led the troop detachment out of Washington early that morning, the streets hummed that many in the North applauded Brown's "courage," "daring," and "alacrity." That, Lee—considered America's finest individual soldier at the close of the Mexican War, following his legendary exploits in leading his countrymen on their victorious surge from Vera Cruz to the City of Mexico—could not fathom.

But more immediate danger pressed. Jeb Stuart crouched near the firehouse, imposing Navy Colt drawn, ordering Brown and his men to emerge unarmed, hands on their heads.

Stuart himself had no time to worry, nor think of his beloved wife and daughter. His answer was a bullet that sang inches over his head. Crouching had indeed been a good idea. He grimaced, then gave the signal for his men to advance. The next moments were a chaotic blur.

Stuart remembered the thick oaken front door finally giving way to a telegraph pole cum-battering ram. Two of the men carrying it fell wounded in his path. He stumbled and fell over one, which saved him from the swath of a double-barreled shotgun blast that would have removed his entire head. In the dark, smoky firehouse frenzy around him, he rolled over, leveled his Colt at the shotgun wielder as the man came at him swinging the weapon like a club, and squeezed off two shots, knocking the man down and driving him, lifeless, into the wall behind him. Then a trooper and one of Brown's men tumbled over Stuart, one of their boots thumping the Virginian in the jaw. The two rolled on the hard dirt floor, struggling for possession of a huge old Sharps pistol. Stuart leaned over and placed his Colt against the renegade's head, just as another soldier fired twice into the man's chest from a few feet away.

Stuart blinked as a ferocious volley ripped behind him. He turned to see several men, soldiers and bandits, shooting it out at close range. One of Brown's men fell screaming to the ground, then another. Then a soldier fell to his knees, clutching his side. He looked up, sighted tall, rawboned Brown himself, and pulled the trigger of his own Colt. The shot knocked Brown, firing at another trooper, off his feet. Another soldier kicked Brown's gun away and dragged him to his feet by his collar. When other bandits saw their leader bloodied, disarmed, and cornered, the fight was over.

Lee looked heavenward and thanked his Lord that justice had prevailed. Then he looked again at the smoke-enveloped firehouse and heard the agonized cries bleating from the wounded within. One foreboding thought would not leave his mind: *What has been wrought today, Almighty God?*

Jackson ate supper with Dr. Junkin and Julia just over a month later in the Washington College president's dining room that held so many memories for him. It had been quite a spell since he had done so. He did not often visit the president's home anymore. Ruthie was glad to see him and had just dolloped out an extra chunk of steaming apple pie for him when Preston tramped in, clad in his blue VMI coat, his majestic face carrying an urgent look.

"Father," he said respectfully, bowing, "Julia, Tom. I've been ordered to Charles Town with Colonel Smith—tonight. John Brown is to hang in one week. Tom, you'll be coming with Major Gilham and the cadets in two days. Robert Lee is coming with four companies of government regulars from Fortress Monroe. All tolled, there may be two thousand troops present for the execution, counting militia."

Junkin wiped his lips with the fine linen napkin, then lowered it slow as molasses to his lap.

No one spoke for a moment. Jackson caught Julia's expression, her paleness standing in particular relief against the requisite black mourning attire. *She doesn't need this now,* he thought, *with her fine husband, Julius Fishburne, only a month in the ground.* "Father," he said, standing and rounding the table to the frail twenty-four-year-old widow. He bent to her and hugged her. She grasped his arm and clung to it. He felt her quivering.

"Must they make such a to-do about it?" Junkin groused.

No one answered, but Preston pulled a newspaper from under one arm. He handed it to his father-in-law. "The latest edition of the abolitionists' publication *The Liberator,* Father."

Junkin scanned the front page, a white sheet spreading across his creased sixty-eight-year-old countenance. Slowly, he lowered the paper and shook his head, just as Ruthie entered again from the kitchen with a silver pot of boiling coffee.

Preston turned to Jackson and Julia, the color in his normally staid countenance rising. "The Sumners and Garrisons of the world are hailing Brown as a providential martyr, such as such heathen would know about Providence or martyrs." He pointed an accusing finger toward the paper. "That," he cried, fury dripping from the word, "while brave Virginians and government marines lie fresh in their graves, *that* puts the South on notice that expeditions from the North are being launched to rescue that vile murderer who would have unleashed the lowest nature of honest faithful blacks on defenseless women and children across Virginia."

Preston trembled with anger. That disquieted Jackson, who had never seen the man so. Jackson released Julia and stepped toward Junkin, whose head remained downcast. The professor lifted *The Liberator* from the table. He could not believe his eyes. The paper reported organized efforts by Northerners to monitor Southern military preparations for Brown's hanging. No less than the great transcendentalist essayist-poet Ralph Waldo Emerson lauded Brown as a selfless hero in a just cause.

Jackson lowered the paper and glanced at Junkin, who met his eyes. An icy chill braced the Virginian, and for the first time he could not escape the fact that armed civil conflict—section against section, state against state, brother against brother—might eventually force itself on a people who almost universally did not want it. Then his gaze took in Junkin and Preston—*No, there are too many sober, decent men in the Union,* he thought with relief, *a great majority like that, in fact. A nation that does not allow itself to fall into war will not!*—and as quickly as the frightening specter had gripped him, it passed from him.

But indeed, both Junkin and Preston flared with anger.

"Just you remember, my dear sons," the old patriarch warned, now pointing his own long bony finger, not at Preston, but at the younger man, Jackson, "whatever ensues, Virginia and the South must never break the Lord's sovereign compact of this Union. Else I swear to you by the holy name of Christ that He shall visit devastation upon this fair land and all who have sprung from her loins."

Jackson saw that Preston wanted very much to reply, as often he wanted when such conversations sprang forth, but, as always, he held his peace in order to honor the man of God who had sired his wife.

Then silence encompassed the room and all lost themselves in thought. All the whites wished for the presence of their beloveds. But Julia's and her father's were dead; Maggie was cloistered in her room at home with cold packs over her aching eyes; and Anna would be at the Rockbridge Baths until after Jackson's departure for Charles Town, taking steam and water for her ailing respiratory system.

Jackson himself felt his inflamed throat grip him, and he grabbed for the jar of glycerine next to his table setting and drank from it. He hoped the throat, as well as his aching, nearly deaf left ear and his hurting right eye, would not trouble him too terribly on the trip north to Charles Town, in which he would command two institute howitzers and help preside over the hanging of a man who represented many things to many people across a troubled land.

CHAPTER 28

HOW COULD SHE GET IT ALL DONE BY THE WEEKEND? MAGGIE flavored the last of a tardy batch of autumn apple butter and eyed the colorful swatch of broadcloth brought to her from Trenton by her brother John on his recent visit from the North. That sublime material would make for a fine season of sewing. She smiled as she thought of the new sweater with which she would surprise dear Willy. She would begin that sweater, perhaps, even tonight.

Amazingly, her skill as a needlewoman had become almost proverbial through the extended Preston clan. "As great," feisty old statesman-orator Colonel William Preston of South Carolina had marveled, "as if she had never the first sonnet penned!"

Maggie glanced back over her shoulder at the ovens heating her secret recipe mince pies and crullers. *Oh, the love this endless line of Preston children, cousins, aunts, and uncles parading in ceaseless waves in and out of this home has developed for my mince pies and crullers, and my jellies!* she marveled. And all now acknowledged that not even the most flattering of visiting Tidewater guests could entice her and her delicate but iron-set jaw from the preserving kettle until the fruit was ready to be put into the jars.

Still, she thought with a twinge, leaving the kitchen for a moment to Hannah and Rahab and crossing the few feet to the smokehouse to season the winter supply of sausage—with her own hand always, she insisted, *that* being something the sainted Sally Preston never did— words, inflections of words, and poorly-disguised expressions had cut her to the quick time without number in the two-plus years she had now been Mrs. John T. L. Preston, wife of a true Virginia scion and descendant of English aristocracy.

Among the worst, of course, had been old Carolinian Colonel Preston and his disapproving slights on her appearances in print.

"Unseemly," he called it, not always with inordinate effort to hide his comments from her own ears. And how often had she heard, or been informed, of his disfavor of "the little redheaded Yankee's want of style and presence." *Oh!* What did they expect of her? Sally Preston *had* been every bit the saint, and she had had twenty-three years to win the family. Sometimes Maggie thought it enough to return her to her previous condescension of heart toward the "gentle" South and its "gallant" men.

Finishing the sausage, however, she smiled, remembering the day the previous summer when, with nearly all the Preston minions assembled in the orchard back of her own home, she had stilled and won forever the Colonel Prestons of the family. Thinking to demonstrate to Maggie her proper place, the old boy had challenged her on the relative merits of Hawthorne as opposed to Poe, the latter having been a close and long-standing Preston family friend. When her soft, melodic response had concluded a half hour later, the dozens in enthralled attendance sat hushed. Had they not been good Presbyterians or Anglicans all, spontaneous applause would have erupted. As it was, old Preston confided afterward to his nephew John, "Hark, little Margaret is an encyclopedia in small print!"

Everafter he would be her most ardent champion among the family and beyond.

Difficult, too, had been reigning her quick torrid temper against the admonitions of the old house servants that "Miss Sally never did so." Here Maggie sought deliverance through the Scriptures, remembering the tongue as "an unruly evil, full of deadly poison" by which men praise God and curse other men made by God in His image, and that "the fruit of righteousness is sown in peace of them that make peace." Slowly so did her angry impulses melt into the response she had given her father earlier this very day, that the servants "meant it kindly."

But undoubtedly the most trying of all the circumstances of marrying at thirty-seven into an immediate family of seven children and an enormous extended family of dozens and dozens, then adding her own motherhood with the arrival the previous year of little George, was her own dear husband's difficulty in supporting her God-bequeathed literary gifts.

Only the day before, she remembered with pain, she had come to Preston flush with the excitement of having won the *Baltimore Sun*'s annual short story contest, which drew entries from as far away as California and England and was worth one hundred dollars. He had affected happiness, but she saw the lift of his eyebrows, the slight slackness in his jaw, the general *surprise* on his face. It cut her more than any words could have, for words were words, even for a gentleman, and the honest expressions of an honest man carried much import.

She consoled herself with remembrance of how God worked to establish holiness in the life of every Christian, and worked specifically so when He brought two sinners together in matrimony, especially those who had had several decades to cultivate that sinfulness. And she knew her husband loved her and had to overcome his own sharp reluctance to having a pen in his wife's fingers and her name in very public print.

But she also remembered the joy she had shared over her literary ideas and successes those many months with Tom Jackson. *My old kindred spirit,* she thought with a twinge of regret. But such thinking would neither effect holiness nor prepare for the weekend arrival of the North Carolina Prestons, so she turned back toward the kitchen, where it sounded as though Hannah and Rahab were raising a ruckus with one another.

Just then, Jackson kissed Anna good-bye and strode out the front door, down the steps, and into the mild afternoon sunshine. First he saw Elizabeth and John Preston, with their older brother Willy, then John Carlisle's little son and daughter and their nanny. These joined Jackson on the wooden sidewalk at the foot of his own front steps. He blushed as he looked around at them, tousling little master Carlisle's thick brown hair.

"Why have y'all gathered here?" Jackson asked shyly.

"We're going with you to see that mean man hang," Elizabeth blurted out.

"Actually, they wanted to accompany you to the VMI, Major Jackson, sir," Willy said.

Jackson was at a loss for words. "But—why?"

"Because we love you, Major Jackson, sir," Elizabeth said, affixing herself to Jackson's leg like a leech. All he could see of her were black curls and pink ribbons holding them.

Jackson blushed anew and his throat tightened. He felt a strong urge to launch an arm skyward, but resisted it.

Upstairs, Anna raised the shade and pushed aside the creamy lace curtain, then watched as the group turned to move up the street in the direction of the VMI. She balled a soft white hand and pressed it hard against her lips. Up the street, three more children, one white and two black, and their black nanny, joined the group.

Anna released the curtain and turned away from the window. *What manner of man?* she wondered.

When Jackson arrived at the institute parade ground, he regarded the throng of little people gathered around him, all huffing and puffing from keeping up the several blocks with his long quick strides. *Such as these John Brown would have murdered if necessary to achieve his aim,* Jackson thought. Then he winked at the smiling Willy and hugged each of the twenty children, black and white, thanked them for their support, enlisted their prayers for a safe journey for the assembled cadets and faculty and himself, and exhorted them to lead their guardians home and return to their regular duties.

John Brown's gallows rose on a high stand of ground that commanded the valley between the twin mountain ranges that enveloped it both east and west. As Jackson peered through the early morning semihaze, the white clouds to the east that sat atop the purple mountains like balls of eiderdown reminded him of the snow-peaked Alps he had once viewed from afar.

No drums, no music on this day, despite the assemblage of fifteen hundred federal and state troops. Jackson sensed that, Northern intrusion or not, this day brought more than a hanging. He ordered the howitzer he would personally command swung into place no more than twenty yards to the left of the gallows. He glanced across the plateau and observed VMI Lieutenant Dan Trueheart supervising placement of the other howitzer. As Superintendent Smith purposed, the two could sweep the field if trouble arose.

Jackson glanced across the VMI cadets lined directly behind the gallows. Along with the various Virginia flags snapping and popping in the breeze around the perimeter of the ground, the boys presented the day's most vivid color. They wore gray greatcoats, open in the front, over bright red flannel shirts. And the boys looked ready, even anxious, for action. *Pray God it does not come,* Jackson thought, closing his eyes. Mexico had etched itself deeply into the recesses of his memory.

Flanking the cadets on either side were the best two militia infantry units in Virginia, the Richmond Grays and Richmond's Company F. Some of the state's finest sons comprised their colorful dashing columns. The Grays also included on this day one John Wilkes Booth. Contrary to the later assertions of Carl Sandburg and other Northern writers, Booth was not and had never been a member of any militia unit. This once, he had talked his way into accompanying the Grays so he could witness the hanging.

Best as he could with his poor eyesight, Jackson scanned the hundreds of other Virginia militia and Federal troopers that covered the field. The great majority were infantry. But across the way he sighted Smith, whom Governor Wise of Virginia had placed in charge of the entire event, mounted with John Preston, Robert Lee, and other officers, both state and federal. Jackson offered silent thanks to God for the show of solidarity between the Old Dominion and the Union.

He also noted an imposing troop of militia cavalry, mounted—to the man—on sleek, huge black chargers. At their head, one man sat astride a peerless warhorse brilliant white as the winter snow atop the Blue Ridge in the sun at noonday.

That man was Turner Ashby of Fauquier County.

Then Jackson heard a rumble in a left oblique direction behind him, back toward the town. He turned and saw three companies of Lee's regulars marching toward the gallows. In a few moments they arrived, followed by a wagon drawn by two white horses. The entourage turned to pass directly in front of Jackson and his howitzer en route to the gallows. As the wagon neared, he saw seated in it several law officers and soldiers, along with a tanned, rawboned man, his hands and feet chained together, who sported a great shock of gray hair atop his head. *John Brown,* Jackson realized.

Brown conversed with the sheriff seated next to him and gestured with his manacled hands toward distant objects. As the wagon moved in front of Jackson, within fifteen feet of him, he heard the condemned man say to the sheriff through the hushed stillness, "This is a beautiful country. I never had the pleasure of seeing it before."

Then, as the wagon passed Jackson, Brown proceeded momentarily into the Virginian's line of view. The two locked eyes for an instant, then Brown was gone. Gilham, standing some yards away from Jackson, noticed Brown's gaze linger on the stern, rigid, expressionless artillery commander.

When the wagon arrived at the gallows, the sheriff unlocked Brown's feet manacles, but not those for his hands. The prisoner climbed down off the wagon and moved to the steep steps of the gallows, which he ascended to the platform. All of this, Jackson noted, Brown did with aplomb and without hesitation.

Jackson studied Brown's face. *It is serious, but unflinchingly firm. Death is no matter of gaiety and merriment,* the professor thought, recalling the gay attitude of many of the militia the past twenty-four hours. Some had talked of war as an entertaining pastime, and many looked upon it as an altogether glorious endeavor.

The sheriff placed the white cap over Brown's head and tightened the noose around his neck.

"Do you wish a signal when all is ready?" Jackson could hear the sheriff ask Brown.

"It makes no difference, just as long as I am not kept waiting too long," Brown replied, the calmness of his voice surprising Jackson.

Then the sheriff attached the noose to the hook above and moved Brown forward a few steps. The prisoner advanced his feet with great caution.

Odd, Jackson marveled, *how his instincts caution him in putting out his feet, as if afraid he might fall a few feet off the scaffold when he, without wish for minister or prayer, stands facing the brink of eternity!*

After a few more moments during which Brown's troop escort was redeployed, Smith called to the sheriff that all was ready. Despite the extraordinary silence of the convocation—no galloping horses now—the tense sheriff did not act as though he heard the order, and Smith, after consulting briefly with Preston, repeated it. This time the sheriff heard it, and a moment later he descended the steps, took a hatchet, and with one swift chop of the rope, dispatched John Brown to eternity.

As the abolitionist dangled between heaven and earth, his arms drawn up to a right angle at the elbows and his fists clenched, Jackson closed his eyes and considered the awful thought that Brown might within a few minutes receive the sentence, "Depart from me, ye cursed, into everlasting fire!" *I hope he is prepared to die, but I am doubtful.* Jackson then offered God a passionate petition that Brown's soul might be saved.

For minutes, Brown swung, his body quite still. The enormous throng watched the momentous event in silence. Only the fluttering of the flags sounded. So long did everyone remain silent and unmoving that Preston finally cleared his throat, adjusted his collar, then turned to Smith, Lee, and the other officers around him and proclaimed, with no animosity, "So perish all such enemies of Virginia, all such enemies of the Union, all such foes of the human race."

The cofounder of the Virginia Military Institute could not know how many would perish before the American states had ceased their terrible fierce dealing with the enemies of Virginia, the Union, and the human race.

That evening in Richmond, Jackson sat erect over a lamplit old wooden desk in the cramped hotel quarters he shared with several other officers. Twin currents of thought swirled through his head as he pondered what to write Anna. At length, he dipped his quill in the small tub of gooey ink.

"Viewing things at Washington from human appearances," he wrote, "I think we have great reason for alarm, but my trust is in God; and I cannot think that He will permit the madness of men to interfere so materially with the Christian labors of this country at home and abroad."

Indeed, Jackson thought, immigrants from spiritually sagging Europe continued to stream into the nation. The American population itself burgeoned. And increasing westward migration confronted white Christians with legions of pagan red men. All boded well for a bountiful harvest of souls for the Lord.

Again, Jackson reasoned, the Lord would not allow a military conflagration to interfere with this most critical of all endeavors. He would sustain the requisite number of thoughtful, circumspect minds in all the sections—North, South, and West—to sustain a peace *"that we may lead a quiet and peaceable life in all godliness and honesty."*

CHAPTER 29

VIRGINIA MAY HAVE HANGED JOHN BROWN, BUT HER LEGIONS of other enemies grew as 1859 became 1860. The Jacksons traveled North to Vermont, then Massachusetts early in the summer in search of hydropathic water relief. Both had recurring intestinal irritation, and his eyes experienced frequent pain and some deterioration of sight. During the travels, Jackson winced at the realization that he had failed to experience good health for any period beyond a few days since the Mexican War!

Like other Southerners, the Jacksons experienced rudeness and bigotry from some of the Northern locals. His calm demeanor and refusal to participate in the increasingly frequent and rancorous arguments regarding the sectional disputes over states' rights, slavery, tariffs, culture, and economics and politics in general kept the Jacksons' trip less stressful than those of many Southerners.

However, the trip, in light of the looming fall elections, where presidential hopes shined for Abraham Lincoln of the young, strongly antislavery Republican Party, prompted Jackson to confide to Anna a horror he had never before considered, even within himself: "I fear now that our differences, on top of the coming elections, may portend armed civil war."

Anna gasped at the suggestion, then dismissed it. In fact, she decided to remain North for further treatment even after her husband returned to Lexington for the fall VMI term.

As the carriage pulled away from their hotel for his solo return south, the curious thought struck Jackson that though he loved his wife dearly, he could not imagine ever having parted with Ellie, by choice, for months at a time, as he had already done several times with Anna. For a moment, he wrestled with reconciling those contrasting situations, before his attention was captured by the conversation of two other passengers. Their accents revealing their Northern heritage, one read to the other from an article in one of the Boston newspapers. The words chilled Jackson as none others yet had.

"Here are the words of the abolitionist senator from Pennsylvania, Thaddeus Stevens," the man with the paper said, "'If the South's whole country must be laid waste, and made a desert, in order to save this Union from destruction, so let it be. I would rather, sir, reduce them to a condition where their whole country is to be repeopled than perpetrate the destruction of this people through our agency.'"

Nor did matters calm upon Jackson's return to Lexington. Most of Lexington, Rockbridge County, and Virginia, including Jackson, remained staunchly pro-Union and opposed to splintering from the Union. Secession talk blazed red-hot across the Deep South Cotton Belt, however. And the majority of men in Rockbridge County and Virginia—women not yet being entrusted with the vote—favored the conservative new Constitutional Union Party and its proslavery presidential candidate John Bell of Tennessee. But unanimity was not the order of the day in the South, at least not yet. Jackson and most of his colleagues belonged to the conservatively inclined Democrat Party. Even they were split. The larger group backed Governor John Letcher, a Lexington native, and his support of old Lincoln nemesis Stephen Douglas of Illinois. Jackson, Preston, and others stood with former U.S. vice president John Breckenridge of Kentucky, a staunch backer of the expansion of slavery, not for its own virtues, but for the attendant political punch to protect Southern culture and society in the halls of Congress.

The disputes grew closer to home than Jackson desired, especially after Abe Lincoln won the election. The tall, sad-faced Illinois lawyer garnered only 40 percent of the national popular vote, but he easily carried the determinative electoral vote, his strongholds being the electoral-rich Northern industrial powerhouses.

Abraham Lincoln received exactly one vote in Rockbridge County and none at all in ten Southern states.

Now secession became the only course remaining in the eyes of planter-controlled South Carolina and several other Deep South states. Lincoln! Though he had promised repeatedly never to infringe on the rights of slaveholders, and in fact said he would not abolish the practice even if he could, if to retain all of it or part of it would better ensure the continued health of the Union, Southern Democrats heard the death knell of their political and economic leverage with the ascendancy of the Republicans.

Events began at long last to outrun the efforts of any man to slow them.

One crisp November evening, shortly before Anna's return from the North, Jackson's servant George pulled the professor's buggy up in front of Dr. Junkin's home. There, Preston was to join Jackson for the ride to the evening's Franklin Society meeting, which promised to be a lively one.

His eyes bothering him, Jackson decided to fetch Preston himself, thinking to clear his head a bit with the walk.

He heard the shouting from outside, even before he reached the door.

Inside, Preston and Dr. Junkin were engaged in very unparlorlike debate in the parlor. Their powerful voices echoed through the large house. As Jackson walked through the front foyer, an odd sound drew his attention to the staircase. Several Preston children clustered near the top of the carpeted steps, their eyes wide.

Next Jackson nearly ran into Ruthie, who had appeared from out of nowhere. She shook her head from side to side, her face a mute portrait of sadness, then peered over her shoulder in the direction of the shouting. Jackson proceeded to the parlor entrance and stopped, not in the least desirous to enter the fray. The two towering combatants stood on the lush Oriental rug only a few feet from one another in the center of the room. Only after a moment did Jackson notice Maggie cowering on the sofa to the side. Rarely in the nearly ten years he had known her had he seen her face so ready to dissolve into tears as it was at this wrenching scene.

John Preston had received the last bellowing lecture he could stand from his father-in-law, whom he loved and, truth be known, idolized. For more than a decade the strapping Virginian had held his piece during the periodic outbursts he witnessed from the old theologian-educator. Even had Maggie finally scolded her husband for not speaking up, and she a Pennsylvanian and former loather of the South.

But this night was the fourth anniversary of Sally's death and also the tenth anniversary of the painful death of Preston's eldest son to typhus. Two of his children were now ill and so had he been of late. And he had just returned from a trip to the North, where everyone from a train porter to a hotel manager had made certain he knew in their eyes he, scion of one of Virginia's finest families, former best friend of Edgar Poe, and descendant of General Washington's secretary of state, was no more than a subhuman Southron slaver.

So when the old patriarch once again lit into the "imbecility and supreme foolhardiness" of the South's political leadership, Preston, aching in body and spirit, stood and, respectfully at first, begged to differ.

"I'll not stand silently while depraved mercenary lunatics rend this sovereign Union to pieces," Junkin now roared as Jackson observed, the old warrior's chin thrust forward and his eyes blazing like Moses come down from Mount Sinai to find his people worshiping a golden calf.

Before Preston could respond, Junkin spotted Jackson. "My dear son," he said, moderating his tone and waving Jackson in, "come, Son, come. Please, try to reason with John. He takes umbrage at my defense of God's sovereignly established Union. Please, please, Tom, talk sense to our brother." With this last, Junkin managed the winning smile and sparkle of eye that had helped win Rush long years ago and many a congregation and student body since.

Blood scaled the top of Jackson's high forehead as all eyes bore in on him. Preston fumed, clearly not wishing to relinquish the floor, whatever Jackson's position might be. But Maggie sat up straight, her pale face a shade whiter than normal, even her painted lips pale. The blue eyes were wide like those of a deer realizing he has been sighted. *She is looking to me in hope for an answer, an answer that will please all,* Jackson realized. Alas, he knew, sighing audibly, he had no answer that could satisfy all.

"I . . . " Jackson began, his eyes uncharacteristically blinking several times. He had never backed off from a scrap in his life, but the thought struck him that this might be the first time. His lips moved, but the well from which he drew his words seemed dry.

"Come on, Tom," Preston urged, in a contentious manner Jackson had never before seen, "I've never seen you set store by a man not speaking his mind when the question is put to him. Tell him what you think."

Junkin's eyes were hopeful as Jackson cleared his throat. Jackson had never dared take issue with the old man during his Unionist tirades either. Usually he agreed with him, at least with most of what he said.

"The union of states is a divine compact constructed by the Lord Jehovah Himself," Junkin said, sounding now more like the firm but reasonable Scots-Irishman behind the pulpit or lectern. "Those who seek to destroy that compact shall only bring down upon themselves the wrath of He whose fury swallowed the hosts of Egypt and Syria, the Amalekites, the Philistines, the Canaanites, and all the others who sought to stand in defiance of the Almighty's sovereignly ordained plans and purposes." Then he turned his again-burning gaze back to Preston. "And all those who would seek to do so."

Preston blanched, but before he could speak, Jackson's gentle voice sounded forth: "I believe Christians should not be disturbed about the dissolution of the Union. It can come only with God's permission, and will only be permitted if for His people's good. I cannot see how we should be distressed about such things, whatever be their consequences."

Spoken like one true Calvinist to another, in the witness of other Calvinists.

Junkin seemed to grow very old in that instant when the shadow of Satan's ancient dark vision of the breaking apart of loving families fell again. The proud old war horse saw so many dreams dissolve before his eyes and so many hideous nightmares flash into view that he leaned from the import of the statement.

Preston, who had won the moment, seemed no happier than his father-in-law, for he too began to apprehend the first terrifying glimmer of what he might have to lose.

Jackson, who felt suddenly ill, allowed himself a glance at Maggie. Though she agreed with the Virginian's words, her head was bowed, scarlet tresses tumbling into her lap.

Junkin turned back toward the chair where he had sat, then thought better of it and pivoted toward the door. He let out a deep sad breath and trudged very slowly out of the room, muttering as he went, "I fear I have now lived too long."

The pearly snows of Christmas descended on Virginia with South Carolina no longer a member of the Union. Stoned hearth fires toasted the airy rooms of the Jackson home. A happy and secure home it was, though still bereft of the squeals, laughter, and foot patters of children. Sometimes Jackson dreamt of little children, lots of them, following him as on the day he left for John Brown's hanging. But in his dreams, all the children were his. When he awoke from such dreams, he always found a way to steal some time at play with at least one of the village's delighted little people.

One dark evening a few days before the Lord's birthday, Anna read a letter by the light of the sitting room fire to Jackson from Laura.

As always, his heart beat quicker in anticipation of her latest news. His anticipation contained mixed parts hope for her happiness and her spiritual deliverance, and disappointment at the inevitable sadness hanging over the letters like a soupy winter fog.

This night, however, he sprang to his feet as the tone of the letter indicated a sea change in Laura's spiritual temperature. No longer did the words drip with disappointment, longing, and despair. Rather, despite one or two curiously strident remarks against secession supporters in Beverly, they spoke of present and future hope—in the Savior! Temptations and challenges to her faith aplenty, yes—but though she did not say so directly, her words implied trust and belief in Christ.

"You speak of your temptations," Jackson said, the letter Anna held in her hands the object of his words, as though Laura could hear each and every one of them. "God withdraws His sensible presence from us to try our faith. When a cloud comes between you and the sun, do you fear that the sun will never appear again? O, pray for more faith."

"How wonderful," Anna said, her cherub face rent in two by a heartfelt smile.

Jackson, booted, jumped straight up in the air and screeched a shrill "Yee!" that hurt Anna's ears. After landing with a thud that shook the house, he lifted her out of her chair, into the air, and swung her round and round. "My *esposa,* my *esposa!* My baby sister has come finally to the blessed cross!"

She giggled and it looked as though the gymnastics would proceed presently to the boudoir when Jackson placed her back on the rugged floor in midswing.

"I've an idea, my love dove," he said, his eyes alight but seeing something else, not her. "I've got to go see Pastor White. Now."

Her face crinkled in disappointment. Yet, she knew he would not interrupt such proceedings for less than something of great importance.

Five minutes later Pastor White ushered Jackson into the cozy parlor of the Lexington Presbyterian parsonage.

"So what does my hardest working deacon have on his snow-dusted mind this evening?" White asked, his gray eyes twinkling.

Jackson cut to the chase. "If the general government should persist in its threats to suppress South Carolina by force of arms, there must be war, sir. It is painful to discover with what unconcern they speak of war, and threaten it. They seem not to know what its horrors are." Jackson's eyes narrowed. "I have had an opportunity of knowing enough on the subject, to make me fear war as the sum of all evils."

The horrific specters of sacked cities, torn families, widows, orphans, and rotting corpses, assaulted White's mind and he winced. But then Jackson's face brightened, and he leaned so far forward in his chair that White thought he would topple out of it.

"But do you not think," Jackson asked, "that all the Christian people of the land could be induced to unite in a concert of prayer, to avert so great an evil?" Now Jackson's face blossomed into the brightest smile White had ever seen grace it. "It seems to me, that if they would unite thus in prayer, war might be prevented, and peace preserved."

White stared at the beaming face, which seemed intent on securing permission to launch an immediate call to national prayer. In fact, White had for months been engaged in informal discussions by letter with clergy colleagues North and South on just that subject. Yet no one had mustered the fortitude to translate words into action. *How often it takes a practical-minded layman to light the fire the pastor himself has, at best, merely stoked,* White thought.

The white-haired minister stood, rubbed his chin, and walked to the fireplace. He took a poker and jabbed at the already flaming logs. After a moment, he turned back to Jackson. "Son, I believe I have the men that can engineer, with God's help, a concert of prayer that might reach from one end of this nation to the other and help forestall this madness. Meantime, let us this moment begin to pray."

Indeed, Dr. White set about with the most furious effort to marshal the Christian leadership of the nation. His Southern friends Robert Dabney of the Presbyterian Church and John Broadus of the Southern Baptist Church possessed national stature in both preaching and theological circles. Their influence proved invaluable in the quick marshaling of Southern ministers as well as Northern, though the two stood in vigorous contention with many in the latter group concerning a host of the day's volatile political issues.

Within a few weeks a national day of prayer was set. One of the few names unknown in theological circles that attached itself to the missives that furiously crosshatched North, East, South, and West was that of Major Thomas J. Jackson of the Virginia Military Institute. "Who is this Jackson?" denominational leaders asked as bulletins arrived in their far-flung towns by telegraph, stagecoach, and mounted postal rider. Most of the names were known, at least to those in the same section. But no one other than William White of the Upper Shenandoah Valley, Virginia, village of Lexington had an inkling of the identity of the military academy professor.

When the big day finally came, it found Jackson fresh but bleary-eyed. The immortal influence of Ellie on his destiny continued. He had remembered a few occasions in which she rose from her bed in the middle of the night and left the room for lengthy periods of time. The final time this occurred, just two nights before her death, he had arisen two hours later and found her in the parlor on her knees before an end table on which sat a gas lamp and her mother's old family Bible. "For what are you praying?" he had asked her. "For the baby's soul," she said, "my honoring God—and for you, my darling Tom, should anything happen to either of us."

So had Jackson begun, infrequently at first, to feel a strange but powerful compulsion on the nights before momentous occasions to rise from the warm comfort of his bed and go to his little office to pray, in the dark, of course, because he never read anything, even the Bible, other than by natural light.

But he meditated upon lengthy passages of Scripture he had committed to heart, lest total blindness ever overtake him, which he feared it would.

When the sun dawned on the national day of prayer, Jackson already had five hours of prayer behind him since the day began, though he would never tell a living soul. Anna knew it though, and silently thanked God for a man as strong in his faith as she was weak and lethargic in hers.

Every church in town brimmed over, especially the Presbyterian. Willy and Lylburn raced all the way to that building—Willy in his suit, Lylburn in his cleanest shirt—from the fishing hole where they had dropped an early line. Lylburn had caught the only fish of the morning, but Willy had won by a few steps the race to reach the church before the final bell pealed for services, partly because he was fast as the wind and partly because Lylburn kept trying to add new endings to the sermon he had preached for Willy at the fishing hole. Lylburn knew whenever he grabbed ahold of a sermon that both Big Sam and Willy went to shouting about, that was a sermon that would preach.

Lylburn also knew he could scream and shout with the best of them from behind pulpit, under tent, or next to river. But what he needed was to know more powerful words and how to use them, words that would not only move his people to their knees in broken-hearted repentance over their sin, but would help them understand with their *minds* about the eternal God who had created them for good works and to glorify Himself. Like what was talked about, Lylburn suspected, in those books in Pastor White's office. Only then, Lylburn believed, would the sermon he preached by sunlight help fortify his people through the devil's urgings in the darkness.

Lylburn was beginning to draw groups of blacks to hear him preach, at odd times at first, but increasingly at regular times like on Sunday afternoons and Wednesday nights in his slave cabin as well as other cabins around Rockbridge County when he was able to go. On Sunday mornings, however, he insisted on planting himself in a tiny closet just behind the sanctuary altar at Pastor White's church. Only four members of the Lexington Presbyterian Church knew he was there—Maggie and Willy Preston, and Anna and Tom Jackson. The latter had secured the space and given his approval for Lylburn's occupancy of it while Pastor White was in the pulpit, for the "betterment of the young man's mind and soul, and the improvement of his ability to serve his own people."

Jackson, in his accustomed seat four rows back on the right aisle, noticed Willy's late entrance, and that of—*Could that be Wayne Marley?* The professor knew that both his eyes had been worsening over the past few months, and he could barely see to the entrance of the sanctuary. But surely that was an eye patch the man wore, and Jackson knew of no one else in the church who wore an eye patch.

After the service, where Lylburn was blessed by hearing the finest calls to repentance of the congregation by both the Reverend Dr. White and the Reverend Dr. Junkin—the former warning of the potential destruction if the North should persist in its vain imaginings of godless economic and political conquest; the latter warning against the futility and arrogance of the South's seeking to sever God's sovereign compact of Union—Jackson learned that Marley had indeed attended the gathering. The thirty-year-old, bathed and clean shaven for the first time Jackson could remember in a couple of years, hailed him on the steps outside the church.

"Hello, Tom," Marley said, offering a hearty hand before turning to Anna and tipping his hat. "Miz Jackson."

"Good to see you, Wayne," Jackson said with a warm smile, noticing that the younger man clutched a bound volume under one arm, "Very good to see you within these walls again, friend."

Marley nodded and glanced down as they stood at the foot of the steps. Then he eyed the swarm of people emptying onto the street.

He seems a bit nervous, Jackson thought, *but it's good to see that gray-green ring gone from under his eye.*

"Are you going home?" Marley asked.

"Yes, we are," said Jackson.

Marley cleared his throat. "May I walk with you and visit about something?"

"Certainly," Jackson answered.

Marley caught Anna's uncertain look. "It's nothing the three of us can't discuss," he said.

She smiled. "And we'll insist you stay with us for Sunday dinner, Wayne Marley."

Memories of intoxicating aromas and savory dishes at an earlier Jackson household stole into Marley's memory. But somewhere along the way, people died and the invitations stopped coming and even the desire to accept them if they did come and . . . . *I wonder if this lady is as kind and sweet as the first Mrs. Jackson,* Marley mused.

Over steaming ham and chicken and a colorful spread from the Jackson garden—corn, butter beans, onions, squash, turnips, and wheat bread (stale only for Jackson, of course)—Marley felt again the goodness and tranquility of being among God's people. For he realized, pain and regret flooding through him, that it had been a very long time since he had been with anyone other than the wrong sort.

Jackson sensed his friend did not wish to delve deeply into events of the past few years, so he channeled the conversation toward gardening, VMI cadet stories, and the day's preaching. The professor did not know if Marley had ever embraced God through faith in His Son—he certainly had not in his more "respectable" days—but Jackson felt the time might be a fragile one to broach the subject.

At length, he asked Marley about the book he had brought, which now lay on the table next to him. Marley's eye flickered, then he looked down. After a moment, he grasped the book and leveled his gaze at Jackson.

"You once told me I had become—," he turned to Anna, "excuse me ma'am—," then back to Jackson, "a drunkard, a whoremonger, and a ne'er-do-well, and that my father was Satan. Well, the last part may be right, I don't know, but your words set me to thinking. Oh, I don't know if just the words, but the fact it was you saying them—because you're one of the few men I know who lives what you say, whether I agree with what you say or not, which I sometimes don't."

Amy listened just outside the closed door to the dining room. Marley handed the book across the table to Jackson. The sweet scent of new leather filled Jackson's nostrils. *Narrative of the Life of Frederick Douglass.* His surprised eyes darted to meet Marley's gaze.

"You are reading this?"

"I have stayed up all of the past two nights reading it."

The two men stared at one another. Neither had to tell the other that Douglass was a Northerner and a famous abolitionist. And a free black man. A thought he had nearly forgotten snuck back into Jackson's mind: *Wayne Marley is a Northerner as well,* he remembered, *and at least some of his family, Unitarians, are ardent abolitionists.* Marley had never said much about them, and had evidenced no desire to return north to live amongst them. *Yet why,* Jackson pondered, *with no presaging, has he appeared with* this *book?*

Jackson leafed gingerly through the crisp new pages. "Did some member of your family send this to you?" he asked quietly.

Marley looked back down at his plate as he replied. "It has much in it that—," again, he returned his gaze to Jackson "that gives me cause for reflection and a certain amount of uneasiness." Once more, his eye turned downward.

All that Amy, shushing Hetty's son George, who had wandered by the dining room door, could hear from inside the room was Jackson's hand flipping pages.

After a moment, she heard Marley's voice speak again from inside the room: "Sir, would you favor me by reading a certain passage I have marked for you?"

Jackson indicated a page where Marley had inserted a bookmark and noted with light pencil a certain passage.

"Yes sir," Marley nodded, "that is the one. You are one of the few—you're one of the churchmen I respect, and I need your appraisal of Douglass's views."

Jackson read the passage. Some of the words he had heard. Eloquent and impassioned words they were, but profoundly disturbing.

> I love the pure, peaceable, and impartial Christianity of Christ: I therefore hate the corrupt, slaveholding, women-whipping, cradle-plundering, partial and hypocritical Christianity of this land. The man who wields the blood-clotted cowskin during the week fills the pulpit on Sunday, and claims to be a minister of the meek and lowly Jesus. The man who robs me of my earnings at the end of each week meets me as class-leader on

Sunday morning, to show me the way of life, and the path of salvation.

He who sells my sister, for purposes of prostitution, stands forth as the pious advocate of purity. He who proclaims it a religious duty to read the Bible denies me the right of learning to read the name of the God who made me. He who is the religious advocate of marriage robs whole millions of its sacred influence, and leaves them to the ravages of wholesale pollution.

The warm defender of the sacredness of the family relation is the same that scatters whole families—sundering husbands and wives, parents and children, sisters and brothers—leaving the hut vacant, and the hearth desolate. . . .

The dealers in the bodies and souls of men gives his blood-stained gold to support the pulpit, and the pulpit, in return, covers his infernal business with the garb of Christianity. Here we have religion and robbery the allies of each other—devils dressed in angels' robes, and hell presenting the semblance of paradise.

Jackson closed the book and stared at it for a moment, his jaw tightening. Powerful and thought-provoking words they were, that could not be denied. But he thought of the legions of pathetic black souls who would wander in hellish chaos and destruction without the provision, security, and shelter of their masters; the many Negroes, some old, some young, some unable or unwilling to work who would never prove the financial worth of their masters' outlay of resources, but who would be kept for their own well-being even until their owners had no breath left to support and defend them. Certainly, the professor reflected, the occasional sad case occurred, perhaps with men such as Sam McDowell and Will Russell, as it did in the Northern industrial furnaces, where owners and bosses—in contrast to the typical God-fearing Southern slaveowner—cared nothing for their workers and would discard them as soon as a new immigrant came through the door. *With whom has this man been?* Jackson wondered. *This is not the land I know.*

Jackson eyed Marley. "You're troubled, aren't you, Wayne?"

A pause. "Yes, sir, I am."

"About the South?"

"About much, sir; some of it myself."

"Have you become an abolitionist?"

Anna gasped.

Marley glanced sideways at her, then said, "I—I don't know, sir. I have lived in the South for many years, and I believe I know what it would do to the Southern economy."

"Do your Northern relatives concern themselves with that?"

Marley blushed, then shook his head. "No sir, not really."

"Dr. Junkin," Jackson said, "himself a Pennsylvanian like you, believes the blacks in America should all be removed at the government's expense to Africa, where President Jefferson and the others established the land of Liberia for their benefit and to keep them from having to compete in the white man's world." He hesitated. "I understand our new president Lincoln would favor such a course if the decision were left to him." Hearing her stir, he glanced at Anna.

"Forgive me for intruding into a man's discussion," she squeaked, "but I must say in my dear husband's defense that he is a strict but kind master, with the result—," she swelled with pride at this, "that our slaves have become as polite and punctual as that race is capable of being. In addition to providing for their every need and requiring little work of them, he insists they attend daily family worship in the morning, church on Sunday, and his Negro Sunday school."

Marley noticed a trace of flush on Jackson's high bronzed forehead, but knew the man to be too much of a gentleman to correct or reprove his wife in front of a visitor. Still, he thought perhaps the time had come to take his leave.

"I admire you greatly, Major Jackson," Marley said, with meaning. "And I thank you for, hopefully, helping bring me to my senses. I sought no disrespect toward you, your hospitality, or your friendship. I am searching for resolution on certain matters and desire your wise counsel. But perhaps that is for another day."

The two men stood and each moved to assist Anna in rising from her chair, just as Amy rushed in with tea that was not now needed.

"I do hope I was not unladylike," Anna began.

"No, no, dear," Jackson assured her. Then he stiffened. "Hold there, Wayne. I've something to give you. But I must go to the office and fetch it."

In a moment he hustled back, handing Marley another thick new leather volume. The words *Holy Bible* gleamed in gilt embossment on its cover.

Marley stared at the book and shifted from one foot to another, then opened it. Soon, he felt his throat tighten to where he had to gulp down air to clear a passage through it. Inscribed in a flowing hand on the inside cover were the words, "To the finest young man I know, with my fervent prayers that your bright future shall soon be illumined as will that holy city of which the sainted apostle wrote, 'had no need of the sun, neither of the moon, to shine in it: for the glory of God did lighten it, and the Lamb is the light thereof.' Your ardent friend and supporter, Thomas J. Jackson."

CHAPTER 30

MAGGIE HAD SEEN ENOUGH PRAYERS ANSWERED IN THE LIVES of her mother, father, Ellie, Jackson, and even, occasionally and haltingly, in her own life, that she knew the Bible's promise—"The effectual fervent prayer of a righteous man availeth much"—to be trustworthy. But she knew the same book did not promise to answer every prayer, at least in the manner sought by the petitioner, and that sometimes it was because he who offered up the petition did so with the wrong motivation.

Even knowing this, she watched with increasing horror as America's national day of prayer, repentance, and fasting was indeed answered, within five days—by the secession of Mississippi. Within three more weeks, Florida, Alabama, Georgia, Louisiana, and Texas followed.

What will come of us? she thought with a shudder, looking out her window as the winter sun poured its pale thin light over the orchard to the north. *I cannot fathom that what appears about to take place actually could, in this Christian nation!* Then the rare blue eyes narrowed and focused on the pad before her as she took pen in hand.

On the paper, she wrote: North—John, George, Father, and Julia. South—Me, Ebenezer, and William. *John, George, Father, and Julia.* She lowered her head to the old desk and nestled it in her arms. The searing anguish of homesickness lanced her very heart. *For what is home but where all the family is, and with love and affection and tender caring?* she thought. *What is this monstrous demonic force that could wrench a person's very loved ones from her grasp and care, that could turn those who should offer home, hearth, and shoulder upon which to weep, to—oh, it can't be, it just cannot be!—enemies in a war between kingdoms of the world? How could this low cosmos ruled by Satan rend asunder the sublime high chords of Christian love and*

*family? How can up be down; wrong, right; darkness, light; and fool-
ishness, reason?*

She jumped to her feet. Now the pounding ache around both eye
sockets that had bedeviled her since before dawn was joined by a
palpitating heart and such shortness of breath that she thought she
must surely faint. She flung back the lacy curtains and threw up the
window. Crisp cold late February air rushed in, filling her nostrils and
returning vitality to her addled brain.

She walked to a shelf of her published poetry and leafed to a
page entitled *A Year in Heaven.*

Her pulsing eyes scanned line after line written in honor and
memory of her mother. The tears began to flow as she cried out
across the years to Rush. *What would you do, Mama? What would you
say?* She wept as she read, seeking her mother's heart in words she
herself had written to her. Finally, Maggie's frantic rushing thoughts
became crystalline. *I know what you would do, even though I am more
Papa's than yours. Because I know what Ellie would do, and she is
yours from start to finish.*

Gradually, her sobs relented and a wry thin smile crept across her
face. *If Papa were alive, you would return north—or anywhere else—
with him. And if not, you would stay and minister to those who needed
you where God had placed you.*

And so no one ever thought more of Margaret Preston's staying in
the South in the days and years to come than, "She was a loyal wife
and would have stood with her husband to the death."

She read the closing words to *A Year in Heaven,* one of her greatest poems:

> *A year of tears to me: to thee,*
> *The end of thy probation's strife,*
> *The archway to eternity,*
> *The portal to immortal life.*
> *To me, the pall, the bier, the sod;*
> *To thee—the palm of glory given;*
> *Enough my heart—thank God—thank God!*
> *That thou hast been a year in Heaven!*

Just then, Maggie felt so close to her mother it was as if the
deceased woman were in that very room with her.

Across town, Dr. Junkin had had his own remembrances of Rush during his daily pilgrimage to that precious spot just northwest of town. The remembrances warmed him against the frosty early morning. But as his carriage neared the foot of the hill that led up to Washington College, a sight filled his eyes that struck a polar chill clean to the bone.

Though still a couple of hundred yards away, Junkin could see hanging limply in the early morning calm from the top of the campus's highest point—the statue of General Washington that adorned the summit of the main academic and administrative building—a flag, which, unless Junkin's tired old eyes betrayed him, sported the blue and white of the Palmetto flag of South Carolina, one of the many current banners of secession.

A rage like no rage he could ever recall began to kindle in the man who had fought major campaigns at every college he had led. For in all the battles he had fought—theological, educational, and political—never had anyone dared defame him, an institution he served, or the nation that had borne, succored, and sheltered him for seven decades as had now, evidently, been done.

"Hah!" Junkin called to his horse, lashing him with the whip in a manner he had never before done. The stunned animal pulled up, snorted, then burst into a gallop.

Oh Lord Jehovah, what have they done? Junkin agonized to himself as a throng of students came into view in front of the main building. Junkin slammed the dashing carriage to a skidding halt in front of the building, spraying gravel and dirt in all directions.

A moment before, the youthful male throng had been a merry, even a rambunctious, one. Now, the one man whom they had inwardly ridiculed had appeared, the man they had thought just moments before they wanted to see so they could show off their new *Southern* flag and claim their youthful inheritance as mockers and defiers of that which was older than they. Yet when that grand towering old visage emerged from the carriage, veins bulging from forehead to neck, the great snowy shock on top itself seeming to attack in all directions, the rebellion and defiance in most of the young assembled hearts seemed to vanish like the mists atop the Blue Ridge in springtime.

Junkin stomped to the foot of the statue. A slight breeze rustled the brittle branches of nearby oaks and maples. The old man's eyes narrowed as the flag uncoiled ever so slightly. *The Palmetto.*

"Yes!" his voice rang out as he whirled toward the gathering. "I thought so. You know not what you do, young men. This great state of Virginia, I shall remind you, still stands in the Union. And I still serve as president of this august institution—named, I might remind you, for the very man from whose loins that Union sprang." He shot a quick glance up at the again-limp flag. His jaw tightened and fire flashed in the dark eyes. He looked straight at the students. "Bring it down now."

An eerie silence befell the gathering. Never before had anyone defied, had anyone wished to defy if he could, old "Doc" Junkin. Most of the boys loved him as they did their own fathers. But here was something—different. No one spoke, moved, breathed. Somewhere back toward town, a dog with a deep bark took issue with someone or something in his wake. But on the grounds of Washington College, nothing or no one made so much as a peep.

Junkin ground his teeth together. *How far will such temerity extend?* he thought. When he spoke again, the words came cold and with an edge of danger: "I order you to take that flag down." This time his gaze bore in on the student body president, who stood just a few feet away. The young man blushed, but did not blink. And his eyes remained locked with Junkin in an epic show of will, young versus old, North versus South. Another moment passed. Still no one flinched, and the group's nerve appeared more to steel the longer the impasse wore on. After all, many told themselves, *We are many and he is but one, and we in the right, and he, a Northerner, after all, when all is said and done.*

Then Junkin's mouth twisted and he started to say something else. Before he could, a voice blasted through the hush from high atop the main building's colonnade.

"Boys!"

"Look," someone said, "it's Willy Preston."

Junkin's eyes, with everyone else's, trained on the handsome, lithe figure, as the boy stood on the roof near the flag. Though a VMI cadet, Willy, a Lexington native, had many friends in the Washington College student body.

Lord Jesus help me, Junkin prayed, staggered. *That wonderful boy, favorite stepchild of my eldest child.*

"Boys," Willy repeated, "Dr. Junkin is right. Virginia is still in the Union. And he is still president. We must wait a few days." Then Willy shuffled his feet a bit. "I am going to take the flag down."

No one doubted where Willy's allegiance lay. For he himself had helped raise the flag.

Yet, pandemonium broke loose. The crowd's pent-up frustration, fear, and anger burst forth. They begin seeking stones to throw at

Willy! Fortunately, few could be found on the smooth sward. The limber boy, unharmed, scurried up the statue and grabbed the flag. He lifted it aloft and, to the shock and everlasting consternation of Junkin, called for three huzzahs for the Southern Confederacy. The crowd below, which had multiplied since Junkin's arrival, screamed the cheers, the sound echoing off the walls of the nearby buildings and drawing Maggie's attention in her home on the other side of Lexington.

Willy, grinning ear to ear, rolled the flag up with care, deposited it in the bosom of his coat, and clambered back down to the applause of the crowd.

Forgotten and ignored in the rumpus was Junkin, his face grim with horror at the calamity he now saw unfolding before him and, incredibly, unavoidable without God's supernatural intervention. *But how can I leave those, alive and dead, most beloved in all the world to me?* he wondered as he walked, quite alone, toward his office.

A few hundred yards away, Jackson strode toward the VMI complex to supervise a thirteen-gun salute in honor of General Washington's birthday. The long-legged professor relished particularly the use of the splendid new Parrott rifled cannon in the ceremony. Taking Jackson's counsel over that of several others, the state—virtually on the professor's advice alone—had just purchased a dozen of the cannons from their namesake's New York manufacturing plant.

The gun had been discovered by Superintendent Smith when he and other Virginia leaders went north ten months before to purchase enormous amounts of arms and military equipment and stores. Both buyers and sellers knew the purchases were in preparation for possible war, and the sale, which enriched various Northern businessmen, would eventually widow and orphan the families of thousands of their countrymen.

However, Jackson at the moment concerned himself more with whether his eye, ear, throat, and digestive problems would ever desist from their torment of him. When the weather warmed, he would have to return north for more hydrotherapy and to see Dr.— *What?*

Now he moved at the quickstep, his aching eyes opening wide. *It is,* he realized as he neared the institute buildings. The flag flying atop the barracks, apparently made from a sheet, brandished the goddess of liberty display from Virginia's state shield and the state's motto, *Sic Semper Tyrannis.* And over it all someone had written "Hurrah for South Carolina."

"A flag of secession," Jackson breathed to himself as he arrived at the barracks. Near the entrance of the building was a guard. "You," Jackson called to the cadet, "bring that flag of treason down at once. We still defend the United States of America."

"Sir!" the boy responded with a salute, spinning around toward the barracks. "Cadet O'Neal!" he called to another guard as he rushed inside.

A couple of cadets—both hailing from South Carolina—happened out the front of the barracks as Jackson marched past them, his countenance grim. They stared at him, their own expressions sullen. Jackson wheeled toward them. "You men know which traitors raised that banner of treason?"

This is not the Professor Jackson of the section room, the cadets thought to themselves. *This is not a man with which to trifle.* The resolution of youngsters who had been brave in the chill wind of predawn darkness dissolved under the heat of Jackson's scorching cobalt gaze.

"Uh, no, sir," one of the Carolinians stammered.

"Then assemble the cadets for the ceremony," Jackson replied, turning to go. The two cadets remained frozen in their places. "Now!" he hollered, turning back to them. They burst back into the barracks, the day's secessionist inclinations doused.

But flags, like words and music, represent ideas and currents larger and more powerful than themselves. The lowering of flags did not prove sufficient for the quenching of convictions and sentiments that grew more potent with each passing day as peace uttered its death rattle in fractured America's spring of 1861.

Flags flew again in Lexington as a warm spring sun chased the Valley's sweet nocturnal canopy of mist away the morning of April 13, the day before Easter. Two flags predominated—the Palmetto of South Carolina, flown by those sporting secessionist sentiment, and Old Glory, still supported by the majority of Rockbridge County residents.

Meanwhile the town, and the rest of the South and most of the nation, waited breathlessly for the resolution to a standoff at some fort far south off the South Carolina coast in Charleston harbor, an unfamiliar island fortress called Fort Sumter. There, a Federal detachment had refused to relinquish control of the property to the South Carolinians, who wanted them and everything else Northern *out* and returned north.

Heightening the tension were rumors that President Lincoln had ordered a large force of Federal troops from Washington City south to Fort Sumter to defend the post by force if necessary.

Will Russell's loathing of all things Northern had grown in the past months until the vast storehouse of venom and hatred swelling his tortured lonely soul streamed into an ever growing tower of loathing and revulsion. For Northerners wanted his business at deflated prices, they wished to stymie the European sales of his cotton, they wanted his darkies, and they wanted his political influence. In sum, the greedy grasping mercenaries, most of whom had never set foot in Virginia, wanted whatever *power* he had labored so long to garner. For the first time in years, since his wife's death actually, Russell prayed. He prayed for the destruction of all things Northern and, as McDowell wished, a slave empire stretching to the Pacific Ocean and south into Mexico.

Still, though, Russell thought with a grimace as he squinted through bloodshot eyes at the late morning as he left Taylor's Barber Shop, it was hard to decide whom he detested more greatly, the Yankees or *them*—those insolent snot-faced little VMI scoundrels. He growled aloud as he watched a group of cadets flirting out in the crowded street with two pretty, bonneted and challis-dressed young Lexington lasses. *Saturday. Lot of them in town today, arrogant spoiled curs,* he thought.

Russell stepped down onto the street and glanced over at Lylburn, who waited with the buggy. Even that small action felt like a club drumming against his tired brain. He brought a thick brown hand to his temple and rubbed it. *Who had put him to bed last night—had it been Lylburn?* He glanced at the young man, who waited quietly, but with a steady gaze.

Then he heard the high urgent sound of an ardent young male voice: "Hurrah for the Union—the Union forever!" Russell looked back to the flirting cadets and saw a couple of other young men, about the same age, imposing on their gaiety. One of the newcomers waved a small Stars and Stripes in the air near the cadets.

Lily-livered town-bred urchin, Russell thought with a low grumble. The fleeting specter of yanking the flag from the young man's grasp and thrashing him if he resisted in the least flitted through the planter's awakening mind. Before he could complete the thought however, another, more ominous clamor began down the street in the opposite direction. Before even his eyes located the noise, Russell's long years of witnessing man's brutality to man in saloons, on ships, and in battle told him that this was that strange distinctive sound of physical clashing.

The courthouse, he saw. *Some of those cadets are raising a Secesh flag.* He had to chuckle. *At least those young ingrates are going to get me war started for me.* A small crowd of cadets and townspeople stood cheering around the flagpole. Russell's whiskey-dulled eyes could not make out, but Lylburn's razor-sharp ones could: two or three other townies crawling injured away from the ceremony on the hard-packed dirt.

Lawdy, Lylburn thought with shock, *white folk gonna fight each other.*

Then another rumpus caught Russell's and Lylburn's attention at the courthouse's other flagpole, twenty yards or so from the first. Now it was Old Glory being raised. The planter's square jaw tightened. *This hangover is going to disappear fast at this rate,* he thought. But this time the cheering stopped as, halfway up, the flag suddenly fluttered to the ground. "What? What happened, Lylburn?" Russell cried out.

"It's the pole, sir," Lylburn said, pointing toward the courthouse, "the pole done broke in two, sir."

Now a wild cheer erupted from the crowd surrounding the first flagpole. Over the pandemonium carried a man's shout, "They fixed the pole. The traitors doctored our pole—it's broke!"

Even Russell shook his head in surprise at the next thought that formed in his mind. "The kindling is gathered," his old da had used to say, "and the match is ready. Now it just needs a spark to light it." Russell intended to be that spark. *If war is to begin,* he thought to himself, *let it begin here.* While Lylburn still craned his neck to observe the gathering tumult down at the courthouse—now a fistfight had broken out near the secessionists' pole—Russell marched out into the street and weaved his way through the mass of bodies toward the cadets, the bonneted girls, and the small flag waver.

When he arrived, one cadet was at the point of swinging at the taunting flag waver. Swift as a cat, the stocky planter clenched his fist and slugged the Unionist hard in the jaw, then grabbed the surprised cadet by his ear and jerked him from the throng, then dragged him away.

"Hey, wait, you!" Russell heard from behind him. Then he heard the sound of fist striking face and that old sound of physical combat, accompanied by the expected shouts of females whose wooing had been interrupted by the hot blood of competing courters. Russell smiled without looking back. Just the same, he kept his other hand on the six-gun tucked into his belt.

"What are you doing, mister? What are you doing?" squealed the cadet Russell had in tow.

The older man offered no reply, until he had the boy up on the sidewalk in front of the barber shop.

"Mr. Taylor, Mr. Taylor, sir, come quick," Russell shouted from just outside the door. The barber and a couple of customers quickly emerged. One lanky callow customer had just begun shaving the year before, as he breezed through Judge Brockenbrough's local law school. A Marylander by birth, strikingly handsome, and an opponent of secession and slavery, Henry Kyd Douglas had known John Brown and pronounced him "cruel, bloodthirsty, and unscrupulous." Now Douglas, a twenty-year-old St. Louis lawyer visiting friends in Lexington, observed the unraveling of a nation.

"Mr. Taylor, sir, run and fetch the sheriff. A group of hooligan Unionists just made a play to dry-gulch this dear lad and his mates," Russell said. "I managed to spirit him away, but I fear for the other fine cadet lads."

Taylor, an ardent secessionist—due primarily to Russell's coercing—stared dumbly.

"Are you all right, lad?" Russell inquired of the squirming cadet, still pinching his ear.

"Yes, I'm fine," the cadet shrieked, "if you'll let my ear alone!"

Russell looked back to Taylor and the other men, and the crowd—mostly secessionists—now gathering, with a beneficent knowing look. "Brave lad here, like all the fine lads at the VMI," he said. "Wanted to fight them, wanted to take them all on himself."

Suddenly the man to Taylor's left, Campbell, pointed behind Russell and called, "Is that them? Is that the rascals?"

Russell whirled and saw three men coming toward him, their faces grim. He had never seen any of them before.

"Yes, that's the curs what attacked these fine young boys," he blurted.

"Get 'em boys!" Campbell shouted, leaping down onto the three and crashing to the ground with them.

In a flash, half a dozen other secessionist barber shop loiterers piled into the frenzy. None of them had any plans for the day anyway, other than hitting the tavern by noon, and this would ensure that that task would be all the more enjoyable.

As women screamed and the frenzied mound of fighters grew, Russell jerked his hapless prisoner up close. "Sorry me lad, looks as if we're going to need a spot of assistance on this one. Didn't want to tell you for fear of stirring you and the other lads up, but Lylburn over here caught sight of a couple of your mates over by the courthouse taking a fearsome beating. Said guns were in evidence as well. Perhaps you'd best hotfoot it back to the institute, rally the boys, and bring them down the hill, muskets at the ready, to restore order. These crazed Unionists are obviously too much for the mayor and constable, Unionists themselves, to handle. And I fear for the other cadets if you don't get help here quick. Meanwhile, I'll try to rally some of the good men of the town 'til you get back with aid."

The cadet's eyes nearly popped out of his head. They registered pain, then fear, then deadly resolution. Satisfied, Russell released the boy's ear and without a word the cadet wheeled, leapt off the sidewalk, and sprinted down the street, knocking aside whomever and whatever had the misfortune to be in his way. As he raced toward the VMI, he heard gunfire. His keen country-weaned ear correctly assessed the sound as a .22-caliber rifle. But his shocked mind proved not as adroit as his ear, and what was actually Old Man Richter popping a bunny on his spread just north of town, the boy wrongly appraised as gunfire from the direction of the courthouse, probably against one of his embattled fellow cadets. He began screaming, and some of the cadets were already scrambling for their firearms by the time cadet A. J. Summers of Gap Mill reached the parade ground.

The intent expression on Russell's face dissolved into a look of merriment, and by the time he turned to the incredulous Lylburn, his deep rolling laughter could be heard from one end of the noisy street to the other.

He did not know that the Unionist mayor indeed had plans of his own.

"The Rockbridge County militia is drilling out on Simmons' Common," the mayor said to his fifteen-year-old son as the two witnessed the burgeoning debacle from the elder's office. "Run and fetch them, Son. All of them. These blasted cadets have finally torn it, and if we have to call in the marines again like at Harper's Ferry and assault the institute itself, I'll see order restored to Lexington today."

CHAPTER 31

SUPERINTENDENT SMITH LAY IN HIS BED ON THE VMI GROUNDS fevered with pneumonia. He first heard shouting from the barracks area. When drums began rolling, he struggled to his feet and hobbled to the window. *Trouble is brewing,* he thought to himself as he saw cadets pouring from the barracks, throwing on jackets, strapping on sabers, and shouldering firearms. Others on horseback galloped across the yard and out onto the parade ground. Then a quick knock sounded at his door.

"In," Smith gasped weakly.

It was Gilham. "Sir, there's been trouble in town. Some cadets have evidently been shot by Unionist locals."

"What? Who said that?"

"Well, one of the cadet officers reported that Cadet Summers reported that."

Smith scoffed as he stripped his robe off and moved toward the armoire and his uniform. "Lots of reporting going on around here today."

"Sir, you're not in any condition—"

"Help me get this blasted uniform on," Smith interrupted.

Jackson, gardening on his plot that overlooked the VMI, had heard the distant sounds of conflict coming from the town. Too far away to discern the nature of the activity, he knew intuitively something was amiss. The rear axle on his buggy needing greasing; he had ridden up on his horse today. For this, he now thanked Providence as he dropped his gardening tools, mounted, and raced down the hill toward town.

Maggie was supervising Elizabeth in her daily piano exercise when her eldest stepson, Frank, rode up to the house at full gait. She saw him leap from his winded horse and rush across the door yard. *Quiet, steady Frank . . .* she thought. She stood at the front door as he burst through it.

"There's trouble in town," he blurted to Maggie. Then he turned, breathing heavily, to his father as Preston appeared from his study. "There's a scrap, Father, more than one, between Unionists and Secesh. Willy said to come get you."

Preston and Maggie exchanged a furtive glance. *Is this what it will be like?* she thought with a stab in her heart. *Surprise? Fear? Loved ones in who-knows-what danger?* She prayed just then to God with all her heart that He would provide a political solution to the cataclysm that seemed to lurk just over the next day's horizon.

"I'll take your horse, Frank," Preston said, grabbing his hat as he headed out the door. "You stay here with the ladies."

"But Father—"

The slamming shut of the heavy oaken front door provided Major Preston's answer.

Down the hill the cadets streamed, more than a hundred of them, for a different reason than ever before. Now, months, even years, of anticipation, anxiety, anger, and heroic adolescent fantasizing had crystallized into the duty to confront whatever might face them at the bottom of this hill as they came to the rescue of their besieged comrades. By the time word of the crisis had reached the youngsters, few if any of them had an inkling that no one had actually seen any cadets shot down in cold blood in the streets, though they knew full well it had happened.

As the surging ranks, sans any faculty or adult officers, neared the bottom of the hill and the road into town, those in front saw eighteen-year-old Willy Preston approaching from town on his great black steed.

"Who's been killed?" a half dozen voices rang before Willy could draw rein.

"Why, no one, far as I know," Willy replied, a quizzical look on his face.

"But didn't you hear?" one of the cadet leaders asked. "Some cadets have been shot, likely killed."

Willy's face screwed up and his horse reared, nervous at the large and uneasy throng coming down the hill. "No, no that's not right," Willy protested. "There's been some fistfights, but—"

"Boys!"

All eyes turned to another cadet approaching on horseback from town at full gallop.

"There's a fight going on, boys," the second horseman gasped, his horse throwing dirt as he jerked rein.

"We know; that's where we're headed," the cadet leader said.

"No, down in Carolina at that fort."

"Fort Sumter!" a voice shouted from somewhere in the cadet throng, still growing as reinforcements continued to surge down the hill from the institute.

"The Yankees," the horseman continued, "the blasted Yankees have fired on us."

"Fired on Charleston?" someone shouted.

"Well, we're actually firing on each other, the telegraph in town says so," the horseman said.

"But have they fired on Charleston?" the other voice persisted.

The horseman felt a hundred pairs of eyes on him. He could not disappoint. "Think so."

"Let's go, boys!" screamed an ardent redheaded cadet from Charleston as he shouldered his way out of the crowd and past the speechless Willy.

"Let's go!" chimed twenty voices.

"For South Carolina!"

"For Virginia!"

"Death to the Union traitors!"

Willy winced as a guttural roar rose up from the entire crowd. "But no one—," he started. It was no use. He saw a dozen mounted cadets thundering down from the top of the hill. "God save us all," he muttered. As his friends, his brothers, rushed past him, he realized he had only one course. If there was to be a fight, he had better be there with his brothers.

Just then, two hundred Rockbridge County militiamen appeared at the opposite approach to Lexington, their lean faces grim. Word had reached them that what at first had presented itself as a minor police action might now prove to be a martial encounter with the Virginia Military Institute. Many had friends—a few, brothers and even sons—among the cadets. Some shared Will Russell's view of the corps as a haughty band of spoiled privileged youngsters, worse because few of them hailed from the county.

Holy cow, one militiaman fretted to himself, *what if they've brought cannon with them into town? What if they've brought Old Jack?* The ancient deeds of Mexico cast a long shadow.

"Here they come!" shouted a Union sympathizer standing near the broken courthouse flagpole. He spotted the militia rounding the corner onto Washington Street, marching six abreast, arms shouldered—but loaded.

The owner-editor of the Rockbridge County *Valley Star* newspaper, viewing the proceedings from the courthouse steps, felt like leaping in the air for joy. Just last week he had changed the paper's masthead slogan from "The Union and the Constitution" to "The Union must be preserved." And now the saner, more quality substance of the county was coming to insure that preservation. Plus, what a great story this would make!

Across the street, watching from the doorway of the *Lexington Gazette,* that owner-editor cursed the militia under his breath. His masthead now read, "Let us cling to the Constitution as the mariner clings to the last plank when the night and the tempest close around him." *And now these men from our own county are doing Abe Lincoln's dirty work for him!* he thought. *Brazen serfs, hapless heathen charges in the federalist blasting away of our Constitutional rights.* The scribe possessed more weapons than his printing press. Quietly, he stepped back into his office and pulled his old double-aught buckshot Remington down from behind his desk.

Several shouts and screams sounded over the pandemonium as 175 Virginia Military Institute cadets appeared in formation at the north end of Washington Street, marching toward the courthouse square. Now they carried rifles and muskets at the ready.

A satisfied smile crept across Russell's face as he watched from the barber shop. The smile spread when he spotted the militia far down the street to the south. Russell had wearied of Lexington's ambivalence about disunion. Why continue the charade? North and South were no longer the same people, if indeed they ever were. After the rude treatment he had received the last time he ventured north, he knew he would never return there anyway. So why delay the inevitable? Forcing Lexington to decide once and for all where it stood on the Union should help expedite the process. So what if he had to use those detestable cadets to do it? He only marveled at how stunningly efficacious had proved his brief little actions with the hapless cadet and the flag waver. Best to move back inside for some cover now, however. It looked like shooting might break out any minute.

Wayne Marley still had some big decisions left to make, but the number was decreasing. One he would make right now by jumping off the sidewalk, squirrel gun in hand, and taking a place in the ranks of the advancing militia. He knew many of them probably leaned Secesh, but between them and that hornet's nest of fire-eaters down the street, he had but one choice.

Lylburn waited with the buggy out of sight behind the barber shop. He knew many of the men among both the militia and the cadets. Some he did not like; most had been only kind to him. He went to his knees in prayer, beseeching the Almighty to intervene before folks were hurt, and asking especial protection for Willy.

Just then, Willy sat astride his horse to the right of the cadets who advanced on foot, and pulled the Colt six-shooter his father had given him a few months before on his eighteenth birthday out of its soft leather holster. His hand trembled slightly as he loaded a sixth bullet into the one empty chamber. Then he looked down the street. Suddenly it was empty. Not a soul appeared between him and the courthouse two hundred yards hence. But beyond that edifice rose a plume of dust. *The militia,* he realized, his heart pounding. *Oh God, what is happening? Why have we come out like this?* He glanced around. A few of the marching cadets' faces betrayed fear. But the jaw lines of most were set in hard sober resolution. Willy nearly fell out of the saddle when a large mongrel dog erupted from the sidewalk with a ferocious series of barks directed at the cadets. A brief urge to silence the mutt with a single .45-calibre bullet prompted a subsequent feeling of guilt and amazement in Willy at how quickly and easily he could be tempted to shoot a dog, something he had never once done in his life.

Now the militia were in clear sight. *What are we doing?* Willy cried out to God. *Some of those men are bound to be my friends. Bound to be.*

"Column—aten-hut!"

The VMI's youngest professor, twenty-five-year-old Johnny McCausland, had emerged from nowhere at the front of the cadet column.

"Men, we cannot do this," McCausland said with as much authority as he could muster.

"They killed cadets!" came a shout.

"We don't know that for sure," McCausland responded. "We've just heard rumors."

"A. J. Summers done saw two cadets shot down in cold blood with his own eyes!"

The ground started to shake with the cadenced marching of two hundred Rockbridge County militiamen. They were less than one hundred yards away, rifles at the ready.

"Join us or get out of the way, Mac," a cadet yelled.

McCausland bit down hard on his lower lip, then turned toward the sound of orders being shouted by the militia leader. It was Jed Staley, from over Buena Vista way. McCausland knew him and liked him. Staley halted the militia fifty yards from the cadets, rifles readied but not yet aimed. The two groups stared across the short space on the main thoroughfare of the remote sleepy little village of Lexington. The mongrel's barking grew louder and fiercer. The next move was Mac's, and he did not know what to do.

"Men, men stop," rasped another voice from the opposite side of the cadet infantry ranks from Willy. Superintendent Smith brought his horse around to the front of the cadets.

He looks really ragged, Willy thought.

Smith gazed over the assembled cadets. They stood motionless, most of them ready to go right over or through the superintendent if he tried to stop them. He started to speak, but the mongrel was now out on the street and roaring straight at Smith.

"Cooper, deal with that animal," Smith ordered a senior cadet in the front rank.

"Sir!" Cooper shouted. Then, with one ferocious kick of his boot, he lifted the mangy canine up off the ground. The stunned animal squealed, then fled with a velocity that surprised those witnessing his abrupt exit from the scene.

Smith turned back to the cadets. A glint appeared in his gray eyes.

"Men, I don't know what has brought this on," he spoke, his voice growing more steady and strong as he went. "But I am your commander. And if you're going into a fight, it is I who shall lead you. And if I am to lead you, you must obey my orders."

"Yeah!"

"Huzzah!"

"All right!"

Even Willy thought, *OK, it makes more sense to fight if Colonel Smith says so and leads us.*

Smith dove in. "Right face!" The heartened cadets turned as one. "Forward, march!"

Thus they did, back down the street from whence they had come, back toward the institute. But few if any of them realized, yet, that Smith had no intention of leading them into battle, at least today.

Russell caught that part right away, however. He burst forth from the barber shop and out onto the street, chasing after the superintendent. "Hey, Smith, where do you think you're going?" he shouted.

But Smith had cantered to the front of the retreating cadets and did not hear the angry planter.

"Smith, come back here, you yellow-livered cur," Russell bellowed, stalking through the startled ranks of cadets, shoving one out of the way, then another. He knocked one small fourth-year plebe sprawling in the dirt. "I know you're Secesh, Smith, so get back here and see to it the right flag flies over this scummy town."

Russell emerged from the cadet ranks on the opposite side of the street from whence he started and saw Smith ahead. "I'm talking to you, Mister High-and-Mighty Head Bast—"

From out of nowhere, Jackson reined his horse up right in front of Russell, forcing the planter to a sudden halt in order to escape colliding with the snorting animal.

Russell's eyes widened as he looked up and saw his old enemy sitting stiff-backed and glaring down, the blazing cobalt eyes spitting fire.

But Russell breathed fury as well. "Get out of me way, you slow-witted pretender of a teacher," he growled, attempting to move around Jackson's horse. But the Virginian adroitly backed the bay into Russell's path. And when the man tried to move the other way, Jackson maneuvered the animal forward, again cutting him off.

Now Russell's nostrils flared like a brazen bull stabbed through in the ring. "Get down off that horse, man, before I drag you off."

Jackson swung down and faced Russell so quickly that the planter blinked.

As the last of the cadets, few of whom had witnessed Old Jack's arrival, turned a corner and disappeared from the street, Jackson stepped into Russell, butting chests. The planter bounced back, his face raging. "Why, you—," he began, clenching a fist. Jackson stepped into him again, his tall lean frame repelling his shorter muscular foe.

Now laughter broke out from a few of the militia, who had begun to disperse at the exit of the cadets. Some of them stayed to observe Jackson and Russell. The latter spun to face them, his face crimson. He reached for his pistol.

"I wouldn't." Russell turned to see Marley, from the other side of the street, clicking the hammer back on his rifle and placing the sight in the middle of the planter's barrel chest.

Russell's jaw dropped and he turned back to Jackson. The major kept coming, wading again into his adversary. This time Jackson did not stop, and Russell had to backpedal, stumbling and nearly falling. Jackson stretched his long legs into their normal extended stride, and Russell began to pump his short legs quickly, nearing a run, to stay away from his mad fellow churchman.

"You," Russell stammered as he tripped backward and fell onto the sidewalk, then jumped up as Jackson came up off the street after him, "You—"

But Jackson had had his fill. He walked straight into Russell, pinning him against the front door of the barber shop.

"No, you!" Jackson cut in, his visage a furnace blasting fiery breath down into Russell's terrified countenance. "You clear out for home right now. And if ever you cross me, any of mine, or anyone who wears VMI gray again, I'll put you six feet under, you whited sepulchre."

For a moment, Russell could only stare dumbstruck up into the sheet of fury that was Jackson's face. Then from somewhere he gained the vigor to squeeze out from between the soldier and the wall and bolt to escape. Far back in his bullying mind he knew that he hated Major Thomas Jackson, but he also knew that he feared him, and he knew that he feared him more than he hated him and that he would not cross him or his again.

Others besides Russell still wanted a fight. Many of them wore the blue jackets and gray trousers of VMI cadets. Marching back up the hill to the institute, they still did not know what all had happened in town. What cadets were hurt? Who had been shot? The cadets, initially crisp and responsive under Smith's orders, grew increasingly sullen as they neared home.

Bang! Willy's horse nearly bucked him off when a cadet musket cracked just behind him.

"Keep your weapons shouldered, gentlemen," John Preston ordered as he rode up to Willy from behind. As the younger Preston regained control of his mount, two more muskets discharged from up ahead, then one from behind, and another, and another.

"Anyone else fires his weapon is on report!" Major Preston bellowed, causing heads to turn. Rarely had a cadet ever seen his anger. But even rarer was a show of anger from the cadets toward a faculty member, especially the lettered, venerated cofounder of the school. In his heart, the typical cadet saw John Preston as the embodiment of what he someday wished to be. Yet seething faces of rage now surrounded Preston, chilling his blood. Faculty and cadet settled into an uneasy truce for the remainder of the return home.

Willy glanced at his father, who rode beside him. His face conveyed the question Preston knew to be in his son's heart.

"I rode through town," the elder man said in a low voice, shaking his head. "I looked around, asked questions. No one was shot, Son. Nobody even heard gunfire. Some bloody noses, a couple of bruised heads, yes. But no gunfire." He trained his gaze on his son, whose countenance questioned him for a moment, before the boy looked away in confusion.

"It's what happens when men spread stories without checking the facts," Preston added. "It's what's happening all over the country right now, I fear. And it's what's happening most regrettably in Washington City."

Smith led the cadets to Preston's section room, the only one large enough to contain the entire corps. The cadets had again grown restive. As Willy took his place against a side wall, he heard more than one oath uttered, and more than one cadet discussing the possibility of eminent departure back to town to rescue lost cadets and finish the job they had earlier started.

Try as they might, not Smith, nor Gilham, nor Captain J. W. Massie, nor even Preston could quell the cadets' smoldering tempers.

Jackson sensed the tension when he strode in from his business in town and marched to the front of the room where he took an empty seat on the faculty rostrum.

By now, the cadets' fuses were burned just about to the quick. A couple had crossed the line to irreverent temerity, had crossed past the point of concern for the consequences to insubordinate behavior.

"It's Jackson," one crowed.

"Hey, Old Jack," said another.

"Old Jack, give it to us," said another.

Now the room rumbled with anticipation. Somehow, the atmosphere had changed with the arrival of the awkward dreary professor who had been the decade-long butt of cadet jokes and ridicule. Some cadets whispered hurried phrases about Mexico. Others recalled the calming effect Jackson provided the night of the slave insurrection scare. A few had seen Jackson deal with Russell back in town. The sum of these patches of recall resulted in a strange tenor enveloping the gathered throng, faculty included. First one, then a couple, then a few, then more than a few, and finally the entire cavernous room erupted in a chorus of "Old Jack! Old Jack!"

Cadets clapped their hands. Cadets stomped their feet. Truth be known, no one had any idea what Jackson would say, or even what they wanted him to say. Just that they wanted him.

Smith, at the lectern, turned slowly back to Jackson. The major, thin lips tight and jaw set, shook his head. Smith cleared his throat and looked back at the corps. The chant grew louder and more raucous. After a moment, Willy felt the glass window beside him shaking. A slow crafty smile began to sneak across his handsome peach-fuzzed face. *They do not know the greatness—and potential greatness—of the man, but I do,* he thought. *But they begin to suspect there is more to him than perhaps they had supposed.*

Nonplussed, Smith turned again to Jackson. Again, "Old Jack," chin thrust out and eyes steady, gave a quick shake of his head. This time, as the chorus resounded, Smith walked to him. Jackson noticed tiny beads of perspiration across the superintendent's forehead and upper lip.

"I have driven in the nail, but it needs clinching," Smith said. "Speak with them."

Jackson stared at him. From Smith, Preston's disciplined VMI cofounder, the words constituted an order. The professor stood, and the room erupted into cheers and more chants. When he reached the podium, the company quieted. No one listened more attentively than Willy. He prayed that his earnest friend would not stumble.

"Military men, when they make speeches, should say but few words and speak them to the point," Jackson began, each word exuding the confidence of a well-thrust rapier. Preston smiled as he thought of how the rugged years of Franklin Society debates had honed and polished his friend's oratorical skills. Many of the cadets thought it odd how much taller than normal Jackson seemed as he continued.

"I admire, young gentlemen, the spirit you have shown in rushing to the defense of your comrades, but I must commend you particularly for the readiness with which you have listened to the counsel and obeyed the orders of your superior officer."

Then a spark from somewhere deep within Jackson's soul set the blue eyes ablaze, and they flashed like the fiery mouth of the cannon that turned the day at Chapultepec.

"The time may be near when the state needs your services, but it has not come yet." Jackson bore his gaze in on the group of first-year class leaders sitting at the front of the room.

"If that time comes, then draw your swords and throw away the scabbard."

With that, he returned to his seat. The room lay hushed, transfixed. Not a man among them who wore shoe leather that day would but take those words to the grave with him.

How strange, mused Preston, the husband of Maggie Junkin and who of all men thought he knew Jackson, *that we should today have found in this quiet self-effacing professor our leader.*

That night, word arrived that the South Carolinians had thrown the Federals out of Fort Sumter.

The next day, Easter Sunday 1861, Dr. White, a stout Unionist, his voice quavering, called the overflow Presbyterian church congregation, which included the Jacksons, Prestons, and Dr. Junkin, to prolonged prayer and petition for the mercy of the Almighty. President Lincoln had called for seventy-five thousand volunteers—the largest military force in the history of the Republic—"to execute the laws of the Union; and suppress insurrections." Yes, Virginia would be expected to offer her men to march by force of arms against their brothers and cousins in South Carolina.

Word had already reached Lexington that its native son, Virginia governor John Letcher, another ardent Unionist and opponent of secession, had rejected Lincoln cold.

"Our militia will not be furnished to the powers at Washington for any such use or purpose as they have in view," Letcher thundered.

Thus was sown the destiny of the sons and daughters of Virginia.

CHAPTER 32

SATURDAY'S NEAR-PITCHED BATTLE IN THE TOWN SQUARE mere hours before the annual celebration of Jesus' resurrection, in the shadow of the Presbyterian church no less, featuring representatives in both contingents from that congregation and every other one in town, had shaken Lexington to the ground. But no one's blood ran colder than Dr. Junkin's.

During the special after-church prayer and testimony session Easter Sunday, he persisted in trying to reconcile the drifting Southerners to the Union that seemed, to an increasing number of them, more and more like a menacing foreign power. "Remember what President Lincoln said in his inaugural address," Junkin pleaded, "when he begged all Americans not to destroy 'our national fabric, with all its benefits, its memories, and its hopes. We are not enemies,' he said, 'but friends. We *must* not be enemies.'"

But Southerners were no longer friends of Lincoln. And many in Lexington were not to Junkin. The grand old patriarch pleaded, chided, and stormed to no avail. Conversations were growing shorter; expressions, icier. Anyone less beloved and formidable than Junkin who had persisted in such vehement Unionist talk would have been told by now to leave town.

No one else could have gotten away with shouting, "God Almighty can't do without this United States government in His work of evangelizing the world, and He won't let you break it up!"

Still, as he left the president's home at the sweet-scented dawn of April 18, 1861, he chastised himself for not having pressed his case harder through the years. *These Southerners are so wrong-headed; if only somebody, if only I, could have properly explained to them God's sovereign purposes in the sustaining of the Union He created, they would most surely have turned from this madness and villainy.*

He did not realize, stopping to drink deeply again of the intoxicating aroma of his home's verdant environs, that had he pushed his fellow Lexingtonians any harder through the years, he would not still have been president of Washington College.

"Dr. Junkin."

Junkin's eyes focused on the lean tall frame of fifty-year-old William Nelson Pendleton, rector of Grace Episcopal Church, Lexington's second largest congregation; graduate of West Point; and lifelong Virginian. Junkin respected Pendleton, but did not find him a particularly likeable sort. The predilection was mutual. Today, though, Pendleton dismounted from his big bay and came to Junkin.

They shook hands, then Pendleton said, "The Virginia Convention has adopted an ordinance of secession from the Union."

Junkin felt his knees go weak. He thought for a moment he might fall, but steadied himself. He had feared this, but nothing could have prepared him for reception of the news. His eyes filled with tears.

"We have had our differences, sir," Pendleton said, "but I should like to pray alone with you for a bit if you could manage."

Junkin could not speak, but he nodded and motioned Pendleton to follow him into the president's home.

Inside, Pendleton did most of the praying. For he and many others, the day, while regrettable, bore grand significance, honor, and purpose. Junkin went through the motions and appreciated his sometimes-adversary's reaching out the hand of fellowship and brotherhood, but his mind was stalled.

After Pendleton left, Junkin trudged slowly across the greening lawn toward his office. Then he saw it. Another flag had been raised atop General Washington's statue, this one the Bonnie Blue Flag with a single white star centered in a field of sky blue. He stopped dead in his tracks, thunderstruck. As he stared at the flag, however, an odd event transpired. From somewhere deep inside him, a rumbling fury began to rise. Now it all came quite clearly to him, as it had already done to many of his townsfolk. *That despised banner has replaced the Union's,* he thought. *It would seek to remove the Union itself from the starry throne upon which God has placed her!*

Dr. George Junkin moved more quickly than he had in years, straight toward the flag. Several students stood observing it, expressions of satisfaction evident on their smooth young faces. Junkin approached them, already pointing up toward the flag. His fierce countenance prompted the students all to take a step back.

"That," he said, his voice coming from somewhere low and fearsome, "you shall remove that abomination now."

The cluster of young men stirred nervously. But no one moved.

"I said remove it now!" Junkin boomed. Now the students turned and walked away, but not in the direction of the flag, and not out of sight. Soon, other students began to appear from doors and hallways and dormitories. Again Junkin pointed toward the flag. "I order you to bring down that banner of treason now!" His blazing eyes scoured the mounting numbers of students, even as a voice from somewhere far back in his head whispered to him that nowhere near this number of students should be assembled this early in the morning.

A murmur ran through the throng, which now faced Junkin on the lawn from all four sides, at distances of at least twenty yards. Still, no one moved to take down the flag. And now faculty began to appear on the edges of the crowd. His rage escalating, Junkin called to first one faculty member, then another, and another, to assist in the drawing down of the standard. No one replied.

Finally, Junkin stood still in the center of the yard. *No one is going to take the flag down,* he realized, his heart tremulous with anguish. *No one is going to come forward, no one is going to go back. Just as none of us will now move forward to be counted of the Lord, and none of us can now go back to do what we should have done long ago.*

Faces, he thought, turning slowly round, gazing at them all, looking urgently for a flicker of indication that some, *any,* were with him, *faces of strangers, for I now reside in a land of strangers. A strange land of people I don't know, and who don't know me. Who no longer share my hopes, dreams, and destiny—if ever they did.*

They all loved old "Doc" too much to deride him or to revel in any way in his anguish. Their features showed not gloating, happiness, or even satisfaction, but pity, sorrow, and compassion for their revered leader. Yet more they loved their homeland, and all it meant to them, its good and its bad, its sage ancient enlightenments and its dark brutal ignorances. For they were the issue of its green fruited loins. They were of the South, and could not be other.

Junkin's massive shoulders sagged and the flush went from his face. He looked once more around the pleasant arbors and bricks he had grown to love so well over the past thirteen years, the longest period of time he had ever lived in one place and served at one school.

Then, as the entire faculty and student body of Washington College watched without a word, he, being (though he should have died before admitting it) of a different tribe, began the long, long return to his own mortal home.

For weeks, Jackson had looked forward to the Lexington Presbytery's semiannual meeting. He relished the gathering of the area's Calvinist divines, and had seen to it that several of them stayed at his home, the better for personal audiences and exercise in the hobby he so relished: discussing theology with theologians.

But now the professor attended not one of the Presbytery meetings, and he barely saw even the theologians staying in his home. Preparations for war swamped him and all the other VMI faculty, even though regular classes had been dismissed for the year. The professors prepared the cadets for reporting to Richmond for active military duty. Jackson urged Preston (placed in charge of the institute by Smith, who had been called to Richmond) to expedite the casting of more cannonballs, the delivery of ammunition long since overdue. The newly-christened Rockbridge Rifles, the militia force that less than a week before had squared off against the cadets in order to defend the flag of the Union, now rushed down the Valley to fight against it.

It is all happening so fast, Maggie fretted at her writing desk the morning of the nineteenth. Today, her father and sister Julia would leave Virginia and return north to Pennsylvania. Maggie had not slept but perhaps an hour the whole night, and that the one just prior to dawn. Insomnia worsened her eyes, and this morning it felt as though her head was clamped inside a cold iron vice, a vice being gradually ratcheted tighter. She had planned to go north herself to visit the doctor who had aided Jackson with his eye problems, but that journey would not now take place.

She had begun to recognize that some of her best verse flowed in the maelstrom of her worst pain.

She fought to focus her beautiful flawed eyes on the flowing script she had penned a few hours before in the darkest midnight of her pain. For she knew that others besides her father would soon be leaving.

These words were inscribed not on writing paper, but on the flyleaf of the ancient Bible she had carried all her adult life and had had rebound three times. The words came to her as she wept through Psalm 91.

Lean not on Earth, t'will pierce
thee to the heart,
A broken reed at best, but oft a
spear
On whose sharp point peace
bleeds and hope expires.

And the others, written when in the depths of her despair God's comforting Spirit came to her, as He did not for His Son in either the garden or on the cross.

But oh! thou bounteous Giver of
all good
Thou art of all Thy gifts, Thyself
the crown.
Give what Thou canst; without
Thee we are poor
And with Thee rich, take what
Thou wilt away.

She offered another prayer, asking God for strength, then rose for the trek to the president's home at Washington College.

Dr. Junkin already had his new carriage packed when Maggie and Preston arrived out front of the white porticoed home. Julia was climbing aboard, garbed still in black mourning clothes from the loss of her beloved husband, Junius, two years before. In the past twenty-four hours, Junkin had sold his 250-acre farm and furniture, paid all his debts, and purchased the carriage.

Maggie's brothers William and Ebenezer, both now Presbyterian ministers, and their wives and children stood nearby. Maggie and Preston had arranged a happy good-bye party for their children and "PawPaw" the evening before, to preclude sad farewells today. William would himself leave in a few hours to join the gathering Confederate forces in Richmond. The Jacksons arrived just after the Prestons.

Even now, the sight of Tom Jackson always brought at once a touch of euphoria and melancholy to Maggie's heart.

When all was prepared, Junkin began hugging his children and their families. He could not speak, but he hugged each one as if it would be the last time he ever would, which was the case with several of them.

No one else spoke a word either. Only the old mocker on his perch up near the window of the bedroom once shared by Jackson and Ellie.

The Jacksons were next-to-last in the order of farewell. Junkin hugged Anna, then turned to Jackson. The younger man stood ramrod-straight, his eyes misty. When Junkin noticed the blue VMI uniform, a veil of sorrow passed over his face and a choke keened from deep in his throat. "My dear son," he said, speaking for the first time, grief hiking his voice nearly an octave higher than normal. He enfolded Jackson in a massive impassioned embrace that lasted for many seconds. When he released him, Junkin swayed for a moment, and Jackson thought he would fall, but he did not. When the seventy-year-old man spoke again, directly to Jackson, his face was ashen, as if he were staring at a ghost.

"You will not survive this war."

Jackson blinked and Anna gasped. Junkin's eyes filled again with tears and he shook his head slightly, then he turned to Maggie and Preston.

Maggie had started out brave, but now her fine porcelain chin quivered. When Junkin looked at her, he saw all the best of his life before him. Rush, Ellie, a large, loving family that had always followed him wherever he went, from college to college, state to state, and had always stood by him, whatever his disputes, contentions, and tirades. Until now. *Why? What is it that causes the people of the South to stand against all that is cherished and loved, against even their own flesh and blood?* he questioned, the incomprehension of it all contorting his face as he stared at his Maggie. *My eldest child.*

If Maggie hadn't burst sobbing into his arms, he would have. But instead he held the frail small daughter beside whose crib he and Rush had knelt praying for the first week of her life, thinking any breath could be her last. The daughter whose near-death and miraculous survival, after they had offered her back to God, had knit him and Rush more tightly together than they had to that point been. The daughter, his most brilliant, whom he himself had taught Hebrew, Greek, Latin, French, English—and the Scriptures. The daughter whose flashing aqua eyes, the only ones of all his nine children, were a continual reminder of his own mother, who possessed the same. The daughter whose flaming red hair he had so often stroked in love as he now did. *When will I see her again, Lord?* he pleaded silently, again unable to speak. *When will I see any of them?*

"But where will you go, Papa?" Maggie wept. "What will you do? You've given away all the possessions and money you ever owned to students and poor people. It's just not fair. You've done too much. And now you have nothing. Ohh—," she wailed, beating on his strong wide back with her small fists.

He patted her softly, loving to be able to hold her again; in a way, loving having her cry in his arms as she had done as a child. After a full minute, they pulled back from one another, Maggie accepting a handkerchief from Preston with which to wipe her wet face. Junkin shook hands with Preston, then took one last look around his gathered beloveds. He would ever keep close to his heart, in winter and summer, comfort and pain, that image.

Then he climbed into the wagon and drove off with Julia. They would go to his attorney son George in Philadelphia. Maggie, William, Ebenezer, Jackson, and their families would remain in the South. His physician son John was in Trenton.

The hooves of a horse drummed up the hill from town. It was Wayne Marley.

"Wait, Dr. Junkin, sir," Marley called.

"Why, Wayne," said Jackson, noticing that the clean-shaven, fresh-scrubbed man's meager belongings seemed all to be on his back or strapped to his horse. "Where are you headed?"

Marley swallowed and eyed the group and Junkin, who had stopped the wagon some yards up the road. "Back North, Tom."

Surprise and disappointment covered Jackson's face. "But Wayne, we love you here. And you're doing so well now, my brother."

Now Marley's eyes watered. He looked down at the pommel of his saddle, which he clutched hard with both hands, and twisted his hips.

"Ah, well . . . I, uh . . . I have to go with my people, sir," he said, eyes downcast.

"But we're your people—," Jackson began. Anna reached gently for his arm. Jackson turned to her and caught her expression. Then he turned back to Marley, swallowed hard, and extended his hand up to him. "God go with you, Wayne. Read the Book. And know you're welcome back anytime."

Marley bit down so hard on his lower lip as he shook Jackson's hand that he nearly drew blood. He needed to leave, now, quickly, or he would burst into tears in front of everyone.

"Good-bye, sir," he choked, even as he kicked his horse into a gallop away from the group to follow after the Junkins, without looking back.

"It doesn't seem right, Anna, it just doesn't seem right." Jackson spoke for them all.

The faces. Ever would Junkin remember the faces as he drove the carriage across the seven-thousand-person village toward the cemetery. Someone must have spread the word, for people seemed to have posted themselves at spots along his exit route to wait for him as he approached. Others, standing or walking, heard the murmurs and turned, then halted to eye him as he went past.

For the most part, Junkin kept his eyes straight ahead, though the faces still somehow showed themselves. Anger burned in his bosom for the "stupendous madness" of these, his neighbors of thirteen years. Periodically, someone would shout, "Good luck, Old Doc," or "Wish you wouldn't leave, Doc." He would wave back and bid them adieu. But most just watched. Anger simmered just beneath the surface with some of them. More than one felt Junkin a traitor—to his country and, worse, to his friends. Their damning accusatory expressions felt palpable to him.

Junkin could not help but notice a couple of glowering VMI cadets lounging near the carriage block of one of the general stores. He feared for a moment they might force a scene, but when Wayne Marley brushed back his duster to reveal a revolver, they reconsidered and stayed their ground.

Then Mrs. Pendleton, wife of the rector, bustled out into the street, toting a large, and evidently heavy, basket.

Huffing and puffing, her face appeared ready to dissolve into tears as Junkin halted the carriage.

"Oh, Dr. Junkin, sir," she said, "is there nothing we can do to induce you to remain?"

The old warrior's vaunted dash and élan had about played out on him. He stared straight ahead, then down. *Dear Southern woman, whose own husband's church I have so often, at least in my heart, derided,* he thought, ashamed. "Thank you, Mrs. Pendleton, but no, I must return North."

"But—," she began, before realizing she was forgetting herself. She handed the basket up to him. "Well, there ought to be enough food in there to see you all the way to Philadelphia, Dr. Junkin, sir."

Does this entire town know my plans? Junkin wondered to himself.

"I even baked you two of my famous blackberry cobblers, sir," she revealed, leaning closer to him to secret this valuable information.

At this, he stared down at her and, in the full emotion-laden face, beheld anew the quixotic Southron soul that would baffle, anger, and beguile him until his dying day.

"Thank you, Mrs. Pendleton," he said, his strong chin trembling, careful not even to touch her head, though he longed to offer a warmer display of affection and gratitude.

He drove on under the balming April sun. Some angry faces, some quizzical ones, many compassionate ones. "Traitor!" shouted by someone, then several instances of, "We love you, Dr. Junkin."

Marley waited at the carriage with Julia as Junkin opened the squeaky old iron gate and stepped slowly into the Lexington cemetery.

"As I look upon these fair hills and soft meadows, Rush," the old educator began, after doffing his hat, "my heart is overcome with the sudden belated awareness of how they have so subtly and craftily embroidered themselves around my heart with love, tenderness, and sanctuary. These years restored me, Rush. They were not filled with the clamor and rancor, like all our other stations of service, that you so regretted but which you kept silent so well from me in your bosom. And now it strikes me that my—our—happiest years were here."

Junkin shook his massive head slowly from side to side, as if bewildered by stumbling onto the truth of an equation he had long factored incorrectly. "Only now, even as I am leaving this comely valley, do I realize it. And I wonder if, should we have come from this lovely land, I should have stayed and stood as these shall do, come fire, thunder, or the strongest army in the history of the world—all of which I shudder to say I believe shall eventually come." His head dropped for a moment before he looked back up at the marker and nodded at it, speaking softly. "Yes, I believe I should have.

"But Rush, there is so much I need to tell you, so much yet that I need to ask you, and if I go away, if I go back North, and you here, well—" At this, the lion's voice broke and his chin went quivering to his chest. Tears streamed down the long cheeks to water the bright violets that had presented themselves unannounced to early crown Rush's resting place.

He lifted the great tired head with difficulty and sighed. "Oh, I know you're not really in there, never have been, but—but it just makes you seem closer somehow to come here and talk, and right now, with all that is happening, well, they can all turn against me, our sons, our daughters, our friends, but somehow, I just need to know that you— that you're still with me, Rush. If I, if I knew *you* were still with me, that you would stand with me, that I was right just in your eyes, then I could, well I think I could just about stand any—" Now the sobs came, for the first time in the seven years he had come to her graveside.

Julia and Marley saw the huge old frame silhouetted against the azure Virginia sky. She covered her mouth with the back of her hand. She wanted to go to him and hold him. But she did not know, her own pain still numbing at the loss of her beloved Junius, then their only child, her youth slipping away like the faded green of a Shenandoah autumn—she just did not know . . .

Junkin fought to collect himself, smearing tears away with the sleeve of his frock coat. "I guess it's been a long time now that Joseph, our first to go, has been here, and now he's with you, my dear." His eldest son's tombstone, next to Rush's, bore the wear of the dozen years since his passing from typhus. The dark eyes moved to the next marker.

"And Junius Fishburne, you know him well by now. Such a fine, learned young man. Too bad it nearly broke Jul—" Again the tears choked him before he could continue. His eyes moved down the lengthening row of headstones. Julia's little baby, just over a year before—*no, better not think about that one yet.* Then his eyes stopped.

"And Ellie and her baby, well . . ." He bit down hard on his lip. "This—this is just a little bit harder than I had planned on it being, Rush. And much as it hurts about these who are with you now, at least I thank the Father they are living in bliss at the eternal wedding feast. It is those who remain, those who remain here in the South, for whom my heart most frets. What will become of them?"

He shook his head with great weariness and sadness. "Oh what will become of any of us?"

He stood for a moment with his eyes closed, steadying himself. Then he knelt down and placed the posy of jonquils he had brought by his wife's headstone. And he leaned over and gently kissed the marker.

He had first brought Julia Rush Miller a posy of jonquils fifty years before.

When Junkin stood, he drank in the perfumed redolence of his home in the Valley of Virginia one final time. And then the Lord strengthened him for what he must do, and he felt energy course again through his veins and limbs. He turned without looking any more at the graves and let himself out the squeaky old iron gate. Then he strode to the carriage, climbed aboard, and did not stop but to sleep until he had crossed the Potomac River into Maryland. There, he stepped down and made haste to shake the dust of Virginia from his boots.

CHAPTER 33

JACKSON WONDERED IF HE WOULD GET ANY TIME AT ALL WITH his theologian guests. *Tomorrow,* he thought to himself as he strode across the lovely spruce- and maple-festooned Washington College campus toward the institute to conduct afternoon drills on the parade ground, *Tomorrow is the Lord's day, and surely I shall have some time then. I must discuss this millennial kingdom question with some of the good pastors.*

Then he cringed and his right arm shot immediately into the air. When his eyes, ears, nose, throat, and side all hurt at once, he knew it must be unequal blood supply to one side of the body. Hopefully, the raised arm would even the distribution. If not, he might have to procure hand weights from the fitness room at the institute and begin criss-crossing the parade ground, arms pumping, his tall angular form leaping into the air. Oh, the inevitable hoots and shrieks would sound forth from the cadets, but a man must act as he must, despite the reactions of others. *Why, who is that?*

Ahead, perched tomboy-style atop the gatepost to the Washington College president's house, was Preston's twelve-year-old daughter Elizabeth. *Father must not be at home, else—no, Father is indeed no longer at home,* Jackson remembered, as though struck. With not quite as much spring in his step, he reached the slim, tall, raven-tressed youngster. It seemed only yesterday Sally Preston had presented her in swaddling clothes to Pastor White for the symbolic New Testament covenantal sign and seal of infant baptism. Only yesterday that she looked up at Jackson with those same willful but generous brown eyes and blurted, "We're going with you to see that mean man hang." Only yesterday that—

"Hello, Elizabeth," he heard himself saying. "Do your parents know where you are?"

She stared at him, then at his airborne arm, her fair face elegantly faithful to her father's, but now blooming into a ghostly rendering of her mother's beauty. He had not before noticed this. The slight imperious pout registered irritation. He did not care. He stared at her, awaiting an answer. Her gaze wavered, then broke off. "*Nobody* knows where I am," she said, tossing the coal black curls back off her shoulder.

Without a word, Jackson swept her from her pedestal and set her lightly on the ground. Her first thought was to be angry, but then she decided she liked being swept through the air so by such strong arms. So had her stepmother once blushed in the grip of those strong arms. She emitted a quick giggle.

Jackson kissed her quickly on the cheek. "Now you run home to your mama, Elizabeth Preston."

The girl's precocious eyes glittered and she turned and walked quickly away, skipping happily as she went. She looked back at Jackson once, blushed, and giggled anew before waving shyly at him and then skipping away.

As he waved back at her, he thought sadly, *When will children again be free to run and play unattended?* Just then a sudden gust of wind blew in from across the river and the VMI parade ground from the north, sending a couple of errant leaves whisking against Jackson's face. He turned in the direction from which the leaves had come. An old familiar voice sounded amidst the strangely hushed scene from away up near the deserted house. *The old mocker, in his favorite perch, outside* our *window,* Jackson thought with a smile.

Then the professor did something quite rare for him. He turned from one task to another before the first was completed. Opening the gate, he walked, more slowly than usual, up the walk toward the quiet house. He stood outside the front door, remembering the night James Walker had drunkenly called for him from that very spot and Father—Dr. Junkin—had stood the hotheaded cadet down. *Wonder if that high-spirited lad is still alive?* Jackson thought.

Next, he found himself inside the silent dwelling. He stared around. The furniture had already been taken away. The house stood empty of all except a decade—*could it be already that long?*—of memories for Jackson. Memories the like of which could not be put into words. The festive loud suppers in the dining room with Father—*or was it Ruthie?*—holding court. And there, the very room where he had first laid eyes on *her* that wondrous starstruck night so long ago. And now these stairs, upon which he had carried her toward the unspeakable bliss of their first night "home" following their honeymoon. Maggie's room, and Father's, and—

He stood staring for a long while through the open doorway into the modest few feet where had come true so many of the earthly dreams he had imagined, and others he had never imagined. He realized he had not set eyes upon the room in five years. Not since he had moved out. And he realized he had rarely thought about it. With a start, the truth dawned that no, he could not recall having *once* thought about it since that sea-splashed return voyage from Europe. *God, in His inimitable mercy—*

The room . . . the room . . .

> *A simple maiden in her flower*
> *Is worth a hundred coats-of-arms.*

Long did he muse upon and remember that which had been forgotten. At length, the day's dying amber rays fled behind the tall pines, no longer willing to gaze upon that which had been and was no more. Stillness lay over the house in prologue to the familiar welcome lullaby of the grasshopper and katydid.

Jackson started to step across the threshold of the room, but before he could cross it, he realized he was no longer alone. He whirled to see *Ellie*—his heart stopped cold—no, Maggie, never before had he noticed such a resemblance—standing a few feet away in the wide hallway.

"Why, you look as though you had seen a ghost, Tom," Maggie said.

Jackson sighed. They stared at one another, as they had done before. Both wanted to speak, but no words came. Jackson glanced into the room where he had shared his soul with two sisters so very different, shared it as he had never done before or since. The room where order had finally, irrevocably come to his life. Yes, in this room had that happened. So brief in birthing, but sure and strong and permanent in its flourishing. He looked at it because he had to do so. Because he honored it and esteemed it highly, ever more so than he could have imagined he still did. Because the past was not gone, it would never be, it stood now beside him and in front of him, still in fair full bloom of womanhood, and he had stuffed away so much and he wondered now if that had been proper, if it had been perhaps too easy, too selfish . . . and here, in all her ruddy aqua splendor was not a sister, not a peer, not the wife of a friend, but the essence of all that had been so very, very important to him and to his utter shock still was.

She saw his eyes well up and it caused hers to do the same. *Oh, I did not mean for it to be this way,* she thought desperately. *I only wanted to share finally with him what* Silverwood—

And then she was clutching him, holding him, spilling long years of dutiful well-hid tears into his strong breast. She held him as she had once, a very long time ago, dreamt he should hold her. She cradled all that the world could ever offer her with its most lovely evil allure, all that was good but not God's best, all that the ramparts of heaven in their unsearchable wisdom had thrown up between them. She held on for the years she had prayed would be but had finally trusted would not. And then, without looking him even once in the face, because she wanted greedily always to remember him with tears in his eyes—for she felt somehow, in some way, she had claim on at least some of them—she turned and ran away from him as fast as she could, down the stairs, out of the Washington College president's house, and home to her family.

At dawn the next day, Sunday, April 21, 1861, the War Between the American States began for Jackson.

He had told Anna the night before that he prayed the fateful call from Richmond would not come until Monday so that he could "enjoy the privilege once more of communing with God and His people in His sanctuary." But come it had, with a 6:00 A.M. knock on the front door, and he had gone quickly to the VMI to prepare for leading the school's entire corps of cadets to Richmond and their report to wartime duty.

At 11:00, he asked Pastor White to come to the barracks at 12:30 to pray over the departing officers and cadets. Then he returned home. Anna, in her best Sunday dress, her face flushed, had fixed one meal for him and packed another. *Never have I seen her look prettier,* he thought to himself. He ate quickly and quietly. He knew she was scared because not even the staccato chatter normally present in times of nervousness or anxiety evidenced itself. She did not eat one bit.

After the meal, he called each of the blacks into the sitting room. He had special gifts for all of them. *Why, where on earth did he get those?* Anna wondered in amazement. And he hugged and kissed each person: Hetty, Jeff, George, Cyrus, Emma, and Amy.

"I'll expect you, my stalwart brothers and sisters in the Lord," he said as though barking commands at a cadet drill—though Anna knew it was only a pose to cover the great emotion swirling beneath—"to remain faithful in your morning prayers, devotions, and

Bible reading. *Punctually* faithful. And in your own attendance at the Sunday school and the, er, Pastor Downing's Sunday and Wednesday meetings. And most importantly, in your growing sanctification and love of the Lord and your fellow man."

With a rough sound, he cleared his throat. "And you, young George, do have my approval in your courting pursuits with, er—"

George stared at him, gape-mouthed, then spoke. "Miz Hannah Brockenbrough, sir."

"Yes," Jackson nodded, "that's the young lady. And a fine, Christian, house servant, I am told. You do indeed have my permission, young man, provided you acquit yourself at all times as a Christian gentleman."

"Well, y-yes, sir," George beamed, wondering, *How did the old Goober ever find out about Hannah?*

"You'll answer to me personally if you don't," Jackson said, but all in the room witnessed the love and affection resident in his voice. "Mrs. Jackson will keep me apprised of all goings-on in my absence. And I shan't be many miles down the Valley."

Then he turned to Jeff. He had not yet spoken to him or given him a gift. "Mrs. Jackson will have your gift tomorrow, my young brother. I only regret that our burgeoning conflagration with the North has so accelerated as to preclude my having it for you today."

The tightly-wound young man's brow furrowed.

"Why, it's your freedom, Jeff. I'm giving you your freedom. Seemed a good time to do so," Jackson said.

The bright eyes stretched wide. "But, but Major Jackson, sir. As of today, I have twenty-two monthly payments remaining, sir, before I am a freedman."

"No sir," Jackson said with a smile, touching the young man softly on the shoulder, "as of today, you have no payments remaining and you are a free man. My only hope is you shall soon appropriate for yourself the true and lasting freedom available to you by grace through faith in God's Son Jesus and the blood He shed for you."

This last caught Jeff short. He thought he had said all the right prayers and spoken all the right words to satisfy the Goober and his white man's religion. Well, he was pleased with his early manumission, but the only freeing he planned on doing anytime soon was of other Negroes by way of the Underground Railroad. He knew many of them would never go, even if offered the chance, but others would, and he intended to help whomsoever he could, with the help of the Quaker friends he had developed. He only hoped the major never learned of his activities, for the major had indeed always been good and kind to him. Still, just as the major prepared to fight for the independence of the South, he himself would toil for that of his African blood brothers who desired their own freedom.

At the last, Jackson led Anna by the hand into their room. Theirs had been a sweet season together last night, partly because he feared his departure might be on this Lord's Day. He felt her trembling and held her to himself for some moments. Then, holding her in one arm, both of them kneeling by the bed, he opened his Bible to the fifth chapter of 2 Corinthians and read aloud: "For we walk by faith, not by sight. . . . For the love of Christ constraineth us. . . . Therefore if any man be in Christ, he is a new creature: old things are passed away; behold, all things are become new. . . . Now then we are ambassadors for Christ, as though God did beseech you by us: we pray you in Christ's stead, be ye reconciled to God. . . ."

He turned back to her and embraced her with both arms. He closed his eyes and prayed, his throat so choked with emotion that it cracked every few words.

"Lord God, sovereign creator of the universe, seer and knower of all things, we earnestly beseech You that if it be consistent with Your holy and perfect will, that You would still avert the threatening danger and grant us peace."

For a moment, he could not continue. This dear, *dear* sweet woman with whom He had entrusted him. Sweet and pure and innocent as any he had ever known, even Ellie.

"And—Lord," he rasped, "for my darling—Anna, I plead for Your tender mercies and lovingkindnesses to so abundantly abound that in the days ahead, her joyful and trusting spirit would well up as a fountain of life, brimming over with pleased contented godliness. And that my darling would be a beacon of feminine grace and light in these hours of darkness and villainy."

Once more he paused, his breathing so heavy that now she clutched his hand.

"Father in heaven," he spoke, in a whisper, "I entrust her to You for Your safekeeping, as I entrust my own life. Be Thou our guide and friend even until the end."

Then they kissed more passionately than ever they had, and the distinct feeling permeated Jackson's conscious thoughts that here God was sealing what was right and desired and in His perfect will, whatever lay beyond. And in that moment, Jackson felt more powerfully than ever before that indeed, all the days of his life were numbered, and Ellie had been Ellie, and Anna was now his loving, faithful friend and partner, for the remainder of his days.

Their eyes locked.

"I love you, Anna," he said.

She smiled. "Yes, I know you do, Tom. Now more than ever I know you do. And I shall love you for it 'til no breath remains in me."

As Jackson descended the steps of his home one last time, he offered an additional prayer for Anna. *Sweet and meek she is, Father, and unaccustomed to not having family members close by for support. I pray Thee to steel her soul and lift up her countenance before the world.* Her fragile conscience concerned him in a way neither Ellie's nor Maggie's would have.

When he reached the street, a familiar voice called out, "Major Jackson." He turned to see Lylburn Downing and several other black males approaching him. He recognized one as Big Sam, also from Russell's plantation. He knew each from attendance in his black Sunday school.

"Well, afternoon, Lylburn," Jackson said, touching his cap. "Sam, Moses, James."

"Afternoon, sir," several voices responded.

"Sir, we brung you something," Lylburn said, shifting nervously from one foot to the other. Then he handed the professor a small three-legged stool, smooth, polished, and smelling sweetly of new cedar. Jackson looked at it, puzzled.

"Well, sir," Lylburn said, smiling proudly, "the boys here and me, we figuring if this here war lasts very long at all, you gonna be a general. 'Cause . . . ," Lylburn looked around at the others, a couple of whom nodded their support, "it's just that what with all you done for us, sir—and we heard what you done for Jeff—that we expects you be one of the smartest leaders the South gonna have in this here war. And we also figure the Lord a-gonna see fit to shine His face smack onto you, sir, a-causin' you one of the *best* men the South got too."

At this, Big Sam contributed a none-too-inconspicuous cuff to Lylburn's ear.

The skinny preacher glared up at the towering field hand, then looked back to Jackson.

"Anyhows, sir," Lylburn raced on, "we figures as you rides from battle to battle and victory to victory gin' them Northern heathen folk, you's likely to find yourself in some places without proper, er—"

"Accommodations?" Jackson offered.

"Uh, yessir, that be the word—I knew it, it just escaped me for the moment," Lylburn said. "Anyhows, some of them places you gonna be ain't likely to have proper ac-com-mo-da-tions, sir. And we wants you to remember as you winning battles and gettin' glory that we's with you, sir, and we wishes they was more like you, sir."

Lylburn looked as though if he were any prouder he might just pop a button off his gingham work shirt. But his cohorts reveled in his eminence with him.

In days ahead, Jackson would find to his amazement that this assortment of black house and field slaves—who would have collaborated on precious little else—would prove perhaps the only people in Virginia with such prophetic insight into his martial aptitude.

Now the stool took on entirely new significance. Not even Jackson could contemplate the import of that significance, but he ascertained enough of it that it overwhelmed him. He gazed at the well-crafted, but unprepossessing piece of wood.

The fragrant earthy aroma of fresh cut cedar captured Jackson and transported him back to his youth at the mill with wild barrel-chested Uncle Cummins. Then Jackson remembered the deep forest of cedars behind Russell's big house. And he thought of the chance these young men had taken in making this stool—for Jackson of all people. He had no doubt they knew the professor to be the absolute last person for whom the volatile planter would tolerate the making of a stool from his own wood!

Lylburn and the others grew nervous. *Does he not like it? Is he offended?*

But when Jackson looked up from the stool, his eyes misty (*Haven't my eyes been wet a lot lately?* he thought to himself), they knew better.

"Men," Jackson said hoarsely. But he said no more. Instead, he snapped to rigid attention then gave them a crisp heartfelt military salute.

Lylburn, Sam, and the others registered amazement. Then they too straightened their backs and offered salutes.

Jackson said no more. He did not have to. *"But she of her want did cast in all that she had. . . ."*

Jackson arrived back at the institute as the cadets wolfed down their dinner, to a man eager to depart down paths of glory and renown. At 12:30, the professor wheeled his horse to face the cadets and removed the beat-up kepi cap he wore pulled low over his eyes. "Let us pray," he said.

Dr. White, his silver hair gleaming in the warm spring sun, offered up a lengthy and heartfelt petition to God for those about to leave. A lump rose in the old parson's throat as he looked across the assembled ranks. *So young they are,* he thought with anguish. Some he had known since their birth. Willy Preston and others he had held in his own arms and baptized. Now they left for war.

And then there was his most dedicated deacon, Tom Jackson.

"You'll see that my black Sunday school class is looked after, sir?" Jackson asked as White prepared to leave.

"Yes, Tom," White said, his voice thick with emotion.

"And Lylburn—you'll continue the church's, uh, our support of his ministry?"

"Just as we have done," White said with a satisfied smile. He, Jackson, and Preston had secretly provided financial subsidy for Lylburn's own burgeoning work among the blacks of Rockbridge County.

As White walked away, he shook his head at the thought that whatever the new Confederate States of America's need for Thomas J. Jackson's martial skills, it could scarcely be greater than that of the church and community for his spiritual acumen.

Jackson glanced at the barracks clock. Ten minutes until his announced departure time of one o'clock. He retrieved his stool from his horse and sat down on it.

Willy and several other cadets approached him. "Can we go, sir?" their voices echoed.

Jackson eyed them, his face blank, his thin lips compressed. "When the clock strikes the hour we will march, and not until then," he said softly.

Willy more than any of the cadets knew the depth of Jackson's character beyond the professor's awkward, sometimes ridiculous, section room shortcomings. Yet even he was struck by the cool steady demeanor of the oft-abused man. While everyone around Jackson, including the faculty officers, seemed electrified with tense anticipation, the odd thought struck Willy that Jackson looked every bit as excited now as he did during the moments immediately prior to his nodding off in rigid-backed naps during Pastor White's church sermons.

When the barracks clock registered precisely one o'clock, Jackson remounted his horse and barked in his high voice, "Right face! By file left, march! By file left, march!"

Then he led the Virginia Military Institute down the Shenandoah Valley to war.

> *The hour was sad I left the maid, a lingering*
> *farewell taking,*
> *Her sighs and tears my steps delay'd, I thought*
> *her heart was breaking;*
> *In hurried words her name I bless'd, I breathed*
> *the vows that bind me,*
> *And to my heart in anguish press'd the girl I*
> *left behind me.*

CHAPTER 34

JACKSON BELIEVED IN AN OMNIPOTENT GOD OF PROVIDENCE. He also believed man's portion was to do his best. Not that Providence needed a helping hand, only that He pleasured in man's cooperation and favored it, even as He Himself facilitated it.

"Duty is ours; consequences are the Lord's," he wrote Anna from Richmond upon learning he had been granted only a commission of major of engineers, and that not in the Provisional Confederate Army, but in the lesser Virginia Militia.

But a torrent of anger and bewilderment swept over him who had held the brevet rank of major nearly a decade and a half before. *How?* he wondered to himself. *Why? With Superintendent Smith one of the three men on the appointment commission?* He slammed his fist down on the washboard that served as his writing desk in the burgeoning military camp that for days had seen men and youths drifting in small and large groups virtually every half hour, around the clock.

Did he esteem my teaching skills this lightly? Jackson asked himself. His head drooped as he pondered the unthinkable. *Does he esteem me this lightly as a man?* For a long moment his head hung as he sat alone in the tent he shared with two other "officers." His body went slack and he felt the pain that had been absent for days begin to surge back into his eyes, his ears, his throat. Then, volcanolike from the deepest recesses of his soul, the ancient fire that had long driven him and still yet battled with the Almighty for possession of his energies and passion, came rumbling forth.

Jackson flew to his feet. "No!" he screamed, stopping conversations outside his tent. He looked heavenward, pleading his cause before the ultimate tribunal. "I cannot believe You will allow this to happen, Sir!" he shouted. Now heads turned his direction from outside, but the general pandemonium of the camp, and the speculation that an officer was dressing down a green non-com, prompted a few chuckles before the men resumed their conversations.

Still looking upward, Jackson spread his arms in appeal. "It is not finished, Sir. Our fair name is not yet restored. If anything, it is worse!" His ardor flagged. "I, Sir," he said, more softly, gesturing to himself, "*I* am not yet restored."

At times, he now realized, he had grown too comfortable during his years in Lexington. Too comfortable on the church diaconate, too comfortable on the board of the bank, too comfortable with his varied trips to Europe, the North, and the various bath spots. Now he saw just how important this war loomed in establishing his destiny. Had he so easily forgotten his heritage, the pledge he possessed to carry forth that name once renowned and now so—comfortable?

He shook his head as if to brush away years worth of cobwebs from his soul. *Could it be that had this war not come I should have* remained *comfortable?* he asked himself. *Perhaps even growing more comfortable, ever more comfortable indeed, until the laurels and plaudits of the world and its favor smothered the last vestiges of fame, glory, and honor for my people—for* her?

From somewhere far, far away rang a once-familiar refrain: *"You may be whatever you resolve to be."*

A glint charged the eyes whose blue chased into retreat their gray. The brown hair rose on the nape of his neck. His breath came in gusts. His body pulsed with purpose. He looked again into the heaven of which even the Junkins and Whites of the world marveled he had such a clear view and cried, "And so shall it be, so shall it be that, by Christ's name and in His everlasting glory, I shall accomplish the destiny assigned to me and mine by the Lord God Almighty. So shall it be!"

Quick and urgent notification by Jackson of the situation to his longtime friend Jonathan Bennett in Richmond brought swift action. Attorney Bennett, a power in Richmond political circles as state auditor, had the ear of fellow Lexingtonian John Letcher, the governor of Virginia and another fan of Jackson's.

"Who is this Major Jackson that we are asked to commit him to so responsible a post?" one Virginia legislator asked on the floor of the state's Constitutional Convention as it adopted a plan of temporary cooperation with the newly birthed Confederate States of America.

Also under consideration was the promotion of Jackson by two ranks to colonel—in the Provisional Confederate Army—and temporary commander of the key post at Harper's Ferry. That town lay at the northern tip of Virginia and on the southern bank of the Potomac River, which separated the Old Dominion state from South-leaning but as-yet neutral Maryland. It housed a huge arsenal of weapons and ammunition. However, the Federal army occupied the ordnance and the town.

Jackson's ten years of seeming obscurity and vocational frustration in Lexington had prepared him for the work that now was to begin. Rockbridge County delegate Samuel Moore, another friend of Jackson's, rose from his convention seat and extolled the awkward professor.

"Who is this Major Jackson you ask?" Moore boomed. "He is one who, if you order him to hold a post, will never leave it alive to be occupied by the enemy."

Jackson received his new rank and the command of Harper's Ferry.

"It is the post I prefer above all others," he hurried to write Anna on April 27 before rushing from Richmond for his post, "and has given me an independent command."

He had arrived in Richmond only hours ahead of Colonel Robert E. Lee. That Virginian, fifty-two years old and fresh from dusty lonely sentinel on the Texas frontier, had resigned from the American army and arrived in Richmond dressed in civilian clothes, including a tall silk hat. The following day, Lee was commissioned a major general and given command of Virginia's military and naval forces.

Jackson wrote Anna again as he traveled north by train. While doing so, and watching the lush green Virginia countryside roll by, he realized he could not remember feeling physically better than he now did. His sight in both eyes had improved, and the pain seemed in near complete remission. Alike, his ears, throat, nose, and stomach registered no physical displeasure.

Could he have stoked more kindling into the locomotive's hot-burning engine, he would have done so in order to expedite arrival at Harper's Ferry. Beyond the obvious reasons for his favoring the assignment was Jackson's secret desire to utilize the town as a staging point for a raid into neighboring northwest Virginia, land of his birth, to crush out the Union forces he considered as oppressors and intimidators of Southern feeling in the mountainous region.

He refused to countenance the possibility that many in the thirty-one counties of the state lying west of the Blue Ridge and thus removed from the fertile lowland conducive to the propagation of slaveworked cash crops, had no intention of ever leaving the Union. This company included his own troubled sister, Laura, whose marriage he now feared was over.

Jackson had just received the news that a bold contingent of Virginia militia had stormed into Harper's Ferry and liberated the town from Federal occupation. The band included two extraordinary horsemen and leaders of men from Fauquier County, brothers Turner and Richard Ashby, as well as former American army captain John Imboden and Big John Harmon, the blue streak-swearing owner of the thriving Shenandoah Valley Stage Line, which had transported Jackson and the VMI soldiery partway from Lexington to Richmond.

When Jackson arrived in Harper's Ferry he saw lounging, laughing, and frolicking "soldiers." He saw arrogant greenhorn militia leadership. Tinsel, nodding plumes, sashes, and cocked hats teemed. The man who had faced down Mexican cannon and stormed the halls of Montezuma shook his head at the frightening specter of what awaited these undisciplined, unprepared men, mostly in their late teens and early twenties, when the ordered, well-equipped thousands in blue came pouring in from the North.

Immediately, he commenced replacing the gaudy, staff-heavy militia leadership with seasoned men picked for their military aptitude and character, not their political and financial pedigrees. The dehorsed militia chieftains streamed downstate to register their furious complaints with the new Confederate leadership.

Jackson also proceeded to give the entire garrison a kick in the seat of their collective pants. He slammed the door shut on "playing war."

His outward appearance did not impress many in his new command. Even those farm boys and "crackers" who themselves looked ragged and unkempt and naturally recoiled against the authority of their social betters, seemed to expect more in "looks" from the West Point officer and Mexican War hero who was to lead them. One Southern newspaper correspondent wrote that Jackson lacked the "pride, pomp, and circumstance of glorious war."

With his pulled-down forage cap and dingy, well-worn blue uniform, and sans braid and glitter, Jackson plowed headlong into organizing the eight thousand men into battalions and regiments, and worked them at demanding military drilling from sunup to sundown.

When Imboden returned to Harper's Ferry after military business in the new Confederate capital, he scarcely recognized Jackson's revamped camp. *What a revolution three or four days have wrought,* he thought in astonishment as he viewed the sweating, hard-marching soldiers.

Gradually, Jackson cobbled together his staff. Auspicious among them were tall, thin Hunter McGuire, only twenty-five years old but a splendid physician, as chief surgeon, and brilliant young Sandie Pendleton, not yet twenty-one, the pride and joy of Lexington's Episcopal rector and his wife.

The elder Pendleton, himself a West Point graduate, had put together the Rockbridge Artillery, commanded by himself. Its battery featured cannons named Matthew, Mark, Luke, and John, as well as an assortment of pastors, theologians, and seminary students.

And Jackson, the pious Calvinist, appointed the profane Harmon as his quartermaster.

But trouble brewed in the ranks of perhaps the outpost's most dazzling component—its cavalry.

Many Southerners felt the sacredness of their cause—defending home, hearth, and way of life—would ensure victory over the North. Many others felt primarily that God would see them through to triumph because of His holy preference of a Christian people over a mercenary mélange of Unitarians, Arminians, Jews, and Pope-followers.

But more than a few possessed an abiding faith in the ability of a people of the land, a nation of horsemen and hunters, to succeed against a people—albeit more populous, industrialized, and materially blessed—comprised largely of shopkeepers, factory serfs, and wharf riffraff.

And two whose reputations, and personal rivalry, were mounting were Virginians Jeb Stuart and Turner Ashby. No better horsemen rode for North or South than Stuart and Ashby. Both were barrel-chested and blessed with immense physical strength, though Stuart, at nearly six feet, stood several inches taller than the Moorish-looking Ashby. Stuart's tawny beard, broad shoulders, high cheekbones, and glimmering blue eyes made him a heartthrob among ladies of high and low social caste in the South.

Stuart was also an inveterate prankster, a gay reveler at soirees, and a merry flirt with the fair sex. And his sartorial élan, consisting of yellow sashes, great gauntlets, brightly feathered hats, and jingling spurs, buoyed his own spirits and those of his men. But he also possessed a Puritan streak nearly as wide as Jackson's. A devout married

Episcopalian like Lee, Stuart's personal purity and piety were well known in the land.

Ashby, swarthy but dashingly arrayed, was thirty-seven, nine years older than Stuart. Ashby was himself the model of Southern gentlemanliness and self-made wealth in his personal life. But a man to answer to the orders of others he was not, and his vaunted Ashby Rangers vowed to "ride to heaven or hell with Turner, whichever comes first." He had led a cavalry troop since 1859, and helped lead the militia's successful storming of Harper's Ferry.

Ashby had had his brushes with Stuart already, and when Jackson reorganized his outpost's hodgepodge of cavalry companies into a battalion under the command of Stuart, thunderclouds roiled across Ashby's dark face.

"But I am the natural leader of these Valley horsemen," Ashby seethed to Imboden at the Point of Rocks encampment a dozen miles from Harper's Ferry. "Most of them are as upset as I that Jackson has tendered authority over them to this reckless cocky youngster. I intend to resign."

Imboden pleaded with the furious cavalryman to plead his case directly with Jackson in Harper's Ferry. This Ashby did, along with delivering a letter from Imboden supportive of Ashby.

Jackson stared at the stocky horseman inside his command head-quarters. *I don't like reversing an order, especially one I believe good such as this,* he thought. *Yet this Ashby—he looks rather like a pirate, actually, and a dangerous one at that (wonder if he is a believer?)—is too valuable to lose, and the Valley men show ferocious loyalty to him. In fact, if I lose Ashby, I may lose a large number of them.* Valley men were not prone to the fear of orders, regulations, or even laws they deemed unjust.

Then Jackson spotted a half lemon on the rough wooden plank that served as his desk. His eyes widened. *Why, I thought one of the staff had taken that.* A smile nearly broke out across his face as he scooped the unexpected citrus and began sucking it with vigor.

I guess, Jackson thought, humored by the lemon as he relaxed but continued to stare at the tense Ashby, *that the reorganization could be served by splitting the cavalry companies into two units. Might even be easier for me to ride herd over. Yes, that's it. I'll keep Stuart in command of one and appoint old Colonel Angus McDonald over the other, with Ashby shortly to succeed him.*

It was not Jackson the pragmatist whom the ebullient Ashby lauded upon his return to Point of Rocks, but Jackson the magnanimous.

When Ashby returned to Harper's Ferry a few days later with a squad of his men, he chanced to cross Stuart's path, both men mounted.

Ashby drew rein and stared coldly at the one man he viewed as an obstacle to his autonomous marshaling of the fierce northern Virginia horse under himself.

After a moment, Stuart, aware of the bad blood and rather enjoying the gamesmanship of it, removed the wide brimmed, black hat highlighted with a large purple feather he wore and bowed low, sweeping the hat before him with a wide flourish and a winning smile.

The act startled Ashby, whose mouth tightened, then relaxed in a bemused half smile. He nodded at Stuart and tapped the front of his own hat with his index and middle finger before riding on.

Jackson spent hours at his desk writing letters. He wrote to his friend Bennett regarding the potential of a brigadier generalship for himself. He wrote Lee pressing for a mounted expedition to roust the Federal army out of Jackson's native northwest Virginia. And he wrote Anna adoring letters of how he loved his *esposa,* and how his health remained better than he could remember since, well, since the war in Mexico. "My only ailment seems to be lack of sleep," he concluded.

Then Jackson looked out the window of a local residence's spare bedroom that served as his headquarters. There stood, tied to the fence, "my new horse, darling, and what a fine little fellow he is. I have named him Fancy. His gait is as easy as the rocking of a cradle, his endurance is remarkable, and I pet him and feed him apples from my hand."

Outside, not far from the horse, Lieutenant Henry Kyd Douglas eyed Fancy. A natural leader of men and irresistible to women, as well as stubborn, willful, and winsome, Douglas could not brook the name "Fancy" for Jackson's squat new horse, bounty from a captured Union train.

Walking to the thick little horse and stroking his mane, Douglas, as comfortable on a horse as on his own two feet, spoke softly. "You, my friend, are no chestnut. You are a plebeian-looking little beast. You are not even fourteen hands high. And you'll be happy to know we have a new name for you, much more fitting than Fancy. Henceforth, the troops have christened you Little Sorrel."

Then Douglas peered closer at the horse's rounded carriage. His eyebrows arched. "By heaven, you actually appear fat, Little Sorrel."

Then the horse did an odd thing, at least an odd thing for most horses. He had had a strenuous day of riding, and just now he lay down to rest like a dog. Douglas stared at him. *Just the sort of odd creature I might suspect for*—he caught himself and looked toward the home that housed Jackson's headquarters—*such an odd man.*

Jackson had tired of the continual passing of Federal trains along the nearby Baltimore and Ohio lines. For thirty-one miles from Martinsburg to the west of Harper's Ferry, to Point of Rocks to its east, the railroad was double-tracked. The traffic ran heavy. Though three-quarters of the B & O's tracks lay in Southern states and Southerners stood on the company's board, the organization had decided the South could not garner the support it needed from foreign powers such as England and France to win its independence, and thus it kept its lot with the Union.

Jackson seethed every time a B & O train rolled west to supply Yankee troops all the way to the Ohio River, or returned east stocked full of coal for Baltimore and Washington City. His aggressive ideas and disposition of troops up and down the Potomac were causing his superior Lee to pace the floors at night with nervous anxiety. And now he decided, on his own and without divulging his thoughts to anyone, that he would no longer brook the transporting of the enemy's abundant resources and goods through the camps where his men, even this early in their armed struggle, barely had food to eat or clothes to wear.

Early in May, Jackson notified B & O President John W. Garrett that the noise of passing trains disturbed the Confederate camps at night. He requested scheduling between 11:00 A.M. and 1:00 P.M. of all eastbound trains through Harper's Ferry. The befuddled and helpless Garrett had to agree.

A few days later Jackson contacted Garrett again. The westbound trains, it seemed, still disturbed the camps. The Virginian requested that they too be scheduled through Harper's Ferry between 11:00 A.M. and 1:00 P.M.

"What is he up to now?" Douglas half-smiled to himself as he watched the area pulsing with action each midday. "I believe he has constructed for himself the liveliest railroad in America," Douglas said with a chuckle to some of his men.

But Jackson was not laughing. One day in early May he ordered Imboden, east of Harper's Ferry at Point of Rocks, to stop all eastbound B & O trains from eleven o'clock on. To the west of Harper's Ferry at Martinsburg, he ordered Colonel Kenton Harper— one of those Virginia militia generals who had gone whining to Richmond after Jackson demoted him—to halt all westbound trains.

Both scenes were similar. At Point of Rocks, Ashby's Rangers barreled down on either side of the tracks from the enfolding hills, brandishing revolvers and sabers. The Union officer in charge of the train contemplated a resistance from his perch atop the front car. Ashby himself cocked the hammer back on his long gleaming Colt and aimed it squarely at the bluecoat's chest.

"No matter what else happens—somebody dies, everybody dies, nobody dies—you get it, right through the lungs, Yank," Ashby said, his low voice murmuring dread.

The Yankee cursed, then tossed his own pistol down onto the dusty ground next to Ashby.

Jackson, whose only apparent physical involvement in the action was to spend much of the preceding night on his knees in solitary anonymous prayer, won fifty locomotives and more than three hundred cars with his bold endeavor. Men who had ridiculed him as a buffoon—as men had done in the fifties at the VMI and the forties at West Point—now scratched their heads. "Maybe Old Jack has more going for him than we thought," they said.

Kyd Douglas decided his goal for the war was to be attached to Jackson's staff.

Though the Confederates were only able to salvage a handful of locomotives—through the madcap overland hauling of them down the Shenandoah turnpike to Strasburg, where they reached the rails of the Manassas Gap Railroad—an implacable lesson attached itself to Jackson. He realized once and for all that the Christian who devoted himself first to humble pious living bathed in importunate prayer and then, when appropriate and led of the Spirit, to creative and unconventional action, could succeed at endeavors not even contemplated by the worldly man. For none of his peers and no superior above him clear to Confederate President Jefferson Davis would have approved the B & O heist had Jackson submitted it for their counsel or approval.

"Thou through thy commandments hast made me wiser than mine enemies: for they are ever with me. I have more understanding than all my teachers, for thy testimonies are my meditation."

A few days later, Jackson dined with old friend and business partner Preston, for whom he had sent as an adjutant, in the splendid
expanses of one of the town's finest homes, which had been opened
to him for his headquarters.

"Three sons I have now wearing the gray," Preston beamed, "and
as fine a little wife working to keep the old home place running as a
selfish old man ever had."

Preston cut into the tender steak that covered his plate while Jackson washed his entree of stale brown bread down with cold water.

"Oh, but a temper that one has to her," the older man boomed,
laughter spicing his words, "as wicked and unpredictable as a Tidewater hurricane."

Jackson smiled. He remembered that temper. And the sweet feminine grace that ever followed it.

"But never is she more sweet than right after her anger," Preston
continued. "She has won the entire family, even the fire-eating Prestons
in South Carolina."

Just then, Jim Lewis, a handsome free black from Lexington who
had long attended Jackson's Negro Sunday school and who had
accepted the colonel's invitation to come north in the role of his body
servant, entered the room and announced that Jackson had guests.

"Big guests, I reckon, sir," Jim added, then, in a whisper, "with
lots of gold braid, sir."

Jackson and Preston exchanged bemused glances. "All right, Jim,"
Jackson said, standing, "show them in."

A moment later, a short wiry balding man with a beard and a confident rugged air entered, followed by a train of a half dozen staff
officers.

"Why, General Johnston, sir," Jackson spoke, saluting.

Fifty-four years old, Joseph E. Johnston himself was a famed Mexican War hero. He had sustained five wounds there and three battlefield promotions. His dogged heroism had spurred a military career
where he rose to become a brigadier general in the U.S. army, and the
highest ranking Federal officer to throw his lot with the Confederacy.

Such was the man of enormous reputation, a generation older
than himself, who informed Jackson that the new Confederate War
Department had assigned him, Johnston, to take command of the far
northern Virginia region, including Harper's Ferry.

Jackson felt as though he had been decked by a falling tree. He
knew he had been doing the work of a general, not a colonel, ever
since he had assumed command of the sizable forces in the area. He

also knew that their acute strategic significance in the unfolding conflict was far beyond the normal scope of a colonel. Yet, had he not acquitted himself in an exceptional manner? Had he not whipped an undisciplined mob of toy soldiers into a force now ready to war?

The order came not from Lee—*did Lee even know of it?* he wondered. Probably not. Through the reports of his friend Bennett, Jackson knew that influence and intrigue were already swirling around the new national administration in Richmond. Small vain men sought for themselves power and prestige, as always they had. That was why he needed Bennett keeping him apprised of the shenanigans now haunting the halls of state of the besieged new Confederate nation. And that was why he needed that brigadier generalship. Only a rank on that order would allow him such commands as Harper's Ferry, commands he knew, now more than ever, had the ability to handle.

Jackson stood erect and swallowed hard. Preston, a man of great poise, felt none just now. He watched as Johnston grew fidgety at Jackson's prolonged silence.

Then came the answer. "Until I receive further instruction from Governor Letcher or General Lee, I do not feel at liberty to transfer my command to you, sir, or any other," Jackson said, looking straight into his superior's eyes, "and I must therefore decline to do so."

Johnston's face turned ashen and the throng of gray behind him stirred. The one man in the room who saw the grandness of the situation, and of the man central to it, was Jim Lewis, who had seen the same man stand against those who would deny the black man the right to organized spiritual opportunities. And Lewis, through that inscrutable agency of the black Rockbridge County grapevine, knew other names such as Will Russell and James Walker which figured into the Jackson legacy. The fine ebony face hid itself in the shadows of a corner room, that the smile which escaped across it might not be discovered.

"Please be assured, sir," Jackson continued, "that it will give me pleasure to afford to you every facility in my power for obtaining appropriate information relating to the post."

Johnston's eyes widened and the pale countenance of his face turned red. He started to speak. Preston detected the protrusion of a couple of neck veins just above the general's high, crisply starched gold-starred yellow collar.

Just as a serious confrontation appeared imminent, the old warrior's visage relaxed. "Find my saddle bags, Cartwright," he ordered one of his staff officers. "I believe Secretary Benjamin's order is in there."

And so it was. When found, Jackson graciously turned over command.

"Just what would you have done had he insisted on taking charge, without the written orders?" Preston asked Jackson when Johnston and his men had left.

Jackson, outwardly calm but inwardly smarting sharply from his loss of command, did not hesitate. "Why, John," he said, walking toward the door, "I would have thrown him in the guardhouse."

CHAPTER 35

ANTICIPATING THE LARGE MOVEMENTS OF FEDERAL TROOPS toward the Potomac that soon followed, Johnston determined that Harper's Ferry, ringed by steep high hills, could not be defended. He moved his ten thousand men south toward Charles Town, including the brigade he had assigned to Jackson.

Jackson struck the B & O again June 18. Led by Ashby, his men torched the main depot and roundhouse at Martinsburg and destroyed 42 locomotives and 305 cars. Coal packed most of them.

Newspapers North and South broadcast the mass destruction. Twice, Jackson had wrecked huge collections of B & O—and now, Northern—trains. The word from Washington was clear: squelch the Rebel troublemakers in the Lower Shenandoah River Valley.

Anna wrote to Jackson. Could it truly be he, the anonymous, mild-mannered Christian professor, engineering the maelstrom of ruin, as the papers reported?

Jackson responded with regret that it was. "If the cost of the property could only have been expended in disseminating the gospel of the Prince of Peace, how much good might have been expected!" he said.

Then he turned his literary energies back to his friend Bennett in Richmond. The Federals appeared to be running roughshod over northwestern Virginia which, mountainous and not benefited by and thus unsympathetic toward slavery, had been invaded by Jackson's old West Point classmate George McClellan.

"Have me ordered there at once," Jackson pleaded. "That country is now bleeding at every pore." Both he and Bennett hailed from the region.

He also beseeched Bennett again for his assistance in attaining a brigadier generalship.

Jackson received no commission to northwestern Virginia and within two years, despite significant secessionist resistance, the region, which included Jackson's birthplace and Laura's home, declared its independence from the Old Dominion and joined the Union as the new state of West Virginia.

At 4:00 A.M. the morning of July 2, 1861, eighteen thousand Union troops under the command of sixty-nine-year-old Major General Robert Patterson began splashing across the four-foot-high Potomac River from Maryland into Virginia. No Southern troops opposed them, but Jeb Stuart's reconnoitering cavalry detected the crossing immediately and had word to Jackson three hours later.

The Yankees were less than five miles away.

Jackson rode toward the invaders with his Fifth Virginia Infantry Regiment, Stuart and a few horsemen, and the Reverend Doctor Colonel Pendleton and one gun, Matthew, from the Rockbridge Artillery. All told, he had fewer than five hundred men. Coming directly for him were two thousand Wisconsin and Pennsylvania farm boys under Colonels J. J. Abercrombie and George Thomas.

Willy Preston watched Jackson from a distance. He had heard all the stories; now he wanted to see if they were true. He saw Jackson, mounted, issuing orders to various officers, quietly and with economy of words. Jackson moved about slowly on his horse—*an odd stumpy little animal of unsightly appearance,* Willy thought—even as bullets and minié balls began singing around him.

The main road split the wheat field in which they stood. The field rolled gently into woods both left and right. Jackson deployed troops to either side of the road. On came the advance protective shield of Federal skirmishers. Breathing hard, events happening too fast to consider, Willy cocked back the hammer on his rifle and fired with everyone else.

The bluecoats receded from view under what seemed one large puff of gray smoke that rose against the hot noon summer sun overhead.

As Willy reloaded, with efficiency but trembling, he glanced out of the corner of his eye at the major, *er, colonel.* Jackson sat astride his tubby horse—*Little Sorrel, I believe he is called,* Willy thought—straight-backed, one hand holding the reins, the other against his hip.

On came the Federal skirmishers again, more of them. Oddly, Jackson's cool demeanor seemed to calm Willy. As he glanced around, the men near him seemed to respond in a like manner. When Willy fired this time, his hand and eye were steady and he believed that he felled a man.

Again the bluecoats retreated. *Thank You, Lord,* Willy thought.

But now, the enemy moved up in force. Jackson was under orders to fall back on Winchester if he faced such a show, and he dispersed word to do so. But even in retreat, against odds of four or five to one, Jackson, dirty kepi cap pulled low over his eyes, seemed to Willy, and the officers and men on the field, steeled with nonchalant resolve.

Now the Yankees swarmed onto the road and moved forward as one bulging mass. Federal artillery moved into place and began raking the Southern positions.

Confederate officers began to shout. Sandie Pendleton, shaken, turned to see Jackson's reaction. The colonel, unruffled, sat on a large stone next to the road, writing an answer to a dispatch from one of Johnston's couriers. One shot from a Federal battery shrieked overhead, exploding a Confederate horse fifty yards back. Jackson kept writing. Then another shot smashed straight into a large white oak that stood less than ten feet from Jackson. The shot plastered Jackson, and the paper on which he wrote, with a mass of bark, splinters, and trash. Every officer within twenty feet, including Sandie, either ducked or dove for cover.

When Sandie peered up, quaking, he saw Jackson brush the trash off the paper with the back of his gauntleted hand and finish his dispatch, without ever looking up or giving a sign anything was amiss.

Then Jackson stood, coated with fallout from the blasted oak tree, handed the dispatch to the courier, and dismissed him matter of factly. Next he called for the elder Pendleton, who stood nearby with Matthew. "Reverend Pendleton, sir," Jackson said as the clergyman approached, his sweaty face grim but determined, "I see Federal infantry, and now cavalry, rushing at us down this road. They shall be upon us momentarily. Can you do something about that, sir?"

Pendleton's eyes glinted and he shouted, "Yes, sir!" This was certainly much more exciting for a West Point graduate than the average day in the rectory back in tiny Presbyterian Lexington.

Pendleton ordered the gun sighted and aimed. As more shells began to scream overhead, and his own son looked on admiringly, he cried, "May the Lord have mercy on their wicked souls!" and Matthew boomed out his gospel.

The shot tore into the front of the Union ranks, sending horses and riders alike into a screaming heap. In one fell swoop it stemmed the blue tide, as the Yankees cleared the road—though several dead and wounded men and horses lay where they fell. One more crackling volley from the Southern infantry, and Jackson's force began a slow, calculated retreat.

Yankee Colonel Thomas, the future "Rock of Chickamauga," marveled at the tenacious, frustratingly slow retreat commanded by Jackson.

Very difficult indeed to maintain order in a slow retreat under fire, Thomas frowned to himself, *particularly with green raw troops, but whoever that Rebel commander is, he is doing it.* For three miles he did it. Little did Thomas know that his opponent was Colonel T. J. Jackson of the VMI, like the Unionist Thomas himself, a Virginian.

Though he understood the tactics, Jeb Stuart could not brook sitting idly by. He took his few dozen horsemen on a sweep back around the Federal right, dashing, firing, disappearing, swooping back to fire again. Stuart had learned as a Virginian who grew up astride a horse, he had learned more at West Point, and he had learned more still fighting Kiowas and Pawnees. He did not intend to get shot again. Suddenly, racing ahead of his own troop, Stuart burst through a section of brush and out into a clearing—where fifty Yankees stood idle. *Oh, no,* he thought to himself, *both my pistols are empty!* But the momentum was with him, and he was after all a Virginia Cavalier, and before he knew it he was upon them and shouting, menacing Colt brandished, "Drop your arms, men. You are now under the protection of Southern forces."

The men froze, staggered. One started to raise his rifle. Stuart just caught it with the side of his eye and swung the Colt around on him before he could. "You'll be the first man down if anyone makes a play," the Virginian warned, his eyes cold and steady as his hand. But inside he cried, *Where in blazes are my loyal subordinates?*

No one moved for a long tense moment. Finally, Stuart heard brush popping, then multiple hoofbeats approaching behind him. But his relieved breath did not gush forth until he saw, incredibly, two Pennsylvania officers and forty-seven men, dejected at the startling turn of affairs, stack their arms and place their hands on their heads.

Johnston crowed about both Jackson and Stuart in his report of the "Affair at Falling Waters." He recommended both for immediate promotion, Stuart to colonel and Jackson to brigadier general.

Lee sent Jackson his commission. No Confederate insignia of rank having yet been designed, Jackson removed his old blue army jacket long enough to have a star sewn on the shoulders of it. He now looked indistinguishable from a Federal brigadier general.

Lieutenant Wayne Marley slept little in his tent on the green fields north of Manassas Junction, Virginia, the night of July 20. And when he did, a fearsome specter shook him to his soul. Nothing similar had corrupted his sleep in the year since he had sobered. When the dream occurred, he did not wish to resume sleeping.

Only around 3:00 A.M. had Marley slept at all. He did not like the haughty disposition he detected amongst his regiment, the Fourth Pennsylvania. More especially, he did not like what his cherry-cheeked young cousin Joe had reported hearing the day before from the boy's father, an abolitionist Republican congressman.

"It's going to be swell," Joe had said. "Father says half of Washington City is coming out to watch us destroy the Southrons."

"Huh?" Marley asked.

"Yeah, they're coming out, Congress, the Senate, the foreign delegations, the cream of Washington society," Joe said with a nod. Marley could remember seeing the eighteen-year-old on a family Christmas in Pennsylvania a decade earlier, similarly excited at the bounty that had presented itself to him under the Christmas tree. Well, excited for a day or two anyway. Many the Virginia family Marley had since seen whose home was not the worth of Joe's presents that Christmas morn.

"And Father himself told me that May Freiburger's father said she is coming out to the affair just to see me," Joe beamed. "They are all coming together to picnic."

Not only were they going to sweep the upstart reactionary Rebs from the field and the war in one afternoon of work, Marley lamented, but half of Washington City, including sixteen-year-old ingenues, was coming out to watch it, over Sunday dinner.

No, he did not like it at all. The men in his regiment, with notable exception, were not outdoorsmen. They were shopkeepers, smiths, factory workers, a few farmers, and school boys. They were thick-trunked with leaden feet. The Virginians he had known who would come against them were lean and hard, hunters and horsemen, even the rich among them. And, unlike most in the Fourth—and certainly in Joe's hoity-toity Washington circles—many of them, despite their lack of understanding on constitutional and even human decency matters, were, in their misguided way, God-fearing, even pious.

And then there was the dream. *No, the nightmare.* A cold shiver shimmied through Marley. What to make of it? A huge shining black horse, bigger than any he had ever seen, gleaming in the sun, sharp white teeth bared, trampling something into dust—*What was it?* He had strained hard and long but could not make it out. Something soft and white and innocent. What to make of it? *No, nothing, I wish to make nothing of it.* He shook his head with violence and sat up from his cot. Had he heard reveille? *No, only 4:30 A.M.* Sweat drenched him and his bed. *It is not that hot,* he thought. Another horrid image of the devilish black giant and he was on his feet, splashing water on his face from the basin.

Time to get up, anyway, Marley groused to himself. *They say there's to be a fight today.*

Jackson rarely read the newspapers anymore. The words of his old Lexington pastor, Dr. White, resonated in his ears: "There is little, if anything, resident in those pages that matters in God's eternal scheme." Jackson also had little time to read the classic works of theology, literature, and military science. Only the Scriptures could he regularly visit. But occasionally he acceded to Sandie's urgings to listen as the young redhead read potent headlines or story snippets. Such had been the case the morning of July 18 as Jackson and his staff relaxed following breakfast in Winchester, to which Johnston had further retreated from Charles Town as Patterson's much larger force advanced southward.

"Here is the *Tribune,*" Sandie said. "'The hanging of traitors is sure to begin before the month is over. The nations of Europe may rest assured that Jeff Davis and Company will be swinging from the battlements of Washington, at least by the Fourth of July. We spit upon a later and longer deferred justice.'

"Now the *Philadelphia Press,*" he continued. "'No man of sense could, for a moment, doubt that this much-ado-about-nothing would end in a month.'" He looked up at the expressionless faces of Jackson, Preston, the other young staff officers, and Stuart, who had stopped by to breakfast. "It says the Northern people are 'simply invincible', and that 'the rebels, a mere band of ragamuffins, will fly, like chaff before the wind, on our approach.'"

"And how long does the mighty *New York Times* give us?" Stuart inquired, the promise of a twinkle impregnating his blue eyes.

Sandie leafed through the stack. "Thirty days, sir."

"Ah," Stuart nodded, as though enlightened.

"And it says the so-called 'rebellion is an unborn tadpole,' 'a local commotion, not a revolution,' and that it will all happen 'without much bloodshed' because we of the South are 'weak, disheartened, and demoralized,'" Sandie added.

"What do you expect of the Yankee press, gentlemen," Preston said, "when their own Secretary of War Stanton publicly scorned the mistaking of this 'mere casual and ephemeral insurrection' for war?"

"Why, it almost makes a man want to ask where can he turn in his sword to save himself all the fuss and trouble," Stuart said, his eyes merry as usual. Jackson could not remember having yet heard Stuart speak, even on the weightiest of matters, without gently seasoning his words with affable good humor.

Just then, one of Johnston's staffers presented himself with a salute. "Begging the general's pardon, sir, but General Johnston wishes to see you in his quarters at once, sir."

"Ah," Stuart said with a smile, "Could it be we have surrendered?"

Jackson, Johnston's other three brigade commanders, and Stuart learned that orders had arrived to march eastward to Manassas Junction, an important railway link where General Pierre Gustave Beauregard, the "hero of Fort Sumter," had called for immediate help. Advancing on Beauregard was the main Union army under Brigadier General Irvin McDowell. Johnston's job had been to occupy Patterson to the west, then, at the appropriate time, steal undetected to merge forces with Beauregard in a stand against the Federals pouring south from Washington. The tenor of the War Department's telegraph from Richmond indicated that stand would now be a desperate one. Beauregard was outnumbered thirty-one thousand to twenty thousand, his advance outposts had been shoved back, and the only hope of saving what remained of the entire northern half of Virginia was that Johnston could reinforce "Old Bory"—and that before Patterson cut Johnston off or himself arrived at Manassas to support McDowell.

Emerging from the council, Jackson immediately ordered that his twenty-five hundred troops pack three days of rations, fold down their tents and leave them on the ground, and prepare to march.

The order to leave thrilled Willy and most of the men around him. They detested the unsightliness of the camp, its abominable rations, and its dirty water. A number of the men had even begun catching various intestinal and abdominal maladies. Willy suspected these occurred in direct proportion to the amount of a man's food and water intake. Thus, he consumed as little of both as possible. Some of the men had begun to lose weight and color due to the frequency of their trips to the woefully inadequate latrines. He hoped the medical personnel came up with some solution for these unfortunate cases soon. He suspected they would. One item, however, puzzled him. Where were they headed? No one knew, not even the officers.

That afternoon Jackson's First Brigade decamped, marched through Winchester streets lined with cheering men, smiling women, and blushing girls, and headed southeast toward the Blue Ridge. Now mystery truly engulfed Willy and the other soldiers. Wasn't Patterson off to the *north*east?

Little did they know their confusion was nothing to that of Patterson's. That general faced a two-front war. In his front were the Rebels whose recent movements—or lack thereof—had sent conflicting signals. To his back were the infuriating telegraphic insults of veteran Union commander in chief, and Virginian, Winfield Scott, winner of the Mexican War thirteen years before, and behind him, President Lincoln, pressuring Scott for a quick ending of the bothersome disturbance.

But now the Confederates sought to accomplish the very act Patterson had been dispatched to prevent. They headed straight for Manassas Junction to bolster Beauregard. To obscure the movements of Jackson, the other three infantry brigades, and their artillery batteries, Jeb Stuart and his horsemen flew into any gap through which Patterson's skirmishers gave indication of attempting to slip and detect the urgent march eastward of ten thousand men.

A few miles southeast of Winchester, Jackson called his men to a halt. He pulled out a sheet of paper and read from it with loud bold clarity.

"Our gallant army under General Beauregard is now attacked by overwhelming numbers. The commanding general hopes that his troops will step out like men, and make a forced march to save the country."

Never again would Jackson allow his own troops to know the destination of a march. But on this occasion, he smiled when his men shook the earth with a sudden explosion of thunderous cheers. It never occurred to Jackson how surprised these men would have been to have seen his first many, long ago attempts at public speaking at the Franklin Society of Lexington.

Tears filled Willy's eyes as the applause roared on. Something began to dawn on him. He thought of his brothers and sisters. He thought of his dead mother and all she represented to him. He thought of Maggie, who had helped renew his hope and purpose in life, as she had done for the entire family. All the thoughts and memories of home wrapped themselves around him as a hot flaming cape, and suddenly through him pulsed the fierce rage of the Norse berserkers he had read of as a child. Now he realized why he and all the others were here, why his stomach ached, why his feet hurt, why he had to slap away the hordes of lice that in recent days had begun to introduce themselves to him. He was here to defend home and everything dear and blessed to him. *Home.* Suddenly he loved it as never he had before. Suddenly he knew it and treasured it like never before. These—*people*—who would dare to trod down the very ground that had borne him from the womb to manhood, were not they now doing it to others' homes just a few miles north?

Oh, it was all now so very important to him.

Then Willy's lungs joined the roaring chorus and he knew what to do.

When Jackson finally allowed his exhausted men to stop that night, they fell where they stopped, parched but not drinking, famished but not eating.

"Sir," Sandie said to him. "Some of the staff may have to stand sentry. It may take the point of a gun to rouse any of the men."

Jackson stood silent for a moment and pondered the statement. "Douglas?" he said.

"Yes, sir?" came the energetic unseen youthful voice.

"I'll stand guard myself for a few hours."

The assembled officers stood dumbstruck in the dark.

"Fetch me a lemon, lad, that's all I'll need," Jackson said.

And thus did Brigadier General Thomas J. Jackson, with two hours sleep in the past forty, patrol the perimeter of a camp of twenty-five hundred soldiers, himself and exactly three other volunteers, until relieved an hour before dawn by Douglas.

Jackson's brigade, beginning in the afternoon, had waded across the cold rushing Shenandoah River in the dark, scaled the west face of the Blue Ridge, and totaled seventeen miles of tough marching.

Resuming the march at dawn on the nineteenth, Jackson having had one hour of sleep, the First descended the Blue Ridge, then turned south and marched six more miles to Piedmont, a stop on the Manassas Gap Railroad. There, Jackson began loading his troopers onto trains for the latter half of the sixty-mile trek.

Willy overheard his father telling Rev. Pendleton that it was the first time in history a railroad had been utilized to achieve strategic military mobility.

Meanwhile, Stuart and his Confederate horse ran circles around their less-accomplished Union counterparts. It was a full twenty-four hours before Patterson even smelled anything amiss. By the time he figured out that Johnston, Jackson, Stuart, and company had skedaddled, the Rebs were boarding trains thirty miles away on the other side of the Blue Ridge Mountains and heading directly for a fight Patterson was assigned to prevent them from reaching!

Thus, with great confidence in his superior numbers, arms, and equipment, and never suspecting the possibility of facing Southern reinforcements, McDowell began probing moves against Beauregard's outnumbered positions along a small northeast Virginia stream called Bull Run. Even when Scott, then Lincoln, received Patterson's belated news that he had been four-flushed, they still believed McDowell would have his battle—and their war—won before Confederate backup troops could arrive.

So did the thousands of Washington dignitaries and high-society types who streamed out of the capital in barouches, gigs, and phaetons on the morning of the twenty-first. Some most eagerly anticipated the sporting event that lay ahead; others, the picnic; still others, the overall festivity of the day's outing.

But confidence flowed in abundance across section lines. Talk across the South had it that, under normal circumstances, the average Southerner could whip ten Yankees.

Thomas Jackson and his men possessed great confidence that the victory would be theirs, though Pierre Beauregard, whose men had repulsed two Union forays already, was not so sure. Jackson and his men had had a full day of rest as Johnston's thousands of other troops arrived in trainload after trainload at the Manassas Junction depot.

A short distance away, Beauregard prepared to spring a trap on his Northern foe. But McDowell beat him to the punch, circling a large contingent of men, the polished steel of their bayonets gleaming brilliantly in the sun, around Beauregard's front and flanking his left.

For Jackson, it was Sunday, it was Anna's birthday, and it was a good day, he thought, to restore the fair name of the Jackson family.

To that end, he had spent most of the previous night engaged in an activity no other leader on either side had done. Not for minutes, but for hour after arduous hour he had bent on his knees in prayer. He prayed from remembrance, he prayed for the day, and he prayed toward the future. Anna occupied his attentions, as did Maggie, Ellie, and his two dead babies—*Shall I be permitted any more babies, Father, perhaps even one whom I can know?* This last, heartwrenching ordeal of reflection and petition drove him to confession of his sins to his Father in heaven, beseeching of Him, with thanksgiving, for wisdom and courage, pleading for the safekeeping of his men, and inquiring of Him for His mercy, kindness, and blessing on the work that lay ahead.

When Jim saw Jackson emerge from his tent at dawn, he thought to himself, *The general is a great man for praying at all times, but when I see him get up a great many times in the night to pray, I'm beginning to know there is going to be something to pay. . . .*

CHAPTER 36

JUST BEFORE HIS CAVALRY REGIMENT BROKE FROM CAMP, Marley's young cousin Joe had burst into his tent with the confirmation: May Freiburger was indeed coming to picnic with Joe's congressman father and the two families. The congressional page who had carried the note to Joe told him that a line of buggies, barouches, gigs, and carriages stretched from the high ground just to the north of Manassas Junction nearly the entire twenty-five miles back to Washington City.

There are liable to be more spectators than participants in this battle, Marley thought with a jolt. Joe secreted that the courier had even offered him a slug of champagne from a still-cold bottle he had tucked in his saddlebags.

And indeed, all of Washington was aflutter at the comeliness of young May Freiburger as she passed by in the congressman's barouche, the rattle of musketry and crash of artillery sounding in the distance, then took a place, daintily, on the large spread picnic blanket at the site her father had spotted under an ancient huge oak.

"From what Corporal Harding tells me," Freiburger told Joe's father, their wives, and Joe's two teenaged sisters, "this ground is remote enough so as to insure safety, yet close enough that we may sense the drama of this glorious day."

James Freiburger had never fought in combat.

The picnic spread was magnificent—minced pies; cold chicken, ham, and roast; deviled eggs; caviar; pickled pears; sweet cakes; peach cobbler; sarsaparilla; and buckets of champagne. Now all that was needed was a victory.

A mile away, McDowell's brilliant flanking move, set up with a couple of major feints at other points on the line along the small stream known as Bull Run, had smashed into the Confederate left flank. Only the stubborn, profanity-laced leadership of Southern Colonel Nathan "Shanks" Evans delayed the bluecoats long enough at a Bull Run crossing known as the Stone Bridge to prevent a complete rout that would have rolled up the Southern left and swept the Confederates off the field and back across the Manassas Gap rail line.

Still, Shanks Evans was outnumbered ten to one, and despite belated reinforcements from the Confederate right, he finally had to relinquish his forward post. Now the Southerners had more men in position to meet the onslaught from the northwest, but the Federals had the momentum and they barreled through one grayback regiment after another, shoving them around woods, over green rolling fields, and across the Warrenton Turnpike, to the foot of a broad gentle incline known as Henry House Hill.

The Freiburgers and Joe's family joined the wave of cheers that roared forth from the long line of Yankee spectators at word that the Federal assault appeared to be driving the Rebels from the field. May giggled demurely and brought a fan to her face upon hearing the whispers of nearby youths that she would soon be wedded to young Joe. And her father felt barely a twinge of regret that many of the bullets being fired at young Joe and his comrades by the secessionists had been—and continued to be—manufactured from his own New England factories.

But Joe, Marley, and the other mounted hundreds in Colonel William Tecumseh Sherman's brigade felt no remorse at all as they led the infantry into the fray, riding down graybacks, shooting, slashing, and trampling as they went. *Where is the vaunted Reb cavalry?* Marley thought fleetingly as he slashed another screaming foe to crimson death.

"Look!" Joe shouted, not far away, his smoke-darkened face aflush with triumph and manhood. "They're chasing up that hill."

Marley turned and stared into the smoke. Sure enough, it was a hill ahead. In fact it appeared, through his one eye, in the screaming deafening murky roar to be a colony of gray and butternut ants, scrambling for their lives up the grade.

"Colonel Sherman says to press on, men!" a captain rode by shouting, "We're to drive them across the rail line."

Marley paused for just an instant, pinching more bullets into his revolver, as Joe and twenty other riders swarmed after the captain toward the hill. *Could it be that we* are *going to finish it today?* he thought to himself. Then he recognized the sickening sweet pungent aroma of spilled intestines and blasted brains. Not since Mexico had he—suddenly, something swung him around, to his blind side. There, a wounded Reb on the ground raised his rifle to fire at Marley. His gun just loaded, the Yank jerked off a shot that coincided with the Reb's. But it was just a shade quicker, and the other man's bullet took off Marley's hat instead of his scalp. Marley's shot went through the Southerner's heart. But he noticed before he swung around to ride off that the soldier had sustained at least four previous wounds. The Pennsylvanian flinched as the realization struck him, *Those Southern boys are getting licked, but I fear they are dying hard, very hard indeed.*

Then Marley turned and joined the tidal wave of men ahorse and afoot that now swarmed up Henry House Hill. As he rode, he wondered what it was that had turned him to his blind side and delivered him from death and eternity by the scantest instant in time.

For months, since he left peacetime Lexington, Jackson's health had prospered. He feared this day might reverse that condition and not because of war, but the lack of it.

As the morning hours passed, he had been dispatched from one end of the field to the other by his superiors, to support engaged units. He had not so much as glimpsed any action. But he had heard that the day went sore against his people.

As blue-white smoke spread across the sky ahead of Jackson and the earth shook from the rumble of artillery and masses of pounding men and horses, he led his brigades toward the Stone Bridge, point of the main Union assault.

The color in his bronzed face receded and his eyes seemed to shrink into dark hollows as he heard the fury ahead. *O God,* he thought, *two nations and tens of thousands of men come out against one another, and the war may end today, and I not allowed even to participate? Even to witness it? For what have I been prepared? How ever shall our name be righted?*

Then his furrowed brow, nearly hidden by the dusty sweat-stained VMI forage cap pulled low over his forehead, crinkled deeper. *Those guns are not coming from the Stone Bridge. They are closer. The Federals are pushing us back.* He turned to Douglas and Sandie. *They heard it too.* Without a word, he kicked Little Sorrel into action and veered obliquely left away from the direction of the contested Stone Bridge.

Douglas and Sandie traded knowing glances. *He has received no such orders contravening the previous ones to support Evans, Bee, and Bartow at the Stone Bridge, nor does anyone know what he is now doing,* Douglas thought. Weary tatterdemalions in gray and butternut, many garnished with crimson, their lips and faces black with powder, began to emerge on foot from the direction of the fighting.

"Too many," one soldier panted to Sandie and Douglas, "too many."

Then Jackson's young staff officers rode hard after him.

Shanks Evans had succeeded in wrecking the entire brigade of General Ambrose Burnside. That organization sat the rest of the day on the sidelines. But when Sherman spotted a crossing downstream from the Stone Bridge that allowed the flanking and finally dislodging of Evans as well as the supporting brigades of Bee and Bartow from their forward positions after two hours of tenacious fighting, the Confederates were bloody, disorganized, and scattered. Chased by Marley and hundreds of other Union cavalrymen, and thousands of infantry, they scrambled toward the top of Henry House Hill where Imboden's battery of three guns blazed away. There they purposed to stand.

Into the gap flew Wade Hampton, the richest planter in South Carolina, and his volunteer legion of cavalry. Down Henry Hill toward the Federals they flew, firing revolvers and shouting. They drove most of their foes off the hill and reached the Warrenton Turnpike, where they decimated one Union counterattack.

Hampton had no military experience and little training, but he was a born leader of men, boasted enormous innate physical strength, and brimmed with quiet confidence. For a while, his six hundred men stymied the Northern effort along the entire front. Then, the bluecoats' superior numbers produced a withering enfilading fire that forced Hampton back up the hill. Defiant, he tried to stand again, but the Yankees surged around both his flanks. Nearly surrounded, he fought on, until Shanks Evans himself rode into the smoking hellish din and screamed for Hampton to pull back. This he finally did, swarming hordes of Yankees breathing down his backside. In fact, the entire Confederate left front that had opposed McDowell's flanking attack now collapsed, and the men of Bee, Bartow, and Evans, as well as Hampton's legion, all fled across the flat top of Henry House Hill.

Contemptuous of the Northern advance, and angry that Bee's troops were retreating past him rather than supporting his battery, Imboden directed his guns as they continued ripping into the oncoming Northern lines. But two salty Federal career officers, James Ricketts and Charles Griffin, and their rifled twelve-gun batteries of U.S. army regulars, now zeroed in on Imboden's outnumbered placement. As the Union batteries' fire became overwhelming, Imboden noticed fresh new ranks of Federal infantry massing a few hundred yards away on the turnpike. *They are pointing at me,* he thought with a shudder.

"Sir, we are nearly out of ammunition," a sergeant called to Imboden. Blood streamed from the man's right shoulder. Imboden looked around. Half his men lay sprawled on the ground. Nearly all his horses were down in bloody heaps. Equipment was strewn everywhere. One cannon was shattered, another damaged. He wanted to continue, he wanted to keep fighting, but— "D——!" he screamed, his face a raging purple. "Where is Bee? Where is my infantry support?"

Then another shell showered him with turf and elicited a wailing scream from one of his already-wounded men.

"Sir, we've got to retreat," the sergeant pleaded.

Imboden cursed again, then gave a quick frustrated nod. He knew that after he patched together makeshift limbers to transport his two surviving guns back across the flat top of Henry Hill, nothing stood between the Federals and their gaining that high ground and from there rolling up the entire off-balance Southern army. *And thence the Manassas Railroad and Northern Virginia. And thence—*

He cursed again, bitterly.

When Jackson reached the southeast foot of Henry House Hill, his mouth dropped open and he drew rein on Little Sorrel. *Father, can this be so?* he thought with anguish. A tidal wave of his countrymen flooded at, through, and around his startled troops. Some wounded, some defeated, a few cowardly, all outnumbered, outequipped, and outgunned, they had had all the fighting they wanted.

Jackson's thin lips drew thinner. Douglas noticed a muscle twitch in his commander's taut jaw.

"They need help, sir," one retreating soldier, his arm in a bloody sling, said to Jackson. "They need your help up there. The blasted Yankees are cutting them to pieces. Their—" The soldier strained for a word adequately detestable, but failed to find it. "Their artillery is tearing us to pieces, sir, and it's getting closer. Please, sir, you've got to help them."

The man nearly fainted, but two of his mates caught him and helped him along.

Jackson raised his field glasses to his eyes. *Flat terrain behind me, a rising grade ahead, the Yankees still beyond that.*

"Shall we go to their aid, sir?" Sandie asked.

Jackson looked around at his aides, each of whom he had selected after careful study. *Such fair, fresh, honest young faces,* he thought. *And good, so far as men's hearts can be good.*

Then above the din of muskets, cannon, screaming, and shouting rose the booming curses of an angry man. Despite its thick jet coating of smoke and sweat, Jackson recognized the thin frame of Imboden stalking toward him.

Jackson had thought his quartermaster Harmon could swear fleas off a hound dog, but Imboden proceeded to raise (lower?) the art to new heights. The artillery captain did not appreciate being chased off the hill and nearly killed due to lack of infantry support, when he had been doing his job. Jackson's already grave visage grew darker as Imboden's raging, tearful oaths multiplied. Finally, huffing from his verbal exertion, Imboden noticed Jackson's granite stolidness.

"Uh," the artilleryman stammered, remembering Jackson's piety.

The general, his eyes grim slits, stared at his mounted subordinate. His heart urged him onward, to engage the advancing enemy, or at least to support his own embattled comrades. But his girded wits would have none of it.

"I'll support your battery," the Virginian said quietly. "Unlimber right here."

At least you are not beaten, my foul-mouthed friend, he thought.

Imboden's mouth opened in surprise. He turned and shouted for his men to set up shop. When he turned back to thank Jackson, all he saw were Little Sorrel's departing haunches.

Surprise arrested the aides' crestfallen faces. "But our brothers are up there, over that hill, being cut to pieces," each countenance seemed to shout. But Jackson had already left them and was observing a long thick stand of pines stretching to his left. *A thick, dark, tangled stand,* he thought to himself. It curved outward on both right and left from a lengthy straight center. To his right, the hill rose a few hundred yards to where it crested with a wide plateau. At the other end of the plateau sat a two-story frame house glistening white in the smoky sunlight. Out-buildings and a barn flanked it.

"Check that house," Jackson said over his shoulder to Douglas.

Jackson pulled up for a moment. His gaze took in the pine copse. *Protection on three sides from attack,* he thought, *and ahead, good elevation for my guns out front, even better if I shield them by placing them slightly down from the plateau.*

He looked around for Douglas. "I need a lemon, sir." Douglas produced one from a supply in his saddlebags. Jackson bit into it with relish, a fresh juicy mist spraying his bearded dirty face. Refreshed, he thought to himself, if the day is to be won, this is the spot from which it must happen.

"I lived here since the Revolution, sonny—the first revolution," eighty-two-year-old Judith Henry snapped at Douglas as he beseeched her to accompany him to safety behind the Confederate lines. "I ain't a-going anywhere. If them dad-blasted Yankee curs want me out of here, they'll have to blast me right out."

Just then, an exploding shell took off the roof of the Henrys' barn thirty yards away.

Mrs. Henry hooted like an old crow at Douglas and his cowering friends, all three of whom had dived to the floor. Douglas, red-faced, managed a mortified smile and stood up. The old woman hooted again. Douglas sighed and fumbled with the sweat-stained broad-brimmed gray hat he held in his hands. The air outside was rife with smoke and the sounds of heavy- and small-arms fire, which had closed to within a few hundred yards of the sturdy two-story white framed house. He glanced at the two hulking men, no older than he, who flanked him in Mrs. Henry's second-floor room.

"We are prepared to escort you to safety, ma'am—," Douglas said in a wavering voice.

"I never needed no escorts yet, sonny, and I don't need none now," she cut in.

"Forcibly, if necessary," Douglas finished.

Thirty-eight-year-old Ben Henry, as big as Douglas's two mates and much more menacing, stepped out from the corner where he had been observing the conversation. His thick hands gripped a shotgun, which he pointed at Douglas's chest. "And we are prepared to escort you straight to hell, dandy." He clicked back the hammer. "Now you heard my grandmama—move out."

Douglas feared Jackson, but not as much as the wrong end of the shotgun now facing him.

Twenty minutes later, a Union shell made Judith Henry, born the day Lord Cornwallis surrendered to General Washington in 1781, the first civilian casualty in the War between the States.

Jackson, acting on his own counsel, distributed his twenty-five hundred man First Virginia Brigade along the front perimeter of the pine trees, including where they flared forward on both the left and especially the right, the latter at almost a right angle to the concentrated force in the center. There Jackson expected the heaviest attack, so he placed two of his five regiments directly behind his guns. Each regiment lay on the ground in two lines, forming a formidable four-deep formation, plus the guns in front of them.

Many of the men were actually concealed within the tangled thicket. All of them were veiled by the Henry House Hill, including the two cannon.

As the smoke and thunder roiled ahead of him, beyond the plateaued top of the hill, Jackson sat erect on Little Sorrel. His dusty uniform and cap as blue as those of the enemies fighting to get to him, he brought his field glasses to his eyes. *Nothing yet,* he thought. Then he began to walk Sorrel slowly, along a line parallel to his men but out front of all of them. He knew the battle was coming to him. He felt it. Knew it could be no other way. More men streamed past him and his five regiments. The occasional minié ball whistled overhead. Jackson continued to walk the rotund Sorrel, who walked with composure.

From one end of the long line to the other he rode, steady and quiet. For a long while, nothing happened. The sounds of battle grew fainter and the minié balls stopped. He ordered his batteries, however, to launch their own salvo against the distant Federals.

Jackson, piloting Little Sorrel back and forth, waited . . . and waited . . . and waited. *Where have they gone?* he wondered behind his bearded blank face. *Have I erred in posting here? No, the battle must come through here; it must. And it is our best station for standing.*

Then came over Jackson a depression so strong that for a moment he keened in his horse. *But what if I am mistaken? What if it all ends, and I here with my men, out of position, away from where I was sent to support?*

A burning bolt of panic flashed through his body before he straightened back up. *I must stay strong for my men,* he thought.

After a bit the minié balls began to return, with greater velocity.

"Why, lookee there at nonchalant Old Jack," Jake McCullough, laying near Willy, cracked in his easy nasal drawl to those around him, "his chin cocked up as if he was expecting a rain and 'tweren't averse to having a drop of it on his face."

The observation heartened Willy. He was terrified. Lying prone on the hot ground, out front of the pine copse, he peeked up and looked left and right. As far as he could see in both directions, men lay as he did. He was ready to do his part, but nobody had said anything about just laying out under the scorching July sun hour after hour, waiting—and that ornery Jake McCullough and his tales about laying there even while the shells were coming down, why, that couldn't be true, could it?

Willy's answer came with the abrupt crashing of a shell fifty yards out ahead of the front line, of which he was a part. He stared at the flying debris and smoke. *My heavens—*

Then another shell landed far down the line to his right. This one registered hysterical shrieks. The realization crashed home to Willy: *Men are hit.* He had seen very little of that at Falling Waters. Had he even seen a dead man? He did not think so. A couple wounded. No one was hit in the area where he had fought. Then he ducked instinctively as another shell screamed directly over his head before crashing into the pines behind him.

Jackson glanced back at the forest, where men were beating out the flames of a fire that had sprouted from the exploding shell. Now other shells began to pock the field and woods where lay Jackson's brigade. And the infrequent singing of minié balls grew to a chorus.

A mounted aide, ducking low in the face of the escalating enemy fire, reported to Jackson that his orders to gobble up additional four-gun batteries from adjacent commands had begun to produce fruit. One battery was coming now, and another would be soon.

Jackson had scanned his surroundings. He knew just where he wanted the guns placed.

"I'll swan, boys," McCullough said, peeking up from where he had burrowed into the rich black earth to duck the rain of bullets now flying in. "Look at him now."

Willy, clawing even lower than McCullough, adjusted his sweat-stained, dirt-caked face to sneak a peep at Jackson. The general continued to ride slowly and steadily out in front of the line, from one end of it to the other. Willy stared at his friend. *But how—*

"How in tarnation can he do that?" Eddie Drake gasped.

"Why he's riding around in this shower of death calm as a farmer about his farm when the seasons are good," McCullough marveled.

Despite himself, not noticing the dirt sneaking into his parched mouth, Willy raised his head a bit higher for a better look. *Why is he doing it?* he thought. Then, *Why is he not hit?*

"What's he saying?" McCullough said as Jackson neared their point in the line.

Willy's eyes grew wider the nearer Jackson rode. The boy forgot the buzzing fat blue flies that bedeviled his wet face. He even forgot the bullets whizzing past. *What is he saying?*

Then Jackson was passing them, only a few feet away. Willy stared up at him. Just then, the sun hung over Jackson, shimmering down over the general's shoulder into Willy's heated face and putting Jackson into black eclipse. As shot and shell rained around them and the roar of battle escalated, the nearby Confederate batteries belching their own hot metal death, Willy attempted to block the sun with his forearm, but all he could see was Jackson's square lean silhouette. *What is it he is saying?* Willy wondered, straining to hear over the growing din of war.

He listened.

"All's well, all's well."

Over and over, as soothing and sure as a mother with a frightened babe in the crook of her shoulder. When Jackson arrived at Willy's point, the looming giant presence stopped and covered the boy with its cooling shadow. Still, Willy, try as he might, squinting, could not make out the features of horse or rider, though the familiar rustic aroma of the sweaty beast permeated his nostrils.

"All's well, son, all's well."

Then the rider moved on and the sun burned into the boy's face again. As minié balls continued to zip past, Willy turned and his gaze connected with McCullough's. He had heard it too. For once, the grizzled lanky prankster had no joke, no bit of irony to offer. Their eyes met and their thoughts were one: *What manner of man is this?*

Willy watched for a moment as Jackson proceeded on down the line. *All's well.* Then a bullet tore the boy's right collar from his shirt and he slammed his head back to the ground. A deep breath, then, *Indeed it is.*

Up and down the line, hundreds of men, hearing their leader's calm steady words, relaxed and proceeded with their remembered Scripture, prayers, and Catechism, even as death visited itself upon them, and their comrades from beaten regiments raced through and past them for sanctuary in the rear.

Now Jackson knew his soldiers were being hurt. Here a shell exploded and a cluster of men shrieked. There a bullet splatted a man's skull and widowed and orphaned a distant frightened family.

Where is the battle? he agonized. *It should have been here by now.* Everything in his heart tugged him forward, toward the sound of the guns that now visited terror upon his beloved boys of the Valley. Everything in him screamed at him to unleash at long last this splendid array of manhood. These men who for years had been insulted, patronized, mocked, and scorned by many of their countrymen from the North. These men, these boys, who had been called forth from their homes, fields, businesses, and plantations to defend against these "brothers" that had now physically invaded and trampled the very earth upon which they lived and worked.

When a handsome towheaded youngster no older than eighteen screamed and clutched his throat as it pumped forth crimson, Jackson despaired and his shoulders slumped. After a moment, he looked heavenward. *Lord, how long?* Bullets whipped past him. One ripped through the left waist of his blue coat, another nicked his right boot. He swallowed hard. His aching heart pounded. *Father, my men are being cut to pieces, Sir. Are we to be shamed, Sir? Have I shamed us? When shall we be allowed to defend the right?* Then something drew his attention to the west.

There through the haze loomed the distant Blue Ridge, radiant in the clear noonday brilliance. Jackson stared at the long ancient rampart of the Shenandoah Valley. Beyond it lay all on earth meaningful to him. All the people, all the memories . . . the once great name of Jackson. *We are here . . . for all of them.*

Then the Lord strengthened him and he squared his shoulders, sat again erect, and turned Little Sorrel to return back down the line.

Galloping toward him was the only other mounted Confederate in sight oblivious to the fusillade, a handsome familiar face above a strapping build, also a general and also in a blue coat.

"Why they didn't tell me it was General *Tom* Jackson," General Barnard Bee of South Carolina saluted, his countenance momentarily given reprieve from its grimness at the recognition of an old friend.

"General Bee," Jackson said, returning the salute, then shaking the proffered gauntleted hand.

"How is your Spanish, General?" Bee said with a quick wink.

"Fine, sir," Jackson replied, his face serious. "Oh," he blushed, remembering long ago shared days in Mexico.

"General," Bee said, resuming his grimness, "they are beating us back. We are decimated. They are too many, sir." His perfect head of jet-black hair glinting in the sun, he pointed up the hill. "They will be appearing over that crest any minute, sir."

Jackson eyed the smoking scene ahead. Bee noticed the Virginian's eyes flash.

"Then, sir, we shall give them the bayonet."

Bee could scarcely hear the quiet words over the tumult of battle. It was the white-hot cobalt eyes that roared thunder.

CHAPTER 37

JACKSON WATCHED BEE FOR A MOMENT AFTER THE LATTER had ridden toward the flank to rally his men. Just as the Virginian turned back, a long low rumble began toward the other side of Henry House Hill. *There they are,* he thought.

Over the crest of the hill, perhaps four hundred yards ahead, came a shouting, shooting, roaring wave of blue, massive in view of the tattered, paltry men in gray and butternut they swept before them. Then another sound jerked Jackson's head around. *Bee,* he grimaced. A hail of shots had riddled the handsome South Carolinian and his horse, which now pinned him under it.

Douglas arrived with bad news from brigade commanders. "Sir, the Yankees are threatening to flank us both right and left."

In the midst of all, a somber gangly man, sitting straight up in his saddle and wearing all black, including the tallest of Prince Albert hats, appeared from the snarled forest behind, walking his horse toward the front. The prostrate Confederate soldiers, most of whom had not yet sighted the onrushing Yankee horde, stared at the strange sepulchral figure.

The mingled strong odors of sweat, blood, and burning powder meshed with the sweet smell of pine to fill Willy's head to bursting with sensation as the gaunt horseman proceeded directly toward him. So close came he that Willy could see the twin china blue eyes, far away eyes, looking out toward the approaching foe, but looking beyond too. Then rang forth the familiar wry voice of McCullough in comment on the queer specter.

"Good Lord, what have I done that the devil should come after me?"

A wave of hoots and cheers greeted McCullough's shout and Willy thanked God for the buoyant presence of the irreverent soul.

"Would you look at that?" McCullough said, nodding toward Jackson.

Willy turned and saw that his old Sunday school teacher had stopped Little Sorrel out front of his men. The squat little animal faced directly into the storm of fire and thunder that bore down upon him. But Jackson was not even watching the charging Federals. He stared toward heaven, his eyes closed, his lips moving, and his arms spread wide, palms open upward, as if appealing his case to the ultimate arbiter of justice.

Bee, finally pulled out from his horse, lay in pain, coughing his own blood. As one of his men comforted him and his physician did his best to staunch the flow of two deep chest wounds, Bee struggled to focus his gaze on Jackson.

"Why, holy Moses, looks as if he's praying," an aide said. "Right in the middle it all. Looks as if he's talking right to God."

Bee burbled some words, then summoned great will to clear his blood-clogged throat. The tearing pain nearly overcame him, but his words, finally, were clear. And defiant. "Three hours he's stood them off, gentleman. Three hours." The physician noticed Bee's eyes glint with electricity. "There stands Jackson like a stone wall, men. Rally behind the Virginians."

Then he collapsed into a coma, and within five minutes his earthly life was completed.

As shot and shell poured into them, Jackson's still-prostrate regiments, many of their number killed or moaning and shrieking in pain, grew restive to the point of explosion. Imboden and the other batteries—seventeen pieces in all by now—wheeled to the rear, ordered so by Jackson, whose adroit assembling and placement of them had kept the Yankees at bay for hours. So effective had Jackson's defensive stand been, while enormously outnumbered, that Confederate field commander Beauregard believed enough reinforcements had finally been mustered to mount an attack.

Willy stared at the general and shook his head.

"Why don't he fall?" came a voice from behind.

"Why don't he get down before they knock him down?" came another.

"He's protected, yes he sure is, like General Washington with Braddock against them Indians when seventeen bullets tore his clothes. He can't fall."

"Down," Willy said, his quavering voice lost in the din. "Get down, Major Jackson. Get down, sir!"

"You get down, blast you, boy," McCullough growled, grabbing Willy's arm to pull him back to the ground. But Willy broke free as though the lean hard McCullough had no more strength than a soft young Lexington lass. Then the man was on his feet, hollering for his friend to get down.

"Come back here, Willy Preston!" McCullough shouted.

But Willy was walking wraithlike toward Jackson. He did not see a minié ball tear the top of a nearby rider's head off, along with the tall black Prince Albert hat he wore.

"Major Tom Jackson, come down off that horse!" Willy screamed.

He did see one bullet tear through the left side of Jackson's coat, then another his right sleeve. Another blew away the leather strap upon which his field glasses hung over his shoulder. As Jackson remained rigid and erect upon Little Sorrel, the horse as stationery as he, looking straight through the windows of heaven, no cannon, no bullets, no Yankee onslaught, no war, nothing at all, but heaven . . . and God . . . and the Lamb . . . Willy stepped finally around to grab Sorrel's bit and bridle, as McCullough rose behind him, and a score more men around McCullough.

Willy stared up into Jackson's face. The boy's jaw went slack. The general's countenance blazed with an incandescence singularly reflective of . . . the very glories and beauties of the Eternal . . . the Majestic . . . the *Holy.*

And what is it that he is saying? the boy strained to detect.

"O GOD the Lord, the strength of my salvation, thou hast covered my head in the day of battle . . . "

Then two dead Confederates tumbled into Willy, knocking him down. And something went terribly wrong with Jackson . . . "Major Jackson!" . . . Willy screamed.

A musket ball blew a hole in Jackson's left hand, shearing off part of one finger and damaging another. Another bullet tore into Little Sorrel, and when horse and rider had spun around, blood sprayed the air from Jackson's torn hand and dappled Willy's chest. Terror filled the boy's face as he saw blood streaking Jackson's cheeks and cap. But fire blazed across the Virginian's bloodied visage and he raised his ruined hand, raining crimson, and charged his men: "Reserve your fire till they come within fifty yards, then fire and give them the bayonet; and, when you charge, yell like furies!"

And so was born the Rebel yell.

When eighteen-year-old Willy Preston turned toward the north, his smooth face and gentle eyes grown hard as granite, the Southern race turned with him. They raised their rifles, they raised their voices, and, sixty-five hundred against twenty thousand, they stepped out into all the inferno hell's minions could marshal on earth. Then, unharnessed after their long, long wait, they ran, they screamed, and they fired. And even cherished remembrances of wives, girlfriends, mothers, and homes receded before the urgent primal drive to destroy the invader, the wrecker of property, the killer of Judith Henry.

And fled fear.

The Yankees had been jolted by a surprise charge a little while before by Jackson's Thirty-third Virginia Regiment, from the far left of the bedraggled Confederate line. That assault had stifled the Northern advance and garnered the Southerners temporary control of several key forward Union cannon. The Thirty-third, outnumbered and unsupported, had been driven back, but this time the Confederates screeched forward in thousands, not hundreds. They pushed the Yankees back and up onto the tableland of Henry Hill, then clear across to the far side of that plateau.

Willy ran and screamed through the roiling charcoal-gray haze, vaguely aware of stepping on dead and wounded bodies, of comrades falling all around him, of bullets whizzing past. Deaf to the ceaseless roar of artillery and cracking of musketry.

Then he was throwing himself into them, forgetting his training and all sanity, falling to the ground on top of a heap of them, swinging and slashing his rifle butt and bayonet like a vengeful twin-headed monster.

"B——s!" he screamed, not hearing himself or even knowing he used such words. Then no more words came, only grunts, sighs, and other guttural noises as he tried to destroy everything blue that he saw. Destroy, destroy, *kill!* As he finished crushing the second man—boy's—face into cherry jelly, panting, almost laughing, he looked for more. He saw McCullough grab a dead Yankee officer's revolver and shoot a wounded teenager attempting to crawl away, in the back. Then the lean Southerner, draped in a thick cloud of smoke, pulled another Yankee by the hair up off a Confederate, spun him around, and shot him in the face.

Wide-eyed, Willy turned and saw two men rolling among the bodies, fighting for control of a knife. Both had sustained bloody wounds, from the knife or otherwise, and such was their exertion that they squealed like children. Willy dodged a Yankee who fell screaming, shot in the groin, in his path, then charged the knife-fighters, his bayonet dripping dark blood.

With superhuman strength and accuracy, Willy, bellowing the Rebel yell, drove the long knife into the exposed Yank with such velocity that he lifted the man off the ground before driving him back onto it and burying the blade into him again and again. Finally, the bayonet seemed to catch on something and Willy paused. He bent to the grotesque ruined form and pulled from the tip of his bayonet a pocket New Testament. He stared at the bloody little book and opened it, bullets flying all around him.

"To my beloved only child James, from your loving Mother."

Willy shook his head, wanting to erase everything. Something else caught his eye. He looked down. James's trousers were filling with excrement.

Willy stood stunned. Then something loud sounded and he felt a blow in the back knock him across another dead Yankee to the ground.

"You durned fool, get up, before you get yourself killed, boy."

Willy squinted up through the smoke and dust. He saw McCullough, the revolver smoking. Then he felt a weight on him. A dead Yankee. Shot through the lungs and bleeding on Willy's dirty gray jacket. McCullough shoved the bluecoat off Willy with the heel of his boot.

"That man had his bayonet aimed for your liver, Willy boy," McCullough said. He bent to offer Willy a hand. As he pulled the stunned youngster to his feet, McCullough's head jerked. Willy stared as Jake's face twisted into a bewildered frown before he loosed Willy's hand and grabbed for his own throat. Then he choked and staggered backward, giving Willy a last questioning look before falling dead onto James.

"Willy—Willy Preston!" came a shout. Willy turned to see a group of his mates manning a Yankee cannon. "Come on, Willy boy, help us get this piece turned around." Willy started toward them just as a hail of Yankee canister tore them all to bloody pieces.

"Retreat! Retreat men!"

An officer from somewhere, and the trumpeted sounding of recall. Then Willy, without his rifle, was running back toward his lines, over more bodies than before, still bodies, moaning bodies, shrieking bodies. *Running back, why are we running back?* his mind asked him from somewhere afar off.

Then he was back near the pines and Jackson was staring through his field glasses into the fray. The major—the general—rode a different horse and his wounded hand had bled a white handkerchief crimson. Dried blood speckled his bronzed face.

"But General, sir," Willy heard an officer—*A colonel I think*—plead. "There are too many of them. We have twice taken their forward batteries and twice been repulsed. If we had even half—"

Willy stopped to stare.

"Then if you feel that way, sir," Jackson said coldly, staring the man in the face, "you'd better keep it to yourself. And get to the rear. But first, send me your next in command. And tell him, sir," Jackson, standing in his stirrups, shouted after the retreating colonel, "if he doesn't believe we can lick these people, I'll replace him too!"

Then, more shots and lots of yelling, off to Willy's right. He turned to see, emerging from the pines down the line toward the west, a mob of cavalry, nearly all of them astride gleaming black horses, shouting, whooping—and *singing?*

"Go get 'em Jeb!" came a shout.

"Yeah!" followed a dozen cheers.

Willy had heard the strange high frenzied banshee cry several times now, had even howled it himself, but never had it sounded forth with the gusto that Jeb Stuart and his men now sent it as they thundered back into battle.

"Rugged and a dandy all in one, and his men like it, and his dancing eye too," McCullough—*Oh poor, poor Jake*—had chuckled about Stuart to Willy as Stuart and his cavalry had passed by the afternoon before, gaily chanting the memorable lilting "The Girl I Left Behind Me." And Jake had been the least inclined toward fondness of cavalry.

But Jeb Stuart was no ordinary horse soldier, and sure hadn't looked it either to Willy as he passed by the boy, high atop a tall, powerful black steed, tugging on gauntlets of snow-white buckskin that half hid the golden galons on his sleeves. Just as Willy was admiring these, and the purple plume in the horseman's floppy black hat, the brim on one side folded up against the crown, Stuart had winked down at him with that dancing eye. Then he was past, singing and laughing.

"They say he makes you feel good just being around him," McCullough had grinned. "And I guess they're right."

How magnificent he now looked to Willy as he raced his men back onto the Henry House hilltop from whence the Confederates had again been repulsed, Willy with them the last time. His tawny thick beard glistening in the summer sun and his long saber flashing,

Stuart and his three hundred charged into two forward regiments of red- and blue-bedecked Zouaves, New York City firefighters. Stuart had assaulted the firefighters once before, shaking them as they attempted to flank Jackson's men on the left. He intended to shake them again.

Jackson smiled as he observed Stuart through his field glasses and the clouds of smoke and dust that rolled across the field. The Virginians cut and slashed their way through the troubled Yankees, again preventing them from entrenching themselves, and leaving several dozen of them lying dead or wounded.

Jackson's eyes blazed again. *Now we shall finish it,* he told himself. As some of his men returned to the line while others continued fighting in pockets of desperate, sometimes hand-to-hand combat all around the field, he rode his horse again out to the front of the line of men now reforming. Some men came up from the rear, reinforcements pulled by General Johnston from other parts of the field.

Just as he started to give the order to attack again, Sandie Pendleton rode up with orders from Beauregard.

"Widespread attack all along the line, sir," Sandie said. "The Yankees are readying another assault to drive us back to the rail line, and General Beauregard wishes to preempt the move. Some of our prisoners say McDowell and all his generals believe they are about to sweep us from the field, sir."

Sandie and Douglas both spied the flicker in Jackson's eyes as he reined his horse around.

"Men of Virginia and men of the South," he called, walking the horse in front of them and ignoring the singing of bullets all around him. "We shall now drive the enemy once and for all from that flat ground topping this hill. Then we shall drive them out of Virginia whence they are uninvited and unwelcome guests. It is time to give them cold steel, Virginia!"

A thunderous chorus of whoops rumbled along the line, echoing above the clamor off the surrounding forest. Willy, numb for the past several moments, regained his wits. *But I've lost my rifle,* he thought with a jolt. It didn't take him long to find another just like it on the ground a few feet away.

And then he was racing forward again, unleashing the unearthly high shriek that he and all the others had begun this day to utter as they ran into battle. It all happened too fast. He just knew it was hard to breathe and hard to see and then he was into them again, slashing his bayonet—*Oh, my heavens, this rifle has no bayonet*—swinging his rifle like a club, kicking, gouging, fistfighting like he hadn't done since he was twelve out behind his father's orchard. But this was a different sort of fistfighting. It was as a dream, a nightmare, with crushing and ripping and thumping and thudding. He would fight with one man and bash his brains in or be knocked off him, then he would be into it with someone else. He found himself fevered, desperate to find his next victim. At one point, he was about to smash a Yankee's face with a large stone when someone hoisted him up by his shirt and flung him through the air. He landed hard on his shoulder, hurting it, in a pile of dead men, then saw a large swarthy Yank stalking toward him with two huge hands and a murderous demeanor. Just before the man reached him, something exploded nearby and tore the upper third of the Yankee's body to shreds.

"Retreat! Retreat!"

But this time it was the Yankees and Willy intended to help them on their way. He scrambled to his feet, grabbed another rifle—with a bayonet—and chased after the withdrawing bluecoats. He raised the weapon high over one fleeing man's head, then did other things he sought afterward to forget.

Jackson's heart leaped within his chest. Through his binoculars he could see that the Yankees had been driven from the plateau atop the hill. And the Confederates, his men their vanguard, were this time holding fast.

Now Beauregard galloped up as far as the edge of the woods from the right, a raft of aides and subordinates behind him. Jackson rode to him.

"Pray us a good prayer my devout Virginia friend," the elegant South Carolinian said to Jackson. But his eyes, through his own spyglass, were directed toward the west, toward the Blue Ridge, no longer visible through the tumult of battle.

"Ours, General?" a major asked.

Jackson turned and looked through his own glass, but his flawed eyes could see nothing.

"A brigade, gentlemen," Beauregard said, a quaver on the edge of his smooth aristocratic drawl.

All in the group sat silent as the battle raged over the hill to the north. The same thought pressed down like an anvil onto every man: *North or South?*

A gutteral sound escaped Beauregard's throat.

"What, sir?"

Jackson winced as he saw the fiery Frenchman's shoulders slump.

"They are blue," Beauregard said, his voice hollow.

"So am I, sir," Jackson intoned.

Beauregard looked away from the glasses and glanced at Jackson. "More brown and red now than blue, I'd say, Jack," he said, with as much lightness as his heavy soul could muster. Then he looked some more. After a moment his arms fell and his head drooped to his chest.

"My God, my God, had we but one more brigade we could this day save the South," he said, verging on tears.

"What, sir?"

Beauregard could not lift his head. "The flag. It is red, white, and blue."

"Old glory?"

"But our flag too is red, white, and blue, sir," Jackson said. *Do they not know that our God will not forsake us?*

Beauregard managed with effort to put the glasses again to his eyes. *All our plans, all our blood, all our hopes and we are bested by one brigade,* he lamented. He stared at the flag, limp in the sweltering heat. He remembered sustaining serious wounds in Mexico while thwarting the enemy's attempts to capture the same flag. Just then, a moderate breeze from the direction of the Valley lifted the colors and as they unfurled, blood flooded his beleaguered brain. *Lord in heaven, there are not thirteen stripes, only three.*

Jackson did not detect the change in Beauregard's countenance, for the Virginian's eyes were pressed shut in prayer, his thin tight lips moving in rapid concert with one another. It was Jackson's face Beauregard first saw when his head swung round to shout the good—the exceedingly great—news. The sweaty, blood- and dirt-caked face, only half visible under the low-drawn kepi, gave Beauregard pause. He saw also the blood seeping through the soggy handkerchief on Jackson's hand. *Perhaps,* Beauregard thought, *perhaps He really does—*

"What is it, sir?"

Beauregard blinked, then smiled. "Ours, gentleman, it is ours!"

Indeed, the final irrevocable balance of power on the field of Manassas arrived with Brigadier General Edmund Kirby-Smith and his seventeen hundred blue-clad men, the final arrivals of Johnston's lightning rail line troop movement.

Hungry, thirsty, and exhausted, Kirby-Smith's men showed up in a bad temper perfectly suited to plunging right into their first fray of the war. And that is what they did. Kirby-Smith himself was knocked almost immediately off his horse with a near-mortal wound. But his men hurtled into the smoking din of fire and death.

Willy, firing at the stymied Federals from the cover of a captured Yankee cannon he and several other Confederates clung to after repelling two attempts at retrieval by units from a Maine brigade, heard the same shrieking hyenalike sound some of his mates had begun to call the "Rebel yell," from the far left of the line.

He turned and saw Kirby-Smith's troops churning toward him.

"Yeah!" Willy shouted, echoed by the bloodied, weary Confederates around him.

Then something went wrong.

"Why, they're stopping," someone nearby said.

Sure enough, the whole mob had stopped in unison.

"But there ain't nobody around them, nobody firing at them," another soldier said.

Willy looked down the north slope of Henry House Hill. The Federals appeared to be massing for another charge. *Oh, Lord, please,* he thought. *We need those men.* Then a shaft of sunlight broke through. Its reflection off something on the ground nearby caught Willy's attention. *Field glasses,* he realized. He grabbed them. One eyeglass was shattered. Willy peered through the other.

"What is it, boy?" a soldier asked. "What do you see?"

It can't be, Willy thought. *The battle and maybe the whole war hanging in the balance and these men who could win it have stopped—to pick blackberries?* Willy had noticed extensive patches of them in the same area himself the night before. But now—with the Yankees ready to overrun him, his army, and indeed the whole Southern cause—how could they stop now?

He could see officers screaming and waving at the soldiers to move past the blackberry bushes. One even waded into a cluster of soldiers with his horse and sent several of them sprawling. This prompted the yanking of the officer off his horse and the commission of a brawl—all amidst blackberry bushes.

"What fools!" Willy shouted aloud as he watched through the glasses in horror. "Why, such a people as we don't deserve to have our own nation. We can't govern ourselves if we can't even—"

A minié ball ended his sentence by blowing the binoculars out of his hand.

Willy scrambled for his rifle. No more time to watch blackberry-picking fools.

Then, just as he and the men around him resumed their fire and braced for what appeared the inevitable counterattack from the brigades of Sherman and the devout Oliver O. Howard, more shrill noise sounded behind them.

Even as he bit off the wrapping of another cartridge, Willy glanced back to see the blackberry pickers again charging en masse toward the battle, some of them apparently plucking additional berries off bushes as they came!

All across the makeshift front line, the Confederates raised a hurrah so loud it stopped the Yankees for a moment just as they prepared to renew their attack. It was a signal moment, for it stole the initiative from the Federals and particularly spooked Howard's brigade on the far right of their line.

It seemed to Willy that, all of a sudden, the Yankees just decided not to fight anymore. One minute they were firing at him, the next he saw their backs as they, by individuals and groups, began simply to walk away.

Later, he knew who comprised the brigade that finally tipped the scales in favor of the South. The men with blackberry juice smeared over their dirty mouths, chins, and shirts. And he also knew, even as he rose back up on youthful legs so weary they shook, that it was himself and the other men of Jackson's command who had stood in the gap and stayed the seemingly irresistible tide of men and history.

Then he was running again, whooping with lungs that, like every other part of his body, had maybe one more run of whoop left in them.

What on earth do they think they are doing? he wondered as he and the wave of men around him approached throngs of bluecoats who continued to walk away from the fight. Not until the graybacks were nearly upon some of the Federals did they seem to snap from their lassitude and start to run as men possessed. And how they did run. They jettisoned everything attached to themselves—hats, guns, haversacks, cartridge belts. Willy had to duck to miss getting beaned by a flying canteen.

"Excuse me, gentlemen," Jackson saluted to Beauregard and the others before reining his horse around to head out, "General McDowell should be paying call to my left flank right about now."

Indeed, even as the Union right and center melted from attack mode into uncertainty, then confusion, then retreat, then panicked headlong flight, one of McDowell's brigades had already pushed into position on that left flank. But Jackson the old artilleryman had smelled out the maneuver a half hour earlier and had jockeyed Imboden and the other batteries, including, now, Pendleton's new one under Johnston's command, into position to meet it.

The best Marley could tell, the battle was all but won. He was aware of some confusion off to his left as he and Cousin Joe moved into position for the attack on Jackson's left flank, but whatever was happening over there, he thought, this charge would remove the Rebels once and for all from Henry House Hill and begin the rolling up of them back toward the Manassas rail line.

But an unwelcome fact presented itself to him at the outset of the assault. *There should not be this much shelling,* he thought with a jolt. Riding full throttle across the dusty field, he caught sight of Joe, shouting and waving his saber, ahead and to his left at the front of the rank, leaping a stream at full gallop.

Just as he looked away, something blew Joe hard out of his saddle. The boy's horse screamed and fell too. *Canister.* That ghastly reality wrenched Marley's breath away from him. He jerked rein so fast his horse squealed. Then he was on the ground and running toward the boy. A Confederate bullet knocked Marley down. He cried out in anguish. *They have broken my shoulder.* But he got up and staggered to the boy. He found him, dead and dying and wailing Union soldiers all around his cousin. He took Joe's head tenderly in his arms. The boy's chest was shredded. Blood filled his mouth and drained over his cheeks and throat.

"May," he gurgled. And then he was gone.

As men ran past him and at least one horse jumped over him, Wayne Marley thought, *Only now have I finally held the full horrible face of war in my arms.* It was a repulsive and sickening and unacceptable face. And it turned him in that instant into all of those things. He turned toward the South. As if appointed by fate, through the nightmarish gray hell, his one eye caught sight, two hundred yards away, behind the line of Confederate riflemen and cannon, of the familiar awkward silhouette of a lanky college professor astride his horse. It could be only one man.

"You," Wayne uttered as if it were an oath.

Then his comrades were rushing back past him, toward the rear. His gaze remained fixed on Stonewall Jackson, in his saddle. Immovable.

"I shall knock you out of that saddle, you incorrigible butcher," Wayne scowled. He stood and screamed, his voice lost in the roar of battle. "You Joshua! You murderer!"

He began to weep as he picked Joe up in his arms. But his left arm was ruined at the shoulder and he dropped the dead boy. Then he threw him over his other shoulder and began to walk to the rear.

"Black horse! Black horse coming!"

The words visited terror upon the retreating thousands of bluecoats. For months, these men had heard rumors and stories of the fabled Virginia horsemen and their shining ebony mounts. They had been forgotten as events went in the Yankees' favor most of the day. But now their remembrance came crashing home in horror as Jeb Stuart, Turner Ashby, and hundreds of others rode down on their foes like zealous farmers on this awful field of harvest of the Grim Reaper.

But Marley did not hear or care. He walked blithely toward home, numb with sorrow and pain. And even as Jackson demolished McDowell's last aborted attack and the rest of the Yankee line disintegrated into chaos, Marley's path, through no effort of his own, and quite amazingly, remained clear of Confederates until he was well out of reach of any pursuers.

James Freiburger eyed the golden bubbly champagne that filled his glass. *How many glasses has it been?* he wondered. Too many, probably, but not to worry. His social and business stations ever improving under this new "administration" of gullible Republican fools; announcement of lovely May's engagement to the congressman's son imminent; the big contract with that Southern gunrunner not only inked but paid for in full—why, it didn't matter now whether the so-called "rebellion" ended today or not, though it probably would. He would profit from this fight, and he would only profit more if the conflict continued a while longer.

Just as he pursed his lips to sip, a tiny geyser of champagne sprinkled his handlebar mustache and nose. Something seemed to have plinked into his glass. *An acorn?* He looked up, but his blurring vision presented him twice as many branches as it should have. He eyed the glass, his vision swimming. There it is, at the bottom. He reached into the small container with a bear paw and, after sloshing most of the liquid out, retrieved—*Why, it looks like a tiny jagged piece of—metal.*

None of his gay fellow merrymakers had noticed. May's fan swished the chasm of air between her and two handsome Philadelphia scions who might one day don uniforms, though only in an "honorary" sort of way, but today continued their persistent but fruitless wooing of her. For her heart belonged to another.

All in the group seemed happily tipsy. But Freiburger frowned. *If that is what I think it might be—and it might even be mine, at that!—I shall have some general's head for letting the fighting get close enough to—*

The next splash was much larger. It was a Confederate howitzer round landing in Cub Run a couple hundred yards down below.

Freiburger flew to his feet and ran to the edge of the ridge. Washington's most respectable were murmuring and pointing down toward the boiling huge fog of smoke that billowed from the distant field and out of which now appeared—*Our soldiers!*

"Why, I can't believe it," Freiburger stammered. "Our men, the best-equipped, best-fed, best-trained army in the entire—"

No doubt remained when another shell blew a retreating Federal ambulance off the nearest bridge over Cub Run.

This event ended the tense quiet paralysis of the picnicking spectators and generated a series of high-pitched female screams that began at one end of the long line overlooking the ridge and extended the length of the hundreds of vehicles parked along it.

Then all was panic and flight. Freiburger and the congressman crammed themselves and their tipsy families into the barouche and ordered the coachmen not to stop until he reached Washington City. But they knew not what journey awaited them.

As the Confederate cavalry bore down on the tens of thousands of fleeing bluecoats—only General Sykes's cool regiment of regulars remained on the field, firing until ordered to retreat—Jackson hurried as many of his guns forward as he could muster and threw shells at the vanishing foe, not realizing civilians were anywhere near. One ball carried farther than the others and exploded near a carriage hauling the governor of Connecticut and his family. The carriage rolled over. None of its occupants were seriously injured, but a few moments later, two of Stuart's horsemen took the governor prisoner.

Elsewhere, terror turned otherwise mature, even brave, men into savages. Freiburger, now cold sober, watched out his window as the barouche stood stationary on the jammed road to Washington. Time and again, he saw Union soldiers pull men, women, and even children from vehicles, fling them aside, then commandeer the vehicle and light out across a field toward the north. He also saw at least three ambulances forcibly emptied—one at gunpoint by the ambulance drivers themselves—of wounded soldiers, then driven off by fit ones.

Indeed, not a single wounded man in the entire Union army would reach Washington by ambulance. Those who lived would suffer all night the pain of their wounds and insects swarming those wounds. Then they would broil the next day, many of them to death, in the scalding July sun.

Many of their healthier brothers, despite a miserable long walk or ride back to the capital beset with fear, hunger, thirst, and a raging twelve-hour thunderstorm, would not stop at Washington. Some would continue without pause on to Philadelphia, others to New York, others to Boston.

"This is not sport," one exhausted, drenched, and mud-caked soldier gasped to a knot of stunned Washingtonians, "and if it is war, I want no more part of it."

James Freiburger had to shoot one soldier and threaten several others, but his coachman miraculously guided the barouche back to the capital, with all original passengers in tow—along with half a dozen new blue uniformed ones. These were not invited, nor welcome, but Freiburger had not enough ammunition to handle all of them, though none of them were armed, having all ditched their weapons in their flight.

Tens of thousands of Union soldiers crowded the route between Manassas Junction and Washington City that night. But few people besides a shaken President Lincoln realized that absolutely none guarded the capital. The last thought in anyone's mind that morning, which had dawned so sunny and festive, was that Stonewall Jackson—for there had been no Stonewall Jackson that morning—and the Confederate army would come tramping down that same road, flush with devastating victory over the most powerful military force on earth.

CHAPTER 38

"YOU WILL NOT, SIR," STONEWALL SAID AS A RICHMOND doctor ordered him to a nearby chair for the removal of his finger.

"But it is ruined, General," the silver-haired physician exclaimed as Jackson tore a length of fabric from the bottom of his shirt. "You have a hole clean through your hand. If we do not remove the finger, you will lose the hand and maybe—"

Stonewall stood and turned his back to the startled man, then walked out of the tent.

"And that filthy rag will do more harm than good!" Stonewall heard the doctor shout from inside the tent as the general headed toward the small nearby stream of Young's Branch, where he had heard Dr. McGuire had established a field hospital. In all directions came the sounds of men crying, men screaming, men whimpering. Men pleading.

When McGuire saw the bloodied officer, his damaged coat, and his ashen face, he left the man he was tending and came to Stonewall.

"No," Stonewall said, waving him off, "I'm not half as badly hurt as many here, and I will wait." He sat by the stream and thought of dipping his hand in the mild waters to ease the throbbing fiery pain. *Any relief at all will help,* he thought. But the stream ran so scarlet that he pulled his outstretched hand back from it.

McGuire finished working on his patient, then left his tent and the swarm of wounded men and came to Stonewall. When the general, his face more ashen, tried to protest, McGuire cut him off: "I'm the general in this theatre, sir. And you're too valuable to have you adding your blood to that drink there. The good news is, I think I can save that finger, though it will be a painful experiment."

Stonewall stared at him. "Well, of course you can, Doctor, of course you can."

Then a murmur traveled through the sprawl of men lining both sides of the stream for as far as Jackson could see, most of them in his vicinity wounded.

"Look," a nearby private with his arm in a sling said, pointing, "some fool is riding out into this cesspool."

Fifty yards away, an erect, frock-coated man indeed guided his horse expertly out into the middle of the three-foot-high water. He turned in Stonewall's direction.

"Men of the South, I am President Davis—follow me back to the field."

"Who is that man and what did he say?" Stonewall asked McGuire.

"Why, that is President Jefferson Davis, sir, and he wants men to go chase Yankees with him, I believe, sir."

Stonewall's eyes regained their fire and his face its color and he clambered to his feet, nearly kicking McGuire in the face with one big size fourteen boot.

"General, sir, wait," McGuire said, but Jackson was already three steps out into the stream.

Stonewall doffed his filthy blue cap and waved it at Davis.

"We have whipped them—they ran like sheep, sir," he shouted. "Give me ten thousand men and I will take Washington City tomorrow."

Davis's eyebrows arched at the tattered bloodied blue visage.

"Is that man Union or Confederate, Major?" Davis said out of the side of his mouth to a nearby aide.

"I don't know, sir."

Davis stared some more, then glanced back at the major. "Is he an officer?"

"I don't know, sir."

"Please, sir," Stonewall insisted.

Davis's mouth thinned and he pulled his horse out of the stream. "I do not believe these men shall be of much further help to us today, Major. Let us look elsewhere to find men for the pursuit to Washington."

Little did the Confederates know that the Federal capital that rainy evening was not chiefly a scene of shock and sorrow. It was, rather, engulfed in terror and, frequently, panic. Hundreds began to pack wagons, coaches, and horses. More would have, but it seemed the Rebs would be on them so quickly there was no use.

"The capture of Washington seems now to be inevitable, Mr. President," grim Secretary of War Edwin Stanton—abolitionist, industrialist, and despiser and mocker of the agrarian South—told a Lincoln who had not slept for thirty-six hours. "The rout, overthrow, and demoralization of the whole army were complete."

The gangly man with the sad eyes, hollow cheeks, and tousled hair walked to the darkness of his window and stared out into another in a long succession of black episodes in his life's journey.

"Send for George McClellan," Lincoln said over his shoulder. "I know, he is a Democrat, but he is a brilliant officer, his men love him, and he seems to have wrested western Virginia from the secessionists. I believe one day soon it shall enter the Union. Yes, we need Little Mac, Mr. Secretary. Immediately."

Lincoln turned back to Stanton. Now strength shone in the long face. "If we survive this debacle, Mr. Stanton, I intend to insure that the next time war is carried to a capital, it shall not be ours."

Not even this time, however, would the war be carried to Washington City. Few Confederate officers beside Stonewall and Stuart were game for the chase, and Stonewall was wounded and Stuart left with barely a squad of men not riding prisoner escort. Then the rains came, units were hopelessly separated, a Yankee counterattack was rumored, and officers and their men alike were exhausted.

Just as God had steeled Stonewall Jackson on Henry House Hill and sent him as a flaming ambassador of doom against the Yankee nation, the Almighty had thrown down a protective curtain around that fleeing army. The rain, when history became biography, proved the final delicate balance that kept the Confederate army, fully half of which had not even participated in the battle, from storming into the Yankee capital and dictating its own terms of peace—before long years of death and suffering ever followed.

Such a golden opportunity would never again present itself to the South.

To Anna, Stonewall wrote, "The glory is due to God alone . . . my preservation was entirely due, as was the glorious victory, to our God, to whom be all the honor, praise and glory."

To Bennett in Richmond he wrote, "The First Brigade was to our army what the Imperial Guard was to the first Napoleon—that through the blessing of God, it met the thus far victorious enemy and turned the fortunes of the day."

And to the Reverend Doctor William White in Lexington he wrote, "My dear pastor, in my tent last night, after a fatiguing day's service, I remembered that I had failed to send you my contribution for our colored Sunday school. Enclosed you will find my check for that object, which please acknowledge at your earliest convenience and oblige yours faithfully, T. J. Jackson."

Back in Lexington, the initial euphoria of the smashing triumph began to fade as the casualty reports rolled in. Maggie stood at the telegraph office in starched crinolines one scorching noon a couple of days later with Ruthie, who now worked for the Prestons. Two hundred other Rockbridge County folks joined them. The word had circulated that the telegraph would shortly bring a summary of casualties from the Battle of Manassas, or the Battle of Bull Run as Northerners were calling it.

Just after noon, Old Jester Carmichael stepped out onto the wooden sidewalk and tacked the list to the wall. Twelve dead and thirty-five wounded from the county. Some had not been previously reported and drew wails and sobs from the crowd. Others had been reported and drew renewed wails and sobs. In two cases, families with members earlier reported as casualties suffered the news of another member felled.

Maggie, more than most, discerned the horrible future specter possible for Virginia and the South. Jackson had rarely spoken of his war experiences in Mexico. But the handful of times he had alluded to them, the horror and savagery he did not mention but which Maggie sensed, had stolen her breath away.

Already half a hundred dead or wounded men from the small population of this remote county, she thought, as she comforted Eliza Wallace, whose eighteen-year-old son had today been confirmed as dead rather than wounded. *What shall become of us if it continues and the North's industrial combine gears up, and its multitudes of immigrants and teeming urban masses join the war effort?* she wondered. *What shall become of the Prestons? What shall become of—*

It was then that *Beechenbrook* first came to her.

Beauregard emerged as the South's hero of Manassas. Others received praise too, though less. Anna fretted in her parents' North Carolina home, to which Stonewall had directed her to keep her out of harm's way.

"Why, from what the papers say, it is as though you did not even participate in the battle, my darling, when in reality, it was your brigade that turned the tide of battle," she seethed in a letter to him. She took personal affront at the tenor of the reports.

Soon came a reply from Stonewall. "I am thankful, my *esposa,* to our ever kind heavenly Father, who withholds no good thing from me (though I am so utterly unworthy and ungrateful). He makes me content to await His own good time and pleasure for commendation, knowing that all things work together for my good." He had paused that evening in his lantern-lit tent to blow some pesky flies away who were after his wounded finger. He smiled as he thought of his wife's ambition for his reputation. *It pales only in the light of my own ambition,* he realized with a shudder.

Stonewall waved his good hand—the damaged one hurt too much—again at the flies. Then he turned back to the letter. He lifted silent thanks to God that it had been his left hand that sustained the wound. "Never distrust our God, who doeth all things well, my darling. In due time He will make manifest all His pleasure, which is all His people should ever desire."

As the weeks passed and the Confederate leadership failed to press the attack, Stonewall grew agitated. The three Southern division commanders in the theatre, Johnston, Beauregard, and New York native Gustavus Smith, all pleaded with President Davis for his support of an assault on the North to end the conflict before it could worsen.

One radiant September morning that Stonewall called "a beautiful emblem of the morning of eternity in heaven," he made the bold and unusual move to call upon Smith. The Virginian sat on the dusty ground in the rugged old engineer's tent and poured out his heart.

"Whilst we have sat in peace week after week and contracted maggots and disease ten times more lethal than the bullets the Yankees send to us, George McClellan reorganizes the Union army, fortifies Washington City, and encourages the building of their navy, a force that could effectively smother every port we possess, and strangle victory out of us," Stonewall said with passion uncommon for him.

Smith listened, twirling his rust-colored handlebar mustache—the one apparent vanity of this hardy man—as Stonewall proceeded to

explain his plan for storming the North and bringing quick independence to the Southern nation.

"Crossing the upper Potomac," the soft high voice began, "occupying Baltimore, and taking possession of Maryland, we could cut off
the communications of Washington, force the Federal government to
abandon the capital, and beat McClellan's army if it came out against
us in the open country."

Smith ceased playing with his mustache and shifted his hefty
frame in the creaking wooden camp chair. *This man is dangerous,* he
thought to himself, *and what is worse, he has thought through the
issues—my, has he thought through them. How odd, he seemed such
an assuming sort, pleasant but boorish, even disheveled. I would never
have expected such boldness, such initiative, such*—but Stonewall was
plunging ahead, his pitch and volume rising.

"We could destroy industrial establishments wherever we found
them, sir, break up the lines of interior commercial intercourse, close
the coal mines, seize and, if necessary, destroy the manufactories and
commerce of Philadelphia and other large cities within our reach—"
Now Smith's face darkened and he leaned forward, waiting for an
opportunity to jump in. But Stonewall had heard all the objections,
and besides, he was offering advice at this point, not enlisting it.

"Then we could take and hold the narrow neck of country
between Pittsburg and Lake Erie; subsist mainly on the country we
traverse, and, making unrelenting war amidst their homes, force the
people of the North to understand what it will cost them to hold the
South in the Union at the bayonet's point."

At the last, Stonewall came up off the ground and leaned across
the clapboard table. Now Smith leaned back a bit. The blazing eyes—
Weren't they more gray when the man entered my tent?—seemed to
send forth jets of fire. Smith, for once, was dumbed. *This is a normally quiet man,* he thought, *but he has thought through this matter
in great depth and detail and makes a passionate and persuasive case
for it. And durned if I don't think it is his conviction more than what
he says that moves me.*

"Alas, General," Smith said at last with a sigh, "you have painted a
lovely and inspired vision indeed. And perhaps even a reasonable
one. But such arguments and plans have already been laid before the
President and he has determined to stay a defensive course."

Stonewall shook his head, stricken. "But sir. Surely you must con-
cur that with the North's immense advantage in *everything*—population, factories, resources—time is our enemy. Do you not agree that

our chances to sustain our independence decrease in direct proportion to the increasing amount of time they have to regroup, find their best generals, and deplete our meager resources?"

Smith sighed again. He was beginning to like this man, frightening as he was. "Whether or not I agree is, I'm afraid, of no consequence at this point. In the President's defense, hopes are high that England and possibly France will enter the war on our side, or at least begin to support us with goods and material. A defensive posture is best suited to minimizing opposition to us within those quarters."

Smith's eyes narrowed and he leaned against the table. "And the President must contend with the unfortunate reality that we are a band of sovereign states—that's what this scrape is all about, after all—and certain of the states have left no doubt with President Davis that their troops are to be kept close to home to protect their own people."

"But sir, the war is not to be won or lost in Georgia or Florida," Stonewall said. "If we do not muster an assault force capable of smashing the main Union armies in northern Virginia, Maryland, or Pennsylvania, those armies will eventually visit devastation on our other states one by one. Can they not see that?"

Smith raised his hand. "Remember, General, the people of the South are extremely distrustful of centralized government. They have seen what its onerous specter has done to the Republic; they do not wish it repeated in the Confederacy. I'm not indicating my accord, son, merely my acknowledgment of the political realities involved."

Stonewall sat again, stunned. "Political realities," he muttered.

Smith, wondering why he suddenly felt guilty and ashamed, fumbled for his scuffed old walnut pipe.

Stonewall climbed slowly to his feet. He extended his hand and grasped Smith's with an earnest shake. His voice grew soft once more. "Thank you, sir. I am sorry. Very, very sorry." Then he turned and walked slowly from the tent, his head hanging.

Somehow, far from feeling satisfaction at having dealt with a subordinate's objections—again—Smith felt strangely chilled on the warm autumn day. *We do have them on the run,* he thought. *Outgeneraled, outpresidented, outfought, and ready to flee their own capital at the drop of a hat—for now.* He puffed blue smoke and heard his younger visitor mount and ride deliberately away. *Perhaps we shall all be sorry.*

●◇ ●◇ ●◇

Whilst they sat in peace week after week, Stonewall's health, which had been on the ascent since his active military duty began earlier in the year, flowered. His complexion grew ruddy, even when not bronzed by the sun; his physique filled out, his arms, chest, shoulders, and thighs adding layers of muscle. Not only was his physical health improved, but his spiritual maturity continued to blossom. And, he slowly came to understand, spiritual matters were playing an increasingly large role in the life of the army around him as a whole. Many men who had lived vigorous but relatively stress-free lives off the fertile Southland, whether as planters, independent farmers, or backwoods hunters, now recognized an immense need for a power and sustenance stronger than their own efforts could effect.

Some of the South's finest preachers descended on the encampments, many of them by Stonewall's invitation, including his own Pastor White. The general met Robert L. Dabney, the forty-one-year-old Union Theological Seminary professor and theologian whose deep Puritan convictions, powerhouse intellect, and flaming zeal in the pulpit had garnered him fame as a defender of the cross—and the South. They also gave him much in common with Stonewall, and friendship between the two grew quickly.

As Stonewall began to discern the developing situation, he knelt alone one chilly evening in his tent by the lantern. *There is a war larger than that for which we take the field against the Northern invaders, is there not, Heavenly Father? A war for the immortal hearts and souls of men.* He shook his head in contempt at himself. *Oh, late have I grasped Your hand of provision and opportunity midst the calamity surrounding us. Oh how late and sluggardly have I been!* For a moment his head stayed bowed and his throat tightened on him. *Forgive me my unbelief, Father of lights, forgive me my self-seeking and dullness of heart.* Then a feeling of warm joy cascaded over his weary soul.

"What I need is a more grateful heart to the 'Giver of every good and perfect gift,'" Stonewall prayed aloud. "O that my life could be more devoted to magnifying His holy name!"

He looked upward, ashamed of his discontent at missed opportunities for battle. "And how should I complain that rather than taking lives in slaughter, You are taking them for eternity, Lord?"

When he rose, he saw Anna's latest letter open on his small wooden table. For months she had been after him to allow her to come visit. He had demurred; too many men were away on furloughs already; camp life was spartan, rough, even dangerous when moving; and he must set an example of duty and perseverance to his men. Why, just today, a young officer had begged him to be allowed to return home—again—to see his dying young wife.

"I wish I could relieve your sorrowing heart," Stonewall had responded to the young man, "but we must think of the living and of those who are to come after us and see that, with God's blessing, we transmit to them the freedom we have enjoyed. What is life without honor? Degradation is worse than death . . . I am sorry, my friend." A few minutes later, Jim Lewis heard the general alone inside his tent weeping as he prayed quietly for the young officer and his wife.

And Stonewall needed Anna now, in many ways. Not the least was to help stay his mind on pure thoughts. For how could he expect the blessing of Providence if his thought-life became an abomination?

So she arrived, "In the van of her own clothes train," Douglas snickered to Sandie as they observed piece after piece of luggage being carted into the home of the Utterbachs, the Centreville family hosting her.

The Jacksons' reunion, after six months apart, was tender and passionate. Midway through the first night of Anna's stay, Molly Utterbach nudged her snoring husband in the ribs and motioned toward the ceiling, above which lay the Jacksons' room. "I swan, honey, I do believe that big old four-poster is bound to come right down through that wall and on top of us," she giggled.

"I'll never be a Calvinist," her husband replied, adjusting his sleeping cap, "but I'll begrudge them this—they exhibit none of the Puritan sense of duty regarding the marriage bed for which they have been accused."

The next morning, Stonewall bathed his inflamed and swollen hand with spring water near his tent, pitched in the Utterbach's front door yard.

"How's your mitt coming, sir?"

Stonewall looked up. "Hello, Captain Imboden. Nice to see you again. Oh, the hand. It is very painful, sir."

Imboden would never have known, since Stonewall's demeanor held as blank a cast as the whitewashed walls of the Utterbachs' farmhouse.

They sat down together for breakfast, joined by Anna, Douglas, and both Sandie and Reverend Pendleton. Anna reveled in her role as "belle of the breakfast," and the fragrance of sachet bewitched the entire table, triggering rich remembrances among the men of the lady or ladies who had moved their hearts.

Imboden remained silent through most of the meal while the other men dissected the battle at Manassas. At length, he finally blurted out, in a manner indicating that the question had been threatening for some time to boil to the surface within him, "General, how is it that you can keep so cool and appear so utterly insensible to danger in such a storm of shells and bullets as rained about you when your hand was hit?"

All at the table paused in mid-bite and stared at Imboden, then at Stonewall.

The general swallowed his food, and his bronzed face grew grave. His voice sounded soft, slow, and low, intent on offering precisely the correct response. "Captain," he said, "my religious belief teaches me to feel as safe in battle as in bed. God has fixed the time for my death. I do not concern myself about *that*, but always to be ready, no matter when it may overtake me."

Silence shrouded the table, and those around it. Only a nearby whippoorwill refused to keep his peace. Stonewall paused as though deep in thought, then looked Imboden square in the eye and said, "Captain, that is the way all men should live, and then all would be equally brave."

Still, no one spoke. Imboden blushed crimson. He knew to what Stonewall was referring. "Sir," the artilleryman said, "sir, I reckon that doesn't describe me that day on Henry House Hill." He searched Stonewall's face for signs of a reprieve. He found none. "What—what with my poor mouth that day, sir. It has been on my mind, sir, that I offended you that day, sir, you know, cursing in the manner I did."

Imboden remembered Anna's presence and blushed anew, nodding toward her, "Begging your pardon, ma'am." The whippoorwill trilled his amusement. "Anyhow, sir, I am sorry for that poor display. I was hard-pressed, sir."

Stonewall stared at him. When he was certain Imboden had concluded his petition, he said simply, "Nothing can justify profanity."

On October 7 Stonewall received promotion to major general. In less than months, he had risen from the rank of major to that of major general.

On the same day, Willy received a double brevet promotion to sergeant. His superior had put in the requisition days after the battle at Manassas, but it took the Richmond bureaucracy weeks to churn it out, then it had been lost for more weeks. But Willy's battlefield heroism and coolness under fire, as well as his year at VMI, presaged further advancement.

However, Willy did not feel promoted as the rainbow of a Shenandoah fall spread across the Valley. He believed he could trace his malady to the moment he stood on a hill three miles away looking out over the panorama of slaughter the day after Manassas. Even that distance was not enough to lessen the mind-numbing stench of blistered blackened corpses and carcasses rotting in the July sun.

A slight breeze lifted from below and pushed the odious reek up Willy's unprepared nostrils. So strong was the odor that he doubled over in nausea. He did not vomit, but he had to rush behind a nearby clump of mulberry bushes and still barely averted discharging a stream of diarrhea into his trousers.

Willy had retreated back to camp, five miles from the battlefield. Even there, the stench suffocated him. The next day he experienced two more loose bowel movements, as he did the following three days.

By then, the camp had gained the sobriquet "Camp Maggot," so loathsome were its air and water. And by then, Willy's bowel movements had increased to three per day. This posed a dilemma. He knew he risked dehydration with the frequent loose stools. Yet he suspected the apparent remedy for that dehydration—the available water sources—was its cause. Others around him experienced symptoms advanced to his. Some rushed to the bushes four, five, even six times daily. Many of these were discharging unsettling amounts of blood with their diarrhea.

The first week in August, two men, that he knew of, in his company died. The deaths were not pretty and they were not comfortable. The doctors could cite only "intestinal disorders," but Willy and others knew the cause—Camp Maggot.

Finally, Stonewall, (as his troops were beginning to call him, over his unceasing objections) had managed to find a better campsite with cleaner water near Centreville. Willy's condition did not improve, but it did hold steady. Still, between the frequent diarrhea and the gradually dwindling supply of food, his weight dropped precipitously. And he began to contract colds and all manner of minor infirmities he never before had. He also noticed that minor bruises and cuts did not heal as rapidly as normal.

He knew of a half dozen men in his company who died of "intestinal disorders" in September. That number, of those known to Willy, grew to a dozen in October and two dozen in November.

What a war, he thought with a grimace while catching cold in a chill driving rain during another frantic rush to the bushes to relieve an urgent bowel movement. *Hardly a bullet fired on us since Manassas four months ago and men beginning to fall in droves. What shall it be like when the Yankees reorganize and the shooting resumes in earnest?*

He grew more chilled when he saw, for the first time during a bowel movement, the scarlet drops speckling the ground beneath him.

It was the largest colored folks funeral ever in Lexington. But then Ruthie had probably helped more folks, black and white, than perhaps anyone else in her long years there. Glimpses of some of those works, most of which had been anonymous or at least private, flashed across Lylburn's mind as he stood before the mournful throng at the Negro cemetery outside of town. He thought, too, of the last work of which he was aware, wherein she had secretly and at great risk paid two white trash all her meager store of money to transport a young slave and his new wife North in the men's buckboard.

Lylburn smiled. He had long known the struggle in Ruthie's soul on the matter of the Underground Railroad. Her firm belief that she could better help her people from her position of responsibility and respectability working for the president of the Washington College, then, toward the end, Major Preston and his family. Her private turmoil over the potential cost of risking the station she had worked years to attain. All that responsibility, respectability, and, yes, comfort and safety.

Many of Lylburn's people liked the more emotive, less liturgical worship of the Baptist and Methodist churches. But words had always meant so much to Lylburn, even though he had only recently learned to read them, with the help of Ruthie—and the secret help of Mrs. Preston. Words had been his salvation, his deliverance from the drudgery of his work. And somewhere deep in his soul stirred recognition that the God from whose brush came the splendor of the Shenandoah, the God from whose mind came the words in this Bible he held, the God from whose heart came the compassion and love that had kept Lylburn from himself climbing under those crackers' buckboard tarpaulin, even as his two friends urged him to do, even as Ruthie had paid for him to be able to do—that God was too high, too matchless, too holy to be worshiped other than with trembling reverence and awe.

So Lylburn led the assembled in the creeds he knew so well from Major Jackson's Sunday school . . . "We acknowledge and bewail our manifold sins and wickedness . . . Have mercy upon us, have mercy upon us, most merciful Father." He also prayed for his young friends, including the man whose back showed crisscrossed lines of pale scar tissue from his many beatings at the hand of Marse Sam McDowell.

Then he thanked the Lord for the life of Ruthie, who had fought a good fight, finished her course, kept the faith, and now had laid up for her a crown of righteousness.

And he prayed for strength, courage, and wisdom to help him guide the needy flock for whom he had counted the cost and decided to stay the remainder of his earthly days.

Lylburn firmed his now-manly jaw and concluded the recitation. Not as tired rote like many of the white folks did he proclaim it, but with the heartfelt meaning that only someone who had been brought face to face not only with the ugliness of life but with the ugliness of his own sinful heart, then delivered from it all by miraculous grace, could.

"And grant that we may ever hereafter serve and please You in newness of life, to the honor and glory of Your name."

Two weeks before her cancerous end, Ruthie had indeed gambled it all. One of the Prestons' black house servants heard her discussing the slaves' escape with Lylburn one day through a window from her bed and told Maggie. The little redhead wrestled in anguish over whether to report the looming action, possibly without implicating Lylburn or Ruthie. Maggie's Bible told her that slaves were to be obedient to their masters as to God, and that such an escape, even from that vile Sam McDowell, would be sinful, doubly so for others involved in the theft of someone else's property. God-ordained civil law saw it no differently.

Maggie agonized. The pain in her eyes and head grew worse than they had been in months, perhaps ever. "Ruthie!" she shouted, to retrieve for her a cold damp cloth as she had so often done. *Ruthie. Ruthie can no longer do that,* Maggie's pounding brain told her.

Oh, perhaps Robert Lee and the others are right, she thought, *perhaps it is best to emancipate them and let them make their own way. And perhaps President Lincoln—and Father—are right when they advocate their return to that new country in Africa to people their own society. Sometimes it is all too confusing to me.* Then she went mercifully to sleep.

When she awoke, her pain nearly gone, she cleaned herself and went to the church to deliver the remainder of the family's linens for transport to the troops down the Valley. It had been agreed that each person should retain one set of linens and that all else should go to the soldiers.

As she braved the chill December breeze walking to the church (the carriage remained parked in its shed since its horse had been sent north to pull a supply wagon) it dawned on her that the battle at Manassas, bloody and victorious as it was, had in no way ended the war. That had been the supposed saving virtue for Rockbridge County for all its lost men and boys. But the Northern papers were full of Beauregard, Johnston, "Stonewall" Jackson—her heart fluttered at the remembrance of the wonderfully appropriate sobriquet and she glanced guiltily around for any witnesses to the flush that had captured her face—and Tom's old classmate George McClellan, and "Little Mac's" preparation not for a negotiated peace but for *an all-out assault on Richmond!*

Maggie shuddered. *I can see that bawdy baboon Lincoln and his greedy pirates wanting to crush us so, but I thought McClellan was supposed to be a Democrat and a conservative sensitive to us and our needs. Why would he be party to such folly?*

Us, she thought with a wry smile. *I have indeed become one of us.* She had not laughed much for some time, but she laughed now at how her God could do such a thing as make, of all things, a Southerner of her. *And what a time to become a Southerner,* she thought, praying that Ruthie's gamble would succeed.

CHAPTER 39

WILLY HAD BEEN COLD BEFORE. HE HAD BEEN CAUGHT OUT IN the open in a blizzard forty miles from home the previous winter. But never had he even imagined he could be so cold for so long as he had been on this "expedition" to the northwest of Virginia.

Oh, how could he have been so foolish as to leave behind his coat? But New Year's Day 1862, the day Stonewall's new eighty-five-hundred man command left Winchester in the lower Valley to traverse the east range of the Allegheny Mountains to recapture Romney in northwest Virginia from the Federals, had been sunny and warm. The weather was expected to remain that way for the duration of the trip. Full of youthful ebullience and following the lead of others older than himself, Willy had left behind not only the great woolen coat given him by his father but also his blankets, in a supply wagon.

Now, one day later, his feet and hands numb and the pain throughout his body too profound even to allow him to cry, he ground his teeth and attempted to rehearse Scripture and the Catechism.

Willy knew Stonewall's logic. The commander would love to have taken his expedition clear to the western reaches of Virginia and cleaned out the Union forces that successive Confederate generals, the latest of them Robert E. Lee, had failed, while greatly outnumbered, to clean out. He had said so to President Davis himself. Since the Confederate high command had evidently given up on that area, Stonewall had authored and proposed to Secretary of War Judah Benjamin an expedition to run the Federals out of near northwest Virginia before settling in for the winter, to prevent them gaining a foothold in the region and having a staging base from the west against Winchester and the lower Valley.

But was *this* worth it?

Willy gasped and shook his head as he struggled up the ice sheet that had been a road. The whole expedition appeared increasingly to be a folly. Stonewall, as he had done at Manassas, had judiciously managed to cobble together disparate pieces to form an efficient fighting force. But a major portion of this force, under the command of General Loring—who left an arm at the same Mexican battle Wayne Marley left an eye—had arrived in Winchester December 9, weeks after Stonewall expected them.

When Stonewall then issued orders that only general officers could enter the town of Winchester from their encampments without headquarters passes—and posted pickets to enforce the order—all five regimental commanders in the Stonewall Brigade accused him of "an unwarranted assumption of authority" and "an improper inquiry into their private matters."

But the worst remained for this horrific trip itself: horses falling again and again on the steep marblelike frozenness until their knees streamed blood, dozens of them having to be put out of their misery with a bullet to the head; close-packed men tumbling down steep glassy grades on their backsides in groups of ten and twenty; others moaning, wailing, and, in some cases, dying, in the road of pneumonia from the arcticlike elements.

They had indeed chased the Federals first out of Bath, then out of Romney itself. *I guess even the dad-blamed Yankees know this cursed land is not worth the keeping,* Willy grimaced. Stonewall's audacious expedition stunned the winter-entrenched Northern commanders of the area into panicked retreat. But waves of men in the Confederate ranks, then their officers, had begun to turn on him. Others simply left and walked home. One company of "unmanageable Irishmen" in the Thirty-third Virginia had not even made it as far as Winchester with any officers. Stonewall preferred charges of "neglect of duty" against Colonel Gilham, his own colleague from the VMI. Gilham had chased a bunch of Yankees back across the freezing Potomac, forcing some of them to swim it. But, against withering rearguard fire, Gilham failed to take a depot assigned him by Stonewall. Gilham's return to the VMI a week later preceded by two days his receipt of the charges against him. Two days before, Stonewall had chastened his old brigade's commander Richard Garnett for not being on the move by "early dawn" with his frozen troops.

"But it is impossible for the men to march, especially in these conditions, without eating," Garnett said.

"I never found anything impossible with this brigade," Stonewall fired back.

Yeah, Willy thought, for the first time bitter as he watched several of his comrades trying to wrap their freezing blue *bare* feet with rags, *even freezing to death by the dozens.*

Later that day, as a blizzard blew down from the western Alleghenies, Willy watched the surreal scene unveiled before him of a column of men and horses groaning as one up a steep mountain and into the teeth of the worst nature could throw at them. He stopped as Stonewall rode past him, Little Sorrel—recovered from his Manassas bullet wound—somehow maintaining his footing while every other horse in sight seemed to be stumbling or falling. As he neared the high point of struggle for his men, Stonewall stared at them for a moment, blue-gray eyes blazing hot cobalt, then dismounted and threw his own shoulder into a wagon that teetered over the edge of a ditch.

"Those men cannot reach the top of that pass and they are going to quit," Willy's buddy Tucker Randolph gasped while huffing out wild white clouds of air. *"He* cannot will the impossible."

Willy knew who *he* was. As the boy slipped and stumbled up the path, he kept his aching red eyes on Stonewall. And then—*My sweet Jesus, the entire column is going to collapse onto me as a human avalanche,* Willy thought with panic, his eyes growing to large globes. He ducked away. But somehow, Stonewall helped corral the wayward wagon back onto the icy road. Somehow the men ahead of him took the cue and redoubled their efforts. Inch by inch, foot by grunting foot, stung by sleet, whipped by wind, and tortured by cold, they clambered toward the top, pushing, dragging, and just plain cussing animals and vehicles with them.

Holy Moses, he can *will the impossible,* Willy thought with incredulity. Even as Stonewall's own body threatened to burst through his whitened, soggy uniform, he pressed on, his men with him. His eyes bulged out of their sockets, his hamstrings and calves quivered, his shoulders shook, his pulsating lower back bowed outward. *"But they that wait upon the LORD shall renew their strength; they shall mount up with wings as eagles . . ."* the general rehearsed in his mind.

And then they crested the top. Willy looked at Randolph, then whopped his disbelieving friend so hard on his arm that it nearly knocked him down. They both laughed very loud.

Willy looked back to the top. Sandie Pendleton held Little Sorrel as Stonewall gimped toward him, the general's nearly doubled-over frame shouting the pain his countenance refused to betray. It took two men to help him back onto his horse, and they, with those around Stonewall, cheered him as the sleet battering them grew to the size of strawberries. Willy shook his head, marveling. *I love that insane man. And I should be pleased to march on hell itself for him.*

But he already had—at Manassas.

Then the order came down: Stonewall and the his namesake brigade would return to Winchester for winter quarters. The cheers of Willy, Randolph, and hundreds of their mates had nearly ceased resounding off the high arctic walls around them before they heard the rest of it. General Loring and his men would remain stationed in and around Romney, to hold the area for the Confederacy through the winter months.

The latter order set in motion a furious series of complaints, reports, letters, and personal visitations by and on behalf of the "stranded" brigades, as they thought of themselves, that reached to the office of President Davis himself. But Willy knew little of that as he limped out of Romney in the midst of a driving subfreezing sleetstorm. The soles of his own boots had worn through, but since his feet were numb with cold, he knew they were pressed against the ice only when Randolph pointed to the blood Willy left smeared behind him.

Never would Willy forget the cursing and blaspheming of the teamsters he passed who were only then entering Romney for the winter. He had not known such words existed heretofore. What a revelation were the teamsters' oaths to him as to the variety, pith, and eloquence that men of that calling could give to their profanity. The peaks and gorges echoed and multiplied the cursing and swearing into a blasphemous roar that Willy believed must have shocked even the vermin that dwelt in the mountains. *At least the horses and mules pulling their wagons are used to it,* he thought with the closest thing to a chuckle he had mustered in days.

Like Willy, Tucker Randolph praised the God who had made him for his deliverance from the Romney hellhole. But as they descended the granitelike mountain trails, Randolph gazed at the human agony surrounding him, then lowered his voice, "General Jackson has a great load on his shoulders to answer for in *this* campaign."

Anna saw to it that Stonewall had a great load on his supper plate his first night back in Winchester. Never had he been so happy to see her, or a crackling fire such as the one offered him in the parlor of Presbyterian minister James Graham. Three months it had been since he had last seen his wife.

"I intend to thaw every last icicle out of my darling's frostbitten system," Anna giggled as they retired to the Grahams' master bedroom for the night.

General William Loring's one arm was as far from Stonewall's thoughts that night as the moon as he and Anna engaged in the most passionate embraces of their marriage.

"Well," Pastor Graham said, referring to the orchestra of sounds emanating from the master bedroom and nibbling his wife's ear, "I present to you, exhibit A against the case for bluenosed Puritan joylessness."

"Dear," Mrs. Graham said with a lusty smile, "I believe we have exhibited that case six times."

Her husband's dancing eyes precluded the need for him to ask, "Shall we strive for number seven?"

Stonewall Jackson's domestic bliss was of no concern to Colonel William Taliaferro, commander of one of Loring's suffering brigades, as he made the rounds of high officials in Richmond. With Loring's sanction, Taliaferro took the case against Stonewall and his handling of the Romney expedition to judges, Confederate congressmen, Vice President Alexander Stephens, and finally, President Davis.

"No one disputes the man's bravery, nor his abilities as a brigade commander, Mr. President," Taliaferro said, barely able to contain his anger. "But our expedition lost four men killed to enemy fire and twenty-five to the elements, most of them frozen to death. Many who survived were frozen so badly they shall be maimed for life, sir. Not one regiment has more than one third of its men available for duty."

Taliaferro looked down. When he again faced Davis, his eyes gleamed with moisture. "It was, sir," he began slowly, his voice cracking, "a degree of severity, hardship, toil, exposure, and suffering that finds no parallel in the prosecution of the present war, if indeed it is equalled in any war."

Davis, his ashen face blank, eyed him. "Why, Colonel, has no officer in the so-called Stonewall Brigade, which itself irrefutably suffered before returning to Winchester, nor in Anderson's Brigade, under Loring, signed your protest document?"

Taliaferro bristled. *Stonewall Brigade indeed. Jackson's pet lambs.* "I cannot answer for others, sir. I know only that the best army I ever saw of its strength has been destroyed by the bad marches and bad management. It is ridiculous to hold the place, sir."

"Evidently the Federals agreed, Colonel," Davis said blandly. "Despite having their entire east-west rail operations through the area destroyed by Jackson, they fled the whole region, some of them swimming the icy Potomac in their underwear—or so Turner Ashby has wired. General Jackson does seem to have cleared the field northwest of the Shenandoah Valley of Unionist threat."

Taliaferro thought about that for a moment, then rolled the dice. "General Jackson, sir, is incompetent to administer so extensive a district and hold a separate command. It was his vaulting ambition upon which the entire debacle was girded."

"I presume President Lincoln should wish for such debacles as he witnesses his men again sent fleeing across the Potomac by 'Stonewall' Jackson," Davis said.

But Stonewall's "vaulting ambition" was stymied by Secretary of War Benjamin's January 31 telegram to him: "Our news indicates that a movement is being made to cut off General Loring's command. Order him back to Winchester immediately."

The order would infuriate Stonewall's superior, Johnston, whom it circumvented. It would infuriate President Davis's chief military advisor Robert E. Lee, who was not consulted. It would infuriate others, great and small. And it brought a response from Stonewall the same day he received it:

> Sir: Your order requiring me to direct General Loring to return with his command to Winchester immediately has been received and promptly complied with.
>
> With such interference in my command I cannot expect to be of much service in the field, and accordingly respectfully request to be ordered to report for duty to the superintendent of the Virginia Military Institute at Lexington, as has been done in the case of other professors. Should this application not be granted, I respectfully request that the President will accept my resignation from the Army.
>
> I am, sir, very respectfully, your obedient servant,
>
> T. J. Jackson
> Major-General,
> P.A.C.S.

CHAPTER 40

NEITHER SECRETARY BENJAMIN NOR PRESIDENT DAVIS anticipated Stonewall's violent reaction or the firestorm that followed it.

"Is our Confederacy so aflush with brilliant leaders that it can afford for one to languish in his VMI section room?" Maggie flared at her husband, who promptly journeyed to Richmond to weigh in with their opinion.

"Loring is like a scared turkey and so is his command," Stonewall's volatile quartermaster Harmon railed, "They have returned to Winchester in dozens of separate groups and are terribly disorganized."

"I don't know how the loss of this officer can be supplied," Johnston wrote Benjamin. "General officers are much wanted in this department."

"Why have Christians allowed this vile conflict to happen?" the renowned Presbyterian Pastor Dabney, in Winchester to preach to the soldiers, asked Stonewall. "But since we are in it, we had best honor the Lord by winning against that contingent of Unitarians, Arminians, heretics, and Christ-deniers."

Word of the resignation blew through the Shenandoah Valley like a summer prairie fire and the people deluged Richmond, and Stonewall, with hundreds of telegrams.

Governor Letcher decried the situation and rallied waves of Stonewall's political friends to urge him to relent. The governor himself beseeched Stonewall, as did Confederate (and ex-U.S.) congressman Alexander Boteler from western Virginia, State Auditor Bennett, even Stonewall's superior Johnston. So did the newspapers. One of the heroes of Manassas, fresh from a successful winter campaign, returning to the college classroom?

Then reports began to surface from Army of Northern Virginia military officials and medical officers such as McGuire. Despite the protestations of Loring and his subordinates, serious illness and death from illness were only fractionally higher during the frigid Romney campaign than during the preceding, mild, month of December. Indeed, an increase in sickness had occurred—but almost totally from troops in Loring's brigades.

"The diseases in the large majority of cases were very slight," McGuire reported, "and in many did not exist at all. In fact, there were too many of the last class to believe it was altogether accidental. . . . In many cases the officers . . . encouraged the men to return where was no necessity for it."

"There is evidently much moral discontent in the present Romney command, which is Loring's," Johnston conveyed to Benjamin after reviewing the reports of Department inspectors.

Stonewall would not budge. He slapped court-martial charges against Loring for a battery of offenses related to neglect of duty and of conduct subversive of good order and military discipline.

"The authorities at Richmond must be taught a lesson," Stonewall told Anna, "or the next victims of their meddling will be Johnston or Lee."

While a large portion of the Confederacy groaned at the specter of losing one of its brightest lights, Stonewall received a telegram in his Winchester quarters that his old classmate "Little Mac" McClellan, fresh from defeating Lee and the others in western Virginia, had dispatched a Union force that had retaken Romney, seized Moorefield— a staging point just seventy miles west of Winchester—and captured a force of Stonewall's militia in the area, including seventeen officers.

"Such is the fruit of evacuating Romney," he said bitterly to Anna, who had come to his room to investigate his cry of anger. Stonewall crushed the telegram in his fist and his eyes sparked. "Loring should be cashiered for his course."

Meanwhile, in Washington, a skittish McClellan sent a stream of telegrams to his commanders in northwest Virginia. Over and over, they conveyed one message: "If you gain Romney, look out for the return of Jackson. I know him to be a man of vigor and nerve, as well as a good soldier."

But Stonewall faced a different battle. The battle cries downstairs in Rev. Graham's parlor had grown tumultuous. Two neighbors, awakened from sleep, had already come to investigate. The general strapped on his sword and spurs and marched down the stairs.

Before him raged a full-blown war. Mrs. Graham's seventy-five-year-old mother led the furniture forces of tables, ottomans, and couches against "Confederate Artillery Captain" Marye's array of chairs. Swarming over, through, and around them were more than a dozen neighborhood children, whose whoops and shouts—along with those of the several adults—rose to a clamor that brought the constable and was only surpassed by the roar of the children's mobbing their beloved General Jackson, who tumbled to the floor and rolled with the pile of wiggling, squirming, squealing youngsters until his exhausted laughter caused him to retreat his own forces back upstairs.

The next day, after another passionate night spent in his chambers with Anna, he notified Johnston that, if that superior still permitted it, he should like to withdraw his resignation.

McClellan, pressured by Lincoln to produce quick results before twelve-month Union enlistment periods elapsed, had larger designs than Romney. In late February he dispatched General Nathan Banks and 35,000 men across the upper Potomac at Harper's Ferry. Then he launched the main 120,000-man Union army on a massive assault against Confederate capital Richmond. This he did amphibiously, bringing his troops up the Chesapeake River from the east on boats.

Lincoln never liked the McClellan plan, preferring a more direct overland attack that would retain the bulk of the Army of the Potomac between Washington City and Confederate forces in northern Virginia. While the President cast nervous eyes at a now relatively open field—he thought—between him and the vanguard of Johnston's Army of Northern Virginia, Stonewall, alone, sniffed out the strategic possibilities inherent in the near-paranoia of Federal government leadership fears of a Rebel capture of Washington. For the Virginian's Winchester headquarters was indeed *north* of Washington City. *Ah, what mischief might be sewn in the Northern invader's camp by forcing Lincoln to watch nervously over his right shoulder at us, even as he moves the heart of his force elsewhere,* Stonewall thought with a smile as he studied his map by lantern light the evening of March 10, the chill wind outside whipping a birch tree branch against the windowpane.

He smiled and considered how well events were transpiring. The apparent revival among his troops continued to blossom—*And small wonder,* he thought, *with the fire of such preachers as Robert Dabney, James Henley Thornwell, and others.* The system of pouring out the liquor stores that streamed into the camps from both Northern and

Southern sources had soaked the lower Valley with enough whiskey to raise the water table several inches. And now that Johnston had retreated south from Manassas, the rest of the world saw Stonewall's meager thirty-five-hundred-man force jutting out into a fearsome Federal arc that surrounded him on three sides and left him close to a hundred miles from any other significant Confederate force.

But Stonewall Jackson saw opportunity. And that opportunity broadened his smile wider than it had been since those special nights with Anna in the soft bed a few feet from him. *My, that woman came north determined to please her soldier,* he thought, giggling out loud in spite of himself. That woman. He thought back to their parting at the train station a few days before.

"What will my darling do?" a worried Anna had asked him after she climbed aboard a snow-covered, Richmond-bound train full of wounded and dying Southern soldiers.

"I have only to say this, that if this Valley is lost, Virginia is lost," he told her. He stared for a moment down into her apple-cheeked sweetness. *You have indeed given to me the gentlest, sweetest creature on earth, Heavenly Father,* he thought. *Thank you.*

"When my little sunny face has gone out of 'that' room"—they had come to think of the bedchamber as their "holy of holies" so dear were the memories they had created in it—Stonewall told her, "I never wish to enter it again."

Her eyes swelled with tears and she gripped him and they kissed long and hard, especially for a public setting. He did not step off the train until it was already moving and picking up steam.

Somehow she knew as she watched his tall gaunt bearded frame recede from view, and heard the pitiable moans and desperate cries of his wounded men crowded all around her, that it would be a long, long time before she would see him again.

But now he had work to do, *and that work begins tomorrow night,* he thought, shaking off the sweet memory and rising from his desk.

The next day Jackson's thirty-five hundred men retreated south through Winchester in the face of Banks's overwhelmingly superior force. All day the loyal Southern citizens of the town watched their disappearing protectors with gloom. Yet Stonewall's countenance remained cheerful, even jolly. After supper (where the general's willpower regarding food continued to amaze Graham) Stonewall still remained with his guests. The pastor asked him to lead the family's evening devotions. Then the general left the house. But he surprised the Grahams by saying, his cheeks ruddy, "Oh, I'll see you again. I don't expect to leave."

Stonewall whistled "Dixie"—he liked the tune, though he could never remember its title—as he loped down the street to the first senior officers council he had ever called. *How excited they will be,* he thought with glee, *when I reveal my—the Lord's—plan to them.*

And how shocked. Outnumbered ten to one, Stonewall had ordered his wagons and troops to halt just south of Winchester and sup. Then he would order their return north through the town after dark to assault Banks's unsuspecting thousands. A demon for secrecy, Stonewall had revealed his plan to no one, including his ranking officers. He counted on surprise, his troops' ability, the Federals' inexperience, and a full moon for success.

We shall drive these ravagers of Virginia from this fair valley and give Mr. Lincoln and Mr. McClellan pause to consider just which capitol lies in harm's way, Stonewall thought. He knew of no other general who utilized spies in the enemy camp. But Stonewall did, and his spies had alerted him that Banks planned soon to depart east with most if not all his command to support Little Mac's assault on Richmond. The Virginian did not plan to allow Banks such a luxury.

To Stonewall's dismay, his top commanders greeted his audacious plan less than enthusiastically. Worse, Douglas interrupted the meeting to inform him that rather than halting just south of Winchester, his forces had continued on another five or six miles. Ambiguous orders, one colonel said, "presaging certain doom for this unique but frightening idea of a night attack."

"Impossible for our men to traverse such a distance now, even if the attack could be mounted effectively—against odds of ten to one," another said, arching an eyebrow at Stonewall.

The general stood, shaken. He dismissed the meeting and returned to the Grahams. Alternately disconsolate and filled with murderous rage, around 9:30 he finally abandoned his plan.

A few minutes later, he sat astride Little Sorrel on a hill south of Winchester that overlooked the moonlit town. McGuire, a native of Winchester, accompanied him. The young physician, normally the picture of poise and calm reserve, wept openly. "Down in that fair village is everything in this world that I hold dear," he sobbed. Already, stories abounded about the treatment of some Confederate sympathizers' property in areas occupied by the Northerners.

Stonewall seethed in silence, shoulders hunched and dirty kepi cap pulled so low it completely hid his eyes. Another moment passed and McGuire quieted. Shaking, Stonewall rose in his stirrups and screamed with a savagery that sent a chill through the doctor.

"That is the last council of war I will ever hold!"

His words echoed off the nearby hills, and some people in the town heard them. McGuire stared dumbstruck after Stonewall as the general turned his horse and galloped away.

With that retreat began what the history books and military manuals would call the Valley Campaign of Stonewall Jackson.

CHAPTER 41

"IT CANNOT BE," UNION BRIGADIER GENERAL JAMES SHIELDS exclaimed. "No sane commander would risk battle so far from his supports."

"Ah," Shields' adjutant said with a smile, "but this 'Stonewall' Jackson as they are calling him appears not to have great concern for either risk or sanity."

Still, Shields thought to himself, shaking his large handsome head, *the man cannot have more than three thousand troops under his command, less than half what I have. We have chased him halfway up the Shenandoah Valley from Winchester. Why in blazes would he decide to turn on us now?*

Born a half century before in County Tyrone, Ireland, Shields had fought in the Black Hawk War, served in the Illinois Supreme Court, been wounded in the Mexican War, and served as governor and senator from the Oregon Territory. And he had once challenged an Illinois political opponent named Abraham Lincoln to a duel over a series of venomous newspaper articles he suspected Lincoln of aiding a young woman named Mary Todd in writing.

But never had James Shields seen such audacity. No, it was unthinkable. Still, Shields, who would become the only man ever to represent three different states as a United States senator, had heard about Stonewall's stand at Bull Run—and of his bold winter march on Romney. *I shall go see for myself,* he decided.

When the Irish-American arrived in the low hills south of the village of Kernstown, itself half a dozen miles south of Winchester, a Michigan colonel pointed toward the reported Rebel troop presence. Still shaking his head in disbelief, Shields cantered ahead.

Nearly a mile away, Turner Ashby, atop his magnificent white charger, gave the signal to his "horse artillery," which let loose a round.

Shields heard the shell coming in, but not in time to escape being blown off his horse, his chest and shoulder peppered with shrapnel.

The next day, the wounded Shields' commander, Banks, satisfied that Stonewall's main force lay many miles to the south, departed for Washington to proceed with Secretary Stanton and President Lincoln on plans to shift much of Banks's command east, some to support McClellan's assault on Richmond and some to protect the Federal capitol.

But Stonewall had other ideas. Just before he sent his small force crashing into Shields', he pulled a chewed-up lemon from his mouth and smiled his silent laugh at Sandie's biographical report of Stonewall, taken from the New York *Mercury* newspaper. He hailed from the family tree of Jack, the Giant-killer, the *Mercury* reported, as it lauded Stonewall's boyhood accomplishments, the force of his will, and the wonderful abstemiousness that enabled him to live for a fortnight at a time on two crackers and a barrel of whiskey.

The story humored Stonewall, who realized how rarely he found whimsy in, or even respected, the contents of newspapers. He flicked the lemon away and his right arm shot up into the air, the motion unrelated to his command to attack.

Racing forward with the Stonewall Brigade, under the command of Brigadier General Richard Garnett, Willy soon realized the late afternoon fight would be tough. Thankful he now was for the ten-minute rest each hour that Stonewall gave his "Foot Cavalry," as they were coming to be known, during their marches, no matter how pressing the objective. Yet somehow Stonewall still got his men where they headed faster than anyone else. And the word from the officers was that the old ex-professor had insights into physical conditioning and endurance and their importance that was possessed by few if any other general officers North or South.

Willy had chuckled at the disappearance of some of the brigade's most infamous packs of cards and the sudden appearance in their place of pocket Testaments. Also, at Tucker Randolph's newfound concern over his own frequent profanity and lustful considerings. But now all energies turned to survival. The fight blazed in tight quarters, with little room for maneuver. Willy's mind detached him from the observance of splattered body parts and the deafening roar of battle. He loaded, fired, then reloaded, occasionally shifting to a position with better cover, though never moving far.

Once when stepping over a dead friend to take the boy's place of cover behind a splintered oak, he caught view of a Union shell tearing through the two rear horses of a Confederate team, ripping the legs off the driver, and continuing on to shred the trunks of two other men.

The fight raged for two hours. Twice Willy and his comrades threw back charging blue waves. Later Willy would reflect how the Union forces advanced so thickly that it seemed he could hardly have missed hitting somebody unless he had fired straight up into the air. Twenty-eight Confederate rounds ripped through the banner of the Seventh Ohio Regiment.

But the realization closed in on Willy that ammunition grew more difficult to find. First he had loaned it to others. Then he had borrowed it. Then he had pilfered it from the dead. Now, all of a sudden, he had two cartridges remaining, with the Yankees massing for another charge.

He bit off the wrapping paper and poured his powder into the breech. Then he turned and saw Randolph shaking his shoulder.

"We're retreating," Randolph said, his eyes wild and his face covered with brown dirt, black powder, and the red mist of comrades' blood.

Willy shook his head in denial. *No, Tom Jackson never retreats— from anything.*

Randolph read his thoughts. "I know, I can't believe it either, but sure enough it's the truth. General Garnett himself give the order. Now come on, else we'll be fending off this charge by our lonesome."

Then a bullet splintered a branch above Willy's head and he began to back off, firing his next-to-last ball, then reloading the final one as he continued.

No one panicked; they retreated in order, peppering the Yankees whenever they attempted to start a run.

Down the line, Stonewall, unaware of the retreat, brought the large, veteran Fifth Virginia Regiment forward, only to come upon other men heading to the rear. Sandie had informed him just before the commencement of the battle that the usually reliable Ashby's report had grossly underestimated the strength of the Union force. It doubled Stonewall's in size. But *this*—his own men moving away from the sound of the guns, without his knowledge, much less his orders? He whipped Sorrel with the reins, which he rarely did, and galloped toward the break.

He stopped one retreating youngster, shouting to know why he had quit the field.

Raising his rifle, the tawny-headed youth said, "No more ammunition, sir. We used up even the dead's. We was fixing to have to throw rocks."

Stonewall's face boiled like a volcano about to erupt and he rose in his stirrups, great pulsing veins advancing outward from his scarlet neck. "Well then you bloody well should have thrown rocks, son. Now get back there and fight with the bayonet!" Then he saw a drummer boy retreating. Stonewall hoofed Sorrel over to intercept that youth. "Beat the rally," he ordered, his sparking white-hot eyes stunning the boy. "I said beat the rally!" The drummer, more frightened by Stonewall now than by the Yankees, nodded and drummed the call. But Stonewall could not stem the backward flow.

He rode until he found Garnett.

"Why have you not rallied your men?" Stonewall shouted at his brave subordinate. "Halt and rally!"

Garnett was speechless. In his eyes, he had just saved Stonewall's old brigade.

"Why this—this loss of will?" Stonewall said, gesturing to the troops that cascaded around them toward the rear. "Even as I was myself bringing up reserves to support you. Five minutes, General, five minutes longer and this hill would have been ours for the night!"

Garnett had never seen such rage in man or beast. He turned and shouted himself hoarse attempting to stem the retreat he himself had ordered, and which had led to the falling back of the other, now-exposed, Confederate units.

Stonewall managed to erect a line of riflemen that, coupled with the creeping darkness, fended off Union pursuit and enabled an organized Confederate retreat.

Ashby wept when he realized the battle was lost. Only the physical intervention of a half-dozen of his own Rangers prevented him from single-handedly attacking a line of Union horse soldiers.

Willy shook his ringing head and collapsed in an exhausted heap in a fence corner.

And Stonewall ground his teeth together, already pondering what disciplinary action to take against Garnett. For the hero of Mexico and Manassas fought for his God, his country, and the good name of Jackson. The latter he no longer realized was so, though it was.

But on this day, he had lost his first battle.

CHAPTER 42

"HE HAS ALWAYS RIDDEN SEVEN WAYS FROM SUNDAY," Douglas said, "but of late—and this, this is—"

He could not think of a suitable adjective as he watched Ashby emerge galloping from the mist a half mile away on the magnificent milk-white charger. Stonewall had sent the enigmatic cavalier across the North Fork of the Shenandoah with a small squadron of cavalry to observe the Federals as they pursued the Virginian's scrawny battered division up the Valley.

The rest of the squad had returned several minutes before, leaving only Ashby across the river—and the bridge, upon which combustibles had been stacked by the Confederates to burn it.

"I believe it was his brother Robert," Sandie, the only voice among the hushed hundred gathered, said. "The Yankees cornered him and killed him—some say, well, Ashby seems to have friends everywhere, and some got word to him that his brother gave a whale of a fight but finally ran out of ammunition. Then, Ashby believes, they murdered him."

Douglas turned and stared at Sandie, who did not return his gaze. *No,* Douglas thought, *I should not want either to acknowledge the unthinkable—that we have fallen so far as to now be murdering one another. Land sakes,* he thought, lowering his head and shaking it, *I know boys in my neighborhood fighting on both sides. My Lord, I know boys living under the same roof fighting on both sides. Can it have come to this?*

"Look!" someone exclaimed.

Douglas looked up. "Why I didn't know Ashby took so large a force in with him," he said.

"He didn't," Sandie said, his voice hollow.

Then the sun broke through and Douglas saw better the color of uniforms emerging from the haze behind Ashby—*blue*. So close were the Yankees that Ashby appeared to be riding at their head.

Douglas's heart pounded and a claw gripped his throat. One hundred men and not one man spoke. Not one man emitted a sound. An emotion unvoicable, unutterable seized their hearts. Our man, our flesh—our *honor*. But they would never know the words. Only the feeling, many times before the long ordeal ended.

Ashby veered off toward the bridge and hammered across it. Faster was his horse than any of those chasing and he lengthened his lead as he crossed to the near side of the bridge. Puffs of smoke speckled the entire area as the bluecoats launched a hail of fire at the Southerner.

Oh, no, Ashby, Douglas thought, cringing, *do not stop to fire the bridge now, make haste for your life, sir!*

But before Ashby could, the lead riders were upon him, sabers drawn and pistols blazing. Bullets flew everywhere in the wild melee. One shot punctured his canteen. Another tore into his boot, took out a hunk of his leg, and buried itself in the side of his charger. Then Douglas saw Ashby's sword flashing down in the sunlight and a Yankee fell, the scream carried on the wind to Douglas's ears. More bullets, more sabers flashing, then—no Ashby. As one, the whole company of Confederate witnesses rose in their stirrups, squinting down into the smoking haze. One man fell over the bridge lifeless into the water. Douglas could not tell from the distance the color of his uniform. *Oh, Jesus, please,* Douglas pleaded.

And then, like a centaur of old, Ashby and horse appeared from nowhere, thundering out of the smoke and across the plain. A chorus of shots rang out from the Yankees.

Then the first Confederate voice sounded, Ashby's favorite lieutenant Jack Thomson: "Sergeant, load!"

The Confederate cannon boomed fire. One took out the front rank of horse soldiers who pursued, shooting, after Ashby. The second threw up a geyser of water a few feet from the bridge. The Yankees thought better of pursuit and wheeled around to recross the bridge. They had no time to spare, for just behind them the Southern cannon's next shots tore the bridge in two.

Ashby raced up the hill, to a raised-hat chorus of Rebel yells and cheers. *How?* Douglas wondered, shaking his head, a smile spreading across his boyish face. *How did he do it?*

"Just don't know how I made it out of that one without the dandy James Ewell Brown Stuart here to protect me," Ashby mumbled, dismounting on the run. Douglas and others noticed the emphasis on the twin middle names.

He fights ceaselessly, Douglas thought.

Then the grand stallion, bathed in mud, foam, and blood, sank with a cry to the ground. Like his rider, the beast proved the warrior to the end. He seemed to fight even against the inevitable fall to the earth. Ashby threw off his wide-brimmed hat and knelt over the horse, stroking his mane, saying not a word, but staring into the animal's dilated eyes.

A strange thought flickered across Douglas's mind, a Bible verse about the suffering death of the Christ. *"Knowing that all things were now accomplished . . ."* *Oh, to die so well,* Douglas thought, as Ashby sobbed, the only time any present would ever witness a tear shed from his eyes.

Stonewall heaved a sigh of relief bigger than anyone in his division at the news of Ashby's daring escape—and at the valuable scouting information the dauntless horseman's audacious foray provided him.

But two items troubled him. One, the extremes of danger to which Ashby now subjected himself. Since news of his brother's demise, it seemed nothing would satisfy him but joining Robert.

The second item seemed dicier. Ashby stood unsurpassed as a cavalryman. And no one on God's green earth—Russian Cossacks, Mexican vaqueros, Plains Indians—were, man for man, the measure of Ashby's Rangers. Certainly not the United States Cavalry. Stonewall had read of and seen them all, and he knew. But his initial concern over the individualism of Ashby and his men had broadened. That individualism, while possessed of greatness and capable of smashing the Union foe in his teeth and sending him reeling, had also begun to exhibit disturbing patterns. Pursuits were not made with the desired punctuality and force, as in the Romney campaign. Couriers often did not deliver their messages. One group of Rangers had failed even to post a picket, and had been scuppered by Union cavalry. Far too many men came and went for duty will-o'-the-wisp fashion; thus Ashby rarely had even two-thirds of his Rangers on hand. And now faulty information from Ashby himself had led Stonewall into battle against a much larger foe than reported. A losing battle. Stonewall ground his teeth together in anger. *No one—not Turner Ashby, not the War Department, not Jefferson Davis himself—will I allow to compromise our duty.* He glanced at other papers on his beat-up desk. *And not even the Sabbath?* he thought, rehearsing in his mind the written scolding Anna had given him not just for fighting the Battle of Kernstown on Sunday, but for himself initiating the fight. *Could our loss in any way be attributed to that act?* He shook his head, thinking, *Even Jesus broke the Sabbath when circumstances so necessitated. I shall place Ashby under the umbrella of General Charles Winder and my old brigade.*

Ah yes, the Stonewall Brigade they now call it, Stonewall mused. But his dry grin evaporated as he thought of the brigade's previous commander, Garnett. *Such a brave and noble soldier,* Stonewall thought, looking over the court-martial papers and arrest orders he had prepared against the man. *A pity to see a man's career ship-wrecked on the shoals of indecisiveness and lack of will.* He sighed and leaned back a bit on the camp stool his black friends in Lexington had given him. *But such shipwrecks must needs occur, else our independence will be lost. We are outnumbered better than three-to-one, out-equipped, and outgunned. We are blockaded by sea. We haven't factories, railroads, ships, nor foreign allies. And my command. My courageous, valorous, tiny, tattered command.* He placed the Garnett papers in a pouch and sealed it, thinking with resolution, *Yes, many more Kernstowns and Virginia shall be ruined.*

"'Stonewall Jackson's men will follow him to the devil and he knows it,'" President Lincoln read. His gaze shifted through his bifocals to Secretary of War Stanton and two key Republican congressmen sitting before him in the Oval Office. "The words of one of our boys formerly imprisoned and recently paroled." He lowered the paper, removed his glasses, and rubbed his reddened eyes. "But they are only an echo of the words of many others."

"But Mr. President, sir," another man said, "General McClellan will be furious, and we need his party's support for the proper prosecution of this war."

Lincoln rose and strode to the window Stanton so often had witnessed to be his refuge. *His face looks longer and tireder all the time,* the secretary thought. *If his boy Willie dies, I honestly believe the fool might commit hari-kari. And he seeks to engineer the nation's military along with everything else.* Stanton had always detested Lincoln as an opportunistic political opponent; now he detested him as a fool playing toy general. But the secretary grudgingly conceded that the president had set his course to preserve the Union, whatever that took.

And that course now meant protecting Washington City from the rampaging Shenandoah Valley army of Stonewall Jackson.

No, Stanton did not like Lincoln, but he had to suppress snickering at the expression that would be painted on Little Mac's cocksure face when the general learned that the President had established three commands wholly independent of McClellan, all in northern Virginia and all reporting directly to Washington.

The actual implementation of these strategic moves did not humor Stanton, however, for they worked against the hope that fueled his heart each and every day—the early crushing of Confederate capital Richmond and the bringing of the rebellious band of Southern traitors to their knees. Of course McClellan still had at his disposal the most mammoth military force ever seen on the North American continent. But oh, how that Jackson and his men—*How many were they,* Stanton wondered, *twenty-five thousand? Thirty-five thousand? Who knew?*—had upset the apple cart.

First, Lincoln transferred the German General Blenker's entire division to General Fremont and his new Mountain Department in the Alleghenies, west of the Shenandoah Valley. Temporarily, though, Blenker would aid Banks. Second, he held McDowell and his thirty-seven thousand men—bound for McClellan on the peninsula near Richmond—near Washington in the Manassas area, to protect the capital in case Jackson broke through. And third, he ordered Banks and his seventeen thousand men, also slated to support McClellan's Richmond assault, to stay in the Shenandoah and deal with Jackson.

"The most important thing at present is to throw Jackson well back and then to assume such a position as to enable you to prevent his return," Lincoln told Banks.

Meanwhile, George McClellan's howls upon receipt of all this news could be heard nigh to Washington City. After all, he merely faced the task of storming the bastion of the Confederacy. And because of Old "Tom Hick" Jackson (Little Mac still remembered smeared chalk covering the mountaineer's sweaty face as he attempted to work the simplest of equations on the section room chalkboard) more than fifty thousand men had been shifted away from the potential war-ending attack on Richmond.

Stonewall's embarrassing tactical defeat at Kernstown was proving to be one of the great strategic victories of the war for the Confederacy.

As physical death visited itself in ever-greater numbers across the Confederacy, spiritual life did the same. The unparalleled potential for the propagating of the gospel continued to impress itself upon Stonewall. With greater vigor than any other commander on either side, he continued to bring in pastors to preach, to hold camp church services, and to blanket the army with a sea of gospel tracts that presented man's need, Christ's sufficient, accomplished work, and the promise of eternal life for God's elect through Holy Ghost-generated repentance and new life.

As the historic revival of the Southern armies began picking up steam and Stonewall discerned potent spiritual tidings in the wind, he took a thick clump of tracts one rainy afternoon in late April, 1862, and moved bareheaded among his men. Another factor encouraged him that day, one that he anticipated arriving in camp any time.

Indeed, Douglas and Sandie spotted the Reverend Dr. Robert L. Dabney, the theologian-pastor, whom they had heard declined to accept the offered high teaching and leadership position at Princeton Theological Seminary, entering the camp at that moment.

"What in blue blazes is that?" Sandie said.

Stonewall's young staff officers stared gape-mouthed as Dabney approached them.

His sleek long Prince Albert coat, high beaver hat, and immaculately polished boots received the perfect *coup-de-grace* with Dabney's large wide umbrella, which shielded him from the burgeoning rain.

Douglas had heard Dabney's powerful preaching at Manassas, and at this point in the young man's life, he did not wish to hear more of it. This conviction, coupled with the rumor (it was never news with Stonewall Jackson until it happened) that the general's new chief of staff was to be a well-known Presbyterian pastor, prompted Douglas to holler, as the rain turned into a downpour on everyone except Dabney, "Come out from under that umbrella! Come out! I know you are under there; I see your feet a-shaking!"

The gathering crowd erupted into laughter. Dabney, who had tried every argument he knew to resist Stonewall's determined admonitions for him to take the chief of staff position, peered out under the lip of the umbrella. Bristling, he took note of the man who had launched the sarcasm.

Stonewall, too, took note. After he had welcomed Dabney, shown him around the officers and camp, and supped with him, the general called Douglas aside and told him he would be riding across the Blue

Ridge Mountains immediately to find General Richard Ewell and deliver him new orders.

That boy clearly has an excess of energy, a stockpile of spirit, and it is time he proved himself, Stonewall thought after sending the astonished soldier into the rainy dark for a destination the young man had only a hazy idea where existed. *Plus, if that new map maker Jedediah Hotchkiss's calculations are correct, it is only a matter of days before General Shields will be back on me. I shall defame my own mother's grave—God rest her soul—before James Shields shall send my boys packing again.*

Fifty miles away, Nathaniel Banks leaned back and smiled, accepting the offer of sherry from his aide. *Yes, indeed,* he thought to himself, *General Jackson—General "Stonewall" Jackson—your rambunctious behavior in this fair valley has come to naught. If by some quirk you remain here, we are about to "bag" you, sir. But you are reduced, demoralized, and on half rations, and I speculate you are already east of your beloved Blue Ridge.*

"Jackson is flying from this department," Shields, recovering from his wound, proclaimed, "and there are no Union troops needed in the Shenandoah Valley but those who are necessary to garrison the different outposts."

"Jackson is on his way to Richmond," General McDowell reported.

"Bring your men back north down the Valley to Strasburg," Stanton wired Banks, "and send Shields east out of the Valley to reinforce McDowell."

Abraham Lincoln heaved a long sigh of relief as he left his office to visit his sick son Willie. Yes, it had been a good month for the Union, the best yet in this terrible conflict. New Orleans captured, and the whole of the Mississippi River back in Union hands, slicing the Confederacy in two. McClellan and over one hundred thousand men laying siege to the beleaguered and outmanned Confederate capital Richmond. Key Southern forts in Georgia and Tennessee captured.

The secessionists on the run in Arizona and New Mexico. And Grant's stirring victory at bloody Shiloh, which cost the South nearly eleven thousand casualties. The South was reeling, perhaps mortally, and not even "Stonewall" Jackson, the man who turned the day at Bull Run, was going to change that, Lincoln thought, thanking God.

"Darkness seems gathering over the Southern land," Maggie wrote the same day. She could no longer write at night, as the Prestons' small remaining supply of candles and kerosene oil had to be kept for emergencies. "Disaster follows disaster; where is it all to end? My very soul is sick of carnage. I loathe the word—*War*. It is destroying and paralyzing all before it."

And Stonewall Jackson, after spending most of the night on his knees with an open Bible in vigorous prayer, hustled his filthy little column out of its hiding place in a safe corner of the Valley southeast of any Federal forces. He marched it west through rain, sleet, and muck toward the Alleghenies to pick a fight with the quite unsuspecting Union General Fremont. No one knew where Old Jack was nor what he planned, including hair-triggered Confederate General Ewell, who had found only smoking campfires when he arrived at a supposed junction with Stonewall.

"Colonel Walker, from your acquaintance with General Jackson, did it ever occur to you that he might be crazy?" Ewell raged to one of his choice officers. "I tell you, sir, he is crazy as a March hare. He has gone away, I don't know where, and left me here with instructions to stay until he returns, but Banks's whole army is advancing on me and I haven't the remotest idea where to communicate with General Jackson."

"I don't know. We used to call him 'Tom Fool Jackson' at the institute, but I don't suppose he's really crazy," the colonel replied. Then James Walker, commander of the Thirteenth Virginia, Ewell's division, saluted and returned to his regiment for a game of stud.

CHAPTER 43

CAPTAIN WAYNE MARLEY'S BLOOD GREW COLD MAY 7 WHEN he heard the news that Stonewall Jackson was coming after the brigade of Robert Milroy, in which he now served, near the town of McDowell. Milroy led Fremont's push west out of Virginia through the Alleghenies to converge with other Union forces in Knoxville, Tennessee.

Marley's appreciation for the direction of Stonewall's in his spiritual rebirth had been submerged in his growing bitterness toward the Virginian and his key role in the death of Cousin Joe. The hardened horseman got a fight the next day with Stonewall's men, an all day fight. But in the end, Milroy's outnumbered force was driven from the field and Fremont's drive to Tennessee was derailed by Stonewall. Marley's fury deepened when two of his closest friends were killed by Confederate sharpshooters, and when he learned Stonewall himself had not even arrived on the field until the battle had ended.

Stonewall chased Milroy through the Alleghenies. Heading toward Franklin, a nearly palpable presence came over him. He stopped Little Sorrel and gazed around the beautiful spring foliage. He saw a stand of towering pines and a blue pool of water fronting them. Now he remembered. He and Ellie had giggled together at that same pool upon passing it during their journey to see Laura years before. They had giggled how the next time they passed the pool they would not be riding a stagecoach, and would stop for a long "swim" together in the crisp clean water. He stared at the pool.

I know Laura has gone with the Union, he thought with a twinge. *I wonder how she is. And Ellie. I wonder if she is waiting for me.*

Back across the Shenandoah Valley to the east, Ewell, ordered anew to stay put at Swift Run Gap, boiled over again, this time to his cavalry commander. "This man Jackson is certainly a crazy fool, an idiot. General Lee at Richmond will have little use for wagons if all these people close in around him and we are left out here in the cold. I swear, my ulcer will never survive this war or this looney General Jackson."

Cavalry commander Tom Munford chuckled, remembering how "Tom Fool" Jackson looked dodging bricks dropped out of windows and wives' hairpins in church. He also realized for the first time just how much he had learned about war and the military on the artillery drill ground with "Tom Fool."

Stonewall eventually let the retreating Yankees go, and turned back into the Valley. General Richard Taylor of Louisiana, son of former U.S. president Zachary Taylor, and a graduate of Yale, joined the Virginian with his raucous Louisiana Tigers as the leader of the Army of the Valley crossed eastward again across that lush spring expanse.

The urbane and intellectual Taylor could not figure Stonewall. Mile after mile he rode next to him, clear across the Valley. Yet neither Taylor nor any of Stonewall's other commanders had any more idea where their leader proposed to take his army than did the lowliest Irish or Cajun criminal that had been conscripted into the Confederate army off a New Orleans wharf (and spread as much terror among the Southern populace as among Northern soldiery).

Such an ungraceful horseman, Taylor thought to himself as he watched Stonewall gnaw on a lemon for hours on end, *mounted on a sorry chestnut with a shambling gait. Our new commander is not prepossessing.*

Mid-May came and went and Stonewall, unbeknownst even to his closer advisers, prepared to lead his army east out of Harrisonburg and turn it north into the Luray Valley, the easternmost of two parallel north-south valleys comprising much of the northern half of the Shenandoah Valley and separated by the fifty-mile-long Massanutten Mountain. While Taylor and other officers fumed at Stonewall's total secrecy, Ewell, at Swift Run Gap, received a flurry of telegrams and dispatches from Johnston, Lee, and other War Department administrators in Richmond. Varying in content, they all ordered him in one direction: east. Ewell was to cross over the Blue Ridge from the Luray and head toward Gordonsville to help fend off McDowell. Subsequent communiques ordered Stonewall himself not to attack General Banks, entrenched at Strasburg, just north of the Massanutten.

Still furious himself at Stonewall's mysterious ways, Ewell none-theless spoiled for a fight. And he had an odd intuition that "that enthusiastic fanatic" had a method to his certifiable madness. How-ever, the orders from highers-up—*highers-up across Virginia who don't understand the situation here,* Ewell thought with a grimace—were crystal clear. He did not know what to do.

Most of all, he had had his fill with being treated like an old yard dog by that mystical "Ironside" Presbyterian. As he slung himself into the saddle, the old Indian fighter thought, *I'll have me some answers this night or that loon will have my resignation and I'll go soldier with Loring, Taliaferro, Garnett, and all his other unfortunate victims.* Despite an aide's warnings of an approaching storm, Ewell galloped cursing out of camp, taking only his Apache sidekick Friday with him, toward Stonewall at Harrisonburg as night came on Saturday, May 17.

Trouble marked Stonewall's soul as well. Late the previous evening he had read a heartfelt letter from Maggie. Drawn from a conversation of hers with her husband, who had been in Richmond, her portrait of the capital rent his heart. Certain parts of the beautiful old city had become impassable due to roving bands of criminals, some of them army deserters. Foreign speculators, swindling subtlers, and houses of ill repute, seizing the opportunity to gain at the expense of others' suf-fering, with a lack of armed good men to preserve sufficient law and order, had sprung up in various sections of the city. And their tawdri-ness spawned additional evil. *Sin begetting sin . . .*

For the decent and upright folk, Maggie said, even the essentials of living—flour, coffee, sugar, soap, cotton for clothing—grew difficult to obtain, and when found, their prices proved exorbitant. Stonewall's heart sorrowed as she explained the paucity of any sort of medicines.

And the controversial scuttling of the South's ironclad warrior ship *Virginia*—which had taken on all comers in the vastly superior Fed-eral navy and sent most to the bottom of the sea—by its own crew, had left the River James open to the enemy's fleet, up to the very wharves of Richmond! Only now were the Confederates frantically attempting to mount guns and barriers before the Yankees realized their opportunity.

McClellan and his one hundred thousand, flanked by other war-ships on the Chesapeake River and by heavy field guns, had stormed up the peninsula and stood at the eastern gates of the city. Lee and less than half their number stood against them. General McDowell's thirty-seven-thousand-man Fredericksburg force sat poised north of Richmond, with little more than scattered Confederate guerilla units between it and the ramparts of the city.

In the face of this terror, Maggie wrote, came the fevered removal of military stores to the southwest, the packing of Confederate government archives, and the departure south of scores of government officials and employees. It all told a signal story: Richmond would be deserted to the enemy.

At the last moment, however, she continued, the people of Richmond had risen up and demanded the State Assembly present a resolution to President Davis proclaiming their desire that he defend the city, if necessary, until one stone was not left upon another, and proposing to lay it as a sacrifice, with all its wealth, upon the country's altar.

"The people of Richmond have purposed," Maggie went on, "that if the city cannot be successfully defended, it should only be yielded to the enemy as a barren heap of rubbish, at once the sepulchre and glorious monument, of its defenders.

"We know other Union forces under Fremont and Rosencrantz lie to our own west," she concluded, "that could march on Lexington at any time. Most of us have determined in a like manner not to abandon our hearths and homes even if the Federals burn them down over our heads."

Stonewall sat staring at the letter for a very long time. *Maggie. Dear Maggie, a Yankee nearly your whole life. And my dear Virginia. My land. My people.* Outside, thunder crashed, and rain cascaded in under the sides of his tent. The water drenched his trousers as he knelt for the next three hours before his heavenly Father, in much weeping and with many tears, confessing and asking forgiveness, begging mercy for himself and his people, and beseeching the Almighty's wisdom and direction on what to do.

So was he postured when Ewell shoved Jim and a white guard to the side and flung open the tent flap, the torment and chagrin of his long ride having brought his angry soul to a boil.

Ewell's mouth flew open and the first profane words were halfway up his throat when he realized that his commanding general, in pitch dark and three inches of water, illuminated to Ewell only by the fulguration of lightning, was not dispensing orders to aides in his quick firm voice, but was imploring the mercy and intervention of Almighty God.

Ewell stood, dumb, thunder crashing and the storm raging harder. Jim and the guard backed away and found cover.

As water poured down Ewell's large bald pate, a single realization came home to him. *If that is religion, I must have it.*

He turned and walked away, Stonewall never aware of his presence. Jim approached Ewell. "I just don't understand that man," the general muttered.

"Well, sir," Jim said with a smile, "General Jackson, he pray a lot. But when he go to spending a whole lot of a night praying, then I know something big's fixing to happen."

Dabney's soul-searching sermon the next morning, drawn from Jesus' text "Come unto me, all ye that labor and are heavy laden, and I will give you rest," led to several men trusting Christ as their Savior, and numerous other "backsliders" voicing sorrow and repentance over recent wickedness, and turning back to Christ. And it buoyed Stonewall. He needed it when he heard Ewell's news.

"But I have telegraphed General Lee, clarifying our opportunity," Stonewall said, the color rising on his high forehead. "He is still officially President Davis's military advisor, and I am requesting him to preempt the no-fight orders with Banks. Since I am your commanding major general, surely you can remain in the Valley at least until we hear back from General Lee."

A muscle in Ewell's jaw twitched and he shifted from one booted foot to the other.

"I'm sorry, General," he said finally, "that could bring the wrath of Hades down not just on you and me, but on Lee. And that's one man I would never do that to."

"Then Providence denies me the privilege of striking a decisive blow for my country," Stonewall said. The picture of Maggie and her houseful of children and servants suffering without the comforts of medicines and basic food items filled his mind's eye and his head drooped. "I must be satisfied with the humble task of hiding my little army about these mountains, to watch a superior force."

So soft were the last words that Ewell could not hear them. Then, seeing Stonewall for once, evidently, defeated and vulnerable, and sensing the justness of the man's convictions—convictions shared by Ewell—his heart swelled and he blurted out, in spite of himself, "Sir, sign me an order commanding me to stay with you until Bobby Lee gets us back an answer. I bet he'll side with us. He's forgotten more about soldiering than that whole band of fools in Richmond will ever know."

Slowly, Stonewall's head rose. When he again faced Ewell, that general saw for the first time the eyes that had given rise to another of Stonewall's sobriquets: "Old Blue Light."

If Stonewall's own commanders had been in the dark regarding his plans, Banks and the remaining Yankees in the Valley had not even a clue as to his location. Rumors flew from one Union camp to another, placing Stonewall everywhere from western Virginia to the Tidewater peninsula. But the old college professor knew all about the Federals' disposition. He knew that Shields had himself "flown from the department" to join McDowell between the Blue Ridge and Washington at Manassas. He knew that Banks's forces no longer boasted their formidable numerical advantage. Following the military philosophy espoused by Clausewitz, the Virginian largely ignored the other players on the field and drew a bead on what he felt to be the decisive point—the first decisive point.

Ashby and his Rangers proved so effective at screening the movements of the Valley army as it moved north toward Stonewall's target of Front Royal that the Yankees did not know of their presence until the Confederates had virtually arrived at the town. Then, helped by the "scouting" report of comely eighteen-year-old Belle Boyd, a childhood friend of Douglas's, Stonewall unleashed his men on the outnumbered Federals and routed them.

After this, he turned toward Strasburg, ten miles west, and Banks. That Union general could so little believe that Stonewall would actually bring the Valley army to his doorstep that he barely left Strasburg in time to avoid being captured himself. As it was, Stonewall's cavalry barreled into Banks's mammoth, miles-long supply wagon train five miles out of Strasburg at Middletown. They cut it in half. Banks and most of his infantry got away to the north to Winchester, but some infantry, the cavalry, artillery, and most of the wagons were caught in Stonewall's vice grip. They fought for a while, then lit out in a hundred different directions. Hundreds were killed and hundreds more taken prisoner. And the Confederate haul of guns, ammunition, medical supplies, food, and other equipment proved staggering.

Willy had fought and marched for two solid days with nothing to eat or drink besides water. Finally, that evening, he obtained the reward of gorging on the bounty of abandoned Union wagons. Cake and pickled lobsters, piccolomini and candy, canned peaches and cheese, pickled crab, honeyed ham, coffee, and condensed milk. He consumed until he could barely walk, anticipating the order to bed down for the night to come at any moment.

Willy's continuing intestinal disorders disallowed him from enjoying the banquet for longer than it took him to ingest it, then discharge it right back out again. He had lost twenty pounds in six months, from a lean and taut frame. At least the bloody discharges seemed to have receded into intermittent episodes.

When the order came to close ranks and march for Winchester after Banks and what was left of his command, the boy nearly dissolved into tears. No one part of him hurt. A horrible all-consuming (he could not even classify it as pain) suffering possessed his body.

His own colonel, Samuel Fulkerson, pleaded with Stonewall to let the men rest, both to ease their suffering and to enable them to fight well at Winchester.

Stonewall answered quickly, his face firm, but his tone gentle, "Colonel, I do not believe you can feel more for your men than I do. This is very hard on them, but by this night march I hope to save many valuable lives. I want to get possession of the hills of Winchester before daylight."

Stonewall could not pray on his knees in his tent, so he applied himself silently and wholly to communion with his God as he rode through the dark, praying for the grace to ignore his hurting back, buttocks, and legs.

As You restrained and diminished Israel's enemies in preparation for the time of David and Solomon so that they could be enabled opportunity to bring glory to You through the suppression of those—weakened—adversaries, and not themselves, Almighty God, he prayed, *I see how, even in the face of our initial victory against McDowell, you have allowed the enemy to* weaken *his force in this sweet valley for a season, that we might accomplish for Your glory in a succession of actions what we could never do against his fully arrayed forces. I do see how only You have enabled us to honor and glorify Yourself, not through the winning of military battles, but so that those triumphs might allow a broader platform upon which to trumpet the salvation message of Your dear Son's death. O great God in heaven, affix my heart and mind to the remembrance that without spiritual victories for Your kingdom, earthly accomplishments ring hollow and lay spread before us as so many whitewashed sepulchres. May our gallant little army be an army of the living God, as well as of its country.*

For a moment Stonewall rehearsed in his head what his "sources" had informed him had occurred in recent days. *Blenker gone west from Banks to support Milroy, after we have already stopped that force and driven it across the Alleghenies; Shields gone away east from Banks and out of the Valley just when he is needed here. Lord, these are not ignorant men, no matter what the quaking bureaucrats in Washington City spew about them. And it is certainly not our woefully small band that is to credit for their confoundedness. Keep me, keep us all, mindful that without Providence's kind restraining hand, we must certainly have been swallowed whole by this multitude.*

Just then, the unmistakable sound of bullets whistling past Stonewall's ears jolted him, followed by the crackle of rifle fire. *That was close,* he thought. Douglas and Sandie awoke from slumber. They could not understand Stonewall's determination that he and his staff, including his cavalry chief Ashby, should continue to ride at the head of the entire Confederate column—*In the dark, most of them sound asleep in the saddle!* Douglas thought with incredulity.

The ambushers, perhaps twenty of them, fled into the trackless night. Then Stonewall himself dozed off, declining to alter the position in the column of himself or his staff.

The column, most of it exhausted and footsore infantry, many of their feet now bare and bloody, moved past scores of burning wagons the Federals had fired to deprive the Rebels of food, medicine, ammunition, and other stores. The fires gave temporary light, but soon another ambuscade sounded, close by this time, knocking a couple of staff member's horses out from under them. Again, Stonewall heard a couple of the unseen messengers of death sing past, inches from his head.

Ashby, whom Douglas had noticed never closed his eyes, but rode silent, brooding, rose in his stirrups. He unleashed every cartridge of the Spencer repeater he had taken off a dead Yank cavalryman in the direction of the fleeing ambushers.

This time, Stonewall sent a party of infantry ahead. And he moved himself and his staff farther back in the line.

When another ambush sounded a few minutes later, Stonewall's advance party swarmed on them, killing every one, with bullets, bayonets, knives, and in one case, a heavy rock to the skull. Thus ended the night's bushwhacking.

Stonewall did not need Jed Hotchkiss to tell him the topography around Winchester. And he knew where the Yankees would make their stand. As he suspected, they formed atop the hills on either side of the Valley Turnpike. But they were outnumbered and shaken from the previous days' drubbings.

The Virginian rode to the crest of the ridge where the shot and shell flew thickest. With him rode three colonels, one of them thirty-year-old Johnny Patton. Stonewall ignored the musket balls and shell fragments zinging all around the little group and raised his binoculars to his eyes to scout the Yank positions. The fusillade knocked the colonel to Stonewall's left out of the saddle with a gaping chest wound. Shrapnel tore a hole in the sleeve of the colonel to Stonewall's right, prompting a streak of excited oaths from that man. Patton, whom Stonewall had acknowledged seeing for the first time in a decade with an immediate nod of recognition and a "My compliments, Mr. Patton," sat silent and erect. He knew he had been lucky to escape "Tom Fool" Jackson and graduate the VMI. He did not intend to give the new "Stonewall" Jackson any cause to dampen his chances of graduating this war. But fear clawed his insides and if anyone but his old professor had been present, he would have thrown up, or turned his horse and raced for cover, or both.

Patton marveled at how Stonewall could ignore the screaming, the shooting, the soldiers falling around him, the ordnance flying sometimes within inches of his head, even the other colonel's cursing. But this he did, gazing all the while through the glasses and barking tactical orders for the attack.

When Stonewall raised his old cap and shouted, "Let's holler!" Willy and his fellow sons of the South, hurt, tired, and weary to the bone, rose to the occasion, loving him whom they had cursed, and advanced with a thousand shrieking yells on Winchester. They took back the town of their brothers and sisters, where Yankee subtlers had placed their own goods for sale in the finest shops, and they received the hoarse shouts and tears of appreciation from the once-again liberated folk.

"General, sir," Douglas opined that evening to Stonewall during a rare moment when the two sat alone next to a crackling fire in the Grahams' parlor. "Am I right that had the cavalry done its job—er, been more efficient today, that perhaps Banks's *entire* command could have been bagged?"

Stonewall hesitated, poking a stick at the fire. He knew Douglas's suggestion was correct as it applied to both the Middletown and Winchester encounters, as well as, earlier, at Romney. "In his way, Colonel Ashby is a great soldier," the general said, his voice soft. "And, I suppose Washington will find precious small consolation in the day's events."

The Virginian had found great consolation in the response of the women of Winchester to his request that they knit socks and other garments for his tattered soldiers. The ladies had swarmed him, their adulation scarcely allowing him room to breathe. His request had delivered him from their collective grasp, if only for their desire to please him through providing the desperately needed items for his troops. Already, piles of garments streamed in.

"Sir?" Stonewall looked up to see McGuire. "Sir, I have found something I believe you should see."

Stonewall and Douglas accompanied the doctor to one of the largest storehouses in Winchester. Captured Union medicines, surgical instruments, and hospital appliances filled it to overflowing. The three men stared in speechless stupor.

"This building contains more medical stores than are to be found in the entire Confederacy," McGuire said, his voice lower than usual.

From around a corner came Rev. Dabney. A strange expression contorted his face. Stonewall could tell from wet streaks down the great theologian's face that he had been crying.

"Reverend Dabney, sir, are you well?" Stonewall asked.

Dabney stopped and looked him full in the eye.

"My good friend, as I observe this, this mountain of priceless treasure, I am filled with loathing for a people who would perpetrate an inhumanity unknown in modern history," Dabney said, his teeth clenched and his voice a growl unlike Stonewall had ever heard it. "I see this, and I think of the blockade they have imposed to all medicines and hospital stores for the Southern people."

For a moment, Stonewall thought Dabney's voice would break, but it did not.

"With this blockade, sir," the preacher continued, "they can only hope not only to make the hurts of every wounded adversary mortal, where brave men would have been eager to minister to a helpless foe, but to deprive suffering age, womanhood, and infancy of the last succors that the benignity of the universal Father has provided for their pangs."

Now, the strong voice did crack. "I tell you, sir, it is a cold and malignant design."

Dabney turned, head bowed, and stepped back into the shadows.

"Uh, sir," McGuire said, "the Yankees have cleared out the First Winchester Bank building and made it into their own hospital. They left behind seven hundred sick and wounded, doctors, and—a lot more of what we see here. It is a completely self-contained hospital, sir."

Stonewall pondered that. He saw the rage painted on Douglas's handsome young features. And the deadness in McGuire's eyes.

He knew what he wanted to do. He wanted to torch the whole bloody "hospital." Or drag every manjack out of it into the street and allow the good folks of Winchester to take turns shooting them. He thought of little George Preston, who Maggie wrote had nearly died of a slight cough because not even the simplest medication could be found to help wash out his tiny lungs. But then he remembered his Savior's words. Oh, the fools who campaigned him that the Old Testament and its Law was the more difficult of the two books to live by! They had forgotten, "Love your enemies, bless them that curse you, do good to them that hate you, and pray for them which despitefully use you, and persecute you."

The pained expressions on Douglas's and McGuire's faces when they heard his response did not bother him in the least. "Make sure the hospital has plenty of food and water, Doctor," Stonewall said, "then leave them alone—and leave their stores alone—and allow them to do their work for their people. As the soldiers are able to leave, have them paroled, not to fight again until they are exchanged for prisoners of ours."

The warm late spring sun bathing Washington City belied the cold pallor enveloping President Lincoln's chambers the next day.

"Mr. President, I am sending forth telegrams immediately to all the governors of the Northern states, imploring them to send forward every possible soldier they can muster," Stanton said, a bead of perspiration perched on his normally steady brow.

Lincoln stared out the window for a long time before he spoke. "The weight of this entire nation thrown against the Southern capital and this one Rebel is about to descend on our own capital with his own army. I just do not understand it, man. With Richmond about to be overrun, why have they such a detachment storming down the Shenandoah?"

"Sir," Stanton replied, "now that Johnston has been wounded and Lee is in charge of the Army of Northern Virginia, there is no telling what the Rebels might try."

"Yes," Lincoln nodded with a frown, "that is precisely why I wished him to be leading my army. But this Jackson—who knew anything about him? Tecumseh Sherman told us it was Jackson who turned the day against him at Bull Run. And by combining the reports of our other generals, it appears this "Stonewall" Jackson has now thrown three separate Union army forces back across the Potomac in the past ten months."

Lincoln turned to Stanton. Fatigue and sorrow etched their deep marks in his honest midwestern face. "Yes, Mr. Secretary, send for those troops. And I want McDowell, Shields, and every blessed Union soldier between the Alleghenies and Richmond descending on Mr. Stonewall Jackson. Before, God forbid, he gets across the Potomac and descends on us."

CHAPTER 44

AT MIDNIGHT MAY 27, SANDIE RECEIVED THE FIRST REPORT that the Yankees were converging on Stonewall's forces. He decided not to wake the general. The next morning, with Dabney and Douglas, Sandie delivered the frightful news: McDowell was marching west toward them from Fredericksburg and away from Richmond, with Shields and a ten-thousand-man advance column making forced marches and only a day east of Front Royal. Fremont would march east by way of Moorefield and Wardensville. And Stanton had ordered the governors of Massachusetts, Rhode Island, and Pennsylvania to send forward every additional troop they could muster to join with Banks in a return up the Valley after Stonewall from Maryland, with Harper's Ferry as their staging point.

"Of course, sir," Sandie concluded, "if Shields reaches Front Royal before we leave Winchester, he'll be south of us and closer to Strasburg and our only route of escape, down the Valley turnpike, than we are. We would be cut off, with Fremont closing from the west, Banks from the north, and McDowell with more men behind Shields from the east."

The Confederates' course lay too obvious even to state: escape south, back up the Valley.

Stonewall thought. Long had he pored over Hotchkiss's new maps the night before. Because of those charts, Stonewall knew the topography of the Shenandoah Valley better than any other general in the war. And after the maps, long had he pored over the Scriptures on his knees in his tent, and communed with God in prayer. *Lord,* he asked, *have I a wise accounting of the men I face? Shields is probably the best of them, though it was his tough subordinate Kimball who commanded at*—the remembrance of the day still galled him—*Kernstown.*

He rose from the now-scuffed camp stool.

"We shall proceed to Harper's Ferry," he said, as though he were ordering an extra piece of stale black bread for breakfast. "Order the troops into motion immediately."

Sandie blanched. Douglas gulped. North? *North?* To the Maryland border? As though all those blasted Yankees coming from four directions just weren't there? The hint of a wry smile appeared at one corner of Dabney's mouth.

"You have your orders, gentlemen," Stonewall said, walking past them and out of the tent to find Jim. "Get cracking."

"Unsearchable and inscrutable indeed are the ways of the Lord, my friends," Dabney bellowed, touching Douglas's shoulder, "and of our Stonewall Jackson."

The two younger men saw nothing humorous in the assertion. After Dabney walked out, still chuckling, Douglas growled to Sandie, "I think I should like to find another umbrella for the good reverend. But rather than keeping the rain off him, I would like to beat that fire-breathing Bible thumper's big black gentleman's hat down around his ears with it."

"God in heaven, Mr. President, Stonewall Jackson has taken Harper's Ferry."

Stanton's countenance shown grimmer than the fearful words he delivered President Lincoln.

The American commander in chief stared across his desk at the Secretary. Stanton did not like him, and Lincoln knew it. This well-circulated fact added to the Republicans' dismay that the president would choose a Democrat as his secretary of war. But as Lincoln looked on the man, he knew his choice had been right. Stanton feared neither man nor God, and no amount of Confederate victories would intimidate him, even if they cowed every other administration official and military leader in the Union. Lincoln prayed he would have the opportunity to share better days with this unlikable stalwart.

"McClellan and more than a hundred thousand men, even aside from McDowell, along with the United States Navy, pounding on Richmond's front door, and Jackson storms up the Shenandoah Valley to take Harper's Ferry," Lincoln said.

"Perhaps, Mr. President, it is a bluff, a ruse to draw our forces away from the Rebels' capital to our own," Stanton said.

"I believe that result is not in dispute," Lincoln said, standing and crossing to a large war map spread across a planning table. "The question right now is what Mr. Stonewall Jackson plans next."

"Every source available to us insists he cannot have more than fifteen thousand men with him, sir, twenty thousand at the outside," Stanton said. "Even Jackson is not crazy enough to cross into Maryland with that, much less move on Washington City."

Lincoln eyed the map, then peered at Stanton. "He's been crazy enough to give us fits in northern Virginia for a year now, Mr. Secretary, to empty the Shenandoah of our troops, and to drive to our border at a point this here map tells me is thirty miles *north* of where we stand this minute."

The cavernous cheeks colored; Lincoln turned back to the map and its sprinkling of Federal and Confederate flag pins. He studied it, then Stanton thought the president's mind seemed to move somewhere else, though his eyes remained on the map. After a moment, Lincoln looked up again.

"Whatever this enemy's force," he said, "he has driven Banks before him and I think the movement is a general and concerted one, such as could not be if he was acting upon the purpose of a very desperate defense of Richmond. I'm ordering McClellan today to attack Richmond in force or return to defend Washington."

Stanton's eye twitched. "With—all his men, sir?"

Lincoln's eyes blazed and he pounded the table, crushing a cluster of flag pins beneath his big bony hand. "I'll not let the seat of American government be shamed by the invasion of an enemy army, no matter how many of them are barefoot, lice-ridden, and underfed," he roared.

"By thunder, we've got him now," Shields crowed to subordinate, newly promoted Brigadier General Kimball when he heard his prey had stormed north clear to the Maryland border. "He'll never get past us this time. Look at this map, Nathan. And three armies we've got, converging from different directions." Shields clenched his teeth, remembering the still-painful wound that had absented him from his first clash with Stonewall. *This time I'll be there and we'll allow no 'orderly retreats' at dusk. We shall have ourselves Stonewall Jackson for breakfast.*

Willy's continuing diarrhea now hampered not only his endurance, but his overall muscle strength. Each day, during the march to Harper's Ferry and now heading south with the rearguard Stonewall Brigade back up the Valley toward Winchester, severe cramps in one or both of his legs would sideline him for an extended period of time by midafternoon. But pride and the heritage of his name drove him relentlessly onward to catch the main van of the brigade before he halted for the night.

Pride, heritage, and not a little fear.

"Willy boy," Randolph said, terror etched across his face as the evening shadows of May 31 reached across the Valley, "The lieutenant said the whisper is that the Yankees are already in Winchester. What are we gonna do now? Old Jack and the rest of his men are already south of Winchester. We're surrounded, outnumbered, hungry—"

"Yeah," Willy growled as he stumbled along, his shoe soles nearly gone, and weary of "the whisper." "The lieutenant also said Banks would be all over us before we left Harper's Ferry. Well, if you'll listen real close, Randolph, that's Yankee guns still firing on our positions at Harper's Ferry. Except we left there this morning. Old Jack got us into this fix, and with the blessing of God, he'll get us out."

Still, he felt a lump grow in his stomach. *What* will *we do when we get there if they beat us there?* he wondered. But his fatigue, his disease, and his youth allowed him undisturbed sleep.

The hurrah just after dark when the Stonewall Brigade entered Winchester and found no Federals lasted only as long as the order came down to keep marching right through the town toward Strasburg, thirteen miles to the south—which some reports placed in Union hands under Shields and others under Fremont.

"Willy," Randolph said, fear enveloping his young voice, "Shields has taken Front Royal, and that ain't no whisper. He drove out one of our regiments and took a bunch of prisoners. It happened this morning, and Front Royal's only nine miles east of Strasburg."

A white sheen covered Randolph's grimy, peachfuzz-laden face as he stared wild-eyed at Willy. "We're cut off now, Willy boy. It's all up with us."

Willy's exhausted constitution strained to interpret Randolph's words. A reply, even in thought, was impossible. And Willy, like his comrades, had heard the artillery fire earlier in the opposite direction, to the west, indicating that unless Ewell's men and Ashby's cavalry held, Fremont might be in Strasburg too.

"The desperate state of near-insane detachment that we all felt during seemingly endless days' travel under the clouded doom of anxiety is impossible to adequately describe to someone who has not experienced it and the accompanying lack of sleep, rest, and food," Willy would write to Maggie.

"Such is the lot of Jackson's Foot Cavalry," his letter continued, "and, God bless him as he rides sucking his lemons, the old arm occasionally shooting skyward, and his prayers to the Almighty emanating from him even in the saddle, in full view sometimes of the men, we love him."

But Willy and the Stonewall Brigade reached Strasburg, before the Yankees, collapsing after midnight to sleep in the road where they stood.

Shields and Fremont still thought Stonewall was up north in Harper's Ferry. How could he be otherwise? He might be moving across the Potomac River into Union Maryland. He certainly could not be very far south of Harper's Ferry, for he was in that town just the morning before, and reports indicated he had nearly ruined his men with the days of fighting and marching that got them that far.

So while Shields, Fremont, and Banks plodded toward Strasburg to squash their Rebel antagonist, Stonewall's ragged band escaped on bleeding bare feet and empty stomachs through their grasp and up the Valley.

Marley stared through his field glasses and a pouring rain from atop a Massanutten Mountain ridge as the last of the gray-and-butternut column across the swollen North Fork of the Shenandoah River disappeared to the south. Then he turned and peered east through the glasses. The far-forward troops of Kimball, Shields' advance force, appeared faintly, meandering toward a Strasburg now barren of Confederate soldiers.

Marley had not read his Bible in several days, nor uttered more than passing prayers, and could not stifle a vigorous stream of his most faithful old curse words.

Panting in the downpour, he screamed, "Gone again! You've escaped again!"

Marley had proven himself a superb horseman and soldier, but the independent streak native to so many of the Southerners among which he had lived for a decade had rubbed off on him, and that, coupled with the cynicism that had grown in him since Cousin Joe's death, had rendered him less successful as a leader of men. So he leapt at the opportunity his commanding officer "arranged" for him to become a Union scout. His assignment: penetrate Ashby's formidable cavalry screen and learn the location and movements of Stonewall Jackson.

Marley could scarcely contain himself from leaping into the air and shouting in the presence of Shields and Kimball when he received his assignment. Yet a small still voice pestered him: *How can I be consumed with bringing about the destruction of the very man who held the lantern for me in the dark night of my soul and pointed me toward the saving Christ?*

He quashed the voice, and it spoke less and less as the days passed.

A couple of rainy days later, June 3, Stonewall stood under the partial protection of a leafy oak and looked over Hotchkiss's newest set of maps. Nearby, the miserable drenched column ceased the day's march, most of them falling to the soaked ground where they stopped.

A few miles back, Confederate engineers blew up the bridge across the North Fork of the Shenandoah River. That would delay Fremont's pursuit, as the river had flooded, rushing along at its highest point in decades.

"Ashby says Shields is coming up the Luray Valley on the east side of the Massanutten, while Fremont and whoever else chases us here on the west side of the mountain," Stonewall said.

Dabney, Sandie, and Douglas waited as Stonewall's forehead crinkled in thought. "Shields will try to beat us to the south of the mountain, seize the bridge at Port Republic, and cut us off from moving east to hide in the Blue Ridge like we did before," the general said. He looked up at the men, his eyes glowing. His rapt subordinates awaited his next words: where to? But disappointed as they were, they knew by now not to expect to know Stonewall's mysterious plans until they unfolded.

"Major Dabney," Stonewall said, "bring me the papers concerning Colonel Conner's arrest. I shall begin proceedings to have him cashiered."

The three subordinates exchanged a quick glance. Georgian Zephaniah Conner had lost Front Royal and a portion of his regiment to the Yankees. His misfortune grew when Stonewall learned Conner had lost no men killed and few if any wounded in his flight from the town. It did not help that Shields' advance force under Kimball, Stonewall's nemesis at Kernstown, had executed the surprise attack.

Within weeks, Stonewall would see the brave and faithful Conner disgraced and drummed out of the Confederate army. The fate of Garnett, who had retreated at Kernstown, hung in the balance as the Southern high command transferred him to a new assignment away from the Valley, attempting to wait out Stonewall's persistent demands that he too be cashiered.

"Loring, Taliaferro, Garnett, and now Conner," President Davis lamented to Lee in Richmond as the Yankees stood at the gates of the city. "How does this brilliant commander find time to stay after these men like a hound dog after bloodied game? In some ways, even as he bedevils Lincoln, Banks, and McClellan, he bedevils me."

After dismissing Dabney, Sandie, and Douglas, Stonewall received Patton, who offered a report on rearguard activity against the pursuing Fremont.

"Something troubling you, Colonel?" Stonewall asked when Patton had finished.

"Well, sir, it is just that one particular party of Federal cavalry displayed extraordinary courage," Patton said, "and, well, sir, I regret our need to kill the whole lot of them."

"Colonel, why do you say that you saw those Federal soldiers fall with regret?" Stonewall snapped.

"Well, sir," Patton said, wishing he had not mentioned the episode, "I wish that men who fought so bravely, refusing to surrender, might have survived the fight."

Stonewall shook his head, crumpling the Conner papers in his fist, his eyes blazing. "No, shoot them all," he said. "I do not wish them to be brave—shoot the brave and the cowards will lose heart and flee. I wish them to leave our homeland, Colonel. Have you heard of what they are doing in northeast Virginia? Their own General Milroy has issued a statement decrying the deeds of certain Union divisions. Colonel, in certain areas, they have entered and sacked every house for miles around on their marches, stealing what little food our women and children have, emptying drawers, trunks, and bureaus, stealing every earthly treasure possessed by our unfortunate families."

Patton swallowed hard, wishing the rain would stop and wishing he were anywhere but in the way of Stonewall Jackson's righteous wrath.

"Leaving women and children crying behind them," Stonewall stormed on, "but no feminine or infant tears or entreaties stop them, Colonel, that is what their own Milroy writes. He says that General Blenker's Dutch will be as celebrated in history as the vandals who raped Rome. No sir!" At this, officers and men fifty yards away in the marching column looked up. "By the might of Almighty God, we shall drive these pillagers, these looters, these plunderers from this valley."

Now Stonewall's voice grew low, "So we shall shoot them, Colonel, until there are none left in Virginia to shoot."

The next day the rains lifted and Patton reported that Fremont had thrown a pontoon bridge clear across the river. Stonewall ordered his exhausted men forward. Their number had decreased by one thousand the previous few days just by those who had collapsed along the way.

"We cannot outrun them this time," Randolph said to Willy, who wondered if Stonewall would finally be forced to make a stand.

That night, Jim knew "something was really about to happen" because he spotted the lantern flickering late in Stonewall's tent. *He be visitating with the Lord,* Jim thought.

As Stonewall visited and Fremont's cavalry crossed the pontoon bridge, the most enormous thunderstorm yet formed out of a crystal clear sky, then broke loose. Two feet the river rose, then five, then ten, all in four hours. Fremont's bridge began to break up, and he had to cut the southern end of it loose to keep from losing the whole thing.

The next morning, as Stonewall continued south, Fremont stood with his infantry staring across the swirling river at his stranded cavalry. "It's enough to make a man wonder whose side God's on," he snorted.

Meanwhile, Stonewall and his men marched on, toward Harrisonburg, just west of the southern end of the Massanutten. Ashby and his cavalry pestered what they laughingly called Fremont's "a la carte cavalry," and also wiped out all the bridges across the Massanutten from the east. The latter action penned Shields up in the Luray, not allowing him a shot at Stonewall until one or both of them emerged in the open land south of the Massanutten near Port Republic.

Near Harrisonburg, Dabney reported to Stonewall that one of his brigades had become disorganized and fragmented, and now threatened to bottle up the whole column's march.

Stonewall galloped to the trouble spot.

"Colonel, why do you not get your brigade together, keep it together, and move on?" he barked at the brigade commander.

"It's impossible, General," the man answered, "I can't do it."

"Don't say it's impossible," Stonewall said, his face reddening under the old low-slung kepi. "Turn your command over to the next officer. If he can't do it, I'll find someone who can, if I have to take him from the ranks."

Within minutes, under a new brigade commander, the logjam cleared and Stonewall's Foot Cavalry burst through.

"I am again retiring before the enemy, my *esposa*," Stonewall wrote with a weary hand that night in his tent just before retiring. "They endeavored to get in my rear by moving on both flanks of my gallant army, but our God has been my guide and saved me from their grasp."

A gentle nudge from Jim awoke him a few minutes later. He had fallen asleep where he sat, his head plunging onto the page he had written. His face smeared with ink, he shook his head before adding a final line: "You must not expect long letters from me in such busy times as these, but always believe that your husband never forgets his little darling."

His last conscious thought as he fell onto his cot, still cloaked in uniform, boots, and spurs, was of the strong urge that pressed him sometimes to mount Little Sorrel, ride straight south to Anna, and "lay with her." How long it had been since he had been able to do that.

Oddly, the urge came sometimes during the day, even as he rode in the saddle. Often, it came as rain poured. Other times, it came when he saw the tearful pretty women heaping praise, food, and gifts upon him as he passed through their towns. And sometimes it came at this time of night, and he gave thanks to God for the exhausted sleep that covered him before his mind could dwell too long on it.

CHAPTER 45

DOUGLAS FIRST NOTICED THAT STONEWALL "LOOKED AS IF HE were without much sleep," but Sandie agreed. Dabney, overhearing the two discussing their concerns (they disliked the pastor, who they felt was stiff, overbearing, and not a fit with the rest of Stonewall's youngish staff, and therefore would never have included him in such a discussion) asked the general if he had been getting sufficient rest.

Stonewall dismissed the suggestion, blinking his bloodshot eyes. But even the loyal Dabney wondered, with others, why their commander had not loosed Ewell to turn back and wipe out Fremont's stranded cavalry south of the North River. Ashby begged permission to pounce on the weary Federal horsemen, but Stonewall said no.

When Fremont finally got his infantry, artillery, and wagons across the North River and entered Harrisonburg on June 6, the day after Stonewall had left it and moved southeast toward Cross Keys, Port Republic, and his Blue Ridge haven, Ashby took the initiative and bedeviled the Union general's advance cavalry. Playing his confused foe like a Stradivarius, Ashby danced his Black Horse troops in and out of the Yankees' clutches. If the enemy advanced against him, he retreated. If they pulled back, he plunged in, himself and his men shooting, killing, and hauling in small groups of prisoners with each thrust. The actions frustrated, angered, and frightened Fremont. He felt helpless to staunch the systematic destruction of his own cavalry, whom he—even more than Stonewall—needed to alert him to what lay ahead. To no man but himself, he admitted that the Black Horse, whom he had once derided as overrated and bound for doom when faced with United States Cavalry regulars, were proving more fearsome than even their reputation had suggested.

As the afternoon grew late on the sixth, Ashby reported to Ewell that only one significant pocket of Union cavalry appeared to remain anywhere on Fremont's front. He requested infantry support, which Ewell supplied. But Fremont had sent his own infantry reinforcements, and they drove the Confederate pickets in and cut down the forward rank of Ashby's Rangers.

The Black Knight, as the Yankees had begun to refer to Ashby because of his dark swarthy countenance and long flowing ebony hair and beard, saw this and remembered what he had just learned of Blenker's depredations in northeastern Virginia. His younger sister lived in the region worst hit. What had become of her and her little home?

He also remembered that it would have been his little brother Richard's birthday. Brave, loyal Richard, shot in the back by a gang of Yankees after running out of ammunition.

Ashby ignored Sandie's advice from earlier in the day to expose himself less to fire and rode out front of the Confederate infantry, which was wavering under the blazing fire and appeared ready to retreat.

A series of Yankee rifles crackled, knocking yet another horse out from under Ashby. As the bluecoat infantry rumbled toward him, he sprang to his feet and unsheathed his sword. One speedy little Yank raced toward him, bayonet bared. Ashby jerked out a revolver and pulled the trigger. *Click.* Empty. He slung it aside and pulled out his Colt .45. He shot the Yank between the eyes, blowing the man backwards onto the ground.

Bullets whizzing past him on all sides, Ashby waved the long blade and screamed for his comrades to take heart.

"For God's sake, men, do not turn your backs on Virginia!" he screamed. Some of his own Rangers, nearby, blinked in surprise. Never had they heard their revered leader, who smiled often but rarely laughed, shout so. "For God's sake!" Ashby shouted, tears appearing at the corners of his eyes.

But as quickly as he had appeared from nowhere to rally his men in a skirmish that within a matter of minutes had evolved into a key frontline battle, he vanished. Jim Thomson, his second-in-command, blinked, wondering, *Where did he go?*

Turner Ashby lay dead in the dust, shot through the heart by an errant slug from one of his own men—no one could know which—who did not know he had been hit until after they rallied to his heartfelt challenge by rending the surrounding hills with a deafening cacophony of Rebel yells and thundering through the Yankees with rifles, bayonets, and knives, sending them back riddled and bleeding to a shaken Fremont, who now pondered whether he might even retreat back north.

"Have I the entire d—— Rebel army in my front?" he had gasped to his aides. "I have no cavalry left to my whole command to tell me, so I do not know."

Morning's summer sun cascaded through the parlor window onto the ivory keys where ten-year-old Martha Preston practiced her sonata for Maggie. Martha's instinctive deft touch on the pianoforte had come to provide one of Maggie's prime reprieves from the inexorable dull pall of gloom that chilled her blood and pressed more achingly upon her with each new message of death or maiming from the war front.

Martha's nimble long fingers helped remind Maggie that decency, beauty, and dignity still existed in a world rent by barbarous savagery on a scale her mind still could not comprehend.

The look on Phebe's face as she entered the room told Maggie more woe had arrived.

Just two days ago, news of Willy's older brother Frank nearly killed at Winchester and his arm lost. And now—oh, how can it be? Maggie shuddered and strained to digest the horror that Phebe sobbed out to her. *Ashby? Dark Knight of the Shenandoah? Is anyone immune to destruction?* Her skin crawled with terror as other faces flashed before her—Willy . . . her husband . . . Tom . . . .

She consoled Phebe, sent Martha to check on four-year-old Georgie, who from the sound of it seemed intent upon rearranging the diminishing supply of canned produce in the basement, then departed to her writing desk.

Through tears, tears that came less frequently now as her system hardened to nightmare piled upon nightmare, she took pen in hand and wrote upon the used wrapping sheets that now served as her only stationary, the war having vanquished writing paper in the South.

> *Saw ye the veterans—*
> *Hearts that had known*
> *Never a quail of fear,*
> *Never a groan—*
> *Sob mid the fight they win,*
> *Tears their stern eyes within*
> *Ashby, our Paladin,*
> *Ashby is gone!*

She could not know that generations of Virginians would write, recite, knit, carve, and grieve those famed words.

After moving through Harrisonburg, Stonewall, jolted by Ashby's death like none other yet in the war, ordered Hotchkiss to post the division's best set of eyes atop the southernmost peak of the Massanutten. Straddling the Luray and the main Shenandoah Valley, the man could spot the approach of Shields from the former or Fremont from the latter.

But Marley, alone, relentless, wearing out horse after horse as he rode in and out of the enemy's lines, had detected the gleam of the scout's long spyglass. He raced back toward Shields at Conrad Store, a day's march north of Port Republic in the Luray, running another horse into the ground, then stealing a new one from a Confederate farmhouse occupied by a war widow, her six-year-old daughter, and two slaves. He did not even bother speaking, much less brandish his pistol on the mute assembled group. He had stolen Virginia horses before and he would steal them again. He only grumbled that the horses seemed to be growing more thin and haggard as the months passed. He did not know nor would he have cared if he had known that he had taken the widow's last mount.

What he did care about was helping Shields' boastful prediction of "bagging" Jackson come to pass. Marley's scouting prowess had spread through the Union ranks. Now, when he had important findings, Shields and Kimball both turned out in person to hear them.

And important findings were these, coupled with Marley's earlier information that Jackson had reached Port Republic.

Shields smiled and ordered a box of his finest cigars, a snifter of his best brandy, and a comfortable tent provided for Marley, then turned to Kimball. "Send Colonel Carroll and a company of horse south to Port Republic. Let us pay a surprise visit to the good general and see if he hasn't left at least one bridge open across the South Fork of the Shenandoah."

"A general," Kimball reminded him with a sage smile, "whose 'eyes' were plucked from him yesterday near Harrisonburg."

Shields' majestic ruddy Irish face lit up with another thought as he remembered not only the stunning news of Ashby's death, but the scout with the spyglass. "And General Kimball," he said, "have them ride tonight—after dark. We would not want our surprise spoiled, would we?"

Sunday morning, June 8, dawned clear and luminous over the Shenandoah. Stonewall had bivouacked on the southeast edge of Port Republic near the home of a Virginia family named Kemper. Typically, he had declined their offer to quarter him in their main house. He preferred to camp among his troops unless the weather, his health, or campaign planning absolutely prevented him doing so.

He rose before any of his youthful staff, as he usually did, refreshed from the first full night of sleep he had had in two weeks. He did not realize that the cumulative effects of long-term fatigue and loss of sleep could not be slept off in a night, or even a week.

Stonewall spent extra time on his knees in his tent in prayer. He thanked God for the unspeakably happy blessing that had been shared with him in a letter from Anna the evening before. She was again pregnant. Oh, how long had he waited; how many times had tragedy and loss struck him numb. He remembered Ellie, her baby, Anna and her first, and another that had miscarried.

He prayed for the baby, the mother, and also that God would give him the grace to entrust the child to Him, and not make an idol of it. He prayed this partly for protection against the grief that, should he lose yet another child, he feared might overwhelm him. General Longstreet had lost three children, and others had lost even more.

And then he prayed for divine protection for himself and those many charged to his care, and that they might accomplish that which would cause them to be known as a righteous Christian army, doing the Lord's bidding only. For they would indeed need the Lord's aid, as President Davis's note denying Stonewall the reinforcements he had for weeks pleaded for, had arrived with Anna's.

As Stonewall rose, he heard a commotion outside. He threw back the tent flap and walked out, the sun's radiant beams causing him to squint.

"Sir," Douglas said, "this rider begs to report that the Yankees are just north of Port Republic."

"Well," the mounted youth stammered, "that is the report of one of our couriers, and I thought I should report it—"

"Did you see them yourself?" Stonewall asked.

"Well, sir . . . "

"Then go back and find them, son," Stonewall said, turning away. Then he sent orders to Ewell, near Fremont north of town toward Cross Keys, to hold his position until clarification came regarding the position of Shields' forward elements.

For a moment, Stonewall had been truly worried. His entire force was separated from him by the North River that bounded Port Republic on the west and north. That meant if Shields or someone had men that somehow got across the South River, which bounded the town on the east, Stonewall, his staff, a few cavalry, and his entire train of hundreds of wagons would be cut off and swallowed up.

A cold day in Hades it would be before Turner Ashby would let Yankees sneak in this close, Stonewall thought. Then remembrance jolted him. *Ashby—*

Another rider appeared in a cloud of dust, his horse slinging foam.

"The Yankees, sir," he shouted at Dabney, "the Yankees have snatched the bridge across the South River and are in Port Repub—"

A cannon shell exploded a few hundred yards away in town, drowning the rider's words.

The first thought of several of Stonewall's troops across the North River to the northwest of Port Republic: *He must now* prefer *to fight on Sunday!*

For an instant Stonewall, Douglas, Dabney, Sandie, Jim, and the few other staff and officers nearby stood mute. Then all exploded into action.

"Take my horse, sir," Douglas said, offering Stonewall the reins, "he's ready."

"No, I'll wait on mine," Stonewall said as rifle fire broke loose in town. He walked past Douglas into the middle of the road and peered down its length, which became Port Republic's main street. No more than two hundred yards away, directly ahead, he saw a wall of Yankee cavalry thundering straight toward him.

He spun around and took his horse, now readied by an aide, and swung into the saddle. Then he charged directly toward the Yankees.

"General! Sir!" Douglas screamed, spurring his mount and racing after him.

Chaos enveloped the town as Stonewall hit the main street. Gunfire resounded all around him, windows shattered, civilians screamed, some of them trampled in the dirty road, and the Union cavalry was everywhere, riding down the scattered Confederate defenders.

Douglas charged after Stonewall, six-gun in hand. He saw the general disappear into a swirling mob of Federals. *He's gone,* Douglas thought frantically, *he's gone.*

To Stonewall's amazement, most of the way through the town, no one paid him any heed. He had, after all, forgotten the color of the uniform he still wore—blue. Finally, as he cleared the town and galloped toward the bridge across the North River, a Yank shouted, "Hey, you— what are you doing!"

"Lord, that's Stonewall—"

Then shots rang out all around him. He heard one zing past him, felt the death breath of another whistle by his neck. As he approached the bridge, a bluecoat on foot stepped out into his path and drew down on him with a revolver. He spurred Little Sorrel, who charged for the man, forcing him to dive into the South River for safety before he could squeeze off a shot.

A mounted trooper aimed his Spencer repeating carbine at Stonewall as the Virginian rode away from him across the bridge. A burst of fire from Douglas's Smith and Wesson knocked the Yank out of his saddle.

Stonewall reached the crest of a hill across the river, Douglas galloping up behind him.

They looked at each other for an instant, and darned if Douglas didn't detect a bit of a smile flicker at the corners of Stonewall's mouth.

Nodding toward a hole in Douglas's gray coat, he said, "Looks like your colors earned you the worst of it."

Before Douglas could respond, Stonewall turned back toward the river. He saw Confederate infantry swarming in from their camps. Without another word to Douglas, he kicked Sorrel into motion and galloped toward Sam Fulkerson, the infantry commander.

Stonewall jerked off the dirty old kepi and waved it in the direction of town. "Charge right through, Colonel, charge right through."

Then he hustled over to other approaching Confederate units and ordered them ahead. One battery of cannon he told to stay and set up shop. As Stonewall's Foot Cavalry streamed down into the smoke-swallowed town, Rebel yells blaring off the surrounding hills, Stonewall spotted a blue-clad battery unlimbering down by the bridge. Remembering that he had seen a Confederate battery in camp wearing blue, he rode forward and called, "Bring that gun over here!"

The artillerymen stared at one another, then appeared to swing their guns around toward Stonewall.

Douglas rode up and said, "General, that's a Yankee battery."

Stonewall ignored him, rising high in his stirrups and shouting, "Bring that gun up here, I said!"

The bluecoats then fired one cannon, the shot sailing right over Stonewall's head and exploding fifty yards behind him. Dirt flew over him, Douglas, and the Confederate battery.

Stonewall's eyes blazed white and he called out to his own battery, "Let 'em have it!"

They did, splintering one Union cannon and sending the other artillerymen running. Fulkerson's men scuppered them, and commandeered the remaining cannon.

Across town, the Yankee cavalry churned toward Stonewall's encampment, realizing they had the whole Confederate wagon train, and possibly its commanding general, in their grasp. As they came within thirty yards of the wagons, which had begun to retreat south away from Port Republic, Dabney appeared with the blue-clad Confederate battery Stonewall had seen. When the ambush broke, the reverend had raced on foot to retrieve the artillery and order it placed in front of the wagons.

The battery commander was down, and Dabney took charge: "Give it to 'em, boys!"

The four cannon burst forth in fire, tearing down the whole front rank of horsemen, who fell in a screaming, tangled heap of men and beasts. The survivors wheeled and fled back through town, where Confederate foot soldiers unleashed on them with muskets and the captured Union cannon at the bridge.

Those Federals who could splashed across the South River to the east and, dodging shot and shell, made it back to the lead elements of Shields' advancing column, under General Erastus Tyler.

These men had hung Stonewall Jackson's only defeat on him, at Kernstown. Now they intended to finish him and his Valley Campaign, spurred on the more by the news that Ewell, spearheaded by Patton's brigade, had just thrown back Fremont's larger force northwest of Port Republic at Cross Keys.

CHAPTER 46

STONEWALL GOT VERY LITTLE SLEEP THAT NIGHT EITHER. HIS dazed state of near collapse, which he did not discern, now manifested itself to his entire staff. And Douglas and Sandie blamed it for his rash throwing of his men against Tyler's oncoming thousands east of Port Republic the next morning, June 9.

Even Stonewall's chief of staff, Dabney, with his limited military acumen and himself near exhaustion, thought as he watched the vicious battle unfold, *He has both rushed his men in unprepared, and done it in a piecemeal manner, without proper coordination of his men either with one another, his artillery, or his cavalry.*

And Tyler's men proved an obstinate foe. In no way did they believe their Kernstown victory a fluke. Willy, weary and chilled from his months-long diarrhea, had never seen such gruesome carnage. For hours the battle raged, transitioning into desperate hand-to-hand combat as the day wore on. Again and again Willy and the Stonewall Brigade, Patton's men, and Taylor's Louisianians plunged into the sanguinary inferno. Ashby's martyred memory drove more than one Confederate beyond the bounds of normal human endurance. Yet, as the afternoon wore on, the Yankees gradually seized the advantage, pushing the desperate Southerners' backs against the woods fronting the Blue Ridge.

Willy's eyes sighted men without arms, legs, and heads, men with only torsos from the furious cannon fire, men who existed as nothing more than a crimson mist over the fertile Shenandoah bottomland, but he did not see them. He fired his musket, then emptied the revolver his father had sent him into two Yankee cannoneers. He, Randolph, and several others turned the captured cannon around and pointed it into the faces of their onrushing foe. The gun's smoking blast melted the men away.

Then Willy felt a crushing pain across the back of his head and all went black, though he retained consciousness and could still hear the din and roar around him. After a moment, his vision returned as he knelt on the ground. A Confederate flew past him, landing face-first in the turf, two bullets through his chest. Willy could not digest the horror of the scene, but it entailed a swirling, grunting, screaming mass of men in blue, gray, and butternut hacking one another with knives and bayonets, swinging rifle butts and cannon ramrods, and smashing one another's faces with rocks, fists, and anything else they could grab, unless a bullet, blade, or blast stopped their actions.

Willy stared into the teeming insane throng, then dove headfirst into them, swinging his fists at first, then a long bowie knife he pulled out of the chest of a soldier so bloodied he could not tell the color of his uniform. No longer did fear or any other emotion possess him.

A short eternity later, he found himself running as fast as he could after the Yankees, who had begun a retreat that became a rout. The Confederates raised a shrieking mighty Rebel yell that pierced the ears of Shields and his men a few miles away.

General Shields had heartily claimed credit for the victory at Kernstown where he had not been present on the field. He now blamed the hard-fighting Tyler for this defeat, in which he was again not present. And from Shields down to the lowliest private under his command, which was the finest Union division in the Valley and one of the finest in Virginia, the Federals sat mute that night around their campfires. They had not expected, nor could they fathom this defeat. True, the Union had for once been outnumbered, but "I just cannot believe he has licked us," Shields said to Kimball, shaking his head and pouring extra whiskey into his coffee.

So upset was the defeated Fremont at eventide that he posted cannon on a ridge overlooking the Stonewall-Tyler battlefield and the South Fork of the Shenandoah, which he could not ford because the Confederates had torched every bridge across it for miles north and south. With these guns, he began lobbing shells toward the ruined, body-strewn field—just as Dabney, McGuire, and other Confederate clergy and medical personnel began attending to Union wounded. The Confederate wounded had already been tended to or removed.

When one shell splintered a Confederate ambulance, killing two wounded Union soldiers but sparing two Confederates, Stonewall's eyes narrowed and he said to Dabney: "Leave the rest of them for the swine."

Now Stonewall had his entire force east of the South Fork and near the Blue Ridge, where he wanted to be, so that he could wheel and deal further in the Valley or slip through the mountains in escape or to aid Lee in Richmond.

The next night, no Union troops remaining in the area, the Confederates rested around their own campfires under a light drizzle.

"A strange man, that," General Taylor said to Sandie and Douglas when the two had a moment alone at their campfire. "I shall never forget the portrait I saw etched in his face, no, just in his eyes, when I appealed to him on the basis of magnanimity from his glory and brilliant triumphs to relent and allow Colonel Charles Winder, the Stonewall Brigade commander, to take the personal leave he requested to attend to a dying child."

"What portrait was that, General?" Sandie asked, swapping a wink with Douglas.

But Taylor meant no humor. "The portrait of ambition, gentlemen, boundless as Cromwell's and as merciless. A vast, absorbing ambition. What is compelling is that I believe he loathes it, even fears it. But he cannot escape it."

The three sat as a harmonica played at a nearby campfire.

"I have been round him long enough to know that he fights it—with prayer," Taylor continued, poking the fire with a stick. "Constant and earnest. Apollyon and Christian in ceaseless combat."

Taylor watched Stonewall, not far away, as Ewell presented to him the brigade commander whose charge had turned the day and saved the lives of Willy and many another Confederate—Colonel James Walker.

"Well done today, Colonel," Stonewall said, shaking the red-bearded man's hand, "perhaps you learned your lessons better than we thought you did."

Walker and Ewell, joined by Munford, whose cavalry had pursued Tyler's defeated troops for miles, and Patton, broke into hearty laughter as they walked away from Stonewall, who had turned into his tent.

That evening, drunk quartermaster Harmon complained to Hotchkiss that in the previous six months, Stonewall had court-martialed two brigadier generals and two colonels, including Gilham, one of his best friends from Lexington. What's more, his treatment of numerous other officers, Harmon himself included, had pushed them to the brink of resignation.

"Why," Harmon bellowed, launching a belch so offensive it made Hotchkiss wince, "The old fool even resigned once himself!"

And in his tent after the clouds had unleashed a downpour that drove everyone else to turn in, Douglas wrote in his daily journal, "The past thirty-two days Stonewall has defeated four separate armies; relieved Staunton of Milroy and Schenck; run Banks out of Virginia; suckered McDowell and thirty-five thousand soldiers away from McClellan and Richmond; beaten Banks, Fremont, and Shields in turn; broken into pieces their triple combination; and driven the Federal Administration in Washington to the verge of nervous prostration."

A gunshot not far off jolted Douglas. When all remained quiet, he fished more ink out of the well and continued. "In thirty days this army has marched nearly four hundred miles, skirmishing almost daily; fought five battles; defeated four armies, two of which were completely routed; captured about twenty pieces of artillery, some four thousand prisoners, and an immense quantity of stores of all kinds; and done all this with a loss of less than one thousand killed, wounded, and missing.

"Surely a more brilliant record cannot be found in the history of the world," he closed with a flourish.

As Douglas fell into deep slumber a few moments later, the realization struck him that perhaps Stonewall's most amazing feat was that he never lost his cool, even when the battle grew hottest. Anger and frustration, yes, but never, ever, had Douglas seen or heard of him losing his poise under fire.

Lincoln, sleepless and without food due to worry over the war situation and the worsening condition of his beloved boy Willie, stared out over the Potomac from his Oval Office window. Behind him, scattered across his huge oaken desk, spread newspapers from the greatest cities in America—New York, Philadelphia, Boston. The words varied, but the message of Stonewall Jackson's Valley Campaign blared as one, sad and foreboding as unexpected death. In no case did Lincoln feel the publications came even close to articulating the shock, confusion, and distress revealed by the tone of their stories.

The president sighed a long tired breath. "Mr. Stanton, call them back from the Valley. Call them all back."

●◇ ●◇ ●◇

In the Shenandoah, Stonewall placed a gentle hand on Ewell's arm. "General," he said, his eyes wider and his voice more animated than usual, "he who does not see the hand of God in this is blind, sir. Blind!"

CHAPTER 47

STONEWALL RODE TO RICHMOND TO MEET LEE. EVERYWHERE HE went, men cheered, ladies swooned, girls giggled, and fellow officers looked on in awe. Basketfuls of food, drink, and assorted gifts pursued him at every turn. He assigned Douglas the duty of disbursing the bounty—without disclosing that it came from Stonewall—to the troops and to hungry women and children.

Exhausted, he broke into his first smile in days when the marvelously handsome, barrel-chested, snow-bearded Lee told him of Jeb Stuart's latest exploit.

"The 'Ride Around McClellan' they are calling it," Lee, who was the only man Stonewall had ever seen who looked not just worthy of having a statue made of him, but of being one himself, said, his gray eyes twinkling. "I sent young Stuart and twelve hundred of his horse on a heavy reconnaissance of McClellan's positions. Well, our young cavalier determined that rather than backtracking home over old ground, he would push on across McClellan's lines of communication and ride completely around him and his nearly one hundred thousand men."

Lee seemed to derive great joy in relating the story. "He rode one hundred miles, fought skirmishes with Federal cavalry commanded by his own father-in-law, General Cooke, and returned into Richmond after three days with one hundred sixty-five prisoners and two hundred sixty captured animals. He lost one man killed."

Stonewall nodded, thinking to himself, *I believe I have found my replacement for the gallant Ashby.*

He also had to find himself a replacement for Dabney, who tendered his resignation as Stonewall's chief of staff. Illness and exhaustion from the rigors of war and the open camp drove him home. Tears filled Stonewall's eyes as the beloved pastor departed. He never returned, which brought no small pleasure to Douglas, Sandie, and the other young staff members, who had never accepted Dabney and had mimicked and derided him the more as his misery increased.

After all of McClellan's immense preparations, it was Lee and his Army of Northern Virginia, outnumbered eighty-seven thousand to seventy-five thousand even with Stonewall's troops, who crashed into Little Mac's mighty Army of the Potomac, beginning a series of gory battles June 26 to July 1, 1862, that became known as the Seven Days. The clashes began northeast of Richmond at Mechanicsville. Blow led to counterblow, and thirty-seven thousand casualties later, Lee had driven McClellan south to the James River and run him out of Virginia.

The Confederates could claim only one decisive victory, and they suffered thirty-five hundred more casualties than the Federals. More importantly, a series of missed opportunities, leadership bungles, and narrow misses kept Lee from not only saving Richmond and chasing McClellan away, but from destroying his entire force and perhaps ending the war. But Lee had humbled the Union army in front of the whole world—and captured fifty-two Federal cannon and thirty-thousand shoulder arms.

Stonewall did not shine at the Seven Days. He brought his men to the initial fray late, and generally performed as only an average general, far below average for Stonewall Jackson. Longstreet and others, weary of the continued praise and plaudits heaped on him, privately muttered that the swamps of central Virginia had proved a sterner test for Old Jack than the rolling hills of the Shenandoah.

But Douglas, Sandie, and others close to Stonewall knew that his exhaustion and lack of sleep had grown more acute. He went more days without close to appropriate sleep. At times, his aides saw him sitting ramrod-straight in his saddle with his eyes wide open, but unaware of anything transpiring around him. Even other Confederate generals asked Stonewall's aides if he was ill. He had pushed himself beyond the bounds of his human constitution. As he recuperated following the Seven Days, he wrote Anna that he had not been well. "I confess to suffering during the battle from fever and debility, but through the blessing of an ever-kind Providence I am much better today."

Stonewall Jackson's brilliant Valley Campaign had very nearly killed him.

Fortunately, the brilliance of Lee and the valor of the individual Confederate soldier carried the day—and confirmed Lincoln's reservations about McClellan being the man he needed to win in the East. Out West, generals like Grant, Sherman, Sheridan, and Pope were winning the Battle of Shiloh and snaring New Orleans, the Mississippi Valley, and the Ohio and Mississippi Rivers from Confederate forces who had no Lee, Jackson, Longstreet, or Joe Johnston to command them.

A few days after the close of the Seven Days, the Union placed Pope in charge of the newly organized Army of Virginia. Puffed up from successful campaigning in the West, he insulted the ability of Federal troops from the East. Then he thrust America into a new era of war with itself—officially sanctioned war that spared not civilian property or even civilians.

Through a series of proclamations, Pope announced that, unlike McClellan, he would live off the food and property of Virginians. Virginians had their own term for the practice—stealing. Worse, anyone offering the least resistance would have their home burned. Males age sixteen and over who did not swear allegiance to the Union would be driven from their homes into the wilds, to be killed if they attempted to return.

After hearing one (false) report that Confederate guerrillas had shot a Federal trooper, Pope had every home for five miles in all directions put to the torch. As the summer wore on and Stonewall heard multiplied such stories, his anger rose, even as he championed a heavy program of preaching, Bible study, and evangelism among his troops.

One day, Douglas reported to Stonewall that Pope had brought another enormous Federal army, comprised of the former commands of Banks, McDowell, and Fremont, as well as thousands of newly conscripted recruits, down into central Virginia, perpetrating outrages against civilians all along the way.

"This new general claims your attention, sir," Douglas said.

Stonewall's eyes grew dangerous. He spoke, his voice low and full of murder.

"And, please God, he shall have it."

A chill pierced Maggie when she heard her husband's account of Richmond at the close of the Seven Days. Over twenty thousand wounded Confederate soldiers had streamed into the capital, whose total population at the beginning of the war had been only twice that number. Wagonload after wagonload of maimed soldiers rolled in, spilling rivulets of crimson onto the streets until loads of dirt had to be thrown over them to keep the horses from slipping and breaking legs.

Nearly every church, warehouse, and business in the city, and many homes, bulged with bleeding, often dying, men and boys, writhing, groaning, and whimpering in agony.

"We live in one immense hospital, and breathe the vapors of the charnel house," Stonewall's friend Jonathan Bennett told Preston.

"I think continually of Father and Julia, and long to hear from them," Maggie wrote in her journal. "Thank God they are not suffering the apprehension—the undefined fear—the constant dread—that I am never free from."

Several more Rockbridge County men had died in the Seven Days. A terrifying voice whispered to Maggie, *How long before someone else close is maimed—or killed?* She shuddered as she realized that unless the rate of killing slowed, numerical law must assure that the Grim Reaper would come soon near her door, or perhaps even cross its threshold.

One evening, as his troops rested and recuperated from the Seven Days gauntlet in camp north of Richmond, Stonewall rode alone to a tranquil pond he had taken to visiting for at least a few minutes every day.

The new division commander that Lee had just assigned him occupied Stonewall's thoughts. *Of all people in the world, that General Lee should assign me that Tidewater snob,* Stonewall ruminated, *that immoral, venereal-ridden Tidewater snob, A. P. Hill.* The sting of ridicule from those long-ago first days at West Point rose up in his memory like a returning unwelcome guest. Who exhibited the coolest demeanor, the most elite attitude, the greatest unwillingness ever to accept a mountaineer, no matter that man's progress and development? Stonewall remembered whom.

And Lee's gentle admonition to Stonewall when he presented Hill to him as a general "with whom you can consult, and who by being advised as to your movements can save you much trouble in arranging details, as he, and your other division commanders, can act more intelligently" did not humor Stonewall. The old professor considered secrecy—from everyone—one of the keys to his success.

He did not realize that though Lee himself prized secrecy and surprise, that man considered corps commander Stonewall's failure to communicate his plans to his division and brigade commanders a serious leadership flaw. He attributed Stonewall's clash with Garnett at the Kernstown defeat to this.

Neither did Lee enjoy assigning a traveling military court to Stonewall's command just to deal with the stream of charges he brought against his own high-level subordinates.

Plus, Stonewall knew Hill had been assigned to him chiefly because the little commander had so tangled with his previous corps commander, Longstreet, that the two had scheduled a duel of honor with pistols, averted only by Lee's last-minute transfer of Hill.

Objective observers knew Ambrose Powell Hill as moody, sensitive, petulant when angered, the red color of his hair and his temper equally fiery. They also knew he commanded of one of the hardest marching and toughest fighting units in the whole Southern army. Lee ranked him right behind Stonewall and Longstreet as the Army of Northern Virginia's best general.

Hill . . . Pope . . . Stonewall turned his mind to prayer. He petitioned the Lord on behalf of Laura, still to his knowledge not a believer, despite his earlier hopes, from whom he had not heard in months, and who he knew had become an ardent Unionist.

Then he prayed for Anna and the baby. After several minutes, he pulled writing materials from his saddlebags. He sat on a large rock next to the water and drank in the sweet elixir that was Virginia. The silence astounded him. *Can we truly be just a few miles away from the fighting of the bloodiest war in American history?* he thought. He wished he were back in the Shenandoah. He thought of his friends, his family . . . Maggie. And the slender smooth white ankles he had spied years ago. He shook his head and began to write to Anna.

"I love to stroll abroad after the labors of the day are over and indulge feelings of gratitude to God for all the sources of natural beauty with which He has adorned the earth."

He looked up and listened, then resumed writing. "The morning caroling of the birds, and their notes in the evening, awaken in me devotional feelings of praise and gratitude, though very different in their nature. In the morning, all animated nature (man excepted) appears to join in active expressions of gratitude to God; in the evening, all is hushing into silent slumber, and thus disposes the mind to meditation."

Himself stilled and calmed by God's lush creation, as so often he had been, Stonewall closed his entry. "How delightful it is, thus to associate every pleasure and enjoyment with God the Giver! Thus will He bless us, and make us grow in grace and in the knowledge of Him, who to know aright is life eternal."

Lee ordered him north against Pope's advanced corps the next day. The Federals had captured Culpeper and set their sights on Gordonsville, a key east-west and north-south railroad junction near the center of Virginia. Strategically, Lee knew he would eventually need to deal with Pope's entire seventy-thousand-man force. He believed McClellan's army would soon sail north from the James River along Virginia's Atlantic coast. If so, it could reappear in northern Virginia and offer a second threat.

But more trouble brewed within the Confederate ranks. Stonewall led his three divisions, commanded by Hill, Ewell, and Charles Winder, respectively, out of Orange Court House on August 8 toward Culpeper and the Yankees. Ignoring Lee's advice, when Stonewall changed his order of march, he failed to alert Hill. Thus, "Little Powell" Hill, who had peeled his gray jacket in the ninety-degree heat and wore a blood-red shirt whose sleeves he rolled up to his elbows, lost hours of time trying to figure out where to march his division.

Hill had just moved out when Stonewall galloped up.

"Why is the Light Division just getting under way?" Stonewall asked, his expression black. Before Hill could answer, Old Jack barked, "Why are you following Winder's division and not Ewell's?"

Hill bristled, attempting to contain his own boiling anger. "I was not informed that Ewell was ordered to a different route of march, nor that I was to change the Light Division's route."

"You were ordered to follow General Ewell," Stonewall said, seething that timing and the element of surprise were lost. He jerked Little Sorrel's reins around and rode off without allowing Hill a chance to respond.

Hill stared after him, his ruddy complexion scarlet. *I'll not be shamed by that backwoods fanatic,* he thought with venom, marking the incident well.

He did not know that Stonewall had himself given the episode great weight.

Stonewall's force slammed into Federals under his old Valley adversary Banks the next day near Cedar Mountain, north of Gordonsville toward Culpeper.

The Confederate force in the area was twice the size of Banks' corps, but getting the bulk of them into the fray proved difficult. In fact, the Federals had the upper hand as the fight wore on. Winder was killed. The hand-to-hand fighting for Willy and the other Foot

Cavalry grew more vicious than at any time in the war. Both sides were by now battle-hardened. Grudges had developed, not the least of them the Confederates' awareness of what Pope was doing to the land and property of Virginia.

Stonewall, "much prayed up" in Jim's words, sat on his camp stool writing an order for Douglas to present to a courier. Shells fell all around him.

"Sir," Sandie said, "perhaps you might wish to move farther back, as the Federals have attained good range."

Stonewall did not even acknowledge hearing the statement. A moment later a shell splintered a pine tree a few feet away, showering him with bark and other debris. Douglas and Sandie stared as Stonewall brushed the mess from his paper and completed writing the order.

"He did the same thing back at Falling Waters," Sandie told Douglas later.

But events turned against the Confederates, and some began a retreat from the hot, concentrated Union fusillade. When Stonewall realized the situation, he called for Little Sorrel and swung into the saddle.

"Sir?" Sandie called.

Another exploding shell drove the young officer and the other aides for cover.

Stonewall galloped through the smoky, roaring din, flying limbs and branches whipping his bronzed face, every few seconds hearing the distinctive *sizz* of passing minié balls. He knew war and he knew what he had to do.

There they are, he thought, spotting individual Confederates limping, walking, and trotting away from the ferocious fight.

"General Jackson, sir," a rider called, approaching him. Before Stonewall could turn toward him, shell fragments ripped the man and his horse and they fell in a bloody heap.

Stonewall rode on. Ahead, more men, a large number now, were streaming back, many of them wounded and bleeding. Another rider attempted to reach him, but a bullet through the throat tore the man out of the saddle. A few yards away, another shell exploded, shredding a cluster of retreating Confederates.

Stonewall looked heavenward and raised one arm. Of all people, his civilian mapmaker Hotchkiss had come after him. Hotchkiss read the words on Stonewall's lips: "Almighty God, creator of heaven and earth . . . " Then a shell exploded, throwing another dead Confederate rider and horse into Hotchkiss, knocking him to the ground.

When Hotchkiss rose, shaken, he saw Stonewall trying to pull his saber from its scabbard. The general shouted at his retreating men.

"Ah!" Stonewall blurted, giving up on the sword, which had rusted or bent inside the scabbard. He jerked the sheathed weapon off his belt and swung it high.

"Sons of Virginia, Sons of the South," he screamed, "do not turn back from this heartless foe who would turn your wives and children, your mothers and fathers out of their homes and leave them hungry!"

Another shell exploded, showering Stonewall with bark and dirt, as well as human and horse flesh, bloodying his blue coat, and nearly knocking him out of the saddle. For the first time, Little Sorrel reared up, almost dumping Stonewall off his back.

Then Hotchkiss's eyes widened as Stonewall began swinging the steel scabbard like a lasso and whipping it down on the heads of his retreating men, all the while screaming so loudly that Hotchkiss heard every one of his words over the deafening din of the fight.

Other officers watched Stonewall from a safe distance, behind trees and wagons.

"Why does he not fall?" one marveled.

"Look—look at how his eyes flash and his cheeks flush red," said another.

One youth ducked Stonewall's flailing rod and fell to the ground. Stonewall looked down on the boy from atop his horse, his eyes softening. "Get up, son," the Virginian said, "get up. What do you wish to say that you did on this great day to your grandchildren some distant year as you rock by the fire?"

The frightened, emaciated youth blushed and looked down in shame, beginning to sob. When he looked back up, Stonewall had thrown away his reins and grabbed a Confederate battle flag, which he proceeded to wave back and forth, still shouting.

Such did Douglas and Sandie see when they galloped onto the scene. They looked at one another.

"I won't ride into hell, but I'll go afoot," Douglas said, fire in his eyes.

Sandie said nothing, flying out of the saddle, whipping his pistol from its holster, and rushing on foot toward the fight, shouting over his shoulder, "I'll beat you!"

Douglas dismounted and chased after him. Both yelled the singular "Ai-ihh!" of the Rebel yell, which they had seldom had the opportunity to do, but if Old Jack could rally his troops by waving the battle flag, why couldn't his aides do their part?

Others, too, including A. P. Hill and one of Stonewall's newest aides, Anna's younger brother Joe Morrison, pushed, bullied, and urged those retreating to take heart.

The young soldier who had ducked Stonewall's swing of the scabbard looked around him, as his general continued to wave the banner. *It is true,* the boy thought. *Who will protect my people if I don't?* He looked up again at Stonewall. Minié balls tore one after another through the flag, but Stonewall's eyes burned like anthracite coals. *Who will protect Maggie?* the boy thought. Then Willy's heart returned to him and he rose.

"Sir?" he said to Stonewall. "If you please, may I have the honor of carrying those colors back into the fight, sir?"

Stonewall looked down at the boy's face, smeared with blood, dirt, gunpowder, and tears. The blazing eyes cooled and Old Jack's throat grew tight. For an instant, that innocent face was again asking him for permission to lead the prayer in the black Sunday school class. *From where do we get such noble men—such noble boys,* he thought, his head nodding ever so slightly. *For I am not worthy of them.*

He handed the flag slowly down to Willy, who smiled, then turned and raced back into the cauldron, shrieking the Rebel yell. Others saw him and followed.

And so did the Confederate retreat become a countercharge that, along with the arrival of Hill's ferocious Light Brigade, drove the Yankees again from the field, with a loss of fully a quarter of their nine thousand men. And so did Stonewall Jackson's renown grow North, South, and even to the far corners of the "civilized" world.

As every Union general who ever faced him would do, John Pope underestimated the audacity of the kindly Christian general Robert E. Lee. He knew not the thunder and lightning resident in the soft-spoken gentleman's heart. He perhaps forgot the Southerner's father, George Washington's legendary cavalry chieftain "Light Horse" Harry Lee of Virginia.

So Pope could not have expected Lee to break every military maxim in the book and keep his force separated in the face of a better-equipped foe potentially three times his size. This Lee did. As reports continued to stream in of the toll Pope's campaign of destruction visited on northern Virginia, vengeful feelings began to boil in Lee like they never before had. "That man must be suppressed," he wrote Stonewall.

Lee, with Longstreet, moved north to the Rappahannock River to occupy Pope. Meanwhile, Lincoln having ordered McClellan back to Washington, Stonewall's men, the majority of them barefoot or wearing rags on their feet, disappeared from Union observation.

Even Wayne Marley, who had been shadowing Stonewall since the Seven Days ended, lost track of his old mentor, narrowly dodging a hail of bullets from an aggressive Confederate cavalry patrol that served as part of the Foot Cavalry's screen as it marched northwest, around Pope.

When Marley realized he had lost Stonewall, he screamed curses at God until his throat grew so hoarse it could scream no more.

But Stonewall's displeasure with A. P. Hill grew when, on August 20, he himself ordered Hill's waiting division to begin an early morning "moonrise" march he had told Hill to commence a couple of hours earlier.

I'll not let some arrogant shirking insubordinate aristocrat hinder our success, a silent Stonewall brooded, his cap pulled low, as Hill's men moved out. *Arrogant Tidewater—his name and destiny may have peaked, but I'll not suffer him as Pete Longstreet did.*

But he spoke these words to no man.

On August 25, Stonewall's corps marched twenty-six miles. The next day they marched twenty-five more. As Randolph marched, his feet bled. As Willy marched, his rectum bled. Similar plights plagued thousands of other graybacks—a name affixed to them by the Northerners not because of their colors, for few now wore gray, but because of the lice that swarmed them. They carried nothing other than muskets, ammunition, more than a few pocket Testaments, and the scantiest of rations. For days they had nothing to eat but green corn and unripened apples.

But the Foot Cavalry brimmed with hard confidence. Lean and sinewy, tawny-locked and -bearded, they chewed up the miles. When they came upon their leader, himself dust-caked and ever with them, often on foot, lemon in hand or mouth, they raised their hats and voices to cheer him. This time, he waved them to silence, to protect their secrecy.

Stonewall turned to speak to Douglas as one particularly ragged band of tatterdemalions tramped by, their gaunt faces sun-burnished and cocksure. Douglas detected tears in his commander's eyes.

"Who would not conquer with such troops as these."

Riding more horses into the ground, Marley—and other Union scouts—located the Foot Cavalry as it churned north. But Pope believed Stonewall headed back to the Valley. Thus was the Federal commander's stupefaction the greater the night of the twenty-seventh when he spotted a horrific red glow lighting the sky to his north and learned that the entire Union army supply base at Manassas Junction had furnished the kindling. Stonewall had circled behind him to capture the base, near the Manassas battlefield where "Stonewall" had been born.

Willy and Randolph stared gape-mouthed at the scene before them. Warehouses filled to the ceiling with stores. A two-mile-long train of loaded railroad freight cars. More ammunition than the entire Confederacy could produce in a year.

Knowing his ruined intestines could not keep it down long, Willy nonetheless ate until he ached, as he had a few months before at Middletown. Then he laughed as Randolph pulled silk undergarments on over his sunburned, vermin-splotched skin.

The two noticed a stream of dark liquid flowing past them down a hill.

"Old Jack's busted all the whiskey barrels and smashed the brandy bottles!" shouted a haggard soldier with a long stringy beard dressed in faded butternut as he rushed to the rivulet, knelt, and began to slurp from it.

"I fear that liquor more than Pope's army," Stonewall told Hotch-kiss.

The Confederates consumed and took what they could carry in their bellies or on their backs, then Stonewall burned the whole depot (including the vast liquor stores, which he had kept under guard) and vanished from sight.

Now Pope raged. He turned as a wounded lion and rumbled north after Stonewall, spreading his huge force out like a net. Knowing he could not proceed against Richmond with his supply base destroyed and Rebels astride his communications artery with Washington, Pope's desire to destroy Stonewall turned to obsession.

Again Sandie and Douglas and the other staff officers wondered how Stonewall would escape from the tightening noose. To their consternation, with the Federal capital only thirty miles to the east, Pope approaching from the southwest, and McClellan's advance corps already back ashore at Aquia Creek to the southeast, Stonewall sidled his troops into the woods north of Manassas at Sudley Springs and waited.

Late the next day, near Groveton, he ambushed Union troops who had appeared in the woods. For two and a half hours the two forces stood facing one other, mere yards separating them, and blazed away. Two of the war's greatest brigades—the Stonewall and the Wisconsin and Indiana Iron Brigade—went head to head. Neither side flinched as faces, heads, and chests exploded all around them. *The magnificent stubborn courage of the American character when it believes it is in the right,* Stonewall marveled. Finally, at dark, the Yankees, undaunted, drew back. Of Stonewall's three division commanders, two were put out of action with serious wounds, including Ewell, who lost a leg.

Only Hill remained in service, and he again displeased Stonewall the next morning. Jaw set and eyes sparking, Stonewall watched with mounting irritation the slow and sloppy manner in which Hill's division formed ranks, then failed to close up on the division next to it. Stonewall said nothing, but he continued to compile the "case" he had now determined to build against Hill.

Groveton proved only a prelude to what history would call the Second Battle of Manassas, or Bull Run.

Pope found Stonewall entrenched on the edge of the old Manassas battlefield. So fevered to destroy the Virginian was the Union commander that he did not wait to consolidate his spread-out force of nearly seventy thousand men. He threw separate chunks of his command against Stonewall's stout earthworks in piecemeal fashion.

But Stonewall had only twenty thousand men and the onslaughts were terrific. On came the thousands of bluecoats, wave after wave, until five times they had rushed the Southern positions and been repelled.

Hill's men took the brunt of the assaults. They fired and fired, stacking dead Federals up like cordwood. But as the sun sank in the west, with a sixth charge forming in the swirling dust and smoke, Hill, the blood-red flannel shirt he wore sans jacket soaked through with sweat, told Douglas his men were down to their last round of ammunition.

"Tell General Jackson we shall do the best we can, but I am not sure we can withstand another attack." Hill said.

When Douglas reported this to Stonewall, the general's face darkened. He pointed a gauntleted finger at Douglas. "You tell him if they are attacked again, he must beat them back again. You tell him!"

Douglas wheeled his horse around and hurried off. Before he got fifty feet, Stonewall took out after him, riding with him to Hill's beleaguered position.

"General, your men have done nobly," Stonewall told Hill. "If you are attacked again, you will beat the enemy back."

As if on cue, a rippling cascade of musketry opened up at that instant from the Union lines.

"Here it comes," Hill shouted, turning his horse and breaking toward his lines.

Stonewall rose in his stirrups. "I'll expect you to beat them!" he yelled after Hill.

As courageous bluecoat masses marched into the Confederate firestorm, Willy found himself out of ammunition. He had used all his own and every cartridge he could find from his dead comrades. He had ventured out into the Union dead at one point. Now no ammunition remained anywhere around him. Nor did Randolph or any of the others nearby have any left.

Willy looked out. *Lord God, they're less than fifty yards away. Help me, Sir.* He looked at Randolph. "What do we do now, Tuck?"

Tucker Randolph, his face blackened from powder, smoke, and dirt like Willy's and most of the others, gave Willy a wink. "Peas, peas, peas, peas, eatin' Goober peas," he sang, "I like nothing better than eatin' Goober peas."

For some reason, Willy remembered how when he was a boy, Lylburn and the other Negro boys had called Stonewall "Goober."

Then Randolph grabbed a large stone, rose on dirty bare feet, and hummed it into the face of a Yankee rushing toward him with a bayonet only a few yards away. It cracked the man's skull and dropped him like a fat cock pheasant shot out of the sky.

Willy stared for a moment, but then the Yankees were all over them. He saw Randolph grab the dead Yank's rifle and plunge the bayonet into another bluecoat's heart. Then a Union officer stuck a horse pistol against Randolph's back and pulled the trigger, blowing his lungs out the front of his chest.

"No!" Willy screamed, leaping out of his ditch and lunging for the officer. The man swung the gun on Willy and fired, but the youngster's quickness helped him deflect the shot and it just grazed his shoulder. He drove the Yankee to the ground and clamped one hand on his throat, the other on his gun. They struggled, swallowed in a nightmarish swirl of gunfire, shouts, and smoke. All the months and months of killing and suffering, dead friends, savaged farms and homes, widowed mothers and orphaned children seized Willy, and he saw this one man who had killed his best friend from behind as the cause of it all; he hated him now, yes he hated him, and he tore the shrieking man's throat out with his bare hands.

Blood-soaked, Willy grabbed the dead man's gun and shot the first Yankee he saw. As though his body were being controlled by someone or something else, taking it to a level of physical performance it had never before attained, he spun around and shot another man between the eyes whose bayonet was inches away from piercing his back.

A dead Confederate fell into Willy, knocking him over another dead body. He hit the ground with a thud, and another body, blood pouring from where the top of its head had been blown off, fell across his chest. Several Yankees converged on Willy now and he fired the gun up at them as fast he could pull the trigger, blowing one man off his feet, then another, their screams drowned by the cacophony.

Then he heard a loud explosion very close by and everything went black, though he could still hear for a moment, then he couldn't hear either. And then he didn't know anything.

One of Hill's staff rode up to Stonewall and saluted. "General Hill presents his compliments and says the attack of the enemy was repulsed."

A rare battlefield smile dawned across Stonewall's bronzed face. "Tell him I knew he would do it," he said.

The next day Pope had two additional corps from McClellan's force. Again, he threw the weight of the Union army against Stonewall's damaged, outnumbered lines. But Pope had no idea that Longstreet, whom Lee called his "Old War Horse," had arrived on the field with the other, larger, Confederate corps. Longstreet unleashed them on Pope's unsuspecting troops. Backed by a ferocious artillery fire and still outnumbered by twelve thousand men, Longstreet and Stonewall now had the Federals caught in a murderous enfilading fire.

Marley, alone as usual, watched through binoculars from a hill. Tears of anguish filled his eyes. "Curse those Rebels," he said. "Their hoarse roar, their 'Rebel yell'—I swear, they sound like cages of wild beasts at the scent of blood."

"We slaughtered them like hogs," Douglas wrote in his journal that night. The statement brought him no joy as he listened to a torrent of rain thump against his tent. "I could have walked a quarter of a mile in a straight line without putting a foot on the ground for the bodies."

Mad we are, he thought, shaking his head. He dipped his quill back into the ink tank and wrote again as the rain poured. "The heavens weep over every bloody battlefield."

The Union army again found itself fleeing from a Manassas battlefield in a driving rainstorm. Pope had been relieved of command almost before he staggered back across the Potomac to the Federal capital. Adding insult to injury, Jeb Stuart and Robert E. Lee's son Rooney had themselves sacked Pope's personal tent of his baggage, books, papers, and uniform when they raided his headquarters camp a couple of days before the pitched battles that came to be known as the Second Battle of Manassas, or Bull Run.

In ninety days, the Army of Northern Virginia had routed Union forces out of the Shenandoah Valley, defeated McClellan's army, defeated Pope's army, freed Richmond from attack, cleared the state of Federal forces, and carried the war to the Union border.

Stonewall went straight to his tent to write Anna, which he had not been able to do for a few days. "May He ever be with us, and we ever be His devoted people is my earnest prayer. It greatly encourages me to feel that so many of God's people are praying for that part of our forces under my command. The Lord has answered their prayers.

"I pray that all the glory will be given to His holy name, and none of it to man. God has blessed and preserved me through His great mercy."

Stonewall's exploits now demanded global proclamation. London *Times* reporter Francis Lawley painted them on a European canvas. English, French, and German alike shared what Lawley described as "universal wonder and admiration" for Stonewall's exploits.

"They who have seen and heard him uplift his voice in prayer, and then have witnessed his vigor and prompt energy in the strife, say that once again Cromwell is walking the earth and leading his trusting and enraptured hosts to assured victory," Lawley wrote.

And lift his voice in prayer Stonewall did later that evening as he walked alone to a dense wood near his camp. *Oh, Heavenly Father, what shall be done for this wicked and deceitful heart? Victory upon victory, the utter protection of my staff and aides, deliverance after deliverance from our oppressors by Your righteous omnipotent hand, the preaching of Your gospel to the entire army, thousands trusting and believing in Christ, and I—I in my vain darkened imagination consider my own name and glory and how they will ascend with this victory.*

Trembling, he gazed up through the leafy tangle. A few silver stars twinkled through. *Cast my name—the Jackson name—and all my abominable earthly ambitions once and for all into outer darkness, Father—*"Oh, be done with my infernal conceits!" These last words careened through the forested area and flushed an array of creatures from comfortable hiding spots.

He felt oddly like he had the time when as a boy he hid in the woods outside his cabin upon learning he would be taken from his sick mother.

Again on this night he felt cold and alone upon hearing from Dr. McGuire that Willy Preston lay close to death from his wounds.

CHAPTER 48

LYLBURN SMILED. THE GRAPEVINE SAID THE YANKEE PRESIDENT Lincoln would issue an order any day freeing the nation's slaves. Though the Confederates would reject any such action, Northerners, he believed, would not. The Fugitive Slave Law would be voided. Northerners would thus allow slaves escaping from the South to remain in the North, free.

He had long pondered the issue of escape. Big Ben McDowell and others, including a couple from the Russell plantation, had made it safely to the Yankee states already on the Underground Railroad established years before by Harriet Tubman and others, and many had made it on to Canada. Now that Russell was back from the war, minus an arm and badly scarred, he had been a terror to be around. Lylburn believed that if old "Goober" or someone like that owned him, he would not be so eager to leave. In fact, the specter of cross-country travel in the middle of a war terrified him. But he had had his fill of Russell. And that vicious Sam McDowell had made that girl Hannah over on his plantation pregnant. Hannah had been the only girl for whom Lylburn had ever caught a fancy. Now McDowell had spread the word he wished to sell the girl and her child, devil take her parents.

I have had enough, Lylburn thought as he strode down the road to the Prestons', where Russell had sent him with money for a mule. Russell had one gimpy horse and one old mule left on his whole spread. Lylburn knew the Prestons did not like his master, but they had been the only ones kind enough to part with an animal they themselves sorely needed. Lylburn believed it was more because of his and some of the other slaves' well-being than Russell's that John Preston had acceded to his wife's request to practically give the animal to Russell.

But within the next few days, he planned to be headed north, Bible in hand, on the Staunton Quakers' buckboard.

Ahead, he saw several horses tied out front of the Prestons'. *Hey, maybe Mr. Willy come home to rest up and heal from his wounds,* Lylburn thought, his countenance brightening. *Yea it'll be good to see Willy Boy one more time before I pushes north.*

Whistling, Lylburn pushed open the white picket gate, flecked paint fluttering off onto the ground. He scurried up the walkway toward the large house when Mrs. Pendleton came out, covering her red face with a kerchief. Her eyes looked dark and wet.

"Oh, Lylburn," she said, sobbing and touching his shoulder. "Oh—" She burst into tears and rushed away.

Lylburn stood there for a moment, unsettled. He had never before seen Mrs. Pendleton cry, even as the bitter roll calls of the dead and wounded cascaded in from the war. He walked slowly up the steps to the portico. Pastor White came out of the house, his expression grave and his eyes watery.

Then it was like a dream. Lylburn hurried into the house. He heard sobs from a sitting room to one side. He went from room to room. In one corner, he spotted an old fishing pole. *Where is Willy?* he wondered, becoming frantic. From upstairs, the brittle frightful sound of a crying young girl—no, a weeping young girl—penetrated the back of his mind. Willy's brother Frank, minus the arm he had left at Winchester, came around a corner from the back staircase, his eyes rent with sorrow.

Lylburn found himself staring out the back door. Alone, in the yellow dress he had always adored—frayed though it now was—sat Maggie. On a table before her appeared to be a letter. And a cluster of yellow flowers brighter, now, than her dress—jonquils, Lylburn thought. She sat still and stared out into the fields that sloped gently down into the Valley of Virginia.

Lylburn lowered his head and walked slowly from the house. No one had told him anything. But he knew. And if he had not, he would have when he glimpsed through a doorway Colonel Preston sitting at the desk in his office, his head on the desk, wrapped in his arms.

Lylburn staggered numbly down the front steps. "Willy," he whispered. Then he began to run, faster and faster. He ran the five miles back to the plantation. He did not care about the Underground Railroad. And he did not remember the mule. It did not matter; Russell had drunk himself into another stupor. He would retrieve the animal the next day.

Maggie did not feel like writing a few nights later when she sat in near darkness at her desk, but in her numbness, something persuaded her the time had come to write out what thoughts she could bear to record.

Oh, poor Thomas, she thought with grief, reading again the letter that had arrived that day. "He was in my very first Sabbath school class, later he was the first person who volunteered to help with the black Sabbath school class," Stonewall wrote, "and I have loved him since he was a little boy. I planned in but a few days to name him one of my aides, but God in His providence has ordered otherwise."

Smudges stained the writing in a few places, though the outside of the letter and envelope were crisp. *Tom's tears,* Maggie thought with a pang.

Never had she realized just how much she loved Willy. God had used him to open up an entire new world to her that she had before kept shut tight. She heard her two little boys giggling in the next room as Phebe put them to bed. *I can love them . . . because of him,* she thought.

Her chest felt like it would burst through the yellow dress as she inked her pen.

"Willy, the gentle, tenderhearted, brave boy, lies in a soldier's grave on the Plains of Manassas," she wrote. "My heart is wrung with grief to think that his sweet face, his genial smile, his sympathetic heart are gone. My eyes ache with weeping."

She sat up and tried to clear her clutched throat. She could not, so she continued writing.

"Dear Willy was the darling of this entire family—I daresay of this entire village. Selfless, without guile, and ever concerned more about the other person was he. His love and care for his father had a womanly tenderness in it. He was ever gentle and kind to me, and loving to my children."

"Slain in battle."

The words jolted Maggie and she looked out the window down onto the darkened veranda. With her poor eyesight—*Oh, how they ache tonight*—she could not see her husband, but down there he was. Her blood ran cold at the sound of the words. Over and over he had repeated them, ever since returning from Manassas and his attempt to retrieve Willy's body.

He had not known for certain which grave was Willy's, and had opened the one he supposed to be the boy's.

"Alas! For our poor humanity!" she wrote on the used old Christmas wrapping paper. "When he opened the blanket in which the body was wrapped, he could not distinguish a feature of his boy on the despoiled face—he tore open the shirt, and there where I had written it was Willy C. Preston!" She began to weep her own tears onto the paper, "He thought to bring a lock of his hair—it crumbled to the touch!"

Outside, another haunted refrain of "Slain in battle" wafted up to her. For a moment, she thought she could not go on. *But I must,* she thought, *I must tell of it so others will not forget.*

"Such pictures of horror as Mr. P. gives!" she continued. "Unnumbered dead Federal soldiers covering the battlefield; one hundred in one gully, uncovered, and rotting in the sun; they were strewn all along the roadside."

Horror upon horror struck her. *They, too, are some weeping mother's boy, some shattered widow's life, some frightened little boy or girl's—* Then came long racking deep sobs from somewhere deep inside her pained tiny body. "Oh, God, oh Jesus," she wept, her pen continuing in its own power.

"Dead horses everywhere, by the hundred. Hospitals crowded to excess, and loathsome beyond expression in many instances. How fearful is war!"

She bowed her head for a moment, before finishing. "I cannot put down the details he gave me. They are too—horrible."

Willy's clean, kind visage returned to her. "And how brave was he, so full of manly courage! Dr. McGuire says he died trying to save one of his friends. Thomas himself said when Willy grabbed the flag from him at Cedar Mountain and charged, that it spurred his whole regiment into action and turned the day—and thence, we now know, the entire campaign of Second Manassas, which has thrown another Federal army out of Virginia.

"And additional letters relate how when others of his friends gathered heartstruck with sorrow around him, he said, 'Don't distress yourselves about me, I am not afraid to die.' He told Dr. McGuire just before he passed into the upper sanctuary, 'I am at peace with God and with all the world.'

"Alas! What sorrow reigns over the land! There is a universal wail of woe. Dr. Paine's son has been killed at the same battle, as well as the Patricks' boy, and our own Pastor White and his family have lost their most cherished one, Hugh. It is like the death of the firstborn in Egypt. Who thinks of or cares for victory now!"

Maggie stopped for a moment, remembering the boy's sweet open freckled face, gooseberry pies, his clear pure voice singing "Away in a Manger" to the little slave children at Christmastime. Remembering his left-behind tears on her bosom that long ago day of a different summer.

"A more faultless character I think I have never known," she finished. "And he was so consistent a Christian, even through the tribulations and temptations he faced in this world of woe; *that* is the crowning blessedness of all."

"Slain in battle."

Pity etched her face as she glanced again out the window toward where those mournful words came from the darkness. She put down her pen. Then, her throat thankfully clear, she began to sing, softly, the final verse of that hymn of the Savior's birth that Willy had sung so well to little black boys and girls he knew Jesus loved no less than himself.

> *Be near me, Lord Jesus, I ask Thee to stay*
> *Close by me forever, and love me, I pray;*
> *Bless all the dear children in Thy tender care,*
> *And fit us for heaven to live with Thee there.*

She sang it for Willy. She sang it for herself.

CHAPTER 49

LEE DECIDED TO INVADE MARYLAND. MANY FACTORS prompted the decision, which reversed Davis's normal Confederate strategy of fighting a defensive war. The smashing string of Confederate victories in Virginia's Eastern Theatre battleground gave the Southern army momentum; Virginia farmers needed peace over their ravaged lands to bring in the summer's meager crops; Lincoln had had to declare martial law on contentious Maryland to keep it in the Union, and such an offensive might bring the state to the Confederacy, thus enveloping Washington City in enemy territory.

Further, Lee hoped a decisive victory on Northern soil would encourage England and/or France to recognize the Confederacy as a nation, and perhaps even assist it. Without such a victory, in view of Southern defeats and loss of land to the west and a stifling Union blockade on all Southern ports, Lee expected no such help.

Most of all, however, he hoped continued carnage would weary the North and allow the South to be allowed to go its own way.

Gaunt, filthy, tattered, often barefoot, and ridden with lice and other unsanitary critters, the Army of Northern Virginia arose, as per Stonewall's instructions, at "early dawn" September 3. On that day, they would for the first time cross the Potomac into Maryland.

Stonewall's personal dawn came earlier than anyone else's. He arose in the cool dark, lit his lantern, and set about praying and reading the Scriptures. Not a sound came from outside his tent.

"Almighty God, I pray Thou wouldst cover these noble men, veterans of so many deadly encounters, with Thy feathers, and that Thy truth might be their shield and buckler," he prayed aloud on his knees, his eyes closed and his hands clenched so tight his knuckles glowed white.

Fired, he rode from camp to camp, personally supervising the readying of the various units. Then he gave the order to march.

Douglas looked at his trusty gold watch, illuminated by moonlight. *Exactly four o'clock,* he saw. *To the minute as usual.*

Stonewall's satisfied countenance turned to a frown a little while later. *Hill,* he thought with a start, *Where is Hill's division? They should be in the lead.*

Spurring the game horse he rode in place of the temporarily lost Little Sorrel, he galloped over to Hill's camp. Stonewall smoldered as he observed the men standing idly. One brigade had not even broken camp.

He found Hill and barked, "General, your brigade commanders have not carried out your orders, sir. Your men are to lead this van, not trail it. Move them out now, sir."

Hill glared back at Stonewall, but said nothing. He wheeled and gave the order.

From that point on, Stonewall kept his eye trained on Hill's division. They moved out in the lead, but Stonewall noticed their ranks failed to stay tight and compact as he liked. Then the division began to string out, with a growing number of stragglers unable to maintain the accelerated pace.

He is speeding his pace to elude further criticism for foot-dragging, Stonewall thought, his temper rising. Douglas and the other aides knew their chief was steaming. They stayed away from him.

At noon, when the other divisions observed the customary rest period ordered by Stonewall, he noticed that Hill's men did not stop. That did it. Stonewall raced his new mount to the head of the column and ordered it to halt for rest. Then he dismounted and waited for Hill to show. *An irreverent, arrogant man he was the day twenty years ago I met him, and an irreverent, arrogant man he remains. Such are the snares of the ungodly,* Stonewall thought, seething.

When Hill arrived, hatless, his long red hair and beard blowing in the breeze, he flew off his horse, demanding to know why the column had stopped. Pointed toward Stonewall, Hill, eyes blazing, flung off his gray jacket, revealing the customary blood-red battle shirt and stalked toward his commander, unfastening his sheathed sword and thrusting it at Stonewall.

"If you take command of my troops in my presence, take my sword also," Hill said, his words dripping with venom.

Stonewall stood nonchalantly. "Put away your sword," he said mildly, "and consider yourself under arrest."

Hill's jaw dropped and he thought of demanding satisfaction of the insane Roundhead, as he had with Longstreet. Before he could, Stonewall had mounted and ridden off.

Major General A. P. Hill walked across the Potomac River into Maryland, at the rear of his own troops, not knowing the fate of his military career.

Lee again split his force in the face of the vastly superior foe, this time into three parts. Stonewall took the largest third and overwhelmed the unsuspecting Union force at Harper's Ferry. He captured twelve thousand soldiers.

"If we had you, Stonewall, this would never have happened to us," an unarmed Ohio farm boy shouted as he marched past with his entire regiment, guarded by Confederates with bayonets and loaded rifles.

The capture of Harper's Ferry cleared an escape route back into Virginia for Lee's army. The other two wings of invaders maneuvered to sucker McClellan, whom Lincoln had reinstalled as commander of his army after firing Pope, out into the open for battle, and awaited Stonewall's return once he had secured Harper's Ferry.

Lee had McClellan chasing shadows and the entire Federal government to the point of apoplexy over his intentions.

"My Lord, Mr. President," Stanton shouted, "Robert E. Lee is in Maryland, Jeb Stuart and his cavalry are in Pennsylvania, and we do not know what they intend!"

But now the tides of destiny, the hand of the unsearchable Providence that Lee, Stonewall, and Jeb Stuart loved, intervened. An obscure young Indiana private found in an abandoned Confederate campsite, wrapped with three cigars, General Lee's actual orders for the Maryland campaign.

McClellan, staggered by his good fortune, converged on Lee, who had only twenty thousand troops with him. Stonewall had another twenty thousand, and between ten and fifteen thousand had fallen ill, dropped by the way, or deserted for home. Barefoot, vermin-ridden, sick, and hungry, even malnourished, the latter could not continue forever. Many trudged home just long enough to gather crops for their hungry families, to return within a few weeks.

But McClellan, though bedeviled and hampered in his performance by the relentless attacks of his Republican political foes in Congress and Lincoln's administration, had nearly ninety thousand well-fed and well-equipped troops, including two corps that had not as yet suffered any losses at all.

They found Lee, backed against the Potomac, near the Maryland village of Sharpsburg.

Stonewall marched his men all night to arrive from Harper's Ferry hours before the bloodiest day in American history, September 17, 1862, dawned. When it did, the horror was unspeakable. Whole rows, complete columns of men, North and South, fell where they stood or charged, cut down by thousands of muskets and roaring artillery.

One entire corn field, standing six feet tall that morning, was left without a stalk rising more than a few inches from the ground.

Stonewall commanded the Confederate left, which suffered devastating casualties in the battle's early hours. But they destroyed twice their loss. General James Walker led a contingent of reinforcements that helped Stonewall hold his position.

Then McClellan attacked the Southern center, which bent under the weight of dead bodies piled like cordwood, but did not break. Over half the men in the lead Union division were cut down.

Finally, the Federals assaulted the Confederate right. Now the weight of sheer numbers told. As the sun began its descent, the Northerners slugged their way to within a half mile of the Confederates' line of retreat to the south.

At this juncture, A. P. Hill, released by Stonewall from his arrest just long enough to fight in Maryland, his hair, beard, and shirt shining through the smoking sunny hell, led the last division to arrive from Harper's Ferry, two thousand starving, half-crazed, Rebel-yelling men, crashing into the Union force. They proved just enough to drive the Federals back, even as the bluecoats were cutting off the Confederate line of escape.

The day ended with the armies in roughly the same positions from which they had started the battle. And both sustained more than twelve thousand dead or missing men. Over twenty-two thousand casualties. More Americans died during the twelve-hour battle of Antietam, or Sharpsburg, than in the War of 1812, the Mexican-American War, and the later Spanish-American War combined.

Lee determined to stand firm, even as McClellan brought up more reinforcements. The next day the armies faced one another again. The pitiable moans and pleas of the wounded rose up like a howling chorus from the lowest chambers of perdition to fill the stench-ridden air. Stonewall, reconnoitering in person, determined that attack was folly against the massive and growing Union force. But neither did McClellan advance.

That night, Lee took his men out by cover of darkness.

"Funny," one rotund Union officer told some associates the next day, looking off toward the south, his crisp leather accouterments crackling as he walked among the carnage. "They say you can follow their line of march by their bloody footprints. Most of them don't have shoes, you know."

Marley smiled as he viewed the Confederate retreat back across the Potomac through his field glasses. The epic battle appeared to him, McClellan's bleatings of sweeping victory notwithstanding, to be a tactical draw. But it was irrefutably a strategic victory for the Union.

Only "Jackson's God" could have allowed the Rebs even to escape from this one, he thought with a twinge. *The Potomac should have run red with their blood.* Still, he knew the War of Southern Secession was far from over. So was his personal war with Stonewall Jackson, whose troops, Marley now knew, had wrecked two entire Union corps in the battle.

CHAPTER 50

HOW DRAMATIC THE CONTRAST FOR THE REVEREND DR. GEORGE Junkin. The day before, standing on thick pile carpeting, warmed by gas mantle heaters, and preaching to the well-heeled Congregationalist church congregation. And now—this. He gazed around him. *Most of these men were scarecrows when they arrived, and prison life has done little to put meat back on their bones,* he thought with regret.

Junkin had taken to making frequent visits to Union prisoner-of-war camps like Fort Delaware. Following the Bible's admonitions to visit and minister to prisoners, he did it for the men. But he did it for himself as well. As he looked into the hollow-eyed, disease-ridden ragamuffins, his enmity for the South melted away. How often the realization seared his mind that *they could be my boys.* For two of his own sons, and his two sons-in-law, wore Confederate gray. And word had reached him that his boy Ebenezer even now sat wasting in a prison somewhere in the North, but he did not know where.

Forgive me, Father, he prayed, *for the hatred I have harbored in my heart, and me supposed to be a man of God.*

"Some stick you got there, Parson," rang out a game but wispy young voice.

Ah, Junkin thought to himself, swinging up the gold-headed cane Stonewall had given him years before. *Still, my dear son gives through his loving gift.* Junkin had found that the cane served well as a conversation stimulator with the lonely suffering soldiers. Many had been the boy, or man, who had wept for the Virginia farm, South Carolina plantation, or Texas cotton patch that he might now never see again. Junkin knew the survival rate in some of these prisons was no better than that out on the bloody battlefields. Yet he praised God, seeing how the Almighty had used his years in Lexington to prepare him to minister to these brave men, with whom he now had an esprit de corps through their shared familiarity with the Southland.

Junkin found a corner and sat on the floor next to a cluster of lethargic soldiers who wore nothing but rags and lice. He glimpsed a rat scurrying for cover. The vermin appeared much healthier than the men. Coughing and hacking echoed through the enormous room. Junkin opened the large knapsack, bringing out sandwiches and apples, toothbrushes, clean underwear, socks, and blankets. He distributed them as fairly as he could. Mostly, the near-starving men reached for the food. Nearly every man in the large room managed to get something into his stomach. They could not have known that, refined and well dressed as this tall dignified old preacher appeared, he was giving away most of the few earthly goods he still owned. Since his son John's family in Trenton had taken in Julia, the money for his furniture, extra suits of clothes, and theology books went now to provide comfort and sustenance to these pitiable soldiers.

Of course, Junkin had found that the way to a hungry man's soul was through his stomach. As the men around him ate and made use of the other items he had brought, some of them weeping with joy over the tiny treasures, he opened the "book of life" to them. Some of the men already professed Christ as their Savior, though a few had "backslid." Others needed to hear the gospel message anew.

As he read to them all from the apostle Paul's prison epistles, he silently thanked God again for the blessing of serving Him. And he felt Rush's strength coursing through him, knowing she was proud of him.

"Thank you for teaching us, Parson," one of the scarecrows said at day's end.

Junkin swallowed hard. "No, son, it is I who am the pupil."

Despite Hill's heroics at Sharpsburg, Stonewall decided not to drop the charges against him. The man, he felt, had established a pattern of insubordination and poor discipline that must needs be addressed by the assigned traveling court. When Hill caught wind that no pardon was in the offing, he took the initiative on September 22 and requested a court of inquiry on the charges.

"The general must acknowledge that if the charges preferred against me by General Jackson were true, I do not deserve to command a division in this army," he wrote Lee. "If they are untrue, then General Jackson deserves a rebuke as notorious as my arrest."

Lee's pacific temper prompted him to advise Hill against a court of inquiry and to suggest that both Hill and Stonewall drop the matter. After much prayer, satisfied that the issue had received the attention and consideration it deserved, Stonewall agreed to do so. Hill did not.

Going on the offensive, the Tidewater warrior renewed his request for a board hearing of Stonewall's charges.

"Why?" Stuart asked him.

"Because he abused his authority to punish and then sustained his punishment by lodging loose charges against an officer who has done aught but his best to make his troops efficient and help the Confederacy," Hill said, fuming. "And you know what else I'm going to do? I'm going to draw up countercharges against him."

When Hill made good on that declaration, Stonewall's hackles rose, and he turned his attention back to the matter, pointing out to Lee in his endorsement of Hill's countercharges that his subordinate's "continual stirring of the matter constitutes further neglect of duty, and buttresses my earlier case against him."

Lee, bearing the patience of Job, leaned back in his headquarters tent chair and sighed. Two of the best three commanders in the Army of Northern Virginia, he thought, both of them stubborn as a mule, which is part of why the Yankees can't lick them. Well, the Yankees are going to have to continue to deal with them, because I can't afford the loss of either.

Especially since President Lincoln had electrified the world a few days before with his Emancipation Proclamation, deeming the continued ownership of slaves in the Confederacy, but not Union border states, illegal effective January 1, 1863. Lee knew this action elevated the war to the level of a moral crusade for some in the North—though many Unionists decried it—dampened Confederate hopes of aid from England or France, and steeled the South for a fight to the death.

He forwarded the entire thick folder to the confidential files at headquarters, hoping it would go into permanent hibernation.

Meanwhile, Stonewall devoted his personal energies, and those of his aides, to procuring clothing and supplies from any source imaginable. From Richmond, from Winchester, from Lexington, socks, shoes, and blankets came pouring forth in response to his exhortations for aid to his troops. Every item of the hundreds and hundreds that came to him personally from admirers all over the South, Canada, and Europe, he passed on to his men.

He continued to fan the flames of religious revival that now began to sweep through the ranks. He prayed, he brought in the South's best preachers, he passed out tracts, he scheduled as many worship services as he could.

"I greatly desire to see peace, blessed peace, and I am persuaded that if God's people throughout our Confederacy will earnestly and perseveringly unite in imploring His interposition for peace, that we may expect it," he wrote Maggie and her husband. "Oh! that our country was such a Christian, God-fearing people as it should be. Then might we very speedily look for peace . . ."

And he prayed many hours that God might somehow be pleased to bring him forth the child for which he had long wished, and safeguard the dear mother. *Nevertheless, Thy will be done,* he always added.

One sweet sunny afternoon in early October, Stonewall, alone in his tent, opened a letter from Major General Richard Ewell. Recuperating from his lost leg, Ewell expressed his profound gratitude to his superior. Angry, profane, now crippled "Old Baldhead" had become a follower of Jesus. More, he had married a godly, middle-aged distant cousin who had prayed for years for his conversion, always believing he was the man for whom the Lord was saving her.

"Blessed be the Lord," Stonewall said aloud, closing his eyes, "with whom nothing is impossible." He opened his eyes. "Now we must be about getting Bull Paxton saved. I believe he is getting close."

Stonewall had just named Paxton, who in the past had exhibited not the least interest in Christianity, as commander of the old Stonewall Brigade. This further infuriated Hill, who felt one of his own best friends had been snubbed by Stonewall in favor of the relatively inexperienced Paxton.

Then a joyous baritone voice filled the air around Stonewall's headquarters with the lilting Celtic refrain of "The Girl I Left Behind Me."

That voice can belong to only one man, Stonewall thought, a smile spreading across his face as he hopped up from his stool. No man did he more enjoy seeing than Jeb Stuart.

"Look, sir," Douglas said, "General Stuart's brought you a gift."

Stuart, all jingling and jangling and magnificent in his new cape, sash, and ostrich-plumed hat, swung his big body nimbly off his black charger.

"It is my distinct honor and privilege, General Thomas Jackson," Stuart said, approaching Stonewall, "to bestow upon you a matchless gift that at once recognizes your unparalleled ability to wreak havoc upon the general officer corps of both the Northern and Southern armies, and your peerless dearth of sartorial splendor."

As the gathering crowd of men chuckled, Stuart gently tugged on the front of Stonewall's frazzled coat. "See, gentleman? Nary a button remaining on this disturbing garment."

"Yeah, cause all his female admirers at Martinsburg snitched them off'n him," one soldier shouted.

Stonewall blushed crimson. Children had taken more of the brass buttons than had women.

Stuart presented him the box. It impressed Douglas that Stonewall's smile came easier when Jeb Stuart was around than at any other time.

Out came a sumptuous new woolen uniform coat of dark gray cloth and cavalry cape, adorned with gilt buttons and sheeny facing in gold lace.

The men began to cheer, but Stonewall folded the coat and reboxed it. "It is much to handsome for me, Jeb, but I shall take the best care of it, and shall prize it highly as a souvenir."

"I warn you, General," Stuart replied, tweaking his beard, "I'll not be able to return to my duties of warning you about approaching foes until I at least have the honor of seeing how it fits."

"We shall see," Stonewall said, with the closest thing to pure audible laughter that Douglas had witnessed from him in months.

A bit later, a hush befell the officers and aides as they dined at tables in the front door yard of the farmhouse that played host to them.

"Is that General Jackson, boys, or his long-lost nephew?" someone shouted.

Even Stonewall joined the laughter, as the soldiers stared in amazement at their transformed leader. No one even noticed the big turkey Jim had just brought up. Word spread through the camp like wildfire, and dozens, then hundreds of troops swarmed to the area to glimpse their leader in his new finery.

As the thunderous applause, hooting, and Rebel yells reached a crescendo, Stuart raised his hands to quiet everyone. In mock confusion, he scratched his head. "In all the hubbub, boys, I seem to have forgotten the most important element of our esteemed general's new kit."

As the troops roared for Stuart to reveal what was missing, he reached into one of Stonewall's front coat pockets and pulled out—a shiny yellow lemon.

Surprise covered Stonewall's face. "How did you do that? It wasn't there when I put on the coat—"

But his protestations were drowned out by the laughs and hollers of the crowd, whose consensus seemed to be something along the lines of, "Sure, Old Jack, you probably snuck that old lemon in there yourself to get an early start on it!"

The ceremony failed to amuse A. P. Hill. He caught Stuart a little while later as the latter climbed into the saddle, spurs jingling, headed off to mail his little daughter Flora a bevy of birthday presents, his voice booming "Jine the Cavalry."

"The Almighty will get tired, Jeb, of helping Jackson after awhile, and then he'll get the d——est thrashing," Hill ranted. "And the shoe pinches, for I'm sure to get my share and probably all the blame, as the people will never blame Stonewall for any disaster."

Stuart's eyes twinkled and he doffed his hat and bowed in his easy way. "Powell Hill, sir, as fine as that man looked tonight in his sartorial splendor—and fine he did look—he could not hold a candle to you and your sweaty blood-red battle shirt, sleeves rolled to the elbows. And upon that, sir, I take my oath as a Virginian."

Hill cocked his head. "Jeb Stuart, you alone among all men in the world could maintain a friendship with both Fool Tom Cromwell and me."

Within a month, the beloved young daughters of Lee and Stuart died. Both children were the apples of their fathers' eyes. Stuart's wife had written him repeatedly, begging him to come to little Flora's bedside in Lynchburg. Though he loved the little girl more than he loved life itself, he did not go, believing his duty to defend and preserve the safety and honor of life for all the little Floras in the South disallowed him such a personal luxury.

Now his aides caught glimpses of him in his tent late at night, his work completed, head in his arms at his desk, his powerful shoulders quaking with grief, little Flora's photograph and the same old prayer book, opened, beneath him.

"In the hours of night, when there is nothing to lighten the full weight of my grief, I feel as if I should be overwhelmed," Lee wrote his wife. "But 'the LORD gave, and the LORD hath taken away; blessed be the name of the LORD.'"

Hearing these heartrending events, Stonewall's petitions to God for Anna and the child that had been in her womb nearly nine months multiplied. When a desperate tide of anxiety would assault him and grip his heart with the specter of burying another wife, a third baby daughter, he would cry out to God, "Everlasting Father, visit unmerited mercy upon me, upon us, Sir, unworthy sinners. For I do not know if I can bear it again."

Then the Holy Spirit would move over him, silencing his doubts, soothing his fears, and reminding him of the infinite benefits of heaven for his loved ones and that he should praise God for taking them to Himself whenever He would, and Stonewall would again sleep in peace.

"He is the happiest man I have ever known," Dabney told many a person.

Maggie raced to finish her journal entry before the last dying embers in the fireplace rendered her room dark. No candles remained in the house, save one stub to be used only in the direst emergency. She and her husband had determined that light in the house could last only as long as the few logs that lay in the fireplaces at sundown provided it.

Only because of the colonel's lands did they still have any firewood; most of the other families in town did not. *Oh, such presumption we take in times of plenty,* she thought, *dipping the rusty nail back into the bowl of persimmon juice.*

"Ouch!" she yelped, squinting in the near-dark to see if the nail's prick of her index finger had pierced the skin. *Oh, I don't mind writing on wrapping paper and family album pages, I don't mind doing so in the dark, and I don't even mind using pokeweed or persimmon juice darkened with a rusty nail for ink,* she thought. *But Lord, please, spare me from leaving orphaned children because I caught my death in the dark from the poke of a rusty old nail!*

A wry smile creased her face as she thought of the gallows humor emanating these days from Richmond. "A new development in Richmond," her husband had deadpanned on his last return from the Confederate capital. "The rats now come out in the kitchens to beg for food, while the half-starved cats stagger around the house because the rats aren't worth eating anymore."

My poor, poor husband, she thought, wincing. Away to Richmond again that night, he had lost two sons and had a third maimed in the past year. In a few months, his lustrous jet-black hair had turned silver. As his fortune evaporated, he worried for his family and the VMI, for both of which he was now responsible.

Richmond, she thought. *What the horrors of war are visiting upon it and upon the South in general.* She shuddered as she thought of her husband's continuing accounts of the transformation taking place in the beautiful old city. Swindlers, speculators, gamblers, prostitutes, Federal prisoners, wounded Confederate soldiers, and government officials had swelled its population from forty thousand to over one hundred thousand.

While the cost of even basic foodstuffs and necessities—the few remaining available at any cost—continued to climb to impossible levels, Preston saw men, women, and children on the street in tattered dirty clothes, some of them gaunt and pale with hunger. Wounded soldiers filled the hospitals, warehouses, and sometimes the sidewalks to overflowing. His eyes had narrowed as he had related how all the while, an elite class of speculators and thieving quartermasters and commissaries grew fat, comfortable, and rich.

"A reckless spirit of money-making seems to have taken possession of the public mind," Governor Letcher told Preston. "Avarice has become a ruling passion . . . patriotism is second to 'love of money.'"

This seemed so far from her world of dressing her baby Herbie through all the weeks of cold in calico dresses made out of the lining of an old dressing gown.

And another pain pressed in on Maggie that she could share with no one but God, not even her husband. Only could she write of it in her journal.

"I feel so lonely and isolated," she wrote. "How often I long to fly to dear Father and Julia for a little while, have a good cry on their bosoms, and then fly back! It is very sorrowful to be so utterly cut off from them. They are in my thoughts every day, and almost every hour. So are my brothers and their families. When I am compelled to hear scorn and loathing predicated of everything Northern (as is continually the case), my heart boils up, and sobs to itself, for among these 'enemies' are my own people, whom also I love and honor, whom also I know to be honest and true. But I must be silent."

Then her aching eyes discerned the outline of her husband's visage in the photo on the desk near her. *Slain in battle.* Maggie sighed. *His own hell, infinitely worse than mine, has he experienced,* she thought, a tear dotting her eye. Deep and rich had her love grown for him through the long ordeal.

She looked toward the ceiling as the last orange ember died and darkness reigned.

How long, Lord, how long shall we Thy guilty people who deserve all this fierce wrath, continue to suffer it! she thought. *Oh, how right was Thomas when he said that war is the sum of all evils.*

As Maggie wrote the words, more than one hundred thousand Federals, under new Army of Potomac commander Ambrose Burnside, advanced across the ravaged countryside to perpetrate more of that evil on Virginia.

For Burnside had snuck past Lee's army, still northwest in Winchester, and gotten himself between the Army of Northern Virginia and the capital of the Confederacy.

CHAPTER 51

LEE, WITH LONGSTREET'S NEWLY CHRISTENED FIRST CORPS OF the Army of Northern Virginia, rushed to Fredericksburg on the south side of the Rappahannock River in central Virginia. By November 19, the 35,000 Confederates had 115,000 Federals within a day's march of them across the four-hundred-foot-wide river. The other half of Lee's army, Stonewall's Second Corps, lay 140 miles to the northwest in Winchester.

But Burnside's stellar strategy bogged down when pontoon bridges he needed to ford the Rappahannock did not arrive on time from Washington. Meanwhile, Stonewall, left to his own discretion by Lee to an extent no other general on either side in the war had been, marched his suffering men straight across Virginia.

Through snow, sleet, and icy rain the Second Corps slogged, many of them wearing nothing at all on their feet.

Stonewall dispatched Douglas to command the rearguard as the force crossed the frigid Blue Ridge. His duties included orders to allow no stragglers to remain behind.

Tears streamed down the youthful captain's face as his men rounded up one party of stragglers. Some he recognized as mean-spirited shirkers, but most were barefooted, their feet cracked and bleeding on the ice. Forcing them on up the bitter mountain road at the point of his sword, he thought, choking back his feelings and growing into manhood, *No more admirable march was ever made by any body of troops.*

Stonewall's push beat Burnside's pontoons to the Rappahannock. The Virginian rode past streams of refugees who had been driven from their homes out into the open of the nightmarish arctic frozenness, and established his headquarters at the home of a local pastor.

A wad of mail awaited him. One letter began: "My own dear Father, I trust that you are rejoiced to hear of my coming, and I hope that God has sent me to radiate your pathway through life. I am a very tiny little thing . . . my only desire in life is to nestle in close to my mama, to feel her soft caressing touch, and to drink in the pearly stream provided by a kind Providence for my support. . . . Your dear little wee daughter."

He stared at the letter for some minutes. The years of yearning, hoping, losing, and suffering flowed through his mind. He went to his knees on the dirt floor and clasped his hands. "Thou who continually showers blessings upon me; Thou who has spared my wife and given us a darling little daughter. My heart is filled with overflowing gratitude. I know the desire of my unworthy self is to live entirely and unreservedly to Thy glory. Help me, Heavenly Father, to do so."

Then he stood and walked outside. He spoke of the birth to no one as he made his way to the river and strolled along it until Jim caught him and wrapped the new coat Jeb Stuart had given him around him, along with a scarf. Stonewall had not noticed the sub-freezing late afternoon air, made the worse by the raw wind blustering in from the river.

"Do not spoil the child," he wrote Anna that night, "and don't let anybody tease her. Don't permit her to have a bad temper. How I would love to see the darling little thing! Give her many kisses from her father."

He continued about his duties, thinking continually of the little child but not telling a soul about her. For he had lost two others, one—Mary—who lived for some weeks after her birth. He prayed it would not happen so again; but if it did, he thought he could endure it better alone, not having to discuss or explain the loss to others. Still, he wrote for himself as much as he did Anna, "Do not set your affections upon her, except as a gift from God. If she absorbs too much of our hearts, God may remove her from us."

He knew Stuart felt exactly that that had been the case with little Flora.

"And may this unspeakable blessing be to us a reminder," he closed, "of how our lives and energies should ever be applied toward the preparation of a splendid future place for those who come after us. Be the temptation strong, we should not allow our attentions to be turned to the past. It is the future for which we live, temporally and eternally. The Christian should be a man or a woman of the future, not the past."

The shelling began around 1:00 P.M. on December 11. Burnside wanted his 115,000-man army across the Rappahannock so they could deal once and for all with the Army of Northern Virginia, arrayed in the heights south of Fredericksburg, then forge on to storm Richmond.

A thin sheen of ice topped the frigid river as Federals laid pontoon bridges across it down river to the south. They attempted to do the same thing in front of Fredericksburg, but Confederate General William Barksdale had sixteen hundred sharpshooting Mississippians and Floridians dug in. As the morning fog lifted, the riflemen shot every bluecoat who showed himself into the water.

Incensed, Burnside ordered every piece of Union artillery within range to unleash on the historic little town in order to drive the Confederates out.

With no warning at all to the civilian populace, many of whom had already refugeed out, the cannonade began. Lee, stunned by the bombardment of a civilian enclave, refused to allow the Confederate artillery in the hills to respond, not wanting to further endanger the defenseless populace, and hoping the shelling would prove only a momentary burst of rage by the Union high command.

Stuart, who had returned from a second successful "Ride Around McClellan" that helped spur Lincoln to sack the cautious commander, rode down into town to scout the situation. The merry countenance long laughed into his wide bearded face evaporated. He watched gape-mouthed as walls and chimneys fell, bricks and mortar flew, buildings exploded, and metal blew about like a fiery cyclone.

As shells crashed and solid shot rained like hail, Stuart saw the town burst into flames in several places. Remembering that women and children remained in Fredericksburg, he drew one of his big Colts and started to ride forward. But the fusillade proved staggering. He drew rein, his face and beard coated with dirt and black smoky grime, knowing that to proceed meant death.

Stuart's head dropped to his chest in despair. He could watch no more. He reined his horse around and rode back into the hills as over one hundred Union cannon reduced much of the sad little village to rubble.

To the southeast of town, Stonewall, his face grim as he observed the horrific barrage, looked upward, closed his eyes, and raised one arm toward heaven, petitioning God to encircle the aged, infirmed, women, and children in the little town with His protective angels. He prayed so hard that Kyd Douglas saw sweat beads break out on his forehead in the twenty-five-degree air.

The final accounting of the Union barrage registered one dog killed and one slave wounded. Barksdale and his men held fast and, enraged, shot bluecoats off the pontoons faster than they had before. The Federals finally drove the Confederate troops from the town after filling the pontoons with men and paddling across the corpse-strewn river, eschewing the bridge altogether.

Lee and his army had two days to think about what they had witnessed done to Fredericksburg. Fifty thousand graybacks, half under Stonewall and the other half under Longstreet, and half the number of the foe they faced, arrayed themselves through the hills to the south of Fredericksburg.

Lee, Stonewall, Longstreet, Stuart, and Stonewall's old friend and brother-in-law Harvey Hill, commanding one of Stonewall's divisions, sat their mounts and gazed down on the endless blue columns positioning themselves to charge up the hills. Legions of Union drums resounded in unison off the surrounding hills.

"Old Pete" Longstreet, the brooding Dutchman who had lost all three of his children to scarlet fever, ignored the gravity of the panorama. He enjoyed poking fun at Stonewall when he had the opportunity. "General," Longstreet said, pointing a thick gauntleted forearm out toward the blue masses, "don't those multitude of Federals frighten you?"

Stonewall, resplendent in new coat, hat, trousers, and boots, eyed the Northern masses, then Longstreet. "We shall see very soon whether I shall frighten them," he replied, his eyes simmering blue.

For a moment, the other three commanders sat quiet. Then Stuart took off his hat, waved it in the air, and shrieked a Rebel yell, holding it as he whipped his horse around and galloped off down the line.

Three hundred Union guns opened fire on the two-mile-long Confederate position. Then the Federal infantry came teeming up the heights. First they attacked Stonewall's area to the right. His men slaughtered them. The one close call came when the Northerners poured through an opening in the line left through an oversight by A. P. Hill. Stonewall bristled at the mistake and made a large mental note of it.

After Stonewall's Second Corps repulsed them, with A. P. Hill in blood-red battle shirt personally and heroically rallying his portion of the line, the Federals turned to Longstreet's First Corps, on the left directly south of Fredericksburg. Fourteen times they charged gallantly up Marye's Heights. Fourteen times the Confederates, the smoking ruins of the town hazily in view below fortifying them, shot them down, stacking the corpses so high in some places that those behind could barely climb over them. No Yankee got within one hundred yards of a Confederate position.

As Lee viewed the butchery, he silently cursed foolish generals and the politicians who forced them into such slaughter and turned to Longstreet. "It is well that this is so terrible," he said in his soft gentle way, "or else we might grow fond of it."

Over twelve thousand Federals fell dead or wounded.

For two more days the Northerners remained encamped around Fredericksburg. Then they disappeared back across the river under cover of darkness. Stonewall Jackson and the dogged Rebels had thrown back another Union army and dethroned another Union commander.

Later in the day on December 16, Lee, Stuart, and Stonewall stepped through the still-smoking wreckage of Fredericksburg. None of them uttered a word until Stuart, bending over and retrieving something from a pile of smashed stone said, "Look."

He held up a battered, shredded little pink rag doll, its blue eyes and smiling candy cane mouth seared black. Stonewall saw Lee's eyes flicker and the grand old general hurried to Stuart and took the doll from him. He held it in a bent hand, still damaged from being broken in a fall several months before, and stared at the little soft character. He swallowed hard. "An . . . " The words choked off and Lee cleared his throat. "My—my daughter Annie had one just like it." Stuart and Stonewall exchanged glances as Lee's eyes watered over. "But it was left behind when—those people—took our home." Lee swallowed again and bit at his lip. He gazed around the devastation. "What?" he said quietly, hurt. "What are we to do about this?"

Stonewall pushed over a pile of crushed bricks with the heel of his boot. Under it was the smashed daguerreotype of a young couple and a baby. He stared out toward the river. The words of King David, the psalmist, toward the enemies of God filled his mind: *"I hate them with perfect hatred: I count them mine enemies."*

"Kill them," Stonewall said. "Kill them every one until they return forever from whence they came."

Four-year-old George Junkin Preston and his little brother Herbie had learned well the language and operations of war. George marched his little stick soldiers around each day, beating "the Yankees" with them, carrying off prisoners. All day Maggie sewed socks and underwear for the soldiers in the old rocking chair of Stonewall's that Anna had left her, watching George build hospitals with blocks and corn-cobs, drive ambulances with chairs, and administer pills to his rag-boy babies, who laid up in bed as sick and wounded soldiers.

One day he broke form, grabbing a large stick as a crutch and hobbling about, regaling his mother and Herbie of how he had lost his leg at the Second Battle of Manassas. Maggie winced at the mention of the name and what that day had taken from her. Seeing her countenance sadden, George hobbled over to her and assured her he had cut off Yankees' heads and bayoneted them.

Each day, sporting an old cartridge box and haversack, a stick for a sword, and various items stuck in his belt for pistols, he bid Maggie good-bye with gravity. "My furlough is out and I must go to my regiment again."

Two-year-old Herbie would then charge into the breach, promising to kill his share of "Lankees" and talking about pickets, cavalry, cannon, and ambulances.

Maggie's smile upon watching them faded as she realized how war had come to frame her little boys' very lives.

Christmas Eve night she stood alone in her home's dark library. Her husband had gone on another assignment to Stonewall. *Can it be just last Christmas that every one of the children was here? Such a beautiful Christmas tree we had,* she thought, turning in the darkness toward the corner where it had stood. *Green and fragrant it was, filled with innumerable presents for everybody, servants and all. This very room was a scene of innocent gaiety, dear Willy distributing the contents of the tree, as his father had done the year before. Everybody pleased and happy and together. A family.*

She sighed and sat in a chair.

Now the sadness of the household forbids any recognition of Christmas in this Christian home. We are scattered to our own sepa-

rate rooms to mourn over the contrast. Willy, whose genial loving face rises so brightly before me in this blackness, lies in a distant grave—cut off by a violent death.

And now the coffin of his soldier brother Randolph, killed not by a bullet but by measles, has been carried out of the house. No sunshine has yet come back to us following this blow. Frank is here with his one arm, making me feel perpetually grieved for him. Still I hear my dear husband moan in the night watches, "Slain in battle. Slain in battle."

She heard George and Herbie laughing upstairs. *Forgive me, Father. How can I complain? I have nothing to what many others have suffered. My husband and children are spared to me, so that I have peculiar cause for gratitude. I have been permitted to hear of my father's and sister's and brothers' welfare too. Surely it does ill become me to utter lamentations. Rather let me bless God that His rod has been laid on me so lightly.*

She rose and put George and Herbie to bed, her mind fixed on the brave men she knew shivered on cold distant fields. She scoffed at Northern accounts of the Southern soldier's "desperate fight to cling to his human chattel." She knew that at most one out of ten Confederate soldiers owned even one slave. *Why, President Lincoln's own wife, and General Grant himself, own slaves,* she thought.

She smiled as she recounted the numerous stories that had relayed to her the efforts Stonewall continued to make to provide shoes and clothing for his frosty troops. *Oh, and other Christmases I remember with Thomas—and Ellie and Father and Mother.* She remembered to silently thank God for providing little Herbie with a pair of coarse shoes from his Aunt Agnes. He had no others, nor could she prevail upon any shoemaker, for any money, to make a pair of child's shoes.

Then she took pen in hand and wrote, with the aid of her trusty friends the rusty nail and the persimmon juice, "The Bivouac in the Snow," whose multiple verses would long outlive her as a testament to "Spartan soldiers, Stout and brave and bold."

> *Shivering, 'midst the darkness,*
> *Christian men are found,*
> *There devoutly kneeling*
> *On the frozen ground—*
> *Pleading for their country,*
> *In its hour of woe—*
> *For its soldiers marching*
> *Shoeless through the snow.*

CHAPTER 52

THE EMANCIPATION PROCLAMATION TOOK EFFECT JANUARY 1, 1863. Marley entertained mixed feelings about it. Of course he favored freeing the slaves from bondage and whatever it took to accomplish that. But as he sat nursing his own thoughts by a blazing fire in the Union camp next to the Rappahannock one evening in early February, his old cynicism grew. *Lincoln does not care one way or another for the slaves, else he would have proclaimed those in the border states and elsewhere free. He did it for political gain, especially to keep England and France off our backs. Then he kowtows to those pirates in Washington and fires McClellan, the best general he ever had, the only one the men will ever love, and the one that saved Old Abe and his government's backside when he cleared the Secesh out of Maryland. How quickly they forget,* he thought, anger filling his heart.

Marley unfolded the yellowed page of an old *New York Times* and read Lincoln's own words by the firelight: "My paramount object in this struggle is to save the Union, and is not either to save or destroy slavery. If I could save the Union without freeing any slave, I would do it; and if I could save it by freeing all the slaves, I would do it; and if I could do it by freeing some and leaving others alone, I would also do that."

For that, we shall utterly destroy the South and waste the flower of the North, Marley thought with a wince. *For now we shall have to kill Tom Jackson and every man in the South like him if we even hope for victory. When will I ever get back home?*

What had at one time seemed to be a holy mission to champion God's glory now seemed like . . . Over and over Marley saw again the coal black cloud rising from Fredericksburg. He knew civilians remained in the little town and that no warning had been given by Burnside before the withering salvo began. He remembered a girl he once knew from Fredericksburg. Was she there when his brave comrades leveled her town from across the Rappahannock?

Marley shook his head and stared into the fire. The night before, he had taken his first drink in years. His first dozen or so drinks. Now he wanted more.

"Lookee here, boys" Jimmy Flanagan called, running up from the direction of the river. "I got us must be near half a pound of tobacco from one of them Johnny Rebs. All for a spot of sugar and a mite of coffee. He said he ain't had no sugar nor real coffee in over a year. And," Flanagan grinned, producing a small amber glass container, "he give me this."

"Golly," the other soldier at the fire exclaimed, "a Johnny give you that? Give me a pull."

Flanagan tossed it to him, a bewildered look sprouting on his face. "Yeah, said he had no more use for it 'cause he got hisself religion. Said they got churchlike deals every day over in the Reb camp. And guess who makes 'em do it? Stonewall Jackson hisself. What do you make of that, Marley? That man kills us by the thousands, but the Johnny told me he brings in grayback preachers from all over the South to preach at 'em. Said Stonewall leads some of the prayers hisself."

Flanagan caught the flask back from his buddy and sucked down a long drink. "Ahh, that's better. Sure cuts the chill. Yeah, he offered me his cards too, but I told him I already had two packs. Sounds like all sorts of funny things is going on over in them Reb camps. Want a pull, Marley?"

Marley looked at him, but his thoughts were elsewhere, thoughts more bitter than the cold. *"Stonewall" Jackson. I've been trying to get a shot at that—that man—for two years and now he's leading a revival. Boy, a touch would sure taste good against this cold.* He stared at the bottle. Marley could not know that Stonewall knelt in his tent at that moment, praying for Wayne Marley if he was still alive, that he would remain true to God and stand firm against sin.

Without a word, Marley turned away and pulled his blankets over him, tears glazing his eyes. *It is so hard,* he thought, *so bloody hard. I need some—help.* Then remembrance came to him of the man they called "Old Prayer Book." Major General Oliver Otis Howard, commander of the Union Eleventh Corps, ardent abolitionist and defender of the Christian faith. Marley knew that Howard was laboring, with less success, for what Stonewall, Lee, and others were accomplishing in the Southern army—religious revival.

God, Marley prayed, silent sobs racking him, *if You have not turned Your back on me, Sir, please help me find a way to come into this righteous man's company.*

Lylburn stared down the two roads. Over one would come the buckboard beginning his journey north to freedom. The other led back to his "home" on the Russell plantation.

With Russell maimed and drunken and his white overseer gone to fight the bluecoats, Lylburn's escape would be easy. He truly believed if the Quakers' vehicle did not arrive, he could walk all the way down the Shenandoah Valley to Maryland and his freedom. And now no one would return him. Nor was anyone able to come to get him.

Big Sam and several other slaves on the Russell place had already left—so had many of those on the McDowell plantation, and a few others around the county. But most stayed, and in the words of fellow slave Booker T. Washington: "To defend and protect the women and children who were left on the plantation when the white males went to war, the slaves would have laid down their lives."

For rare was a white man between the ages of sixteen and sixty with a whole body seen in Rockbridge County anymore.

Yet something gnawed at Lylburn. He knew hard times lay ahead in Virginia, regardless of the war's outcome. He had seen Maggie Junkin—Maggie Preston—walking the whole town on foot collecting clothes to send to the soldiers. And Maggie wore the same faded yellow dress, winter and summer, she always wore it. When times got tough for white folks, they could only be tougher for black folks.

And so Lylburn came to wonder if God might not desire him to stay and minister to the coloreds in the county. Despite the law against it, Dr. White at the Presbyterian Church had taught him to read and write the Book he so loved. He had thus learned to love it more. And with the white men killed, the fields grown over with weeds and trees, and even food maybe hard to come by someday, he could not escape the fact that many without his youth, his health, his wherewithal, might never make it to the "Promised Land" up North. Try as he may, he had to face the truth—he would be needed, in Virginia, win or lose the war.

It had begun when he lost Willy. Oh, how he had grieved. He had never known how much he loved the boy. And yet Willy's loss had borne life for Lylburn. Life to realize how much he loved the people around him, black and some white. He was warm, fed, healthy, could read and write, and he had met the Living God. He had come to realize that slavery was wrong and hurtful to master and slave, but maybe, if it was ended, he could build a life in Lexington that could be special. And maybe God could use him in a mighty way. For Lylburn Downing so wanted to be used by God in a mighty way.

Maybe, he thought, hanging his head, he was running away from something more than bondage. Maybe God would have him stay and face the destiny He had given him, difficult and trying as it might be. Maybe it was right for Big Sam and Ben McDowell and all the others to head down freedom's road. But maybe it was right for Lylburn to remain where God had placed him and be used to lead others to that true spiritual freedom that alone is everlasting.

How often he had suppressed feeling like Jonah, not wanting to preach to the Ninevites but to go his own way. How often— Suddenly Lylburn heard something in the distance. He ducked behind a thick oak and watched as a buckboard neared. *Lord, please help me, Sir, it's time for me to make my decision.*

Lylburn bent low and scurried behind some brush as the buckboard pulled up to the appointed spot and its two white riders waited.

Oh, it looked so appealing, so inviting! *Lord,* Lylburn prayed, *I need a word from You, Sir, or I'll have to climb onto that wagon and leave.* When one of the white men called out his name, Lylburn instinctively started to go forward. Then a small silent voice said, *Feed my lambs.* He stopped. Then, the same silent voice, *Feed my sheep.* Lylburn knew the words. He knew who had said them. Shaking, he knelt down in the thicket. Again, *Feed my sheep.* Now he knew he was to stay. But he did not believe he had the strength, the courage to do so. Then the Lord brought a deep sleep over him and when he awoke it was night and the buckboard had long since departed.

Stonewall stared thunderstruck at the man. A quarter of the army's once-magnificent horses dead of sickness or starvation in the three months since Christmas; half-naked soldiers grubbing for wild onions and sassafras roots to keep from starving themselves; pneumonia, scurvy, and diarrhea devastating the ranks, the Union's well-fed Army of the Potomac, under yet another new commander, growing stronger all the while.

And now this.

"You are saying, Captain Adams, that General A. P. Hill, whom you serve as signal officer, ordered you and other officers to take orders only from him," Stonewall said, his voice even higher than usual, "and to pass all information—whether going up or coming down the Second Corps chain of command—through him, General Lee's orders to immediately send intercepted Union signal messages directly either to himself or the corps commander notwithstanding?"

"Yes sir," Adams said.

Stonewall pursed his lips, the color rising on his high bronzed forehead. "And you are saying that General A. P. Hill particularly specified that no attention be paid to any orders coming from the corps commander?"

Adams swallowed, wishing he were anywhere but in this tent before this inquiry with his corps commander, Stonewall Jackson. "Yes sir," he said finally.

In a way, Stonewall appreciated Adams' startling revelations. Combined with Hill's persistent defiance of Stonewall's actions against "Little Powell" and Hill's unrepentant pursuit of countercharges against Stonewall, he felt the case had grown so overwhelming that even the magnanimous Robert E. Lee could not but agree with his request.

Hill's oversight at Fredericksburg, which left a six-hundred-yard gap between two of his brigades and allowed the Federals temporarily to breach Stonewall's line at that point, further strengthened Stonewall's confidence that he would soon have himself and the Army of Northern Virginia relieved of this troublesome officer.

"I want this man relieved of duty again," Stonewall said to Lee of the Confederacy's best division commander, "and this time I shall prepare the paperwork for a court-martial."

Maggie walked home in the rain from the empty store that now served as a sort of hospital for the twenty or so wounded soldiers who had wound up in Lexington but had no home nearby to take them in. The pitiable sanguinary sights and reeking odors had at first rent her nearly prostrate with dread and revulsion. As the months progressed, however, the experience became almost ordinary. This presented its own peculiar horror to her.

Severed arteries, lost limbs, every manifestation of disease and fever, capped by the lice ubiquitous among the Southern soldier—*all now so common,* she thought. *What fearful times we live in!*

She ate a simple supper of beans, onions, and cornbread with the family and played for a while with George and Herbie before tucking them into bed. Then she retired to her room to write a bit before the late-April sun died.

She thought of her father and sister. The remembrance of how many friends and kin had already died or been exiled from her cut a cold chill through her that prompted her to wrap a frayed old blanket around her. A knot grew in her stomach. The loss of loved ones. The loss of dear faces. *Such a sobering, cold feeling,* she thought. *Who shall next be taken from me?* Then she shamed herself, remembering the tide of refugees flooding town, some of them losing their homes to the devastation of war, some to the depredations of the Yankees, others just starved out from trampled fields or no one to harvest the crops.

"In fact," she wrote, "we hear much of the danger of the army itself being starved out of Virginia. Mr. P. has given the government every pound of bacon he can spare and put the family on the smallest of rations. Still, how can I complain? I heard of four new refugee families in town today. One is a mother with eight children, one of them twenty months old, and one four weeks; they had to fly from their home onto the open road, penniless and without father or husband."

Her eyes filled with tears as she wrote, "Such distresses do we hear of continually; it is a wonder we dare to feel anything like happiness. Oh! When will the war cease?"

She sat for a moment, not certain she could continue. Then the Spirit of the Lord, having work for her to do, encouraged her heart, turning it toward her old friend "General Jackson," from whom she had received a letter the day before. In it, he promised to try and get a letter from Maggie across the lines to her little sister Julia.

"His note had hardly anything else in it than earnest breathings after heavenly peace and rest," Maggie wrote. "He surely is a most devoted Christian. All his letters to Mr. P., and he writes right often, are full of religious experiences and utterances, and pleadings for prayer for himself and his country. He is quite absorbed now in trying to provide chaplains for his army."

She stopped for a moment, contemplating for the first time the heartfelt words Stonewall had written in his letter about Ellie. Then from out of the shrouded mists of the past the old times rose up anew and her heart swelled and she wondered, *What if—*

But just then Herbie screamed out in fright. *Oh,* she thought with dread, *more nightmares.* She laid aside her pen and rushed from the room to comfort the small child. He would need much consolation and soothing. He would need the arms and love of his mother.

Sandie Pendleton had not been able to resist distributing the copies of the *Times* of London and the *Illustrated London News* after a now-daily morning prayer meeting in Stonewall's mess tent. "19th Century Joshua," "The American Cromwell" they crowed. Then Stonewall had received from Dabney, who had recovered from his physical ills and lately preached in Second Corps camps, a letter complimenting him on an evident increase in his own personal "spirituality and Christian activity."

President Davis's March 27 "day of humiliation, prayer, and fasting" had generated a more vigorous response from Stonewall's divisions than the Virginian had ever seen. Beginning with the old Stonewall Brigade, many of his units had built their own log chapels. Soldiers packed them and encircled them on Sundays. Many units now held their own daily prayer meetings and Bible classes. Even the attendance of Bull Paxton, Stonewall's respectably irreligious gentleman planter friend from Lexington and new Stonewall Brigade commander, had grown regular at the morning prayer meetings in Stonewall's mess.

The enormity of success Stonewall experienced on his two-front war of the world and the spiritual realm drove him to his knees in extended prayer in his room at the William Yerby farm west of Fredericksburg one night at the end of March. He struggled afresh with his old nemesis. At times during the night, he felt that Jacob's wrestling with the angel of heaven could scarcely have been more desperate. His thoughts turned toward the Junkins, and especially Ellie. At one point, slumber poured over him, his head fell forward into his arms, and he slept. And in his dreams she came to him again, as she used to do, on a bright peaceful Lexington Sunday long ago when all was as well as could be on troubled earth. He saw her shining face, felt her warm touch, heard her angelic voice.

"Major Jackson, I love you and I'm so very proud of you. I know you'll be faithful to please Him by working on the two *A*'s."

"I know, I know," Jackson nodded, exhaling. "Ambition and anger."

"The one does prompt the other," she said gently, turning him to her. "And you are so much better than the both of them."

Jackson's throat tightened.

"You are so many things to me, I don't know where to begin," he said finally.

Stonewall stirred awake. The brilliant noonday autumnal sun of Lexington was now the gloomy apricot of his night lamp. The realization came to him urgently. After all, most of the other generals' wives were already in camp with them. *I must be with my wife. And I need to see my daughter.*

A few nights later, a letter arrived from Anna. Tiny Julia, just four months old, had a serious case of the chicken pox. They could not come. Instead, they desperately needed his prayers. Stonewall's blood turned to ice. *Not again, Lord. Please, Sir.* He fell to his knees in his room. *I would ask in Your sufferance toward your miserable infirmed servant that You would spare this tiny child, that she might be a declaration to the world of Your mercy and goodness.* His throat tight, he whispered, "I have not even seen her, Sir."

In the next days, he lavished his affections toward Janie Corbin, the precocious, and flawlessly beautiful, five-year-old daughter of a neighboring family. She had golden strawberry tresses that tumbled into her eyes, which shone wistful and wise beyond her years. Though every officer in the surrounding area became solicitous of the sweet charismatic young darling's affections, she and Stonewall developed a mystical bond. They shared a unique blend of solemnness and, in safe surroundings with trustworthy friends, merry abandon.

Hordes of admirers besieged Stonewall, many of them young and female. He never once exhibited irritation through the hundreds and hundreds of autographs he signed, though he could never understand why anyone could covet his scrawled signature.

One day, Douglas and Sandie watched as two comely lasses in their late teens badgered him for locks of his hair. Expecting Stonewall to courteously greet the young women, then find a quick escape, the two young staff officers thought their eyes and ears were playing tricks on them when Stonewall replied with a glint in his eye to one of the girls, a tall one clinging to his arm, "Well, you may have a little if you promise not to take any gray hairs."

"Oh, General Jackson," the gorgeous admirer cooed, her Southern drawl rich as molasses, "you are a young man, you have no gray hairs."

Stonewall blushed, then blurted, "Why, don't you know the soldiers call me Old Jack?"

The girls got their wish, snipping locks from his hair, which had grown quite long and down onto the bright canary collar of the uniform Stuart had given him.

When he had had enough, Stonewall would shut the door to his office, order his favorite guard (one from the Irish Battalion of the Stonewall Brigade) posted, and for hours play with Janie, the slender little girl with the face of an angel. *She looks as Ellie must have looked as a child,* Stonewall thought. He would regale her with stories. She would cut legions of stalwart Stonewall Brigade veterans out of paper for him. He would hold her to himself as though never to let her go, as though he would never have another little girl to hold.

One day Ellie and Maggie's brother William, a Presbyterian minister and captain in the Army of Northern Virginia, surprised Stonewall with a visit. They walked and talked for an hour about old times, about the letter William's brother John, a surgeon in the Union army, had gotten through the lines at Fredericksburg to Stonewall for Maggie, about old Dr. Junkin's growing fame in the North as a preacher and speaker at political rallies.

Finally, Stonewall stopped under a cherry tree whose fragrant blossoms seemed ready at any moment to burst forth into color and new life. His right arm shooting into the air, he turned toward William and told him what he would not tell any man in his own corps.

"You cannot imagine how I long to be out of the field and home once more," he said, the earnest blue eyes more plaintive than William had ever witnessed them. "I have not seen my wife in over a year. And I have never seen my child."

The two men returned to Stonewall's tent in silence. There, Sandie entered and alerted Stonewall that a firing squad for two deserters was taking the field. "This is the last opportunity, sir, for, uh, a revocation of the order."

Stonewall stared at him, the cobalt eyes growing steely. "Widowed women and orphaned children are being turned out of their homes into the cold for want of more men to defend our country, Colonel. Let this sentence serve both as the just recompense for cowardly selfishness and as an example for others whose lower natures might be deterred from pursuing a like detestable course."

Sandie had no sooner left the tent where Stonewall and William sat than a tall thin man of forty-five wearing a cleric's collar shoved his way past the guard and into the tent.

"General Jackson, sir," the beet-faced minister blurted with nary a by-your-leave, thrusting a long bony finger of accusation at Stonewall, "these men you are taking pause from your revival to kill have no conception of the bonds of military discipline. They are young, they are scared, and they have their entire lives roamed the land like nomadic Indians."

The man stalked across the tent toward Stonewall, the finger remaining thrust forward like a charging bayonet. "I am their chaplain, sir. Do you know you are sending these men's souls to hell?"

Stonewall rose to his feet, the finger no more than three inches from his face. William winced, fearful the raging chaplain would poke Stonewall's eye out with it.

But the general shocked both men by grabbing the chaplain by the shoulders, turning him around, dragging him across the tent, then hurling him headfirst out the tent flap that Douglas, Jim, and the Irish guard had pulled open.

Outside, Catholic priest Paul O'Dwyer stopped in his tracks as the unfortunate chaplain landed face first at his feet in a cloud of dust.

Oh me, the Irishman fretted, *if this is how the man deals with Protestants . . .*

O'Dwyer genuflected, then strode past the confused throng into the tent like Jesus passing through a band of angry Pharisees and Sadducees.

"Father O'Dwyer?" Stonewall asked. "Yes sir, I was expecting you. This is my brother-in-law, Captain William Junkin, Father."

William forced a smile, his mind asking him, *Is this a typical day at Stonewall Jackson's headquarters?*

O'Dwyer proceeded quickly to business.

"General Jackson, sir, I understand that not a tent will be taken once the Second Corps is again on the move." His voice trembling, O'Dwyer continued. "Knowing your religious persuasion, sir, and respectful of it, I would ask your indulgence that I might have one tent for the taking of confession from the few soldiers in this army who adhere to the Church. The Church of Rome, that is, sir."

Hail Marys cascaded toward heaven as recollections of past ill treatment from Southern Protestants filled O'Dwyer's head. *And of this man I must ask this thing, one of the staunchest Calvinists on the continent.*

I am glad it is not I who must refuse this honorable man, William thought to himself as Stonewall stared at O'Dwyer.

"Very well, Father," Stonewall replied in his high squeaky voice, "you shall have the one tent in the Second Corps for the purpose of doing the Lord's work as you see your way to do it."

O'Dwyer stifled a frown. "Thank you, General, for at least hearing me out. I knew it would not—" The Irishman's ruddy face lit up. "Did you—did you say yes, General, sir?"

William's face showed no less surprise than O'Dwyer's.

"I see through a glass darkly, Father," Stonewall said, "and though I may see through a different color of glass than you, I fear to tread upon any work that could conceivably be of the Lord."

O'Dwyer's eyes, even bluer than Stonewall's, misted over. "Is there any matter for which I may be praying for the general, sir?" he asked.

"We do not approach the number of preachers we need, Father," Stonewall said. "I want preachers, of all denominations. I would like no questions asked in the army as to what denomination a chaplain belongs, but let the question be, does he preach the gospel? For that you may pray, if you would not be offended, sir."

"Bless you, General," O'Dwyer said. As he left, he turned back. "General, I must say that this so-called 'revival' in the Army of Northern Virginia that seems to be sweeping even those fallen away from our Catholic Church—well, General, from what I can discern, the credit due you personally in this historic movement of repentance shall far outlast your many and deserved military laurels, sir."

"It has been—an experience, Thomas," William laughed as he left a few moments later.

Late that afternoon, as Stonewall was leaving to visit little Janie Corbin, whom he had not seen for several days, Douglas stopped him with the news that she had died of scarlet fever.

It rained all the next day, as often it does in central Virginia in April. Over and over again Janie's sweet visage appeared to Stonewall. The news that A. P. Hill had kicked up more dust against Stonewall with General Lee did not even faze him. The rain stopped after dark, as Stonewall found a campfire where, out of character, Jeb Stuart sat alone.

A chill spiced the evening and Stonewall tossed more kindling on the fire, the better light revealing that Stuart held a little cameo of his own daughter.

Stonewall sat across from his friend. Soon he fell lost into thought of Janie . . . and Ellie's stillborn baby . . . and little Mary Graham

Jackson . . . and a tiny infant down in North Carolina whom he had never seen and who had fallen victim to a dangerous case of chicken pox. *Oh Lord,* he thought, his heart clutching, *oh Lord.*

Sometime later Lee walked up, greeted the two men, and poured himself a cup of coffee. The old warrior noted the sullen mood of his younger lieutenants, Stuart staring at little Flora's cameo and Stonewall gazing into the fire. And he remembered his own deep losses in recent months, which now included his treasured baby grandson.

"Daughters are God's most precious creation," Lee announced.

Stonewall's eyes, shaded by the new kepi, pulled low down his face like the old one, darted at Lee, then back at the fire. He kept his own counsel. Stuart turned to Lee and watched him, feeling as though, without knowing it, the older man were throwing him an emotional lifeline.

Then Stuart broke into a smile, as tears filled his wide honest eyes. He nodded his agreement as he spoke. "When I see the sunbeams in spring, it's like her yellow hair. And when I see the pretty blue cornflowers—well, it's her eyes."

Lee cleared his throat. His big shoulders and barrel-chested upper body shifted around on the cracker box upon which he sat. He seemed struggling to maintain his composure. Then he straightened his back and the rich deep voice sounded clear and sure.

"I believe in the Resurrection. And I believe we shall one day stand together again with them."

Stuart smiled at him, his eyes still full, nodding. Stonewall stared into the fire, his jaw set and his eyes unseen, inscrutable.

Even as Major General Oliver Howard's benediction closed his Eleventh Corps chapel service and buoyed the resurging spirits of Marley, and many other homesick Federal soldiers, Marley found reason anew to seek the utter destruction of Stonewall Jackson.

Over the past few months, Howard's earnest dark face had time and again helped restore Marley's flagging soul. Beginning with their first "chance" meeting when Marley delivered a scouting report to Howard's staff and accepted an invitation to remain for supper and a prayer service, the two had developed an increasing esprit de corps. They shared geographic heritage, family friends, abolitionist sentiments, and the faith to which Howard had clung but Marley had virtually jettisoned. And they were born the same day in 1830, just thirty miles apart.

The mere incredulity of their meeting and common backgrounds and perspectives helped resurrect Marley's once vibrant faith.

Now he watched as Howard came toward him. The general's manicured beard hung in a stately fashion from the long, curiously somber face that belied Old Prayer Book's tranquil inner spirit. So did his right coat sleeve hang down. He had left his right arm at Bull Run. The day fame bestowed upon Tom Jackson the sobriquet "Stonewall," his counterattacking Confederates had routed Howard's division and nearly killed the pious Union commander.

As Howard grew familiar with Marley's talents, and his struggling faith, he had the horseman transferred to his own staff as a scout *aide-de-camp*. Under Howard's encouragement and godly example, Marley resumed reading his dusty Bible and grew into one of the most consistent attenders of religious functions in the entire corps. He found that even his performance as a scout improved with his rehabilitated attitude and sense of purpose. For once again he did very much believe in what he was doing. He remembered that the uniform he wore represented ideals and beliefs so different from those he fought that he could scarcely understand how both sides could be Americans.

Howard's words to Marley as they walked alone along the Rappahannock a few minutes later stirred his heart. "You have been a great encouragement to me, Wayne," the general said, placing his one strong hand on Marley's shoulder. "As you know, the general spiritual climate among the current field leadership, shall we say, leaves much for us to direct our prayer efforts toward."

That is understating it, Marley thought, remembering how one devout officer, a Baptist minister in New Jersey before the war, had commented that morning on the dramatic contrast between "The Christian General," as many referred to Howard, and the "combination barroom and brothel that constituted new Army of the Potomac commander Joseph Hooker's headquarters."

Marley knew most of the ambitious Hooker's fellow officers did not like the commander, nor respect his varied pleasures in women. Marley had overheard one refer to him as "little better than a West Point adventurer."

"I would beseech your continued prayers for me, Wayne," Howard said, "that I might accomplish my duty with honor and efficiency, while bringing the salty seasoning of our Lord's gospel to all levels of our ranks." Howard shook his head. "And the Germans—my, I believe the majority of my corps is German or of German descent. I believe the Lord has brought these men to America and to us, some of them not even speaking our language, that we might be His instruments in reaching them with His saving gospel. Such an opportunity we have, my friend. And of course . . ."

Howard's voice drifted off as he looked out across the river to the South. "To reach those in spiritual bondage while seeking to liberate those in physical bondage." The general's honest almond eyes shined as he looked back to Marley. "A high privilege our Lord has given to us, Wayne, if we shall but stand fast in the gap before the company of enemies that confronts us from both within and without our own camp."

At that moment, the sounds of drunken revelry coming from the direction of Hooker's mess erupted anew. Neither Howard nor Marley knew the noise emanated from Fightin' Joe Hooker's celebration of his complex, just-completed, and still-secret plan designed to do what his parade of predecessors had not—surround and destroy the Army of Northern Virginia, which he now outnumbered by more than two-to-one.

CHAPTER 53

JOY FILLED STONEWALL'S HEART AS ANNA WALKED INTO HIS room, carrying Julia. Between them lay a table. Somehow, the five-month-old baby broke from her mother's arms and began to crawl across the room toward Stonewall, moving under the table, then reaching his feet. He stared dumbfounded as she began to crawl up his leg, pulling herself all the way up to his face, where she gave him a big kiss right on the cheek. His face beamed as he stared into her cherubic loveliness.

But then it was not Julia's countenance into which he was staring, it was Sandie's, with a dispatch from Lee. Stonewall lay prostrate in his bed as the morning sun flooded in through the open window. Sleep still in his eyes, he could not listen to Sandie, so crushing was his disappointment. *I need my family,* he thought, near tears.

After disposing of only his most pressing business, he rode to a nearby wooden chapel and went inside to pray for the health of mother and child, and that they would soon come to him.

An hour later he emerged, his heavy heart lightened. He drank in the spring air and praised God for his bountiful blessings. Before he could mount, Douglas came pounding up. "General, sir," the younger man shouted, "your wife, she's coming, sir, her and your little girl. They'll be at Guiney's Station this evening!"

Stonewall said nothing, but looked toward heaven, where was his true communion and fellowship. *"Thou hast put gladness in my heart, more than in the time that their corn and their wine increased."*

That night he stood at the stagecoach depot in Guiney's Station, rain pouring off his new hat and the rubber cape he wore. He ignored the chill that shivered through him. Then the stage from Richmond was pulling up and passengers stepping from it. *Where are they?* he wondered when no one else appeared. *But—but Sir, they were supposed to be on this stage.* His shoulders sagged and he felt a hard cold surge of air sweep down his throat into his lungs, hurting him. He turned slowly away, slogging through the swirling muddy road. *You know what is best, Sir.*

"Thomas?"

He turned back and saw Anna standing there, with the baby. She had to walk to him, for he could not move. And then his wife's sweet happy face was before his and he was kissing her and holding her hard before he even took note of the baby in her arms but then he was holding the baby and it had been so long that he had waited for his baby, forever really, and he was holding the little baby, who laughed and gurgled at him and he saw himself and his beloved in the tiny angelic features and finally he knew without knowing he knew that here now were his beloved and the fruit of his beloved's loins, and the ancient words of Jesus' mother Mary filled his heart: *"My soul doth magnify the Lord, and my spirit hath rejoiced in God my Saviour."*

The men of the Second Corps could have welcomed the Queen of England no more resplendently. As Stonewall escorted Anna the next afternoon to the well-appointed Yerby home, a regimental band (several bands actually, come together to celebrate the arrival of Old Jack's lady) burst into the lilting Southern-Celtic strains of "Bonnie Blue Flag." Hundreds of soldiers raised their hats and shook the earth with the chorus:

> *We are a band of brothers, and native to the soil,*
> *Fighting for the property we gained by honest toil;*
> *And when our rights were threatened, the cry rose near and far,*
> *Hurrah for the Bonnie Blue Flag that bears a single star!*

A few moments later, the Jacksons sat down to a luncheon spread with staff and other corps officers. Stuart, his spurs and saber clanging, directed the party's attention to the gallant rooster shape imprinted in the large cake of butter that adorned the center of the table.

"A fighting cock, that is, dear friends," Stuart regaled them, chomping and munching his food. "Symbolizing the sporting spirit of one of Stonewall's favorite western Virginia recreations."

Stonewall blushed crimson, his mouth dropping open to reveal a large half-eaten chunk of stale black bread.

"And," Stuart continued, discouraging the table's raucous laughter, "most importantly, a perfect rendering of the Jackson family coat of arms."

Even Stonewall had to laugh at that one, though his hips still ached from where a slumbering Stuart had dug his spurs into him after falling exhausted into bed with him in his tent a few nights before following an all-day scouting sortie.

Anna and little Julia filled Stonewall's next days. *Is it possible these days are even more special than that winter in Winchester?* the joyous wife wondered to herself. She sensed a more complete spiritual devotion in her husband, and his conversation, than she ever had. *He seems to be giving utterance to those religious meditations in which he so delights,* she thought. She watched him for minutes on end as he played with little Julia. *Oh, Lord,* she thought, *never has he appeared in better health, never have I seen him look so handsome and noble.*

She marveled at the sweep of his mind and interests. "How can a nation that defamed the Sabbath by choosing to deliver the mails that day expect the blessing of God on its pursuits?" he asked her. "Please continue to pray earnestly and importunately for our efforts in bringing physical relief to the men through improved clothing, supplies, and equipment. And pray the more for the efforts to bring spiritual relief to them through more chaplains. I believe each denomination should provide a supply of its best clerics in proportion to its size."

And, quietly one evening: "How well I have learned the scriptural precept that 'Vain is the hope we place in man.' For every time I think I have found a man I need and am about to rest satisfied, something turns out to be lacking." He sighed. "I suppose it is to teach me to put my trust only in God."

"Your husband," Hotchkiss told Anna one afternoon after pulling her aside, "is the most humble and devoted Christian I ever saw."

Dozens of Stonewall's staff and other Second Corps officers gathered for what was shaping up to be the royal coronation of the season—tiny Julia's baptism.

One of the greatest preachers in the Confederacy, Rev. Tucker Lacy, who had fought the year before in the Army of the Valley and now served as de facto Second Corps chaplain coordinator, would preside.

At the appointed hour, all had convened except Anna. *Some things never change,* Stonewall thought with mixed irritation and affection, harkening back to the early morning family Bible studies where he sometimes locked his wife out of the room when she failed to arrive at his decreed time.

He marched out of the Yerby parlor, scooped up Julia, and brought her to Lacy.

"Press on, sir," Stonewall said, his eyes beaming with pride at the little girl.

The little girl. He spent hours at a time with her, mostly in late afternoon and evening. (He would not shirk his duty during the day even for his wife and child.) In her were all the other little girls who had ever been taken from him—Janie, little Mary, Ellie's baby, and, yes, his sister Elizabeth. When he would think of them, he would hold Julia to himself as snugly as he felt he could without injuring her. *Oh someday, my little princess, they will never ever take you away from me again.*

He would carry her in his arms, push her in the strolling cart, and walk with her perched atop his hard strong shoulders. Mainly, he would just be *with* her. Little Julia amazed everyone with her buoyant comfort among the staff and officers. Stonewall longed to take her through the entire corps, but the omnipresent smallpox, typhoid, and other scourges disallowed that.

"He sure loves that little girl," Douglas said to Anna early one evening as they watched Stonewall play with Julia on a blanket under a blooming peach tree.

"Yes," she replied with a smile, her attention seeming to Douglas to be somewhere else, "he has for a long time."

The sound of musket fire jolted her.

"What is that?" she asked.

Douglas canted his head, his forehead furrowing. "Well, ma'am, those are deserters, men who not only fled their posts, but went over to the enemy. The general, he shows no leniency in such cases."

Stonewall rose early the morning of April 29. Anna and Julia did not stir. He raised the window and looked out to where the sun had just crested the hills to the east. It shone brilliant and golden over the spring-splashed Rappahannock River valley. He thought for a moment of his own valley, the Shenandoah, and how he should like to return there soon and walk the quiet streets to the VMI, return home for lunch with Anna and play with Julia, then ride up to his little farm and work among the onions, leaks, and corn. He had to admit his physical health had never been better than it had the past many months of war. *But it is not right to be continually away from one's loved ones while wreaking death and destruction,* he thought.

He turned toward his family. He walked to where Anna lay. *So loving, so loyal, everything a wife should be,* he thought. *How blessed I am.* Then he turned to Julia, asleep in a cradle. On bended knee, he brought his face within inches of her and marveled at God's handiwork. The miniature but perfectly crafted ears, the button nose, the tiny fingers and toes. He stared at her for quite a long time, treasuring up in his heart even the tiniest freckle he spotted on her left hand. He considered himself of all men, most blessed.

His head swung around at the sound of rapping on the door. It was Kyd Douglas.

"General Early's adjutant is downstairs, sir, with an urgent message," the young man said.

Stonewall knew what that meant. Hooker was crossing the Rappahannock on the Second Corps' left, near where Stonewall had stood at the battle of Fredericksburg.

A few minutes later, after receiving the report downstairs that Stuart had spotted Hooker coming across the river, and that "as usual, the Yankees are not cleaning up after themselves," he spoke to Anna as he buckled on his sword.

"I've got to go forward immediately and you must prepare to leave at a moment's notice," he told her. "I'll get back to you if I can. If not, I'll send your brother to take you to the train at Guiney's."

Joseph Morrison had developed into one of Stonewall's most dependable aides.

Stonewall looked at her, then at the baby, still asleep. He bent over and kissed Julia softly on the cheek.

"I'll walk down with you," Anna said before he could say anything.

When they got outside, Douglas had Stonewall's splendid new charger Superior ready for him. Stonewall had specified that he ride Superior, a gift to him from a family near Fredericksburg, rather than Little Sorrel. He wanted Anna to see him once on the towering bay.

He held his wife close to him and looked deep into her gentle brown eyes. "Take care of our baby," he said, his voice raspy, "and remember that I love you very much. I shall return as soon as I am able." Then, before his emotions could get the better of him, he kissed Anna long and with much love before stepping away, swinging up into the saddle, raising his cap to her, and bowing.

Tears of pride filled her eyes as he wheeled Superior around, gave a Rebel yell, and galloped away, Douglas and Sandie on his flanks. The horse ran like Pegasus and Stonewall's hat flew off, but he did not stop.

He is flying like the wind, she thought to herself, loving him more than ever. *Who ever said Stonewall Jackson could not ride a horse as well as any man in the Shenandoah Valley?*

Then the crashing of cannon fire shook the ground upon which she stood as well as the house behind her that for nine days had been her Eden on earth.

"I have the rebellion in my breeches pocket," Fightin' Joe Hooker announced to the dozens of officers surrounding him amidst a haze of cigar smoke as his Union juggernaut of 134,000 men, the largest and most powerful military force ever arrayed on the North American continent, prepared to march. "And God Almighty himself cannot take it away from me."

CHAPTER 54

THEN DID MARGARET JUNKIN PRESTON, FORMERLY OF PENN-
sylvania, in all the mixed swirling sorrow and joy that was her
redeemed fallen humanity, begin to write her greatest work. *Beechenbrook* would mark her North and South as one of America's finest
living poets, man or woman. It would bring her to the attention of
the great Longfellow, who himself would one day ask permission to
include three of her pieces in one of his own books. And it would
emblazon her name into history's flaming pages as "The Poetess of
the Confederacy."

"To every Southern woman who has been widowed by the War, I
dedicate this rhyme as a faint memorial of sufferings, of which there
can be no forgetfulness," she wrote, the pain and fear and anguish of
two years metamorphosing into power as they flowed from her pen
onto the waiting inside cover of a scuffed old yellow book.

Then, unable to see her own writing because of her aching ruined
eyes, and breathless at the epic torrent unleashed to her by God, she
shouted stepdaughter Elizabeth to her room, thrust pen and book at
her, and spoke page after page to her, as the girl lay on the rug next
to the fireplace and wrote, the dying embers nearby her only illumination. Maggie spoke as fast as she could, as she never had, pouring
forth sentences, rhymes, and stanzas she did not know, until the
incredulous girl's wrist, arm, and shoulder throbbed with pain. Maggie laughed and cried and praised Him for His goodness and provision, and prayed that the words would not cease of how the brave
farmer, husband, father, and Southern everyman had put down plow,
left family, and gone forth to defend his country and his honor.

> *And if never round this altar*
> *We should kneel as heretofore,—*

If these arms in benediction
Fold my precious ones no more,—

Thou, who in her direst anguish,
Sooth'dst thy mother's lonely lot,
In thy still unchanged compassion,
Son of Man! forsake them not!

Chancellorsville was not a town nor even a village. A half-century old mansion with white columns, it housed the family of Virginia farmer Melzi Chancellor and served as an inn to travelers. At the edge of a large area of wild forest and tangled scrub, it also sat astride a key central Virginia road junction eleven miles west of Fredericksburg and just over fifty miles north of Richmond.

By the final day of April 1863, Chancellorsville's strategic importance had become paramount to the combatants of the War between the States, entering its third year. Army of the Potomac commander Fightin' Joe Hooker knew which side his bread was buttered on—the Richmond side. President Lincoln had made that clearer to him than the peels of the Liberty Bell that rang in Philadelphia, even journeying in person to visit Hooker's headquarters in the field. Lincoln wanted the war ended, and taking Confederate capital Richmond, a package that doubtless would include the destruction of the Army of Northern Virginia, was how he wanted it done.

But two formidable obstacles stood in Fightin' Joe's way: Lee and Stonewall still held the high ground opposite Fredericksburg, which blocked Hooker's best route of march to Richmond; and the Confederates had fortified the few available crossings of the Rappahannock in the Fredericksburg area.

The handsome Hooker, whose cocksure manner and organizational skills made him the most popular commander among the soldiers of the Army of the Potomac since McClellan, devised a brilliant scheme to force Lee into a fight the Virginian would not want.

Hotchkiss, weary and dust-caked from riding and mapmaking, presented the chilling picture to Stonewall and Lee that evening as they sat atop hardtack boxes. A sea of Union horse (twelve thousand) under Stonewall's West Point roommate George Stoneman had rumbled south toward Richmond, behind Lee, wreaking havoc on the defenseless countryside and attempting to cut the main Confederate army's supply, communications, and retreat lines. Meanwhile, a large force (fifty thousand) of Federal troops under General John Sedgwick stood a few miles to the east at Fredericksburg. Other Union divisions were moving on both the United States and Banks Fords of the Rappahannock just north of Chancellorsville. The Yankees had several observation balloons up over the river, as well as, reportedly, an electric telegraph station transmitting messages among the various corps commanders.

And finally, Hooker's main force (over seventy thousand) had stormed across the Rappahannock upriver from Lee and moved southeast to Chancellorsville.

"Our line is flanked to the west, sir," Hotchkiss said, his voice sounding like an open grave. "And if Sedgwick succeeds in crossing the Rappahannock in force at Fredericksburg, we shall be flanked on the east."

Lee eyed Hotchkiss, then spoke. "Our erstwhile mapmaker's countenance betrays strong emotions he wishes to share."

Rarely did Jed Hotchkiss render editorial opinion to his commanders, but what he had heard from scouts and what he had himself seen in the past twelve hours compelled him to speak, even as he blushed at Lee's unexpected perceptiveness.

"Sirs, I do question whether it is possible for our brave men to attain victory in the present circumstances," Hotchkiss said. "The few officers with whom I have spoken who have sufficient grasp of the tactical and strategic situation, brave and tried men all, have rendered to me their sober opinions that we would be wise to effect an escape further south to a position of our own choosing."

Both Stonewall and Lee saw their predicament. If they came out and fought, they sacrificed an impregnable defensive position to face overwhelming numbers, while outflanked. If they retreated, they must pass in front of Hooker's main wing, which itself outnumbered the entire Confederate force by nearly twenty thousand men and would surely win the day in open field battle.

Without speaking a word, the two Confederate commanders both recognized the painful truth and knew the other did as well. At length, Lee sighed and made the call: he would again defy the classic maxims of military theory and split his force in the face of a larger foe. Jubal Early and ten thousand men would stay on the river at Fredericksburg to face Sedgwick. Stonewall would march the remainder of the command out to "make arrangements to repulse the enemy."

Most commanders would have interpreted such an order as an indication to strengthen the Confederate earthworks already begun to the east of Chancellorsville. Yet to Stonewall Jackson it meant one thing: attack the rampaging Hooker in the Wilderness.

The Confederate move stunned Hooker, whose lieutenants had to that point executed his multifaceted strategy brilliantly, and who had surprised and unsettled the Army of Northern Virginia's high command. But when the lean, filthy, lice-ridden veterans of Robert E. Lee and Stonewall Jackson, whose towering reputations had attained near-mythic status even in the Union army, smashed into Fightin' Joe's forces a mile and a half east of Chancellorsville in the Wilderness's near-impenetrable undergrowth, the Federal commander's blood ran cold. He remembered the fate of all his successors, who likewise each had more men, more guns, and better equipment than the Rebels. Alcohol, women, and all the power the world could offer could not buoy Hooker. Over the fury of several of his subordinates, he ordered his main force, driven back on its heels by Stonewall, into a defensive posture to slug it out with Lee in the miserable tangled woods.

Riding far forward with Stuart late the afternoon of May 1 to look for vulnerable points in Hooker's positions, Stonewall found a spot for a battery on the extreme left, or west, of the Confederate line at Catherine's Furnace, a civilian ore smelter converted to the production of Southern munitions.

Pointing to a compact timbered knoll, Stonewall said to Stuart, "Place the cannons there, and I believe we can enfilade the Union line."

Stuart supervised the placement, but the brush proved so thick that only one cannon could be set up. As soon as it opened fire, half a dozen unseen Union guns erupted from close range.

A volcano of shot and shell tore through Confederate horses and men alike. Stuart sat astride his charger Chancellor in a cluster of four men. He felt the air grow hot and wild as one blast killed everyone in the group except him, including his handsome young assistant adjutant general, Channing Price.

Ignoring the scalding fragments exploding all around him, Stuart lifted Price's lifeless ravaged body up like a mother finding her treasured baby fallen out of its crib, and laid it across the pommel of Chancellor's saddle.

"General Jackson, we must move from here," Stuart said as he remounted, tears filling his eyes and an uncharacteristic sharpness tinging his voice. He did not even bother to draw his pistols as dirt, branch fragments, bark, and human and animal flesh splattered the Virginians.

Stonewall scowled as more blasts from the Union batteries filled the air with burning metal and the screams of wounded and dying men. "All right, but we're coming back later for that gun," he said, canting his head toward the lone Confederate cannon, whose crew had been blown to pieces.

Stonewall Jackson was not about to lose his first field piece to the Yankees.

That night, the thumps and thwacks of axes resounded for miles around Chancellorsville as Union and Confederate soldiers strengthened their positions. Stonewall again met with Lee over the campfire, this time in a stand of pines near the Plank-Catherine crossroads. They sat atop hardtack boxes and pored over Hotchkiss's latest map rendering. Though Stonewall had roughed up Hooker's main force, an unsavory prospect faced the two Confederate chiefs: attack—at once—a much larger foe, before it came crashing down upon them.

"Jubal Early has done yeoman work against those people today at Fredericksburg," Lee said, "but with several times his number, they must surely fall upon him on the morrow, driving him into our back, with Hooker growing ever stronger and likely to attack our front."

Lee considered the map, deep furrows slicing his forehead. "I fear a frontal assault in either direction would be fruitless," he said in his soft way. "How can we get at these people?"

He stared into the fire, then at Stonewall, whose eyes fixed on the map. The thought struck the white-haired commander of how different this corps commander was from his other, Longstreet, whose jealousy for Stonewall had become as evident as his dislike of taking orders from Lee. *Such a fine, candid, and fresh expression Jackson has,* Lee thought, *so charming to see and so attractive to the beholder. How often his resolute pious example has strengthened my own as it flagged. And how he has lit the fires of revival and reformation in this suffering army.*

Stonewall and Lee sat in silence, neither knowing what next to say. Both commenced, independent of the other, to pray to God for wisdom.

Galloping hoofbeats and the jangling of steel broke the quiet as Stuart galloped right up to the Confederate chieftains' secluded campsite. His booted feet hit the soft ground with barely a thump before Chancellor had even halted.

"Gentlemen," Stuart said, the merry eyes twinkling from their keep behind hat and beard, "General Hooker's right flank is unprotected." Lee and Stonewall stared at him, wondering if they had heard right. "It is, gentlemen, if you will, hanging in the air."

The identical thought striking both Lee's and Stonewall's minds was: Jeb Stuart has continued to run circles around the Yankees through this entire campaign, as he has the entire war, and he must surely be the greatest cavalry commander on the continent.

Now the plan crystallized for both Lee and Stonewall. The latter spoke, even as his commander's yellow-gauntleted finger traced a route on Hotchkiss's map around the Union right. "General Lee, sir," he said, "the Yankee cavalry, in its plundering ride toward Richmond, has succeeded in stealing more of our crops and frightening more of our women and children, but General Stuart here has indicated they have done little more—other than leave him and his men free to roam and scout the back roads of the Wilderness at will."

Stonewall looked Lee straight in the eye. "Therefore, sir, I would propose to march my entire corps, beginning at 4:00 A.M., west past Catherine Furnace and then north, around Hooker's flank, and get at him from behind."

No other lieutenant on the globe would have proposed such audacity. And no other commander would have countenanced it.

"What will you leave me, General?" Lee asked.

Stuart, rarely out of the saddle throughout eighteen straight hours, raced off to locate a suitable road for Stonewall and his men to follow.

"I have no less confidence that General Jackson can flank Oliver Howard and rout him than I have that the dogwoods will bloom in Virginia in springtime," Lee had said, "but we must find a route through that jungle by which he can get there."

"You may have the Confederacy's only foot cavalry, Old Jack," Stuart had said, "but not even you can fly your men to their destination."

A few hours later, Presbyterian pastor Lacy, whose credentials included having preceded Dr. White in the Lexington pulpit, joined a frigid Stonewall, shaking atop a cracker box and trying to warm himself by the fire.

"I once had a church in the Wilderness, and I believe a road exists out there on the precise route you wish to take," Lacy told Stonewall.

"And the man who owns Catherine Furnace is a friend. He can tell you for sure, and his son would make an excellent guide."

Stonewall did not hesitate. "Pastor, sir, would you please take Jed Hotchkiss and go find this road?"

As Lacy rose, a loud clang jarred both men. They turned to see that Stonewall's sword, positioned securely against the stump of an ancient oak, had crashed to the ground, without apparent cause.

A shiver ran through both men. Only the night before, Lacy had regaled Stonewall's staff with the tale of Charles I of England, whose standard had blown over at the beginning of the English Civil War two centuries before, and how he had subsequently lost his head on the block after Oliver Cromwell's hosts had defeated him.

Sandie heard Stonewall cough and sneeze. "Sir," the younger man said, "you are catching a cold. Please accept my coat."

Stonewall waved him off.

"At least take my cape then, please, General Jackson," Sandie insisted.

Stonewall looked up at the clean honest face. *His dear parents should be very proud of him,* the general thought. He wrapped the proffered cape around him, coughing again, a deep racking cough this time.

I must go to write Anna, he thought. *She will be lonely, and if I hasten, a letter might be gotten to her father's home in North Carolina and be awaiting her arrival.* He looked around and saw a dying campfire not far away, the men around it having left on patrol.

"I'd like a few moments alone," he told Sandie.

Stonewall got up and buckled on his fallen sword, then walked to the other fire, lugging along the bag containing his papers and writing materials. He pulled Sandie's cape closer to him and chunked a cluster of kindling on the ebbing embers. As he sat down on a fallen log, the contents of his leather bag spilled onto the ground. *Oh,* he thought with a start as he gathered the bag's contents, *I had forgotten, a letter from Laura.*

He tore open the missive. As he read, his eager expression dissolved into a portrait of sorrow. *Could this vitriol, this venom, be the heart of my sweet baby sister?* he wondered, his heart aching.

"I would rather my brother be dead than a Rebel," she wrote.

When he had completed the sad letter, he knew three things: despite the earlier indications to the contrary, Laura now exhibited no evidence of being a follower of Jesus; the dark despair in that Christless heart had consumed her; and she had disowned Stonewall as a brother.

"The dear brave Union boys I nurse have taken to calling me 'The Angel of Mercy,' and I wish never to see you—their butcherer—again," she wrote, etching two bold lines under the word *never*.

For a moment he sat motionless. Then slowly his head drooped down until his chin hit his chest. He remembered Jesus' lament over the stiff-necked city of Jerusalem: "How often would I have gathered thy children together, even as a hen gathereth her chickens under her wings, and ye would not!" Now the tears came.

He had prayed for Laura's soul, urged her, exhorted her, tried to help her for so long, for years and years. And now . . . he remembered . . . a precocious, headstrong little girl who was the apple of his eye, a sweet, eyelash-batting pixy with yellow pigtails who idolized him from the start.

He remembered holding her for nearly a full minute the day Uncle Bob Neale took her away to Grandma's, and longing for reunions and homecomings that would forever supplant good-byes, and running to the woods and, despite himself and his vow never to cry again, weeping many bitter tears.

But then he remembered rushing through a field with her and along a wooded path to a beautiful patch of mountain clover. And how her mouth was not able to move fast enough to tell him of all that was new in her life: of all the nice relatives and friends, the bully Billy Joe Tolliver, sweet Jimmy McGuire over by the ford who brought her lilies of the valley.

But of course, none of the boys were as cute or as smart or as strong as Tom.

And most of all he remembered a clear shining autumn day up in the Allegheny Mountains and her shouting, "Oh, Tommy, you're wonderful!" and leaping up to hug him and kiss him on the cheek, causing him to blush. Then he was off across the meadow, Laura trilling behind him, to eat gingerbread cake with Warren, gingerbread cake she helped make.

Weeping now, he reached down into the bag. There were more of them he had to see. Men had taught him about war and the gospel, but it was the women, always the women, who had given him heart, shown him what love meant, and taught him about . . . life.

He must find them, he must find them all—*Yes. There she is.* Ellie. *Ellie.* The old daguerreotype. He leaned back, holding her likeness and looking up at the pines and the twinkling stars above but seeing the sweet glow of a beautiful young maiden's face with twinkling hazel eyes staring up at him as she wrested a drenched towel from him. He had just doused the old biddy at Dr. Junkin's sixtieth birthday party.

And then she was riding with him, teaching him the truths only the lifelong devout daughter of a Bible-believing Presbyterian minister could impart . . . marrying him . . . and helping him discover the supreme temporal bliss given by God only to a husband and wife who have known no other . . . .

He smiled, remembering it all. Then he found Maggie's picture. Scarlet tresses, flashing blue eyes, and . . . *my friend* . . . he was sitting again with her on the Lexington lawn, fearing that they were parting but staring with her in wonderment as the shadow of a church cross instead bound them together forever. He gazed at Maggie's face. *She never did tell me what* Silverwood *meant,* he thought, tender sentiments flooding his heart. Then he allowed himself the query he never before had. *What might have been, Lord—what might have been?* He shook his head as if throwing off a spell. *I must pray and then write my* esposa, he thought. The first he did. Before he could do the second, more hoofbeats sounded.

It was Jed Hotchkiss and Lacy.

"We found it," Hotchkiss said, breathless and brandishing yet another map. Sandie, Douglas, and Dr. McGuire sipped coffee from a short distance away and watched as the mapmaker revealed the hidden route that would lead Stonewall and his men around the Union's right flank.

"I never liked old Blowhard Dabney any better than you boys," Douglas said, "but one thing he said made sense. He said Old Jack and General Lee were just alike—religion, duty, and serving God, that's all that's important to them."

Sandie nodded, shivering against the early morning chill, sans his cape. But McGuire's eyes narrowed. "I don't think so, Douglas," he said. "General Lee, he genuinely loves folk, even Northerners, cares about them, about their souls." As a nearby fire crackled, McGuire pondered his next words for so long that Sandie had opened his mouth to say something by the time the soft-spoken doctor finally continued.

"But Old Jack," he said, "he told me once that when they came down and stole our property, ran off the slaves, burned down the houses and barns of his people, insulted our defenseless women, hung and imprisoned our helpless old men, and behaved like an organized band of cutthroats and robbers, that they—"

McGuire, native of the oft-captured and much-abused town of Winchester, cleared his throat as Douglas and Sandie stared at him in surprise. Whether his words or the tone of them most surprised them, the gentle doctor did not know—or care.

"He believed they should be treated like highwaymen and assassins. He told me he hates no individual Northerner—but he hates the whole Northern race."

In the name of Christ, Douglas thought with a shudder, *what has this cursed war made of us?*

As the sleepless night wore on, campfires by the hundreds flickered. Here a harmonica whined the sweet lament of 'The Yellow Rose of Texas."

> *She cried so when I left her, it nearly broke my heart,*
> *And if I ever find her, we never more shall part.*

There a young soldier wrote home to his wife of how he missed her and the little ones. The number of Bibles, Prayer Books, and catechisms in the corps had grown as the number of card decks had decreased, both in direct proportion to the increase in destroyed homes and fields, shattered families and dreams, and dead fathers, brothers, husbands, and sons across Virginia and the South.

Nearly one hundred thousand unbelieving Confederate soldiers, most of them hungry, ill, and barely clothed, would by God's sovereign choosing believe in the risen Christ as their Lord and Savior before war's end.

Stuart, alone for a few moments at a campfire while preparing to catch an hour or so of shut-eye, his staff all asleep, stared at the cameo of little Flora, as he did every night. He thought of his wife's pain. She had lost her only daughter. She had to suffer from afar the constant jeopardy of her husband's life. And that husband had sworn to kill on sight her own father, a career soldier who had forsaken Virginia and led Union cavalry against Stuart and his people.

Silent tears began to stream down into Stuart's rich tawny beard as, after a pause, the harmonica finished the night with "Lorena," the elegiac anthem to lost Southern love.

> *We loved each other then, Lorena,*
> *More than we ever dared to tell;*

And what we might have been, Lorena,
Had but our loving prospered well.

It matters little now, Lorena,
The past is in the eternal Past;
Our heads will soon lie low, Lorena,
Life's tide is ebbing out so fast.

There is a future! O thank God!
Life, this is so small a part!
'Tis dust to dust beneath the sod;
But there, up there, 'tis heart to heart.

CHAPTER 55

"GOD IN HEAVEN," MARLEY GASPED, SIGHTING THROUGH HIS binoculars what one of his picket riders had spotted: the front ranks of Stonewall's column emerging from thick scrub underbrush near Catherine Furnace. "How could he be that far west? He was supposed to be"

But Marley had no time to speculate. He knew Howard's position left Old Prayer Book's far right—the far right of the massive Union line—vulnerable if anyone could flank it, which no one from the high command down had considered possible. *And if Old Jack pushes on another couple of miles . . .*

"I'm going to General Howard myself," Marley said, leaping up onto his horse. He had galloped away before the other two scouts could speak another word.

A breathless courier from Lee galloped up to Stonewall early in the afternoon as he and his twenty-eight thousand men moved westward through the Wilderness on the Plank Road south of Chancellorsville.

"General Jackson, the Yankees have forced the heights at Fredericksburg and are driving General Early back upon General Lee's rear, sir," the courier sputtered. He paused while Stonewall digested this. "They are coming this way, sir, behind you."

Stonewall as usual kept his own counsel, his eyes hidden by the visor of his gray cap. His own couriers had already reported movements directly against his rear flank by closer Union forces.

"Press up, men," he said, spurring his horse ahead. He leaned far forward on Little Sorrel, as if by doing so he could arrive at his destination quicker. To his rear, the crackle of musketry grew louder.

Marley flew off his horse and ran to Howard. "Sir," the scout blurted, barely remembering to salute, "it's General Jackson, sir. He's circling round the Plank Road to flank us to the west."

Howard stared at him. The surprise and orders to action Marley had expected did not come. Over a dozen men stood near, awaiting Howard's response. Finally, glancing in Stonewall's direction, he said, "Jackson can only be moving southward to protect the railroad to Richmond.

"But sir," Marley insisted, "why would General Lee send half his men to an area where there is no fight, when our thousands are here astride him?"

Howard's handsome countenance darkened.

"Sir," a nervous colonel spoke in a German brogue, seeming to Marley to be continuing a previous line of discussion, "please let me at least reinforce your right, in the unlikely case that the Rebels do attempt to flank you."

"I shall not be flanked!" Howard exploded, fire in the normally pacific almond eyes. "Thank you for your enterprise, Colonel von Gilsa," he continued, checking his temper, "but you and your men may return to your assigned duties. You will put your trust in God." Howard turned to Marley. "And you, Captain Marley, may resume your surveillance of General Jackson."

Marley saluted and left without a word, his stomach hollow. *I fear soon nothing shall be left to survey,* he thought bitterly. *D—— Thomas J. Jackson, d—— him to Hades.*

Meanwhile, Stonewall's rearguard of Georgians raised such a rumpus at Catherine Furnace, as the van of the Confederate column turned northwest toward Howard's flank, that the Federals sent twenty-two thousand men to quell the disturbance. That they did, not realizing that Stonewall had sucked them miles away from his proposed attack point, and effectively denuded Howard of his reserve force.

A mounted courier from Stuart raced up to Stonewall and his circle of aides and officers with a dispatch. Stonewall tore open the seal and read Stuart's familiar flowing script. "After significant hardship, the cavalry has come around Hooker and positioned itself to protect your left flank. I will close in on the flank and help all I can when the ball opens." At the bottom of the page appeared one additional line in thicker bolder ink and underlined: "May God grant us victory."

Stonewall grabbed a quill from Anna's brother Joe, dipped it in an inkwell the boy held, and scrawled his response for Stuart on the back page: "I trust that God will grant us a great victory. Keep closed on Chancellorsville."

The Federals overwhelmed the Georgians guarding Stonewall's rear. The Confederates fought with such a fury that the fight ended only when their regiment nearly to a man was killed or captured. Two of A. P. Hill's brigades had to go back to fend off the surging Yankees. Now the Union had Stonewall completely cut off from Lee.

When Lee's nephew, strapping cavalry brigadier Fitzhugh Lee, rode up to Stonewall, Douglas's gold watch told the time as two o'clock.

"General," Fitzhugh said, "if you will ride with me, halting your column here, I will show you the enemy's right."

Douglas saw the blue eyes spark fire. *Old Blue Light,* Douglas remembered the legends calling Stonewall, even back to Mexico. Then Douglas was riding with Stonewall, Fitzhugh, and one courier through thick woods and undergrowth, dismounting and climbing a hill.

Fitzhugh motioned to Stonewall the appropriate place to part the boughs of a thick cluster of trees. He did, and there stretched before him lay a staggering vista. Hundreds of feet below, as far as the eye could see, lay the Eleventh Corps of the Union army. Looking through his field glasses, Stonewall saw that the Federals had stacked arms and were preparing their evening meal, dealing cards, playing baseball, and singing. *Not so much as a skirmish line deployed,* he thought, barely believing it could be true until he remembered that God diluted the strength of the powerful gentile nations during the period of King David's life so that David could be successful and at the same time God could get the credit for tiny Israel's victories.

And Stonewall knew he looked upon Oliver O. Howard's command. *A Christian brother,* he thought with regret. *And an honorable man.* Then he realized the vast expanse of Virginia land on which Eleventh Corps resided, and he remembered all the land and dreams that the multiple Northern invasions had laid waste. *But he is on the wrong side and he is where, by God in heaven, he should not be!*

Stonewall continued to stare out at the mind-boggling tableau. When he said nothing further and the color began to rise on a countenance that exuded sorrow, Douglas and Fitzhugh looked at one another. Minute after minute it went on, as Stonewall's eyes burned, finally almost white with fury. Fitzhugh and the courier stepped back. Never had they witnessed so fierce a glow on the face of a human being.

Then Stonewall's lips began to move in silent petition, his eyes still open, his head now cocked up toward heaven. One arm shot up. Douglas backed away. *He is not with us,* the young officer found himself thinking. He remembered with a chill a Scripture verse his pastor father had taught him as a child: "And I looked, and behold a pale horse: and his name that sat on him was Death, and Hell followed with him."

By five o'clock, as shadows stretched across the Wilderness, Stonewall had managed to line up nearly twenty thousand Foot Cavalry (they had begun to call themselves the Barefoot Cavalry) in a double line of battle 150 yards apart that stretched for two miles across both the Old Turnpike and the Plank Road.

Though more than 130,000 Federals lay within a few miles, the Virginian had finessed himself into position to attack a right flank that actually numbered fewer men than his force.

Stonewall sat astride Little Sorrel, his gold-chained watch in hand, near the spot where he had viewed the spectacle of Old Prayer Book's exposed corps.

Around him were General Robert Rodes, ex-VMI student and professor, and commander of the division that would lead the attack, Douglas, and Sandie. Just then Colonel Tom Munford rode up and saluted.

Stonewall eyed him. "Something bothers you, Tom."

Munford hesitated. "Well, sir, it's those da—" The cavalryman blushed. "It's those people again, sir," he said, retreating to the term Lee gave the Federals. "Word has it they've roughed up some of the Chancellor family. I don't know what's true and what's rumor, sir, but the Chancellors are cousins to a couple of our men, and the troops are, well, sir, they've got their Irish up, sir. They're hungry and tired and they've had just about . . . " With that, Munford's voice trailed off and he shook his head wearily.

"Just about their fill of Yankee depredations, Tom?" Stonewall asked.

"Yes, sir, just about their fill," Munford said. Exhausted from twenty-four hours without sleep, Munford's mind darted to another subject and he spoke again. "Sir, have you noticed the preponderance of graduates and former professors from the VMI in Second Corps? They seem to be everywhere."

Stonewall looked at him. He remembered Munford as cadet adjutant on the day he arrived at the VMI as a professor twelve years before. *Such a fine, earnest boy he has always been,* the general thought. *Even young Patton—even Walker—so many of them have turned out all right. Most seem to be followers of You, Lord, though many of them have come to you late in the day.*

Stonewall's lips parted and he said, "The Virginia Military Institute will be heard from today."

It impressed Sandie that Stonewall spoke the words with no less conviction than he proclaimed at morning prayer meeting a couple of days earlier the sure and certain resurrection of the saints.

Stonewall sat still and silent for a moment, his eyes closed. *"O GOD the Lord,"* he prayed, *"the strength of my salvation, thou hast covered my head in the day of battle."*

Then he opened his eyes and looked at Douglas. "A quarter past five by your watch, Captain?"

Douglas pulled out the timepiece and looked. "Yes, sir. On the nose, sir."

Stonewall turned to Rodes and asked, so quietly that the man nearly requested him to repeat the question, "Are you ready, General Rodes?"

"Yes, sir."

"You can go forward then."

CHAPTER 56

HOWARD'S WORDS BOTHERED MARLEY. "I'M VERY PROUD OF you, Wayne," he had said as he shut his Bible in his officer's prayer meeting a few moments before. "You have done well as a cavalryman, as a scout, and, most importantly, as a Christian. Your example and your faithfulness are helping draw others to the cross of our Savior."

Marley loved and respected Oliver Howard, and those emotions prompted him all the more to feel guilty for the thoughts he had harbored against the man during the day. *Fool . . . blind man . . . arrogant pompous ass . . .* Marley shuddered as he remembered them all. *Pray God I have overreacted,* he thought, dismounting near a fire where thick beefsteaks were cooking.

The mood of the soldiers all around him seemed jovial. The Rebs had confined their actions to other corners of the field, and while everyone had expected a big fight today and certainly expected one tomorrow, no one seemed to expect anything for this remote station.

A burly redheaded sergeant poured steaming coffee into Marley's tin mug. *I think what I need is some sleep. Tonight I'm hitting it early,* the horseman promised himself. *That's odd,* he mused, as the largest covey of quail he had ever seen appeared out of nowhere from the direction of the woods to the west of the far right of the Union line. No sooner had the quail flown over his head than Marley spotted a second wave of birds, more quail and partridges too, hundreds of both, setting sail from the same woods.

"Would you look at that?" the redheaded sergeant said, pointing to where a wave of deer had sprinted from the woods, directly for the Union position, chased by a virtual army of rabbits, squirrels, and other small creatures.

"That whole field's alive with critters," someone else said.

Marley lowered his coffee.

At first, he thought it was the sound of distant shells shrieking through distant woods. *This time of day, especially,* he thought, *battle-field sounds can carry mighty strangely. No, it is too close—and too long,* he thought, a small voice whispering from way inside him that something was terribly wrong.

"Lieutenant," Marley said to a man who stood nearby staring at the woods, baseball glove and ball in hand. "You'd better rally the—"

Then it came over them as when Moses called the black clouds of locusts to swarm Pharaoh and the Egyptians.

Marley could not hear his own next thoughts, so deafening was the horrific sustained shriek. *From which direction is it coming?* he wondered, his eyes darting all around, confused by the earsplitting echoes. *It must be coming from the—*

Then the entire woods erupted into a sheet of flame, and men, horses, and everything else fell around him, a chorus of howls rising now from the Union line.

A long gray cloud of smoke shrouded the woods, but the terrifying high shriek—*Is it human?* Marley wondered—persisted. Then from within the smoke, invisible to the Federals, a second roar of musketry sounded, splintering men, animals, and objects as far as Marley could see in every direction.

God, there they are, Marley thought, dread filling his heart.

Thousands of Rebels, in a line that stretched left to right beyond the limits of his vision, charged as fast as their legs could carry them, screaming, rage distorting their faces, straight at Marley and the Union line.

Like the Celts of old they are and always have been, Marley thought, his last thought before he slung down his coffee cup, jerked out his revolver, and ran back to his horse. *Got to warn General Howard.*

As the Confederates stampeded through the Union pickets and over the main line's breastworks, slaughtering men where they stood as they grabbed for their stacked arms or as they ran, Marley galloped away.

All was chaos, gunsmoke now enveloping the entire field as drums, bugles, and the screams of men filled the air. *Holy Moses,* he breathed, his heart pounding, *I'm heading the wrong direction.* He reined his horse around and raced toward headquarters. Suddenly a Rebel horseman appeared, shooting at him. They traded shots back and forth, no more than a few feet apart as they passed. Marley's horse screeched, hit on his left just in front of Marley's leg. The Reb fell from his horse to the ground.

Marley started to ride on, knowing he should. But now his own anger boiled up and he swung his gasping, sagging mount around, took aim at the fallen Confederate, and fired more bullets into the defenseless man. From out of nowhere, another Reb rider screamed, "You b——s!", flew off his horse, and tore Marley out of his saddle, the two of them sailing to the ground with a crushing thud.

Marley landed on the bottom, the air punched out of his lungs. Hurt and scared, he tried to crawl away, but the furious Confederate caught him by his collar, slung him around onto his back, and began to pound his face with his fists, spewing venom and spit from his mouth. "You miserable Yankee butchers," the man railed. "You scum of the earth." Marley tried to deflect the blows, but could not. Pain surged through his head and he heard and felt the bridge of his nose crack. The raging grayback jerked Marley's sword out of its scabbard and raised it to cleave him just as more shots sounded nearby and the man fell across Marley, blood gushing from his pierced lungs and chest.

Marley crawled away, soaked with the man's blood, and stumbled over to where Jimmy Flanagan sat mounted on his horse, smoking revolver in hand.

"Get on," Flanagan said, extending his hand.

Is every manjack among the Southern race a raging animal? Marley thought with anger as he climbed up. *Every blasted one of them?*

Just as Marley got aboard, the Confederate who had nearly killed him shocked both him and Flanagan by rising from the ground and turning toward them. Crimson blood drenched the man's entire front torso, yet rage streaked his ashen face and he came for them, unarmed, breathing murder.

"You murdering Yankee sons of—"

Flanagan emptied his revolver into the Confederate. It took every bullet to put him down. Still, lunging, the Reb tumbled hard into the horse, bruising the animal and causing it to rear up.

"Those boys just don't stop coming," Flanagan said, shaken.

Marley stared at the dead heap laying at the foot of the spooked horse. *No, they don't stop coming . . . and win or lose this war, I don't believe now that they ever will.*

"Men! Soldiers of the Union, come back with me and fight!" General Howard shouted with bared head from atop his horse as Federal troops retreated past him like a tidal wave rushing in from the sea.

"Please, men—do not shame yourselves and the Union!" Howard screamed. But so deafening was the roar of battle and the panicked retreat of thousands of men that he could not even hear his own voice. One man passed by him carrying the colors of a New York regiment. With superhuman effort, Howard spurred his horse through the sea of humanity, leaned over, and snatched the brightly colored banner from the man, who reacted as though the loss of the flag was good riddance.

Howard pushed his horse back around to face the oncoming surge. Waving the colors back and forth with the arm maimed by Stonewall Jackson's men at the First Battle of Bull Run, he wailed, "In the name of the Union, in the name of Christ, I adjure you, men of America—come back with me and let us give battle to these heathen!"

But his voice had gone hoarse and his troops, many of them German and not even able to understand English, had but one thought gripping their souls: to run as fast as they could away from the slaughterhouse that had engulfed their entire line and reach safety, if indeed a place of safety existed on that harrowing field of death.

Stonewall Jackson rode toward the front of the Confederate line. His men had rolled the Yankees back nearly three miles. The one-sided battle had destroyed much of the land through which he rode. Everywhere were dead bluecoats and horses, smashed wagons, caissons, limbers, and small fires.

Every few moments, Stonewall closed his eyes, his arm shot toward heaven, and he prayed for God to receive the soul of a fallen son of the South who lay nearby.

Douglas, riding with A. P. Hill, spotted Stonewall at the head of his entourage near the extreme front of the line. *Joshua could have been no more fearsome riding through the ruined Canaanites,* Douglas thought as he watched his commander coming on, straight-backed, his visor pulled low over his eyes. *Nor could Charles "the Hammer" Martel after his destruction of the Islamic hordes that saved Europe, nor even Alexander after completing his conquest of the known world.* Even Hill seemed to Douglas a bit awed by what his old nemesis had accomplished.

The general shall not outlive the legend here berthed, Douglas thought.

The sun had set and darkness loomed. Douglas glanced at his watch. *After eight o'clock.* Then he turned and rode to a nearby clump of trees. He had needed for hours to relieve his bowels. If he waited any longer, he would mess his pants.

"General," Stonewall said when Hill, shirt-sleeved in his blood-red fighting shirt, reached him, "did you receive my order to get your reserve division into line and move promptly against the Yankees?"

"Yes, sir," Hill said. "They are moving."

In the gathering dark and from under his visor, Stonewall's eyes blazed anew to the exhausted men surrounding him. He pointed with a yellow-gauntleted hand toward the northeast.

"The United States Ford is less than half a mile from where we sit, General. It is the sole line of retreat for the entire Union army, sir, and they have no organized force between here and there." Stonewall's eyes burned white-hot, the thick veins in his neck bulged, and he rose in his saddle. "Press them, General Hill! Press them and cut them off from the United States Ford!"

Douglas, wiping himself with leaves, could not make out Stonewall's words, but he had never before heard the general so shout.

Hill blinked. For a moment, neither he nor the other two officers within hearing range understood. Consistent with his practice of secrecy, Stonewall had shared his strategy with no one else. He alone of any man on the entire field recognized the opportunity for the Confederacy. Slowly, the sense of the master stroke illumined Hill's face.

Why, if we get to the United States Ford before Hooker gets back to it with his main force, we'll have him caged between our men and cannon, and the Wilderness, Hill thought. *He will have to overwhelm us or starve on the vine, surrounded by Virginia and the Army of Northern Virginia.*

A tiny smile spread across Hill's face. *Maybe God does talk to the old fool.*

"The entire Union army, sir," Hill said.

"The entire Union army, sir," Stonewall nodded.

The main Union army, destroyed. Hill knew the Northern public clamored already for an end to the carnage. Many if not most of them now wanted the Southern states released to go their own way rather than preserve their unwilling "Union" with the North through fire and steel. *If we accomplish this, and the unimaginable slaughter that will ensue,* Hill realized, *Lincoln and his mercenary Republicans are finished, and this cruel unnecessary war with them.*

"Sir!" Hill shouted, saluting and riding off to deploy his men.

"General Jackson," Sandie said, riding up, "we're getting reports the Yankees are massing for a charge back down the Chancellorsville road at us."

Without a word, Stonewall spurred Sorrel ahead. *I must make certain a road exists to connect us with the United States Ford.*

"General," a nervous colonel in the eighteenth North Carolina Regiment said, squinting to recognize Stonewall as he passed, "don't you think this is the wrong place for you?"

"The danger is all over," Stonewall said, "the enemy is routed. Go back and tell A. P. Hill to press right on!"

Now nothing but the commands of Federal officers and the ring of Yankee axes biting into wood to be used for erecting barricades remained ahead of Stonewall.

"General Jackson," Stonewall heard one of his aides, whom he could not see, say, "General Hill's chief engineer just rode into a Yank battery and got took prisoner. We best be getting back right now, sir."

Twenty yards ahead, a bleeding Union officer's ears perked up. *Can it be?* the man thought, incredulous. *No, it must be another General Jackson.* But he craned his neck around the trunk of the scrub oak against which he leaned. He could make out only the silhouette of a tall, rigid-backed man topped by an army forage cap.

"You have come to me," Wayne Marley uttered, barely able to fathom the staggering sight before him. He glanced around him. Jimmy Flanagan—dead, a Rebel bullet through his throat. Flanagan's horse—dead, riddled with shrapnel. Marley's own left shoulder packing the bullet of one of Jeb Stuart's reckless horse soldiers, his broken nose a throbbing bloody mess. And the shrill bloodcurdling sound of the Rebel yell still ringing in his ears.

Marley grabbed for the Spencer repeating carbine he had taken from a dead Union cavalry colonel. He had no time to waste. He had not a doubt in the world as to what he must do. He could do only one thing, and God be praised for the impossible opportunity only He could have provided.

Marley leaned his quivering left shoulder against the tree to steady his aim, and drew a clear bead on Stonewall. He cocked back the Spencer's hammer, single action, then double. His index finger squeezed against the trigger. Then he noticed that Stonewall had raised his arms and eyes toward heaven. Normally, the sight would have incensed Marley. But for some reason, it touched him. Howard's words in the prayer meeting came back to him. "We must fight for the right, we must defend the defenseless, but we must never forget our humanity or that of those whom we come out against."

And the words of Stonewall Jackson returned to him. As the Virginian tossed him a strip of his own shirt to stem Marley's bleeding face the day he lost his eye and gained his manhood at Chapultepec: "You'll thank yourself one day as you rock by the hearth that you missed not a moment of this day, soldier." And, "To the finest young man I know, with my fervent prayers that your bright future shall soon be illumined as will that holy city of which the sainted apostle wrote. . . . Your ardent friend and supporter, Thomas J. Jackson."

Slowly, even as Stonewall remained in his view, Marley lowered the rifle. He sat for a moment marveling at how the darkness now enveloping the bloody field of Chancellorsville paled before the darkness that had so long rent his heart—his redeemed heart. He dropped the rifle and buried his head in his arms, sobbing—with exhaustion, pain, and grief, but moreso with joy that perhaps the long night of his soul had at last departed.

"Help me, Lord Jesus," he said, "help me to start a new life, a life where I can once again be clean, and love and not hate."

Stonewall turned his horse back toward his own lines. *We shall bury whoremongering Joe Hooker, pagan headquarters brothel and all, in this Wilderness.* Then the sharp crack of a single musket cut through the night air. A volley of rifle fire from the spooked eighteenth North Carolinians followed. Stonewall sought cover, only to hear a volley of shells from Union artillery scream overhead, smashing trees and eliciting screams from the Confederate lines.

Off to Stonewall's right, Hill hurried his horse toward the Tarheel position. "Cease firing! Cease firing!" he screamed.

"Who gave that order?" twenty-three-year-old North Carolinian Major John Barry, nervous and sweat-stained, called out. The woods were crawling with Yankees, shelling had just ripped through the Eighteenth's ranks, a Federal counterattack was rumored, and Stonewall, Hill, and their thirty-man contingent sounded in the darkness like a brigade of cavalry—coming straight from the Union lines. "By thunder, it's a lie," Barry shouted. "Pour it into them, boys!"

"No!" Hill cried.

But it was too late. The Tarheel line exploded from the darkness into a yellow sheet of fire. Piercing shrieks filled the night air, horses pitched to the ground, riddled riders flew to the turf or reeled in the saddle as their mounts bolted in all directions.

Hill was closest to the firing line. Cat quick, he leaped from his horse, an instant before a half dozen minié balls knocked it down, and lay face down on the ground, miraculously unhurt.

Stonewall felt a searing pain tear into his upper left arm. The force of the blow, severing the main artery and splintering the bone, knocked him around just as another ball ripped through his left forearm and came out his wrist. A third tore into the palm of his right hand.

Little Sorrel went wild, racing straight for the Union lines. Pouring blood, Stonewall used every ounce of strength remaining to rein the horse, but succeeded only in slowing him. Unseen tree branches slashed bloody stripes across the Virginian's face, knocked off his cap, and bludgeoned him nearly senseless.

"Oh!" Stonewall sputtered when a thick oak bough cracked the side of his head. Dazed and blinded, he felt himself falling from the saddle when strong arms grabbed him and Sorrel's reins.

Another man rode up and braced Stonewall from the other side. He could no longer hold his horse's reins, his left arm hanging limply and his right hand shot.

"Wild fire, that, sir," Stonewall said with a grimace. "Wild fire."

When one of the men touched Stonewall's arm, he nearly fainted from the pain. "You had better put me down," he said.

Meanwhile, Hill grabbed someone else's horse and charged toward Barry. "Madness—you have shot my friends! You ignorant band of fools, you have destroyed my staff and General Jackson's too!"

"But sir," Barry started, stunned.

"You shut your mouth," Hill shouted, thrusting a finger at him. "If you're the man who gave that order, you're lucky I don't kill you myself." With that, he whipped out his pistol. "If you say another word, boy, I may. Now all of you—keep your mouths shut about General Jackson."

With that, he turned and galloped to where a couple of staff officers stood over Stonewall, lying at the foot of a pine tree.

Sandie rode up, unhurt. Seeing Stonewall's bloodied condition, he himself swooned in the saddle and fell off his horse, awakened only when he crashed against the ground.

Nearby, Union artillery opened fire again, shells streaking through tree branches overhead.

Hill rushed to Stonewall's side. When he saw his old nemesis's bloodied, bullet-torn body, he gasped. A surge of guilt coursed through the Tidewater general as he realized how much of his thought and energy had come to be directed against his fellow Virginian, his fellow Confederate. Just that afternoon, Hill had practically giggled as he forwarded to Lee a new sheet of accusations that he felt certain would leave the old chieftain no option but to publicly reprimand Stonewall.

Now Hill's face shown nearly as ashen as Stonewall's as he cursed himself for wishing upon a man the ill that had come to pass.

"I—I am so sorry . . . General . . . Tom," Hill stammered, kneeling beside the wounded man. A maddening feeling of helplessness filled Hill. "I have been trying to make the men cease firing," he said in a plaintive tone. His brows crinkled, Hill peered at Stonewall. "Are—are your wounds painful?"

"Very painful," Stonewall replied in a steady voice. "I think my arm is broken."

Hill stared at him, then gently removed Stonewall's gauntlets. Hill gasped again as blood poured out both of them. Gentle as a nursing mother with her baby, Hill removed Stonewall's saber and belt. Now tears filled Hill's eyes as he realized just how badly wounded was his old foe. As musket fire opened not far away from the Yankee lines, the Tidewater aristocrat sat on the dirty ground and cradled the mountain man's head in his lap. Gingerly, Hill tore open Stonewall's left sleeve and tried with handkerchiefs and cloths to staunch the hemorrhaging.

"Thank—thank you, Powell," Stonewall said.

"I—I'm . . . ," Hill began, staring at Stonewall. Then he looked away. "Captain Leigh, fetch a surgeon and an ambulance. Captain Adams, how about a pull off that brandy."

When signal officer Adams, whose testimony in Stonewall's dealings with Hill had so infuriated him, offered the flask, Stonewall hesitated. Would it be honoring to God? Then he remembered the apostle Paul's admonitions regarding alcohol for medicinal purposes and took a small swallow, which eased his suffering.

A moment later, Stonewall, his head swimming, heard Adams call out, "Halt! Surrender! Fire on them if they don't surrender!" Hill squirmed out from under Stonewall and whipped his pistol back out. He saw two Federal soldiers standing a short distance away, holding rifles.

"Drop them right now, gentlemen," Hill said, cocking back the hammer of his revolver.

The bluecoats looked at one another, then obeyed, just as Anna's little brother, Joe Morrison, rode up. "The Yankees are only fifty yards away and they're headed straight for us!" he shouted.

"We've got to move you," Hill said to Stonewall as Union artillery began to rake the area around them.

"No," Stonewall said. "If you will help me, I can walk."

When Hill and Morrison got Stonewall to his feet, his wounds pumped so profusely that they drenched the two men's uniforms. *Oh, what will dear Anna think?* Morrison thought sorrowfully.

After a few steps, amidst the sounds of shrieking shells and screaming wounded men, a litter mercifully arrived.

"I shall try to keep your accident from the knowledge of the troops," Hill told Stonewall.

"Thank you," Stonewall said as Morrison and others loaded him onto the stretcher. Behind them, Stonewall could hear the crackling reports of massed arrays of muskets.

Hill watched for a few seconds as the men carted Stonewall off. *What will become of him?* he thought. *I fear I have been an unforgivable bore in the entire matter.* He thought back through the long years. *Never have I understood that man.* An explosion nearby and the bloodcurdling cries of mangled men jolted him back into action. He now commanded the Confederate Second Corps.

Pistol still drawn, Hill made his way to where the Southerners had established their line to stand against the expected Union assault. He supervised some positional adjustments, then rode, now with Douglas, to again find Stonewall.

"How is he?" Douglas asked, dumbstruck at the news of Stonewall's condition.

"He is wounded several times, in both arms," Hill said, his face drawn. "And badly, I fear."

Douglas gasped. Then a shell tore through the woods and exploded just a few feet away. It blew both men off their horses, killing Hill's. Douglas's boot was damaged and he was stunned, but otherwise just bruised. Hill's boots were shredded and one leg bloody.

So great was the searing pain he thought he would vomit. He tried to rise but could not.

"Oh," Hill cried, lying on the ground and clutching his bleeding leg. "Go tell Pendleton." He cringed in pain. "Go tell him I cannot continue in command."

Douglas stared at him as another Yankee shell brought screams of anguish from a cluster of Confederates a few yards away. "Stuart?"

Hill nodded. He saw his pistol in the dirt a few feet away. "Give me my gun and get going."

Douglas found Sandie and gave him the news.

"General Rodes is next in command," Sandie, who had pulled his wits together, said. "But . . . "

Douglas nodded.

In unison, they said one word: "Stuart."

And so Jeb Stuart took command, with his whole heart and his formidable talents ready to defend his beloved Virginia against its invaders. But no one now knew to tell him of Stonewall's plan, sheathed as ever in secrecy, to grab the lightly guarded United States Ford and trap the entire main Union army in the Wilderness. That brilliant idea drifted quietly away like the smoke over the Chancellorsville battlefield, along with its fellow traveler: the dream of an independent Confederate nation.

CHAPTER 57

THE NEXT HOURS WERE A BLUR TO STONEWALL. PAIN RACKED his body. After a few moments, he rose and walked for twenty or thirty feet as bullets whistled through the jungle around him. Then a stretcher arrived. All around him, flaming patches of the Wilderness burned through Stonewall's hazy vision. And he heard the crashing of shells, the shrieking of horses, and the moans and cries of damaged men.

Then a round of grapeshot blew down one of the men carrying Stonewall's litter. Another man caught it before Stonewall could hit the ground.

"Let me walk," Stonewall said. The men carrying him, noting his blood-drenched uniform and ashen countenance, hesitated, but Stonewall got to his feet. He trudged only a few feet before the pain proved overwhelming and he sagged into the arms of one of the soldiers.

Then he saw one of his brigadiers, Dorsey Pender, who had sent the surgeon now accompanying Stonewall. The Virginian gasped as he saw Pender's own bullet-torn, blood-stained coat. "Oh, General, I am sorry to see you have been wounded."

"And I you, sir," Pender said, grimacing in pain and leaning against an adjutant for support. "And now the lines here are so much broken that I fear we shall have to fall back."

Stonewall, about to collapse back onto the stretcher, his blood trickling onto it, firmed himself and rose back to his full height.

"You must hold your ground, General Pender," he said in a low growl. "You must hold your ground, sir!"

With that, Stonewall accepted the aid of the men who lowered him back to the ground and replaced him on the litter.

As they passed by Pender, that bleeding general steeled himself as a flaming tree bough crashed to the ground just a few feet from him. Above the hellish din of battle, he ordered, "Take me back to the front, Captain. We shall give not another inch of ground."

Stonewall's pain grew as the minutes passed. The irregular bouncing journey through the chaotic Wilderness intensified the agony. Then another shell screamed past, within a few feet of the Virginian and his group. One of the exhausted stretcher-bearers flinched at the sound, got his foot tangled in a vine, and fell headlong to the ground, Stonewall and his litter thudding hard just behind him.

Stonewall's full dead weight and the momentum of falling several feet landed him brutally on his side against what a felt like a tree stump. The pain seared through him. For the first time he groaned, thinking he would faint. Tears filled his eyes. He cried silently to God for escape from the unbearable agony. Then he lay back, looked heavenward, and remembered the words of another man of war and man of God. *"He delivered me from my strong enemy, and from them that hated me: for they were too strong for me."* A sweet peace cascaded over Stonewall, and he felt as though he would at any moment be standing before his Lord at the gates of heaven. *"They prevented me in the day of my calamity: but the LORD was my stay."*

On and on the sweating soldiers carried Stonewall. Sometime later he felt them lifting him into an ambulance. Then Anna's little brother Joe was holding him, sniffling back tears, whispering, "I'm trying to keep your arm steady, Tom," as the springless wagon jolted along the rutted, war-battered road.

Later, the vehicle arrived at the Chancellor inn, whose flames lit the black night for miles around. The Federals had begun the day in possession of the surrounding structures. Stonewall had rolled them back miles to the east.

McGuire stepped forward. He knew of Stonewall's wounding, but gasped at the grisly sight.

"Oh, I hope you are not badly hurt, General," the doctor said.

Stonewall forced his swimming eyes to focus on McGuire. "I am badly injured, Doctor. I fear I am dying," he said calmly. "I am glad you have come. I think the wound in my shoulder is still bleeding."

The young doctor climbed into the ambulance and inspected his commander's wounds. He pressed a finger on the artery that continued gurgling a dark stream of blood from the ruined arm, then poured a long slug of whiskey down Stonewall's throat.

"Get going," McGuire ordered the ambulance driver.

As the vehicle lurched west toward the Second Corps field hospital, McGuire wondered silently at Stonewall's patient calm. *His cold hands, his clammy skin, his pale face, his compressed, bloodless lips— this man is suffering physical torment. And yet not a groan escapes him, not a sign of suffering except the furrowed brow, the fixed rigid face, and his thin lips, so tightly compressed, that I can see the impression of his teeth through them.* Yet, McGuire marveled, *Through his iron will he remains polite, controlled, and calm, not given to the restlessness usual to such a huge loss of blood.*

"*I called upon the* LORD *in distress,*" Stonewall prayed silently, his eyes closed, "*the* LORD *answered me, and set me in a large place. The* LORD *is on my side; I will not fear: what can man do unto me?*"

More than two hours after his wounding, the ambulance brought Stonewall to the Second Corps hospital. The surgeon in charge, Dr. Harvey Black, stared at the wounded general as Joe Morrison and others carried him to a warm tent.

"How is he still alive?" Black whispered to McGuire. "He should be stone dead, Dr. McGuire."

McGuire stared at him. "I honestly do not know, Doctor."

Two and a half hours later, at around 2:00 A.M., McGuire sawed off Stonewall's left arm, two inches below the shoulder. Stonewall, chloroformed, felt nothing but a pleasant floating sensation before he lost consciousness.

About an hour later, Sandie arrived.

"I've got to speak with the general," he told McGuire. "A. P. Hill is down too, the troops are confused, and Jeb Stuart is now in command. He says the safety of the army and the success of the cause depends on my ascertaining Old Jack's plans."

The two men, upon whose young shoulders so much of their country's destiny pressed, peered at one another. Both knew they shared the same thought: *He told no one of his plans, and now those plans are in danger of being lost to us.*

"Make it quick, Sandie," McGuire said, "very quick."

"Well, Major, I am glad to see you," Stonewall said, his face brightening. "I thought you were killed."

Sandie could not conceal a brief stricken expression at the sight of Stonewall's pale, mauled face. Several of the facial wounds were deep and oozing and looked as though they needed suturing. Composing himself, Sandie inquired as to what course of action Stonewall wished Stuart to take. The general fired several questions back, as of old.

Ah, McGuire thought, *Old Jack.*

When Sandie had answered, Stonewall stared at him, deep in thought. *Yes,* he reasoned, *it seems quite clear. The way should be open still . . . the way . . . yes, the way . . .*

Tense anticipation filled the tent as every man in it waited for Stonewall's reply. He crinkled his brow. *Oh, it is just outside my grasp,* he thought, *floating, but I think I can reach it.*

Sandie saw the blue eyes flash their old fire as Stonewall's head came up off the pillow.

Oh, Stonewall thought, *the road, I see the road, and the river, but . . .* Then the road and the river and the Wilderness all became scrambled in his drugged, sapped mind and he sighed. *I cannot reach it, too tired, I'll think of it later perhaps.*

His features relaxed and his head rested back against the pillow. With all in the tent hushed and waiting for his answer, Stonewall closed his eyes, swallowed, then looked up at Sandie. "I don't know," he said, the feebleness of his voice stunning the young adjutant. "I can't tell; say to General Stuart he must do what he thinks best."

Sandie felt as though he might faint as he had earlier in the night. He wanted Stonewall's plan so badly he started to step forward and press the issue. Then he took stock of the man who lay before him: nearly dead, his right hand shot, his left arm amputated, his right side damaged from a fall, his face beaten nearly to a pulp. *He has very nearly given his life,* Sandie thought, ashamed of himself. Lowering his head, he turned and walked sadly from the tent, mounted, and rode to Stuart, a dark foreboding cloud enveloping him.

A couple of hours later, Stuart turned to his young aide just before giving the signal for thousands of dirty, hungry, exhausted Confederates to assault Hooker's new position, which lay through the morning mists several miles east of where his position of the previous day had. The boy, a recent VMI graduate, showed great promise, but he shook with fear.

"Remember, son," Stuart said, a merry twinkle in his eyes—the only ones the youngster had seen up to this nine o'clock hour of the day that evidenced no trace of blue rings under them or bloodshot lines through them—"remember that cavalry gallops at an enemy and trots away from him. No other gait is worthy of a cavalryman. A good man on a good horse need never get into trouble."

The boy's countenance brightened. *I can follow this man,* he thought, heartened.

But on this day, Jeb Stuart would prove in the face of his critics and doubters that he was not a leader of cavalry, but a leader of men. He looked up and down the long line of tatterdemalions who stood poised to go forth into fire and steel for him. *How grand they are,* he thought, his soul stirred. *And I myself shall ride before them.* He reached back to his saddlebag. He had not time to retrieve his prayer book and read from it; just to feel its trusty bulge helped calm him. Besides, he knew every line in it, and in the Bible that rested in the other saddlebag. He had carried both with him his whole life.

Stuart drew his sword and thought of his beloved brother Stonewall Jackson, lying savaged and near death and unable to complete this consummate victory, which would belong to him. *How can I do less?* Stuart thought. He spurred Chancellor out to the front of the entire twenty thousand assembled graybacks and rode back and forth across their front, shouting a song to the ancient fiddler's breakdown, the "Old Dan Tucker" tune:

> *Old Joe Hooker, won't you come out' the Wilderness—*
> *Come out' the Wilderness—*
> *Come out' the Wilderness—*
> *Old Joe Hooker, won't you come out' the Wilderness—*
> *Come out' the Wilderness now.*

Then fire and a fierce rage filled Stuart and he stood high in his stirrups as Stonewall's boys roared, lifted his sword aloft, and screamed so that the Foot Cavalry he himself would lead into battle could hear and understand, "Remember Jackson! Remember Jackson!"

The Federals had regrouped during the night, erected sturdy if hasty breastworks, and brought up thousands of reserves. Across the field to the east, Sedgwick led them up and over the skeletal remains of their own comrades fallen the previous December at Marye's Heights, and drove Early back onto Lee's rear.

But Stuart and his thousands could on this day be stopped by only one thing—the wholesale slaughter of every last one of their number. They knew not fear, they knew naught else but the taking up of the gauntlet for the man who had led them to victory after victory against the strongest and best the Union could throw against their skinny, vermin-ridden, half-naked columns.

"Remember Jackson! Remember Jackson!" resounded the hoarse throaty shouts of the Sons of the South through the tortured burning Wilderness.

The Yankees fought hard, smashed back against their foe, and died in heaps and piles as the Confederates thundered forward, their gaunt, cartridge powder-blackened faces masked in rage, honor having become more cherished to them than life itself. This lesson had their fallen leader taught them.

For five hours the battle raged. On the right, along a front less than a mile wide, one hundred guns roared. Once, twice, the Southern infantry, riddled red battle flags fluttering, charged out of the woods and up to the Yankee breastworks, only to be thrown back by a withering storm of cannister and musketry.

Stuart, his heart burning for his brave men, galloped to the front of the army, still singing his song. Blazing gunfire cut Chancellor to ribbons. Stuart fell hard to the dusty ground as a whole section of muskets along the Union line drew down on him and fired. Unhit, he leapt onto a riderless horse, a big blood bay, dashed into a shattered regiment fleeing from the relentless Northern riflery, and snatched the regimental battle flag from the staggering, gut-shot color bearer, then turned back toward the Yankees.

"Boys! Sons of Virginia!" his voice rang out, "leave us go forth amongst them, boys! Remember Jackson!"

Then Stuart headed alone through the smoke, fire, and hail of lead into the teeth of the flaming breastworks, Confederate battle flag in his hands.

The first man to gallop after him, despite his own aides' attempts to restrain him, waving his sword, his long red hair flowing in the wind, screaming "Remember Jackson!" was thirty-year-old VMI failure James Walker, soon to be commander of the Stonewall Brigade.

Then dozens of men, hundreds, half-starved, exhausted, homesick, and heartsick, gained their hearts back watching the splendid strapping general in the fancy hat, ostrich plume, and red sash, disappear into the cauldron of hell itself. And so there remained nothing for them to do but follow, *for he is rich and famous and has much more to lose than I do*, one diarrhea-ridden scarecrow from the North Carolina mountains thought. *I have only my life to give.*

Stuart rode through the thunderous cacophony, heading straight for a Union flag in the middle of the line. He heard and felt minié balls singing by him on all sides. The very gates of hell could not prevail against him. He jumped the horse over the forward breastworks, trampling a nest of soldiers in various stages of firing their rifles at him. Then the Yankees were retreating and his own men were pouring through the lines.

Stuart turned the big bay around and stood him atop a smoldering earthwork, the magnificent animal's nostrils flaring and his lathered flanks heaving above the dead and wounded and the splintered debris, between two silent guns.

Then other battle flags appeared from the east, and Jeb saw that Lee's divisions were uniting with his own. *We have licked them,* Jeb thought, pride in his boys—Stonewall's boys—and thankfulness to God swelling his breast.

Fightin' Joe Hooker did not come out of the Wilderness to meet Stuart. A Confederate cannonball had crashed into a porch pillar against which he leaned at his headquarters. The explosion nearly killed him. It did knock him senseless, and for several hours the Union army had no commander.

Sunday, May 3, dawned bright and fresh. Stonewall felt little pain and his mind seemed clear. He ate a bit. That afternoon, Douglas came to his tent with news of the Confederacy's smashing triumphs, and in particular the bloodstained valor of the Stonewall Brigade.

"It was just like them," Stonewall said, his eyes moist and his voice quavering, "just like them. They are a noble set of men." He pondered the news for a moment, then looked back up at Douglas. "The name of Stonewall belongs to that brigade, not to me."

"He looks very good, very good indeed," McGuire told Douglas as he left. "I believe his recovery, other than the loss of the arm, will be complete."

But Sedgwick's push through Fredericksburg threatened the rear of the entire Confederate line so Lee ordered Stonewall removed to the safety of Guiney's Station, a rail station twenty-four miles to the south.

That night, as Stuart rode to meet Lee, raging fires in all directions lit his way like a torchlit parade. No songs came to his lips as he saw, with horror, scores of men being cremated where they had stood or fallen, their charred shapes hugging trees, protecting faces, or stretching forth their hands, as if to ward off the flames.

In Richmond, Anna anguished over the news of her husband's wounding. Yet Confederate authorities would not let her leave the city because Stoneman's Federal cavalry were wreaking havoc throughout the area, the railroad north to Fredericksburg had ceased operations, and the stagecoach she begged to board was denied for fear the Yankees would capture it.

Hotchkiss chose the route for Stonewall's ambulance ride to Guiney's Station. The incomparable topographer rode ahead and supervised the clearing of obstructions and the filling in of the road's worst holes. Masses of men cleared the crowded way amidst cries of "It's Old Jack!" Choruses of cheers resounded into the fresh Virginia spring air. Other troops doffed their hats and stood showing quiet respect.

As another spring thunderstorm roiled, McGuire found quarters for Stonewall in a low frame building near the Chandler house at Guiney's Station. Only a sharp pain that periodically visited Stonewall's side where he had landed after being dropped from his battlefield litter concerned the doctor, who beamed at the general's rapid overall recovery.

The next day, Lee dispatched two more divisions to Jubal Early, who proceeded to muscle Sedgwick's Union force back through Fredericksburg, then throw the whole bunch of them back across the Rappahannock.

On the morning of May 5, Lacy, the Presbyterian minister, came to visit Stonewall, carrying a message from Lee.

"Could I have directed events, I should have chosen for the good of the country to be disabled in your stead. . . . I congratulate you upon the victory, which is due to your skill and energy," the letter read.

What the letter did not include were Lee's comments to one of his aides: "Such an executive officer the sun never shone on. I have but to show him my design, and I know that if it can be done it will be done. No need for me to send or watch him. Straight as the needle to the pole he advances to the execution of my purpose."

"General Lee is very kind, but he should give the praise to God," Stonewall said.

"And General Lee gave me an additional message for you from his own lips," Lacy said, his eyes filling with tears. "He said that you have lost your left arm, but he has lost his right arm." Then Lacy bowed his head. Stonewall eyed him.

"Dear Pastor, sir, you must not fret, for you see me severely wounded, but not depressed; not unhappy," he said. "I believe that it has been done according to God's holy will, and I acquiesce entirely in it. You may think it strange; but you never saw me more perfectly contented than I am today; for I am sure that my heavenly Father designs this affliction for my good. I am perfectly satisfied, that either in this life, or in that which is to come, I shall discover that what is now regarded as a calamity, is a blessing. And if it appears a great calamity—as it surely will be a great inconvenience, to be deprived of my arm—it will result in a great blessing. I can wait, until God, in His own time, shall make known to me the object He has in thus afflicting me. But why should I not rather rejoice in it as a blessing, and not look on it as a calamity at all? If it were in my power to replace my arm, I would not dare to do it, unless I could know it was the will of my heavenly Father."

Lacy stared at him. *And who is the supposed minister here?* he thought to himself with a wry smile. Then he queried Stonewall regarding his nightmarish retreat from the battlefield, including his painful fall from the stretcher.

"It has been a precious experience to me, that I was brought face to face with death, and found all was well," Stonewall said. He thought for a moment before continuing. "I have learned an important lesson, that one who has been the subject of converting grace, and is the child of God, can, in the midst of the severest sufferings, fix the thoughts upon God and heavenly things, and derive great comfort and peace: but, that one who had never made his peace with God would be unable to control his mind, under such sufferings, so as to understand properly the way of salvation, and repent and believe on Christ."

Still feeling robust, Stonewall requested that Lacy and other chaplains visit him each morning at ten o'clock for prayer and Scripture reading.

Then the wounded general caught a glimpse of a clear olive face under mounds of dark brown hair, tied into long twin pigtails, peaking around the doorway at him from the hall outside. As soon as the little girl realized her detection, she fled without a word. *Why, I believe I know that little girl,* Stonewall thought. *I think her name is Lucy. I believe she is one of dear Janie Corbin's friends.*

As Lacy turned to leave, Stonewall said, "Already I have heard the stories building about our recent successes on the field. Most men will think that I had planned it all from the first, but it was not so," he insisted. "I simply took advantage of circumstances as they were presented to me in the providence of God. I feel that His hand led me."

In Richmond, two hundred Confederate soldiers, armed to the teeth, boarded a train with Anna to take her north to Guiney's Station. Among their number were Kyd Douglas and Joe Morrison. Stonewall's wounding shook them. That his wife and baby could not even travel to see him because of the rampaging Yankee invaders enraged them.

"What will happen?" a sleepless, frightened Anna asked Douglas as tiny Julia, sensing her mother's uneasiness, wailed.

Locking a bullet into the chamber of the carbine repeater he had snatched from a dead Yank on the Chancellorsville field, he looked her in the eye, his words soft, but his gaze, surrounded by tiny crow's feet she had not before seen, steady. "We shall shoot our way through to Guiney's Station if we have to."

But Hooker had had all of the Wilderness he wanted. Upon hearing reports that Lee was about to throw his thirty-five thousand remaining men against Fightin' Joe's entrenched seventy-five thousand around the United States Ford to drive them into the Rappahannock, Hooker saved him the effort.

As a thunderstorm blew through the area the night of May 5–6, the Federals retreated back across the river. They would continue retreating, not again clashing with the Army of Northern Virginia until July, far north in Pennsylvania at a small town named Gettysburg, their backs against the wall, their national capital flanked and threatened, their string of calamitous defeats lasting over two years, and their outnumbered, ragamuffin Southern foe led by Robert E. Lee hailed on every continent as the most dangerous fighting force in the world.

The Chancellorsville campaign proved the bloodiest in American history. The Federals suffered more than seventeen thousand casualties; the Confederates, more than twelve thousand. But the Southern army, less than half the size of the Northern, lost nearly 22 percent of its force.

Nonetheless, it was the Confederacy's greatest victory, and it marked the zenith of the electrifying union of Lee and Jackson.

Maggie trembled at her desk the morning of May 6 as she considered the news that had dribbled through to Lexington in bits and pieces from Chancellorsville: Stonewall and A. P. Hill wounded, Stonewall's arm amputated, Stonewall Brigade commander and Lexington native "Bull" Paxton killed. *Ah, Bull Paxton,* she thought, squinting her eyes in pain, even though she now wore eye shades whenever she wrote. *A good man, though without Christ his entire life, until coming under the pious brave influence of Thomas. Then, recently, professing his faith—and reading from his Bible even at the very moment the order came for the charge where he would forfeit his earthly life.*

Maggie petitioned God silently for Stonewall's safety, and for Anna's peace of heart. Then a thought struck her. *Why, I shall invite Thomas to come recuperate here! Yes, that is what I shall do.* The thought buoyed her soul as it had rarely been in recent months. *But first, I must put down these thoughts before I forget them.*

And so, the carnage of Chancellorsville weighing on her mind, she continued *Beechenbrook,* her heartfelt elegy to the suffering wife and mother of the Southern soldier, on the back inside cover of a book of Virgil:

> *The flight and pursuit, so harassing, so hot,*
> *Have drifted all combatants far from the spot:*
> *And through the woodlands, and over the plain,*
> *Lie gorily scattered, the wounded and slain.*
> *Oh the sickness,—the shudder,—the qualing of ear,*
> *As it leaps to her lips,— "What if Douglass be here!"*

CHAPTER 58

STONEWALL'S TRANSFORMATION IN THE EIGHT DAYS SINCE SHE had seen him pierced Anna's heart with dread and apprehension when she stepped through the door the cold, rainy morning of May 7 and saw his empty left shirt sleeve, his bandaged right hand, his pummeled unconscious face, and the desperate pneumonia that had come upon him the previous night.

But Lord, she pleaded silently, forcing her countenance to hold together, *can it have been only a week since he was in the full flush of vigorous manhood? I never saw him look so handsome, so happy, and so noble.*

She winced at his flushed cheeks, labored breathing, and benumbed senses. Gathering her sensibilities, she walked to the bed, sat next to him, and kissed him. His eyes opened and he said, "I am very glad to see you looking so bright." Then, to her disappointment, he lost consciousness again. She did not want to cry, especially in the presence of McGuire and Jim, both of whom looked as if they would at any minute burst into sobs. Then she caught sight of a little brown-haired girl whose sweet face disappeared from the doorway as quickly as it had appeared.

My poor darling, she lamented, turning back to Stonewall, *my poor, poor darling, you did not even get to see your little girl.* Nor would he for the next three days, insisting that tiny six-month-old Julia not see him until he could make a better presentation of himself. Anna detected with terror the growing gloom darkening McGuire's countenance as Stonewall's pneumonia worsened.

Once, rousing from a sedated sleep, Stonewall frowned at her. "My darling, you must cheer up, and not wear a long face. I love cheerfulness and brightness in a sick room." Then, tenderly, the blue eyes glinting with sentiment, "My darling, you are very much loved."

Other times, it was "You are one of the most precious little wives in the world." Never would she leave his side, day or night, and never would he wake without the first words from his mouth being words of love for her. He spoke more while asleep. The names of two men more than any others graced his lips: "Order A. P. Hill to prepare for action . . . Major Pendleton, send in and see if there is higher ground back of Chancellorsville, between it and the river . . . "

Several times, standing hat in hand at the door to the room, young Sandie had to excuse himself upon hearing his name. Little Lucy Chandler would see him duck behind a huge ancient live oak behind the building and kneel over, his whole body shaking with grief.

Stonewall seemed for a time to rally later in the morning of Anna's arrival. Though McGuire, and now head Confederate surgeon Samuel Morrison, Anna's cousin, cautioned him not to exert too much energy, he could not help but wax eloquent upon seeing the constellation of friends and family arrayed around him: Anna, Sandie, Douglas, McGuire, Jim, Lacy, Joe Morrison, young seminary student and aide James Smith, and old Dr. Morrison. Just outside the door, Mrs. Chandler grabbed little Lucy away by the arm as she eavesdropped.

"You have accomplished great things, General," Lacy said.

Stonewall shook his head. "Not I, not I, sir. I have no doubt that prayer and my Christian beliefs make me a better general. They calm my perplexities and anxieties, steady my judgment, and prevent me from leaping to rash conclusions. But the Christian should carry his religion into everything. Christianity makes man better in any lawful calling; it equally makes the general a better commander, and the shoemaker a better mechanic. In the case of the cobbler, or the tailor, for instance, religion will produce more care in promising work, more punctuality, and more fidelity in executing it, from conscientious motives; and these homely examples were fair illustrations of its value in more exalted functions. So, prayer aids any man, in any lawful business, not only by bringing down the divine blessing, which is its direct and prime object, but by harmonizing his own mind and heart. In the commander of an army at the critical hour, it calmed his perplexities, moderated his anxieties, steadied the scales of judgment, and thus preserved him from exaggerated and rash conclusions. Every act of man's life should be a religious act."

He accepted a drink of water from Anna, then continued: "Like Doldridge, I try to picture myself as spiritualizing every act of my daily life; as thinking when I wash myself of the cleansing blood of Calvary;

as praying while I put on my garments, that I might be clothed with the righteousness of the saints; as endeavoring while I eat, to feed upon the Bread of Heaven."

Then Stonewall peered at the contingent of young aides—Sandie, Douglas, McGuire, Smith—in the far corner of the room. "The Bible furnishes men with rules for everything. If you will search, you will find a precept, an example, or a general principle, applicable to every possible emergency of duty, no matter your calling. There the military man can find guidance for every exigency."

He looked straight at the younger men. "Can you tell me where the Bible gives generals a model for their official reports of battles?"

Sandie and Douglas laughed. "It never entered my mind to look for such a thing in the Scriptures," Smith said, blushing.

"Nevertheless," the ex-professor held forth, "there are such, and excellent models too. Look, for instance, at the narrative of Joshua's battle with the Amalekites; there you have one. It has clearness, brevity, fairness, modesty; and it traces the victory to its right source, the blessing of God."

But the pneumonia worsened. By Friday, May 8, Stonewall, in his rare moments of clarity, agreed with McGuire that the brutal fall from his litter on the Chancellorsville battlefield had done more damage than anyone had dared fear.

"I believe the fall punctured his lung, allowing blood to hemorrhage into the chest cavity," McGuire told Anna that evening. "Shock and blood loss from his wounds delayed the full effects of the blow, but they cannot prevent them."

The next evening, May 9, his breathing more difficult, his energy further flagging, and the throbbing ache in his chest worsening, Stonewall smiled at the circle of sad faces ringing him. "My dear friends," he said, "I am not afraid to die. I am willing to abide by the will of my heavenly Father. But I believe that my time has not yet come and that the Almighty has yet a work for me to perform."

Anna and Lacy both noticed Stonewall's judicious use of his favorite names for God—"my heavenly Father," when expressing his acquiescence in the Divine will concerning himself, and "the Almighty" when speaking of the work he expected God, as the Ruler of nations, to assign to him.

Once again, Anna caught sight of little Lucy's face peering in from just outside the doorway. She turned to her husband. "Please, darling," Anna urged, "please see Julia."

"Tomorrow," he said, "tomorrow I shall feel better. I do not wish to disappoint the little dear."

Anna wrung her hands, her heart crying. Feeling if she did not speak, she must burst into tears, she asked, "Might I read us some psalms?"

Stonewall closed his eyes and said, "I fear I am in too much pain to pay attention."

Her eyes widened. Never in her life had he refused the reading of Scripture. "Oh, darling," she cried, pressing her cool smooth cheek against his. "Oh, you must be hurting so badly. Please, allow them to administer more sedative."

"No, I must have my wits about me if I am soon to—I must keep my senses," he said. "And yes, we must never refuse Scripture. Get the Bible and read them."

As the evening wore on, the pain in Stonewall's chest grew fierce, and he had to fight for every breath. "Please, Anna, would you call for the chaplain," he said.

"Dear," she said, "the doctors fear that any conversation will harm you—"

"Please, my *esposa*," Stonewall cut in, "please call for my chaplain."

A little later, Lacy returned.

"Kind sir," Stonewall gasped, fighting for the words.

"Dear, please," Anna said, trying to stop him from speaking.

"No," Stonewall insisted, "must—say it. Are you fighting to defend our view of the blessed Sabbath day observance, that it might be kept—holy? Are you—sir?"

Lacy nodded, his throat tight. "Yes, General, and I shall continue to do so."

Stonewall closed his eyes and smiled. "That is good, dear pastor, that is very good."

Someone, long ago, had taught him how important was such an observance.

Late in the evening, Anna, nodding in exhaustion next to Stonewall's bed, heard him groan, "Oh."

"What is it, dear?" she asked.

"Please," he mumbled, barely audible, pain creasing his brow, "please, could you sing some hymns?"

She, her brother, Sandie, Douglas, and the others did so. After a few moments, Stonewall whispered, "And Isaac—Watts' hymn about the Fifty-first Psalm?"

"Yes, darling," she said. Then they sang, to the tune of the "Old Hundredth," as the expression on Stonewall's face relaxed.

> *Show pity, Lord; O Lord forgive;*
> *Let a repenting rebel live;*
> *Are not Thy mercies large and free?*
> *May not a sinner trust in Thee?*

Sunday, May 10, 1863, dawned as had spring mornings in Virginia all Stonewall Jackson's life. Bright, clean, fresh, cool.

Joe and Dr. Morrison nudged Anna, sleeping at Stonewall's side. "Dear cousin," the doctor said after he drew her aside, "that great man shall not live out this day."

Her bloodshot eyes blinked, but she did not flinch nor tear. She looked back at Stonewall, sleeping, his irregular breaths coming forth in great gusts. Then she turned back to her cousin and Joe, both combat veterans, their eyes welling over. "He has always wished to die on the Sabbath," she said.

When she returned to him, he awoke. She stroked his matted hair and kissed him lightly on his hot cheek. "Dear Thomas," she said, "do you know the doctors say you must very soon be in heaven? Do you not feel willing to acquiesce in God's allotment, if He wills you to go today?"

He stared at her, his eyes confused.

"Thomas," she repeated, stroking his hair, "do you know the doctors say you must very soon be in heaven?" Still he did not answer. "Thomas, do you know the doctors say you must very soon be in heaven?"

Opening his dry, cracked lips, he said, with great difficulty, "Yes, I prefer it." She stared at him. He looked her in the eye and repeated, "I *prefer* it."

She drew a breath. "Before this day is over you will be with the blessed Savior in His glory," she said, her voice sure and clear.

He looked at her, then closed his eyes. He breathed loudly for a few seconds, then said, "I will be an infinite gainer to be translated."

Just then, Sandie came in. "The whole army is praying for you, General," he said, his ruddy face streaked with tears.

"Thank God," Stonewall said softly, "they are very kind." He turned and looked out the window at Virginia as she bloomed again. He drank in her sweet elixir, glad he had refused further medication, despite the pain that coursed through him. "Bury me in the Valley of Virginia," he said gently, still gazing at the green fields. "In Lexington. That is home."

"Darling," Anna asked, "are you quite certain that the Savior is present with you even now?"

He turned back to her. "Yes." She kissed his lacerated hand and asked, "Is it your will that we reside with my father?"

Fading now, he mumbled, "Yes, you have a kind and good father; but no one is so kind and good as your heavenly Father."

For a few moments he rested. Then Anna saw his nostrils twitch. He opened his eyes again. "What is that?" he asked.

Anna turned to spy a tiny clump of purple irises set on the small scuffed stand next to his bed. Several strands of brown hair held them together. Anna grabbed the flowers, then looked around at the men in the room. No one had any idea from whence they had come. Then her gaze went to the doorway, where once again a small little girl with mounds of brown hair tied down in pigtails, darted from sight.

She leaned to whisper into his ear. "My darling Thomas, I should be ever so jealous, the way you have always had with the girls."

His thin colorless lips produced a feeble smile before his eyes widened. "Julia, bring in sweet little Julia, darling."

A moment later, the happy baby appeared.

"Little darling!" Stonewall all but shouted, growing more alert than he had all week.

A beaming smile lit up his battered face. Anna sat Julia on the bed next to him. He stretched out his remaining arm, hampered by the hand wound and the formidable bandaging, and caressed the infant's soft little face with his bandage, which was all that he had. *Long I have waited,* he thought, tickling the tiny chin—*my mother's chin— and You Lord, You have blessed me plenteously. Hide this sweet darling in Your breast, Heavenly Father, she and her mother.*

Now the good and brave men in the room could no longer staunch the tears that had fought all week for release. Soldiers who did not cry before man or God wept like children.

Stonewall glanced at Douglas. Summoning his breath, he said, "Don't look so downcast, Mr. Douglas. Duty is ours; the consequences are God's. Never forget that."

So he played with the little girl, the little girl who, so late, was finally his, who seemed enamored of everything about her father—his scarred face, his thick long beard and hair, his clump of bandages, his high gentle voice—until his earthly life began to ebb, his arm grew numb, and he could no longer keep open his eyes.

Over in the main Chandler house, Lucy apprised the tears moistening her mother's cheeks. "Mama, why have you been crying for two days?"

The woman stopped in her tracks, then turned to the little girl. She tried to think what to say, but could not.

"Mama," Lucy continued, "will General Jackson die?"

"Yes, Lucy," Mrs. Chandler said. "The doctors say they cannot save him."

"But when will he die?"

Choking back tears, the woman said, "General Jackson began this day on earth. He will end it in heaven."

Lucy considered that for a moment, fingering the back of a chair against which she leaned. When she looked back up at her mother, her eyes shone large and solemn.

"Oh, I wish God would let me die for him, Mama, for if I died, you would cry for me; but if he dies, all the people in the country will cry."

Now Stonewall sank into a deep restless slumber. For a long, long time he uttered no sound. Then, as distant church bells tolled and as his beloved wife Anna held his arm and kissed his damaged hand, with his eyes closed, he said, quite audibly, "Let us cross over the river, and rest under the shade of the trees." And then did Thomas Jonathan "Stonewall" Jackson pass down beneath the shadow of the portals of death from his earthly life.

☆ ☆ ☆

Kyd Douglas, tears streaming down his face, thought, *I'll swan, he really did believe it; he believed everything he always said, right up to the end, even when words weren't cheap at all.* He pulled out his grand old gold watch to measure the time of Stonewall's passing. Fifteen minutes past three. He started to put the watch back, but something caught his eye. He stared at the time piece. Ticking the minutes, the hours, the days, for a hundred years without fail, it had stopped forever the moment Stonewall Jackson's heart had ceased to beat.

Maggie heard the rider approaching and sealed her letter of invitation for Stonewall to convalesce with the Prestons. Frayed crinolines bustling, she rushed downstairs to find a handsome young Confederate officer climbing down from his gaunt mount and tying him to the gate.

"Please," she began, holding out the letter, "this must get to General Jackson as soon as—"

But the handsome young officer's tan face ran wet with tears. He had his own letter for Maggie. She took it, knowing something was dreadfully wrong.

Never had the stairs inside her house seemed so steep. *Oh, there are so many of them!* she thought with terror as she gazed upward. *But I must go to my room. I must be alone, just for a little while. I cannot let the children see me now.* Maggie began the long dark climb, each step steeper than the previous one. She had no strength, no will remaining.

Oh, how fearful the loss to the Confederacy, she thought. *The people made an idol of him, and God has rebuked them.* But it was in the quiet, secret place of her heart where she cried out loudest, her heart bursting with sorrow and loss. *How much of my life he was. Just knowing he was always there, Father, was so important. But now—oh now I have lost him forever!*

Somehow, when she reached her room, her remembrance of him and all that he was quenched the blackness from her soul. She pulled back the curtain and watched her children at play across the road as God berthed another spring in his Valley. In her Valley. *No more ready soul has ascended to the throne than was his,* she thought. *Never have I known a holier man.*

She sighed and walked to her desk and sat. She would in time finish *Beechenbrook,* its sad stirring pages raising her to acclaim North and South. But now she must record her true feelings about a most remarkable man that she had known as well, perhaps, as anyone. Putting on her eye shades and dipping her pen in a cup of persimmon juice—*Oh, blessed persimmon juice!* she thought with a tearful laugh—her eyes landed on the mantel above her fireplace. There they were. There they all were. Her mother, her father, Willy, Ellie, and Stonewall. *I shall write for them. I shall write for those who follow. I shall write for him.*

And then she wrote with inspiration, not understanding that her words would outlive her and hers. "Never have I seen a human being as thoroughly governed by duty," the lines flowed. "He lived only to please God; his life was a daily offering up of himself. All his letters to Mr. P. and to me since the war began have breathed the spirit of a saint. In his last letter to me he spoke of our precious Ellie, and of the blessedness of being with her in heaven. And now he has rejoined her, and together they unite in ascribing praises to Him who has redeemed them by His blood."

Across the room, unnoticed by Maggie, a scarred old rocking chair hewn from Ulster trunks and left with her by Anna Jackson, began again to rock, no one near it, as the generations passed.

And no more would darkness and fear visit the soul of Margaret Junkin Preston.

No one in the room had noticed when Stonewall again opened his eyes. Anna sobbed on his still breast, and the soldiers, doctors, and other friends stood stone-faced or wept, some on one another's shoulders, some alone, some sitting on the floor.

But why are they all crying? he wondered. *Do they not know that everything is going to be all right?*

Then he turned and saw other friends and family. But these were not sad. *Over there, just across . . . a river . . . Oh, it is more beautiful even than the Shenandoah—clear, clean, sparkling, new.* Surprisingly, he crossed it with ease. And then, just as the most pleasing fragrance he had ever scented reached his nostrils, a strong hand reached out to him.

"W-Warren," he stuttered. Strong, brown, alive, the winsome smile never brighter, never broader.

"What did I tell you, little brother?" Warren said, flashing his grin.

Stonewall remembered. "That you'd be the first," he said, laughing.

And so were they all laughing, and loving him. Dear sister Elizabeth, Granny Nancy, Uncle Robinson, Ruthie, Willy, and lots and lots of others, and the sentiments that flooded over Stonewall were stronger and more profound than any he had ever had. He felt he should be shedding tears of happiness, but—no tears would come, only giddy, joyous laughter and mirth.

And then he was face to face with his mother.

He stood stunned for a moment, then knelt and kissed her hand, looking up in surprise. No longer were her hands cracked and calloused. No longer did creases of worry and sorrow etch her face!

"So proud I am of you, Son," she said, her voice and words meaning the whole world to him. "You finished your course, Son, even when it was so hard, and you kept the faith."

He hugged his mother; he hugged them all. He barely noticed yet that all about him shown with indescribable tranquility and splendor.

Then he saw her, radiant as even she had never been. He stepped toward her, believing all the others, even Mama, but not able to believe it could be her.

"And I am so proud of you, Tom," Ellie said, smiling. "And I have waited for you for so long."

He stood before her beauty and grace, beyond what it had ever before approached. Only then did he notice, cradled nearby, a tiny giggling infant, her hazel eyes—Ellie's hazel eyes—beaming for all creation to see.

Stonewall opened his mouth to speak, but the wonder was too great. Ellie touched her finger to his mouth. "Shhh, my Tom. There is forever now."

Then he smiled and held her hand. "I simply cannot believe it, Ell. That it's really you."

"Oh, but you've not seen anything, Tom," she said in her sweet way.

And then a beautiful light cascaded over him, over them all.

A NOTE TO READERS

I have always been drawn to men standing on principle against fearful odds. Men for whom, as in the tale you have just read, honor became more cherished to them than life itself.

And so it was that years ago, when Thomas J. "Stonewall" Jackson rose to life for me off the pages of Sir Winston Churchill's epic book *The American Civil War* (a small section, actually, of Churchill's magnificent multivolume *A History of the English-Speaking Peoples*), he and his story—and that of Margaret Junkin Preston—presented themselves to me and demanded to be written.

I would hope it might be understood that in my attempt to convey both the facts and the sense of time and place of *Stonewall,* I have tried to place the reader in the shoes of those who lived the historic events this tale chronicles. In that regard, my narrative has often spoken through voices which seem alien to the contemporary culture of late twentieth-century America, a culture which teaches looking out for one's own self over others. Sometimes, my narrative has spoken through voices with which I personally disagree. For instance, I am not an apologist for slavery. Nor am I an apologist for the belief that the ethnic stock of any group is superior to that of another, which is the definition of racism, as rendered by the *American Heritage Dictionary of the English Language.*

Yet some of the theories traditionally offered for why the American Republic fought one of history's most desperate wars with itself are more informed by our contemporary sensibilities and agendas than a historical record that, as life itself, often defies the simplistic explanations we should like to assign it. It is oh-so-easy from the comfort of our big-screened living rooms and air-conditioned, government-subsidized lecture halls to criticize those who have come before us. I shudder to think what will be thought of *us* a century or more from now.

I hope I have succeeded in demonstrating to the reader that some of the pat, easily packaged explanations for the War Between the States/American Civil War upon which nearly all of us were weaned are, at best, incomplete in their historicity, and, at worst, part of an indoctrination of intolerant political correctness. The latter has for some time been foisted on Americans by institutions such as government, education, and entertainment/media that once served to promote rather than mock the concept, as espoused in the opening question of the Larger Catechism of the Westminster Confession of Faith, that "Man's chief and highest end is to glorify God, and fully to enjoy him forever."

Which brings me to the overarching purpose of this tale: that an ordinary life, even one rent by chaos, suffering, and loss, can be brought to order and used by God in extraordinary ways and for extraordinary purposes when that life is submitted to the Lordship of His Son Jesus Christ. To that end, my challenge to the reader is to investigate the message of God's written revelation in the Bible, from the beginning of Genesis to the end of Revelation. Like Stonewall Jackson, I believe that book to be one seamless, cohesive unit, bound tightly together by both the first and second comings of Christ, and revealing God's eternal holiness, as well as His calling out of a people for Himself. And like Stonewall, I look to the writings of Calvin, Owen, Edwards, Dabney, Spurgeon, and others in the Reformed tradition to best elucidate the glories of those sublime Scriptures.

I hope that this saga has engendered in the reader a thirst for more knowledge about the life of Stonewall Jackson. To that end I suggest in particular, among numerous quality volumes, *The Life and Campaigns of Lieut. Gen. T. J. (Stonewall) Jackson* by R. L. Dabney, *I Rode with Stonewall* by Henry Kyd Douglas, *Mighty Stonewall* by Frank E. Vandiver, *Stonewall Jackson* by Lenoir Chambers, *Stonewall* by Byron Farwell, *Stonewall Jackson's Verse* by H. Rondel Rumburg, and *Stonewall Jackson* by James I. Robertson Jr. And about Maggie Preston, *A March Past* by Elizabeth Preston Allan, *The Life and Letters of Margaret Junkin Preston*, and *Margaret Junkin Preston, a Biography* by Mary Price Coulling. I have drawn both directly and indirectly from each of these fine works, and others, in the telling of *Stonewall*.

I should add that, unlike these works of non-fiction, mine is a historical novel. Where the historical record speaks, I have attempted to reflect it faithfully. Where it does not, I have exercised dramatic license.

The number of people who are due my thanks for their contributions to this effort, which began nearly a decade ago, are legion. A very few I shall mention.

From my earliest memories, my mother stoked in my brother Paul and me a desire for reading and learning, especially about the heroic men and women of the past who sacrificed of themselves that our lives might be better.

At a couple of key junctures, when I found myself on the verge of giving up on my writing, the encouragement of my good friend, seminary professor at Dallas Theological Seminary, and writing mentor Reg Grant kept me going.

Highly regarded content editor Lonnie Hull DuPont, whom my publisher Broadman & Holman wisely brought on for *Stonewall*, proved a gracious and patient tutor to this rookie author.

B & H Publisher Ken Stephens, Vice President of Trade and Academic Books Bucky Rosenbaum, Marketing Director Mark Lusk, Project Editor Lisa Parnell, and others in that organization believed in *Stonewall* and that rookie author.

William D. "Bill" Watkins, a successful author in his own right, who at various stages in this adventure has been my agent, my editor, and finally the acquisitions editor for *Stonewall* at B & H, has forgotten more about writing and editing than I likely will ever know. Never shall I forget his belief in me and his direct contributions to this project.

My six-year-old daughter, Katie, has too often heard the words, "Daddy is still working" as day transitioned into night and she wanted to play. Yet she continues to love me and is already starting to write—and sing—her own stories.

Last and most, Grace, "the wife of my youth," has never given up on me, and suffers long a husband who is much more adept at writing about noble principles than living them.

Withal, my fervent prayer is that the work now completed would prompt all its readers to consider the magnificent promises from the tenth chapter of the New Testament Book of Romans, "That if thou shalt confess with thy mouth the Lord Jesus, and shalt believe in thine heart that God hath raised him from the dead, thou shalt be saved."

John J. Dwyer
Texas
5 April 1998